Silvertongue

REMNANTS OF MAGIC
BOOK ONE

More from Casey White

The Flameweaver Saga
Chosen
Charred
Nightsworn
Ascendant

-

Reverie

Remnants of Magic
Silvertongue
Wanderer

Halfway to Home
Without a Trace
Into the Black

This is a work of fiction, and the views expressed herein are the sole responsibility of the author. Likewise, certain characters, places, and incidents are the product of the author's imagination, and any resemblance to actual persons, living or dead, or actual events or locales, is entirely coincidental.

Silvertongue (Remnants of Magic, Book 1)

*As always, my first thanks
go to Shaun for his unending,
unrelenting patience.*

CHAPTER ONE

Be careful what you choose.

Generally, people are expected to ponder their decisions carefully. We spend months working through the important moments in our lives. Years. We're expected to be thoughtful when we pick a job, when we decide who to date, when we find a place to live.

I wasn't any different. I'd thought that I was a pretty cautious person, overall. Not exactly the high-risk type, you might say. Others would probably have just called me boring and been done with it.

But sometimes, sneaking in when you least expect it, a single decision can change everything.

"I already told you, Keira. I'm tired. I just want to come home. Today sucked."

"Yeah, I get that. But I don't want pizza. It's right on the way, so why's it a big deal? Just swing through and pick us up something." My sister's voice had all the smug confidence I'd long since come to expect, even over the phone.

I swallowed a groan. The road flew past under my tires, leading me from the run-down office I worked at back towards home. I gripped my cell phone a little tighter, scowling. "I don't *want* McDonald's. I just want to sit on the couch and have dinner brought to me for once, okay?"

"That's lazy."

"So?"

"So I want a burger. You should bring me home something."

1

I rolled my eyes, feeling my teeth grind together. She'd win. She *knew* she was going to win, which was why she sounded so damn happy with herself.

Fine. So be it. It was just food, after all, and if I didn't bring anything home I knew she'd just whine and complain for the rest of the night. Shutting her up was worth the hassle, I decided.

"Whatever. Okay."

"Great. Don't forget the fries." She didn't even wait for me to say goodbye before she hung up.

I shoved my phone back into my pocket, muttering darkly to myself. The plaintive chirp of the low-battery warning fell quiet under the thick layers of fabric. Hitting the brakes, I turned back towards the few restaurants clinging to life along the edge of town.

It was *just food*. If I'd have known the mess it'd make, maybe I'd have decided differently. Maybe I'd have put up with the complaining and gone home, settling in with the box of delivery pizza I so desperately wanted. Maybe I'd have approached the whole situation with a little more care. But I didn't know - and there was no way that I could have ever guessed the chain of events that we'd set into motion.

My mind was a blur as I slid out into the cold, walking towards the front door. Drive-through would have been faster, almost certainly. But if my sister was going to make me play personal chauffeur, then it was my obligation to at least make it painful for her. She could wait while I ate my dinner. Fair was fair.

Chuckling to myself, I made my way through the motions of ordering, operating entirely on automatic. My head ached. It had been a long day. There had been not one but *two* irate clients, all demanding total reworks on their projects. I hadn't spent years in school so that I could deal with assholes all day. Reality didn't seem to have gotten the memo.

"What did you say?"

I paused, my card already jammed into the receptacle and deducting the bill from my bank account. The world spun around me as I blinked myself back to awareness. "What?"

The clerk stared at me, his green eyes narrowed. I drew half a step back almost unconsciously, trying to remember exactly what I'd been doing or what I'd said that somehow had set the man off. "Uh. I asked if I could have my drink cup. You guys keep making us wait and it's kind of annoying."

2

The man stared at me, his lips pressed into a thin line. "What are you doing?"

All right, the guy was clearly crazy. I tore my debit card free, shoving it back into my wallet. "I'm trying to get a Big Mac. Is that a problem?"

"Are you insane?" he hissed, leaning forward across the counter. "What are you *doing*?"

"Greg?" someone called from across the store. A manager, judging by the color of their uniform. Their voice was carefully cheerful. "What's going on?"

"Nothing! Just helping this gentleman out," Greg said, his face snapping back to carefully neutral as he smiled at me. The cashier shoved a plastic cup into my hands, along with the paper slip of my receipt. "Look - don't be an idiot," he said, his voice dropping low enough I had to lean in to hear him. "I don't know what game you think you're playing, but you can't walk in here talking gibberish. Leave me alone."

I stared at him, my mind racing, but the customers behind me were already pushing forward. I stepped back to join the others waiting for their food, my mind churning.

I had a bit of a gift. Well, that's how I liked to think about it. It had taken a few years to figure out - all languages sounded exactly the same to me. No matter if I was speaking to someone blabbering on in French or chattering in Italian, it all came across as plain old English.

My parents had been freaked out, understandably. It had taken a bit of doing to convince them I wasn't just crazy. And as soon as we'd pieced together what was going on, we'd begun hiding whatever it was I was doing. It wasn't as though I could suddenly start spouting off Spanish and German, after all. We couldn't even just leave copies of Rosetta Stone lying around meaningfully. The instant someone I actually *knew* called me on it, the secret would be up. I kind of valued living a normal life too much to allow something like that to happen.

Tray in hand and my mediocre food steaming, I filed back to my seat. I could feel Greg's eyes on me the whole way - staring.

What was his problem? Had I stuttered? And what had he meant, gibberish? Maybe he spoke a different language, sure, but why would that be a problem? He should be happy that I'd spoken Polish or Swahili or who-gives-a-fuck. Maybe a bit surprised, but not *angry*. His reaction wasn't normal at all.

I couldn't shake the feeling that something was wrong. Normally I would have lingered, taking my time in eating. With the feeling of Clerk Asshat's glare boring holes in the back of my neck, I just wanted to leave. I shoveled my meal down as quickly as I could, hardly tasting it. My phone lit up with notifications, friends and family blabbering away in text messages and group chats. All of them wanted to know where I was. When I'd be finished with the day's chores. Keira pinged me again, still asking after her damn burger.

I ignored all of them. The wrapper crumpled instantly in my hand as I pushed myself upright, dumping the whole lot of it in the trash. Grabbing the to-go bag with her food, I turned for the door.

The guy wasn't at the counter anymore. A sigh of relief slipped out of me as I saw his station replaced by a tiny, grinning brunette. Good. Maybe his manager had finally taken him down a notch.

The lights on my sedan blinked across the parking lot at me as I stepped out of the store. The cold air snapped me awake, back to reality in an instant. I was letting that guy creep me out for no reason. He was just a jerk, that was all - trapped in his minimum wage job. Probably just a crazy, when I thought about it. He was probably just-

I yelped, my eyes widening as fingers buried themselves in my hair. The bag of food fell to the pavement. Someone had me. There was something cold at my throat - cold and *sharp*.

"Ok, asshole," Greg hissed in my ear, his voice wild. "We're going to go for a walk."

"What the *fuck* are you-"

"Shut up."

The blade dug into my neck. I could feel a hot line of blood dripping down my skin. My mind raced - this was insane. He really was crazy. A lunatic. He was-

There was nothing I could do to fight him as he turned me, forcing me towards the rear of the store. A dingy, beat-up station wagon waited in the back corner, the lot unlit and dismally dark. I scanned the scene even still, ready to bellow for help at a moment's notice.

It was useless. There was no one around. No one was going to hear.

He slammed me into the back of the car, my face pressed painfully against the glass.

"How stupid do you think I am?" he spat.

"What the *hell* are you talking about?" I cried. My fingers trembled.

"What, you think you're being subtle? You'll just walk in, talking the old tongue like you were born to it, and I'll roll over for you?"

"Look, dude, there's been some mistake," I moaned. "It's-It's just something that I can do, all right? It's not-"

"Right," he said with a laugh, his fingers still pulling painfully at my hair. "Like I'm going to believe *that*."

"I speak a lot of languages, all right?" I said, craning my head until I could look at him. "That's all. I don't know what you heard. All I know is-"

"How long until they get here?"

Confusion bubbled up in my mind. "What?"

"I'm not *stupid*," he spat. "I'm not going to sit idly until they come to finish the job. How long until the rest of them show up?"

"The rest of *who*?" I said, trying desperately to keep from crying.

"You know damn well who-" he said, but stopped abruptly.

I blinked, my breath catching in my throat.

Somewhere in the distance, sirens were approaching.

My heart leapt. Police. *Yes.* Someone must have seen him, someone must have called the cops. I was saved. He'd-

He let go of my hair in an instant, leaping away. Abandoning the car and I, he vanished into the underbrush of the woods behind the McDonald's. I fell in a crumpled heap, my heart still pounding in my ears.

Tires screeched as the cop car pulled up moments later, a pair of officers piling out.

"Sir! Sir, are you all right?" one yelled, racing over to me. His dark hair was in disarray, in contrast to his short-trimmed beard. "Can you tell me what happened?"

"There was- a man," I said, glancing back at the woods. 'H-He had a knife. He was crazy. Thought I was speaking some funny language or something."

"Why would he think that?" the cop's partner said, his brow furrowing. He stared at me, leaning closer like he could see straight into my soul.

"I-I don't know," I said, instinctively clamping down. The cops paused, eerily quiet.

"What, that's it?" the first said.

"I'm sorry," I muttered, unable to meet their eyes. My gaze drifted, needing to find something, anything else to look at. The flashing lights of their cars drew my eyes in, holding my gaze.

I froze.

"Well, look. I'm sure this has been a traumatic event. Why don't you come back with us, and we'll talk about it?" the second said, smiling blankly at me. One hand dropped to his belt. He was a heavy-set man, short and broad. I wouldn't have expected an officer to look like him, the thoughts in the back of my head whispered.

Neither of them was wearing a radio. There was nothing hanging off his waist but a gun and a pair of handcuffs. The details of it stuck out like a lightning flash in my mind.

I took a step back.

"Don't worry, all right?" the first said, beaming at me. "You're safe now, right?"

The insignia on their car was wrong. I'd lived in the town my entire life, and it was *wrong*. It didn't even have the right *name* on it. It just looked...

Generic.

I took another step back.

The smiles were beginning to fade from their faces.

"Come on," the first said. "Just take it easy, ok? We'll just go for a ride."

His hand reached out, grabbing for my elbow. I skittered away before he could touch me, suddenly sure of two things.

Whoever those two were, they were *not* police officers.

And I was in a mess of trouble.

CHAPTER TWO

I took another step back, my eyes snapping back and forth between the two officers.

"Would you just calm down?" the bearded cop said, smiling at me as he stepped forward. "No one's going to hurt you, all right? What's your name?"

The sound of a door shutting drew my attention back to their car. A third officer - a third *man in an officer's uniform* climbed out, his eyes fixed on me.

"Look, I'm fine," I said, shaking my head. "I just want to go home. Sorry to- I didn't mean to waste your time. Thanks. Bye."

"Just slow down," the newcomer said, chuckling. "Why don't we just talk a minute, then you can go?"

"We don't have to go anywhere if you don't want," the first said, sliding his hands into his pockets. That dumb smile was still spread across his face "We just want to know what happened."

"What *happened?*" I said, spitting the words out. "That asshole pulled a knife on me, that's what."

"Who?" the third man said. His eyes were a bright, piercing blue behind his glasses as he looked at his friends, as though seeking confirmation.

"Why would he do something like that?" the second said, leaning back against the car as he yawned. "Do you know where he went?"

I glared at them, still feeling the cold ice of adrenaline in my veins. This was wrong. This was all wrong, and the fact that I didn't know any of the rules they were playing by made it all the worse. "I have no fucking idea why he'd do something like that. He probably wanted my wallet."

The bearded man shook his head, stepping closer. "That's not what you said earlier."

I could feel the last of the blood drain from my face. "I-I'm just trying to figure out what's going on, all right? Just- stay back."

They stopped obediently, although I saw them exchange tolerant smiles.

"So where'd he go?" Blue-eyes said, chuckling. "Where'd he run off to?"

A bit of the tension slid from my shoulders as the trio of men relaxed imperceptibly. Something had changed. I'd passed some test, clearly. Said the right words, had just the right amount of fear in my voice. Whatever had convinced them to leave off, I didn't care.

"I don't know," I said, frowning. "He took off back there." I pointed quickly, gesturing back towards the dark woods. It was a small town, nothing to write home about, and you didn't have to go more than a few blocks in any direction to wind up outside the city. "If you hurry, you can probably still-"

A harsh, strident ring cut me off. I stopped almost by habit, falling still as the bearded man dug in his coat pocket. "Yeah, it's Matt," he said, rolling his eyes as he lifted the phone to his ear. "What do you need?"

I stayed right where I was, resisting the urge to kick the pebbles covering the asphalt parking lot as the silence dragged on.

"Uh-huh."

Whoever he was talking to, I wished they would hurry up. I just wanted to go home, to be done with this already.

"You're sure?"

It was cold, too, halfway through fall and too frigid to be standing out in the night air. There were a few people passing by, sliding out of the McDonalds and looking towards the lights of the police car, but the wind was too brisk for them to do more than cast a curious glance our way.

Swallowing a sigh, I turned back towards the three men. "Is this going to take-"

I blinked, shocked into silence. They'd already crossed half the narrow distance separating us, eyes fixed on me and accelerating

8

rapidly. I didn't even have the time to cry for help before their meaty hands were wrapped around my arms, pulling me forward.

For the second time that night, I hit the glass window of the car with a grunt. "W-What the-"

"Where is it?" Matt said, his tone all business. Not smiling anymore, I noticed through the haze of terror sweeping across my mind.

Squirming desperately, I shook my head. "I have absolutely no idea what you-"

An arm slammed into the back of my neck, pinning me in place. "Search him. It's on him somewhere - it wasn't Aedan. Recon's sure."

"What do you mean, sear-" I gasped, my words dying as the one of them punched me in the eye. Dots flew across my vision.

Someone was pawing at my ears, like they were looking for earrings I didn't have. Rough hands tugged at my jacket, my sweatshirt, the pockets of my jeans. I twitched, unsure if I should struggle for all I was worth or let them look. I didn't even have anything. They could rifle through my pockets all day, it wasn't going to change the outcome.

The pudgy one made an irritated noise in the back of his throat, clearly reaching the same conclusion. I managed a smile, relief coursing through my veins.

His hand grabbed mine a moment later, settling around my little finger. I froze.

"Where is it? Stop playing games, kid."

I shook my head desperately, straining against the man even then holding me down. "I-I don't even know what you *want*."

The crack of bone snapping echoed in the frigid night air. I screamed. One of them had my mouth covered a second later, muffling the sound. My hand was on fire, my finger pulsating with heat.

Where were the people, dammit? There had to be someone around, someone to come and help. They couldn't all have vanished. Something like that wouldn't-

"It'll be easier if you just tell us," Matt murmured, his voice low. "No one wants to drag this out."

I squeezed my eyes shut, still gasping from the waves of agony radiating off my broken finger. What the *fuck* was happening?

"There's no time, Matt," the heavyset man gripping me said. "There's only so long I can hold the barrier."

"Fine," Matt said, sighing. Whoever was holding me eased up enough that I could straighten, looking around.

9

Matt was staring at me, his face long. One hand slid down to the gun holstered at his side.

"We don't have it yet," the one holding me said. "Checking the body will take time, and we won't *know*. Recon won't like it. And hiding a gunshot is going to tire me out."

"He was resisting arrest," Matt said, looking at his partner with a crooked grin. "That's all anyone will see. Isn't that how it works? The rest is just noise. It'll be fine."

I flinched, my breath freezing in my lungs as the barrel of his pistol swung up. It was too dark for the weapon to be more than a black mass of metal, but that was plenty.

"Recon'll still be mad."

"Recon's mad at *everything*, Dan," Blue-eyes said, turning back to us with a chuckle. "Doesn't mean a whole lot anymore." He'd been staring off into the woods, letting his friends do their thing. I stared at them, feeling my hands shake.

"I don't want to transport him still fighting us if we don't know what he is," Matt said, stepping closer. His eyes flicked down to mine. "Sorry, kid."

I should have kicked the man holding me - Dan. I should have tried to pull free, to fight, to throw him off and get clear. But all of the common-sense options I might have had drifted away, evaporating in the face of the pistol still pointed at me.

Shit.

With my pulse thundering in my ears, adrenaline shooting through my system, I saw it all happen in slow motion.

I saw Greg come running out of the woods, still wearing his red and black crew member uniform. His teeth were gritted, his eyes wide with fear, but the knife in his hand was steady as he swept it out to the side.

I saw Matt flinch, half-turning despite himself as the blue-eyed man bellowed something completely inaudible. The barrel of his pistol dipped, turning away from me at last.

I saw Dan move, following behind his two friends as Greg launched himself at the trio of police officers. The arm pinning my neck slipped free. Dan's hand fell away.

Reality returned in a flash as Greg slashed down hard, catching the blue-eyed man across the face. The not-officer shrieked, slapping a hand up as blood dripped down from the fresh cut on his cheek.

"No! Get him- Don't let him-" Matt yelled, stumbling over his

10

words as Dan grabbed him by the collar of his shirt, pulling him backward as easily as he'd manhandled me. Greg's knife split the air where he'd stood.

I could hear Greg mutter something dark and foul from across the fight. And then his green eyes fixed on mine, red hair flying.

"Run."

One word - that was all. And it was a *good* word. Running was a good plan, really. But with as much adrenaline flooding my veins as there was, running just sounded...cheap. There were three of them, and only one of Greg. And Greg had a knife, while they had guns. If I left, if I ran, Greg was going to die.

The guy was an asshole. I still had absolutely no idea what his problem was. But right in that moment, he was fighting the guys who'd been about to shoot me. If that didn't make him an ally, it came pretty damn close.

I straightened, squaring off against the three faux policemen just in time to see one of them take a swing at Greg. He ducked the blow like a championship prizefighter, rising again with a lunge and a stab that sent Dan stumbling away.

Matt's eyes were on me, though. I could feel it, could see him staring at me from the corner of my eye. I faltered, seeing the determination there - a determination I had no rational explanation for.

His arm dropped, the gun sliding down to his side as he leapt for me again. I shuddered, my arms coming up to a ready stance. I'd never fought a day in my life, but if he was going to start one, I'd-

Greg's fist slammed into Matt's cheek, hard enough that I saw blood and spittle spray from his mouth. Matt stumbled, on the verge of losing his balance. The crazed man twisted around in the same motion, bringing his knife to bear. Matt was expecting the follow-up, though. He swiveled just in time, robbing Greg of the solid blow he clearly wanted. Even still, his arm erupted in red from where the knife had torn a gash from bicep to wrist.

Greg's fist buried itself in my sweatshirt a moment later. He pulled me close enough that all I could see were his eyes, burning green and furious. "Did I ask for your help, asshole?" he hissed. "The longer you hang around the more likely you get *shot*. Run. The fuck. Away."

When he pushed me, his lip curling in a sneer, I didn't wait. I'd seen enough. I was done. It wasn't like I could help, anyway.

My shoes slapped hard against the pavement as I took off running, heading straight for where Greg had vanished mere minutes before. The woods. Whatever was going on, the three imposters didn't seem to be worried about people interfering - people who had mysteriously vanished, anyway. I needed distance, I needed somewhere to hide. I was safer out there than hoping they wouldn't find me cowering in the gas station bathroom.

As I turned, I saw Matt's eyes fix on mine. His mouth opened, like he was yelling something to his colleagues. Greg was there to cut him off, his foot sliding out just as casual as could be. Matt went flying, tumbling to the asphalt.

The pavement under my feet vanished, giving way to hard-packed dirt and dead leaves. I grinned, hearing my breath come ragged in my ears. Nearly there.

They were still bellowing. I could see Dan and his blue-eyed friend staring after me, making as if to follow, but my new ally was relentless. None of the fake officers seemed badly hurt, but even still, his knife glistened red.

I smiled over my shoulder, even as the trees began flying past me. I was well out of the dim glow of the street lights by then - completely invisible to them, I knew. Nearly there.

My steps slowed as I glanced back. Greg was still fighting. He was holding his own, and he'd certainly been firm enough that he wanted no part of my help, but even still-

A low chuckle rippled through my form as I saw him duck again and again, pressing in ever-closer on Matt. The fake officer looked terrified. Good.

I blinked. No. He didn't look terrified. He looked like he was trying to wave someone off.

My eyes widened as I saw Blue-eyes rise up behind Greg - a gun in his hand. My feet were frozen, pinned in place. Maybe if I ran, I could- I could do *something*. Maybe I could-

The crack of the gunshot echoed across the block, loud enough to make me flinch. I stared, open-mouthed.

Greg fell, streaming red from his- from where his head had-

My stomach churning, I turned and ran. All of my earlier hesitation had disappeared. Fuck. *Fuck* that. They shot him. I wasn't looking to see if they were following, or if they were lingering to clean up the *person* they'd just killed. I had no idea where I was going - I just needed to get away. Anywhere.

12

The sound of twigs breaking underfoot rang in my ears. It was pitch black, away from the lights of town. More than once I stumbled, falling headlong as a log or stump caught my leg. Here and there I could see the distant outline of a house, a glimmer of light peering from a window. I didn't care.

I ran. I ran, feeling blisters form with every step as I pushed my feet far beyond what they'd experienced in years. I ignored the screaming complaint of my legs, pure terror keeping me going long after my strength had worn itself out.

When I could go no further, I collapsed, dragging myself over to hide behind the broad, sturdy trunk of an oak.

And I waited.

The seconds ticked as I gasped for breath, a hand pressed over my mouth to dull the noise. My other hand hung limp in my lap, white-hot with agony from the mess they'd made of my finger. I strained for the slightest bit of noise, the faintest indication that someone was following me.

I heard only silence and the distant sound of a bird crying in the night.

The seconds melted away into minutes. I had no idea how long I sat in the cold, trembling and listening for the tiniest sound of pursuit. As the excitement dwindled, the pain in my hand somehow managed to ramp up further. It was like my broken finger was screaming extra-loud to make up for the time it had been quiet. My legs were blocks of lead, my muscles completely frozen as I closed my eyes and waited, teeth gritted.

I should call the police. I should tell them what was happening. Someone probably already had, but even still, maybe they could come get *me*.

The screen lit up bright enough to blind me. I shoved it back down into my pocket, swallowing a curse. Again I waited, listening. I was an idiot. If someone saw, if they were looking, I'd just made myself a beacon in the darkness.

More carefully, I tabbed the screen on once I was confident I was alone.

A heartbeat after I turned it on, though, I was greeted by the familiar sight of an empty battery.

Fuck. I was supposed to charge the damn thing while I ate. I'd-

I sighed. I'd been so distracted by the asshole staring at me that I'd totally forgotten.

Sliding it away, I glanced around carefully. I'd lived here for years. The woods on the edge of town were laced with trails, forming a network of paths that'd take you most anywhere you wanted to go in the park, if you were patient. I'd been in the forest hundreds of times. Even if I'd gotten myself a little bit lost, I'd probably find a landmark if I just kept going.

My legs had stopped their shaking enough that I could stand, if a bit unsteadily. Bracing myself against the tree with my good hand, I gave one last furtive glance around.

And then I started walking.

My confidence grew with every step. With the cold night air on my face and the stillness of the woods around me, it was almost like being in a different world. Everything that had happened back at the McDonalds - it was just a bad dream. Something like that. Yes. I'd just head back, and everything would be fine. I'd head to the emergency room, get a cast or something, and-

The sight of Greg falling hard to the asphalt rose up in my mind, bringing me back down to reality in a single sickening heartbeat.

Nothing was fine.

My head hanging a little lower, I trudged onward. Somewhere around here, I'd find the way out, and I'd find my way home - and then I'd have to explain. Would they still be looking for me? Would they know where to find me? What were they looking for in the first place - and why did they think I had it? Why had-

Lost in thoughts, I didn't hear the footsteps in the leaves behind me until it was too late. My head snapped up at the sound of someone crashing towards me, but every muscle in my body ached. I couldn't run. I could barely *walk*.

A pair of hands latched around my shoulders as someone launched themselves into me. The start of a yell slipped from between my lips-right up until a hand slapped over my mouth. I twisted, fighting, but they wouldn't let go.

"Fucking stop already."

I froze, the blood draining from my face. I knew that voice, even if I'd only heard it a few times before. They leaned closer, until their face was just a dark mass in front of my own.

"I swear to god, if you say a single word, I'm going to kill you myself," Greg said.

CHAPTER THREE

Greg stared at at me, his eyes wide enough to glow white even in the dark. I stared right back. My mouth was hanging open. I couldn't quite bring myself to care.

It was him. Somehow. But- that was impossible. I'd watched him fight the not-officers. I'd watched him get shot. His head had just....*exploded*. So how was it he was standing here in front of me, not even an hour later? He didn't have a scratch on him - hell, his clothes weren't even dirty.

He leaned back, his hands sliding free of my shoulders as he groaned. "Thank fucking god. Did you *have* to run halfway across the damn forest? Why would you run, just to hang around here?"

I drew breath, starting to respond, but his hand slapped back over my mouth before I could. "No, no, no. What did I just say?" he snarled.

He was the one who'd asked the question. I twisted away, throwing my arms up, and he let me go. "Not a single word," he said, folding his arms. "They're close. We can't risk it."

That wasn't stopping *him* from talking, I thought sourly. My still-broken finger throbbed painfully, reminding me that I had yet to get that cast. It was beginning to look like it would be waiting a while.

Greg shook his head, half-turning to scan the pitch-black woods. "Where is it?"

I blinked, confused. Where was what?

When I didn't immediately answer, he turned back, rolling his eyes. "I'm not an idiot, you know. And I heard the gang of assholes when they were giving their little welcome speech. They know, you know, I know. Everyone knows. Whoop-de-fucking do. So where is it? You need to withdraw, before they find us again."

A groan rippled out from between my clenched teeth. After everything that had happened, after him pulling a knife on me and then saving my life and getting shot and coming back from the dead, he was *still* making exactly zero sense. What were they looking for? Why wouldn't they all leave me alone? And if I could run, I'd have 'withdrawn' a long time ago. But my legs were still trembling under me, the little strength I'd managed to find washed away by the adrenaline and terror of his reappearance.

He'd been *shot*. In the *head*.

Before I so much as shake my head, his palm snapped out. "Give it here. I want to see it."

My mouth dropped open again, exactly where he could stick that hand rising to my lips.

I hit the ground hard as his fist plowed into my nose, cutting off the unkind things I'd been about to say. His weight dropped down on top of me a heartbeat later. I gasped for breath that wouldn't come, his knee pressed into my throat. No matter how hard I squirmed, he didn't hesitate. My hands slapped uselessly at his elbow as he slid a worn backpack from his shoulders.

"I *warned* you," he muttered, glaring venomously down at me. "What are you trying to do, anyway? What did I ever do to you?"

What? He held me at knifepoint, for starters. I couldn't manage the words while fighting for every breath, though. My eyes snapped open as he tapped my cheek.

"Here. Open up."

I blinked. He was still sitting on top of me, the bag open and waiting beside him, but he wasn't empty-handed anymore.

He thrust the wad of fabric he clutched in one hand towards me. "Put this in your mouth, then. Hurry up. We don't have the time for this and I'm tired of arguing with you."

An insane giggle slipped from my throat as he waited, his brow furrowed. It was a sock. He'd pulled a sock from his backpack, and wanted me to put it in my *mouth*. Hell, no.

Catching the look in my eyes, he frowned. "It's clean. I think. I mean, everything got a bit jumbled in there, but- just do it, would you?"

I shook my head furiously. No, no, no. There was no way I was going to-

A metallic click rang through our little clearing. I froze. The knife from before was back in his hand, clean and ominously reflecting the dim light of the moon.

"Did I ask if you *wanted* to?" Greg said, leaning in. "Put it in your fucking mouth, or I'll finish what they started."

My eyes were still fixed on the blade of his knife. Shit. Try as hard as I might, I couldn't think of a way to get myself out of this insanity. Slowly, hating myself and my cowardice, I let my mouth slide open.

He didn't wait for an invitation. Before I could slam it shut again he'd pried my jaw open, stuffing the sock in.

I gagged. He was wrong. Totally and completely wrong. There was no way that sock was clean.

The sound of tearing plastic filled my ears, oddly loud in the silence. Before I could turn my head and spit the sock back out, he'd stuck something to my face, pinning my mouth shut. Tape. Duct tape, judging from the size of the shadowed roll in his hands. I eyed his overstuffed backpack with distaste. Exactly how much did he have in there? And why was he-

"Don't even think about touching it," he said, his face still dangerously close to mine. "I told you to be quiet and you didn't listen. Now, *be quiet.*"

I could feel the tension in him, the pent-up anger and frustration. His hands trembled, the blade of his knife shaking as he sat back. "All right. Just let me see it already. I'm not going to *take* it from you. Probably. I just want to look."

I shook my head more desperately, my own frustration building by the second. He sighed. "Use your goddamn phone. Technology is immutable, as you know perfectly well."

My phone. Uh. Right. I was suddenly grateful that it was as dark as it was. It kept him from spotting the way my ears were burning. I inched clear of him, reaching slowly for my pocket. His knife was still too close and ready for me to even consider taking off the makeshift gag. Easing my phone out of my pocket, I tabbed the button, looking away.

"You didn't charge your phone. What are you, ten?"

It wasn't just my ears burning anymore. He was chuckling, and I didn't get the feeling he was laughing with me.

My heart skipped a beat at a sudden flash of light. And then I looked down.

He was holding a phone out for me to take. At least…

I snorted. It was a flip phone - straight out of the 2000s. My mother had had one just like it for years. From what I'd seen in the store, he couldn't have been older than 22 or 23. It had to kill him, to be stuck with something like that.

He frowned, the expression dimly lit by the light of the screen. "Are you *really* going to sit there laughing at me?"

The low laugh that had been building in my chest died before it could slip out. My hand closed over the phone before he could change his mind.

A bead of sweat dripped down the small of my back as I worked the keyboard desperately. I hadn't had to use a numpad to type a text in ages. Until I'd started hitting the buttons, I wasn't entirely sure I'd remember how. With his knife leveled at me, though, I managed.

What do u wnt

Greg stared at me, eyes narrowing. "Don't play stupid. I told you. I *know*. Your relic - oh, you kids are calling them your 'focus', now, aren't you?"

I paused, eyeing him. You kids? Really? Unless I was totally misreading things, there was no way he was older than me. Certainly not old enough to be patronizing. What an asshole.

don't know wht tht is

"Really? That's your story?"

My pulse quickened. What else could I say? What could I tell him? It was the truth.

Really

His hand latched around the collar of my jacket, tugging. He was trying to get my coat off. I squirmed, kicking him away, but before more than a second or two had passed he stopped. Had he reconsidered?

I risked a glance back. He was watching me again - and this time, the look in his eyes was contemplative, not angry.

"Are you serious? You don't know?"

I reached for the phone again, trying to pretend my fingers weren't shaking.

know what

Greg groaned, apparently finding whatever answer he was looking for in my eyes. Probably the rampant, uncontrolled confusion and fear.

"You've got to be kidding me."

Before my fingers could start tapping away on the keys, his hand closed over mine. I looked up. He was staring at me unhappily.

"All right. What's your name, idiot?"

I fought with the urge to throw his phone into the woods for a long, challenging moment.

Jon

"Nice to meet you, Jonny. When we met, you were speaking the old tongue. Where'd you learn it?"

The clicking of keys seemed far louder than it should have in the quiet.

the fuck u talking about

He sighed. "You said it's just something you do. Don't play stupid. You know what I'm talking about. What can you do, exactly?"

My fingers were frozen in place, hovering over the keys. I'd never told someone else about my oddness. No one knew but my family - my immediate family. I was supposed to keep it to myself, by their instructions, but it wasn't something I'd wanted to share regardless.

And yet, with him scowling at me and that knife waiting at the ready, I didn't know what else I could be expected to do.

i speak langages

He didn't so much as blink. "What languages?"

I snorted, through the gag.

any

"What do you mean, an-"

I was already typing.

whoever Im talking to. Their language.

"So you just walk up, and bam, there it is?"

kinda yeah.

He ran a hand through his hair, still half-shadowed. "Fucking hell. Okay. Look. There's people out there looking for us right now."

duh

My fingers were already tapping it out before I could stop myself.

He glared at me. "I saved your life. Don't bitch at me."

you got shot.

He grimaced. "Ah. Yeah."

how

"How what?"

I didn't bother typing a response. I just stared at him. He smiled crookedly back, knowing it had been a stretch. "It would be easier to show you, but….We'll just say I've got talents too."

you died

It was hard to convey my anger in a text, but I did my best. I'd seen him fall, seen his blood covering the McDonald's parking lot. That wasn't something he could just play off and pretend to be done with.

He seemed to know it too. Pinching the bridge of his nose, he sighed. "I...guess. Ok. Fine. Have you got-"

His words fell away before he could say anything else. He stood, turning in a slow circle. I shrank down into the leaves where I sat, all of the fear of earlier returning instantly. What? What did he hear? The forest was black as far as I could see in any direction, and I couldn't hear anything, but he certainly seemed to.

He turned back to me as I rose, his face beginning to pale. "Just listen. They're close. They'll know I popped out somewhere in the woods."

Popped out? I was already typing, but he shook his head violently. "Stop that. There's no time. Just...You've got something, all right? Something that makes you different. They know that now, and they want it - badly enough to do all this."

I shook my head slowly, my feet sliding away, but he grabbed my shoulder, pinning me in place. "When they're this close, they'll see it every time you use your gifts. They're watching. You need to *stop*. Withdraw, and you'll be safe."

This time he let me pull free when I tugged away from him. My eyes flickered between the dim screen of the flip phone and his face.

withdraw

?

"Jesus fucking christ," he muttered. "Pull out. Stop casting. Whatever. Stop triggering your focus. Once you do, we can talk."

how?

He groaned. "Okay. Never mind. We don't have time for this game. Just...keep your mouth shut and leave the tape on. I'm not getting shot again for you. Say a word, lead them to us, and I'll leave you behind." His eyes were fixed on mine. Somehow, I knew that leaving me to our pursuers was worse in his mind than just stabbing me and letting me bleed out. "Can you do that, Jonny?"

I nodded slowly, still unsure but without a better option. The more he said, the more he tried to explain, the more lost I was getting. That wasn't good. He was already stepping deeper into the woods, glancing around nervously. I keyed in one last message, following close behind. If I lost sight of him, I knew he'd be gone before I found him again.

thanks greg

"Gr-" he spluttered, eye twitching as he came to a stop. "Where'd you- oh. No. Don't call me Greg."

I paused, eyeing him. My brow furrowed, the confusion plain on my face.

He sighed. "It's a piece of shit name, but I had to put *something* on my ID. Not really a good disguise anymore, though, is it?"

My next message came slower, more unsure.

then what

He ran a hand through his hair, ruffling it up as he kicked at the dirt. "Aedan. You can call me Aedan."

Aedan. The fake officers had said that name. Not that that meant anything to me, but even still. I nodded cautiously, following behind as he crept through the darkness.

"We need to get out of here," he muttered. "We're straight up shit creek if they close the net. I mean, well. *You're* up shit creek." He chuckled, shaking his head.

I didn't see the humor in it.

"You've led us on quite the run, haven't you?" he muttered, turning back to the trees. "Any genius ideas? Got a four-wheeler stashed nearby?"

I chuckled, the sound muted behind his sock.

no. cars back there. thats it

His steps slowed. "You...left your car there."

I nodded, not quite sure why *that* was what he was interested in.

"With your registration in the glove box, no doubt," he said, rolling his eyes at the look on my face.

I faltered, slowing nearly to a stop before Aedan dragged me on. Shit. Shit, shit, shit. Well, maybe- maybe they wouldn't know which one was mine.

Right. Mine was just the one sitting there unlocked and waiting, with the lights on. The one that would be sitting there long after the last of the customers left for the night.

Somehow, I was pretty sure they'd figure it out.

"Got any family in the area?" he said, a more serious tone underlying the joking lilt he'd had thus far.

I grimaced. Apparently, that was enough of an answer for him. He turned away without another word.

The world spun around me. What was I supposed to do, then? Were they going to go after Keira, still waiting for a burger that wasn't coming? Would they try and wait at my apartment for me to come home? Should I run? No, no - I couldn't run and leave her behind. It wasn't going to happen.

"Keep up," Aedan snarled, glaring back at me. I flinched, left seeing only the faintest outline of him as he vanished into the night, and crept closer. His hand slid into his pocket, gripping something there. "Start thinking, Jonny."

About what? I didn't even have to type it. He chuckled humorlessly, still glaring. "You have something. Something on you *right now*. Something you never take off, until it feels like it's part of your identity. You already know what I'm talking about. Now you need to realize it - fast."

He stormed on without another word. I followed as close behind as I could, my mind racing.

They'd been looking for something too, hadn't they? Searching my pockets, checking the studs in my ears. They hadn't found anything, clearly, so apparently it wasn't my earrings.

But they'd been in a hurry. They'd been less than thorough, hadn't they?

If the criteria was 'something I kept on my person at all times', then there weren't that many options.

My hand slid to my chest, my fingers sliding over the rough surface of my jacket. It was dark enough that Aedan wouldn't see. I didn't know what he was getting at, what crazy idea had popped into his mind, but I didn't want to encourage him.

All the same....

The necklace was warm against my skin as I traced its outline, my thoughts whirling.

"Take this."

I flinched, reality returning in the span of a moment as Aedan spun on me. There was a knife in his hand. I stumbled back, tripping over a tree root.

Still trying to push myself away as I pressed a hand to my aching head, I froze. He muttered darkly to himself, stepping closer.

"Get your shit together, Jon," he hissed, crouching down. His hand

22

was out again. I blinked. It was a different knife - a second one. He wasn't threatening me. He was arming me.

I wasn't sure I liked that any more. The feeling only grew as he turned, eyeing the distant forest.

Clutching the knife to my chest, I stared, wide-eyed. My pulse thundered in my ears.

Blindingly bright, a narrow beam flicked this way and that across the woods, pausing here and there. We weren't alone. Someone was in the woods with us - or several someones. Distant still, yes.

But getting closer.

CHAPTER FOUR

The sight of the forest cast into harsh light ahead brought my mind back to a perfect, crystalline horror. They hadn't left. They were still looking - of course they were. As much as I'd hoped they'd just wander off, giving up on us, that wasn't going to happen. Even if I didn't know exactly what they were looking for, I knew they wouldn't go to all the trouble they had for no reason.

Could we run? I raised Aedan's phone, moments from starting to type, but stopped. I couldn't ask - not without the light of it putting a target on our heads. Aedan had been very clear on me not talking. And I was still holding a knife - the knife he gave me. Somehow, I didn't think he would have given me a knife if the plan was to run.

The quiet sound of leaves rustling brought my attention back front and center. He was creeping forward, slowly and carefully. I grabbed for him, my pulse thundering. What was he *doing*?

He only glanced back over his shoulder, a dark shape in the night. "Come on. Time to get a move on."

I shook my head desperately, but Aedan grinned. "What, you don't want to?"

I stared at him.

He chuckled. "If we leave, they'll just come looking for us later. These two are separated from the rest of their group. Now's our chance. Stop whining."

I wasn't whining. I had a knife I didn't know how to use, and I just wanted to go *home*. But he was already crab-walking forward, inching closer and closer to the pair. A bead of sweat dripped down the back of my neck, but I was well and truly stuck. After a moment's hesitation more, I crept after him.

The sound of their voices carried over the night air the closer we got to them.

"It's fucking *cold*," the one out front said, the flashlight in his hand sweeping across the forest around him. He had to push aside the branches to keep from whacking his head on them, muttering curses all the while. "Think you can convince Matt to just give up already?"

"No," his friend said with a chuckle. He was shorter, his frame delicate in comparison. "There's no way." I could see his hand tremble from where I crouched, half-hidden behind a tree. His eyes flicked this way and that as he scanned the woods.

"Probably right," the first said. "Have to say, I've never seen him so excited."

"Lucky us."

Aedan was continuing on, his steps soft and inaudible as he picked his way through the woods. I eyed the darkness ahead of me apprehensively. There was no way I could do that. I knew at any moment, I'd step on a stick or a pile of leaves and the game would be up.

He seemed to recognize I wasn't behind him anymore. I heard him sigh, the sound muffled and barely louder than a whisper. Before I could muster up the nerve to keep moving he'd circled back, heading straight for me.

The two men were walking right past where we crouched in the treeline, I realized. They'd missed us completely. I held my breath as they trudged past, until we were staring at their backs.

"I know these two," Aedan whispered. I flinched. He was right beside me, murmuring in my ear. "Well. One of them, anyway. Real asshole. The little guy's new."

He knew them? I swallowed my questions, glancing sidelong at him. He smirked, the expression faintly visible in the half-light left by their torches. "Big one's an elemental-type. Gravity, if I remember correctly. Let me handle him."

I could only blink. Elemental-type? That made it sound like-

"Listen," he said, his words still almost-inaudible. His hand clamped down on my shoulders. "We're special, you and I. They're special too. That's all you have to know. Focus on that." I could hear the smile in his voice. "You can hang back. Don't get yourself killed or anything. Just keep an eye on the little guy for me. I have no idea what his relic is."

Relic. That word again. I could feel the necklace hanging around my neck, its presence like a weight. Was that what I had, then? A relic, or a focus, or whatever? That was what everyone was after?

He stared at me a moment longer, as though gauging my expression. "You'll be fine," he said, a hand pressed to his lips to hide his chuckle. "Just watch my back." His eyes tightened, the smile fading from his lips. "Jon."

I nodded slowly, caught off guard by the sudden shift in his tone.

"I...don't know what contract you made. But, remember." The ghost of a smile tugged at his lips. "You're only limited by what you need, when it comes right down to it. What you ask for, and what you asked for." His hand tightened on my shoulder. "It'll provide. Trust it." He drew back, half disappearing into the dark. "I'm pretty sure speaking fancy languages isn't all you're good for."

I sat in place, completely taken aback. What exactly was he trying to say? What was he expecting? Before I could say a word or ask him to explain himself, he turned. Within moments it was just me and the forest. I was alone again.

Cover his back. Right. I eyed the two men, gripping the knife he'd given me. I could do that. Probably.

They stood side by side, bickering as they continued on their way. I stared as they went, my eyes flicking between the two of them. The little one, then. The one he'd told me to watch. He was off to one side, peering out into the trees anxiously. Slowly, carefully, I slid off into the dark, doing my best to avoid stepping on anything. I needed to get in a better position, if he was going to start something.

Finally, with one last mutter as I almost ran headlong into a tree, I eased the phone out of my pocket. They were ahead of me, and the risk of me falling flat on my face outweighed the risk of them happening to turn around unexpectedly.

Even with a light, it wasn't comfortable. I clutched my knife, my heart thundering in my ears. At any second, I knew-

I never heard him, never saw him approach. Out of nowhere, Aedan lunged at the two, holding his knife at the ready just like when he'd saved me before. I froze, adrenaline coursing through my veins as he threw himself at our pursuers.

They were every bit as caught off guard as I was. The little one didn't notice him at all, his attention too focused on the brush around them to note the insane man jumping out of the trees with a knife.

His friend noticed, but it was too late. He turned, zeroing in on the sound of approaching footsteps, but Aedan was already too close. Aedan's knife flicked out with practiced ease, cutting straight for the man's throat.

That split second of reaction time from the 'elemental type' might not have been enough to run, but it was just enough to get an arm up and in the way. The sound of his pained yelp rang out across the otherwise silent night all the same as Aedan slashed a line of red across his skin.

The elemental-type lashed out a moment later, grabbing for my new friend, but Aedan was already on the retreat. His hands closed on empty air. I heard our opponent curse, the words too quiet for me to hear. His fist clenched a moment later.

The world seemed to groan, the trees creaking perilously. I froze where I was, my heart in my throat. The forest around us trembled, like something was building under the surface.

The sound of branches snapping was the only warning we got that the moment was over. I stared, wide-eyed, as the forest in front of the man erupted into a mess of broken, collapsing trees. The limbs from overhead came crashing down in a cloud of dust onto where Aedan-

Onto where Aedan had stood a moment before. He was already running, putting distance between him and the bigger man. They had flashlights on him, following his movements - and giving him the light he needed to keep going, I realized with a crooked smile. He was circling back around, racing along a roundabout path back towards the pair.

Whatever the elemental-type was doing, he wasn't stopping. Everywhere Aedan ran, the world seemed to shiver. Branches fell a scant few feet behind him no matter where he went, along with the occasional dead tree.

My breath caught in my throat. The smaller of the two was standing stock-still, even as his friend stepped closer to Aedan. He was motionless, staring at my ally.

Aedan stumbled, shaking his head as he pressed a hand to his face. It was just a momentary hesitation, but the sound of the elemental type's chuckling rolled through the woods. It was all of the pause that he needed, apparently. Just like that, the air around Aedan shuddered - whatever was happening, it had caught up at last.

Aedan leapt forward, pushing himself even harder as he jumped clear of whatever it was, but something was wrong. His leg was caught behind him. Even as I watched, his knee hit the ground hard, as though someone had stomped on the back of his calf. With a muffled cry he tumbled, faceplanting in the dirt.

The air hummed, crackling with barely-contained energy. I pushed myself upright, rising to my feet even as the bigger man held his hand out. Lit up by the little one's flashlight, I could see the brush around Aedan flatten, pinned down by some invisible force.

A gravity type, Aedan had said. I could only stare at what I saw, my mind working through it chunk by chunk.

I'd always been different. What I did wasn't normal, and there wasn't a rational explanation for it. I really shouldn't be surprised, then, when I came face to face with something else unexplainable. All I knew was that it looked for all the world like magic - and given what I could do, the tricks I had, I wasn't able to push away the notion so easily.

Abandoning my preconceived notions about what was possible and what wasn't, my thoughts whirled in that single, frozen moment. If Aedan was right, and this guy was harnessing some sort of elemental...magic...then it really did look for all the world like gravity itself was warping out of control in the woods around him.

Even as my mind was focusing on that, my feet were moving under me. Aedan was in trouble. I couldn't just stand around and watch. The part of my mind thinking logically was shrieking, trying to put a stop to my flight, but the rest of me had already focused on the pair of men walking towards him.

"Don't kill him," the little one said. "Matt was pretty clear on that."

I tucked the phone into my pocket as I squared off, my steps gathering speed.

Aedan twitched, one eye cracking open as he glared daggers at the elemental type - who only chuckled, his fingers tensing. I could hear Aedan wheeze as the air was forced out of his lungs.

"Hey - Hey, knock it off, Paul," the little one said, faltering. "Are you listening to-"

"I'm not going to kill him," Paul said. "Fucker's cut me too many times. He's not going to die just like that." He grinned down at Aedan.

"I got faster, asshole. Nice try."

Whatever Aedan's response was, it was lost to the sound of leaves crunching under my feet as I abandoned any hopes of being stealthy. I charged, clutching the knife with my unhurt hand as I tore the tape off my mouth with the other. Aedan hadn't wanted me to give away the element of surprise by using my ability - well, the fight was on. The element of surprise was well past us, and I needed to breathe.

The two men spun, eyes going wide. I winced as their flashlights shone into my eyes, but plowed onward. They weren't expecting me. That gave me a single instant to work with.

The gravity-user was his - that's what Aedan had said. Even as I sprinted in, pushing my way clear of the trees and onto a hard-packed dirt trail, I could see him turn over, coughing for breath.

The little one was my problem.

The skinny man yelped as I bore down on him, but there was no way for him to recover in time. I gritted my teeth, pushing aside the last of my fears and doubts, and plunged my knife into his shoulder.

He screamed, grabbing at me. The sound was almost enough to ruin my resolve. I had *not* signed up for stabbing people. The two of us tumbled to the dirt and leaves, rolling. My hand was still wrapped around the knife buried in him. He grabbed for my face, trying to push me off. His eyes met mine, going unfocused.

I blinked, caught off guard by his sudden and apparent lack of resistance. Should I stop? Was he surrendering, or-

A moment later, a wave of exhaustion swept over me. I shuddered, my head drooping as my fingers slackened on the knife. I shook my head blearily, trying to blink it away, but it was persistent.

The memory of Aedan stumbling as he ran rose up in my mind. A wave of adrenaline washed through my body, overcoming the fatigue just long enough to begin piecing things together.

The little one was still looking at me. I could feel the drowsiness returning, sweeping over me again. I shook my head, desperation taking hold. He'd be armed - the rest of them were, after all. It was too dark to get a look at him or to try and find his weapon, and I was too tired. My mind was foggy. They'd said that they weren't supposed to kill Aedan. The same did not seem to apply to me.

Grasping at the fleeting tendrils of my awareness, I pulled the knife free. Droplets of blood splattered across my other hand, turning my stomach. I didn't care. Even as the blade came free I twisted the hand that was buried in his shirt. My still-broken finger screamed at the motion, erupting into searing agony all over again. The waves of fresh pain were enough to banish the last dregs of my opponent's magic.

He'd been trying to kill me. I seized on the fact, even as I raised my borrowed knife over my head. He squirmed, trying to pull free, but I wasn't about to let him go. With one last indrawn breath, muscles tensing, I-

The concussive blast hit me hard. I gasped, the knife sliding from my fingers as an inexorable force slammed into my shoulders. Before I could so much as twitch I was flat on the ground, my once-victim pinned under me.

It was like being at the bottom of a lake, with the weight of the world on my shoulders. The air itself felt thick - or maybe it was just my lungs, fighting for every breath I could get.

"P-Paul," the man under me gasped, trapped just as surely in whatever this was. I couldn't see him - I was blinded by the light in my eyes. The gravity-worker stalked towards us, muttering under his breath. His other hand was a dark shape in the dim light, palm-down and out to the side.

"Sorry, Jake," he said, chuckling. "Warned you - crew's hard on first-timers, and that was awful sloppy. We'll make sure your focus goes to a good home." His head swiveled this way and that as he spoke. He was good, I realized. Even while he killed us, he wasn't going to lose track of his surroundings.

The man under me - *Jake* twitched. I could feel him trying to speak, trying to force words out of lungs that no longer had air in them. It was useless. The pressure was building moment by moment, straining until I could hear my joints cracking. I felt around desperately with my suddenly-free hand. Jake had a gun, *somewhere*. He had to. Maybe if I found it, I could do something.

I knew it was probably hopeless, but I had to try anyway.

The pressure lifted in an instant when Aedan lunged out of the shadows again, jumping onto the gravity-user's back. Screams split the night as he buried his knife in the crook of Paul's neck. The air shimmered around the two of them as the bigger man pulled at his power instinctively, still reaching for Aedan. Aedan clung to him with every twist and flinch, pulling the knife free and driving it back into his chest.

I could see his satisfied grin from across the distance, illuminated in the shadow of a dropped light. The gravity-user couldn't cast properly - not with Aedan clinging to his neck, not with a knife stuck in him.

Jake thrashed under me, his eyes wide and terrified. I blinked, coming back to reality in the same instant that he threw me off with a burst of adrenaline-fueled energy.

I rolled clear, coughing for breath.

Jake wasn't wasting any time. Even as he gasped he was staggering back, reaching into his jacket. Blood had soaked into his shoulder where I'd cut him. It had to hurt, but he didn't seem to notice.

My hand closed around the hilt of my dropped knife at the same moment he pulled his gun free. I stared, the world falling away as he swung it towards me.

My legs screamed, too-tired and aching as they gathered underneath me. I was rising, straightening, but he was faster. He had distance, he was more prepared than me, and he had a gun. He knew it, too. I could see from the victorious light in his half-shadowed eyes that he knew he had me.

All the same, I had to try. None of this made sense, despite the pieces that were beginning to fall into place. And there was no *way* I was going to roll over and die before I got some answers.

Something inside me hummed gently as I stood, feet breaking into a run. It burned, like embers lighting on a gentle breeze. All of my attention was fixated on Jake - on the gun he held in his hands, the barrel trembling as he leveled it in my direction.

I could see it. I could see all of it, the way his chin lifted, the tightness in his wrist. The ragged breath he took, solidifying as his lips pressed together into an obstinate line. The way his barrel veered away a fraction of an inch as he squeezed.

Now.

I lunged, throwing myself to the side as something in my mind screamed. My arm exploded into pain. A line of fire tore across it, burning brightly even as my ears rang with the sound of the shot.

My mind was blank, dumbfounded by what had just happened. I had no *idea* what had just happened, actually, but I didn't have the time to ponder through it. Jake's eyes widened as I hurtled towards him. Clearly, he'd been just as surprised by my sudden dodge as I was.

For the second time in as many minutes, we fell hard to the ground. His back arched as he swallowed a cry, my knife digging deep into his arm. His fingers quivered, resisting a moment, but I gritted my teeth, twisting the blade. The gun fell from his hand as he screamed.

Any reservations I'd had about killing him had vanished somewhere in the flood of adrenaline pouring through my veins. He'd tried to *shoot* me. People kept trying to kill me, and I didn't fucking deserve that. I'd just wanted to get some dinner, and here I was in the forest, covered in blood and with some asshole shooting a gun at me.

He struggled when I pulled my knife clear again, shaking his head. His eyes were wild, wide and afraid. I didn't care. My hand was on fire, my arm was on fire, and he'd been trying to kill me. I was done. With one clean motion I raised the blade, muscles tense, and-

"Hold on, there," someone said. I flinched as a hand wrapped around my wrist, holding me in place before I could finish the job. I glanced back over my shoulder.

Aedan grinned. He was covered in dirt and more than a little blood, but seemed well enough.

Paul's body lay still and unmoving on the ground behind him. I stared. In the patchy light, I could see Aedan's knife sticking from the dead man's eye.

"Think I might have gone overboard with that one," he said, actually managing to sound chagrined.

Jake thrashed under me, still squirming. Aedan didn't look down, didn't react at all. He just put his foot on the man's still-bleeding shoulder, leaning over until the man froze, whimpering.

"Well. Anyway. See, I think we need to talk to one of them, and Paul's a no-go. So, looks like Sleepy here's up," he said, smiling crookedly.

I swallowed hard. Aedan chuckled, patting me on the shoulder.

"Besides, I think you could use some answers."

CHAPTER FIVE

It was amazing, really.

I'd only been out here for, what, an hour? Two? Less than half a day before, I'd been going about my business, doing the things a normal college-grad kid did. The high point of my night would probably have been sitting down in front of the TV with a beer - maybe something stronger, if I was feeling *really* adventurous.

So little time had actually passed, and yet, my mind was treating all of this as...well, not *normal*, but I was coping a bit better. The fact that there was a man on the ground in front of me, bleeding and hurt with my new friend standing on his wound, didn't shock me the way it should have. The fact that there was another man lying dead a few paces away should have sent me screaming from the clearing.

But those few hours that had passed were important ones, dammit. And with things beginning to quiet down for god only knew how long, my mind focused in on Aedan's words like a beacon in the night.

"Answers, please," I said, nodding vigorously.

He chuckled. "Right. Well, then, *Jake*." He crouched down, sliding his standard issue no-skid shoe free of the man's arm. The man whimpered, shuddering in pain at the motion. Aedan didn't seem to notice. "You good and awake? Ready to chat?"

"Fucking *hell*," Jake said, his eyes flicking up to Aedan's.

Aedan chuckled. "Good. Glad to hear it, Jake." He glanced over to me, his eyes dipping to the dark, shadowed shape of the gun lying in the leaves. "Come on, Jon. Don't litter. It's rude."

33

I gaped for a single second, staring at him, but he only jerked his chin towards the gun. His intent was clear.

I really, really didn't want to have my fingerprints all over a gun. Not with the trail of bodies we were beginning to leave. Every fiber of my being screamed that this was a horrible, horrible idea.

But every second I waited, he looked a little more irritated. His eyes narrowed as I hesitated.

I picked up the gun, settling it into my hand gingerly. My finger burned still, aching. I tried to ignore it, to mixed results.

I'd shot rifles before - I'd been in the Boy Scouts just like every other kid in town - but pistols were new. Pistols were for killing people. I mean, sure, Jake had tried to shoot me, and I could understand Aedan wanting to make sure he was as under-control as we could make him. I *did* feel a little better, knowing I had a gun of my own just in case those other crazy assholes came back.

I still didn't like it.

"Bet you already know what I'm going to ask, don't you, Jake?" Aedan said. His tone was bright and cheerful, but there wasn't a trace of good humor in his smile.

I could see Jake swallow hard as I stepped away, going for one of the flashlights they'd dropped. Paul's body was a dark mass alongside me, one I was doing my best to pretend didn't exist.

"I-I...I don't-"

"Come on," Aedan snapped, his voice losing all of its friendliness abruptly enough that a shiver ran down my spine. "You tracked us to that shithole, didn't you? I'm not stupid."

"L-Look, I just joined, and-"

"Where are they?"

I stepped up beside Aedan, trying to watch as closely as I could without looking too eager. He was still crouched down alongside Jake, who had clearly figured out that lying still was better than trying to run. Aedan had pulled another knife from somewhere - I had no idea how many of the things he'd stashed on his person, and I really didn't want to know.

Jake swallowed hard. "They're n-not really..." He shook his head. "There's no one..."

"Who, now?" I said quietly, glancing between Aedan and Jake. "What's going on?"

Aedan sighed, glaring up at me. "It's simple, Jonny."

"It's Jon."

If Aedan heard me, he didn't so much as hesitate. "There's a whole cluster of these fuckers, right?" He raised one hand, ticking off fingers. "You've met Paul there. Jake. Dan and Christian, back at the store - and Matt." He grinned. "Can't forget Matt, can we?"

I eyed him. "What do you mean?"

"Matt's been on my ass for almost five years now," Aedan said, rolling his eyes dramatically. "Guy just can't let it go. Doesn't know when to quit. Thought he'd give up after the last time he sent his thugs after me - I cleaned his crew out just to be sure." His nose wrinkled as he eyed Paul's body. "Well. I *thought* I cleaned him out."

"Yeah, still not making sense," I muttered.

Jake snorted from his place on the ground. "Holy shit, man. Never pictured you as the type to shepherd a new-blood. Stories really didn't-"

Aedan cast me a tolerant look, even as his foot tamped down on the man's arm. Jake shuddered, hissing in pain. "Yeah, well. Shit happens, Jake." He glanced back up at me. "Anyway. It's simple, Jonny. These guys keep following me. That means they have to have some way of finding where I am - and unfortunately for you, you were unlucky enough to get caught in their net too."

I leaned back, my stomach churning. That much had been obvious. They'd only been interested in Aedan, after all, until they got that phone call. From-

"Recon," I said abruptly, my eyes snapping over to Jake. "They said Recon told them it was me."

"Yup," Aedan said, grinning again. We'd both seen the way Jake's face had hardened, his guard rising. "They always have one - a finder. Someone who can distill the information they need." He tapped Jake's knee with his free hand. Jake shuddered. "Try and run without taking out the finder, well." He shrugged. "You won't be getting too far."

"So you want to know where they are," I said, nodding slowly. "So we can-" I stopped, the words dying on my lips.

Great. More killing. Just what I wanted.

"Relax, Jonny. You're going to be fine," Aedan said, chortling.

"I can't go to jail," I mumbled, shaking my head. "I can't-"

"No one's going to *jail*," he said, laughter rippling through his voice. "Calm the fuck down."

"How can you say that, when-"

"Where are they, Jake?" he said, ignoring me completely.

Jake swallowed hard. He was trembling, more than just from pain. "Can't. They'll-"

"That Paul guy already tried to kill you, didn't he?" I interrupted, the memory flashing into my mind. Me, on top of Jake - and both of us being slowly crushed by gravity, like an invisible hand slamming into my back. "What, you're worried they're going to take it out on you?"

"Kid's right, Jake," Aedan said, nodding. Again, with the kid thing. I glared at his back, but knew it wasn't exactly the time to argue it. The man continued on, completely unaware of the look I was giving him. "Seems like they already decided you're not up to snuff. Your relic will be easy pickings for them, don't you think?"

"I- That's-" Jake started, but the fight slipped out of him almost immediately. He wilted like a flower, letting his head fall back into the dirt and leaves. "*Assholes.*"

Aedan shrugged. "Pretty much. Not really worth protecting - and, I might remind you that they're not here." The knife in his hand scraped against the dirt idly. "We *are*. Pick your battles, Jake."

The man eyed us a moment longer, tight-drawn and trembling. "Fine. Sure. Fuck 'em," he finally said, the words falling out of him in a rush. "Just- I'll tell you what you want, okay? And then-"

"We'll see," Aedan said.

Jake's eyes tightened, like he was thinking about arguing the point, but he drooped again a moment later. "Okay. Yeah. Recon's set up in a truck. She was supposed to stay just outside the park, ready to go if she felt you pop up somewhere else."

Aedan stared at him, expressionless. "You can do better than that, Jake."

Jake swallowed. "R-Right. Uh. Well. That way," he said, pointing out into the darkness after a moment's hesitation. "I think, anyway. East side, there's-"

"There's a little parking lot there," I said quietly, glancing at Aedan. "For the trailhead. You know. A trash can, water fountain."

"I know what a trailhead is," he said. I could *hear* him roll his eyes, even if he didn't look back at me. "How's she work, Jake?"

"I-I don't know," he said shaking his head violently. "Really. I don't. They wouldn't even tell us her name."

His back arched as Aedan leaned on his shoulder again, a pained gasp slipping out of him. "P-Please! I'm serious! I don't know!"

"Aedan," I said, staring at Jake as my pulse thundered in my ears. "Stop it."

"He might be-"

"He's telling the truth, ok?" I said, tearing my eyes off him. "So lay off."

Aedan eyed me sidelong. "Jon, look. The world is an ugly place, and I know you-"

"Just trust me, all right?" I snapped, glaring at him. "Move on." I didn't know why I was so confident on the matter - something about the tension in every line of Jake's body, the sheer terror and pain in his eyes...I knew he wasn't lying, and I couldn't bear to see Aedan hurt him right in front of me.

My new friend hesitated a moment longer - and then he drew back ever so slightly. Jake licked his lips, his gaze flitting between the two of us.

"Who's she got with her, then?" Aedan said, tapping his knife against the ground impatiently. "I know Matt's probably breathing down her neck, but he can't be-"

"She's got a bodyguard," Jake said hurriedly, as though he was trying to reinforce how helpful he was being. "Came with her. Uh. Name's Clark. H-He's an energy-shifter."

My mouth was hanging open, I just knew. Aedan glanced back at me, a smile tugging at his lips. "A healer," he said. "Usually. Or a vampire."

"Don't let him touch you," Jake said, grinning uneasily. His humor died as Aedan turned back to him with a glare.

"And has Matt-"

"Oh, uh, Matt's not there," Jake said, reddening gently as he interrupted Aedan.

Aedan stopped, freezing in place. For once, he actually looked surprised. "What, now?"

"Matt's not-"

"I heard you the first time," Aedan snapped. "Jesus fucking Christ. After what I did to his finder the *last* time he rode my back, he's leaving this one out to hang in the breeze? *Why?* What's so important that he's run off?"

Jake faltered, brow furrowing as he tried to piece together an answer. "W-Well, he said there was somewhere in town he wanted to check out. Thought you might have a backup plan, since you had an ally this time."

"An al-" Aedan began, pinching the bridge of his nose. "Fuck. Great. No, this asshat's not my ally."

"Matt seemed to think he was," Jake said softly.

"Where did he go?" I heard myself say. The words sounded hollow, like it was someone else speaking. "Where is he?"

"Said there was an apartment on the outskirts of-"

"Eastwood Cove?" I said, interrupting him. "4811, unit-"

"I don't know," Jake said, beginning to whine. "Something like that. Didn't really hear."

Aedan was watching me. "You *did* leave your car right where-"

"*Fuck*," I said, running my hand through my hair. "Jesus. I- What does he want?"

"He's probably going to toss your apartment to see if you've got anything on me," Aedan said, his voice oddly gentle. "I'm sorry. It's a pain, but it'll be fine."

"It's not *fine*," I snapped. "I have a roommate. God *damn* it, Aedan."

He paused. "A roommate."

"My little sister," I said, shaking my head. The panic was rising hot and furious with every second that passed. Shit. It was bad enough that my whole world had been thrown into chaos by the events of the night. I didn't have words to express exactly how little I'd wanted to be assaulted and attacked and to have fingers broken and to be shot at.

All of my anger at the matter was a pale shadow of the rage that blossomed at the thought that the people who did that were really in my apartment - that they were in my apartment with *Keira*. It had seemed like a bad dream before that. Horrifying, but unlikely. All of that had changed in a single second.

"Well....shit," Aedan muttered. "Let's pick up the pace then, shall we?"

"You think?" I snapped.

"All right, Jake," Aedan said, turning away from me. "Let's see. You already told me where your finder is, I already know Matt's a dick..." He paused, lips pursing as he seemed to stew on things in his head. "How'd you guys find me, anyway?"

I glared at him, all of my patience gone. "You just explained to me-"

"Their finder would have sealed the deal," he interrupted, looking back over his shoulder. "If there's a finder out there that could track me across the continent, I'd have heard of them by now."

"Y-You're not exactly hard to find," Jake said, stammering again. "H-He's been tracking rumors and reports going out from the passive finders whose territories you've crossed."

Aedan's scowl deepened. "See, I'm pretty sure I made certain-"

"Rumors said you went south to cross the border into Mexico," Jake said. "When Matt heard that, he turned the crew north. Took a little bit, but..." He shrugged. "Found the trail again."

Why was Aedan such a big deal? I stared at the back of his head, my eyes boring holes in his skull. I filed it away as yet another question that needed an answer - but if Keira was in danger, I couldn't very well wait for him to get around to giving me one. With how things had gone, it would take days to get a straight answer out of him.

"Right. Last thing, then," Aedan said, patting his knee. "Relic. Now."

Jake stiffened, going pale. "No."

Aedan *snarled*. Actually growled at the man. "Fucking hell, Jake, I do not have time for your bullshit. Show me your relic, right now."

The man's jaw was set stubbornly, even though his lip was trembling. "N-No. I won't. I don't want to-"

"Just *give* it to me," Aedan hissed, lunging for the man. Jake rolled, covering his head. I watched the two wrestle, my mind racing still.

"Both of you stop right *now*," I finally bellowed, my voice echoing through the darkened forest. "We don't have *time* for this."

They froze, as though my voice had shocked the fight right out of them.

"Jake. No one is going to hurt you. Right, Aedan?"

Aedan hesitated, shoulders rising as my eyes settled on him. "Now, Jon, you have to understand. He's seen me. I can't-"

"I-I won't tell anyone," Jake said, pushing himself away from my newfound ally. "Serious. I won't. Dead silent. I didn't even want to chase you in the first place."

A humorless grin tugged at Aedan's lips. "Right."

"I'm serious," Jake said, shaking his head. "It's Matt's game, not mine. I-I didn't want to wind up- you know. Like all the rest. Dead. I-If you just let me go, I'll never tell a *soul*."

Aedan twirled his knife, settling his hand around the hilt at last. "I'm sure. If you won't give it to me, then I'll-"

"Aedan, let him be," I snapped, one foot tapping anxiously.

The man paused, his arm relaxing, and glanced back over his

shoulder. "Oh?"

"I think we can trust him," I said. "Stop killing everyone. He said he won't tell - he won't."

"You think?" Aedan said. I would have expected the words to be sarcastic, and there was definitely that rough, abrasive tone to his voice, but there was also a sincerity there I hadn't expected.

I eyed Jake again, hesitating a long moment before finally looking back to Aedan. "I think. Come on. We don't have time for-"

"All right. Jon says you're cool," Aedan said, tapping his knife against Jake's leg. "How about you just *show* it to me, like I asked, and we'll see about letting you walk away with it at the end of the night?"

Jake froze. "W-What....really?"

"Hurry the fuck *up*," I spat.

He burst into action, as though my words had snapped him back to wakefulness. His hand snapped over, pushing his sleeve up until we could see-

A bracelet. That was all - a bracelet, wrought from silver chain and gold discs. Was that it, then? A relic, or a focus? That was what all of this was about?

I realized my fingers were brushing against my necklace again. Was all this because of a stupid necklace? Really? What were they, exactly?

"Let me see it," Aedan said, his fingers wiggling with impatience.

Jake hesitated. "I don't-"

"I'll give it back."

Jake still didn't look happy about it, but Aedan had a knife, after all. Slowly, cautiously, he held his hand out.

Aedan had the bracelet off and in his grasp in an instant.

I straightened, glaring at him. "So now what-"

"Quiet," Aedan breathed, not taking his eyes off the piece of jewelry in his hands. Jake watched him, lips tight and arms crossed.

For a long, still moment, there was only the quiet sound of the forest around us.

And then Aedan crumpled, just a little bit. "Damn."

I resisted the urge to stamp my foot. "Are we about done here?"

Aedan thrust the bracelet back into Jake's hands. "We're done," he said sourly.

Jake blinked, surprise written across his face. "W-What? That's it?"

"Get out of here before I change my mind," Aedan said, pushing himself upright. "If I hear a single word about anything that happened here tonight, I'll know."

"No, no," Jake said, shaking his head so hard I thought he might hurt himself. "Not a word! Really. Not a word. Not one." He pulled his sleeve down even as he stepped away. His eyes darted to the gun I still held in my hand, but he seemed to know better than to ask for it back.

Aedan and I stared as he vanished into the night. He didn't look back.

"So…" I began, glancing sidelong at him, but he groaned, running a hand back and forth through his hair.

"Fuck."

I stopped, waiting, but he didn't say anything for the longest time. Finally, right when my impatience was ready to burst again, he glared at me. "Come on. We'll have a quick lesson."

I furrowed my brow, confused, but he was already walking - towards Paul's body.

"Aedan, hurry up. We have to-"

"Get *over* here," he snapped, already crouching down.

We should be moving. Sitting down was not what I wanted to be doing. Sitting down next to a dead guy was the very *last* thing I wanted to be doing, in fact. But he had that irritated, stubborn look on his face, like he was on the edge of exploding again.

I sat down.

"Right. Crash course in relics," he said, spitting the words out as fast as he could. "They're all different, each and every one."

"And they give us *magic*," I said, resisting the urge to snort.

Aedan glanced over at me. "Well, something like that. It's a crude comparison, but sure. It's very straightforward, Jonny."

"Jon."

"They're old, see. Very old. And they have a way of changing the people who bond with them."

"Bond," I said dryly.

He smiled crookedly. "Right. It's a matter of finding a relic a person is compatible with - past that, it's all up to what the person wants, and what their relic can provide."

"So, what," I said. My hand was trembling. I was high enough on adrenaline that even my broken finger was quiet. "This Paul guy has some sort of gravity charm?"

"Probably," Aedan said, reaching for the dead guy's hand. I drew back, cringing as he lifted his arm. "For Paul here, anyway. Someone else, maybe...fuck, I don't know. Maybe it would have made people depressed or something. But for Paul it was gravity." He pointed to Paul's hand. I didn't need the help. I could already see the fat, ugly gold ring squeezed around one of his meaty fingers.

"And that's it," I said.

Aedan grinned, reaching for the ring. "Pretty much. You get one relic, kid. That's the one big rule of the world. It changes you - try for two, and you'll just break."

"And you think mine is something about languages."

He pursed his lips, struggling with the man's finger. "Probably? It's not an exact science, and what you put in determines what you get out. So, yeah. Probably. But, more important than *that*..." His words died as he tugged, furrowing his brow.

"What exactly do you think is more important than-"

The ring came free with a pop, flying free of the man's skin all at once. Aedan landed on his ass, wincing, but hardly seemed to notice. He was too busy staring down at the ring, lost in his own thoughts.

I had other things on my mind - staring at Paul's body in horrified fascination, for one. The instant the ring had left his skin, his whole form had...shuddered. Shivered. And now it almost looked like-

I inched closer, eyes widening. No, it didn't just *look* like it. There were...cracks. Spreading across his body like wildfire.

"Damn," Aedan said, making like he was going to throw the ring aside before stopping himself. Almost absentmindedly, he started digging through his backpack.

"Uh," I managed, seeing the cracks deepen.

He glanced up, a crooked smile touching his lips again. "Right. So. Watch close. Once you've bonded with a relic, or a focus, or whatever you kids are calling them these days, it's done. Permanent. No take-backsies."

Something was happening. He was...Paul was *glowing*, like there was a faint magenta light down at his core finally revealed by the cracks running through his body.

"What the *hell* is-"

"It changes you, Jonny. You can't un-change. And if the owner and relic are split for too long-"

Paul *shattered*. I fell over myself in my need to get away, gasping as his form just crumbled in front of my eyes. Within seconds, the fragments of...of *him* were falling apart further, until he was just a pile of rapidly dispersing dust.

"Any questions?" Aedan said.

I glanced over to him, wide-eyed and staring. Questions? Did I have *questions*? "What the *hell* just happened? Is that going to happen to me? What the *fuck*, Aedan?"

"Calm down," he said with a sigh. He was pulling something from the depths of his bag - a box, steel-sided and utilitarian, maybe a hand's breadth across on each side. It looked heavy, more than anything else. He pulled the top free, tossing the ring inside a moment later and closing it right back up. "You'll be fine. A collapse only happens if you're separated from your relic for long enough for your bond to decay, or if you die. It'll happen eventually, after the wielder passes. We just sped the process up a little by separating them."

"B-But you took Jake's and he didn't-"

"You're not going to die the moment you stop touching it," he snapped, glaring at me as he zipped his bag back up. "Don't be stupid. Normally it would take a couple of days. Maybe two, three."

"Oh, that's so much better," I hissed, doing my best not to scream.

"Would you calm down?" Aedan said, standing. Paul was already mostly gone. Now I knew why he wasn't worried about going to jail. There wouldn't be any evidence of a crime in the first place. "Do you want to stay here, freaking out, or do you want to go take care of things?"

Keira. My mind latched onto her like a life raft keeping me afloat in the shitstorm things had become. Before I even realized I was moving I was on my feet, still glaring daggers at him.

"Fine. Let's get moving," I said, spitting each word out. "But keep talking. You're not done yet."

He chuckled, shaking his head. "Yes, yes. All right. So." He glanced out into the dark, gripping his knife again.

I waited patiently as he stared out into the night, his mind clearly working through something. As much as I wanted to be moving, to *go*, I knew we had to be smart about things. Finally, he nodded.

"Here's what we're going to do."

CHAPTER SIX

"No."

"I wasn't asking, Jon. I was telling."

I glared at him, tight-lipped. "Fuck you, Aedan. No. We're going to-"

"Calm down and think about this rationally for two seconds, Jon," Aedan snapped.

"I *am* thinking about-"

"Jon."

My jaw shut with an audible clack as I fell into a furious, fuming silence.

Aedan smiled gently. "You need to stop freaking out. I know you're worried, but your sister will be fine. Just fine. Trust me."

"You can't possibly say something like that."

He straightened with a sigh. "What good is killing her going to do, exactly?"

"I don't fucking know," I said, spitting the words out. "Maybe they're just pissed off."

"She's worth more to them as a hostage," he said, hands spread placatingly. "They wouldn't just get rid of her like that. Right now we know where their finder is - but not for long. Once she moves, we're back to square one."

"I-" I started, but stopped. What he was saying made *sense*. It didn't make me like it. "I'm not just going to play around while they're hurting her," I said instead, my chin raising stubbornly.

Aedan grinned crookedly. "Think of it this way. Recon's got a truck. That's what Jake there said, right?"

"...Right," I mumbled.

"Well, just think of how much faster we'll get to your place with some wheels." His hand slapped my back, not unkindly. "Come on, Jonny."

"Jon," I grumbled halfheartedly, still completely unsatisfied with his answer, but when he jogged off into the dark, I followed.

My heart pounded in my ears as we slipped through the woods, our path lit by the dim light of our flashlights. The shadows were thick around us, smothering the sound until we were wrapped in a cocoon within the night, totally alone. I was just *sure* that someone was waiting behind every tree, pointing a gun my way or ready to spew fire from their hands. I'd meet some horrible, gruesome end, and that'd be that.

"Am I going the right way?" Aedan said, pulling me out of my thoughts.

I jumped. "Uh. What?"

He glared at me. "Jake there said their finder was at a trailhead. Are we going the right way? Does any of this look familiar?" He swiveled his stolen flashlight, aiming it out into the forest around us. "He was pointing this way, but even still-"

"Y-Yeah. Yeah," I said, gaining a bit of confidence as I eyed the woods. "I think, anyway."

Aedan snorted, shaking his head. "You think. Great."

"I'm pretty sure," I said darkly. I was. We were walking on a trail by then, not stomping through the leaves and branches, and that meant we were getting close. The forest looked...familiar. That didn't mean a whole lot, but it was all I had to work with.

"Fine."

The silence stretched on between the two of us as we slipped closer. We were probably headed the right direction, but there was still a ways to go. The longer the quiet pressed on, the more paranoid I could feel myself getting.

Finally, when I couldn't take it anymore, I cleared my throat.

Aedan glanced back at me, eyes narrowed. "What *now*?"

The question I was going to ask died at the irritation on his face. I glared at him instead. "What, going to stuff another sock into my mouth?"

He groaned. "What do you *want*?"

"I mean, it's a valid question," I muttered. "You were freaking out about me talking a few minutes ago. Why aren't you now?"

"A few minutes ago, their finder didn't know where we were," Aedan said, shrugging. "I'm pretty sure they do now. And besides." He locked eyes with me for a moment before continuing on. "Most finders, they can't look at something like what just happened without being blinded. Too many powers get used in close quarters, it's just...overload." He shrugged again. "Most finders."

"So, to you, I'm still talking in some other language?"

"Hurry the hell up."

I shut up, quickening the pace until I was right behind him. But I couldn't help it. My mind was going crazy, churning through everything new that I'd had thrown at me that night. One thing still stood out over all the rest, screaming for my attention.

"Aedan?"

I heard him sigh, heavy with frustration. "What."

"What's *your* ability?"

"My relic."

"Yeah. That."

I counted the seconds as we picked our way on, the seconds of silence as he chewed on my question. With every moment my confusion grew. It wasn't that hard a question.

"Let's...just worry about getting through this, all right?" he said at last.

I scowled. "What? That's bullshit. You got shot."

"I didn't-"

"I *saw* you."

He conceded the point with a halfhearted nod. "A little."

"A-" I spluttered. "A little? How do you get shot a *little*? Would you stop-"

"If I start going into it, you're going to have questions," he snapped, eyes narrowed against the light. "We don't have time for all that bullshit, and I don't have time for you to try all the stupid shit you're going to want to."

"What do you mean, try something-"

"Everyone always does," he muttered. "Come on. Hurry the hell up. I think we're almost there."

I could see the trees thinning out around us, but it wasn't enough. He hadn't told me *anything* - in fact, I had more questions after his little subject-dodge than I'd had before. "Can you at least tell me-"

He spun on his heel in an instant, his hand covering my mouth even as he pulled both of us to the ground. I flinched, caught off guard, but knew better than to fight. I'd seen how Aedan operated, and didn't think he'd have many qualms about taking me out if I became a burden to his own chances.

"Quiet, now," he breathed, inches from my ear. I bobbed my head in a nod, understanding what he was saying - be quiet, *and* don't talk. Something was wrong.

The sound of leaves crunching was almost deafening in the anxious quiet. I lifted my head an inch, peering out into the dark.

We'd made it. The sight of the trailhead - and the truck parked in the lot - was an almost palpable relief. We'd made it in time. I could see two shadowed figures in the dim light of the cab. That would be that finder woman, then, and her bodyguard.

A shiver went down my spine. If that was the finder and the bodyguard, who was the man strolling idly through the woods at the edge of the parking lot?

"Fucking Jake," Aedan muttered under his breath.

I swallowed hard, staring at the third man - the man who wasn't supposed to be here. Had Jake lied? Had I been wrong about him? Or had he simply not known? Maybe plans had changed on their end. The why didn't really matter. What were we going to do now?"

"We can still slip away," I said, keeping my voice to a near-whisper. "Get back out to the road, hitch a ride or walk or something. It's not really *close*, but my apartment isn't-"

"The truck is what matters," Aedan said, no hesitation at all in his voice as he gathered his legs under him. "One of these assholes is the vamp. The other one...well, I don't know." He glanced at me sidelong. "One more round, then. Still got that gun?"

My finger throbbed as I wrapped my hand around the grip, but yes, it was still tucked into my waistband. I pulled it free, trying to pretend like my hands weren't trembling, and nodded.

"Good. Good," he said, patting my shoulder reassuringly. "See, you'll be fine. Just stop the truck from leaving, and I'll be right there."

I opened my mouth to argue further, but he was already sliding his knife from his pocket. I stared. Well, Paul hadn't had a gun, I supposed, but exactly how many people was Aedan expecting to go all Jack the Ripper on in one night?

47

"I-I don't know if I can-"

"I'll get you past the guy at the treeline, all right?" Aedan said, flashing me a grin that was probably supposed to be comforting. It just looked crazed to me. "Just keep them here. You've got this, Jonny."

I *had* been a little worried about how I was supposed to get by the guy, but I was *more* concerned about how I was supposed to stop two freaks in a truck - a way that didn't involve killing anyone, ideally. That would be just fucking great.

Before I could say another word, Aedan was moving, jogging casually towards the new guy. I was out of time.

"Who the- Nate!" the guard bellowed. I could see the two in the truck snap to attention, their heads swiveling as they searched for the new threat.

"What's that?"

"It's them! Get clear!"

The sound of the truck's engine starting echoed around the trailhead. I had one chance. Before I really knew what was happening, I was sprinting, dodging trees and bushes as I burst into the gravel parking lot.

The truck's transmission thudded hollowly as the man behind the wheel - Nate? - threw it into gear. His eyes danced between Aedan and his companion - and the road ahead. He squared off, turning away from them as he focused.

My mind wasn't involved in my decision-making at that point. If it were, it would have told me exactly how stupid I was being. This was a bad plan, a horrible plan, something that was going to get me killed. But as little as I knew about fighting, I knew a few things about people.

And no one wants to hit something.

As the driver's eyes snapped back to the road, I threw myself in front of the truck. My hands slapped down hard on the metal hood, palms flat as I stared wide-eyed into the windshield. If I was wrong, if he didn't react like I thought he would, he'd-

"Shit!" I heard him scream, slamming on the brakes as his instincts kicked in. The truck hadn't even really been moving, but the whole frame shuddered as what little momentum it had was stopped in its tracks. A bead of sweat dripped down my back. The grill was pressed into my chest - but I was still alive. That had to mean something.

The woman in the seat next to him stared back at me from behind delicate glasses, her eyes narrowed. She didn't seem afraid at all - just a

48

bit surprised.

With every heartbeat that passed, I knew that Nate there was going to figure things out. He'd realize that I was Aedan's ally and the people they were trying to run from - and he'd run me over without a second thought. I had to- I had to stop them before that.

These were the people trying to hurt me. The ones who had Keira. They weren't innocent. They'd put themselves in the position where it was them or me - and I wouldn't give in so easily.

As the truck revved, I hurled myself to the side. I'd jump clear, a-and do what I had to, and-

I fell like a rock as the front corner of the truck slid past me. My world spun as I hit the ground hard, gasping for the breath that was knocked clear of me.

He smirked down from the truck window at me, two fingers raised. He wasn't revving the truck anymore. It purred along quietly, idling.

I tried to push myself upright again, but something had me.

"Nice try," I heard him say, over the sound of the country music on his radio. "Stay there."

His face was growing more pale by the second, but I could feel it - and see it, when I raised my head the few inches I needed.

The gravel underneath me had erupted into roots, tendrils and vines spreading out of the ground like some sort of jungle resurgence. They threaded their way between the stones, wrapping my limbs like a web.

People kept trying to break me. First gravity, now this? And I had, what, some vaguely unusual skills with languages? What a crock.

My thoughts stilled as the first vines crept up the sides of my neck. I thrashed, shaking them free as quickly as they grew, but they were relentless. My leg was hopelessly caught, pinning me in place, and my torso wasn't far behind. The weight of it on my ribs was fast becoming unbearable.

With the icy rush of adrenaline casting my world into quiet stillness, I reached over with my still-free left hand, tearing at the plants spreading across my other arm. My fingers ached with every rip and shred. I could feel the skin splitting around my nails. It didn't matter.

Any hesitation I might have had burned away as my arm swung up, clearing the vines and roots growing around me just enough to level my pistol at the driver's side window.

His eyes widened, the smile falling from his lips in a single, breathless moment. He hadn't seen the gun - of course he hadn't. It was

49

dark, and with everything *they* could do, he'd probably expected me to fall back on my ability. No one would expect a universal translator to jump headlong into a firefight.

The roar of the gun going off filled my ears with the dead, lifeless sound of ringing, wiping the sounds of the night away. The light was blinding in the dark, sending me reeling.

I'd seen him fall back, though, the window shattering between us. He was bellowing something, his arms thrown up around his face. I hadn't hit him, then. Not entirely surprising, given my position on the ground and utter lack of skill with a pistol, but I would have preferred to finish it quickly.

The vines around me fell away as their owner flinched, too caught up in his own pain and fear to control them properly. I seized the chance I was given, jumping upright before he could regain his composure. Aedan bounded about in the corner of my vision, dancing around his opponent like a man possessed. He didn't *need* a gun, I realized. That was his secret, the reason people kept underestimating him. He seemed to have pieced together that he was fighting Clark, the foretold bodyguard. Good.

The bloodied mess I'd left of Nate's shoulder seemed to have finally settled the matter, I saw as I turned back to him. He fumbled with the column, trying to set it into gear, but his hands were shaking. He must have wanted to hang around and savor the kill - right up until I'd stolen it from him. More likely he'd wanted my focus, I thought sourly. Joke's on him.

With my ribs still aching from his grip and the feel of his vines on my neck still fresh in my mind, I didn't feel any guilt at all about leveling the pistol at him. Fuck him. Fuck him and his friends, the ones who'd done all of this. If it was them or me, I chose me.

I'd missed before - when I was on the ground, half-wrapped in vines and gasping for air. That wasn't the case anymore.

And I didn't miss.

Underneath the deafening sound of what was probably going to be a great case of tinnitus, I could hear the sound of little miss Recon screaming. Her second bodyguard crumpled onto the wheel, his face-

I swallowed hard, forcing myself to look away. The truck's engine revved, his lifeless foot still pushing the gas, but he hadn't managed to get it back into gear.

The sound of a car door opening brought me out of my internal monologue. I blinked, head snapping up in a second.

The finder half fell from the cab, her face bone-white in the headlights. Blood coated her face, her arms. Probably her partner's. Every breath she took came out a ragged gasp. Part of me sympathized with her. It had to be a shock, and if Aedan was right about her abilities, she was as helpless in all of this as I was. Aedan had given me no reason to think he was wrong - but it didn't mean that I could just let her run off. He had a point, after all. The longer she was out there, knowing where to find us and having the skillset to track us, the more danger we were in. I couldn't very well let her run.

My feet ached underneath me as I pushed myself into a run, taking off after the woman.

She glanced back over her shoulder - just once. Her eyes widened further than they already were, her mouth hanging open as she sobbed. I swallowed the bitter frustration that was welling up again. It wasn't right. None of this was right. It didn't change anything, but I just felt the need to acknowledge it.

The sound of a fight drew my eye as I sprinted after her. Aedan had Clark down on the ground, his jacket off and wrapped around his hand as he pushed the guy's face into the ground. His other hand clutched a heavy, disgustingly-ornate pendant fixed around the man's neck on a leather cord. He was strangling him with it, in fact, all the while inspecting it with a look of utmost interest.

Fucking Aedan. I tore my eyes away, hearing the woman ahead of me falter.

She was running out of road. Ahead lay only more forest - the forest we'd just come from. And while she was reasonably dressed for the season, she'd clearly been planning on sitting in the truck for the whole evening. Her quite-stylish shoes were tearing themselves apart with every thundering stride she took.

Two more steps. It took two more steps for me to close the distance between us, wrapping my arms around her shoulders as I launched myself at her.

She screamed as we hit the ground hard, a shrill, pained sound. I forced it away, refusing to acknowledge the pang of guilt that shot through me at it. She struggled, trying to wrestle away underneath me, but I had the advantage of size and adrenaline. She wasn't going anywhere.

The gun was heavy in my hand as I pulled it free again. And then I stopped.

"Good work. Much better," Aedan said, walking up behind us. The finder squirmed, twisting her head enough to get a look at him. Her eyes widened at the sight of him grinning down at her. "You'll figure all this out in time."

"Shut up," I said, no venom in the words. I didn't want to get better at killing people. I wanted to go *home*.

"Right. Just...finish up here, and we'll-"

"Or we could *not*," I said, glancing back at him.

Aedan stopped, scowling down at me. "This isn't the time to grow a heart, Jonny. She's one of them - a totally willing partner in all this. You can't-"

"They've got Keira, right?" I said, staring at him.

"You don't know-"

"You have her, right?" I shook the woman underneath me.

She shuddered. "M-Matt hasn't said anything about-"

"Come on, Jon," Aedan said, folding his arms.

"If he went to my apartment, then he's got her," I insisted, glaring at him. "She didn't have work tonight."

"Even so, I can't-"

"If they have a hostage, then it only makes sense for us to have one too."

Aedan stared at me, his expression unreadable. And then he threw his hands up, rolling his eyes. "Fine. Fine! Do what you want. But she's on you, understand?"

I grinned, satisfied. "Right." I glanced down. She was looking back up at me, her breathing slowing somewhat as she figured out that she'd gotten a reprieve. "Come on. If you make trouble, he's *going* to kill you. Fair warning."

She stumbled to her feet as I rolled clear, pushing myself upright. Her glasses had fallen clear as we tumbled, coming to rest in the dead grass nearby. She reached out as she stood, her eyes fixed on-

Aedan's hand whipped in, closing around the glasses before she could touch them. She visibly flinched as he stood again, inspecting them.

"Nice, nice. Awesome. Finders' relics are rare, you know, Jon," he said, glancing at me with a crooked smile. "Always hold onto them when you find them." His eyes flicked over to Recon's. "And I *will* be holding onto these."

Her face was drawn and tight as she stared at him, but she seemed to know better than to argue. She didn't fight when I pulled her upright, or when I tugged her over to the truck a few moments later. Her eyes were fixed on Clark, cracks already shooting through his form where he lay. As I watched, they flicked to Nate, who Aedan was trying to leverage out of the cab. Behind the fear in her eyes there was something that might have been sorrow.

Truth be told, I didn't really care. She was marginally more harmless than the others on her crew, but she'd been with them all the same. Without her directing them, they'd never have found Aedan, and thus they'd never have found *me*.

I didn't feel bad at all about zip-tying her hands together - another gift of Aedan's backpack, which I was beginning to suspect was bottomless. She shuddered as we sandwiched her into the truck's bench seat between us, her eyes still fixed on where her glasses had vanished into Aedan's jacket pocket, but wisely held her tongue.

"All right," I said, glancing over at Aedan. "We did your thing. Now-"

"Calm down and drive," he said, motioning towards the road. "Time's a-wasting. You're the one who wanted to-"

My foot stomped down on the accelerator, cutting off whatever inane argument he'd been about to follow up with. A grin slipped onto his face and vanished as quickly as it had come as the truck lurched forward.

Gravel sprayed out from under the tires as we shot out of the trailhead lot. My eyes were fixed on the road. I'd lived here my whole life. I knew every street, every route and shortcut.

And right then, I was just mad enough to make it count.

The brilliant, achingly brief light of the two bodies shattering into dust behind us lit up my rearview mirror as I tore back towards town.

CHAPTER SEVEN

The truck bounced along the beat-up, broken road as I drove us on. The woman sitting next to me had her hands folded in her lap, tightly zip-tied together. Her knuckles stood out white against her skin even in the dim light of the cab.

Perhaps I was going a *bit* too fast. But it wasn't my truck, and I wasn't in any state of mind to worry about a little thing like traffic laws.

"So can I see it yet?" Aedan said, breaking the uneasy silence. The 'Recon' woman might terrified into silence, but he seemed entirely at ease. He wasn't even wearing a seat belt.

"What?" I said, tearing my eyes off the road just long enough to glare at him.

He smirked back, flipping his knife over and over in one hand. "Come on. Sharing is caring. Let me see it already."

"See *what?*" I said again, resisting the urge to snap.

"Your relic. Hurry up. I want to-"

"I don't even know if I'm right." I muttered, feeling my ears go red for what seemed like the hundredth time that night.

"Bullshit. You've got a pretty good idea. I can tell."

My eyes flicked over to the woman between us. She hadn't said a word, and yet the image of those men exploding into shattered, fragmented piles of dust was frozen in my mind.

Aedan chuckled. "Her?" He grabbed her by the back of the neck. She yelped, eyes squeezing shut as he shook her, but he didn't seem to care. "Oh, she's not going to try anything. She's smarter than that.

Aren't you?"

"Y-Yes," she said hurriedly, ducking her head. "I w-won't-"

"Good, good," Aedan said, releasing her as fast as he'd grabbed her. "You heard the nice lady, Jonny. Now show and tell."

I gave him a look from the corner of my eye as we careened around another turn. I still wasn't quite comfortable with letting her know anything about me. According to Aedan, information was her specialty, and she was with *them*. Giving her information about something that could kill me was even lower on my priority list.

But he was still glaring at me with those furious green eyes, narrowing more and more with every second that I delayed. Swallowing a groan, I tugged the top of my coat open.

"See, I don't *know*, but I got to thinking." My fingers found the thin-worked chain around my neck quickly, pulling it out from under my jacket. The strap was light and delicate enough that it lay nearly flat against my skin, completely invisible under my jacket. That must have been what kept them from instantly finding it, back in the parking lot. "If it's something I always keep around...It's got to be this."

Aedan stared at the necklace I pulled from around my neck, watching it bounce in the half-light.

I eyed him sidelong. "So what exactly-"

His hand snapped out before I could say another word. The rings on the chain vanished into his palm as he pulled it away from me, holding it up closer to his face.

"Hey!" I yelped, my heart skipping a beat as it left my skin. "Give that-"

"I'll give it back," Aedan said, pausing in his inspection long enough to glare at me. "Stop whining and drive. You're going to kill us."

"No, I'm going to kill *you*," I muttered, but I turned back to the road like he said. It flew past in the darkness, faster and faster. My apartment was on the other side of our little town - not far, exactly, but not close, either. Every second we delayed was like a knife in my heart.

With each passing breath, though, the tension in me seemed to build. It was like there was a thread inside me that had been broken the instant he'd taken the necklace from my hands. I shot him a look, tearing my eyes away from the street long enough to fix my eyes on the charm he held.

It was simple - just two old rings that looked like they might have been wedding bands at one point, laid side by side and entwined with delicate, silvery wire. And it was *mine.*

My eyes flicked up to his. "Can I-"

He opened his mouth and said….something. It just came out a mess of gibberish. I blinked, taken aback. I'd never heard someone speak another language, I realized. Not in person, not that I could remember, anyway - something like that was just the domain of TV shows and movies and the occasional video game.

"What?" I said slowly, feeling like an idiot.

He grinned. "Yup. Good guessing, Jonny."

"What was that?" I said, reaching out to grab my necklace back. He held it farther away, taking the rings in one hand.

"Oh, nothing you have to worry about," he muttered.

"You said you just wanted to see it, now give it-"

"Eyes on the road," Recon said, her voice tight.

I turned back around, wrenching the wheel as I pulled the truck back off the shoulder. My skin itched, like there were bugs crawling all over me. Aedan still held my necklace - my relic, I supposed. My focus. Whatever.

"Aedan, if you don't-"

"Stop whining," he said, dry amusement lacing his tone. Before I could say another word he reached out, sliding the cord back around my neck. The instant the warm, smooth metal of the rings touched my skin, it was like a weight lifted from my shoulders. The itching vanished.

I wasn't sure I liked what that implied about the necklace and I - and what would happen if we were separated.

"So…." I said slowly, glancing over at him more cautiously. "That didn't feel good. At all."

"Well, no," Aedan said, rolling his eyes. "It wouldn't, would it?"

"Is that what happens when-"

"Like I said earlier," he said. "If you're separated, it can trigger a collapse. But that won't happen just by letting someone else hold it a minute." A sardonic grin tugged at the corners of his lips. "And you'll keep it around instinctively. It's just one of those things. Don't worry about forgetting it and leaving on a three-week vacation."

"Wonderful," I said darkly. "So, why did you want it, then? You trying to steal my power?"

"Weren't you listening at *all*, Jonny?" Aedan said, beginning to chuckle. "One per person. It's just a pretty trinket to me."

"So why, then?"

He eyed me, not responding. The silence dragged out anew. Recon squirmed between us as though giving form to the awkward, uncomfortable air.

"So, we should figure out-"

"What, you're not going to tell me?" I said, the words flying out of me. "That's bullshit, Aedan. Don't just ignore me."

"I'm not ignoring you. Like I said, I can't-"

"Can I see *yours*, then?" I snapped. "Fair is fair, right?" Truth be told, I wasn't entirely sure what seeing it would get me, especially if it was true that I couldn't try and steal his power. All the same, it would make me feel better.

But Aedan just gave me a stern, superior look, a hint of amusement in his eyes. "Maybe later, Jonny. We should figure out what the plan is when-"

"That's bullshit."

"Jonny. Please. When we get there we'll-"

"You never tell me anything."

"Jonny. Please."

"It's fucking Jon."

Aedan only grinned, reaching over to pat my knee. I considered taking a swipe at him in return, but I knew my chances of hitting him were slim to none. It would only encourage him. Without a good alternative, I fell into a quiet, simmering rage.

"Good. Now that that little tantrum's over-"

"Fuck you."

"What are we doing?"

His question brought me up short. What were we doing? They had guns, and whatever fucked-up magic had sprung into my life, and they had my little sister. They were willing to kill.

What were we going to do?

"I...don't know," I said at last, letting each syllable roll off my tongue slow as molasses. "I haven't thought that far ahead."

Aedan ran a hand through his hair, making a face. And then he turned to Recon.

"All right. See- ah, damn. What's your name?"

"I'm-"

"Fuck it. They called you Recon, right?"

She was going white. Not surprising, given the way Aedan kept waving his knife around her face, but I had to feel a little bad for her.

"R-Right."

"You're Recon, then," Aedan said, grinning. "All right. You're with them, right? One of Matt's crew?"

She stared at him a moment, as though debating if she should lie, but nodded.

"Good. Good. Now. We're going to talk, you and I - you're going to tell me all about what Matt's been up to since we parted ways." His grin widened. "If Jonny there likes what you have to say, then maybe we'll make a go of this."

He didn't say what would happen if I didn't,and he didn't need to. Everyone in that truck understood perfectly. She crumpled, but I was too busy trying to wrap my mind around the idea that Aedan was treating me like some sort of....magical polygraph machine. That's how it came off, anyway.

There was something in her expression that didn't sit quite right with me - a bit of hesitance, a guarded air at odds with her captive situation. But she nodded at last, still jammed in between us.

We were close. Whatever Aedan was hoping she'd tell him, I just hoped they made it fast.

The buildings raced past, more familiar with every block as we sped into town.

***

How, exactly, had I let Aedan convince me that this was the best plan?

I crept towards the back of the apartment building, fighting the urge to swear. It was still night, of course, but the lights fixed to the back wall every porch-length were blinding. In theory, they were supposed to keep thieves away.

That wasn't working in my favor.

My heart pounded in my throat as I pushed free of the treeline at last. Aedan hadn't given me much time to argue, when we'd slammed to a stop half a block down from the apartment. Just a *get out*, and that was it. He was already out of the truck, leaving me no time to offer an alternate plan.

Keira was just collateral damage to him, I knew - an unfortunate victim, and one that he probably wouldn't mind helping, but far from his first priority. I just had to trust that he'd pitch in, since I didn't exactly have a better idea.

Unlike him, I didn't care why these assholes were chasing him. I didn't care why they were pretending to be cops, or why Aedan was so damn special. I just wanted my sister back.

That fact alone was enough to keep me moving. My hands shook as I crept across the grassy yard behind our building, but I crept onward. Looking casual was the trick - I had to look like I belonged, like I was just another neighbor headed in for the night.

I couldn't resist it, though - I lifted my head, rising up on my toes for a second as I slipped across the dying grass. Our apartment was on the middle floor, just above the half-sunken ground units. If I stretched, from this angle, I could *probably* peek in the-

My mouth went dry. The lights were on. Keira was a night owl - she didn't like the harsh, sterile lights of our apartment. She'd never keep them all on. And if I really stretched my eyes - and possibly my imagination - I could see figures inside, half-hidden but moving.

I forced the thoughts from my mind. I didn't have time to worry. Aedan had promised he'd do what I asked. He'd promised that he'd stick to the plan, rather than just run in with his stupid knife and try to gut everyone he saw.

He'd said he'd buy me time. But that time wasn't going to last forever.

Despite the fear still rising, I relaxed a fraction as I reached the wall of the structure. They couldn't see me. Good. All I had to do, then, was find a way in.

I scanned the yard hurriedly, trying to find something, anything that I could use, but our neighbors were irritatingly thoughtful with their possessions. I knew there was no *way* I was going to be able to pull off a movie stunt like climbing the drainpipe.

Swallowing my complaints, I headed for the neighbor's grill instead. It was a big thing, heavy and metal and almost certainly against fire code to have outside his apartment. Its wheels screeched with the strain of years of rust as I leaned into it. Slowly at first, but gaining speed, I worked it from his patio over to under our balcony.

That was the simple part. Already feeling a bit unsure about what I was doing, I made myself keep going. The tired, ancient metal frame of the grill groaned as I clambered up on top of it, but it held.

The balcony railing was an easy reach from my new perch. My ears rang with sounds as I pulled myself up - footsteps, and the floor inside shifting, and doors closing. I flinched at each one, certain that it was someone walking past, someone who'd see me.

But no one came racing out the door, gun in hand and screaming at me. It was just my imagination. I repeated it over and over to myself, as though the repetition would make it true somehow. They couldn't see me unless they came out on the balcony. They didn't know I was there. I was invisible. Probably.

The sound of a harsh crash was enough to make me jump. Stone on wood. I knew what it was, but that didn't make me feel any better.

Aedan had said he'd get their attention. He'd been a bit nonspecific as to how. Apparently, he'd decided that hurling rocks at our apartment's front door was the best way to get his message across.

"Hey! Matt!" I heard him bellow a moment later, his voice echoing around the block. "Open up! I've got something of yours!"

I hoped that Recon would cooperate with the probably-insane man. For her sake.

For a long moment there was only the sound of crickets - and low, quiet voices from inside my apartment. The windows were sealed shut against the chilly fall air, but it was an old building. I didn't quite know what they were saying, but I could hear enough to get the picture.

I fixed the sounds in my mind. They were in her room. I eyed her window, trying my best to silence the little voice in the back of my mind that whispered how far it was, how hard it would be to make it without just falling.

The voices weren't moving, though. I held my ground, staring at the leaves and grass below. One more. I just needed one-

The sound of a second *boom* nearly sent me toppling from my perch on the edge of the balcony. Aedan had found a bigger rock, it seemed.

"Come *on!*" he screamed again. "Let's talk, shall we? Unless you're cool with losing another finder."

He was around the front still, standing at the front door. I couldn't see what he did - but I heard Recon scream, the sound muffled but filled with unmistakable pain.

Tough. She'd known what she was getting into. I wasn't about to worry after her well-being.

And there were footsteps from inside the apartment. A door clicked open - and shut again.

I was moving before the sound had died out, reaching my fingers towards the windowsill and throwing myself from the railing.

It groaned under my weight, loud enough that I was sure that everyone inside would hear it and come running. The wood was cold, icy enough that I nearly lost my grip. Worse still was the burning pain of my hand. Putting enough pressure on it to keep myself up *also* meant twisting it hard enough pangs of agony shot down my arm. The night was just a gift that kept on giving, apparently. The fall wouldn't kill me, but it would slow me down. I wasn't going to fall.

Gritting my teeth and fighting down the urge to vomit, I swung my legs up onto the ancient wood facade and grabbed at the glass frame. Thankfully, we hadn't used a screen in years - a distant casualty of a party gone wrong.

The window slid open at my touch. I grinned, pushing myself through. The sound of Aedan's furious bellowing continued all the while.

My arms screamed as I levered myself in, settling to the carpet in a heap.

"Jon?"

I spun around at the sound, my pulse thundering. Keira was there - just like I knew she would be. They had her duct-taped to her desk chair. My eyes tightened as I stared at the bruises covering her face, her neck, her arms.

"Hey," I whispered, forcing my legs to move as I crept closer.

Her eyes were wide and unfocused as she stared back at me - her blue eyes, piercing and intense, the perfect match to my own. I'd never seen her look so lost. She'd always been so sure of herself, confident in everything she did.

If Matt and the others were lucky, Aedan would beat me to them.

They were still exchanging screamed words with each other out in the entryway. I still had time. I dug in my pocket, trying desperately not to let my vision go white with rage. Aedan had slipped a folding knife into my jacket pocket, patting it with another of his patronizing, infuriating smirks. I had it out in a second as I tore at the tape holding her down.

"Jon? What's- What's going on?" she stammered. Her eyes were red and swollen.

I swallowed another pang of rage. "Bit too much to get into, Keira. Let's get you out of here first."

"But, Jon, those men kept asking about-"

"It's okay. They're gone. We just have to leave - now."

"They were asking about *you*," Keira whispered, her face half-hidden behind a mane of dark brown hair. "And some guy named-"

"Come on, Keira," I said, ripping the blade free of another strip of tape. "Let's stay focused, ok? We can talk in a minute."

Jesus Christ, I sounded just like Aedan. Fucking perfect.

But she only nodded, taking one deep breath after another. "Okay." Her shoulders straightened, as though she was getting her feet under her.

It wasn't that simple. I couldn't expect that much of her. But all we had to do was climb out the window again, and-

I froze, the final piece of tape clutched in one hand. Keira shivered, goosebumps standing out on her skin where the cold air was drifting in from the window. She was already pushing herself out of the chair, nearly throwing it aside in her hurry to be free of it.

But there were other voices, hushed and quiet and standing in the living room. I could still hear Aedan screaming at Matt, but the men in my apartment were having a side conversation all of their own.

I didn't like the sound of that.

My heart leapt into my throat at the sound of footsteps, echoing down the hall as they strode towards Keira's room. The place had always been creaky. I knew every pop and screech of the plywood floorboards.

Someone was coming.

CHAPTER EIGHT

I stared at the door, my mind racing. Shit. They weren't stupid, it seemed.

Just our luck.

The sound of footsteps continued despite my growing panic, moving ever-closer to our room.

I'd hoped that they would be so focused on Aedan that they wouldn't give any more thought to their captive.

I'd hoped that they'd forgotten about me, that I'd been enough of a background figure to their get-Aedan crusade that I'd simply slip their minds.

Apparently, all those hopes had fallen short.

Keira was a warm presence clinging to my back. She trembled gently, but seemed to recognize the need for quiet. I took her wrist and shoved her towards the window as quickly as I could without bowling her over outright. We'd only have seconds before they burst into the room - not long enough for both of us to clamber down the outside of the building, but we'd have to make do.

She hesitated for a single moment, her eyes fixed on mine as she faltered. She didn't want to leave me behind - and she didn't want to be alone in the night with all of *them* around, no doubt. I couldn't blame her, but we didn't have time to debate it. I forced a smile onto my face, hoping it looked at least a little bit reassuring, and nodded more firmly.

I was out of time - I'd have to hope that she was listening. I threw myself flat against the wall behind the door where I'd have at least a little bit of cover, praying that whoever was coming wouldn't be able to see me from the doorway. I clutched the knife with my good hand, trying desperately to pull the bits of tape still clinging to it free.

The door slammed open a moment later as one of the men stepped into the room. He was tense - that much was clear from the tightness of his shoulders and the way a muscle in his jaw was twitching. I swallowed a chuckle as I tightened my grip on the knife. That *did* seem to be the standard reaction from someone who'd recently spent time around Aedan.

He froze, his eyes fixed on Keira. She crouched half out the window, pinned in place by his angry gaze.

"What the-" he began, gaping. Reality seemed to return all at once as he realized she was free. I could see his chest rise as he drew in breath. My eyes tightened, following the motion. In another moment he'd scream, and everyone would hear. She'd never make it out of the complex without being caught. I couldn't let that happen.

His cry came out a pained grunt as I launched myself across the room, throwing my weight against him with all the force I could muster. He bucked, trying to throw me off, but I'd latched my arm around his neck. I gritted my teeth, clutching the knife in my unhurt hand and swinging down as hard as I could.

It glanced off a zipper in his jacket and sank in an inch. He yelped in pain, eyes narrowing. His arm swung around, trying desperately to latch onto me.

"Jon!" I heard Keira gasp, her voice still hushed.

I didn't respond. Stabbing a human was harder than I'd thought, and things hadn't exactly gone as planned. Whoever he was, sticking a knife in the man just seemed to have made him even angrier than he was before.

What's his power? The thought hung in my mind with crystal clarity. Everyone else had such cool, strong abilities, and I had *nothing*. If he triggered his power - whatever it was - then I'd be well and truly fucked. Under no circumstances could I let him-

The thought slipped away from me as his hand latched onto my belt, finding purchase at last. He pulled me free with a muted roar, throwing me to the ground.

The air left my lungs in a rush as I bounced to a stop. I wheezed, trying to pull myself back together, but there wasn't a whole lot I could do while the room spun around me. My knife was still sticking out of the man's chest. As I watched, he reached up with one hand and tore it free.

What next, then? Would he burn me to a cinder in a cloud of fire? Suck the water itself from my body, leaving me a dry, leathery husk? Maybe he'd-

His hand latched around my throat as I tried to force myself to stand. My head slammed back down into the carpet. Even the meager breath I'd managed to work back into my lungs vanished as his grip tightened.

Oh. That worked, too.

Over his shoulder, the shadowed form of Keira lunged at him. She wasn't running. Why wasn't she running? My lips fluttered as I fought for air, needing to tell her to leave, to get *out*, but nothing came out. The pressure on my neck shifted as he let go with one hand long enough to backhand her roughly. She hit the ground hard, smacking into the dresser by her bed.

The pressure resumed an instant later as he went straight back to it, as though this was just another chore to be finished. I tried to bat his hands away, feeling my face burn red as I strained, but he didn't hesitate. His grip was like iron. The edges of my vision went grey as he knelt on my chest, bringing his weight to bear.

After everything that had happened, all the crazy, impossible tricks that I'd seen, he was just going to kill me with his bare hands. I was that helpless. The thought burned like a brand, one last piece of humiliation on top of the shit sundae that the night had been. I'd never felt so weak in my life.

20/20 hindsight, stabbing him was probably a bad idea. The thought circled in my mind, eerily clear as the rest of the world faded into an indistinct blur. Little by little, my feeble attempts at breaking free weakened. My fingers fell away from his hands, my strength fleeing rapidly.

My desperate, burning lungs cried their relief as they filled with air a moment later. I coughed, cracking my eyes open just in time to see the man rear back, hands grasping something about his neck.

Keira. As my vision cleared I could see her standing a pace away, red-eyed and panting with exertion but glaring at him with razor-sharp focus. She'd found a belt somewhere - with how much laundry she left around her room, it could have been anywhere. The leather flexed and strained around his neck as she pulled it tighter and tighter. I grinned weakly despite the danger of the game we were playing. She'd always had a vicious streak a mile wide when we were kids. Just then, I didn't mind so much.

He struggled against her hold, still trying to pull free, but she cinched it tighter every time he flinched. Slowly, the light left his eyes.

It seemed like an eternity had passed when he finally drooped, even though I knew it had probably only been a few seconds. Keira shuddered, dropping his weight to the floor. Her hands came up a moment later, covering her mouth as she realized exactly what she'd just done. Her eyes were wide and staring.

I pushed myself upright, crossing the room to her in an instant. "Shh," I whispered hoarsely, pulling her into my arms. "Come on. It's ok. You saved me."

She shook her head violently. I knew she was still staring at the body lying on her floor.

I swallowed a sigh, not feeling any more confident about things than she did. This whole matter was still fucked up - I'd just had a *little* more warning about things than her. But we hadn't exactly been quiet. Even assuming the others were still occupied by Aedan being Aedan, they'd be coming to check on their friend soon enough. There was no time to waste.

Keira flinched as I turned the two of us back towards the window. "Jon, I-"

"You need to get out of here," I snapped, my lips pressed close against her ear. "Just…Just run. Get as far away as you can. Find somewhere safe to hole up."

"You're not coming with me?"

At her words, I paused. What *was* I doing? I'd certainly planned on getting as far away as I could, and the two of us should stick together, but…If they could track me by my necklace, then me being with her wasn't a good idea.

Somewhere behind me, I could still hear Aedan bellowing, too. Something about things didn't sit quite right with me, as my mind raced through everything that had happened. These pursuers of his, Matt and his gang. Over and over again they'd come face to face with Aedan. They'd killed him, yes - but Matt there had tried to stop blue-eyes, at the McDonald's.

A man who puts people to sleep. A man who controls gravity to immobilize his opponents. A man who binds people with roots and vines. I was no expert at this new world I'd fallen into, but I could follow well enough to pick up the trend.

They weren't trying to kill Aedan - far from it, in fact. They wanted something from him. And right now Aedan was right in the middle of them. If I took off with Keira into the night, leaving him behind with his hostage, what would happen to him?

I wasn't quite sure why I cared, exactly, considering everything he'd done to me, but I found that I *did* care - just enough that I wasn't hot on the idea of leaving him to get tortured or shot again or whatever they had in mind.

My hand was on Keira's back, pushing her out the window. She swallowed hard, eyes wide as she clung to the wall, but didn't fight me on the matter. Within seconds she was out, her feet scrabbling against the brickwork.

I could just follow her - climb out behind her and vanish into the dark. Maybe I'd have to split from her for a little bit, but we'd work something out. Maybe I could give her my necklace and-

"Josh!" a voice bellowed. "You good? Matt wants the girl out front!"

Shit. They'd noticed after all. As Keira froze, eyes wide with sudden fear, I smiled down at her.

And then I slammed the window shut, closing the blinds with a flick of the rod. There. She was completely invisible. That was about as good as I could do for her.

Whoever was looking for Josh, they were close. The options left to me raced through my mind, but I was tired of fancy plans.

The weight of the gun I'd collected in the trailhead fight pressed against the small of my back. I took it out, hands trembling. Shooting inside an apartment was a bad idea. That had been pressed into me over and over again from the first time I learned how to shoot. Never shoot inside, never shoot around people, never shoot *at* people. I'd seen all the YouTube videos about how many layers of drywall a bullet would go through. It was why a knife had seemed the safer option than a gun to begin with.

But the longer this dragged on, the less I could view the situation with cold logic. Their footsteps pounded down the hall, for the second time that night. I clicked the safety off a split second before the door popped open again.

My system was full of adrenaline as I leveled the gun at him. My finger exploded into pain with the motion. The crack of gunfire was deafening in the tiny room. The wall over the man's shoulder exploded into a cloud of white dust.

"Shit!" he yelled, throwing his arms over his head as he stumbled to the side. And then his eyes fixed on me. "Who the-" Recognition washed over his face. I could see it, see the gears in his head slowly turning. His hand twitched to his side - to where a gun waited, I knew. I could see the way his fingers tensed, as though gripping some ghostly copy of its metallic shape.

No. No way in hell was I going to give him the time to shoot me. I pulled the trigger again, clinging to the pistol desperately. My arms shook with the force of it as it exploded into light and noise. Despite myself, I flinched. It was *loud*, dammit. My ears were already aching from the first shot - with the noise of the second still ringing through the room, I could hardly hear at all.

The man's arm erupted in red as the shot clipped him. He roared in pain, the sound still oddly dim and quiet as my ears buzzed. And then his hand snapped out.

His intention was again all too clear to me. I knew exactly what he was trying to do - I just didn't have it in me to stop him. My body was in the process of informing me that enough was *enough* when his hand latched over the slide of my pistol, twisting the gun out of my hands. I let it go, unable to keep myself from screaming as my already-broken finger shrieked its complaint.

Shit.

I reached for the gun, eyes widening as I realized that without it I was helpless again, but he stepped away. His hand twitched towards his jacket, but it seemed almost like an afterthought.

His real plan made itself apparent a moment later as I gasped. It was as though the air around me was dwindling out of nowhere, as though my second-floor apartment had suddenly been relocated to the top of a mountain. My lips fluttered as I struggled, pulling for all I was worth, but there was no air left to breathe.

He grinned.

So that was his relic's power, then. Shit, shit, shit.

Even as I fought for a single breath of air, my mind zeroed in with an ironclad focus. I needed to breathe. To breathe, I needed to get him to *stop*. Could I separate him from his focus?

My mind dismissed the idea almost immediately as my vision began to blur. No, no, no. That wouldn't work. I didn't even know what it was, or where - and wrestling with him would just be a good way to get shot, even if I had the strength for it. Which I didn't.

A single memory flashed through my mind - Aedan, running through the woods for all the was worth.

He might have had the right idea - He'd also clearly been fighting these assholes for a while. I didn't have a better plan to go with.

Clinging to what little breath I had, I launched myself towards the man before I could rethink what I was doing.

He grinned, his hand coming up to grab at me - but I wasn't on the attack. As his arm lifted I threw myself wide, skidding straight past him. My eyes were fixed on his chest, watching the way he moved, the way he turned. I had to get this right. I had to be *perfect*, despite the dull ache in my lungs and the fire in my still-hurt hand and the burning of my crushed windpipe.

His fingers closed on empty air as I slid past, a satisfied smile settling across my face. I rose just as quickly, my legs pumping underneath me as I flew down the hallway of my apartment into the dingy living room. The man bellowed from behind me, his words lost to the sound of my pulse thundering in my ears.

I couldn't go out the window. Keira was escaping that way, and I had to buy her time. I had to lead them away. I'd have nowhere to go from the window in my room, no balcony to conveniently leap to.

That left only one option. I didn't have the gun anymore, either - and I'd stuck my knife into the man's chest. This wasn't a good plan. It wasn't a good plan at *all*. I didn't like it, but I just didn't see an alternative.

A handful of men lingered in my living room as I charged in. I recognized several from the scene where all this had begun. There was Mr. Blue-eyes, who both Aedan and Recon had identified as Christian. He lingered by the still-open doorway, his hand wrapped around a pistol and his eyes narrowed.

I recognized Dan, the one who'd held me against the car and broken my finger. He sat at my kitchen table, eyes squeezed shut and deep in concentration. He'd said something back then, worrying about keeping us hidden - about hiding the sound of gunfire. Was it him, then? The reason why we always seemed to be left alone, no spectators doing pesky things like calling the police?

They were all still dressed like officers themselves, I noted sourly. Christian and Dan - and Matt too, distantly visible standing on the front porch of my building. Why? Was it all just a ploy to let them move around a little easier? Were they trying to fool someone? Or was this all just a perverse game to them?

The air-sucker was right behind me, though, moving even as I bolted for the door. Christian leapt to his feet as I ran into the room, but I didn't slow. With Keira out of the apartment and gone, our reason for staying was gone. I just had to get clear and we could regroup. Aedan would have to find his own way out, with the help of the distraction I was in the process of providing him.

He didn't look happy as I caught sight of him over the railing. Not happy at *all*. His hand still clutched Recon's arm, and he glared up at me as I sped towards the entryway.

Matt spun, his eyes widening as he saw me racing towards him.

A third gunshot split the night - accompanied by a searing, blinding pain. I screamed, tumbling as I fell. I could see the air-sucker from the corner of my eye as I hit the ground. My leg - he'd shot me in the leg.

"Well," I heard Matt say. "This changes things a bit, doesn't it?" His tone was cheerful. Jovial, almost, as though this was just some sort of party.

I couldn't so much as look at him. My hand was pressed to my thigh, trying to stem the flow of blood there. It didn't look all that bad. All right, that was a total lie - it looked awful. There was no way that I could look at my leg, covered in nearly-black blood, and think it looked anything but horrible. It just didn't look like it'd kill me, if I got it taken care of quickly enough.

My finger throbbed with pain, as though taking the opportunity to remind me exactly how well the night had gone for me so far in terms of medical care.

The ground moved under me, though, shifting as someone grabbed me by the arm. Matt. I could see his face as he heaved me upright, the air-sucker grasping my other elbow so hard I was sure there'd be bruises.

Together they dragged me over to the railing. I tried to at least cooperate, unwilling to face yet more pain, but my leg wouldn't listen to me. It was all I could do to stay upright, letting the two manhandle me until I stood at the edge.

Aedan looked even less happy than he had before. He glared at me, green eyes narrowed. I thought about waving, or trying to apologize, or making an excuse. It all came out as a bland, pained grimace.

Recon grinned. Aedan glanced over, seeing the pleasure in her eyes, and scowled. His knife was already at her throat - it pressed in even tighter, until a line of red dripped down her skin. Her smile vanished.

"Now, now," Matt said, smug satisfaction dripping from every syllable. "I don't think you want to do that."

Aedan glared up at him, his lips pursed. "Go fuck yourself, Matt, unless you want to see her-"

"Kill her and I'll kill your ally."

A grin played at his lips. "He's not my ally. So, again, go fuck-"

I heard the click of a safety flipping off, an instant before something cold pressed against my temple. My blood froze. I could hardly breathe - and I didn't dare turn to confirm what all of us already knew. Matt had a gun. Of course he did. And of *course* it was pointed at me.

Distantly, I could feel my hands shake. I expected Aedan to keep laughing, or to tell Matt to go fuck himself again, or to just cut Recon's throat and be done with it. He'd certainly showed he had no lost love for me, after all. Right then in that moment, I was just a burden to him getting away, and he didn't seem to have any patience at all with burdens. He'd even said it - I wasn't his ally.

My surprise was all the greater when he stopped, his arm relaxing a fraction. I could see Recon begin breathing again, her lips tight.

Matt chuckled, the sound loud in my ear. "Good. Well. You've got something I want, and I've got something you want. So why don't we talk, like civilized human beings?" Despite his words, the gun at my head didn't move.

My eyes flicked towards Aedan. He was watching us, chewing on Matt's words. It would have been nice if there was something I could do besides for just stand like a lump, but I had no weapon and almost no mobility. It was his fault we were in this mess, anyway.

Keira had gotten out. I clung to the thought, savoring my one victory.

"I suppose," Aedan said at last. I blinked, caught completely off guard by what sounded too much like his acquiescence. He was smiling, although it looked more like a snarl from where I stood.

Recon shifted from foot to foot, clearly uncomfortable, but he tightened his grip on her arm again. I could hear the others moving in behind me, closing off any hope of finding another escape routes. I was stuck. The irony of us being right back in the same scenario that we'd started in had not been lost on me.

His knife glittered in the dim glow of the streetlights as Aedan tapped the blade against Recon's skin. He was still smiling.

"Fine. Let's fucking *talk*."

CHAPTER NINE

I stared at Matt, still latched onto my arm with an ironclad grip. He stared at Aedan, frozen like our mirror image down in the grass below. And Aedan stared at me, his eyes narrowed and disapproving.

It wasn't my fault, dammit. It *wasn't*.

"So what now, Matt?" Aedan said, finally tearing his gaze away from me. "What's the plan, huh?"

"We can both win," he said simply in response, his fingers tightening further. "Give me my finder back, and you can have your friend."

Aedan snorted. "My friend?"

I swallowed hard. If Aedan didn't speak for me, if he wasn't even interested, then I didn't have a snowball's chance in hell of making it through this mess. Even as we stood there talking, I could feel Matt's eyes on me - searching. Scanning for something, as though he could find it if he could just look hard enough. I didn't have to strain too hard to figure out what he might want from me.

Just as quickly as he'd spoken, though, Aedan's shoulders rose a fraction of an inch. He rolled his eyes, fixing them back on Matt a moment later. "So, what. You're trying to convince me that you're *not* just going to turn around and come after me if I do that?"

Matt shrugged broadly. The gun pressed to my head bobbed with the motion. I shivered, feeling the cold metal scrape against my skin.

"That's life, Aedan," he said, chuckling. "There are no guarantees. But if you're not going to cooperate, then I won't either."

The look Aedan gave Matt would have peeled paint from the walls.

My eyes bounced between the two, straining to keep Matt in the corner of my sight. Whatever there was between the two of them, that was their own business - but having seen Aedan fight, I would *not* want to have him glaring at me like that.

"Fuck," I heard Aedan mutter under his breath, the sound nearly lost to the night.

"What's that? I didn't quite-"

"Go fuck yourself, Matt," he said, straightening. There was no venom left in his voice, though. Recon didn't look so worried anymore, despite the blood trickling down her skin.

"Are you really going to-"

"Fine," Aedan snapped. "We'll do it your way."

"Good," Matt said, the word dripping with satisfaction. "Let her go. I'll give your friend back when-"

"I'm not a fucking moron, you shithead."

The others clustered in behind Matt and I. I could hear them shifting uncomfortably as Aedan and their leader traded verbal blows. Dan stood quietly, focused on whatever it was that he was doing, and Christian was waiting by the door, but the air-sucker was there on my other side too. I really, *really* didn't want him next to me again, but it wasn't as though Matt was giving me any sort of choice in the matter.

Matt sighed, right on cue. "So what, then?" he said.

"What do you think? Together."

There was only silence again as Matt considered Aedan's deal. My not-friend's eyes were on me the whole time, pinning me in place with rigid intensity. *Don't get shot again.* He didn't have to say a word out loud for me to understand what that look was telling me.

I'd do my best, dammit.

My thoughts were rudely interrupted as the world tilted out from under my feet. Matt hauled on my arm again, his friend doing the same on my other side. Decision made, apparently. They were trying to get me towards the stairs, I realized, closer to where Aedan and his captive waited. I gritted my teeth, doing my best to follow along.

I made it all of a step before my leg gave out underneath me. A pained hiss slid between my lips as I stumbled, but they didn't hesitate. They just dragged me on, no matter if I could walk or not.

Somehow, all three of us made it down and onto the concrete sidewalk without me falling and breaking my neck. Aedan quivered visibly, the point of his knife tapping rapid-fire against the woman's throat. Her eyes were fixed on Matt's, firmly enough that she hardly seemed to notice her captor's anxiety.

Aedan offered me the tiniest fragment of a smile, even as his foot beat out a rhythm against the earth. "All right. That's close enough, asshole."

I eyed the distance between us. We were closer, sure, but with my leg still erupting into pain at every trembling step, I wasn't sure I'd call it close enough.

And they had weapons. I had to remember that. Guns. Guns they could *shoot* me with, no matter if I was safely out of arm's reach.

Matt clung to my arm a moment longer, hesitating for a fraction of a second, and then he straightened alongside me. "Fine. Give our girl her glasses back."

Aedan leaned over to spit in the glass, his eyes never leaving Matt's. "Don't remember that being part of the deal."

"I'm sure I can find his," Matt said. "Is this really the hill you want to die on?"

A laugh rumbled out of Aedan's chest. I blinked, caught off guard by the crooked grin on his face. "Oh, Matt. You're an idiot. After so long spent stalking me like a slighted lover, I thought you might've-"

"Just give the focus back," Matt snapped, the last of his patience clearly beginning to dry up. I was pretty sure there was going to be a circular imprint in my temple where the barrel of his gun pressed in. "I'm not going to ask again."

Aedan's eyes twitched to mine again, leaving Matt's for the tiniest fraction of a second. I knew the math that had to be going through his head. Without her relic, Recon was useless. Worse than that, she'd be toast inside of a few days.

Giving her relic back, though, meant that the whole shitshow we were stuck in wasn't going to end anytime soon.

I could almost hear Aedan's teeth grind as he stared across the grassy yard at me. The edge of the complex was so *close* - just like it had been at the McDonald's. Only this time I couldn't run. I'd gone and done what he'd been so insistent about *not* doing, and got myself shot.

"Fine," he muttered, his voice hardly more than a whisper.

A bit of the tension slipped out of me as he reached into his jacket. Good. Good. I was all for anything that put me a little farther away from getting shot for a second time.

The woman snatched the pair of glasses out of his hand as soon as he held them in front of her, his knife still at her throat. She didn't seem to mind it anymore as she clutched the relic to her chest. Her shoulders slumped in relief. I'd felt the tension and strain of being parted from my necklace back in the truck, and that was just for a few moments. I sympathized with how much she had to be hurting, even if I couldn't feel bad for *her*.

"Better?" Aedan snapped.

"Better," Matt said, his voice cheerful again. "Together, now?"

"Hurry the fuck up."

With one last chuckle, Matt released my arm. I stumbled, nearly falling before catching myself.

"Quick, now," he said, chin in the air as he leered down at me. "Better hurry before he changes his mind. Aedan's like that."

"Again, Matt, I know it's hard to get anything to stick in that pathetic mess you call a brain, but this is important, so try and listen," Aedan snapped, even as he shoved Recon forward. "*Go fuck yourself.*"

I ignored the two of them as best I could, my eyes fixed on the woman stalking towards me. She could move. I tried to restrain my jealousy at that fact. Aedan twirled his knife in his hand, foot still tapping as she stepped towards us.

One foot in front of the other. I could do that. Yeah. Sure, my left leg was just a white-hot mass of pain, and I could only sort of stagger along, but I was making progress little by little.

I had to. Something in my gut was screaming that things weren't done just yet. I could have guessed and said it was held in the way Matt's eyes danced from face to face with nervous energy, or the way the air-sucker's breath was coming fast and short. Either of those would have been good clues - but having met both Aedan and Matt, I knew that all it was going to take was time before the violence started again.

That was their problem. Once I got away, once I got clear, they could kill each other to their hearts' content. My worrying about Aedan had ended when a bullet wound up lodged in my thigh.

I blinked, my musings put on hold as Recon's eyes met mine for the barest fraction of a moment. She'd been watching me. That wasn't surprising, really, but that guarded, lidded look was back. She shouldn't look so damn pleased with herself. She wasn't in a position to-

Her quick intake of breath, short and sharp, was the only warning I got before she lunged at me. I yelped, throwing a hand up, but she had

two working legs and a lot less pain to her name than me. I got my hands up just in time, protecting my face as she plowed headlong into me.

The two of us hit the grass hard. Her fingernails clawed at my throat, digging for purchase.

Shit. I could hardly move, and I was suddenly expected to fight? Where was-

Aedan blew past the two of us, his form a blur of motion as he threw himself towards Matt and the air-sucker. Dan's startled cries were a distant sound, only half-heard as I struggled. Great. I wouldn't be getting any help, then.

Recon's face was twisted into a mask of fury as she scrabbled for a better hold. I still had my hands up, thank god. I was in a heap of trouble, but so far I'd managed to keep her far enough away from me that she couldn't latch on.

Her eyes dropped again - to my coat. My relic. I realized what she wanted immediately, even as she grabbed for me again.

I could hear Aedan bellowing all the while. He had to be getting close to his target. Twisting my head to the side as best I could, I caught sight of him tearing towards Matt. The air-sucker waited beside their leader, at the ready. His hands snapped up - and that gun was still in his grasp.

Aedan was going to get himself shot again. I surged, gathering the energy to push Recon off the top of me. He needed help. Fuck. I was an idiot. A gullible, stupid idiot.

The woman yelped as she tumbled clear - but hit the ground rolling, lunging back in. Her hand slammed down on my leg, her fingers digging into the still-oozing gunshot wound.

I screamed, shoulders hunching over as new waves of pain shot through my chest.

"Ben, no!" Matt bellowed from ahead. I squinted through bleary eyes, trying to bat Recon away, but she was all I could see. It was official. I had no idea what was going on anymore.

Recon leapt for my neck again, a victorious light in her eyes. My arms were longer. Her premature celebration died instantly as my fingers wrapped around her windpipe.

The sound of electric crackling split the night sky, odd and unexpected enough that both her and I froze in place.

Aedan was nearly at the foot of the stairs. He'd been that close. The start of a shriek died on his lips as he convulsed.

Matt stumbled backward up the stairs, white-faced. His hands trembled, but one finger was jammed down on the trigger of the taser he clutched.

Aedan hit the ground hard, still twitching as the horrible sound of electricity died away. He didn't get up.

"Shit," I heard Matt gasp. His adam's apple bobbed as he swallowed hard, regaining a little bit of composure.

And then a slow smile spread across his face as he straightened. It grew by the second while he stood, beaming down at his prey.

Recon took another swing at my face, half-heartedly connecting. I swore under my breath, still wrestling to get her under control. This was not good. This was, in fact very, very bad.

"Let's clean it up," I heard Matt say, his voice still breathless.

The air-sucker turned to me as Matt walked past - Ben, he'd been called. He fixed me with an appraising look even as his boss crouched over my friend.

The muscles in his chest tensed as he swung his arm up - the hand clutching his gun. His stance settled, one leg sliding out and back to steady himself.

Shit.

The woman was still thrashing, fighting me every bit as hard as I was fighting her. My leg was on fire, just like my hand, and the first tendrils of nausea were beginning to spread from the pit of my belly at the pain and blood loss.

Somehow, though, I found the strength to pull the both of us upright, twisting to put her in front of me like a shield.

The crack of a gunshot echoed around the yard as the air-sucker fired.

Recon shuddered, her whole frame collapsing in on itself as the round tore through her back. I'd been half expecting it to come tearing out the far side, covering both of us in blood. She only coughed, though, her arms falling to her sides as though all of her strength had fled. Her eyes were wide and confused as she pressed a hand to her lips.

She crumpled a moment later, falling to the grass in a heap. The glasses she'd clutched with such desperation slid from her jacket, tumbling into the green beside her.

I knew what was coming next. Within moments she glowed, lit with a light from inside her.

And then she was gone, just as quickly as it had begun. I shuddered, seeing the dust already begin to vanish into nothingness.

"You...." I heard Matt say as I lay panting. "You absolute goddamn *asshole*."

"You said-"

"What the *fuck* kind of demi are you?" he bellowed. "What was that? What the hell was that?"

"I-I don't feel so good," someone said from the balcony. Dan. He was still standing off to the side, his eyes squeezed shut, but his skin was bone-white. Even from across the yard, even at night, I could see the sweat pouring off him. "Matt, I t-think we should hurry." Someone was beside him, a comforting hand on his back. Blue-eyes. Christian.

I pushed myself up on my elbows, trying desperately to catch my breath.

The air-sucker shook his head vigorously at Matt's glare, his hands held in the air even as he glanced towards me. "Y-You said to clean it-"

"What, so you *shoot* her?"

"I was trying to shoot *him*," he said plaintively.

The sound of Aedan laughing echoed off the apartments. He lay flat on the ground still, Matt's knee in the small of his back. There was a cuff around one of his wrists. Even as I watched, the ringleader was trying to wrestle the other one on. Aedan was putting up about as much of a fight as he could, but from the way his limbs twitched and flexed randomly, his motor control was pretty shot.

"I-I didn't....e-e-even have t-to-"

"Shut up," Matt muttered, kneeing him in the side. Hard.

Aedan hardly seemed to notice. "Y-You killed her *f-for* m-"

Matt slid the lock home with a *click*, turning in the same smooth motion and punching Aedan in the nose. Once, and then again. At the third blow, Aedan finally shut up, curling his head down against his chest.

The sound of footsteps approaching pulled my attention away. The air-sucker was stalking towards me, red-faced but with single-minded intent. I flinched, turning to the woods beyond the lonely structures, but it was too late. I couldn't exactly run, even if I'd started moving fast enough. I was screwed either way.

I gasped, feeling the breath slide out of my lungs, and collapsed from my half-run onto the ground. Ben had taken Matt's comments quite personally, it seemed. A gun wasn't going to be good enough this time. Lucky me. I writhed, trying to worm my way towards the treeline, but his foot slammed down onto my leg. I bit off another scream, doing my best not to throw up as a fresh wave of agony shot through my bones.

"We don't know what his focus does," I heard someone say. Their voice was soft, blurry almost, as though I was hearing it from a great distance. "I think we should-"

"Ben, cool it," Matt called, his tone sharp and irritated. There was a grief hidden underneath the anger, deep and fresh, but it was already fading as he forced himself back under control. "Christian's still shopping. Hold off for a little bit."

"I'm not *shopping*," Christian muttered. "I'm just being-"

"Asinine," the air-sucker said under his breath, but he let up. I gasped for air, trying to calm my racing heart.

I could see Christian glare sidelong at Ben, his lips pursed, but he didn't say anything.

"Are we about done here?" Dan called, still sitting on the stairs. "I'm tired."

"Everyone just shut *up*," Matt snapped. Ben was distracted, still glaring at Christian. I took the opportunity to roll over a little, just far enough that I could see Matt.

He had Aedan on his side, patting him up and down. He was looking for something. Aedan's relic, no doubt. I had no idea what it was, but it had to be worth *something* if Matt was going to all this trouble just to get his hands on it.

Aedan was still dressed in his uniform shirt and black pants, hardly any protection at all against the cold. I could see him shiver from where I lay. Of course, it might have just been the aftereffects of the electricity on his nerves, too. Ben stalked over, leaving me behind with one last irritated look. Aedan's bag lay forgotten on the ground where he'd held Recon. Without a word, the air-sucker tore it open and began pawing through the contents.

"Where is it, you ass?" Matt said, pulling Aedan's shirt up as he continued his pat-down. His face was getting more red with every second they wasted.

"Aren't you going to buy me dinner first?" The words weren't even loud enough to be called a whisper, little more than a breath, but I heard them.

80

Matt did too. A muscle in his temple popped out as he stared down at Aedan - who stared back at him bold as brass, as though he wasn't handcuffed and beaten.

"Hey - It's your lucky day, Christian," I heard Ben say as Matt resumed his search. I tried to push myself upright again, hoping to be at least a little stealthy about it, but as soon as I moved the air pressure around me dropped again. I fell back into the dirt, my head spinning. Ben held a box up as though nothing had happened - Aedan's box, hanging open to reveal the contents.

"Oh, *nice*," Christian said, his eyes lighting up.

"Found it," Matt said. "I found it, you little bastard." His words were rough, falling out of him in a rush of excitement, but there was an odd reverence underlying his tone. I turned my head back to them, trying my best not to do anything Ben felt worthy of another air-draining.

He had a knife. I bit back a morbid chuckle. It was Aedan. It was probably one of about twenty on the guy.

Only, when I looked, Aedan's pant leg was pushed up, and there was a leather sheath strapped to his calf. It wouldn't be an easy reach for him, if this was just another murder-knife.

I blinked, the pieces falling into place. The others were quiet too, coming to the same understanding.

Aedan squirmed closer, throwing himself at Matt as he tried to bite the man's ankle. Matt kicked him in the gut disinterestedly, stepping away. He held the knife up to the light, turning it this way and that.

Somehow, it *did* make sense that Aedan's relic would be a knife.

"Perfect," Matt breathed. "Awesome."

Ben inched closer, simultaneously trying to watch me and check out the knife. "Is that-"

"Fuck all it's going to do you," Aedan said with a groan, rolling over onto his back so that he could glare at them. "You know that, right?"

"Can we go?" Dan yelled down again. "Seriously, guys, I don't know how much longer I can-"

"Is the van ready?" Matt sait without so much as a glance at Dan.

Christian nodded, his attention still fixated on the box of relics. "Uh. Yeah. Should be good to go once we're inside. Brewer said it'd keep him out for at least a day."

"Cowards," Aedan wheezed. "Let me up and fight me like men instead of-"

Matt kicked him in the gut again. Aedan fell silent, turning away as he coughed for breath.

"All right," Matt said, turning the knife over and over in his hand. "All right. Good. Christian, if you want answers out of him, you'd better hurry up. Get the glasses, too. Ben, come help me carry him. Dan, just...keep us covered as far as the van, ok? Can you manage that?"

"Yeah. Just hurry," the man said. He was trembling as he half-fell down the stairs.

He vanished from sight behind the approaching wall of Christian. I hardly had time to yelp before the man had me by the shoulders, rolling me flat. His hands searched my coat pockets, slid around my wrists.

His eyes lit up again as he found the chain around my neck. I heard him sigh as my necklace slid out from beneath my shirt, the silver rings glittering in the streetlights.

"What's it do?" he said, cupping it in the palm of his hand.

He was just window-shopping. What an ass. He was just going to ride around, waiting until he found one that suited his fancy, and steal it?

Fuck that. To hell with him.

"Wouldn't you like to know," I said, my voice tight and strained as I pushed the words past the wall of pain and dizziness slowly creeping over me.

He frowned down at me. And then he grabbed a stick laying in the bushes of our apartment's hideously managed 'garden', slamming the sharp edge into my gunshot leg.

My back arched as I screamed again, every fiber of my being protesting the suddenly renewed agony. He held it for a long moment, the pressure building, and then let me go. I fell to the grass again, my throat beginning to ache.

"Christian. Hurry up," Matt said. Dimly, through the fog that was layered over my vision, I could see him and the air-sucker trying to manhandle Aedan into a better position to carry him from. He was a small man, wiry and lean, and it wasn't going to take them much longer.

Christian scowled down at me, his finger again tracing the necklace. "Look, you little shit," he muttered. "If you tell me I'll at least shoot you before I take it, all right?"

What, *that* was supposed to be his encouragement?

He seemed to see the resentment in my eyes. "If you make me try and guess what it is, so help me god, I'll leave you here," he hissed. "I'll leave you behind to collapse. Don't think I won't. That'll be for Recon."

Oh. I swallowed hard, remembering the sight of those men shattering into dust on the wind. Of *her* disappearing, only a short minute before.

His fingers slipped through the rings, twisting them this way and that as he stared at me. And then he pulled the chain taut, his eyes narrowing as his patience dwindled. Behind him, Matt and Ben were lifting Aedan off the ground, trading curses under their breath while the man kicked and fought as best he could.

"Christian!" Matt bellowed. "Now!"

"Shit," I heard him mutter. "Your choice, kid. Now."

His hand closed around the rings. I reached up, grabbing at the chain, but he just tugged harder. He'd just break it - there was nothing I could do to stop him.

No. The necklace was mine. He wouldn't - he *couldn't*. I wouldn't let him.

My mouth dropped open as I tensed, my grip tightening around the chain. My gaze was locked on his, blue eyes to blue.

Before I could say a single word, he froze.

I'd seen it too, from the corner of my eye - movement, from the trees and brush around our apartments. Someone was there. I could feel a bead of sweat drip down the small of my back as we both searched in the night.

There - a man. My pulse thundered in my ears as I gaped.

It was Jake. He crept along the edge of the woods, hardly making a sound. A gun was clutched in one hand.

What *now*? Why was he- *how* was he here? Had he followed us? What possible reason would he have to do something like that? The thoughts raced in my head one after another as he stiffened, eyes fixing on our little scene.

I tried to pull away as he straightened, bringing his arm up to aim, but Christian still had a solid hold on me.

The flare from the barrel of Jake's gun was blinding, lighting up the night as he fired - again, and again. My head snapped around as I forced myself to the side, taking advantage of my captor's shock.

I spun just in time to see Aedan sag, drooping in the hands of the two carrying him. His mouth fluttered as he crumpled, like he was trying to say something. His chest was a mess of red, though, his throat just….gone. My eyes were wide and unseeing. No. Not now. After all this, he couldn't be-

The cracks spreading across his skin shone with a hot, angry light, every bit as bright in the darkness as the gunfire had been. They rose up from under his skin like morbid, glow-in-the-dark tattoos. Matt and Ben were yelling something, the words jumbled together and incoherent through the flood of sheer disbelief overtaking me.

Before I could blink, before I could move, Aedan shattered into a thousand pieces, dispersing on the nighttime breeze.

CHAPTER TEN

My mouth hung open. I stared, gaping, as the last fragments of silvery dust drifted away.

No. That wasn't supposed to happen. Aedan wasn't supposed to *die*. He was the one keeping me alive, dammit. He'd saved me too many times to end up like…that. He deserved better.

The others were shocked by his sudden collapse too. I could still hear Matt and the air-sucker screaming at each other. I didn't care enough to try and pick out the words.

My mind latched onto a single fact, even as the grief inside me yawned open. Christian was distracted, buried in Aedan's bag still. He'd flinched away at the sound of gunshots, just like the rest of us. It would only last a moment, but I had a chance.

Swallowing the surge of pain that stabbed through my leg at the motion, I threw myself forward and away from him. I wasn't going to be fast, but maybe I could hobble to the-

His hand snapped out as I took another shuddering, staggering step, seizing my ankle. I tipped forward with a muffled cry, every bone in my body complaining as I hit the ground for what seemed like the hundredth time that night.

"Where is he?" Matt bellowed.

Ben was a pale, tight-drawn figure on the edge of my vision. "I-I don't-"

"Find him!"

Find who? I glanced over as Ben took a step towards the trees, hesitating.

Jake was gone. I realized it almost immediately, once I actually took the time to look. He must have taken off as soon as Aedan was- once he'd died.

Something caught in my mind, screaming for attention. Aedan....died?

Aedan?

The sight of him falling in the McDonald's parking lot flashed in front of my eyes. He'd been shot in the head. There was no mistaking it - and no one popped back from a wound like that in an hour or two. I doubted anyone would even *survive* a wound like that.

What exactly was happening? Was it his relic? But Matt took his relic away.

My eyes snapped over to Matt. He stood stock-still, holding Aedan's knife out flat. His fingers twitched on the hilt, tapping a harsh beat against the leather-wrapped wood.

I exhaled slowly. No. Matt had Aedan's relic. Even if his ability was...special, could he even use it? That was the whole point, wasn't it? After Aedan had borrowed mine, he'd spoken some bizarre language that I hadn't understood at *all*. My power hadn't worked.

So that meant that Aedan was...dead. That he'd-

"Get him over here."

Get who, now? My head snapped back up, my thoughts interrupted by the angry, strident tone in Matt's voice.

Aedan's knife was crumbling in his hands, splintering into fragments and chunks and collapsing to the ground. I stared, caught completely off guard. I...hadn't known they would do that. What did it mean? The rest of his things were already gone, the backpack just a pile of dust on the ground.

Even as I gaped, though, Christian's hands wrapped around my shoulders. He had me upright before I could say a word, my leg hanging limp under me. It had finally had enough of me and my mistreatment of it. Perfect.

"Ben!" Matt snapped, spinning on his heel. "I told you to-"

"I'm going," the air-sucker said, rolling his eyes. "But are you sure you're going to be fine with-"

"He hasn't used his focus yet, has he?" Matt said, folding his arms across his chest as the last of the dust drifted away. "I'm fine. Go get that sleepy fucker and bring him back."

Ben nodded, turning and dashing into the forest with one last look at me.

Jake. A surge of mixed emotions welled up at the thought of him. We'd saved him - and he'd come back and shot Aedan? That was how he rewarded us? Did he think that was the kinder option?

I gasped as Christian stumbled, nearly dropping me. The wound in my leg pulsated, seething with agony at the disturbance.

"You good, Dan?" Matt called, tearing his eyes off me long enough to look back towards the apartments.

"Not really," the squat little man said. He leaned against the railing, a hand pressed to his face. "Can we-"

"We're going, so get up," Matt snapped.

Wait, what? I flinched, my steps slowing.

Matt didn't miss my apprehension. He chuckled, his dark eyes narrowed. "Oh, don't look so surprised."

"I don't know if that's a good idea, Matt," Christian said, his hands tightening further. "We still don't know what-"

"If he's got something so dangerous, he would have used it already," Matt said, his chin raising stubbornly. "We're at a disadvantage now, thanks to fucking Jake. A hostage might help."

"I-I know that. But, he's probably long gone. There's no reason to think he'd hang around."

"He's never traveled with allies before, either," Matt said. "Not since we split up. If he's changed the game, we need to adapt with him."

"Are we going?" Dan said, stumbling up to us. His bald head gleamed in the dim light.

Christian sighed. "We should be on our-"

"Yes, we're going," Matt said. "Van's that way. Come on."

"Good," Dan said, relief coloring his words. "Good, good."

Shit. My mind was frozen, a mass of panic as the two began towing me towards the parking lot. They were going to *take* me? Why? What good would come of *that*?

The alternative was probably killing me, the part of my mind still thinking logically pointed out. Even still, this wasn't good.

Christian glanced towards Matt, his lips pursed. "How long are we going to keep him around, exactly?"

"If Aedan doesn't show up in a day or two, then he's long gone," Matt said. He trudged alongside Christian and I. I could see a muscle in his jaw twitching. "At that point we can clean up. He might even be worth something. Sound good?"

"That's fine," Christian said, his voice carefully cheerful. His eyes flicked back to my necklace.

I blinked, furrowing my brow. Well, that made it sound like they thought Aedan was still around. That he was somewhere close. It made it sound like they thought he was alive.

Amber lights blinked on a van in the back of the lot - theirs, then. It loomed, a dark mass in the night alongside their fake cruiser. I swallowed hard, sliding away from Christian instinctively. No. There was no *way* I was getting in some pedo-van with these assholes. They'd kill me. There must be some way for me to distract them, to get away.

"Hurry up," Christian said, tugging me on. I winced, trying to drag my heels, but he didn't seem to notice.

Dan was already there, pulling the door on the side open. He tumbled inside without another word, plopping himself down onto a seat with a groan.

Matt glanced back towards us. "Dan, there's no reason for him to be awake. Find what the brewer made and-"

"Matt!"

My heart leapt as we came to a stop. Christian turned back towards the darkened yard, dragging me along with him. I'd recognized the voice too - Ben. He must have found Jake. I wasn't sure if that made me happy or disappointed. He'd shot Aedan. But if I was reading this situation right and the others thought Aedan was alive, then what did that-

The last remaining blood in my face drained away, leaving me light-headed and sick to my stomach as I stared at Ben. The tall, confident man was scowling as he stalked back towards us.

But it was Keira's arm he clutched in his hand, not Jake's.

"Keira!" I gasped, staring at her. "What- But you were supposed to-"

Her eyes met mine for an instant, and then she glanced away. Her skin was an ashen grey, and I could see the way her hands shook as they approached.

She'd been supposed to leave. To get away. She was supposed to be *safe* by now. But then why was she-

"Found her in the woods behind the yard," Ben said, joining our little group. "Just kind of watching."

Christian dragged me closer, leaning in to catch his companion's words. His eyes were narrowed behind his glasses, wary still.

Keira squirmed, her foot slamming into the air-sucker's ankle as she fought to get away, but he didn't seem to notice. "L-Let me *go*, you-"

"The one you found earlier?" Matt said.

Ben nodded, twirling one finger. Keira's struggles faded as she gasped, her face going red.

"Stop that!" I cried, lunging forward. Christian's hand held me back. My leg collapsed under me at the single step I'd managed, anyway. My knees hit the ground hard.

Ben glanced at me, smirking, but his hand stopped moving. Keira crumpled, panting as her breath returned. She glared at the others from behind her hair, eyes radiating a confused mixture of terror and rage.

"Well, that changes things," Matt said. He glanced between her and I, tilting his head to one side. "Siblings?"

We looked alike. Everyone said it. The connection there was too obvious to deny, so I just nodded reluctantly.

"Right, right," he said, leaning back against the van. "Good."

Keira straightened, glaring at him. "It'll be good when I-"

"Keira," I said, cutting her off before she could say something they'd hurt her for. I knew that look on her face, the obstinate attitude that she always seemed to get when someone pushed her. I'd played with fire, exchanging insults with this lot, so I didn't really have a leg to stand on. But, all the same, I really didn't have a leg to stand on because I got *shot*. I didn't want her getting shot in front of me, either.

Matt looked back to me, one eyebrow arching. "What, can't she speak for herself?"

"She's not involved," I said, pulling my leg out straight as I sat down more heavily. "She's not connected to any of this. Just let her go." I swallowed hard, seeing her stare at me from the corner of my eye. "Please."

"Jon, what the hell is-"

"So she's not?" Matt said, eyeing Keira again. "Interesting."

"I didn't find anything on her," Ben said, his tone almost sheepish. "Might've missed it."

"Or she might just be a mundane," Matt said. "How about it, girl? What's your relic?"

Her eyes fixed on him. "I don't know what the hell you're talking about, but you can go straight to-"

"Keira," I moaned, staring at her. Thoughts of the things they'd done so far ran through my head. Things she'd be tempting out of them if she kept arguing. "Please. Stop."

"What are you thinking?" Christian said. His hand was still on my shoulder, making sure I didn't suddenly heal a gunshot wound and take off running.

"I'm thinking we're down a finder."

I froze.

Christian made an unhappy noise in the back of his throat. "I don't know if that's a good idea, Matt."

"No," I said, shaking my head. "No, you can't." I might be new to this world and how things worked, but I understood well enough. I could see the way Matt glanced at Keira appraisingly, then back to Christian.

"You get those glasses?"

"Uh- No, I didn't get that far," the man holding me said. "Sorry."

"No problem," Matt said. He stepped past where I sat, crossing the lot to where we'd spend the last few minutes. Something glinted in the grass. He stooped to pick it up, carefully holding it in the sleeve of his jacket.

Recon's glasses.

"No," I spat, struggling to stand. My leg wasn't listening, and Christian wasn't letting me move anyway. Somehow, I knew that whatever was going to happen was bad. I couldn't let it happen.

"Still don't think this is a good idea," Christian said.

"Can we hurry?" Dan called from the van's backseat. "Seriously, any minute my screen could go, and-"

"Shut the hell up, Dan," Matt said. "Why are you so worried, Christian?"

"Keeping pets is a risk."

"A pet with a finder's focus?" Matt said, a chuckle dancing under the words. "What's she going to do? Aggressively detect us?"

"I don't want her stabbing me in my sleep. That's all."

"She might not even be compatible," Dan said, glaring out the door at us.

"Relax, Christian," Matt said, eyeing him sidelong as he moved to stand in front of Keira and Ben. "If he's got the potential, she probably does too. We'll be careful. It's a bit of training, that's all."

His hand dropped to her shoulder, patting it companionably. She shuddered.

My blood boiled. "Don't you dare-"

I flinched, the words dying in my throat as the air whisked from my lungs. Ben. He was watching me, his fingers twitching.

"If we've got her, do we really need him?" I heard him say. He almost sounded bored.

"Jon!" Keira screamed.

I couldn't so much as look at her. I hit the pavement, the strength leaving my limbs as I fought for air.

"Well, if Aedan-"

"He's not coming back," Ben said. "You said it yourself. He's never bothered with this kind of thing before. I'm betting he's already halfway across the state. We need to move fast if we're going to catch up."

"We don't need two hostages, Matt," Christian said. "Ben's right."

"Fine. Fine!" Matt said. "Just make it quick."

"Right," Ben said, satisfaction lacing his tone. "I can do-"

His words vanished into a pained yelp. I wheezed, drawing in a great lungful of air as the pressure around me normalized. My chest burned, and I still couldn't walk, but I forced myself back up. I needed to see. I needed to know what was happening.

Keira was attacking Ben, I saw. That's what was happening. She'd launched herself at him in a mess of brown hair and pointed elbows, clawing at his face as he tried to fight her off. She was doing pretty well, too. Bloody tracks were torn down the air-sucker's rugged face, and he had one eye squeezed shut.

"Get off me, you bitch!" he cried, finally lashing out with one great hand. She went flying with a muffled yelp, hitting the ground moments later. He straightened, pressing a hand to his face with a groan.

"All right, then, you two," Matt said, crossing to where Keira was even then pushing herself upright. He took her arm, pulling her upright - and pinning her in place. "That's enough of that."

"I *don't* want her with us, Matt," Ben said, his eyes flashing dangerously as he glared at their leader. "She's-"

"It'll just take a bit more work than I thought," Matt said, pulling the wire-and-crystal glasses out again. "But, we could use a finder. She could help us catch up to Aedan."

"If we need a finder, we could go back, talk to-"

"I'm not bringing in anyone from her crew," Matt said, his humor beginning to fade. "We're fine on our own."

"Does this look fine to-"

"That's enough, Ben. Once we find another candidate we can trade her out, but I'm not letting that snake have the satisfaction of getting her cronies in the door."

Keira was still spluttering, spitting half-formed insults at Matt as he approached. He paused, carefully folding out the arms on the glasses.

"Come on, just calm down. You're fine," he said, sitting back on his heels. "What's your name?"

"Fuck you."

"Guy here called her Keira," Christian said. He had me again - and his fingers were twitching. I could almost feel the weight of my necklace hanging around my neck, dancing out and open for the world to see above my jacket. He was watching it, I knew.

Ben was still wiping at his face, cursing loudly as he mopped away the blood. I had a few more moments - just a little longer, and he'd remember I was here. I had to find some way of ending this before that. Easier said than done.

"Keira. All right, then, Keira," Matt said, offering her a smile. "There's nothing to worry about. We're just going to go on a trip, and you're going to learn a few new tricks. It'll be fun."

She glared back at him, eyes wild. "I'm not going-"

"I've got her," Dan said. He tumbled out of the van, muttering darkly under his breath as he came up behind them. She flinched away, but his hands settled around her elbows. "Let's just get a move on."

"Thanks," Matt said. He lifted the glasses up, hesitating a moment longer. "Really, it'll be fine."

He reached out, his fingers brushing against her hair.

I heard her inhale, a short, sharp sound. Her eyes squeezed shut.

He laughed. He *laughed*, as she shuddered.

"Get the hell away from her," I heard my voice say, loud and strident and filled with rage. "Get your goddamn hands off my little sister, and get the *fuck* away from her." The world spun underneath me as I spat the words out, hardly aware of what I was saying. It wasn't a smart move, I recognized. I was just reminding them that I was here, that they hadn't killed me yet.

Right then, I didn't care. I just knew that there was no way in hell I was going to let him get her hooked on some relic. There was no way I was going to let him keep her around, whisking her off into the night. She wasn't his. He had no business toying with her, and he was going to understand that.

I didn't quite know how, but I was sure of it.

An uneasy silence fell over the little cluster we made in the parking lot.

Dan glanced my way, half-visible behind Keira. He still looked like he was on the verge of collapse, but his expression was scornful. Christian's fingers dug into my shoulders as he tensed, forcing me lower. Ben turned towards us with a sneer, his upper lip curling back. His face was still streaked with blood.

But Matt drew his hand back, sliding free of the mahogany waves of her hair. His other hand twitched, still clutching the glasses, but dropped down to his side.

And then he stepped away from her.

CHAPTER ELEVEN

The world seemed to hold its breath as we stood in place, statues under the dim street lights.

Christian's hand was still wrapped around my arm, pinning me in place. He wasn't about to let me go.

But Matt took another step back, one hand outstretched. Keira's hair fluttered in the evening breeze as at last his arm dropped, his fingers sliding free of her. He held perfectly still for a long, quiet moment, seeming completely frozen in place.

And then he blinked, looking at his hand, and his brow furrowed.

He wasn't the only one confused. Ben gaped, his chin jutted out as he glared at his leader. Dan sat in a crumpled heap just inside the door of the van, but he'd straightened as Matt stepped away from Keira. She didn't so much as twitch, her eyes flicking between mine and Matt's. She had no idea how to react, what to do next.

I couldn't blame her. None of it made sense - only, when I really stared at him, when I really thought about it, it *did*. Aedan had said it, hadn't he? That I was only limited by the deal I'd made with my relic, and what I asked of it.

Maybe I'd just never needed anything enough to figure it out. Maybe I hadn't known to look. But right then I needed everything it could give me and more - and I was paying attention.

Matt was waking up from whatever I'd done to him a little more with every second I wasted, though, and he didn't look happy about the matter. His eyes narrowed, fear and confusion rising up for the first

94

time to match the anger there, and his hand dipped towards his pocket. His gun? A knife? My memory was a blur, the details fading behind a wall of exhaustion, but I knew that whatever he was going for, it was *bad*.

"Don't move," I snapped, fixing my gaze on him. "All of you, stay right where you are." My mind was whirling, centered on one simple fact - he was *going* to listen to me. He didn't have a choice. My words were going to make him stop, because he had to. I needed him to.

He froze in place as though turned to stone. The others were no different - even Christian was as still as ice, one hand holding my arm. I pulled away from him carefully, trying to pretend like my gut wasn't churning, that my mind wasn't a mess of terror.

He didn't move.

My head pounded, thrumming unhappily. I swallowed hard.

"Keira. It's ok. Come here," I said as carefully as I could, unwilling to take my attention off the others. I scanned the group slowly, trying to keep track of each of them in my mind.

Keira pulled free of Matt's arm, slowly at first, but more firmly as he didn't move. Her confidence was hurt, but not ruined, then.

Christian twitched, his frame shuddering as she passed him. His fingers flexed.

"No. That's enough. Stop," I snapped, feeling the tug of him fighting me. He fell still again. My headache ramped up, burning dully.

She was almost to me. I wasn't quite sure what we'd do after that, but she'd be free of *them*. Again. This time I'd make it stick.

Too late, I saw Ben twitch, his chin snap around. His eyes fixed on me, razor-sharp and all too focused.

The first tendrils of air slid from between my lips. I pressed a hand to my mouth a heartbeat later, feeling his power swell. I needed air to talk. I needed to talk to make him listen to me. If he pulled the last of my air out, everything we'd done would be for nothing.

"Stop," I croaked yet again, forcing the words out on the last wisps of oxygen I could muster. My voice was soft and barely recognizable, but it seemed to do the trick.

Ben stopped. His eyes flicked this way and that, fear growing to match the anger in their depths.

I just held my seat on the ground for a long moment, taking one ragged breath after another. Air had never tasted sweeter. With every moment that passed, though, I knew the truth of it - I was stuck. I couldn't move. If I turned away from them, if I allowed my attention to break for even a single moment, they'd get loose. Already as I stared at Ben, reinforcing my intent, I could feel Dan squirming to get free. My head throbbed as I glanced over to him, as though complaining at the sudden exertion.

Even if I had the willpower and strength to keep this moving while we ran, my leg wouldn't so much as twitch under me. The slightest movement sent blades of fire up and down my leg, my back. I wouldn't be running anywhere for a while.

"Take a weapon and run," I said slowly, rolling even word on my tongue as I glanced from face to face. It wasn't an order. She'd see reason. She had to.

"Jon, t-there's no way I can-"

"Stop complaining and go," I said, sparing a single moment to glare at her. Something dripped down my face. I pressed a hand to it, wiping it away. Blood. My nose was bleeding. No part of that seemed like a good sign.

Keira made an unhappy sound in the back of her throat, as though she wanted to argue with me again, but didn't say another word. She was still trembling, but I saw her reach out and slide something from Christian's pocket. A knife. Well, it would have to do.

I forced a smile. "Get clear. I'll see you soon."

She hesitated a moment longer, wrapping her fingers around the hilt so tightly her knuckles stood out white against her skin.

Beyond her, Matt twitched again. I spun to him, my heartbeat accelerating. There were so many ways this could go wrong. Dan seemed to be hiding us somehow - that could stop at any moment, judging by his labored breathing. Someone could pull a gun. A knife. They could scream. And out of all of them, I knew Matt would be the one to seize the moment.

"Sit still," I snapped, glaring at him.

His slow, steady advance halted as soon as the words were out of my mouth. My eyes were glued to his, pinning him in place.

Too much. It was too much. As I fixed my attention on Matt, I could feel Christian squirm, threatening to break free. His fingers pawed at my shoulders, fighting with every second to try and grab at my neck. I spun in the dirt, ignoring the accompanying scream of agony from my still-shot leg, and glared at him. "Don't-"

But as I tried *that*, still reaching towards Matt and doing my best to hold them in place, I felt the rest of my concentration crack. It fell away in splinters as I reeled, my head erupting in splitting, blinding pain.

Ben must have seen his chance. I caught sight of him moving from the corner of my eye as I coughed, a hand pressed against my forehead as though that would somehow make the pain stop. He lunged, one hand already stretching towards me.

I tried. I really tried. But he was faster. Before I could utter so much as a single syllable, the air was knocked from my lungs. My commands came out as a pained, wordless grunt as my lungs deflated in an instant.

My limbs going weak, I keeled over - but not before I saw her move. Keira launched herself at the air-sucker as I collapsed, her teeth gritted and her newfound knife swinging wildly.

Ben was already bloody, a gash torn across his muscular chest where I'd gotten him back in the apartment. He hadn't been expecting my little sister to be the one to go on the offensive - and that gave her a single, precious window of opportunity.

He couldn't dodge as she slashed out with a rough cry, her frame quivering from the effort of it. He tried, stumbling backwards so quickly I thought he'd tumble over entirely, but she was too close and he was too unprepared. A spray of red erupted along his collarbone.

From the way Keira's eyes tightened, her expression darkening, it wasn't the finishing blow she'd been aiming for. In the end, though, it was just enough when combined with the blood he'd already lost. Between her pressuring him and his attempts to get away, he staggered straight back into the curb.

He went down with a muffled cry - and I took another shuddering breath, already hissing commands at the others.

Keira's eyes were wide, her terror all too plain as she stared down at Ben, but she didn't hesitate for long. Before the air-sucker could rise she was on him, the knife in her hand flashing down faster than he could roll over or begin to defend himself.

I should stop her. She shouldn't be killing anyone - but after seeing the bruises covering her, I couldn't find it in me to tell her not to. And I certainly wasn't going to be helping.

"Sit down," I snapped at Christian, feeling his hand sliding across my shoulder again. He dropped like a rock. "Roll over. Face down."

The edges of my vision were going grey. I coughed, a hot metallic taste rising in the back of my throat. I tried to ignore it. We were- Well, we were closer to being through it.

Matt glanced over at me, every movement slow and painful. "You...too," I managed between hacks, putting every ounce of conviction I had into the words. He seemed to hesitate, his frame tensing like he wanted to bolt. And then he sat down on the asphalt, his eyes fixed on mine.

The sound of footsteps was the first warning I had that not everyone was so obedient. I moved on instinct, my head snapping around to spot the new threat.

Dan. Dan was running, somehow finding it in himself to move again. He wasn't what I would call fast, and he wasn't what anyone would call graceful, but I was in no condition to go after him. I bit back a sigh, eyeing his back as he plowed towards the shadows at the edge of the lot.

The shadows that moved when he approached, rippling like they were greeting him.

I stared, wide-eyed, as Aedan buried his knife in the man's throat. His other arm was wrapped around Dan's shoulders, holding him close in a cruel parody of an embrace as the short, squat little man twitched.

He was still wearing his uniform shirt, red with black detailing. And he had his backpack again, the straps digging lines into the fabric around his arms. It was as though nothing had happened, like he *hadn't* been shot, or gone on a hike through the woods, or been tasered. It was all just wiped clean.

Neither Matt or Christian were fighting me, anymore. They watched with me as Aedan pulled his blade free, letting Dan tumble to the ground. And then Aedan was off, stepping towards us with cold efficiency.

Ben was still twitching, still trying to grab at Keira's arm. Tears ran down her cheeks by then, every horrified breath a gasp, but didn't stop.

Aedan snagged her arm on the next upstroke, his free hand settling around her wrist.

"No, not like that," he said. "You'll never get anywhere like that."

I blinked, the ridiculousness of the situation overcoming my fear and pain for a split second. He was just so...clinical about it, his tone perfectly matter-of-fact.

"You're holding it too tightly," he said, a hint of annoyance creeping into his voice as he stared at Keira. "It's not going to run away from you. Stop tensing up."

Ben gasped, still shuddering and bleeding. Aedan slid his hand over Keira's, holding her arm out.

"See? Just like that. Tense too much, and you'll just break fingers."

Her brow furrowed as she stared at him, her mouth sliding further open with every word he said. I didn't blame her at all. In her position, I'd probably look exactly the same.

Aedan patted her shoulder with his free hand, chuckling softly. "You'll be fine, girl. Quick, now. Like *this*."

I hardly saw him move. Keira flinched, clearly not expecting it either. He drove his hand down, still wrapped gently around hers, and plunged the knife into Ben's neck.

The man twitched, his eyes widening- and then he sagged, already going limp.

Keira fell away as Aedan rose, her hands pressed to her face. He didn't seem to notice. She stayed on the ground, kicking herself further away from Ben. Away from Ben's body.

Aedan glanced my way, twirling his knife idly. "You all right there, Jonny?"

I swallowed hard, forcing the taste of blood and bile back down. My finger had pushed beyond 'agony' an hour ago. My head was on fire, and from the pain in my skull I would have thought there was a crack in it. My leg had long since gone numb, but that was better than the searing agony of the gunshot wound.

"Fine," I said, pushing myself farther away from Christian. "Just fine." Things had gotten easier, without Ben and Dan to worry about, but my commands were weakening little by little the longer the silence dragged on.

I realized I had no idea how it worked, this new power that I'd found. The thought was not comforting, when both Christian and Matt were no doubt armed. I just licked my lips, leaning back on my elbows as Aedan patted Keira's shoulder once more.

"You're fine," I heard him murmur. "There, it's done, see? You did well."

Ben's form was already beginning to droop, a dull glow beginning under his skin.

I could see Keira's shoulders shake as she took a deep breath, letting it out in a long, shuddering gasp - but already, she looked more calm. Her eyes were still fixed on Ben, her bloody hands folded in her lap, but she didn't seem like she was about to shatter into pieces herself anymore. Aedan nodded approvingly, a smile touching the corners of his lips, and stepped past her without another word.

The knife in his hand flinted in the dingy light as he snapped it back straight, settling his fingers around it. "Good, Jonny. Glad to hear it. Didn't get yourself in too deep?"

I glared at him. "No."

"Wonderful. Plan went well? Seems you picked up a few tricks, eh?"

The ass knew damn well nothing had gone according to plan. Tonight had been nothing but killing and being attacked, and I hurt, and I was *tired* of it. Matt and Christian were still squirming, still pushing at the edges of my commands, and I wasn't sure how much longer I could hold them.

"Stop fucking around, Aedan."

He chuckled one last time. "Right, right. Stop giving me that look. You're not dead, right?"

"That doesn't seem like a standard worth a damn, does it?"

His smile warped, going crooked for a single second. "It's the one that counts in the end, isn't it?"

I threw my head back, my eyes sliding shut. "Fine. Whatever. Help."

I heard him laugh. "What was that? Did you just ask me for help?"

"Aedan."

"Oh, stop complaining," he said, his voice rippling with laughter. I raised my head again. He was already moving towards Matt and Christian, who were stiffening, drawing back. My hold on them was fraying by the second, but he had to be able to see that.

"I don't know how much longer I can-"

"Don't worry," he said, his voice suddenly eerily calm.

I stopped, the tension in me beginning to fade as he glanced back over his shoulder. And then I faltered, still clinging to the faint hold I had over the two men as his green eyes stared into mine.

"I've got this."

CHAPTER TWELVE

The only sound for a long moment was the crickets, chirping happily away in the darkness outside our halo of light.

Aedan's eyes were still fixed on mine, glowing emerald in the street lights and intense enough to bring me up short. He sounded so confident that there was no way for me to argue it. If he said that he was going to handle things….he would. That was all there was to it.

The sound of his footsteps on the asphalt pulled me out of whatever trance he'd placed over us. His eyes tore free of mine as he turned to Christian - and Matt. They were still fighting, pulling against the hold that my relic and I had on them for all they were worth. I felt another cough ripple up through my chest as they pushed against me. The metallic taste of blood in the back of my mouth was growing stronger by the second, and I could feel the blood trickling down across my lips from my worsening nosebleed.

There was no way I could hold them both. I sagged further, my vision blurring.

"Jon!" I heard Keira cry. She stumbled to her feet, a dark, shapeless mass in the night.

I couldn't keep them both. I couldn't.

Even as I watched my little sister stagger towards me, still trembling, I could feel it - the sudden lurch and release as my power buckled. I gasped, feeling him tear free.

Christian. I saw him from the corner of my eye, twitching as he straightened. His head snapped around, locking on me, and-

"Don't even think about it," Aedan said, the words rolling out of him as he closed the gap between him and Matt's second. I could only shudder, feeling the pressure in my head fall away as half of my burden vanished. If I squinted, I could see them - Aedan, with his hand buried in Christian's collar. Christian was frozen, one hand outstretched and ready to plunge into his pocket.

He seemed to recognize exactly the situation he was in. His arm flexed once, tensing - and then relaxed, falling limp to his side as Aedan pulled him closer.

"You good, Jonny?" he called, one green eye flicking over to me.

I swallowed again, feeling my head spin all the while. "Y-Yup. Hurry."

"No, he's *not*, you asshole."

I jumped. A hand clutched my elbow as someone's arm slid behind my shoulders. They pulled me a little straighter, holding me upright.

"Okay? You've got to be kidding me," they whispered. Keira. I relaxed as soon as I recognized her voice, somehow having lost track of her in the few brief seconds since she'd stood. I didn't like what that implied about my mind, and about the state I was in.

I could feel her turn to me, press in closer. "Where are you-"

"Leg," I whispered, unwilling to take my eyes off the three men still standing across the parking lot. Aedan stalked in to meet Christian, close enough that their noses might have been touching. Neither of them looked happy.

"You little goddamn rat," I heard Aedan hiss, his voice low and cutting. "You know, it's not every day I find someone quite as pathetic as you."

Christian's hands were shaking, but he lifted his chin. "Y-You're only saying that because-"

"Because it's true," Aedan said, his eyes narrowing. "I heard you, you know."

Christian paused. "What a-are you-"

"Have you ever been through a collapse?" Aedan said, his tone suddenly almost...cheerful. "Have you suffered that end - the one you were threatening poor Jonny with?"

My mouth went dry. He shouldn't sound that happy. I just *knew* that anytime Aedan looked that mad but sounded that happy, something bad was going to happen.

I gasped, flinching as a jolt of pain shot through my leg.

Matt twitched, his hand sliding towards his-

"Sit still," I rasped, feeling my throat complain with every word. "Hands on your head."

My eyes ached. My head ached. Every muscle in my body was screaming that it had had enough - but Matt went still again, resting his hands on his head.

"Sorry, sorry," Keira said. Her words were quiet and altogether too thin. She was quivering, her breath coming in ragged gasps, but she'd cut strips of fabric off someone's jacket with her knife.

I blinked. *Ben's* jacket, it looked like. The man lay in a pool of blood, his fingers twitching sporadically. I watched with horrified, morbid fascination. Keira didn't spare him another glance. Another knife of pain stabbed into my leg as she bound the gunshot wound tighter.

"Of course you don't," Aedan said. "How could you?"

I thought he was oblivious to what had almost happened - until his eyes flicked to mine, then away.

Well, it wasn't as though he could die. It certainly didn't look that way, anyway. If he wasn't concerned about the matter...so be it.

Christian squirmed, trying to take a swing at him. "Y-You fucking-"

"See, first, it's like your skin is *crawling*," Aedan said. I saw the knife glint in the dim half-light as he slashed out.

Christian screamed. Aedan's hand was on his mouth a moment later, silencing the cry. A line of red was torn across his cheek, already oozing blood.

The two were stepping backwards, teetering closer to the van.

"Shh, shh," Aedan murmured in his ear. "See, we don't have your friend anymore, do we? So I'm going to have to ask you to shut the fuck *up*."

His knife hand slammed down on the last word, catching Christian in the thigh. The man roared in pain again, his eyes squeezed shut behind his glasses. Aedan rode with the motion, keeping the cry muffled.

And then he tipped him sidelong into the van, taking advantage of Christian's instability as the man fell.

"See, you're just a human," he said, his voice still perfectly casual. "You run with demis, but you're too indecisive to actually make a claim and pick a damn relic. So there's no *way* you could understand what it feels like to have your insides boil within you - and I can't let you escape unpunished. Sorry."

Christian tried to squirm away, but Aedan was done talking. His knife flashed in the hazy light.

Keira was shaking again, trembling as the parking lot echoed with the dim, half-muffled sounds of Aedan putting an end to the threat that had been Christian. Her hands lay across my leg, pressing down hard as she tried to stop the bleeding, but she leaned closer. I wrapped my arms around her, my eyes fixed at the last player on the field.

Matt was fighting my hold harder than ever - and why not? He'd just gotten a front-row seat to Aedan butchering his subordinate. If I were Matt, I'd be struggling to get away, too.

There was no way I was going to let him give me the slip again, though. I clung to him, pouring every ounce of strength I had left into making sure that he didn't turn tail and run. He had nothing - no power to stand against me. I could feel it all too clearly, as I held him in place. If he had a relic, I had no clue what it was. The truth was probably simpler, though - and not hard to guess, considering how hard he'd been pursuing Aedan.

After a few seconds that felt like an eternity, Aedan pushed himself upright, leaving Christian's body crumpled on the backseat of the van.

"Still good?" he said, glancing towards us.

Keira glared back at him, gathering enough of her usual attitude to scowl darkly across the parking lot. "Do we *look* like we're good?"

"Perfect. Just peachy," Aedan said, shooting her a wink. She stiffened further, opening her mouth, but he was already stepping past the two of us towards Matt.

"Was it worth it, Matt?" he said, his voice oddly quiet.

Matt shook, the veins in his neck beginning to pop as he fought against my hold.

Aedan glanced back at me over his shoulder, rolling his eyes. "Look, Jonny, I know you just found yourself a new party trick, but would you-"

"You can talk," I said, spitting the words out as I glanced at Matt.

"Thanks, partner," Aedan said, a touch of his old smirk returning as he fake-saluted me. "Now, where were we, Matt? Oh. Right. Really? All this?"

"Go to hell," Matt said, still squirming like he was trying to push away.

"Stand still," I spat, pressing a hand to my face. My head spun, and even the slightest movement sent waves of nausea through my stomach. I was still bleeding, gushing blood out my nose even as I coughed up mouthfuls of red. Keira was doing her best to remain aloof and out of it, but she was beginning to look disgusted. Couldn't really blame her.

Matt froze, pinned in place with Aedan staring right back at him. "Couldn't give up," he said finally, shaking his head incrementally. "It's- not over."

"It's not over?" Aedan said, straightening as he took a step back. "How do you figure, Matt? Your crew is dead - again. That's another batch of demis you've led straight to their death."

"Only because they were-"

"You know, I'm sorry," Aedan said, his voice conversational. "I let you go, before."

It was Matt's turn to eye him, beginning to scowl. "You didn't *let me go*. I broke both your legs."

"And yet, here I am," Aedan said, waggling a finger under Matt's nose. "And here *you* are, alone again. I would tell you it's time to throw in the towel, but it was time for that two years ago."

Matt's face went paler the longer Aedan talked, his eyes following the point of my friend's knife.

"I thought the cop getup was a nice touch," Aedan said, casting a look back towards the still-uniformed bodies of Matt's friends. "Good use of resources. Very creative. No one would think twice about a cop asking some questions, after all." He snorted. "Well. Just Jon. Don't think either of us planned on that one. You kind of fucked things up, Jonny."

Matt was still trying to ease himself back, to gain another few inches. I put the brakes on, sinking deeper and deeper into the relic as I held him. It hung heavy around my neck, burning with enough heat that I was a bit worried I'd have burn marks across my shirt.

"Aedan," I said, pushing the words out.

His head snapped over to me. "What, Jonny? Bit busy here."

"Jon," I said, locking my eyes onto his. "And stop. Playing."

He sighed, the sound loud and dramatic. "Kids these days," I heard him mutter, shrugging helplessly. "They've got no respect, I tell you."

"Aedan."

"Who knows you were coming this way?" Aedan said, his voice snapping back to a cold, businesslike tone quickly enough that it was all I could do to keep from rocking in place. "Who'd you tell?"

"Everyone," Matt spat, his dark hair hanging limp and matted with sweat around his face. "I told-"

"Wrong," I gasped, seeing the way he stiffened. The curl of his fingers, the way he blinked, as though his eyes were suddenly dry.

Aedan didn't say anything. He just sank his knife into Matt's shoulder, hardly seeming to move.

The man shuddered, not so much as a groan slipping past his lips. I stared, taken aback by his restraint, his composure. That *had* to hurt.

"Jonny says you're lying," Aedan said, heaving him a step back - a step towards the van. "I don't like it when people lie to me, Matt. We're friends. Friends shouldn't lie to each other."

"Fine. It was my secret," he said, his voice tight with pain underlying each word. "No one knows."

"Uh," I said, beginning to sway in Keira's arms. Her grip on me tightened as she pulled me closer, mute and wordless in the face of the spectacle playing out. "Wrong."

"Ok, ok, ok," Matt said, holding a hand up even as Aedan's hand tightened on the knife in his shoulder. "I-I didn't tell anyone. I *didn't*."

"Good," I said, my voice dropping lower by the second.

"O...kay," Aedan said, his brow furrowing as he glanced between me and Matt. "Then, what? Tell me straight, you little-"

"Anke was watching," he said, his eyes twitching as Aedan gripped the hilt tighter. "She was- very interested in the plans I was making. That's- That's all. Swear."

"Anke. That bitch," Aedan said, a crooked grin blossoming on his face. "What's the old hag up to these days?"

"Aedan," I spat.

"Right, right, not now. I get it," he said, holding his hands up. Matt shivered, the tension sliding out of him as Aedan's hands came free of the knife. "Sell her the info, did you?"

"No," Matt said, licking his lips. "Wouldn't sell information like that."

"No, you thought you'd keep it for yourself," Aedan said, nodding. "You almost had it this time, too. Good effort. Good showing, I have to say."

Matt only chuckled, leaning back onto the frame of the van as the strength sagged out of his limbs. I crumpled too, trying to hold onto the world around me as my energy flagged.

"Jon?" Keira said, twisting until she sat over the top of me. Her blue eyes glowed in the dark, staring down into mine. "Just- Take it easy, ok?" She was as lost as I was - more so. Her eyes flicked back to Aedan and Matt, her lips pressing together as she gulped. I gave her a tiny smile, the best I could offer. We'd be fine. We had to be.

I had to wonder - why was Matt saying all this? Why was he just handing Aedan all the information he wanted? Was he hoping that Aedan would bargain with him, agree to turn him loose? Seeing the look on Aedan's face, I couldn't believe that was likely. Of course, with a knife stuck in him and Aedan's fingers tap-dancing on the hilt, it could be a simple matter of pain.

"She's following, then?" Aedan said, patting Matt's shoulder.

He nodded. "Probably. I'd expect it. She- she wanted me to let her men into the crew."

"And you told her no. Good man," Aedan said, still painfully cheery. "Appreciate it."

"Anything for a friend?" Matt said, his voice little more than a whisper. His eyes were fixed on Aedan's, his expression a little more hopeful. "I-I get it. You win. I give up. Really. I-"

"Oh, you give up, *now*," Aedan said, chuckling. "Right. Like you gave up last time. You know, I'd ask why you do this, but I think I know." He was still patting Matt's shoulder, growing in strength with every repetition. It was beginning to look more like a punch than a friendly gesture. "It's because you're a bitter, petty, jealous little fuck, Matt. And that's never going to change."

"Jon. Jon, hey. Eyes on me." Someone was tapping my cheek. Right. Keira. I recognized her voice, although it was too filled with fear to be *her*. Keira wasn't supposed to be afraid like that. "Come on. Wake up."

I couldn't move, couldn't take my eyes off the pair. The strength I had was fleeting, sliding down the drain like a tub with the plug pulled. Aedan was still pressing closer to Matt, and Matt was still backing away. I had no control over either of them anymore, but I didn't think it mattered.

Matt's voice rang out, wavering with fear. "Aedan, I-"

Aedan was already turning, taking Matt by the shoulders as he steered him towards the van. "Come on, then. Blood's messy, and I don't want Jonny getting arrested for murder tonight."

"Please. Aedan, please, just listen, and I'll-"

"Jon! Hey, come on. Wake up. Don't- Come *on*, Jon." Keira's voice was more insistent, demanding that I listen, that I look at her, but I couldn't move a finger.

The sound of a knife tearing through flesh cut across the quiet, unmistakable and horrifying. It was followed by the distant, wet thud of Matt's body hitting the floor of the van behind us. The sound of Aedan going about his work blended together into her fearful tones as I finally lost the fragile grip I'd held on reality and fell away into the black.

CHAPTER THIRTEEN

The world slid in front of my eyes in flashes, half-seen fragments that appeared and went with absolutely no input from me on the matter. I clung to them as best could, trying to pull myself back to awareness, but every time I tried to grab hold they just dissolved away under my fingertips.

"Jon. Come *on*. Don't do this to me." The woman's voice was tight and worried, hovering just on the edge of tears. A face filled my vision, her dark hair hanging in unkempt, dirtied waves.

Keira. I tried to open my mouth, to say something, *anything*, but the world was already blurring again.

There were hands under me, grabbing my shoulders. My legs. The ground fell away from underneath me. My stomach churned, rejecting the idea of 'moving'.

"Don't let him hit the door."

"I've got him. Stop whining. It's fine."

"It's not fine."

Who was arguing? Names flitted at the edge of my memory, names I should know. They vanished behind a wall of pain as my leg slammed into something hard. Something sharp.

"Look what you did!"

"Would you just pick him up higher? Jesus fucking Christ."

"Why can't I just call an ambulance, exactly?" Keira's voice rose over the other two. It was her again - I knew that much. I latched onto the name like an anchor. My shoulders settled against something a moment later, something softer than the ground had been.

Someone groaned, the sound filled with relief, and the pair of hands on my shoulders slid free. "Look, woman. It's not a far drive - it'll be faster this way. Believe me. And if you want the cops to come tear your apartment to shreds, be my guest."

I heard her sigh, the sound lurking on the edge of my awareness. "Who the hell are you, anyway?"

"That's not important. Would you just-"

My head rolled to the side as one of them shoved me. Hard. Someone groaned. It might have been me.

"Woah, woah, stop that. Pull him from the other side."

"Don't tell me what to do."

"Both of you shut *up*," Keira said sharply. I could feel her hands slide across my shoulders, and then I was moving again.

"What's wrong with him?" one of them said.

"He got *shot*," Keira snapped.

"That? That's hardly a graze. And you bandaged it and everything. He's *fine*," someone else said, down by my feet. It sounded like they were laughing. "He's just gone and tired himself out. Poor little Jonny."

"It's *not fine*. He could-"

The sound of their voices drifted away as something slammed shut between me and them. Whatever I was lying on swayed gently in time with it. The tension slid from my limbs as I lay there, feeling the blissfully welcome brush of something soft under me. Fabric.

They were still arguing. Their words were soft and hushed, as though they were trying to be discreet, but emotions were high. I couldn't make out the words. There was no way I was going to be able to summon enough focus for that.

Finally, after what seemed like forever, the argument died away. Distantly, something rumbled - an engine. And another. They revved to life, accompanied by the harsh sound of tires on asphalt, and then vanished entirely.

The sounds of the night filtered back in, accompanied again by the gentle shifting of whatever I lay on.

"Assholes," Keira muttered, the words little more than a whisper. A motor shuddered to life. For a long moment there was only the sound of the engine, and then I felt a hand brush my shoulder. "Hold tight, Jon. We'll get you there."

The fog laying thick and heavy over my mind wouldn't let me respond. She wasn't waiting for an answer, though - moments later, the world spun around me again as I shifted. We were accelerating, and fast.

She was muttering something, the words tight and anxious and completely inaudible under the sound of the motor. I gave up. There was no way I was going to be able to hold on any longer, and the black around me was so tempting. The gentle rocking of the seat under me pulled me in, coaxing me back under.

***

The car lurched. We'd stopped.

Voices. Someone was calling, beckoning. The cold night air washed over my face again. I shuddered.

There were hands - lifting, tugging, pulling.

The feeling of something firm and solid underneath me was a comfort, a reassuring presence after so long spent rocking back and forth.

It was too much. There were too many voices, all calling things to each other, listing off numbers and terms that made no sense whatsoever. The pain in my leg was gone, wiped clean by the cool numbness that was taking over. Something pricked my arm, even as a hand grasped my wrist, pulling me this way and that.

I tried to pull away. I'm very sure of that. What Matt and Christian had said rung clear in my mind - I couldn't go back with them. I wouldn't let them take me.

But no matter how hard I tried to fight, to get away, nothing seemed to work. Someone's hand settled on my shoulder, a comforting warmth.

Something cold flooded my veins, and I was gone again.

***

The soft sound of something beeping rhythmically was the first thing that clued me in that I might not be dead just yet. I was pretty sure heaven wouldn't have something as annoying in it.

Slowly, I cracked my eyes open. Much to my surprise, they actually listened to me. The world around me was painfully bright. I'd no more than slit my eyes when I was forced to squeeze them shut again.

Again and again I tried. Finally, I was left staring at a grid of dingy, off-white ceiling tiles. For a long moment, I could only stare, completely confused. This wasn't the parking lot. It wasn't my apartment. It wasn't even the forest.

The forest where we'd been *attacked*. The forest where we'd killed people. My blood froze as the memories came rushing back - the things that had happened. The things we'd done. That I'd done.

I could still see that man's face, half hidden behind the barrel of my gun before I-

My stomach heaved, threatening to bring everything I'd eaten over the last day back up. I shuddered, half-rolling over. Focusing on keeping it down was effective at keeping the thoughts away, at least.

"Jon!" someone said. I could hear the way their voice lit up, the excitement in their tone. "You're awake! Jesus."

"Keira," I rasped, rolling flat again as I peered across to the foot of the bed.

She was too pale, still bearing the bruises that our enemies had left. But despite the dark circles under her eyes, the smile on her face was genuine. She crossed the room in an instant, flying from her seat to stand beside me.

I smiled back, feeling the way every muscle seemed to stretch at pull at the slightest motion. My head pounded. No, that was putting things too lightly. It thundered, my pulse beating in my ears and sending waves of pain through my body. It was like every hangover I'd ever had in my illustrious college career, rolled together into one spectacular, head-splitting shriek of agony.

"Hey," I said, licking my lips. My mouth was dry, like I hadn't had water in a week.

"Don't 'hey' me," she muttered, beginning to scowl.

"We made it, eh?"

Her eyes softened as a bit of the irritation melted out of her expression. "Just about. How do you feel?"

I chuckled, immediately regretting it as new hurts presented themselves. "Like someone ran my head over with a truck."

"Right. Right. He said that might happen."

I furrowed my brow, staring at her. "Who said what?"

She shook her head. "That guy. Aedan. He told me- well, almost *nothing*, but he said you'd be in a lot of pain."

"Of course he did," I said dryly.

"Who the hell was he?" Keira said, leaning in closer. It was hard to tell if she was trying to be secretive, or if she was angry. Either were entirely plausible, from the frustrated set of her jaw. "What exactly *was* all that stuff?"

I lifted a hand, pressing it to my forehead a moment later - my hand that now had a cast wrapped around one finger. The broken finger was the least of my worries. God, it felt like my skull was cracked wide open. "Look...Keira, just-"

"Oh. Oh, god, you just woke up. Right. Sorry. Hold on. I'll- I'll find someone."

Before I could so much as say a word she was gone, dashing from the room in a blur of brown hair.

I leaned back, the explanations and excuses I'd been about to make dying on my lips.

There was no time after that - it was just a mess of nurses and doctors, all wanting me to take this pill or checking the bandages on my leg. I'd lost a lot of blood, I was informed. As though I hadn't figured that much out already. I sat dutifully and listened to lecture after lecture, tolerating the near-constant flow of people in and out of the wing where I lay. The brief window of opportunity I'd been given to have an honest conversation with Keira had been lost.

I knew exactly how out of reach it had become when I saw the man walk through the door, dressed in the crisp brown uniform of the local sheriff's office.

My first instinct was to shy away - it wasn't my fault, dammit. I'd been burned too recently. But he only held a hand up, seeing me stiffen at his approach. "Relax. Nurses say you've been a while in snapping out of this. Don't force yourself for my sake."

The nurses had been quite puzzled, in fact. I'd seen the confusion plain on their faces, read it in every line of their bodies and heard it in every sentence they said to me. I still had my relic, sure, tucked under my gown. I'd reclaimed it just as quickly as I could, finding it sitting on my bedside table along with everything else I'd had on me. Even still, I didn't need my strange new variety of magic to see how confused my coming to them in a near-coma had made the nurses.

Aedan hadn't seemed surprised. I could remember his voice, lingering on the edges of my memories. And from the few sentences I'd been able to share with Keira without being disturbed, he'd said something like this would happen.

I'd overexerted myself. So Aedan said, and right then, he knew more than I did. The blood loss hadn't helped things, but it looked like it was my own stupid fault for winding up exhausted and feeble.

I put a smile on my face, doing my best to look like I didn't mind the policeman's presence. "S-Sorry. Didn't expect you, that's all. Was there...uh, something I can do for you?"

He chuckled politely, letting it die away a moment later. The humor never seemed to reach his eyes, as though it was unable to breach the crisp, professional front he'd put up. "Well, maybe, maybe not. I just had a few questions for you, Jonathan."

"It's Jon," I said, resisting the urge to sigh. Or roll my eyes. Or both.

"Jon, then," he said, tucking his hands into his pockets. "I'm Officer Baldwin. Really, we just had some questions about-"

"I swear to god, the coffee here is going to kill me," Keira said, stepping back into the room with a cup clutched in each hand. She froze, seeing us both staring back at her. "Oh- uh. I'm, well, I'll-" I could see her swallow, her cheeks beginning to flush. "I'll just leave you two be."

"It's fine," Baldwin said, shaking his head. He had a little notepad in one hand, turning it over and over as he stood awkwardly in the center of the room. "I don't think this will take too long."

"Ok. Well. All right, I suppose," Keira said, her eyes darting to mine. She stepped over to me more slowly, depositing the cup of coffee down on the little table with a soft *clack*.

"Am I allowed to have this?" I said, eyeing the massive cup with more than a little doubt.

She hesitated, her fingers hovering near the cup as she glared at me. "If you don't want it, then I'll just-"

"No, no," I said, taking the coffee before she could snatch it back. My muscles screamed at the motion. "I want it. Thanks. Really. I appreciate it." A bit of caffeine in my system sounded like a great idea, when faced with a headache that grew with every passing second.

"Ok. Well. I'll be right outside," she said, glancing between the cop and I again.

The room was dead quiet as she made her way out, give us one last, unreadable look.

And then it was just the cop and I.

I stared at my feet, just a featureless lump under the blankets. My thoughts raced. Shit. I wasn't quite sure what he wanted, but it wasn't hard to figure out. And given how hard a time I was having believing everything that had happened - *me* with a relic wrapped around my neck - I knew that trying to explain it to a cop was going to be nigh impossible.

More than that, something inside of me seemed to shy away from the thought of explaining our magic to an officer. It seemed like this stuff had been going on for a *long* time, and yet the rest of the world was none the wiser. It wasn't exactly a new concept for me - I could have come forward years ago, displaying my skills for the world to see. I hadn't. My self-preservation instinct had been too strong, and that much hadn't changed.

I fixed him with my best smile, having figured out absolutely none of how I was going to handle this mess.

He ran a hand through his neatly slicked-back hair, that picture-perfect smile still waiting on his face. "Well. I'll get out of your hair here in just a minute."

"Of course," I said, matching him smile for smile. Crap. He might have been saying he'd be on his way soon, but his good cheer still hadn't reached his eyes.

"Well, see, we're just trying to figure out exactly what happened," Baldwin said, folding his arms across his chest. "Your sister brought you in yesterday, shot in the leg."

"Right," I said, feeling a bead of sweat drip down the back of my neck. "I mean, obviously."

"Obviously!" he said.

He laughed.

I laughed.

We both laughed.

"Only, see, it's a bit unusual to see something like that show up around here," he said, the laughter dying out as he got straight back to business. "I've already talked to your sister and heard about your little hunting accident, but I was hoping you could give your side of things."

The coffee cup was already at my lips as he spoke. I flinched, coming dangerously close to spilling the drink all over myself. "U-Uh."

He raised an eyebrow. "That *is* right, isn't it?"

"W-Well, yes," I said, feeling completely out of my depth. Crap. A hunting accident? Keira hadn't said anything about that to me. Of course, I *had* come in with a broken finger and a bleeding, oozing gunshot wound in my leg. She'd probably had to come up with something to give them. But, even still...a hunting accident? That was the best she could do?

Officer Baldwin cleared his throat. He still looked completely unconvinced. "You're sure, then."

115

"Of course," I said, forcing a smile back onto my face. "It's just- a little embarrassing, you know. Just trying to get some target practice in before deer season! You know how it is." I laughed awkwardly, feeling my ears burn.

He didn't join in the laughter this time. He let it fade away on the antiseptic-scented hospital air, still flipping through his little notebook. "Mmhm. Right. Only, there were just a few things."

"Oh?" I said, the words coming out a squeak.

"You got yourself shot, yes, but you've also got a broken finger, don't you? I was wondering if you could tell me how your sister wound up with those bruises?" Baldwin said, letting his hands fall down to his sides as he turned his gaze back to me.

Shit. "Well...that's..." I began, but the words I was reaching for just fell away. What was I supposed to say? She fell and bruised herself on a tree? The branches punched her in the face, covered her wrists in black fingerprints?

"Seems they were a lot more fresh when she brought you in," the officer said flatly. His eyes were cold. "Do you know anything about that?"

Shit, shit. I swallowed hard, doing my best to hold his stare. The man was clearly not buying Keira's little lie - and just as clearly, he seemed to be viewing me as the best candidate for the one who put those marks on her.

"I-I can assure you, I don't-"

"It's just the two of you, is it?" he said, turning back to his notepad. "That's a little odd."

"Not really," I said, rallying a little as we worked our way back to comfortable territory. "The rest of our family's out of state, so it's just us. It was just cheaper this way. We-"

"She seeing anyone?"

"What? No. I don't think so."

"Then what's going on?" Baldwin said. He was still speaking calmly and pleasantly, but there was a steely edge to his tone that hadn't been there a moment before. "Are you claiming the trees punched her?"

Shit, shit, shit. "No! No. That would be insane."

I chuckled nervously. He didn't.

A possibility occurred to me - the only way out that I was likely to get. I didn't like it. I didn't like it at all. But I wasn't entirely sure what alternatives I had, besides for being labeled an abuser.

As he opened his mouth again, drawing himself upright to begin his next line of questioning, I cut him off.

"See - it's like this. Just listen to what I have to say, all right?" I smiled at him, sliding one hand up to rest against my chest. My necklace lay under the fabric, millimeters away. It was warm to the touch. That, more than anything, gave me the confidence to keep going.

He blinked, falling quiet. "All right."

Good, good. "It was a hunting accident," I said slowly, staring him in the eyes. "That's all there is to it - there are no questions. Keira and I were going shooting. Getting back in the swing of things. She tripped, and hit a tree. She shot me in the leg. I fell and broke my finger." I leaned closer, putting every ounce of conviction I had into my words. They were the truth - I just had to believe it, and he'd believe it. He had to. He was *going* to.

Slowly, painstakingly, he nodded. His eyes seemed more distant, somehow. "I see," he said, still nodding.

"You understand, don't you?" I said, unwilling to so much as blink.

"I do," he said, picking up a pencil as he turned back to his notebook. "Well, be more careful next time."

"I will."

"Someone could have got themselves killed."

"I know. I know. We'll be careful. Believe me." Again, I fixed him with my best, most winning smile.

He pushed himself upright, tucking the notepad into his back pocket. "All right, then. Well, here's our number. If you have any questions, give us a call." He handed me a business card emblazoned with the department's logo.

I snatched it from his hand, needing more than anything for him to be on his way. "Right. Do you need anything from me?"

"Your sister gave me your information," he said, his eyes already drifting to the door. "Have a good night, then."

I held my breath. Was it done? Was it over?

Without another word, he turned on his heel. He was out the door within moments. I stayed right where I was, listening to the sound of his footsteps vanish down the hallway until only silence and the soft sound of the hospital remained.

Only then did I allow myself to droop, the tension holding me upright fleeing, and press a hand to my aching forehead.

***

Another step. Another. I stared at the sidewalk in front of me, trying to find something, anything to distract myself from the stupidity that had been my choice to walk to the lake.

You have to get out walking, they'd told me. *The sooner you use it, the sooner you'll finish your recovery.*

Assholes, the whole lot of them. Oh, they weren't *wrong*, but they were assholes all the same. And I was the worst asshole of all of them. It had seemed like a good idea to walk down to the waterfront, to take in the sights of fall at the shoreline. I'd go ooh and aah at the colors, sit on the park bench. It would be *fun*.

It had been fun. And now, on the not-insignificant walk home, my leg was absolutely killing me.

The healing process had gone more smoothly than I could have hoped. After my body recovered from whatever relic-induced shock had come over me, the wound in my leg wasn't *that* hard for them to deal with. It hadn't done any permanent damage, hadn't torn any tendons or ripped any muscle that wouldn't heal. My hand had healed even more easily. That didn't mean I wasn't hurting, but it was a step in the right direction.

Keira had been more of a problem.

She'd been on my back from the moment the policeman left.

"What did you tell him?"

"Who were those people?"

"Why did they *explode*? Were they human?"

"Was this some sort of prank?"

I'd tried to brush it off at first, sweep it under the rug. But in the short time since I'd escaped the clutches of the hospital, she hadn't let up at all. Finally, I'd had to simply sit her down, planting a beer in her hands to keep her at least a little quiet, and tell her *something* to shut her up.

She'd known about me and languages, of course. There was no way she would have missed something like that, through all the tense conversations our parents had had on the matter. The news that there were other people like me out there was a surprise, but not a shock to her.

Even still, the damage had been done. She didn't say anything, but I saw the way she locked the door each night, double- and triple-checking it over the span of the evening. I didn't miss the little bottle of pepper spray she'd taken to tucking into her pocket. And where once

118

she'd leave her window wide open, filling her room with moonlight, now she kept the curtains tight-drawn.

It hurt to see, but I couldn't very well tell her to stop. Both of us needed to be more careful than we had been.

The sight of my apartment building appearing out of the evening haze ahead of me was a welcome one. I masked my pained sigh behind a yawn, forcing my legs to keep moving. Just a little more, and I'd be in.

There wasn't even a mark left on the pavement of the parking lot, no blood splatters or tire marks to show where we'd fought for our lives such a short time before. That seemed wrong, somehow. It was all so...pristine.

I eyed my car with bemused irritation as I walked past it. The same spotless outcome could not be claimed for my backseat. It was soaked through with blood, the evidence that had been left of our drive to the hospital. I still couldn't remember more than a flash here and there of the trip, but my car would bear the marks of it for as long as I owned it. Given that it looked like I'd murdered someone in it, I got the feeling I'd find it pretty hard to pass on to anyone else.

Each step was agony as I forced myself up the long climb to the second floor. One more. Just one more. I repeated it to myself, finally hitting the landing with a sigh of relief.

The handle didn't turn under my hand. I groaned. Right. Keira was covering at work - payback for all the shifts she'd missed to come see me. I was on my own. Digging through my pockets, I muttered curses darkly.

The sound of the door shutting behind me was a palpable relief. I tossed the keys onto the counter, missing the bowl waiting there entirely. Tough. I'd get it later. I went straight to the fridge, pulling a beer out.

And froze.

The TV was on. The sound of one of those mind-numbingly stupid soap operas drifted into the kitchen.

Had I left it on? It wasn't like me to forget something like that, but I *had* been a bit distracted of late. No, no. Even if I'd forgotten and walked away from it, it wouldn't be playing soaps. My blood chilled.

Slowly, trying not to make any noise, I set the can of beer down on the counter. The knife block was waiting by the stove. I wrapped my hand around the hilt of the biggest knife in the set, sliding it free of the wood.

Stepping as gingerly as I could, I slid over to the doorway and peered out into the living room.

Aedan lounged crosswise on my couch, his feet up on the arm. He didn't take his eyes off the TV, but his hand lifted all the same. I thought it was a greeting, until I saw the can clutched between his fingers.

"Hey, Jonny," he said, still not looking over. "You took longer than I thought you would. Also, your taste in beer sucks. Grab me another?"

CHAPTER FOURTEEN

I stared, still trying to process exactly what I was looking at, what I was *seeing*. Cheesy lines drifted across the living room from the TV, tinny and overacted. Everything was right in its place - the television, all of my gaming consoles, everything valuable that I had sitting around. Nothing was *missing*. There was that much to be grateful for, at least.

But there were things in my apartment that shouldn't be. I was still trying to blink away the shock, his flame-red hair stuck in my eyes like a brand.

Finally, I couldn't keep it in anymore.

"What the hell are you doing in my house?" I heard myself ask, my voice oddly distant.

He smirked, chuckling along with one of the actors on the screen. "Coming to check in on you, of course. I kind of thought that much was obvious."

"How did you get *in*?" I said stupidly.

Aedan did take his eyes off his shows at that, casting a derisive look my way. "Really?"

"I've got the key," I mumbled.

His smirk widened. "That's adorable, Jonny."

"Get out of my apartment," I said, my cheeks flushing.

"Let's not rush into things," he said, his eyes drifting back to the TV. "I wasn't joking about that beer. Hook me up?"

"What, you think you can just vanish for however long you want and walk in like you own the place?" I snapped, straightening. I'd asked after him, when I woke up. I'd wanted to know what happened. All Keira could tell me was that Aedan had been there - him and Jake both. And that they'd whisked the bodies of Matt and Christian off, vanishing into the night even as the others exploded into dust where they lay. What they'd done with the bodies, or Matt's cars, no one really wanted to ask.

Aedan groaned, pinching the bridge of his nose between two fingers. "I didn't-"

"You're just going to cause more trouble again," I muttered.

"I thought you'd appreciate some *answers*," he snapped, his tone beginning to rise to match mine. "If you don't, good fucking deal. I'll be on my way." His legs twitched, like he was beginning to stand up.

"Fine. Stay sitting," I said, spitting the words out. "Just start talking."

"Put the knife down first," he said, casting a scathing look at the blade in my hand. "As though you could do a damn thing with it anyway." His voice rippled with amused laughter, lurking just under the surface.

I stared at him a moment longer, mulling over my choices in my head. The thought of just stabbing him and being done with it was oddly satisfying.

All of my blustering aside, I did want answers - badly enough that with a half-muffled curse, I turned on my heel. The knife slid back into its home in the block with a soft *snick*. The can I'd left on the counter was in my hand a moment later, already beginning to drip with condensation. And then, torn between irritation and excitement, I stalked back into the living room.

"H-Hey. I was watching that," Aedan protested as I thumbed the power button on the remote.

I ignored him, throwing myself down into the armchair across the room from him. "Surprised you even came back. But now that you're here, there's nothing else getting in the way, is there? Start talking."

"What about my beer?"

"Aedan," I snapped.

He heaved an irritated sigh, pushing himself upright.

I glared at him as he rose with a muted groan, stretching his arms. "Would you stop-"

"Look. There's just some stuff you should know, all right?" Aedan

122

said, meandering across the room. "Just in case something happens."

"Something like what?" I said, my excitement beginning to taper off. If Aedan was involved, I should have known better than to think it could be anything but bad.

"Oh, don't worry," he said, pausing and glancing over his shoulder, one hand on the frame of the door to the kitchen. "It's not like anything would happen. Just, you know. Have to be careful."

"Aedan," I snapped again, feeling my face redden further. He was already through the door, completely ignoring me. It was absolutely impossible to hold a halfway decent conversation with the man.

The sound of the fridge door slamming shut was followed by the metallic hiss of a can being opened. Aedan reappeared in the doorway, looking almost sheepish as he shrugged.

"It's not really a big deal. I probably shouldn't even-"

He paused, his voice dying away in an instant as his head cocked to one side. A moment before, he'd been entirely casual, as though his mission in life was to make *my* life more trying. Just like that, though, he'd come back to wary attention.

I could hear it too - the sound of footsteps on the stairs outside. My blood chilled. My hand slid towards the pocket of my jeans, lingering over the shape of the knife tucked in there. I wasn't *Aedan*, and after everything that had happened, it was obvious that my own talents were never going to be quite so...brutal. All the same, it made me feel a little better to not be completely unarmed.

After all, one never knew when something was going to happen.

The worry began to fade when the jingle of keys rattling on a keychain echoed through the living room. I knew the voice that was mumbling profanity outside. I just hadn't been expecting it.

I was already sighing by the time the door swung open. Keira stepped through a moment later, hurling her keys onto the counter. They slid across the formica surface, skidding to a halt beside mine alongside the bowl where they were *supposed* to be kept.

She was humming to herself, something bright and cheerful and too catchy to be anything but a radio tune.

It came to an abrupt halt as she turned towards the hall leading off the kitchen, catching sight of Aedan standing by the living room door.

Despite myself, despite the severity of our situation and the fact that I was finally minutes away from getting some actual answers, I had to smother a chuckle. Her mouth hung open, the tune she'd been carrying falling flat and fading out into an ungraceful gulp.

"You," she said at last, still standing in the kitchen like a statue.

"Me," Aedan said, holding one hand up in a jaunty wave. "Cool. That's fine. You should hear this stuff too."

"What stuff?" she said, her eyes flicking to meet mine. "Jon? What's going on?"

"I thought you had work," I said, pressing a hand to my forehead.

"I did," she said slowly. "I got off half an hour ago."

My eyes dropped to the floor. "O-Oh. Right. Yeah." Crap. I'd walked for a *lot* longer than I thought I had.

"What's he doing here?"

"Sit down," Aedan said, turning and flopping back down on my couch. "Get yourself a beer. Put your feet up."

"I thought my taste in beer was awful," I said, glaring at him.

He took a long sip, unblinking. And then he sighed, licking his lips. "Oh, it is," he said at last, holding the can up. "Even so."

"Are more people coming?" Keira said, her voice sharp enough to pull my attention back to her. "I-I mean, are more of *them* coming?"

"What? No. Of course not," I said, shaking my head hurriedly.

Aedan burped. "Probably not."

"Probably?" I said, doing my best not to screech. "What the hell do you mean, probably?"

"Both of you sit down," he said, beginning to finally sound irritated. "You're making me tired just looking at you. Sit down."

I was already sitting - but, all things considered, it probably wasn't worth it to point the matter out. Keira slipped into the room with one last furtive glance at me, sinking down onto a stool tucked up against the wall.

My head snapped back over to Aedan as soon as she was seated. "Explain what you meant by *probably*."

"Jesus fucking christ, let me talk," he muttered. "Look. Like I said. There's a few things you should know. It's just in case something happens - and *nothing is going to happen* - but there are a few ground rules you're going to need to follow."

"Ground rules?" Keira said, folding her arms across her chest as she leaned back. Her brow was furrowed angrily. "Why do you get to set rules? Isn't all of this your fault?"

"Well- Not *exactly*," Aedan said, shrugging again. His ears were red, no matter what was coming out of his mouth. "Anyway. It's not *likely*,

124

but it's not impossible that....well...that more demibloods could be following Matt's little crew."

I blinked, my mind still trying to work through what he'd said. It sounded like he'd said more people like *them* might be showing up, and that couldn't be right. "Excuse me? What?"

He wouldn't quite meet my eyes. "They just tend to follow me around, all right?"

"Why is that?" I snapped.

"If they happen to come here, they probably won't even know you're a demi," Aedan said, waving a hand in front of his nose. "And even if they find you, they won't know you're involved in any of this."

"You keep saying that word," I said, seizing upon the unfamiliar term. "A-"

"A demi?" Aedan said, the words flying from his lips. "Christ. How new are- I mean, why didn't you say anything?"

I glared at him, feeling a muscle in my temple beginning to tick. "I asked you. I asked you *so many times*."

"Well, it's not complicated," he said with a quick shake of his head, breezing past my comment as though I hadn't spoken. "Demi as in someone who's demiblooded. Someone who has bonded with a relic. A focus. Whatever. It would take too long for me to explain the history of the name right now."

"Fine," I snapped. "Why are they going to be coming here?"

"They're not. Really. They won't," Aedan said, continuing to wave his hand dismissively even as he took another gulp of beer. "But-"

"They're looking for you, aren't they?" Keira said, leaning forward to fix Aedan with her beady gaze.

"No. I mean, not *really*. Kind of. Are you going to let me finish?" Aedan said, rolling his eyes.

I rolled my own can of beer between my eyes, trying to get my thoughts under control. "Why are they after you?"

"That doesn't matter. But if any of them should happen to visit town and they actually find you, it's very, very important you listen to me," Aedan said, easing his feet off the arm of my couch as he sat upright. "If they ask about me, you tell them we've never met." His green eyes were fixed on mine. It was strange, to see him looking so serious for once. "You can say you've heard of me, or that you heard I was wandering through, but you never spoke to me."

"I wish I hadn't," I said dryly. "That'd be simpler."

125

"No kidding," Keira muttered.

"Joke all you want," Aedan said, scowling. "Just *remember*."

"Right, right. I've never heard of this Aedan asshole."

"Again. Why are they looking for you?" Keira said. She was getting that stubborn set to her jaw again, her eyes flashing dangerously.

"If all goes well, they'll leave," Aedan said, casting a withering glance her way before turning back to me. "If so, that's that. If they *don't* leave, though-"

"Oh, I love where this is going."

"-Then you should be prepared to kill them," Aedan finished, spitting each syllable out carefully. "You're not quite so helpless anymore, I'll give you that. Although if I could recommend one thing, I find having a gun around makes things easier."

"Now you want us to travel *armed*," Keira said, beginning to shake her head. "What the hell is going on?"

"Jake should have told you all this."

"Jake didn't tell me anything," she said. "He just took off into the night with Recon's truck. That's all."

"God damn it, Jake," I heard Aedan mutter. "Demiblood society is just kind of...dangerous. It's not a big deal."

"If you want us to carry guns, that kind of seems like a big deal," I said. "And people spent the night trying to kill us, Aedan. You need to give us more to work with than that."

He ran a hand through his hair, ruffling it back and forth as he stared at the carpet. I could almost see him working something over in his mind.

"It's not that complicated. You guys are making this harder than it has to be," he said, almost sullenly.

"Aedan."

"I explained the rules to you already," he said, his chin snapping up. His eyes fixed on mine, shocking in their intensity all of a sudden. "You find a relic which you're compatible with. You forge a contract with it. And in doing so, you fundamentally change yourself."

"Like they were trying to do with those glasses," Keira said. "With me." Her shoulders relaxed a fraction as she spoke, as though the edge was coming off her anger.

Aedan nodded, reaching over behind the end table at the foot of the couch. "Just like that," he said, heaving his backpack to the floor between his feet. It was open in a second as he pulled at the zippers, already beginning to dig through the numerous and eclectic contents. "You can only bond with one relic, and it's a lifetime deal."

"You already said all of this," I said, feeling the weight of the necklace hanging by its chain.

"I didn't hear it, though," Keira said, turning to me. "I want to hear."

"I already told you what he told me. Isn't that enough?"

"Use your common sense, kids," Aedan said, his tone sharp enough to bring the two of us to a halt. He set the pair of glasses Matt had threatened Keira with down on the end table with a soft click. I didn't miss the contemplative look Keira gave them.

I eyed him instead of dwelling on it, brushing one fingertip across my relic as the questions I'd never gotten a chance to ask him began welling back up. "Is yours that knife, then?"

"If you only get one shot, and you can't trade out abilities once you've made the bond, then it comes down to strength in numbers," Aedan said, sweeping straight past my question once again. "That's just the way it is. If you have friends who want to help, they need relics of their own - and if you've got a powerful relic, you need an unbonded friend who can use it. The ambitious demis out there travel in groups, and they're always looking for new relics to pass along to their friends and underlings."

I paused. He was still staring at me, as though he was trying to see through to my soul. "Why are you telling *me* this?"

"Because you've got yourself a relic with a lot of utility," Aedan said slowly, still holding my gaze with his own. "It's not particularly strong, but it's got lots of different applications."

"Like mind control," I said, beginning to see where he was going with the whole matter. My stomach churned unhappily.

He nodded. "Like mind control. You'd put a target on your head if anyone heard about it."

"Is that what you did?" I said, seizing on the opening he gave me. "You just, what? Let yourself become too well-known?"

He took another gulp from his beer, his expression entirely unreadable. Keira and I waited, neither willing to move on from the point.

Finally, when it became clear we weren't going to ask a different question, he groaned. "I mean...Kind of. I *am* speaking from experience, even if our situations aren't exactly the same. I know what

127

it's like to have a relic that brings trouble along with it."

I chuckled humorlessly. "Of course. I'm sure you're popular at all the parties. Who wouldn't want to be bulletproof, after all?"

He shot me a look that could have cut glass. "I'm not *bulletproof*." His expression twisted. "Well. Not *really*."

"Stop qualifying everything you say," Keira snapped.

"You do owe us an actual answer," I said dryly, nodding along. "We've earned that much."

"I don't owe you anything."

"You pulled a knife on me," I said, beginning to scowl. "You got me shot."

"That's not-"

"Aedan."

"My body just...reboots," he said, scowling at me. "I'm not bulletproof. It's more like getting a replacement every time mine breaks. I just sort of...snap out of it."

"And by 'it' you mean-"

"The whole 'dying' thing. I just come out of it somewhere nearby instead, back in my original body and ready to go."

Keira and I both stared at him. He was saying it all so matter-of-factly, as though it wasn't a big deal.

Together with that information, though, my memories of everything that happened made a bit more sense.

I cleared my throat. "So when Jake shot you-"

"He did me a *favor*," Aedan said, wrinkling his nose as though the thought disgusted him. "It's not like they could kill me, but spending a few years as the guest of Matt and Christian was not exactly an appealing idea."

"So you can't die," Keira said. Her voice was still doubtful, her eyes narrowed.

Aedan sighed, lifting his beer again. "Everything dies."

I shook my head. "Then what do you-"

"How long have you been doing this, exactly?" Keira interrupted, talking over me neatly.

Aedan rolled his head over to shoot her a tolerant look. "Don't you know it's rude to ask something like that? Have some manners, woman."

She sat back in a huff, falling quiet as a pout spread across her face.

"So that's what Matt wanted, then," I said, pulling Aedan's attention back to me. "Your relic."

"Everyone wants to live forever," he said, holding his hands up helplessly. "That's what we're taught. It's a bit of a problem."

"It's *your* problem," I snapped, my anger rising again. "Don't bring that shit here. We could have *died*."

"Oh, come on, Jonny. You're fine," Aedan said, a bit of his old bluster returning. "Just look at all the fun tricks you learned! If I'd never shown up, hell, you'd probably have just had your throat cut a few years down the road by someone hunting rogues. You wouldn't have stood a chance."

He must have caught the confused look on my face. He rolled his eyes again, chuckling softly. "Right. Jesus. Right. You're a rogue demi, Jonny. Independent. You don't have a crew."

"It's *Jon*."

"Why does that need a name?" Keira said, leaning back farther on her stool. Her gaze was distinctly unamused and fixated on Aedan.

The man didn't seem to mind. He grinned, tilting his head to one side. "Because it's important. Didn't you listen to what I said?"

I snorted. "It *sounded* like a giant pile of-"

"You're alone," he said, carefully enunciating each syllable. "You've got a few cards to play now, but if someone with an offensive relic shows up, you're in real danger."

Keira's eyes darted between Aedan and I, unsure. "So, what, then? He's a target?"

Aedan pursed his lips, glancing to her. "It's unlikely. Outside of the urban centers, it's not quite such a risk. The people are too spread out. It's too hard to find anyone - not worth a crew's time, really."

"But they found Jon once already," she said, her tone insistent. "If they did, someone else could too. Right?"

"Well, that's what I'm saying, yes. It's a possibility. Just not a likely one."

"Oh," she said, going quiet.

I looked over to her, forcing a smile that I couldn't quite feel. "Keira. It's fine. I've had that thing for years and years. No one's ever bothered me until now."

"*He* wasn't here before now," she said, her voice low and sullen.

The two launched right back into their argument, trading insults and quips faster than I could follow. I leaned back in my armchair, feeling the condensation from the beer in my hands soak through my jeans.

Aedan was right. If he hadn't been there to intercede, I would have died. Sure, I could make the argument that without him showing up in my path, I wouldn't have been in any danger in the first place. But excuses like that wouldn't mean anything if someone got the jump on me.

The thought hurt. Without all of this playing out, and without Aedan helping me, I'd never have lasted long enough to learn I could do anything but be a walking Google Translate. If Keira hadn't been threatened, I might never have figured out that I could manipulate people.

Simply because I'd pulled the short straw and wound up with a relic that wasn't deadly at a glance, I would have died. They'd have walked all over me, and I'd have been completely unable to stop them.

As much as it hurt to admit, Aedan wasn't entirely wrong. Being attacked wasn't a good thing, but in the long run, it might have more pluses than minuses.

The creaking of couch springs brought my mind back to reality in a flash. I glanced up. Aedan was standing, pushing himself out of his seat with a groan.

"That's it?" I said, not bothering to try and keep the disbelief from my tone.

"Not quite sure what you're expecting from me, Jonny," he said, stretching. "I've given you the warning I owed you, and you've got those answers you wanted so much."

"That's the worst 'answer' I've ever-"

"You're a big boy. I'm sure you'll manage somehow," Aedan said, smirking. He dropped his empty can onto the table beside him with a clatter, digging in his pocket again.

I frowned. "What are you doing?"

"If any of them *do* show up, you're going to need a way to let me know," he said, pulling out the ancient, beat-up flip phone he'd had back in the forest. "Give me your phone."

There were any number of things I wanted to give him instead. The idea that an explanation like that was going to be enough to satisfy me just wasn't reasonable. But he was wiggling his fingers meaningfully, visibly growing more impatient by the second, and there wasn't a lot I could do to argue the matter.

Slowly, still glaring at him, I slid my phone from my pocket and stood, stepping closer. He snatched it away before I could change my mind and started swiping his finger across the screen with a pleased noise.

"Where's your new best friend?" I said, folding my arms as I waited.

He took his eyes off the phone just long enough to shoot me a confused look. "What, now?"

"Jake. The two of you left together, didn't you? Where is he?"

Aedan chuckled, shaking his head as he continued tapping numbers into my phone. "He's not my friend. Don't be an idiot. We cleaned up the mess Matt and his shithead buddies left, and that's that. Hell if I know where he took off to after."

"He owes me for the damage he did to my car," I muttered darkly, kicking at the corner of the couch. It had been obvious what had happened, once I'd seen the column of the thing ripped open and the wires hanging out. The logical part of me acknowledged that he'd had to find a way to get from the forest to my apartment *somehow*. It didn't change the fact that he'd effectively stolen my car.

And likewise, the fact that all of the demis I'd run into so far seemed to be thieves, murderers, or locksmiths was not giving me any comfort.

"Don't be an ass, Jonny," Aedan said, still focused on the phone. "He won't bother you two, and that's enough. He saved your bacon. Stop bitching."

He flipped my phone back to me on the last word. I fumbled, caught off guard, but got a grip on it before it hit the floor. When I keyed the screen on, my contact list popped up - with his name added.

"Now, Jonny, try to remember this is for *business only*," Aedan said, tapping my nose with one finger. "I don't care how drunk you are or how lonely you get, the answer is no."

I took a swipe at him, fully intending on breaking that finger he was sticking in my face. Not even I was surprised when he ducked my strike effortlessly, skittering back. The sound of his chuckle filled the living room.

"Cool. Later, then," he said, waving jauntily. "If I don't keep moving then more demis really will show up here."

"Not so fast," I said, shaking my head furiously. "You can't just walk off without telling us more. Just *wait*, damn it."

"Have a good life and all that. Try not to die," he said, turning and walking for the door.

Keira stood in a rush, her brow still furrowed and her lips parted like she wanted to ask something. I knew the look - I was wearing one just like it. Aedan, as usual, had done the bare minimum in terms of actually explaining what was happening. It wasn't enough.

A more important issue presented itself as I turned to watch him go, though.

"No, no. Aedan. Get back here," I snapped, snatching up the pair of glasses on the end table.

"What? What now?" he said, glancing over his shoulder wearily.

I crossed the distance between us in three steps, pressing the glasses into his chest. "I don't want these. They're yours. Take them somewhere else."

I didn't need glasses - and I didn't want some stranger's focus sitting around my apartment. With my luck, I'd throw the damn things out or something.

And I'd seen the way Keira's shoulders drooped a fraction of an inch as I passed the glasses back.

Aedan only smirked, taking the relic from me as I pushed harder. "Okay, fine. Sorry. I just forgot." Dropping his backpack to the floor of the kitchen, he started digging through the contents again.

I wasn't entirely sure I believed him, even if I couldn't really come up with a good explanation for why he'd leave them here. All the same, my eyes were more than a little round as he pulled the chest out of the bag.

"Holy shit," Keira said, taking a step closer as the relics inside caught the light. "What are you doing, trying to build an army or something? You're crazy. You know that, right?"

"Why, thank you," Aedan said, flashing a grin at her as he tossed the glasses in carelessly and slammed it shut again. "I'm just being careful. Can't attack me with a relic you haven't got, after all."

His smile didn't fade as he zipped his backpack back up and slung it over his shoulder, but I couldn't shake the feeling it didn't quite reach his eyes. He reached out to pat my shoulder comfortingly.

"There, there, Jonny. Grow a pair. You'll be fine."

"Fine. Get the fuck out of my house," I spat, throwing an arm up to push him off me.

He winked at Keira, stepping backward all the while.

To my horror and disbelief, he took a broad step to the side, pulling the fridge back open, and slid another beer out. Neither Keira or I said a word. There were no words that could express what was going through my mind at that moment.

An instant later he was back at the door, pushing it open. The brisk air was enough of a shock to snap me fully awake, making the conversation we'd just had seem like an odd, bizarre dream.

"Remember not to call me!" he called over his shoulder as he stepped out, tugging his backpack higher.

The door slammed shut again, cutting off anything else we might have said. I didn't have anything left, anyway - nothing but a few choice words I was better off not saying.

Keira and I stood in the suddenly-quiet kitchen, frozen in place in the wake of his passage. For a long while, that was all we could do - stare at the door, and listen to the slow fizzing of the beer in my hand.

Maybe, in another world, that's where things would have ended. We might have kept our heads low, taking Aedan's advice. The events that took place that night would have faded from our minds with time, becoming just another unpleasant memory. An outlier in an otherwise mundane existence.

It would take time, but over the years it would have become the pinnacle of excitement in my life, the sole entry in the folder labeled "Jon does stupid stuff and acts like an idiot, putting himself and everyone around him in mortal danger." We'd move past it and become just normal, stupid adults - and Aedan would become just a footnote, a distant acquaintance soon forgotten.

That's not what we did, of course.

But it would have been nice.

CHAPTER FIFTEEN

Before I really knew what was happening, the time just flew past. I looked up, and weeks had slipped by with me none the wiser.

I'd missed a lot, while I was holed up with a gunshot in my leg. My job had been gracious enough not to complain when I was forced to take a chunk of time off. My boss had only sighed tolerantly, fixing me with the sort of look that made sure I knew he'd be making jokes about it approximately *forever*.

There was no way around that. Honestly, the one I felt bad for was Keira. I just had to suffer the wisecracks, whereas she had the honor of being eternally labeled as the girl who'd shot her brother in the leg. She'd taken the jokes and jabs with uncharacteristic patience and good humor, laughing along as best she could. Each time, though, I saw her expression tighten a fraction.

She still had a lot of questions - so did I. True to form, Aedan had been spectacularly unhelpful. To make matters worse, the careful digging I'd done on my own had been fruitless. It would have been nice if I'd found an owner's manual for my relic lying around somewhere, but no such luck. I'd even tried some cautious google searches, when my patience hit rock bottom. That too had turned up nothing at all - just one single webpage owned by an aging, decrepit historian rambling about old magic and enchanted totems, the whole thing looking like it was straight out of the 90s.

He was close enough to the mark that I tried to give him and his website the benefit of the doubt, but in the end, it was useless. There was nothing there I didn't already know, and the phone number he'd listed was disconnected when I tried calling. From a burner, of course. I wasn't *stupid.*

In the end, we were just doing our best to settle back into something resembling normalcy. I patched over the gunshot holes in my wall before the landlord could catch sight, offering a tiny prayer of thanks that the gunfire had sailed through the exterior wall rather than my neighbors' apartments. Keira continued her post-college job search, plugging away at her boring, mundane job at the grocery store all the while.

There were times when she wouldn't meet my eyes, when her lips pressed together into a thin line as though she was trying to hold something back. Like there were words she was keeping in. I could only stare, confused, but the moods always passed as quickly as they came.

Without speaking a single word on the matter to each other, we'd both known that not a word of this could leave the two of us, that our parents in Wisconsin were never, ever to find out about what had happened. They wouldn't understand, even knowing about my talents. They'd want to start more trouble on the matter, when all either of us wanted was to be left in peace.

She didn't argue when I started looking at other places to live. There were too many memories in that apartment, too many risks and chances and things that had happened. Safer to put it behind us, and find somewhere different.

There weren't tons of options in our sleepy little town, ostensibly named Greenville, but I'd found a few candidates that looked good. My job finally stopped making cracks about the lengths I'd go to to avoid working. More than anything, we'd seen exactly zero signs of anyone on Aedan's trail passing through. I hadn't caught even a rumor of another *demiblood* or whatever he'd called us lurking about the place.

Granted, I hadn't known Matt's crew was around until they'd held a gun to my head. I didn't have the best track record for that kind of thing, but even still.

Things were beginning to look up.

The first glimmers of snow were starting to fall over the forest, coloring the world grey, when the knock came at our door.

I paused, glancing over my shoulder at it. The pot in front of me bubbled gently, smelling like potatoes and garlic and heaven.

Keira was at her best friend's house - Catherine. She was every bit as loud as Keira was stubborn, and with the two of them together I had no doubt she wouldn't be back until morning. Unless the two of them had changed their plans and decided to come back to our apartment, which was something I hoped very, very much was not the case.

The few friends I had in town all had other plans, which they'd extolled to me at great length. They'd at least have *texted* me if something had changed. Heaven knows they always .

Maybe Aedan had come back.

I abandoned the thought almost as quickly as it had occurred to me, shaking my head derisively.

The knocking continued, growing more faint and cautious by the second.

I had no idea whatsoever who it was.

As poorly as I'd taken the idea when Aedan had said it, he wasn't entirely wrong. Getting a gun probably *would* have been smart. I'd thought about it, after he left - and quickly realized that having a gun would put me even more squarely in the sights of Officer Baldwin there. Not that I'd done anything wrong, and in *theory* he should be put off my scent by the relic-infused encouragement I'd sent his way, but I couldn't be sure.

The whole series of events left me weaponless as I slowly walked over to the door. I still had my voice and my words, of course. Somehow, it wasn't a comfort.

The hinges creaked as the door slowly swung open. I stared.

Jake smiled, every line of his face radiating nervousness. "Uh. Hi."

There were no words that came to mind. I just blinked, beginning to gape.

And then reality snapped back into place with a jolt of icy adrenaline that coursed straight down to my bones. Jake put people to sleep - the memories were all too fresh. If I was snoring, it wouldn't matter if I could control someone with a word.

But he only held his hands up disarmingly, taking a step back at the look on my face. "Woah. No, no. No trouble, dude. Serious."

I stopped, the breath leaving me in a limp, formless huff. He wasn't lying. I could read the truth in what he was saying, see the earnestness in his eyes.

"What the hell are you doing here?" I said instead, still feeling hopelessly out of my depth. Aedan showing up had been a surprise, sure, but it wasn't a shock that he'd drifted back to irritate the two of us. I hadn't expected to see Jake ever again.

He glanced around, one foot tapping against the wood of the stairs. "It's- Can I just come in?"

"What? No."

"Just for a minute. I swear."

"Fuck off. *No*. Go away."

"Come on. It's cold. And I'd really rather not have this conversation out in the open." He looked around again, sighing softly.

I stared at him, motionless. "Are you here to attack me or my sister?" His eyes snapped to me. "No."

"Are you here to trick us?"

"No, no."

Both statements came back as true. I racked my brain, trying to think of anything else he might be up to. He waited, not saying a word even as the tapping of his foot grew more insistent.

"Fine," I said at last, taking the tiniest step possible back. "If you try anything, I'll kill you." I hoped that it came off as more than just bluster. I wasn't so sure.

He slid past me before I could take it back, offering me a pale, wan smile. "I'm not- I'm not here for any of that. Really. Believe me."

I pushed the door shut behind him, making an irritated noise in the back of my throat. "Right." And then I straightened, glaring at him. "All right - we're inside. Get talking."

He swallowed hard, looking no more comfortable than he had outside. "O-Ok. So. I won't stay long."

"Good."

"I just- I wanted to give you this." He reached into the inside pocket of his jacket, pulling free a manilla envelope folded in half. And then he held it out to me. "I think...you should have it."

I eyed it, and then him. "Is this any sort of trick or trap."

"No. It's...a gift. Kind of. It won't hurt you."

I watched him a moment longer, but there was no hint of maliciousness in his eyes or words. Slowly, still watching for any sign that he was about to try anything, I reached out and took it from him.

Jake leaned back, nodding with what looked like the first traces of a smile on his lips. "Good. Yeah. Cool." He ran a hand through his sandy brown hair, finally looking away. "That was quite the focus you had, by the way. Why...." He shook his head.

I paused, hand halfway to the flap of the envelope. "Spit it out."

"You held Matt and Christian and all of them in place without breaking a sweat," Jake finally said, his blue eyes snapping up to mine.

A chuckle slipped between my teeth. "Oh, I was sweating."

"I was- I was going to *kill* you. Why didn't you just...y'know." He pursed his lips, looking decidedly unhappy.

"Make you shoot yourself?"

"Something like that," Jake mumbled. "It doesn't make sense."

I sighed, fixing him with a long, solemn look. "I'm...a little new to this. I hadn't exactly known that I could *do* what I did to the others. I'm still figuring this whole relic business out."

Jake froze. "W-What?"

"What do you mean, what?"

He shook his head hurriedly. "Well, you never *tried* before? There's no way. Your focus has too much oomph behind it for you to be fresh-bonded. Who taught you? I know Aedan seemed to think you were new, but really. They should have-"

"No one ever taught me," I said, unable to keep the irritation from my voice. "Before Aedan and you assholes showed up, I didn't even know that I *had* a relic."

"A focus."

"Whatever."

"Shit," Jake muttered, shifting from foot to foot. "Well, I mean, that's just...damn."

"Pretty much," I echoed, looking down to the envelope in my hands again.

"Then what happened to your sibling?"

"Keira?" I said, straightening again with a muffled groan. "She's-"

"No, no. Your *sibling*. The one who gave you the focus." He stared at me again, his brow furrowing. "They're supposed to teach you all this. Make sure you're not totally helpless."

"What? No. No one gave it to me. Is that how you got yours?"

Jake bobbed his head in a quick nod, his hand going to his sleeve. "Right. It was...my older brother. He'd found another one from- on a job. It liked me, and, well, here I am."

On a job. Right. From the tight, shamed look in his eyes, I knew it probably wasn't worth pressing further.

"I didn't get my relic from anyone," I said slowly, holding his gaze. "I found it at a pawn shop. That's all."

For a long moment, Jake just stared at me, his mouth hanging open.

And then he pressed forward, his eyes lighting up. "Are you serious? You found a lost focus? That's- I've never even *heard* of it happening before."

"Get back," I snapped, my hand whipping up to push on his chest. He might have passed my little lie-detection show, but that didn't mean I trusted him.

True to his word, though, he scampered back as soon as he remembered himself. "That's- you just don't know, Jon. That's something that just...it doesn't *happen*, okay?"

"Is it that big a deal?" I said, my brow furrowing. "I mean, how rare are these things, anyway?"

"How rare are-" he spluttered, finally coming to a stop. His face was bright red. "Are you serious?"

I stared at the ground, feeling my own cheeks flush. "If you're going to make fun of me, go ahead and get the fuck out," I mumbled.

Jake ran a hand through his hair. "No, no. Sorry. You're right. It's just..." He shook his head. "It's not like anyone is making the things anymore, you know? So there's only so many *out* there. Every time one gets lost, it's just....gone. Forever, usually."

"Making them?" I said, feeling more and more like an idiot with every passing second. "What do you mean?"

He rolled his eyes. "Where do you need me to start?"

"From the beginning would be great." I wasn't happy about sounding like an idiot in front of someone who had been trying to kill me, but it wasn't like Aedan had given me anything to work with. I needed to understand *something* about what was going on.

Jake only pursed his lips, tucking his hands into his pockets. "Well...I mean, it's not like anyone really *knows*. The things are so old no one remembers how they started. But they're not natural, are they? Someone had to have made them."

"Relics?"

"Jesus, stop talking like that," Jake said, glancing up at me. "You sound weird. It's a focus."

"Oh," I mumbled. "Anyway."

"Fine. Yeah. I mean, it's magic, right?" He wiggled his fingers meaningfully, making a face. "It's some weird shit. People have been wondering how they got started for years. Decades. Centuries."

"And no one knows," I said, my tone skeptical.

139

He reddened further. "It's...not really a priority for most demibloods. Beyond that no one knows how the ancients managed to use magic, or how to make more of them, anyway."

"You're too busy killing each other, you mean."

"And just living," he protested. "A lot of people find ways to use their powers, you know. It doesn't *have* to be killing." He hesitated for a long moment, shrugging half-heartedly. "But...yeah. A lot of the time. A lot of knowledge has been lost."

I kicked at the kitchen tile. "Fucking great," I mumbled.

"What's that?"

"Nothing. So they're ancient tools with some kind of *magic* in them, and you're too busy being vicious, petty thugs to figure anything out."

He didn't have anything to say to that. He just stared at the ground for a long moment. Finally, he broke the silence. "Well. Anyway. Normally they stay in the family, passed from father to son. That kind of thing. So losing them is rare in and of itself."

"Oh," I said, my sarcasm falling away as the conversation drifted back towards something more reasonable.

"Not everyone is even compatible with them, you know," he said, glancing up at me again. "It tends to follow the family line, but even that's not a guarantee. So, I mean, running across another demiblood isn't really common."

"So how'd you wind up with Matt, if it's so rare?" I said, trying not to glare. "Considering you're suddenly all *honorable*."

"Like I said, it was just a job. That's all."

"Right."

"You've had yours for a while, haven't you?" he said, perking up again.

I frowned at him, still trying to figure out what his play was, but it seemed like honest interest more than anything. "I guess. Why?"

Jake shrugged. "It's just...The longer you've got it, the stronger you get. And the bond you've got with yours seems pretty strong. It's pretty unusual to see someone who's had it for so long and yet doesn't have a clue what to do with it."

"You already told me how odd I am. Fuck off."

"Yeah. Sorry," he mumbled, staring at the floor.

The silence stretched out in the kitchen. The ticking of the clock mounted on the wall was deafening, cutting through the awkward atmosphere slowly building.

"Anyway," he said at last, motioning towards the envelope I still held. "That's for you. It was from Matt and them. The rest of their stockpile, their emergency stash. I think it's better if you take it." He was already backpedaling towards the door. I couldn't really blame him for being desperate to get out of there. I wanted him to leave too, when it got right down to it. "Kind of a shitty apology for trying to kill you and all, but...yeah. It'll make me feel a bit better about all this. See you."

I hesitated, suddenly caught by the look in his eyes as he turned for the door. The fact that the only source of information who'd seemed willing to talk was leaving had *nothing* to do with it. "What are you going to do next? That was your job, like you said."

Jake shrugged, his steps slowing. "Well, I've got a good focus. Versatile. There's a chance I can make some cash off Craigslist or something. Hypnosis therapy is pretty popular these days."

"And if not?"

A crooked grin tugged at the corners of his lips. "I'm sure I'll find other uses for it that'll get me by. Don't worry about me. You two...stay safe, all right?"

I lifted the envelope as he inched farther away. The flap came open in my hand as a wave of icy air washed over me. The front door slammed shut a moment later.

He'd find another use for his focus, eh? I wasn't an idiot. He'd be going right back into the thick of things - and from everything I could see, he'd been genuine and honest about the entire thing.

The envelope lay open in my hands as I stared down into it. The neatly-wrapped bundles of bills stared cheerfully back. That was a lot of money. A *lot* of money. The emergency stash from Matt's crew, Jake had said? The last of their resources on the hunt for Aedan?

Hell. There was enough in the envelope to keep me set for a long time, if I was any judge. Long enough to keep our heads down while this mess blew over. Long enough for Keira and I to vanish off to somewhere Aedan and the other demis couldn't find us.

The same frustration as before welled up. Why were we running? Why was I even *considering* that? We'd done nothing wrong, and I wasn't so helpless anymore.

A plan was crystallizing in the back of my mind, taking shape the longer I stared down at the crisp rows of cash. I didn't want to run - and I didn't want to take Matt's dirty money, easing Jake's conscience while we took the coward's way out. I didn't want him to run straight back to the mess he'd come from. He'd just end up killing again, until he got killed himself.

I hardly realized I was moving until the handle of the door was in my hand. The icy air was a slap in the face as it hit me, snapping me back to my senses. What was I doing?

But I was in it by then. Jake was at the bottom of the stairs, already walking towards the parking lot. I swallowed a sigh. This was stupid. I had no business doing anything like this - it was only going to bring trouble, and Keira was going to be *livid* when she found out.

Even still, I couldn't let things go like they were. Gathering breath, I took a step forward. The door to my apartment hung open. I tossed the envelope back through it. It slapped against the linoleum floor, bills sliding free.

"Jake. Wait."

CHAPTER SIXTEEN

The trees flew by alongside us. I stared at the road as it passed under my tires, trying to keep my curiosity in check. The tinny sound of whatever horrible local radio station we'd managed to find was the only thing we had by way of white noise. I wasn't sure it was an improvement over silence, but it was something.

"By the way, your car kind of sucks," Jake said. He was sprawled out in the passenger seat, his hands shoved into the pockets of his jacket. "I was going to tell you that."

My hands tightened on the steering wheel. "So sorry my car wasn't up to your standards as a thief."

"I mean, your suspension is nonexistent. You can feel everything. And your alignment-"

"You didn't have to take it," I muttered.

He shrugged, unbothered. "That's before it got all bloody, too."

"Yeah, I apologize that I got *shot*. Are we nearly there?"

"It's a bit further."

I glanced out the window, beginning to feel uneasy. We'd left the town ten minutes before. The lonely rows of gas stations and not-quite-decrepit office buildings had faded out to cornfields, interspersed with forests. If we had to go much farther, I wasn't entirely sure there would be anything there to *find*.

I'd convinced Jake to hang around, at least for a while. It wasn't like he had anywhere better to go. And, I'd figured, Matt's crew had found us somehow. If I wanted to make sure that nothing like *that* happened again, then I'd better start taking a more proactive role in things.

My car wasn't *that* bad. Sure, the steering column was a bit trashed, and the wires had needed a lot of work, but Jake hadn't argued for more than a few minutes when I'd told him to fix it.

I swallowed a smile, pressing a hand to my face. Well. He hadn't argued at *all*, when it came right down to it. He hadn't had a choice. He'd looked a bit annoyed, after my relic's hold on him slipped, but there was no real anger behind it. Fair was fair.

The sun was still high overhead, but it wasn't going to last forever. I'd thought this would be a quick jaunt - Jake had said it wouldn't be a long drive. The last thing I wanted was to try and have this confrontation in the middle of the night.

Finally, as the fields finally gave up altogether and gave way to darkened woods, I cleared my throat. "Well, maybe we should leave it for now. Come back Saturday, a little earlier."

Jake leaned forward, pulling himself up by the oh-shit handle. "There. The little drive, just past the sign."

I saw what he was pointing to - a giant, safety orange *No Trespassing* sign nailed to a wooden post. Both of us were pushed forward as I hit the brakes, bringing us to a stop.

There *was* a road. A driveway, anyhow. It wound through the trees, half-invisible in the overgrown underbrush. I would never have seen it, if I were here alone. I nodded slowly, even as I stared. "That? Really?"

"Yeah. That's his place. Aren't you going in?" Jake said, glancing back to me.

Every fiber of my being was screaming to *not* go in there, in fact. The wooden post the sign was nailed to was also holding up a gate, ancient and rusted and entirely uninviting. There were matching signs stretching out as far as I could see in either direction, warning trespassers that they'd be met with anything from dog attacks to gunfire. The corners of my lips twitched up despite my trepidation. None of them mentioned the police, I couldn't help noticing. At least I wouldn't have to worry about winding up on Officer Baldwin's bad side again.

"Jon? Wake up, already."

"There's a fence," I said, tearing my eyes off the lonely row of signs. "And a gate. We can't get in." I reached for the gear shift, already turning around to back up. "We'll have to come back when he's here."

"Oh, I don't think he goes anywhere," Jake said, a low chuckle running through his voice. "Rejoining society? Really not the impression I'd gotten from him."

"Then why-"

"It's an illusion. He serves all comers, after all. Payment comes in many forms."

I leaned forward, bracing myself on the steering wheel. The gate looked perfectly solid to me. "Are you sure?"

"I'm sure. Just keep driving."

My eyes drifted sideways to his. "Are you trying to get my car totaled? There was nothing wrong with it before you lot showed up. And if I try and make a claim for damages I got while breaking into someone's property, with my backseat covered in blood and half the wiring taped up, the insurance company is going to have some questions."

"Just drive," Jake said, leaning back again and tucking a hand behind his head. "Calm down and trust me."

I stared at him a moment longer, but it wasn't really a matter of trusting him. It didn't seem like he was lying, and no matter how hard I pushed at my relic, it couldn't find fault with his words. I was still learning, still figuring out how to make it listen to me when I wasn't bleeding and full of adrenaline, but at least *it* was trustworthy enough.

Fine. If he said to drive, I'd drive. Feeling my heart pound louder, I scowled and hit the gas.

More was my surprise when my car drifted straight through the gate. I had a single moment to flinch, drawing back as the steel bars and chicken wire came right through the windshield, but it was behind us just as quickly. I eyed it in the rearview mirror, trying to pretend I wasn't breathing hard.

"Told you," Jake said. A slow smile spread across his face.

"Whatever," I muttered. "So, what? More magic?"

He shrugged. "What did you expect? It takes all forms."

"It looked so real."

"Well, it wouldn't be very useful if it didn't."

"I guess." I let the conversation lapse into silence as I drove on, picking our way down the drive. It had been narrow, down by the main road. The farther in I went, the worse it got. Soon, there were branches sliding across the windows on both sides of the car, screeching and scraping like fingernails on a chalkboard.

I glanced out again, frowning. Inside the forest, it was even darker

than it had been on the drive, and I barely knew where we were.
"Look. I'd really rather not get stuck. Where-"

"Keep going." He didn't elaborate, only waved one hand in the
universal gesture for 'go on'. I rolled my eyes, biting back yet another
snappy retort, and just tried not to hit anything. I could make him
answer, if I really wanted, but somehow I knew the only answer I'd get
would be "It's ahead." And, while Jake probably wouldn't stab me as
payback like Aedan would, somehow the idea of Jake being pissed at
me wasn't really any better. If he left, I'd be alone.

So I just shut up, watching the headlights grow brighter against the
foliage.

Just as quickly as the drive had appeared along the road, though, the
scenery around us changed. A gap in the treeline ahead was the only
warning I got before the woods fell away from either side of us. The
driveway carved a straight path through a meadow - and through the
middle of what looked like a hoarder's paradise.

Rusted-out cars lined both sides of the narrow little road, stacked
five back in any direction. A row of ancient refrigerators waited behind
them, their doors hanging open. A boat. A rotted-out camper. There
was no rhyme or reason to it, and I gave up looking.

I was familiar with the type. They weren't exactly uncommon,
around where we lived. Once you got far enough out of civilization,
there was no telling what you'd find, and it attracted people like...like
whoever lived in the ramshackle little house at the end of the drive. It
glowed in the lights from my car, oddly neat and well-painted even it
looked like half the thing had been built from scratch. By hand. With
scrap wood.

A bead of sweat slid down my temple as we slowed down. "Jake.
Seriously. What are we doing here?"

"You wanted to talk to our contact," he said, unbuckling himself as
we screeched to a halt. "Here we are."

"I didn't want to get *shot* again."

"Just come on."

"We really should just turn around and-" I stopped. It was useless.
He was already climbing out the door, tugging the collar of his jacket
higher against the chill of the evening air. He didn't look interested in
listening to me, and as irritated as I was, I was also oddly curious.
Nothing I'd seen of the demis I'd met would have convinced me to look
for them in a place like this. I reached for the door handle, ignoring the

little voice in the back of my head that screamed its warning.

Jake was already halfway up the drive towards the door when I jogged after him, glancing around nervously. "Jake. Really. This is cra-"

The sound of a muted snarl brought me up short. I jumped back, my spine stiffening as a fresh shot of adrenaline hit my system. There was a dog. Two dogs. It was impossible to pick out anything like a proper breed amidst the mishmash of giant teeth and muscled legs, but what they *were* was unhappy to see us. They crept closer with every passing second, their ears pressed flat.

"G-Good boys," I managed, feeling the blood drain from my face. "D-Don't- uh, s-sit, I mean-"

Of all the times to get tongue-tied, why did it have to been when I was facing down some redneck's guard dogs? Would my relic even work on animals? I'd never tried. I'd never thought it was *important*. Suddenly, staring at those yellowed fangs, it was the most important thing in the world.

"Shit, Jon. Calm down," Jake said, stepping towards the two animals without a care in the world. His hand came up, steady and flat. "What a good job you two have done," I heard him murmur. "Good boys. Take a nap."

The two dogs drooped in place, their eyelids sagging as their snarls turned to whines. Within seconds, both were curled up in the grass, snoring loudly.

A relieved sigh slipped between my teeth at the sight. "Thanks. Yeah. Wow. Your rel- focus really makes things easier, doesn't it?" Dammit. Jake still got irritated with me if I 'talked like a weirdo'. It was easier to work on changing my habit than to try and argue with the low-key but absurdly stubborn man.

He nodded, reaching down to scratch behind one of the dogs' ears. "It does. It's not all bad, you know. Having these things."

"Will it last?" I said, looking down at the dogs.

Jake straightened, brushing his hands off. "Long enough. Come on. He'll be waiting, by now."

I blinked. "You think so?"

He just nodded, stepping off up the drive. The gravel crunched under my feet as I followed.

"How many times did you say you dealt with him before?" I said, eyeing the unpainted wooden door as we approached.

Jake pursed his lips. "Me? Just the once. Stopped in here when we got word Aedan was in the region. Needed to get confirmation, and Recon couldn't feel him." His eyes flicked to mine. "She was an active type, and all that. Aedan wasn't stupid about overusing his powers, at least. Never did leave much of a trail for us to follow."

"So you've been here *once*," I said, unable to keep the doubt I felt from seeping into my voice. This was how horror movies started.

He chuckled softly, glancing back at me. "Once, yeah. But Matt had come here before, apparently. Or Christian had. One of their friends, anyway. He didn't seem surprised to see our crew. Relax. Finders aren't normally the types to kill their customers. It's bad for business."

There were so very many other arguments I wanted to make, holes in his logic I'd have torn open and comments I'd have made about his casual attitude. He wasn't as high-maintenance as Aedan, but he was every bit as crazy at times. We were already at the front steps, though. If the guy really was watching already, I didn't want him to overhear what things I'd have to say.

I just held my tongue, perched on the concrete steps behind Jake, and waited as my new friend raised a hand. There was no doorbell. He pounded on the door itself instead, hard enough that the sound resonated across the meadow. The dogs whimpered, shifting in their sleep, but didn't wake. Jake was good at what he did, I had to give him that.

There was no answer. I shifted uneasily from foot to foot, casting a glance back towards my car, but Jake only shook his head.

"For fuck's sake, man, just calm down," he muttered, rolling his eyes. "Give him time to get to the door before you freak out. This was your idea."

I opened my mouth, ready to tell him I was *done* with it, my idea or no, when the door snapped open. There wasn't even a squeak from the well-oiled hinges - one moment we were bickering on the front steps, and the next there was a man in the open door.

A *big* man. I swallowed hard, taking a step back instinctively. I wasn't exactly short, but he made me feel wholly inadequate. He was an older man, his face heavily lined and what hair he had left silvered and grey. An impressively thick beard curled down from his chin, wiping his neck from sight. I could tell that as imposing as he was, he'd probably been a sight to behold forty years prior. None of that changed the fact that his arms were lined with muscles, or that he was glaring at

Jake and I with suspicion.

The shotgun he held in one hand didn't hurt, either. It was still pointed casually at the ground, but his stance told me all I needed to know about his ability to use it. It wouldn't help him against every demi out there - I was already fighting off the urge to scream *stop*, in truth - but it would certainly give him a leg up.

"Greyson!" Jake said, smiling at the man as he shoved his hands into his jeans. "Sorry to drop by unannounced, but, well, I didn't have your phone number." I had to hand it to him. He almost sounded interested, more so than he had the whole ride over. Maybe he was more nervous than he'd let on.

Greyson just glared at him, his eyes narrowing further. "You're that kid. From Matt's gang, right?"

Jake nodded, half-shrugging. "Well- yeah. I was here a few weeks ago? Buying information on-"

"That old bastard who keeps running circles around you lot," Greyson said, frowning. "I remember. The hell do you want now?"

Jake ran a hand through his hair, glancing to me. "Well...Matt's gone."

"I know."

"You do," I said, unable to stop myself.

Greyson's eyes drifted to me, rolling an instant later. "What? 'Course I know. Don't be an idiot. You wouldn't be here, otherwise."

"Don't mind him," Jake said, shaking his head. "He's new, sort of. Anyway-"

"It's getting late," Greyson said, his voice ominously slow. His fingers tightened around the gun. I was transfixed by the sight, frozen into horrified stillness. "What do you want?"

Jake's mouth slid open, and then he hesitated. He glanced back to me.

I sighed. Fine. I knew that look well enough to understand his message without a word being spoken. *This was your idea, and this is your problem.*

"It's nice to meet you, Greyson," I said, pushing my nerves away as I straightened. His eyes flicked to mine, and I smiled, all of the anxiousness rushing back. "I'm Jon Christensen. I asked him to introduce us."

He didn't move, didn't say a word. Not the worst reaction, but certainly not the best. If no reaction was what I got, I'd have to take it. I held my hand out, trying not to stare at the gun he held.

"I have a proposal for you."

CHAPTER SEVENTEEN

The man stood in the doorway, still glaring at me. His brown eyes were unreadable, but his lip curled back as he looked between Jake and I.

"What's this, now?"

"A-A proposal," I said, feeling the blood continue to vacate my face. "An idea. Something I wanted to-"

"I know what a proposal is, you ass," Greyson snapped, settling his glare on me at last. "I'm not a damn idiot. *What* do you *want?*"

Duh. I knew what he was *asking* - it was just that when I was face to face with him, seeing his hand tighten on his shotgun, it wasn't so easy to string my words together.

"We want your help," I said, forcing the words past the anxiousness I still felt. "I want to make a deal with you?"

Greyson lingered a moment longer, eyeing the both of us warily. And then his gaze settled on me again. "Fine. Say your piece and then get out."

Before I could say a word, he stepped out of the doorway, sliding back into the shade of the house beyond. I hesitated, long since past wondering if this was a good idea. It was *dark* in there - and he had guns. I needed a gun. Aedan was right, damn it.

"Hurry up," Jake muttered, scuffing his shoe on the ground. "Don't make him wait."

He wasn't wrong. As irritable as Greyson seemed, he'd given us the go-ahead. Delaying couldn't possibly make his mood any better.

Swallowing my fear, I stepped over the threshold.

My eyes adjusting to the dim light, I glanced around. The interior was clearly cut from the same cloth as the exterior - cobbled together and clearly homemade, by and large, but solid and sturdy. Every horizontal surface teemed with *stuff* - lighters and books and far too many brass casings for me to feel at all comfortable in the place - but it was all neatly organized in rows, crammed into its proper place.

Like a crazy person's house. Right. That fit the picture so far, at least.

"Get talking, then," Greyson said. He strode through the half-lit sitting room, flicking on lights as he went. An ancient, yellowed glass fixture came alive in the ceiling, giving our eyes more to work with.

"W-Well," I said, seeing him lean his gun against a cabinet and reach for the fridge door. "See, like we said outside, Matt's crew came through."

The old man chuckled, a sound like sandpaper on wood. "And went - none too peacefully, I'm guessing." The hiss of a can opening echoed off the walls.

My eyes dropped to the floor. "Well. No." Something slipped through the edge of my vision. Another dog, white-muzzled and short with wiry hair that stood straight up. Its tail wagged at a hundred miles an hour as it waddled towards me , single-minded.

"Sounds about right," Greyson grumbled. He eased himself into a rocker across from where we stood, beady-eyed and far too watchful for my comfort.

I dropped my hand down onto the head that was thrust against my knee, scratching behind the dog's ears. "It's- well, it's done," I said, unable to meet his eyes. "But it's made us aware that we're in a bit of a bad situation here."

"Does seem that way, doesn't it?"

Jake flopped down onto the couch behind us. I followed suit, the little dog following along gamely. "Right. Anyway. We're on our own out here. I know it's supposed to be safer here than in the cities, but even still, we nearly got ourselves killed."

He chuckled, still looking at me. "How's this my problem, now? Get to the point."

"Help us," I said, folding my hands in my lap as I straightened, facing the older man. "It's not *just* me, for as long as Jake hangs around. Neither of us has an aggressive re-I mean, focus, but we can defend ourselves." I met his gaze as levelly as I could. "I don't think the same can be said of you."

"That some sort of threat?" he said, leaning back in his chair and taking a long draw from his beer.

"No. No. Of course not," I said quickly. From the corner of my eye, I could see Jake shaking his head furiously. "Exactly the opposite. We need your help - and we thought you might need ours. In return."

"Your help."

I nodded slowly. "Ah...yeah. We're not powerhouses, but, well, you're-"

"A finder," Greyson said, his tone flat. "Why does that mean I need your help, now?"

My hands quivered. This wasn't going like I'd hoped. "Well, you can't- if someone attacks you, there's no way-"

"I've been in this game for years," Greyson said, eyeing the dog that was even then rolling on my shoes. "Longer'n years. Decades. Lots of 'em. Wouldn't have made it five if I was stupid."

"I don't think you're stupid," I said, waving my hands helplessly.

"Folks with passive abilities like mine aren't so common, you know," Greyson said, still glaring. "None of 'em want to be the one to kill *that* cash cow. There's no guarantee the next bastard to take the prize'll get the same gift, after all." A crooked grin slowly crept onto his face. "And, well, I can see all of them coming, can't I?" He jerked his chin towards the gun lying against the cabinet. "No one's going to get the jump on *me*."

I clasped my hands together in front of me, the knuckles standing out white against my skin. "Oh."

"Oh," the old man echoed, his voice soft. "But, by all means. *Go on.*"

"I- We just thought, if you felt anyone coming, you could give us a heads up," I mumbled. "Give us a chance to protect ourselves. We were hoping to return the favor as payment."

"And let me guess - you want me to *not* sell your locations to every pack of hunters who comes trolling through."

"That would be nice," Jake said, earning a low chuckle from the man.

"How's a man supposed to pay his bills, hmm?"

"We don't have much money," I said quietly. "We do have some. But, well..." I lifted my chin, meeting his gaze steadily. "If we're sharing this corner of the state long-term, I'd rather know that you're not just waiting for the right price to show up before you sell us out."

Jake elbowed me hard, but I didn't turn. Harsh, perhaps, but also true. I kept my eyes on Greyson, doing my best not to blink. "I know you're confident that you can hold your own-"

"More than confident."

"But you're not as young as you used to be, either," I said, forcing the words out. Jake's elbowing grew to new intensity. I elbowed back, hard enough that he fell away, pressing a hand to his face. "The crew that came after us was, what, seven people? Eight?" I stared at him, trying to make him see that my goal wasn't to *insult* him. "How many can you handle - by yourself, with a support-type relic?

Jake shifted uncomfortably. "What Jon means is-"

I elbowed him again, harder. He shut up, but I heard him sigh.

Greyson was still watching us, his face half in shadow. "It's not often two kids come into my own home and say something like that to my face," he said, his voice carefully slow.

I ducked my head, knowing how red my face must be after that outburst. "I-I don't mean anything. Really. I just think-"

"So, what?" the old man said, swirling his beer in its can. "When folks come by you want me to, what. Lie?"

"Pretty much," I said, feeling a petrified grin spread across my face. "Get them out of our territory."

"Ours."

"You know what I mean. Say what you need to to get them to *leave*. And if they don't leave, we're only a speed-dial away."

He just stared, eyes growing more narrowed by the second. "What's your long-term plan here?"

I shook my head. "Haven't really thought that far ahead yet. But..." I hesitated, trying to put my thoughts in line. "I would have died, not that long ago, because I got caught by surprise and because I didn't have a relic worth a damn. I didn't *know* I had a relic worth a damn, I guess."

Jake was making a face. "My friend means a fo-"

"Shut up. At the least, I'd like to make a place where those of us who don't *want* to get caught up in the murdering and killing and general *bullshit* can have a go of things," I said, not taking my eyes off Greyson. "I thought that'd be something you'd want too." I pushed myself upright, giving the dog one last pat. "If I was wrong-"

"Oh, don't get all huffy," Greyson said, rolling his eyes. "No one likes a drama queen."

154

I froze, feeling my face go incandescent. "W-What?"

He leered at me, one hand rising to tug at the wiry hairs of his beard. "Just what I said. I'm not *uninterested*. I just don't want you two to think I *need* you. I don't. You both have more to lose from this going south than I do, I think."

I settled back down into my seat, feeling a bit like the carpet had been pulled out from under me. "S-So, is that a yes?"

"It's not a no."

"So what would it take for you to agree?"

He sighed, the air hissing between his teeth like wind through the leaves. "Just give me half a damned minute to think, will you? It'll be risky, and all that. What're the foci you lot've got?"

The couch under me trembled from the force with which Jake was shaking his head *no*, but I wasn't an idiot. "Why the hell do you want to know?"

Greyson chuckled. "So that I know what exactly I'm dealing with, of course. For all I know you two've got nothing better than I do, and where would that leave me?"

I narrowed my eyes. His words rang true, and there was no sign of deception to him, but I still wasn't entirely satisfied. "And you won't use this information against us?"

"I won't."

"You're not going to sell it to anyone?"

The old man took another draught of beer, beginning to frown. "Of course not. Wouldn't be a very honorable thing to do, would it?"

"Honor hasn't exactly been what I've seen from people thus far," I muttered under my breath, but nothing he was saying read as even a partial lie. So far as I knew - and the necklace hung warm around my neck as though confirming me it was still there and working - Greyson was telling the truth.

Glancing sidelong at Jake, I nodded. He scowled, his nose wrinkling, but turned to the finder with a sigh.

"I make people sleep," he said, the words flat and unhappy.

Greyson nodded, glancing to me a moment later.

I ran a hand through my hair. "I hold power over language," I said, thinking back to everything that had happened. "Something like that. I can see lies, and translate languages, and command people with my words."

"You're right, those aren't all that impressive," Greyson said, beginning to laugh. My face flushed again. He waved a hand a moment later, cutting our protests off before we could begin. "Fair's fair, though. Like I said, I'm Greyson, and I'm a passive finder." His laughter died slowly, fading into an easy grin. "I can feel when demis cross into my territory, reaching out a good two hundred miles in any direction."

Jake's hands clenched in his lap. "Two hundred-"

"You heard what I said," Greyson said, his chuckle returning. "Reason two no one wants to try and kill me - they'd have to wait another fifty years to get someone with powers like mine. To hell with that, eh?" He shrugged. "Of course, I can't tell you much *about* them, aside from their location and some general impressions about their strength and type, but it's enough to get me by."

The dog was back. I reached down slowly, rubbing the belly it was waving in my direction. "So if you're telling me all this-"

"There are worse ideas. I wouldn't *mind* a bit of stability, going into my golden years," Greyson said, half-shrugging. "Leave me your numbers. A call isn't too out of my way, I suppose."

Jake was smiling. So was I. It wasn't much of a victory - it wouldn't get us much at all - but it was a little in the way of security, and that'd help me sleep a bit better at night if nothing else. I scratched my cell number down on the scrap of paper Greyson threw me, passing it to Jake before the finder could change his mind.

"You know, you're not so bright." Greyson's voice cut through the growing quiet of the little house. I glanced up, a jolt of adrenaline hitting my system at the words, and found him staring at me. Smirking.

"E-Excuse me?"

"You've been here for years. Decades. Told you I have too - for a lot longer."

"...Right," I said slowly, my brow furrowing.

"Told you how far I can see. That I can feel the demis wandering inside that radius."

Shit. I knew my face was bone-white as I stared at him, the final pieces of what he was saying dropping into place, but I was too chagrined to look away. "S-So-"

"You're asking me to not sell your location, hmm?" Greyson said, chortling. "Never have before, have I?"

I ducked my head again, focusing on scratching the guy's dog. "How, uh. How long have you known?"

"From the start, of course."

"Of course you have."

His chuckle grew louder. "Dropped by once, to see who'd moved into the area. Just swung by when you were in town. Really wasn't expecting some preteen kid, running around the playground all carefree."

"Well…" I cleared my throat, still staring at the floor. "Thanks for not selling me out, then." Only the context I'd been given of late told me exactly how lucky I was that the man seemed to have some bizarre code of honor he followed. Anyone *else* would just have probably have seen me as an easy target and made their move.

"That's what neighbors do. So why not. I don't mind covering for you lot, long as you keep your noses out of trouble."

My head snapped up. He was still in his chair, but he nodded towards me. I bobbed my head in agreement hurriedly. "R-Right! Thanks. Thank you." I waved my phone in the air. "And, well, we're around. If you need anything-"

"I remember how to use a phone. Now leave Spike alone and get the hell out of my house."

I gave the dog one last appraising glance - a bit overweight, a bit old, and a bit *happy* - and tried to match what I saw with the name 'Spike'. Jake was already rising, though, glaring at me over his shoulder as though irritated I'd taken another half a second of his time.

"Thanks, Greyson. Appreciate it," I said, standing and making for the door before he went for his shotgun again.

"One last thing."

I froze, glancing back. "What's that?"

The old man was still smiling, but the look he was fixing me with was more admonishing than anything. "I appreciate you two stopping by. Agreements should be handled face to face."

Which was why we'd come. I nodded slowly, trying to look less confused than I felt. "I agree."

"It's good to get my eyes on the both of you, but if we're partners in all this, I want to know *exactly* who I'm dealing with." He raised one eyebrow. "I don't like feeling as though things are being left out. Next time you stop by, bring your friend. I'd like to meet them too."

I glanced sidelong at Jake, my confusion growing. "Ah...what? No. This is everyone." A light dawned. "Oh, well, there was a third here a few weeks ago. Maybe a month? Guy called-"

"Aedan. Like I said before. The old bastard everyone's always chasing after."

"He left," I said, shoving my hands into my pockets. Jake was already at the door, looking decidedly unhappy. "So it's just-"

"The three of you," Greyson said, nodding.

Again, the confusion welled up, but there was a new layer of unease to it. I shook my head more insistently. "No. It's just us."

He scowled, setting his beer down. "Oh, don't go lying to me, boy. This is what I *do*. Felt them appear not three weeks ago, *after* the old coot took off. I'm no idiot. When you lot feel like being honest with me-"

His words died as I threw my hand into the air, pinching the bridge of my nose with the other. "Just- One minute. Just one minute. Please."

Three weeks.

A third member of our little group.

A third demiblood.

Mentally, I ran the weeks back. Again, and again. The answer came up the same each time. The pit of my stomach churned.

Jake leaned against the door, staring at me. "Jon, come on. Let's just-"

"Greyson, I'm sorry," I said, snapping my eyes back to his. "Not trying to lie to you. In fact, I think someone's been lying to *me*."

Jake's brow furrowed. "What are-"

"We'll come back," I said, nodding respectfully to him. "Promise. Jake?

He brightened instantly, coming to life at the promise of escape.

I smiled humorlessly. "Time to go."

CHAPTER EIGHTEEN

The car ride was eerily quiet as we raced back towards Greenville. The scratches the branches had dug into the paint on my horrible little sedan would match the bloodstains coating the backseat nicely, completing the illustration that I was either insane or a serial killer. I couldn't spare them more than an irritated glance. Keeping the car on the road took the lion's share of my attention.

Jake looked even less comfortable than he had back in Greyson's place. His spine was ramrod straight, his fingers curling and uncurling from around the handle beside him. "Woah," I heard him mutter his voice low. "S-Slow down a-"

"We're fine." We skidded around another corner as I spat the words out, narrowly avoiding dragging two tires off the pavement.

"Dude, just-"

"Be quiet for a bit, ok?" I said, glancing at him from the corner of my eye.

He shook his head, his face going pale as the engine downshifted again. "No way. Just calm down."

"I'm calm," I said, flashing him a horrible, plastic smile. "Totally calm. This is fine."

"Watch the road."

"Just let me think," I muttered, tearing my eyes off him and pulling the wheel straight again. Greyson's place was halfway out into the forest. At the speed we were going, we'd be back into the heart of the city within minutes - and I still had no idea what I was going to say.

159

Maybe I was just reading too much into things. Maybe it was someone else, maybe Aedan had people on his tail after all. It was certainly a possibility. And yet, I knew, *knew* that wasn't the case. I'd seen the look in her eyes, the same stubbornness she'd had since we were kids. I didn't know how she'd done it, but I knew what Keira had done.

Jake fell silent at last, clinging to his seat uneasily. He seemed to accept that I wasn't going to listen - and while enspelling him into silence was far from my first choice, it probably wouldn't be a good idea to push me. I appreciated the quiet that fell over the car.

Without anywhere else to go, we'd made a pact with Jake. We had money, thanks to what Matt had left behind. He had contacts, and he had the knowledge that we didn't. By myself, I probably wouldn't make it all that long before getting caught in another mess. I was too new, too green and naive. Both of us wanted to be done with things. Working together, we could almost get there. Probably.

I'd been working a few years. The tech industry was pretty profitable, my company didn't pay badly, and land just wasn't that expensive where we lived. It wasn't like anyone was actually trying to move out into the middle of nowhere, after all. It took a little doing, but I'd found a place out in the hills where I'd hoped to keep my powers to myself - and keep everyone else out. I wasn't thrilled with what I'd had to do to the poor real estate agent to get the rates I'd gotten, but it was for our safety. Just this once, I'd have to put up with using my relic for the crew.

The end result was our house - a one-story thing tucked away into the forest, with a good four bedrooms that were only a *little* in disrepair. It would do, but wasn't ready just yet. Jake had found a sublet nearby for the month or two it would take everything to close out. I skidded to a stop outside his building, holding the car in place just long enough for him to stumble out. He didn't say anything. He'd been in the demi business for a lot longer than I had, and had to know how little I'd wanted Keira getting mixed up in it all. He raised his hand in a half-hearted wave as I hit the gas again, tearing out of the parking lot.

Without even his constant griping to distract me, I was left entirely to my thoughts. I'd already been worried, afraid that we were doing the wrong thing by going to the sullen finder. The more people who knew we were here, the more at risk we were. The discovery that he'd been watching me for years wasn't a comfortable one, even if he hadn't used his information for harm. My mind was already *full* of worries. This was just the cherry on top.

It wasn't far to our old apartment. I threw my car into park, staring at the steering wheel. My thoughts settled one after another, slowly falling away.

And then I pushed out into the cold night air, stomping up the steps to the front door before I lost my nerve.

The sound of laughter from inside rose loud enough that I could hear it through the door. I knew that strident laugh - Catherine. Keira's friend, blonde and big-voiced and full of perpetual excitement. *Lovely.* Just another thing for me to deal with.

The noise built as I pushed the door open, sliding inside. The warm air washed over my face, soothing the chill from my eyes and ears. Sure enough, I could see both of them sitting in the living room.

"Hey, Jon," Keira said, leaning forward to wave at me. "Have a good day?"

Her words died away, her brow furrowing as she got a good look at my face. I was glaring. I *knew* I was glaring, I just couldn't stop.

"Great. Just great. I've...got some groceries to carry in, Keira. Mind giving me a hand?"

She stared at me still, motionless.

"Jon!" Catherine cried, beaming as she popped out alongside my sister. "Long time no see. How's work?"

I forced a smile, trying not to glare at her too. Her exuberance was almost more than I could bear. "It's great, Cathy. Just great."

Little by little, the blood was draining from Keira's face. She knew. She knew that *I* knew.

"You said that already," her friend whined, rolling her eyes. "Jesus. You need a vacation."

"Uh- Cathy popped over for some drinks," Keira said, her eyes flicking between her friend and I. "Sorry. We can go if it's too loud. You've been working. You're probably tired. Why don't we head to your place, Cathy?"

"What, really?" Cathy said, turning back to her. "Can't we just-"

"Jon doesn't want to deal with us," Keira said, grinning at her as though nothing was wrong. It was all so believable. "He's just being polite."

"Oh, come on, Keira," I said, leaning back on my heels. "Don't lie like that."

Her eyes shot back to mine. I smiled. "I don't mind Cathy being here. It's *fine*. Let's not be rude."

"See? He said it's fine. Grab a beer, Jon, you look exhausted," Cathy said, settling back onto the couch.

"Really, though, Keira. Groceries. Car. Help me get everything in before everything freezes."

She glanced at Cathy again, like she was expecting her friend to save her. The woman didn't so much as take her eyes off the TV, chuckling softly to herself at the movie they were watching. She was stuck, and she had to know it.

Slowly, with every motion heavy and weighted down, Keira pushed herself upright. Her footsteps were muted against the horrible carpet of our apartment as she followed me to the door. Cathy didn't twitch. She'd been a few years younger than me, the same grade as Keira, so I'd known her for years. She was a sweet girl, smart as a whip and cheerful, but she couldn't read a room to save her soul. I had absolutely no worries about her catching on that there was anything else behind my sister helping me.

The door slammed shut behind us a few short moments later, and just like that, all of the need to keep up pretenses was gone. I crossed to the stairs in three quick steps, easing myself down onto the wood. My head was aching, pounding with tiredness and worry and all of the fear that had been building since I'd learned just how much danger we were in.

The wood behind me shifted. Keira slipped to the railing alongside me, leaning heavily on the unpainted wood. Her dark hair hung free, drifting in the chill breeze that had set in when the sun had gone down.

"So...I take it things didn't go so well with that finder guy?" she said, her voice cautious. I glanced up. She wasn't looking at me. Her eyes were fixed on the horizon, her jaw set firmly.

She knew as well as anyone that I could see a lie. Of course, there were all sorts of ways to get around telling lies - like distractions.

"Things went fine," I said, turning away from her again. "He doesn't seem all that convinced, but apparently he's already been keeping quiet about stuff. Didn't seem to mind keeping that up." A chuckle slipped from between my lips. "And god *damn*, he's scary. Thought he'd blow my head off. He can see from here to Jackson, too. Still trying to figure out how I feel about that."

"Oh."

"Mmhm."

I fell silent again, toying with the rings that hung from my neck. They glittered in the light from the apartments behind us, glowing bright silver against the grey and black of the night.

She cleared her throat at last. "That seems good. I'm glad."

"Yup."

Staring down at the rings, I counted off the seconds in my head. Finally, when I was about to hit 26, she sighed.

"Shit." Her voice was quiet, as though it wasn't entirely meant for me to hear.

I chuckled again. "Shit indeed."

"Jon, I-"

"Can I see it?"

She froze, her words dying. "That's- look, Jon, there's-"

"I just want to look. Is that so horrible?"

"I know you're probably upset. I shouldn't have kept it from you. I'm sorry about that."

"I just don't get why you'd lie to me," I mumbled. "How can I keep us safe if you're keeping secrets that dangerous?"

"You don't have to 'keep us safe', Jon. Come on. We're both adults."

"I-I know that. But you saw what happened, Keira. That's bigger than either of us. How can I help you if I don't even know you're a target?" I shook my head. "We have to be a team."

She ran a hand through her hair, sending the mahogany waves cascading down across her shoulders. She was buying herself time to think, I knew, trying to find an answer for me. There wasn't an easy out waiting for her.

"Can I-"

"I'd still like to see it," I said, my voice quieter but every bit as firm. Like she'd said, she was an adult, and she made her own choices. I respected that. But when our parents had moved away, years ago, us staying had meant we were alone. She didn't *need* me to take care of her, but I'd just always been the older one. The mature one, I'd thought. It was hard to kick the habit.

And there were suspicions still waiting in the back of my mind. Well. Calling them suspicions meant there was a chance I was wrong - and by then, I was entirely certain I was *right*.

The twitch of her hands at my request, the way her eyes glanced away, was nearly enough to confirm my theories. For a second, I thought she'd continue arguing with me over it.

But the fight slipped from her shoulders as they drooped a heartbeat later. I could see her beginning to shiver in the nighttime air. We couldn't stay out here long. All the same, this was a conversation worth having. Her hands slipped into the pouch of the hoodie she wore a moment later. She hesitated again.

"Don't be mad," she muttered, her ears going red. "It's not his fault. Really."

Before I could say another word, she drew her hands back out - and this time, they were wrapped around a delicate, all-too-familiar set of eyeglasses.

She held them in her lap, her hands open underneath them like a cradle. She didn't say a word. She just waited, frowning as she glared at the ground.

I was all too happy to let her keep her silence right then, for another moment while I stewed. I was nearly there, nearly ready. My mind was roaring, even as I stared at the glasses, tight-lipped. The sight of them brought a few answers - important answers, yes, but ones that introduced a host of new questions.

One thing was absolutely certain. I was going to kill Aedan when I found the bastard.

I forced a smile onto my face as my eyes slid up to meet hers. "And now I'd like you to start explaining," I said cheerfully.

CHAPTER NINETEEN

Clouds of fog accompanied every breath Keira and I took. It drifted off into the frigid air, filing the world with wisps of white. My question hung between us. I could still feel it on my lips as I paused, waiting.

Her fingers curled around the silvered frame of the glasses, gripping them a little tighter. Her lips parted, like she was about to answer, but each time she fell silent again before she could force a word out. I could have interrupted her, demanding an answer, but I just waited, turning my gaze away from her and fixing it on my feet.

"I didn't want to be helpless," she said at last, her words small and quiet. "I didn't want to be the only one left defenseless. It's not fair, and it's not safe." Her chin lifted stubbornly. "And I wanted to know."

"All you've done is-"

"Declared to anyone looking that there's another relic here. Another demi. I know." As quiet as her tone was, there was no hint of an apology in her voice. "They used me as a tool against you last time, Jon. A weapon." She shook her head violently. "I won't let that happen again.

"This won't change any of that," I said, trying to keep from snapping. "Damn it, Keira. This isn't something you can undo."

"I know that."

"It's not something you should decide on a whim. You should have-"

"It's not a *whim*." Keira said, her blue eyes flashing up to meet mine. "You think I haven't spent years thinking about something like this?

165

About you and your *abilities*?" She folded her arms across her chest stubbornly. "I wanted this, Jon. Me. It was my choice."

"I-" I began, but stopped, unable to meet the steel in her expression. There was no hint of a lie in anything she said, no sign of any reservations. She meant it. I wasn't happy about that, but the longer I stared at her, the less I could find it in myself to be angry with her. Worried, yes, and more than a little afraid, but...

"If you'd been open with it from the start, I wouldn't have been so blindsided," I mumbled.

"Sorry. But you'd have argued."

"Probably." I couldn't quite keep the crooked grin from tugging at my lips. "We're still arguing, aren't we?"

She chuckled. "Guess so."

"How'd you even do it?" I said, a bit of earnest frustration slipping into my tone. "I *know* Aedan didn't leave anything in the apartment. I saw him take everything."

Her eyes dropped to the stairs underneath us, her face going crimson in a second. "W-Well, that's...it's not really important, in-"

"Keira."

"You leave your phone *everywhere*," Keira mumbled. "The bathroom, the kitchen, wherever the hell you feel like." The corner of her lips twitched up, her smile returning. "And you've used the same password since we were kids."

"You stole his number," I said, glaring at her. "You went into my phone and you-"

"I didn't know what else to do," she said, her chin lifting. "And you left it lying out, ready and waiting." She shrugged helplessly. "He wasn't that far out of town yet. Easy enough for him to swing back."

"Just like that."

"Just like that," she echoed.

I pressed a hand to my face, feeling a groan bubble up through my chest. Aedan had been interested from the start. He'd baited her into taking a relic, hadn't he? He must have been thrilled to have her call him, going behind my back. Asshole.

"You could have picked anything," I said at last, letting my hand fall. "Anything. Tell me you can throw fireballs, or shoot spikes from your fingernails, or *something* a little more-"

"Sorry," she said, her cheeks flushing further. "I-I mean, he had all sorts of the things. I could have- he didn't *make* me. It's just..." she trailed off.

I fought off the urge to tap my foot, folding my hands in my lap. "Yes?" I said at last, seeing that she'd well and truly stalled.

"I wanted to know. To understand," Keira said, pursing her lips. "None of this makes any sense. I don't want to be confused anymore. I want to know what we are, what we're facing." Her fingers played over the arms of the glasses. They were ancient, I saw, delicately worked in a way that told me they'd never been touched by a factory machine. The lenses looked older still, more like slabs of crystal than prescription lenses.

My fingers itched to lift them from her lap, pull them in for a closer look, but I could remember the constant itch of having Aedan take my necklace from me. I let her keep them, my eyes drifting back up to her face. "And….so?" I smiled faintly. "Anything happening?"

Her head bobbed in a quick nod. "I...Yes. I think so, anyway." She slid her fingertips over the metal one last time, unfolding the arms, and raised them to her face. "I can see things, Jon."

"Finally, some long-awaited confirmation that you're crazy."

She smacked me a moment later. "Ass."

"What kinds of things?"

Keira hesitated, her eyes tightening. And then she glanced back at me. "Well...When I look at you, or Jake…" She shook her head. "It's like you're glowing. There's a sort of...light, under your skin."

I flinched as she raised one hand, tapping against my chest. The rings under my shirt pressed gently into my skin, firmly fixed beneath her fingertip.

"That's brighter than anything," she said, her voice quiet. "I can see it at a glance, Jon."

"That's...cool," I said, my voice carefully neutral. "Well, in the grand scheme of abilities, it's not-"

"It's getting stronger."

I stopped, my words falling away. "What?" I said at last, blinking.

She shook her head again, waving her hands as she tried to find the words. She slipped the glasses from her face, folding them back into her pocket protectively. "It's like...every day, it's a little clearer. The glow is a little brighter. And…" She hesitated for a moment before plowing onward. "I've been seeing flashes, here and there. Images."

"They said that these things mature the longer you have them," I said slowly. "It would make sense that the same would be true for yours." I rubbed at the wood with my toe, not quite sure what to say to her. "I guess...what are you seeing?"

Her eyes dropped, her eyes tightening. "It's not...it's not clear enough for me to make anything out. Just, like, the sort of stuff you remember after you wake up from a dream, you know?" Keira glanced at me. "Wearing the glasses seems to help focus me in, but..." She hesitated a moment longer. "Even without them, it still happens. When I look at you, sometimes I see the house back in Grayling."

"Oh." I fell silent a moment later, letting the quiet stretch out between us again. Our grandparents had lived there for years - when we were kids. Both of us had spent far too long in that neighborhood. "So, like, you're-"

"I don't know," Keira said, throwing her hands up. "I have no idea, Jon. I don't know if I'm seeing t-the past, or just a daydream, or *what*."

"Something important to me?" I said, improvising wildly. "Some sort of insight, maybe?" I drooped a moment later, shaking my head. "Well...we'll just have to wait, I think." I managed a smile, glancing back towards her. "You've only had the glasses, what. A few weeks?"

"Something like that," she muttered.

The sound of Catherine's laughter drifted out through the thin walls of our apartment. We flinched, as though suddenly remembering that the world was going on around us.

Keira half-turned, fixing her eyes on me. "Are you about done?" she mumbled.

I ran a hand through my hair, my mind still racing. "I- yeah. Sorry for going all twenty questions on you."

"I'm sorry too. Should have said something."

I swallowed a chuckle. Her cheeks were still red, and even though her jaw was clenched obstinately, she wasn't yelling. "Dad made me promise to look after you when they left," I said, my voice quiet. "You know that. I just don't want to see you get hurt."

"I'm not going to get hurt," she said, rolling her eyes. "I don't go looking for trouble."

"I didn't *look* for it."

She chuckled. "Right."

I sighed. "Just be careful."

Keira pushed herself upright, only a touch unsteadily. "I will. Stop worrying. I'm going back inside."

"Keira."

She froze, already a step towards the door. Her eyes flicked back to me. "What now?"

I rose, feeling my muscles pull as I levered myself to vertical. "I'd like to borrow your phone. Just for a few minutes."

Her hand dropped to her pocket, held flat like she was shielding it. "I'm not- you can't just delete it, Jon. No."

"You'd just steal my phone again, right?" I said, masking my smile behind a hand. "I just want to borrow it. I'll give it back when I come in. Please."

Recognition lit up in her eyes. She flinched, her hand sliding away from her pocket. "I don't...I don't think that's-"

"Please?" I said again, grinning down at her.

A sigh shook her frame. There was irritation in her eyes, but not enough to keep her from sliding her phone from her pocket, unlocking it with a swipe. "Don't go browsing through any of my stuff," she said, glaring at me. "I'll know."

"I won't," I mumbled, already pulling up her contacts list. The sound of the door slamming shut next to me was loud enough that I jumped, my finger sliding over the screen. Muttering a curse under my breath, I scrolled back to where I'd been.

It probably wasn't strictly necessary to use her phone. All the same, I wanted to make sure he actually picked up. Jabbing my thumb down on the green button, I held the phone to my ear. The tinny, electronic sound of the phone dialing spilled from the speaker. I waited, my irritation growing with every second that passed. One after another, I counted the rings.

Just when I'd begun to think it was going to go to voicemail, a *click* rang across the line.

"Keira!" I heard Aedan say on the other end, his voice bright. "What's up? Running into any problems?"

"Hi, Aedan," I said, leaning back on the railing.

The phone went quiet. I frowned, picking at my cuticles as I waited. Second after second drifted away as white noise purred faintly in my ear.

"Oh, come on, I know you're there," I snapped finally. "What were you thinking, giving-"

The call went dead with a *click*.

I pulled the phone from my ear, swearing under my breath. The words *Call Ended* stared up at me from the screen. He'd hung up on me.

He'd really hung up on me.

Word after frustrated word spilled from my throat as I pulled the screen back up, redialing. Each was more profane than the last, and far more than I probably should have been saying out where anyone could hear me, but I didn't care.

The call rang for a few seconds, and was promptly declined. I glared down at the screen, already putting another one through.

The line connected, after four rings. I pulled the phone back up to my ear, just in time to hear Aedan's exasperated sigh. *"What?"*

"You gave Keira a relic?" I snapped. "Are you serious?"

"She's a big girl, Jon. She asked, and I provided. That's all there is to it. Now if you don't mind-"

"Don't try and end it with *that*. You didn't even give me a heads up. She could have gotten herself killed."

He didn't say anything for a long moment. And then I heard him make an irritated noise, like he was rubbing his face. "Is what it is, Jon. Sorry. I guess. How's she shaping up?"

"Excuse me?"

"The glasses, man. Her relic. How's she presenting?"

"She's seeing things," I said, fighting to keep my temper in check. Aedan's bad attitude was quite nearly more than I could handle right in that moment. "And she can identify demis by sight. And relics. Past that-"

"She's had them less than a month. That's plenty. More than I expected, really," Aedan said, his tone thoughtful. "Interesting. Not strictly a *finder*, then."

"Stop treating her like a guinea pig, asshole."

"Fine, whatever. Anyway. You'll live. Stop whining and act like an adult. Now, I have to go. International minutes are fucking expensive. Pull yourself together and be watchful, and you'll be fine."

I scowled. "International minutes? Where exactly are you, anyway? Don't-"

The line went dead again.

"Got to be fucking kidding me," I muttered, punching at the screen again. I wasn't even a little surprised when it went straight to voicemail. He'd turned his phone off. Asshole.

The sound of voices drifted out again, pulling me back to the present. Aedan being a dick was just business as usual. He'd been exactly no help at all. I didn't know why I even bothered anymore. I mean, sure, I'd mostly wanted to yell at him, but he could have just *let* me. He certainly deserved it.

Muttering one final curse as I let my hand drop to my side, I stalked back towards the door.

CHAPTER TWENTY

My blood roared, screaming in my ears. I lurched on. My legs were leaden weights underneath me, and my once-gunshot thigh was *not* happy about what I was doing to it. It was all I could do to keep running, doing my best not to gasp like a fish out of water. The others would just laugh at me, and right then, I didn't want to deal with it.

"Seriously, though, like, you should really come to the show. It's next week, and I know you'd love it," Mason said. He stood a few steps away, casually leaning against the next treadmill over. We'd been friends for just about as long as I could remember. Going away to school had taken the edge off the relationship, but I knew he'd manage to worm his way back into my life somehow. He was persistent like that. I could see Keira over his shoulder, sitting on a bench pressed against the gym's wall. Cathy was right alongside her, the both of them chattering away at a hundred miles an hour.

"We'll see," I said, doing my best to force the words through lungs that burned with every breath.

A treadmill. *Me.* It was a notion that I would have laughed at only a few weeks ago, but after the way things had gone, I'd realized that there were some parts of my life that would need adjusting.

Mason scowled, leaning in closer until he filled my vision. "What? Come on, Jon. It's one day. I know how *busy* you are, but I think you can find that much time in your action-packed schedule." On his lips, the word was filled with derision. Glancing away from me, he nodded towards the machine beyond me. "You can come too. We'll make an evening out of it."

I bit back the groan before it could escape.

"Sorry," Jake said, just a hair short of a pant. "Busy." He was running just as hard as I was - and showed less wear for it. I tried to keep my jealousy in check.

"You too?" Mason said, shaking his head. "God damn it, guys. And aren't you done yet?"

Another figure slipped up behind him - Dirk, another friend Mason had asked along. "Bet you never expected him to be the one holding you up here, eh?"

Mason held his hands in the air helplessly. "What can I say? I was shocked. There's no denying it. But who am I to say no when a friend asks for my help?"

"I'm just using you to get around paying the fee," I said, spitting the words out. "Don't get ahead of yourself."

"Really, though. You guys know there's other stuff here, right?" Dirk said, coming up alongside Mason. "You don't have to spend the whole damn night running."

I *did* laugh at that. That was easy for them to say. They hadn't gotten to spend a fun-filled night getting shot at. Running was important, I'd learned. "It's good for my leg."

Keira snorted. The sound cut across the roar of the machines and the pounding of our footsteps. So she was listening. I would have said something, if I'd been able to find enough breath.

Despite my best efforts, though, my leg was screaming its protest, and I'd heard the disbelief that filled her little interjection. Trying and failing to mask my relief, I slapped the off button. The world spun under me as I thudded to a stop, leaning on the handrails as I tried to regain a bit of composure.

Dirk's hand slapped down on my back a second after. "Oh, Jon." I could hear him trying not to laugh.

"Shut up."

"It'll be easier next time. Probably."

Next time. Lovely. I forced a smile, stooping further, and massaged the stiff, tense mess that was my leg. The scar left emblazoned across my skin was hidden, but that didn't mean it wasn't there. Which was why I'd asked Mason to help me out in the first place, damn it.

"How's the house going?" Mason said, interrupting my self-pity session. "Got to be pretty rough if even you could afford it. Never figured you for a house-flipper."

"I'm not flipping it," I muttered. "It's ours."

"It's rough," a low voice added. Jake flopped down on one of the benches, a sheen of sweat coating his skin. "It's really rough."

"What, you let him see it?" Mason snapped, standing straight. "After I've been asking all week? What the hell, Jon. I'm going to start thinking you like him more."

"He's the manual labor," I said, raising an eyebrow. "You want to come put a new roof on the place?"

A bit of the color left Mason's skin. "What?"

"It's not so bad. I could use someone to help me carry shingles, with this leg. Or do you want to help with the drywall? I've been meaning to hire someone to do that." I reached over, slapping him on the back. "So kind of you to offer."

"No, thank you," Mason muttered, shaking his head. "But, seriously. We'll come over on Friday. Share a few. You can show us around."

"No."

He scowled. "Why not?"

Dirk groaned. "Mason."

"No, I just want to know why it's such a big deal to want to hang out with you."

"I'm swamped at work," I said, my irritation building by the second. "Everything's piled up after I was in the hospital. I'm busy, and the place isn't ready. Later."

"It was later last week too."

"Seriously, Mason," I said, feeling a headache spring to life. "I'm sorry things haven't worked out. We'll find time, okay?"

"When?"

When I don't have people trying to kill me. When I'm sure that it's safe to have you guys spending time with us, when I'm sure that Greyson isn't going to throw us to the wolves. "I don't know, Mason."

"It's not that big a deal, dude," Dirk said, dropping his hand onto Mason's shoulder. "Come on."

"But he can hang out?" Mason protested, waving a hand at Jake. "Fine. Fine! I see how it is. Glad to see how I rank after all these years." There was a joking lilt to his voice - but I wasn't fooled. It was a thin veneer of humor laid over the top of a giant pile of resentment.

Good god, the man had no tact. I mean, he never had before, but there were limits. "Give it a rest, Mason," I snapped. "He's just a friend f-from school. You'll come over, *later*. Now stop pestering me about it and let's go."

Too late, I felt it - the thin tug, pulling all the way to my core. And the subtle but noticeable ache that layered itself on top of my already-growing headache.

"Right," Mason said, a wall sliding over his eyes. It left him blank, expressionless. "I understand. Let's go."

My necklace was warm against my chest.

I jumped to my feet, horror overcoming my irritation in a split second. Mason was already turning towards the front door of our town's horrible little gym, apparently taking my command entirely literally. I grabbed hold of his shoulder a second later, releasing my hold on the magic in the same instant.

"No. I'm sorry," I said, feeling the blood drain from my face. "That's not what I meant. I'm just- I'm just a little stressed. You guys can come over…soon. We'll hang out. I'll figure something out."

Mason glanced back towards me, the light slowly returning to his eyes. "Yeah," he said slowly, nodding. "I gotcha. I'm just going to keep bothering you, then, okay?" The grin he flashed was small, hesitant, but it was there.

I took a deep breath, trying to steady myself. My pulse thundered in my ears. I *hadn't* meant to cast anything on him. I was irritated, yes, but not to that extent. It wasn't what I'd wanted. And now that I was seeing it with my own two eyes, it brought up a single, horrifying question.

How long had I been able to use my relic like that?

Thankfully, none of my friends seemed to have noticed my slip - or the revulsion I was sure was laid plain across my face. Dirk had already turned towards the locker room, joking with Mason as he led the both of them in. Jake just yawned, still scowling, and watched the TV mounted in the corner of the room.

Only Keira was watching me, wide-eyed and no longer listening as Cathy blabbered away at her. I groaned internally. Of course. Of course she'd have noticed - She wasn't wearing them, but I knew she'd have her glasses close at hand. I must have lit myself up like a damn Christmas tree when I'd cast on him.

I hesitated, totally at a loss as for how to explain myself, but she shook her head, her eyes sad. She knew. Right. She'd seen the whole thing, after all. She turned away a second later, leading her and Cathy towards their own changing room.

Fighting back the guilt wasn't such an easy task as I trudged off with Jake, my mind suddenly circling with doubts.

***

The sun had already gone down when we slipped back outside. I covered my mouth, fighting off a yawn, and waved to my friends. Mason waved back, grinning broadly. He'd entirely recovered from my inadvertent casting, apparently, and seemed none the wiser. That was for the best. Him and Dirk drifted off into the darkness towards the distant shape of their truck, even as Keira pried herself loose of Cathy's hug and pushed the woman towards her car.

My steps slowed, though. I waited, caught in place as their headlights sprang to life - and then faded out into the night, leaving us standing on the sidewalk.

"I'm beat," Keira said, stretching her arms towards the stars. "Anyway. I'll see you two-"

"Actually, do you have a few minutes," I said, cutting her off.

She stopped, holding my stare. "I…guess?" she said at last. "What's up?"

I pursed my lips, glancing back over my shoulder. The lights of Greenville's downtown glimmered a block down from us - small and pathetic, yes, and most places probably wouldn't be open much later, but they were still there. "There's somewhere I want to look into. I'd like your help."

"Cool," Jake said, frowning. "You can just give me the keys, Keira, and I can go home. And then Jon can-"

"What was it you wanted to look at?" my sister said, folding her arms and making no movement towards her keys. "I mean, it's *fine*, but it's getting a bit late." The look she gave me was altogether too knowing. "What's going on? Is something wrong?" She hesitated. "Back in there. I saw what happened. With Mason. Are you-"

"It's not about that," I muttered, shaking my head. "That was…an accident. I didn't mean to."

"Well, I assumed that much."

"I was just thinking. About what Jake and I were talking about, back then," I said, tearing my eyes off her.

Jake stiffened, his brow furrowing. "What?"

I smiled thinly. "Come on. It's not far."

176

I could see their hesitation, the way they glanced at each other, but they fell in line behind me a moment later. I had the keys, after all. Jake might complain, but it wasn't like he could drive himself home. And even if Keira had questions, I didn't think she'd just turn on her heel and leave me in the dark.

"You'd asked me about where I got my relic," I said, glancing over my shoulder. Jake's eyes widened, half-shadowed in the dim light. I shrugged. "I said I got it at a pawn shop. It's right in town here."

"And you want to go there," Keira said slowly. "Why, exactly?"

"You said it was rare," I said, looking towards Jake again.

He nodded. "Ah. Yeah. To put it lightly. No one's going to just *lose* a relic. It's not going to happen."

I turned forward again, watching the sidewalk slide by under our feet. "Right. So how'd it wind up there?"

The other two went quiet. Keira was the first to break the silence. "You think something else is going on."

"I think it's worth looking into how a random pawn shop in the middle of nowhere got its hands on a relic. Greyson kept us hidden from onlookers for years."

"Do you think he's keeping secrets?" Jake said slowly. His voice had gone serious, losing the sleepy, exasperated air it'd had moments before.

I shrugged. "I don't know. We don't really know anything about the guy, that's all I'm saying."

Keira glanced sidelong at me. "Besides that he kept you alive all this time."

"Besides that."

Jake cleared his throat. "Uh...not to be a downer, but if there really is something more going on with this place, do we really want to just charge on in there like we own the place?"

My steps slowed. The storefront lay ahead, shining out blindingly bright in the darkness. I waved my hand towards it, glancing over to Keira. "I mean...first things first, and all that. You said you could see my relic, before. And you saw me cast today. Do you see anything from the place?"

Her nostrils flared, her eyes widening gently. And then she turned towards the pawn shop, her brown hair flicking out behind her. Reaching one hand into her pocket, she pulled the pair of delicate crystal-lens glasses free.

I slid a step back, taking up my place at Jake's side. We waited, neither of us wanting to break the quiet as Keira stared at the building.

"I'm not exactly any good at this yet," she said, a note of strain underlying her voice. "So...I don't know?"

"Do you see anything?" I said, shoving my hands into my coat pockets and trying to look casual.

She shook her head. "No."

"Then let's take a closer look."

Jake muttered something under his breath, too quiet for me to hear. I glanced back. He shook his head, wrinkling his nose, and said nothing.

The doorbell was deafeningly loud after the quiet of the night. We slipped inside, exhaling slowly as the warmth settled over us. The shopkeeper looked up, letting his eyes sweep over us for just long enough to give me the creeps. I heard his warning, even without him saying a word. Don't cause trouble, don't make a fuss.

But he just jerked his head in the barest hint of a nod, picking his magazine back up a moment later. His silvered hair curled out from under a worn, stained baseball cap.

I watched him from the corner of my eye as the others dispersed through the narrow, dark room, digging through every scrap of memory I could get my hands on. He wasn't young. Anyone could see *that* much. But was he old enough to have been the owner back when I'd bought my relic, almost two decades before?

Probably.

I stepped over to the glass cases in the meantime, coming up alongside Keira. She'd put her glasses on at some point during our entrance, and pored over the horrible, cheap jewelry with every apparent sign of enjoyment.

"Lookin' for something in particular?" the owner said, lowering his magazine a hair. His eyes watched me from under the brim of his hat, beady and sharp.

I shook my head hurriedly. "N-No. We were just a few stores down, a-and..." I swallowed hard, rallying desperately. This was my chance. "Well, I'd come here once with my grandpa, and I realized I'd never stopped by again." Feeling like an absolute idiot, I waved dismissively as I returned my gaze to the cases. "That was years and years ago, of course. I'm sure it's changed a lot."

The owner chuckled, the sound rasping through the buildup of what sounded like five decades of hard smoking. "You'd be surprised. Don't much like change. Well, if you see somethin' you'd like to see up close, just yell. And don't touch the glass. You'll leave fingerprints." His last words were sharp. Jake jumped, his hands snapping free of the jewelry counter.

My heart thrummed in my chest. I moved from one side of the store to another, Keira a few paces behind. No matter how hard I looked, I couldn't see anything special about *anything* there. I mean, I couldn't exactly tell a relic from any other antique, so I wasn't quite sure what I was looking for, but…it would have been nice.

Keira elbowed me. I glanced over, mouthing *done?* once I saw her looking my way. She nodded.

The man sniffed as we slipped back out of the store, stammering excuses and goodbyes. His nose was already buried in his magazine again by the time the door slid shut.

"Anything?" I said a second later, unable to wait.

My heart sank as Keira shook her head. "Not a thing," she said, holding my stare with her own. "He's a normal human. And I didn't see any relics in his shop."

"To no one's great surprise," Jake muttered.

I made a face, my steps slowing. "We could…ask him. A little more directly, I mean."

Jake's head snapped around to face me, and the look on it was none too friendly. "Excuse me? What good do you think that's going to do?"

"Probably nothing. You're right. I know that."

"Then don't be stupid."

"I just want to know," I said, a plaintive note slipping into my tone. "I mean, I don't think he's moved from that stool in thirty years. It's got to be the same guy. And how unlikely is it for him to *just happen* to have a relic for sale?"

It was Jake's turn to scuff at the ground with his shoe, not quite able to meet my eyes. "Very."

"But he's not like us," Keira said. "He's *not*. I don't know what to tell you, Jon."

Jake shrugged, shoving his hands in his pockets and pushing ahead of me. The car waited by the sidewalk, dark and welcoming. "Stranger things have happened, I guess. Looks like you won the lottery."

"I guess," I whispered. It wasn't satisfying. Not at all. I'd been convinced there was more to it, more to learn about the messed-up world we'd been thrown into and my own past. I'd *hoped* that I could glean a little more information about my relic out of the guy.

But if he wasn't a demi, then that was that. Asking him odd questions would only put more attention on us, and I'd attracted enough attention for one lifetime over the last few weeks. More than that, even, I knew that playing loose with information about demis and relics was a dangerous game. It wasn't worth it.

So I let Jake and Keira lead me back towards my car, staring at the pavement all the while. I wanted to stay irritated, to keep wondering to myself about what was really happening. The miles Jake and I had put on the treadmills had other ideas. He pressed a hand to his face, masking a yawn, and Keira wasn't far behind.

They were both asleep before we turned out onto the main road, leaving me alone with my thoughts.

**

As the weeks slipped by, I had precious little time to worry about Aedan and his particular brand of assholery. I had a new house to move into - and an awful lot of things to fix in it. I couldn't exactly afford a mansion, after all, no matter how far out into the forest I moved. The place I'd found was solid enough, and it had enough space to house a small army, but it was all but gutted. Between Jake and I we were making solid progress, but winter was closing in. The later the weeks crept on, the more time I spent sealing everything back up.

Jake wasn't surprised by Keira's progress at all. When we'd first all talked about it, sitting around one of the town's less awful bars, he'd only shrugged.

"It's not the same," he'd said, his voice low. "Recon was...well, she didn't say exactly how it worked. Most people don't. You're safer if people don't know all the details."

"But-"

"But it was more like farseeing," he'd said, glancing up at me. "Closer to what Greyson can do, actually. I think. Matt called her Radar a few times. As a joke. She didn't seem to like it."

Keira hadn't said a word as the two of us talked. She'd just stared down at the glasses in her hands, her lips pressed into a thin line.

They'd said it all along. There were no guarantees that a relic would grant someone identical powers after it'd been passed along. There was no reason to think that Keira would wind up being the same as that Recon woman. It would have been *convenient*, but so little of our life had been convenient of late.

All we could do was muddle through it, piecing things together as we went. Little by little, we were figuring her and her relic out, although it was a slow, painful process. Whatever visions she was getting, they were beginning to clear enough that she could make out people. That didn't mean they made any more sense.

The confusion aside, life began to take on a sort of normalcy. The world went on. We still had to go to work, and pay bills, and buy groceries. The fact that it was getting more and more difficult to resist the urge to enspell my boss when he asked me to meet ridiculous deadlines was irrelevant. I hadn't abused my powers. Much. I'd gotten to see too much of Matt and his crew to want to dive into *that* mess.

When the call came through a month later, with the first snow beginning to fall, I'd been confused at first. It pulled me out of my sleep, so early in the morning that the sky outside my window was still dark. I stared down at the phone, seeing the number light up. I didn't recognize it. No one called me, no one except my coworkers - and it wasn't any of their numbers.

Probably just another spam call. I hit decline, tossing the phone back onto my nightstand with a groan. They were getting worse by the day. It took some nerve, calling me before dawn on my day off. Assholes. My eyes slid shut again as I leaned back into the covers.

The shriek of my ringtone split the silence a moment later. I flinched, twitching back out of the sleep I'd been well on my way to falling back into. It was still going, playing its cheesy little jingle and growing louder by the second. Mumbling a curse past lips that hadn't entirely banished sleep yet, I pulled the phone to my ear.

"Jon," I mumbled.

"Morning, kid," a voice said, low and gravelly and awake enough that I wanted to punch them in the face. "Sorry to wake you."

I pressed a hand to my face, rubbing my eyes. "Greyson."

"Real genius, you are. Anyway. Get out of bed and wake up. We need to talk."

An icy bolt of adrenaline shot through my veins. Getting in touch with Greyson had seemed more like a formality, a layer of protection we'd probably never need. If he was calling me in the dark of the morning, pulling me out of bed, then, well.

I pushed myself upright, my feet dropping down onto the worn carpet alongside my bed. "Greyson."

"Still me. You up?"

No. My head was still foggy, fighting against each and every thought that tried to worm its way through. I nodded all the same, realizing a moment later that I was talking on the phone. "Y-Yeah. I'm awake. What's up?"

The sound of his raspy sigh echoed in my ear. "Go get some coffee going. It's going to be a long morning. We've got a problem."

CHAPTER TWENTY-ONE

A problem.

I stared at the horrible, threadbare carpet under my feet, blinking away the last tendrils of sleep. It didn't seem to be working.

"You listening?" Greyson snapped a moment later, his voice tightening ominously. "Don't you dare-"

"I'm listening. Sorry. I am," I said quickly. There was an edge to the older man's voice that didn't allow for any other answer.

"Good. I'm not here to waste my time if you'd rather go back and take a nappie."

"What's going on?" I said, rubbing my eyes. Talking to him when it was...I squinted at the clock. Three AM. It was three AM. Talking to him just then was quite nearly more than I could handle.

"Right. Well," he said, the aggression bleeding out of his tone instantly. "Might be it's nothing. Might be it's something. But I've been feeling a bit of activity down to the south."

"Activity," I said, meandering through my darkened bedroom. The hallway beyond was no better. I kept one hand on the wall, ready to catch myself when I tripped. I didn't think it was going to be an 'if'. "What do you mean, activity?"

"What do you think I mean?" Greyson said, his tone scornful even over the phone line.

I grimaced. "Fair enough. How bad is it?"

He sighed, the sound bleeding away into white noise on his end. "Like I said. It's hard to say."

"Best guess."

"I'm fairly sure there's three of them."

Three. I dropped myself into one of the hard, wooden kitchen chairs, bracing my elbow against the table and cradling my head. Another fight was *not* what I was hoping for, so soon after we'd gotten settled in. Of course, I didn't know that was what was coming, either. "Gotcha. I mean...that's better than with Matt, I guess."

"Yep," Greyson said. "Best guess, mind. Don't hold me to it."

"I won't."

"Anyway. It's not all that unusual, really."

"Demibloods wandering around?" I said, my tone skeptical. "That seems pretty-"

"The hell do you know?" Greyson said, his tone sharp. I thought I might have heard a scornful laugh rippling under his voice, but there was no way to be sure.

"I-I mean, I'm just-"

"Don't get ahead of yourself. You don't know shit."

Part of me wasn't quite so sure about this whole business anymore. How well did we know him, really? How could we be sure he wasn't trying to set us up, lead us right into a trap?

We'd trusted him this far. If he had ulterior motives, I hadn't been able to discern them from his words. He hadn't *lied*.

"Fine," I muttered, giving up and laying my head flat on the table. "I'll take your word for it."

"Damn straight, you will. Folks travel. Sure, some stake their claims in the cities, carving out territories to defend, and some hole up alone like you and I, but there's just as many who wander. It's easier. Not having ties to folks means less suspicion about using your focus to cheat at life. Not so many questions and all."

Begrudgingly, I had to admit it made sense. "Okay. So if this isn't all that unusual, why are you-"

"Let a man talk. It's common enough for me to feel demis wandering. There's a lot of ground under my watch." He sighed again. I could hear him tapping something, like fingers on the table. Or the butt of his gun against the floor. "Only, since this lot crossed into my domain, I've felt two other foci disappear."

I went still. "Disappear."

"You don't really need me to explain, do you?"

"I think I've got it. Shit."

"Shit indeed," he said with a dark chuckle. "They turned north last night."

A shiver rippled down my spine. I didn't want a fight, but if Greyson was right, it sounded an awful lot like this group was killing other demis. And *we* were in the north. "Are they coming-"

"I don't know if they've got a finder," Greyson said. "They're too far off for me to pull anything more detailed than numbers, so I don't know if they've spotted you. And…"

"What's that?"

He made an irritated noise, like he was rubbing his face. "It's nothing. I just can't feel things for sure at this distance. Don't love it."

"They could still go past, right?" I said slowly. "You said people moving around is normal. Maybe they're just traveling. We shouldn't assume."

"Sure. Sure. Unless they know we're here, it's not really an issue. Most demis won't poke around too close to my home. I like my privacy, and *they* like me not charging them out the ass for finder services."

Which was probably the only reason I'd escaped notice for as long as I had. I swallowed hard, feeling a bit more of the sleep leave my mind as fear slipped into its place. I'd been lucky. Very lucky.

Another question was rising, waiting on the tip of my tongue. Greyson said all of this like it was totally normal - three demis passing by, the four of us living in a neat little circle. I couldn't imagine we were the only ones in the state, either. The old man seemed the type to offer the same respect for privacy that he demanded. It was enough to make me think, resting my head on my hand.

Just how many relics *were* there?

"It's up to you." Greyson's voice split through my thoughts, drawing me back to the business at hand. "Can go either way. Just figured now was as good a time as any to put our little deal to use."

"No, I appreciate it," I said, my voice quiet. There were too many thoughts circling in my head, options and possibilities and fears. "So they turned north? How close will they come?"

He made a noncommittal noise. "Hard to say." Despite his casual words, there was an odd note to his voice. He was worried.

"Right," I mumbled.

"Called because they stopped a little bit ago. Were driving through most of the night, but now they're not."

185

I glanced up, my eyes fixed on the darkened sky out the kitchen window. "They're resting."

"Have to sleep sometime. Where they plan on going when they get up, I don't know. Might be they've got wind you're here and they've come to get some foci to sell. Might be they've already got a haul, and they're heading north. There's a good market on the Canadian side of the border. If that's the case, they might not cross paths with you at all."

A market. My mind latched onto the word, rolling it back and forth in my thoughts. A market for what? Selling relics? The logic would follow for that - I just couldn't quite get past the mental image of a flea market for magic. And it suggested a level of organization and culture that was more than a little unsettling. Aedan had been quite clear about the dangers associated with the city crews.

I leaned forward, trying not to groan. I wanted to let them go right past. I wanted to stay out of the spotlight, fly under the radar for as long as we could. But if they posed a danger to us, then ignoring it would just be stupid. "You said they've already killed."

" 'fraid so."

Which meant that no matter what, there was a level of risk involved. I rubbed my forehead again, letting my breath hiss between my teeth. "So what do *you* think?"

"I think it's up to you," Greyson said, his tone carefully neutral. I wasn't quite fooled. There was still that guarded undertone to his words, like there was more he wasn't saying. "Time was, I'd let them go. None of my business, not my place to interfere. Now, it's a choice you'll have to make."

What? Me? My brow furrowed. No, no, no. "There's no way I can decide something like that."

"This is your show, kid," he said, unruffled. "Shit or get off the pot."

I bit off a sarcastic retort before it could fully escape. As much as I completely did *not* want the responsibility of making a choice like this, from his perspective, it probably made sense.

He sighed, the sound fragmenting over the phone line. "Fine. Listen. Think on it - but not too long. If they really are sleeping, this is your chance. You'll want to be on them afore they wake up."

"Right," I whispered, my mouth dry.

"Call me again if you lot decide to move. I'll give you directions." The line went dead before I could think of a response.

I stared at my phone, a thousand scenarios playing through my head. Was it stupid to go on the attack? Or was it more stupid to sit around and wait, hoping for them to waltz on past? If we guessed wrong either way, it would put us right in the line of fire. If we sat around waiting, they might just get the jump on us - or come back with friends.

But if we took a proactive stance, seeking them out, what did that mean for our little family in the long run?

Through it all, the odd note in Greyson's voice stuck out in my mind. He was old, and much more practiced at all of this than we were. Out of any of us, he'd be the one to want to stay neutral with the demis around us. But he was *also* the one who'd called me up.

If this was such a regular occurrence, why had he sounded so worried?

The clock on the counter ticked off the seconds, its display casting a dim green light across the kitchen. I was frozen, pinned in place by the doubts and fears and uncertainties. Just for a single second, it was all I could do to keep from picking up my phone and dialing Aedan. He'd know what to do. He'd never hesitated.

Aedan wasn't here. He was miles off, traipsing across the countryside, and I was an adult, damn it. I didn't need him. We could handle something like this without a babysitter.

Seizing on the momentary burst of confidence, I stood, pushing my chair back with a screech of wood on tile. My footsteps were sharp against the floor as I crossed to the coffee pot, flicking it on with hands that trembled.

And then I picked my phone up.

***

The locks on the door clicked off with a resounding *thud* as I slid to a halt in front of the apartment complex. I hadn't been stopped for more than a fraction of a second before the passenger door popped open. Keira threw herself down onto the seat with the barest of waves. "Hey."

I smiled. "Morning."

"It's not morning yet," Jake said from the backseat, opening the door. "It's not late enough to be morning. I refuse."

"Sit down," I said, glancing back at him over him shoulder.

He just rolled his eyes - and wrinkled his nose, sliding down onto the bench seat. "This is gross. You should have this cleaned."

I eyed the fabric. "I tried. It didn't really come out." It wasn't *my* fault the seat was still stained, the blood long since dried to an ugly brown.

"It's a stubborn stain," Keira said, fastening her seat belt. "I'm assuming you wouldn't have dragged us out of bed if it wasn't important. So. Drive." She was wearing the glasses, I couldn't help noticing. As she had been at every opportunity since we'd had our conversation. It was probably more comfortable than keeping them in her pocket, but I hadn't gotten used to it yet.

My musings on her fashion aside, she was right. It was important - and I'd told both of them as much as I knew, while I drove over. Greyson had said they were south of us. Tossing Keira my phone, I hit the accelerator, sliding us out onto the main road. The freeway wasn't far. We'd be off in minutes, and I could put the doubts behind me. Neither of them had hesitated. I clung to that fact, praying I wasn't making a mistake.

"Call Greyson," I said, glancing over at her as the engine revved. "It's time we got some directions."

CHAPTER TWENTY-TWO

No one spoke after I hung up the phone. Greyson had been helpful enough, so much as he could. He couldn't give us any new information, and he didn't seem inclined to sit around talking about it. He just spat out directions and a quick *good luck,* hanging up as soon as he'd given us the address.

"You got it," I murmured, breaking the silence as I glanced at Keira.

She nodded, already punching in numbers on her phone. "South. Take 75. It's faster."

"Right." I'd been planning on it, but I wasn't about to *say* that. There was a tension in the air, enough so that I didn't want to start a fight by snapping. My fingers tightened around the wheel as I turned down the ramp.

The quiet that had fallen over the car held as we drove. Once we got away from the lights of the town, it was pitch black. With how early it was, there weren't even very many other cars out alongside us. I was left to steer us down the freeway through the tunnel our headlights carved from the night.

My thoughts were none so quiet. What was I *doing?* Was I trying to get all of us killed? If they were in the area, if they were looking for victims, then it'd be safer for us to just pick up and run. Each of us had our strengths, sure, but did that really mean we were ready to go out and kill other demibloods? Sure, it would be self defense - if Greyson was right - but that didn't make the idea of it any better.

We'd just…scout it out, I told myself. We'd see exactly what we were dealing with, while we had the chance.

"What's the plan?" Jake said finally, more than an hour and a half after we'd left Greenville. His tone was light enough, and his hands were shoved casually into his pockets as he slouched across the backseat, but his eyes were fixed on mine in the rear view mirror.

"Honestly, your guess is kind of as good as mine," I said, grimacing. "I don't...Greyson wasn't incredibly helpful. He can feel a handful of demis to the south, and he says that where they go, people start dying."

"Like you said," Keira said, leaning back in her seat. Her fingers stroked the frames of her glasses anxiously.

"So, we're just going to go in and kill them?" Jake said, his voice every bit as at-ease as it had been moments before. "That's all we've got?"

Biting back a sigh, I eyed the two of them. Neither seemed ready to speak up. They were really going to leave it to me, weren't they? "I don't want to go into it trying to kill them," I said, glancing over at Jake. "I really don't. Maybe...we'll just see what they're up to. Maybe we can talk to them. Steer them away from our territory, if they look halfway peaceable."

"Do you think they're going to wear signs declaring they're here to kill us?" Jake retorted, folding his arms.

I winced. He wasn't wrong. "You say you can spot demis, right?" I said, glancing at Keira. "Do you...think you could pick them out? Could you give us an idea of where they are, what they're up to? When we get there. Maybe you can figure something out about them."

She looked up at me, her lips pressed into a thin line. "I mean...maybe," she said, shrugging helplessly. "If they're outside."

"So you have to see them," Jake said, leaning forward. "Right?"

Keira ran a hand through her hair, making a face. "I don't know. Probably? Sometimes I can get a glimmer of Jon from behind a door or something, but...other times, nothing."

"You're still acclimating to your relic," I said, tearing my eyes off her. "That's what Aedan said, right?"

"...Right." Her voice was small.

"So, maybe in time, you'll get there. But it's unreliable right now?"

"Right."

Jake shifted in the backseat. "Wonderful," I heard him mutter.

"We'll make it work."

"Sorry," Keira mumbled. "I'm trying."

"You're fine," I said, flashing a quick smile her way. "Well...so long as they don't see us coming, it shouldn't be a problem."

It was Jake's turn to make a face, his nose wrinkling. "You don't *think*."

"Well, between you and me, we should have a pretty good handle on it.

"Are you going to kill them?" Keira said, her voice soft.

I paused, turning my eyes back to the road. "Well...If they're not aggressive, I'd like to not."

Jake made an irritated noise in the back of his throat. "Again. How were you planning on learning that little tidbit?"

"...I'll figure something out," I mumbled. "Look. If they're killing people, and they're heading our way, then we need to take the initiative, don't we? We're just going to check it out."

"Just be ready to do what we need to," he said. I could feel his gaze on me in the mirror again. I didn't look.

"I know," I said, trying to keep the frustration from my voice. "I will."

"I'm just saying."

"I know."

That was all there was. As much as we might like to try and plan things out, we just didn't have enough to go on. The car fell back into an uneasy quiet as we wound our way south, liberally exceeding the speed limit in our hurry to close the gap. According to Greyson, they were sleeping. Probably. I didn't want to get there after they'd already gone and woken up.

"This is the exit." Keira's voice was quiet. I jumped all the same, caught off guard by the sudden interruption, but caught the ramp before it meandered off.

The light of her phone's GPS lit up the cab of the car as we slipped onto the surface streets, casting an eerie glow over the lines of her face. My heart pounded in my ears as I glanced around, more than a little unsure. It wasn't quite the worst part of town. We'd been taken to one of the neighborhoods built up on the outskirts of the city, far enough out that the woods and fields were just beginning to mix back into the homes and stores, but it was urban enough. There were bars on the windows, spikes on the gutters. Chain-linked fences topped with razor wire wrapped around the parking lots, keeping us away.

"Are we sure about this?" Keira said, glancing up at me. From the way her voice quivered, I knew that *she* wasn't confident about our plan, even if she wasn't saying it. I just cleared my throat, my eyes wide.

"It's what we have to do. We knew they wouldn't be holed up somewhere nice." Not if they were killing people and hunting after demis. I didn't think people who did something like that would be staying in the Hilton.

I hadn't quite expected a place like *this*, all the same, but I wasn't about to tell them that.

"Right on Willow," Keira said quietly. I made the turn, and the next, and the next. We were moving on automatic, our bodies going through the motions while our minds stewed on what was to come.

"Dan kept you guys isolated, right? Kept others away?" I said, glancing back at Jake.

He nodded slowly. "Something like that. I didn't really deal much with him. I was too new, and he was too close to Matt. But...yeah."

"And now we don't have that," I muttered.

"I don't think gunshots and fighting are that unusual here," Keira said, her eyes flicking to the window again.

"We should still be careful. And I don't have a gun in any case." I'd packed a knife, which was pressed into my leg at that moment, deep in my pocket. Remembering the suspicion in the eyes of the cop who'd questioned me, I still couldn't bring myself to try and register a pistol.

Jake shifted uncomfortably. "I mean..."

We glanced back. His face was red.

"Do *you*, Jake?" I said slowly.

"You said we might be fighting," he said, a plaintive note in his voice. "And the old crew were all armed. It would have been a shame to let Aedan get rid of *all* of the weapons."

"That's a yes," Keira said, shaking her head.

I groaned. "Great."

"It would be fucking *dumb* to not," he muttered. "I'm not planning on shooting anyone, but we should at least be *ready* to."

"Fine. Don't get the cops called."

"We should pull over," Keira said, backing out of her Google Maps. "It should be right down the next block."

I nodded. There was nothing to say to that. My brakes creaked softly as I pulled us to a stop, tucking us against the chain-link fence alongside the road. We piled out in silence, each of us doing our best to not slam the door. The sound still stood out far too much in the early-morning calm.

And then we were off, creeping up the street like thieves.

Our destination revealed itself a few brief moments later - a long, narrow motel, announcing itself the Heron Park Inn with a crumbling, rusted sign. The white and grey bird smiling happily back at us was faded and peeling. The building itself wasn't much better, but I'd seen worse. The windows were all there, and I had *some* amount of confidence that the tires of the cars parked in the lot would all be there when they came out in the morning. Not that there were many cars.

We paused, half-hiding behind a nearby store as we peered at the building.

"You getting anything, Keira?" I murmured, glancing at her. "The name matches what Google said, right?"

"Right..." she said, sounding entirely unsure of herself. "I mean...I can't just-"

"No is fine too."

"...I don't see anything."

Jake didn't make a sound. He didn't have to. The uncomfortable way he shifted from foot to foot said everything.

I just glared at him. It wasn't her fault, the way that her relic worked, and she was doing the best she could. If she couldn't see, then we'd just have to find another way.

"Let's just...take a minute," I whispered, settling into a crouch. I cast an anxious eye around, as though expecting someone to pop out behind me. But it was still in the middle of the night, an hour when any reasonable person would be asleep, and we were alone. I tried to swallow my anxiousness, focusing my attentions on the lonely row of rooms in front of us.

My eyes danced across the doors, looking for a sign. Unfortunately, none of our travelers had been so kind as to put a sign on their door saying "Here we are, it's a roomful of murderous demis." Each room had a single, narrow window, but the curtains were drawn tight over each one. We were too far away for me to see in, and there was no way I was going to get closer and peer through each window like a stalker.

My frustration building, I turned my focus to the cars.

And froze.

Given the season, there weren't that many people visiting the state - most sane people went south, once the cold started moving in. That left the motel nearly deserted. Only a few vehicles sat in the lot, dutifully parked in front of the owners' respective rooms.

One was a SmartCar, parked by the office. I glared at it, chuckling under my breath at the thought of the risks its own was taking coming north with snow season right around the corner. Two sedans sat a few spaces down from it, each equally old and worn-down.

I blinked. And one SUV sat in the very back corner - an SUV with Illinois plates. A quick check confirmed it - the other cars were all local, or at least in the same *state*. I stared at the SUV, grabbing for my friends even while my thoughts raced.

"You could carry three or four demis in an SUV, no problem," I murmured, staring at it.

"You could fit them in a Camry, too," Jake retorted, grabbing for my shoulder as I crept forward. "Don't be an idiot."

"He's all the way down there," I said, my voice a little more insistent. "Right on the corner, where he's alone. The others are by the office."

"So?"

"So it's *different*," I snapped, glaring at him. "Do you have a better suggestion?"

"I don't fucking know. My suggestion is we *leave*."

I pressed a hand to my face, wiping away the irritated response that came to my lips before it could escape. "Keira?"

She leaned forward, her eyes narrowed, as though the extra few inches could somehow make the difference. "I'm...not sure."

Jake's sigh was soft, nearly inaudible. "Like Jon said. No is-"

"It's not *no*."

We both froze, staring at her. My sister only shook her head, her attention still fixed on the SUV. "There's definitely something there. I can see the haze, when it's this dark."

"See?" I said, a crooked smile tugging at the corners of my lips as I glanced sidelong at Jake. "I told you. It's there."

Keira grabbed my arm as I rose a little straighter, taking a step towards the SUV. "Jon, no. It's not...I don't really know what I'm looking at. I can't get a good look at them."

"But we've got more information than we did a minute ago," I said, locking my gaze onto hers. "Like you said, you've got some limitations. No one is expecting you to see right through it. This is good enough."

Jake nodded, after a moment's hesitation. His hand slipped into the pocket of his coat, where he'd no doubt stashed his pistol. I resisted the urge to grab for my knife. They needed me to be confident right then. We needed to believe that this could work.

Taking a deep breath, I turned back towards the motel and crept forward.

"Stop walking like you're 90," Jake said, irritation lacing his tone. "It's a fucking motel. Act natural."

My ears burned. Right. Straightening my spine, I walked forward a little more casually, still trying to keep my steps soft.

The sound of it rang in my ears, despite our best efforts. We might as well have been a herd of goddamn wildebeests, for as loud as we sounded right then. It was hard to keep myself from jumping at every sound, at every flickering of the 60's-era lights overhead and every distant thump of a car radio. We were just going back to our room, I told myself. Without a car. And which happened to be right next to theirs.

The SUV crept closer and closer. I paused, my heart skipping a beat.

There was a man in the driver's seat, dimly visible in the side mirror. I mean, I'd *known* that, when Keira saw the glimmerings of a relic from inside the SUV. But it was one thing to hear her talking about it, and another to see a man leaned back in the seat, his eyes closed and his chest rising and falling in the slow, peaceful way of one asleep.

My hand *did* slip into my pocket, then, my fingers wrapping around the hilt of the knife I'd stashed there. My breath was ragged and loud in my ears, filling my mind with the sound of its rasping as I stared at the driver through the car's mirrors.

How should I handle this? What should we do? This was the moment of truth for us - the decision point. Were we going to talk, or should we take the advantage of surprise and attack? Greyson had said other demis had died, that this crew was killing people. Was that enough proof? Should I have Keira get more information out of him? It made sense for there to be a guard, while they other slept, but he was sleeping too - we could have Jake put him under deeper, hold him still while we got what we needed out of him.

The knife was suddenly too-heavy in my hands. My palms were sweating.

"Jon," Keira whispered. "Hold up. Something's not-"

"Let me think," I murmured, frowning.

But if he woke up at the touch of Jake's relic, if he realized what was happening, he might still have time to yell. He could wake everyone up - and then we'd be in the same mess.

I could command him, if he woke up. Make him tell us the truth. We could make our decision then. The possibility of there being some sort of misunderstanding between us and them hung in the back of my head, Maybe it was self defense. Maybe they were like Aedan, being hunted by people who wanted to kill them. Was it really our business to go picking fights?

But Greyson hadn't been pleased. He'd warned me about them - and even if he hadn't said so explicitly, I knew that the older man didn't want us to sit around and lay low. If that's what he'd wanted, he wouldn't have told us about them at all. He'd always ignored them before, hadn't he?

The sight of the guard shifting in his sleep, his face wrinkling as he coughed, sent a burst of adrenaline down my spine. Was he waking up? We couldn't just sit here. We'd come so far - if I was just going to change my mind, then I should have done so when we were all still back home.

"Jon!" Keira hissed, her voice low. Jake shushed her.

I hesitated, waving both of them forward. If he was going to wake up anyway, then we might as well lead with my abilities. He couldn't kill us if I had him in thrall from the minute he woke up. "Okay. We're going to-"

The man in the van shifted again, groaning to himself. He was going to wake up. I stiffened, biting my lip, and reached for the handle to his door. I could feel Keira and Jake's eyes on my back, drilling holes into me with the intensity. We couldn't wait. It was time. We could do this.

But when I grabbed for the handle, my hand slid right through it. The van parted like fog, blurry and insubstantial. I skittered back, my arms wide.

The sound of screaming split the night air a moment later. I whirled, my eyes going wide as my pulse skyrocketed.

There was a man - behind us. He was still standing half inside the van. Inside the *image* of the van. His palms crackled with energy.

And Jake shuddered, held tight by the back of the neck. He tumbled to the ground a moment later as the newcomer released him, still twitching.

The demi grinned at the looks on our faces, jumping back from the crumpled form of our friend as his hand plunged into his pocket.

And then the sound of his voice split the night air as he bellowed "Wake up!" for the world to hear.

CHAPTER TWENTY-THREE

The sound of his words still echoed around the run-down motel, ringing in our ears. I stared, caught in a moment of hesitation. This wasn't the plan. We were supposed to sneak *up* on them.

But Jake was down, cold and still on the ground, and I didn't have time to so much as figure out if he was all right - or still alive. The human taser was already lunging towards me, his palms alight with sparks.

"Sit down!" I cried, one hand going to my chest and the necklace hanging there. It flared to life in a surge of heat. The other demi froze, a look of purest confusion on his face, and crumpled to the ground. His mouth slid open again. "And shut up."

My relic was still working - and I could replicate the miracle I'd worked against Matt and his team. That was a relief. Part of me had been worried it was a fluke, a trick brought on by exhaustion, pain, and blood loss, and that the next time I'd play that card they'd just laugh it off.

All the same, I could feel the pressure begin to build in the back of my head. It was a strong tool, yes, but it wasn't going to last me forever. My hand plunged down into my pocket, seizing the knife I'd pushed aside only a few brief moments before.

"Jon!" I heard Keira gasp, stumbling forward a step.

I fixed my eyes on her, pinning her in place. She'd already killed. She didn't need to kill again. She didn't deserve to have that blood on her hands. Swallowing hard, I gripped my knife tighter, shifting the hilt in my palm.

Aedan probably would have been disappointed with the attack, the lunge and thrust I managed. He'd probably have done just what he'd made Keira do - try the attack again, barely holding back his derision, and tell me to work on my stance. My hold.

But Aedan wasn't there. He didn't get to judge. Sitting still, just like I'd ordered him, the man couldn't even move to avoid my strike. His eyes widened with horrible realization a single instant before my blade hit. The sight would follow me for years, I was sure. His mouth slid open, wordlessly hanging as he fought against my relic's power.

My knife bit deep into his neck. A jolt of energy shot down the blade, as though he'd managed one final attempt at throwing me off, but it was too late. There was too little power behind it, and the deed had already been done.

Hot blood coursed down the steel, covering my hand in seconds. There was so much of it. Even in so little time, I'd forgotten something as simple as that.

But even as the door guard fell, wide-eyed and silent, the screech of hinges cut across the motel parking lot. The door flew open - and a man burst from within, his hair dark and unwashed and messy. The t-shirt he wore bore an ad for Pabst, and besides for that, all he had on were a pair of boxers.

We'd interrupted his sleep. At least we had *that* going for us.

The next problem presented itself to me as my mind finally finished processing and started screaming a warning. Keira had been behind me - and so was the door. That put Keira directly between him and I. Exactly where I *didn't* want her.

She spun on her heel at the sound of the door, though, her arms coming up defensively. I could see the tension in her eyes, the nervousness building just under her skin, but there was no 'run' left in her. Her icy blue gaze was locked onto the newcomer, boring into him as though she could learn his secrets by staring hard enough.

Maybe she could.

Secrets or not, it didn't make a difference. I pushed off hard, my legs surging under me, and threw myself back towards the dark little motel room. I'd seen the recognition in his eyes, the way his arm curled around to the side. It wasn't a natural motion - but he wasn't normal, either.

Keira screamed as his hand whipped back around, droplets of

something flying from his fingertips. Something that smoked as it spattered across the ground, something that filled the air with an acrid tang. My heart froze.

"No!" I gasped, hurling myself past her. "Stop! Freeze!"

His eyes fixed on mine, every bit as cunning and aware as his friend's had been. Some distant corner of my mind noted that this was person number two, the second victim I'd tried to wrest control away from so far. The thought was swallowed up by the first pangs of stiffness, settling through my arms, and the ever-growing ache in my head. These new powers drained a lot out of me. I couldn't keep it up forever.

Keira was still making quiet, pained noises, wiping at her face, her arms. She'd been splashed by whatever the man had summoned - acid, if my high school chemistry classes were any teacher. My anger rose further, focusing down into a narrow, ice-cold point.

My head throbbed. He was twitching, trying to pull free while I wasted time. I raised my blade - and froze.

There was no knife in my hand. I'd buried it in the neck of his comrade, who was even then growing still and cold behind me.

With one last hiss, Keira's eyes fixed on us. She dove to the ground, moving before the light of recognition in her eyes had begun to fade. Jake lay just a few feet away. His fingertips twitched now and again, and he was beginning to moan. The corners of my lips curled up, even as sweat began to soak through my shirt. Not dead, then. Good.

"Keira, my knife."

"Jake had a gun."

"It's too loud," I hissed, tearing my eyes off the acid-thrower to glare more fully at her.

"He already screamed," Keira muttered, still pawing through Jake's jacket.

Something shifted, nearby - the sound of a door creaking. My head snapped up, turning towards the room. A dark whirl of hair told me Keira had done the same.

"Jon, we're not alone," she said, rushing through the words.

"I know," I whispered, glancing back to the acid sprayer - and stiffened. He wasn't moving, but the air between us clouded with mist. I skittered back a few steps, coughing. "N-Never mind. Gun might be good."

"Fucking *listen* to me, Jon," Keira snapped, turning back. "There are other *people* in there. Two. I think."

"Shit," I muttered, stepping back again, and glanced between the door and the rival demi. "Stop that," I snarled, feeling my skin begin to itch. "Stand there and don't do *anything.*"

The acid-hurler froze. The mist lightened, just enough to tell me I was still in control.

"Are they demis?" I said tightly, seeing Keira from the corner of my eye. She pulled the gun from Jake's jacket a moment later, making a pleased noise. Our friend twitched again, as though trying to keep us from taking his weapon, but flopped back down helplessly.

"I don't know."

"What does that mean? And I thought you couldn't see through-"

"I don't know, okay? I don't think they're normal humans, but their glow is so...faint." Her voice dropped off as she went on. I could picture her staring at the door, the way her brow would be furrowed in confusion. There was no telling what adrenaline would do to a person, I supposed. If her power was growing, then we'd just have to trust her. The acid-thrower flinched, his head twitching an inch. His face was red - he wasn't even *breathing,* I realized. His eyes darted up. But not at me, no. It was clear in every muscle of his face, the tiniest slump of his shoulders as a bit of the tension slid away. He wasn't looking at me. He was looking past me.

A brush of air- that's all the warning I got. Just a hint of a breeze, sliding across the back of my neck. After the lessons I'd had so far, there was no way I'd just ignore it.

I ducked, throwing my arm up, and heard the blade slash through where my throat had been moments before. The sound of the steel sliding across the air was unmistakable, but my attacker was still hidden from sight.

"Jon - *left,*" Keira cried, skittering further back. Jake rolled over, groaning. I spun on my heel, wishing for all the world I had a moment to go for my knife, and punched blindly. My mind screamed at me that I was an idiot, that I was acting like a crazy person. But Keira had said left.

My fist collided with the empty air - or rather, with whatever was hiding in the empty air. It wasn't a good hit. Whatever or whoever was hiding under the illusion, I could feel them twist, sliding away as my punch glanced off. They didn't make so much as a peep, and given another moment or two, they'd be off again. I could only assume it was the demi who'd put an illusion up where their 'SUV' had been. With them invisible, and armed, it would only be a matter of time before they got the better of us.

But I'd touched them.

The fabric was still there, under my fingertips, even if it was sliding further away with every passing moment. I surged forward, my hand flying wide, and latched onto them like my life depended on it. It probably did.

I was prepared, when the weight I'd grabbed onto suddenly lessened. My shoulder slammed up, my face curling away protectively. When the knife bit into flesh, it was my arm that took the hit, not my jugular.

It wasn't a fancy move. There was no class to it, no art. I just turned, grabbing their shirt with my other hand, and hurled them to the ground as hard as I could. My foot was a moment behind.

The man attacking hit the asphalt hard, a dull, hollow sound echoing from their chest as the air shot from their lungs. His knife fell from his hand, bouncing off into the shockingly thick weeds and grasses growing at the edge of the lot. The distraction of my blow had been enough. Their illusion shimmered like a bank of fog, dissipating before they could recover, and left them crumpled. My foot pinned their thigh to the pavement. Not my best blow, I thought sourly.

I flinched as something sprayed across the back of my head and neck - something liquid, something that burned like fire at the slightest touch. I screamed, biting the sound off a brief moment after it had slipped out, and turned instinctively.

Keira was faster. She was facing the right direction, and she must have seen that I was losing the last shreds of my control over him. Stupid of me. I mean, I didn't *ask* to have someone try and stab me, but I shouldn't have let my hold slip. She was on the acid-thrower before he could gather himself, her stolen pistol raised.

The crack of it echoed across the motel parking lot, resonating and rebounding off the rows of shabby, run-down homes at the end of the block. My ears screamed, ringing with the force of the up-close-and-personal shot. The sound of something slamming into flesh, wet and fast and destructive, followed hot on its heels.

I looked. I couldn't *not*. It was instinct, pure and simple. I saw the dark-haired demi's face, scrunched up in pure agony. I saw it slacken muscle by muscle as he crumpled, the strength fleeing from his limbs.

Something else. Shoes on pavement, fabric rustling. The illusionist. I spun back around, drawing breath to bellow a command.

Once again, the barest hint of a glimpse saved me. I had just enough time to draw back, teetering dangerously. His fist slammed into my windpipe a moment later.

I gagged, stumbling back farther. My hands came up, cradling my neck as I reeled. I could hardly breathe, let alone speak. My lungs burned, screaming for air. It was growing easier with every second - I'd escaped him crushing my throat completely, then - but there was no way I'd be ordering him around anytime soon.

The illusionist wasn't sticking around to see if I was hurt or dead, and he wasn't going fishing for his knife. He took off running, blazing a trail towards the darkened road at the far end of the lot.

If he wanted to leave, I was all for that. His buddies the taser and the acid-thrower were already beginning to glow, their skin lighting up like the flickering lamps bolted into the horrible, moldering ceiling, and I was in no condition to play tag.

"Jon!" Keira's cry brought me up short a moment later. I was still wheezing, still massaging my neck, but I glanced up. Her eyes were wide and staring, fixed on the rapidly receding back of the illusionist.

"That man - Something's wrong. He's carrying *three* relics. I can see them."

With an icy jolt, the final piece clicked into place. The way Christian and Matt had been talking, back when all of this had begun, discussing training, and pets, and profits. The way Greyson had made a point of calling me this time, when he'd seemed incredibly ambivalent about other demis wandering through before.

And the other, faintly-glowing demis that Keira had insisted she saw inside the motel room.

This was stupid.

My throat hurt. I was getting a bit more air, but still not enough for me to be comfortable. Keeping up with the illusionist was going to *suck*. And leaving Keira behind, with Jake still twitching as he pushed himself to a sitting position, was not anywhere on my list of priorities. I might be wrong. I could have read this situation entirely differently from reality, and I could be leaving them to a whole mess of trouble.

But I knew I was right. And if I was *right*, then lives depended on that asshole not vanishing into the night.

"Stop!" I cried, but the words came out a dull, dead groan. The man didn't hesitate. I shuddered, drawing in a deep breath.

"Cops are probably coming. Get to safety," I croaked, forcing the words from my wounded throat as I eyed Keira. She blanched, raising a hand as though to stop me, but stopped, gripping her pistol a little more tightly.

Not waiting to see if she would listen to me, I broke into a shambling run, slowly picking up speed.

CHAPTER TWENTY-FOUR

The gloomy dark pressed in around me as I pushed forward, feeling every step through my whole legs. I didn't want to be running. I *wanted* to be taking a step back, approaching this whole matter with a bit of caution and waiting until I had a bit of feeling back in my neck before I charged off. But even as I delayed, the illusionist was fading into the murky twilight ahead.

"Stop!" I tried again, pulling air through my lungs in great draughts. But just like before, it fell flat. And I could see it - the pair of headphones the demi I chased pulled from his pocket, slapping onto his head. He was at his phone a moment later, hitting buttons as he ran.

If there was music blasting out of the speakers, I couldn't hear it over the pounding of my feet against the asphalt and the ragged gasping of my breath. I didn't need to hear it to understand what his intention was, though - first, he'd throat-punched me, then he put on headphones to block the sound of my voice. He'd been watching while I dealt with his friends. Idiot. I was a fucking *idiot*. And I'd ignored Keira, too. She'd tried to warn me.

If anything happened, if anything went wrong or if someone got hurt, it would be on me, wouldn't it? The thought was heavy, weighing down on my shoulders as I pulled myself together. I needed to do better.

He was still ahead of me, and I was still in pain, fighting for air. In any other situation, he'd have accelerated into the distance and left me in the dust. But he couldn't just *run* - not without having my spell land about his ears. He was too busy fiddling with his damn headphones to really make a break for it. I seized on the chance, feeling the soreness in my neck settle a little more with every second.

He thrust his phone back into his pocket, glancing back over his shoulders. His eyes widened a moment later at the sight of me. We'd left the motel behind, tearing off into the neighborhoods that surrounded it. Somewhere nearby, I could hear the sound of engines, see the lights from traffic signals and lampposts. Whatever major road was there, the illusionist was steering clear. He turned, skidding in a spray of dust and dead leaves, and sprinted off down a narrow drive.

My frustration welled up as he vanished from sight around the corner, but I couldn't spare the breath it would take to swear properly. I ran on gamely, stretching my legs out and letting my body get used to the run. I needed even more cardio in my life than I'd thought, if everything I did was going to turn into a cross-country match.

When I came around the corner, finally feeling a little more like myself again, I smiled. He was closer. I was gaining on him. He wasn't used to running, was he? Neither was I, I had to admit, but his face glowed red in the street lamps. He was still dressed in pajamas, just like his friend. I just had to hope that no one living in the houses around us would look out their windows - or if they did, that they wouldn't think anything odd of what they saw.

Like that was a possibility, I thought ruefully. We were being *totally* discreet.

There was no point in bellowing again. He couldn't hear me. But the sight of him raising a hand cast a new fear down my spine.

He'd appeared from thin air - and *someone* had cast the working that had put a fake SUV in the parking lot. He made illusions, and right then, he was desperate. I couldn't let him-

With a smirk creeping up the corners of his lips, the demi's form shimmered like a mirage. He winked at me. Actually *winked*, despite the sweat shimmering on his skin and the way his chest heaved with every breath.

And then he was gone, vanishing from thin air at the front corner of a garage.

I'd thought I was going as fast as I could, that I'd reached the limits of my speed. I was wrong. I pushed even harder, racing forward towards where he'd been. It was no use. By the time I reached that garage, I was alone. I skidded to a halt, freezing in place. My heart thundered in my ears as I waited, my eyes scanning the countryside wildly.

He still had to *move*, didn't he? He couldn't possibly wipe away every trace of his existence. With a sinking feeling, I realized that for all I knew, he could. The tattered sound of breathing and the din of my pulse were too loud, surrounding me and filling my ears with the sound of my own growing exhaustion. If there were footsteps, any trace of him running, they were wiped away. There weren't even convenient piles of leaves cast across the asphalt parking lot for him to kick up as he made his escape.

"Fucking *hell*," I swore, feeling sweat drip down my back, and started to run again. And then I stopped.

He could be *anywhere*. If he was invisible, then all he had to do to lose me was turn a corner, and he'd be gone. I had no chance in hell of catching him like that.

I needed directions.

My hand was numb and unfeeling as I plunged it into my pocket, seizing the phone there. Every second was precious, more so than ever. He was *this* close to being gone, and if he was gone, if I was right, then-

The screen keyed on, coming to life in a blaze of electronic light. I winced, already keying the buttons as quickly as I could. My first instinct was to call Keira. What she'd said back at the motel...she'd seen through his illusion, hadn't she?

I was an idiot. The thought shot through my head again, sharp and painful.

But she was too far away, and her powers were too unstable, and I got the feeling she'd have her hands full there with...with everything. He was next down the list from her name. The little voice in the back of my mind pointed out that I needed a speed dial list set up, ASAP.

The rest of me was entirely focused on dialing Greyson's number. I threw the phone up to my ear as soon as the screen went green, turning in a circle as my breathing gradually slowed. The world around me looked just like it should - homes, and cars in driveways, and dark streets.

He picked up faster than I'd expected. I was still steadying my hand, pulling my mind back together, when I heard the line connect.

I *tried* to say something, to tell him I needed his help or ask him for directions. It all came out a formless wheeze.

"I've been watching," he said. His words were short and clipped, cutting right across my pathetic attempts to talk. "Got a runner, do you?"

"Mmhm," I managed, massaging my throat with my free hand. "C-Can you-"

"Get going. Hurry, or he's going to get away."

"*Where?*" I said, desperation and adrenaline finally forcing the word clear.

There was a single, pregnant moment of silence across the air. "Ah," Greyson said. "He's heading north. Start moving."

North? How the hell was I supposed to know what direction north was? I glanced around, my eyes wild, trying to guess which way I should go. Finally, for lack of a better option, I took off straight ahead, towards where the illusionist had been running.

"Fucking *moron*. 90 degree turn to your left."

My arms wheeled as I spun, teetering dangerously for a single moment, and then I caught myself. I was off a heartbeat later, pushing myself just as fast as my legs would go. I couldn't lose this race. I couldn't afford to.

"Better," Greyson said, chuckling dryly. "Keep going. This isn't really my specialty, you know. I'm more big-picture than this. So don't blame me if something goes wrong."

"I know," I gasped, plowing onward.

"Don't talk. Run."

I shut up and focused on running.

If I peered ahead, really squinting and focusing in on it, I could see a dim figure sprinting away from us just as fast as he could. The illusionist. He couldn't keep it up forever, after all. He'd get tired like any of us. The weight on my shoulders lightened, just a fraction. He thought he was away. He wasn't being so careful - and he was slowing down, just a little.

I scanned my surroundings, searching for something, anything I could use. If I just charged up behind him, closing in with my usual lack of subtlety, then he'd just cast another illusion and be off again. He was still wearing those headphones, although they *couldn't* be comfortable, or all that secure on his head. I needed to try something else.

Quick as could be, my eyes flicked to the road ahead. The path he was taking curved gently, meandering through the neighborhood and homes. It was straight, level, and easy enough - at the expense of being indirect.

But the backyards, on the other hand.

My legs were already moving before I'd had a chance to properly think the idea through. I'd already made some stupid choices so far that night - what was a little more? The hedges at the backs of the yards were low and sparse with gaps showing through the foliage, the plants dying off for the winter as the cold moved in. It was the work of a moment to push through, regaining all my lost speed as I hit the grass of the backyard.

"The hell are you going?" Greyson snarled in my ear. "That's- all right, all right. Don't fucking slow down, now. If he gets away, I'm going to-"

I slid the phone from my ear, focusing on the running. His words had hit home, but there was already too much adrenaline in my system. I couldn't add *more* to the mix.

As I sprinted through, stumbling over fences and doing my best not to trip over the toys someone's child had so thoughtfully left in the grass, I gave the backs of the homes an anxious, inspecting look. At any instant, I could just *see* someone come busting out, shotgun in hand and ready to confront the 'intruder'. I couldn't even blame them.

But whatever meager luck I'd been able to find held. I smiled, sweat pouring down my temples as the road appeared in front of me.

The demi appeared in the same instant, visibly flagging as he jogged down the shoulder. His shirt was soaked through with sweat, and his face glowed beet red. He finally came to a stop, dropping his face down into his hand as he peered back behind him.

His head spun around as the sound of footsteps crunching on the dead grass finally registered in his ears, but it was too late.

I hit him hard, tackling him. All of the memories of the single summer I'd spent in football practice before thoroughly deciding it was *not* for me came back in a rush as we tumbled to the sidewalk, hitting the concrete hard. The air shot from my lungs in a rush. From the look on his face, his eyes squeezed shut, he didn't fare much better.

I got my hand up in time to block the elbow aimed straight for my nose. The move was telegraphed through his shoulders, screaming for my attention. His knee came up, faster than I could block, and sailed into my midsection. I gasped, reeling and doing my best not to vomit. He was on his feet in a heartbeat, his eyes wild. The sound of footsteps pounded against the concrete again.

But his headphones lay on the sidewalk in front of me, the cord pulled free by the force of our fall. My mind registered their presence dully, even as I filled my tired, aching lungs with air.

"Freeze!" I cried. "Stop running!" I didn't have the energy in me to chase him down again. I couldn't. There was no telling when he'd pull another illusion, getting away from me entirely. Greyson had helped, sure, but there was only so much the older man could be expected to do from afar.

The illusionist stopped. He overbalanced, in fact, his feet coming to a halt underneath him while his torso tried to keep running. He hit the ground in a pile, unmoving. His eyes flicked back to me, wide and terrified. But no matter how round his eyes were, he didn't make even a single motion to get on his feet.

I stepped closer, wiping my sleeve across my forehead. I was soaked in sweat, and every part of me hurt, and I was still exhausted from the night's interrupted sleep. It was the dark of the morning, but it wasn't going to last much longer. Before we knew it, we'd be surrounded with people trying to go to work and school and go about their lives.

We needed to be done with this business before then.

"No," the demi said. His voice shook, filled with fear. "I-I'm sorry. Do y-you want a cut? I could- we could get the next batch together, yeah?" His limbs quivered as he fought against my hold. They didn't so much as budge, but a nervous smile spread across his face.

And the air started to shimmer.

"Stop using your relic. Your focus," I said quietly. There was no point in yelling - all it would do was draw even more attention to us than we already had. I stepped closer, all too aware that I didn't have so much as a knife on me.

The shimmering stopped.

"I was- I was just about to go to market, too," the demi said. The closer I stepped to him, the faster he talked. "Should be a good haul. Could really set you up nice, yeah?"

"Give me your relic."

His face paled even further. "Please. You'll never see me again. I'll go." But even as he pleaded, his hand reached towards the neck of his shirt.

He was a necklace-type too, I saw as he pulled the delicate gold chain out from under the cloth. But rather than a ring, it connected to a milky white disk of crystal circled with silver. The stone was foggy, clouded with dark shapes.

I could see his hand trembling. He was fighting. But he was just one man, and I was done with him, with this whole damn situation. The voices in the back of my mind were stronger, louder with every second I hesitated.

I could do what he asked. I could let him go, let him run off and vanish into the night. No one would have to die - we could all go about our lives in peace.

But it wasn't that simple.

The crystal was warm in my hand as I slid it into my palm, pulling the chain from around his head. "Now, give me theirs," I said softly.

His eyes tightened. "You can have them," he said, voice wobbling. "They're yours. Not our best run, but we've got a few-"

"Shut up."

His lips snapped closed. He fought the command just like all the rest, his face growing redder and redder, before finally giving up.

When he reached into his pocket, his fingers shaking, I slid my eyes closed. Damn it, I was right. I'd wanted to be wrong, deep down. I hadn't wanted for this to be a *thing*, a part of the world we lived in.

But when I slid my eyes open again, two glittering objects lay in his palm. A ring, silver with gold embossing, and what looked like some sort of pin, bejeweled with sapphires.

And there, right there, was the confirmation of why I couldn't take him up on his offer to just 'vanish'. Oh, he'd meant it well enough. I could see the truth etched into every muscle and tendon, emblazoned across his expression. He'd really go, and he wouldn't come back.

But even though he might promise to leave, that didn't mean that he'd quit his line of work entirely. And even if he promised he would, there was no promise he'd fall back on his old ways given the slightest chance. I couldn't be there to babysit him, and he hadn't earned any mercy. He'd tried to kill me too, after all.

I could try and warn him, somehow. Maim him a little. Send him running, leave his relic in some distant location along our route home and let him scramble to find it. Maybe when he'd felt a bit of the pain and fear his victims felt, he'd be less inclined to do what he did, what I *knew* he'd done. Even that wouldn't work, I knew. He'd just come back with a vengeance and a grudge. It would only create problems down the line for us.

"Just stop," I said, my tone quiet. "Just...stop."

His brows tightened, pure confusion soaking his expression through. And then the fear began again.

I didn't have a knife. More than anything, I wished I had a knife, but I'd left mine buried in his friend and left his kicked amidst the weeds. I'd even settle for a gun, although it would be too loud to use in a neighborhood like this.

But he sat, perfectly still. His face grew redder as he fought against my hold, struggling to breathe. I'd seen the way his friend had reacted to my commands, after all. My head was pounding, and the world swayed gently underneath me, but I had the power to do what I needed to.

Slowly, tenderly, I slid all three captured relics into my pocket. The feel of them on my fingers was uncomfortable, like needles prickling my skin. Aedan's words rang in my head, telling me that trying to bond with more than one relic would just shatter the foolish demi who tried into splinters. I wasn't trying to bond with them - but I didn't want to sit around holding the damn things, either. I set the phone on the sidewalk, crouching next to the illusionist. Greyson's voice still echoed out of the mouthpiece.

And then, with my hands free at last, I slid my arm around the man's neck.

He jerked, pushing against his invisible bonds as my elbow tightened against his skin, but I wasn't about to let go. My stomach churned, threatening to bring up everything I'd eaten over the last day. But I didn't want him to suffer. It was bad enough that I had to kill him, that I *knew* I couldn't let someone like him go. I couldn't make his death as fast as I wanted, but I didn't want to draw it out, either.

He twitched, his limbs stiff with tension as I pulled. I'd thought his face couldn't get any redder. I was wrong. I just swallowed hard, staring at the ground, and focused on taking one slow, ragged breath after another.

Before I knew it, the skin under my arm was warm. Warmer than skin should be. I glanced down.

The illusionist's skin glowed. It was a scene I'd seen play out too many time. I knew what was coming, knew how it would go down. Releasing him, I grabbed my phone, and stepped away.

"Still there?" I said, my voice little more than a whisper as I raised my phone to my ear.

"It's about fucking time. Don't ever call me and then put me on hold, boy."

"Sorry. But I-"

"Yeah, yeah, I felt it. What, do you want some kind of medal?" His tone softened, just a little. "Did you get them?"

"Two relics. He had two relics, on top of his own."

"Good. Go back to the motel and grab them. Bring 'em by the place this evening if you lot need a drink."

Without another word, he hung up on me. I slid the phone from my ear, staring down at it. What, *now* he was going to act like he was the leader? I chuckled mirthlessly. Fine. Whatever. I tabbed down a few rows, hitting the dial button again.

The phone connected on the first ring.

"Jon?" Keira's voice was breathless, filled with fear. "Is that you? Are you okay?"

"I'm fine. Sorry."

"....Good. Yeah. Okay." Her words were soft, with an awkward cant to them, like she was running a hand through her hair. "And you're sure you're fine?"

"I'm fine. Are *you* okay?"

"I'm fine." I remembered the way she'd been splashed with acid. She couldn't be *entirely* fine. But her voice was strong enough that I'd take her word for it. "Jake's still a bit woozy, but he's coming around too. And..." She hesitated.

"I know. I've got two relics here. I'll be back as soon as I can."

"Hurry," she whispered.

"See you soon." I slid the phone from my face, ending the call and sliding it into my pocket in one smooth motion.

The body of the illusionist fragmented, cracking into dust behind me as I turned, beginning the long, painful walk towards the rest of my friends.

CHAPTER TWENTY-FIVE

It had all seemed so fast, when I was running.

I wasn't running anymore, and it didn't seem so fast. I was left to peer out into the darkness, seeing shadows around every corner and from behind every tree. The neighborhood around me was quiet. Now and then I'd see a light inside a window, the residents waking up for their busy morning, but that was all.

I'd been worried that we'd been too loud, that we'd made a scene. Now, looking at it, I realized that we'd just been two people running down the street in the night, out of shape and out of breath.

My legs echoed the sentiment, sore and stiff. The exhaustion that had begun to settle over them a few brief minutes before had solidified into a solid, piercing ache. I ignored it as best I could, taking one stumbling step after another. The hedges I'd run through...I gave them one look, assessing the possibility, before immediately deciding the better of it. They'd looked good when I was chasing someone, with adrenaline keeping me going moreso than any common sense. The road was longer, but better.

There was no way I could relax, though. My ears were pricked, my senses on high alert for the possibility of anything going awry. I'd spoken to Keira just a few minutes before, and she'd have told me if anything had happened, but all the same...I'd feel better when we were all in the car and driving away from the damn city as quick as we could. She'd shot that demi. The motel was mostly deserted, yes, and judging from the homes around me the people living nearby wouldn't be *all* that surprised by the sound of gunshots in the night, but it was still a risk I didn't want to take.

I'd never been so glad to see a cheap motel in my life. The sight of its horrible, moss-covered roof was a physical relief. My shoulders relaxed, even as the ache in my head increased with every second. And then I stopped.

I couldn't hear anything, and I couldn't see anything. If the cops had been called, if they'd arrived, they'd *probably* have made themselves known, right? They wouldn't be hiding. If logic held true, it should be safe to charge right in.

But logic hadn't exactly held out for us so far, and neither Keira nor Jake was stupid. If things went smoothly while I was gone, there was no way they'd hang around waiting to get caught out by the motel owners or the police. Fixing my eyes on where the parking lot should be, peering through a layer of brush and trees and chainlink fence, I began a slow, steady circuit. We hadn't parked all that far away, but it was extra distance they could put between them and the motel - and it wasn't like they could leave without me. *I* had the keys.

The last of the breath I was holding in subconsciously slid from between my teeth as I rounded the last corner and spotted my car - and Jake, sitting on the hood.

Even as I fixed my eyes on the vehicle, something in my pocket started shaking. A grin slipped onto my face, my mind irrationally amused at the timing. I slid my phone from my pocket, lifting it to my ear.

"I forgot to tell you," Keira said. Her voice rang out from further down the road, a perfect match for the words playing in my ear. "We're not at the room anymore. We-"

"I'm here," I said, raising my voice just loud enough that Jake's head swiveled. There was no sense in asking for trouble, after all. Her words cut off mid-sentence, the sound of a surprised exhalation filling the speaker instead. She hung up a second later.

"You made it," I heard her say - and then I saw her dark hair from behind the back corner of the car. "Good."

"Long walk," I said dryly. "But yeah. I made it. Doing ok, Jake?" My eyes flicked over to our companion, who had already returned to leaning back against the windshield.

"My fucking *head*."

I could only imagine. I'd never been tased before, and it wasn't exactly high on my list. "Sorry."

"Got any ibuprofen?"

"Stop wasting time and get over here." Keira's voice cut across Jake's plea, sharp and insistent. The intensity of it caught me, pulling my attention back to her instantly. "You said you had-"

"I've got them." The pain in my legs faded little by little as I resumed my walk, closing the gap between her and I. With every step I could see a little more - and I could see *them*.

There were two of them. A man and a woman. She was short with a head full of mousy brown hair, maybe a year or two older than I. The man looked like he should still be a student at one of the local colleges. And not an upperclassman. His dark hair was shaved off in a tight buzz cut, with a faceful of stubble. They sat on the curb, dead quiet but for the gentle, quiet sound of pained breathing.

Keira crouched behind them. Something gleamed in her hand - a knife. She'd retrieved the one I'd left in the weeds, then. She was sawing away at something wrapped around the man's wrists. A zip-tie, judging from the sound of plastic ripping and tearing. She didn't explain about the pair, and I didn't ask. There weren't all that many options for what had been happening, and none of them were good.

The tie gave way with a snap. The man flinched, falling away. She let him go when he drew back, turning to the woman without a word.

There was no reason for me to wait. I slid closer, digging in my pocket. "Uh...hi," I said slowly, feeling their eyes bore holes into me. The confirmation of what I'd feared wasn't something that made me happy, and I wasn't quite sure how I should approach the pair. But my awkwardness aside, there was something that needed doing. Badly.

Both of their faces turned at the sound of gentle clinking - and their eyes went round at the sight of the two relics waiting in my palm.

"Yours, right?" I said, my voice low as I crouched down beside Keira.

My sister made a pleased noise in the back of her throat as the last of the tie gave way under her knife. The woman hissed, slowly sliding her arms back to her front and massaging her wrists. But even as she did so, she turned, staring towards me with a palpable need in her eyes.

Both of them were sweating, I realized. Their skin was red and flushed, and I could see the man's hands tremble.

I remembered what Aedan had said, to me and to Christian when the man had threatened me - being separated from your relic was a long, painful death. I didn't know how long these two had been stranded, their relics taken from them, but for their sakes I hoped it wasn't too long.

The two tiny, glittering objects shone in the half-light from the street lamp overhead as I held my hand out towards them. They didn't hesitate. The man snatched the sapphire-laden pin from my palm without a word, the woman seizing the ring a moment later. Both seemed to droop, their expressions softening indescribably, even while their breathing continued to come ragged and hard.

"It won't be an instantaneous thing," Jake said. I glanced back. He hadn't moved from the hood of my car, but he watched Keira and I from the corner of his eye. "It takes time, after you've been deprived."

"But it's better," the man still sitting in front of me whispered. "So much better."

I smiled, just a little. "Good." My gaze swept over them all the while, taking in what clues and information I could. There was all too much. Their skin was covered with bruises, with one of the man's eyes blackened and green. Both looked too thin and gaunt. It set my stomach to churning again.

The woman's eyes still flicked between Keira, Jake, and I, the ring she'd taken from me clutched between her hands. She drew closer to the man, pulling away from us as though we were ready to leap for her relic at any second.

"No one's going to take them," I said, as slowly and clearly as I could. I inched away all the while. Keira was a solid, comforting presence at my side, nodding along. "They're yours. Take it slow."

"Maybe we shouldn't take it slow," Jake said, shoving his hands into his pockets. "*Someone* went and shot a gun at a man. We should probably *not* hang around and wait to see if someone gives enough of a shit to do something."

Keira shifted uncomfortably beside me. I wasn't feeling much better about things myself - I really didn't know exactly what was going on or what the goal for the two captive demis had been, but they were clearly struggling to keep up with everything that was happening. I didn't know that shoving them headfirst into the next big thing was the best idea we'd had.

But the little fears in the back of my mind whispered that Jake was right. We could sort through them and their mental state once we were somewhere safe, somewhere we could control. I didn't love the fact that 'somewhere safe' was no doubt going to turn out to be the house we were so carefully rebuilding, but it was the only thing that came to mind.

"My friend's right. It's not safe here," I said, rising with a groan. A chuckle slipped between my lips at the look that passed over Jake's face at my calling him a 'friend' - part incredulous, part amused. The heat rising in his cheeks told me that part of him didn't really mind. "We have a place. It's a few hours away, but-"

Both of them sprang to their feet as I turned towards them.

"Don't *touch* me," the man snapped. The woman kept her silence, tight-lipped and intensely focused. Her fingers clenched and unclenched, wrapping themselves around the ring.

"No one's planning on it," Jake said with a sigh.

The woman inched farther away, taking one hand off her relic long enough to grab at the man's shoulder. "We're leaving. Brendon, come on."

"Just think about this. Where are you going to go?" Keira said, her tone carefully soothing. "Do you have friends nearby? Anywhere you can hide out? Where are you two from?"

I wanted them to say they were from nearby. I wanted them to say that they had friends waiting, people who could fix them up and keep them safe long enough for their relic-shock to fade. But the guarded, hopeless looks on their faces said it all.

"We don't know if there are more of them," I said, opening the drivers' door of my car and leaning against the body of the vehicle. "We've got a finder keeping watch, and he only saw those three. Well, and you two, I'm guessing, but...I don't *think* you've got anyone bearing down on you."

The woman straightened. "Then we'll-"

"But what next? What if they had friends? What if someone comes north after then - or south, checking in on them when they don't show up to wherever they were going? And I'm assuming you guys still want to eat, don't you?"

Her complaints and insistent denials died on her lips as I spoke, following Keira's lead and opting for "soothing" rather than "intense".

"There's no way you can expect us to actually trust you," the woman said at last, her eyes not leaving mine. "Not after all this."

"We killed the guys who had you. The ones who stole your foci," Jake said. *His* voice was entirely disinterested. He hadn't so much as moved, still just sitting on the car picking at his nails.

"The foci we already gave back to you," I pointed out. "Shit, for all I know you could be inches from blowing us apart right now."

"Yeah, that really wasn't your best move," Jake said, shaking his head.

I flushed instantly. "I...I guess. Sorry."

"Look, it's your choice," he continued, dropping his hands into his lap as he turned to eye the two demis. "It sounds like Jon there's willing to put you up while you figure your shit out."

"Put them-" I said, cutting myself off before I could finish. Put them up? I hadn't signed up for *that*.

But, at the same time, it was hard for me to stand there beside the two of them and even think of waving goodbye, casting them off into the shittiest part of town without a prayer. And, well...Greyson had said the demis we'd killed worried him, the ones passing through. He hadn't said they were the only ones lurking around.

Somehow, I didn't think he'd have sent us all the way here to just turn our backs on them.

"We can find somewhere for you two to hole up," I said, running a hand through my hair at last. "For a little bit, anyway. Not forever. Just long enough to get you guys home, wherever that is."

"Fuck off," the woman said, still glaring at me. "I'm not going *anywhere* with you."

"He did give them back, Loren," the man said, glancing down at her. Brendon, she'd called him. "He didn't even ask what they were first."

"That doesn't mean anything."

"So what, then?" he said, more insistently.

"We can-" she said, her mouth sliding open, and stopped. She didn't have a ton of options, and from the look in her eyes, she knew it.

Keira was a dark shape sliding past me, taking a step closer to the woman. "Just trust us," she said quietly, fixing a smile on her face. "Make up your minds, all right? I'm hungry and you're keeping us from breakfast."

Both of them swallowed hard at the mention of food. I smothered a smile behind a hand. Straight for the throat. That was just unfair.

"Fine," Brendon said. His eyes flicked back and forth, sliding between the three of us. His hands twitched, as though he couldn't quite sit still properly. "Please don't- You'd better not be-"

"Dude. In or out," Jake said, rolling his eyes, and popped his door open. I heard him settle onto the seat a moment later with a pained sigh.

"Shit," the man muttered. He crossed the distance between him and the car in two grand steps, whipping the door open.

"Brendon!" the woman hissed, drawing back. Loren. He'd called her Loren.

"Come on. We're still better off, right?" Brendon said, his head snapping back towards his companion.

"I..I don't…" Loren began, wilting, but he was already squeezing himself in alongside Jake in the backseat.

"*Jesus*," I heard him mutter, his voice rising in a whine. "Is this blood?"

"It's mine," I said, swallowing a groan. "Long story."

"He got shot," Jake snapped. "*Short* story. Stop pushing."

"You're on the buckle."

"You don't need it. Come on. You're in my-"

"It'll be fine," Keira said, offering Loren a tiny smile. "Really."

She hesitated a moment longer, biting her lip - and then she threw herself at the car, wedging in alongside Brendon. The complaints from within increased tenfold, vanishing as the door slammed shut behind her.

I could feel eyes on me. I glanced over, finding Keira staring back at me. There was a tiny pattern of red dots down her cheek where the acid must have splashed, all the way across her neck.

"Are you ok?"

Her lips curled up in a tiny, sardonic grin. "Fine. Hurry up. I wasn't joking about being hungry."

There was nothing I could say to that. The arguing from inside the car amplified again as I slid inside, folding myself into my seat. It was already beginning to dwindle, dying out as each of the participants seemed to realize how much effort it took to keep fighting.

It faded away entirely as I turned the key in the ignition, bringing the car rumbling to life and turning us towards home.

CHAPTER TWENTY-SIX

The radio droned on, playing whatever horrible but static-free station we landed on first. Something country. I tuned it out immediately, hardly able to hear the words past the steady, unrelenting ache in my head. I'd overdone it again - not as much as I had with Matt's crew, thank god, but *enough*. I was entirely on Jake's side with the sudden and passionate desire for some ibuprofen to take the edge off.

"Where are we going?" The voice that slipped out of the backseat was thin and filled with worry. I glanced in the rearview mirror, finding Loren staring back at me. For someone who'd fought as hard as she had against the idea of getting in the car, all of her energy seemed to have been used up in that brief surge. Her face was pale, and her eyelids drooped. Brendon was no better beside her, both squeezed in alongside Jake.

"Place called Greenville," I said, tearing my eyes back off her to watch the road again.

"Never heard of it."

Keira chuckled "Not really surprising. There's not much there."

"Quiet is good," Brendon said, joining in at last. "I'm all for quiet."

"We've got...well, my sister lives just inside town, and I live just outside it. It's a few hours off still, but we'll get tucked away and get some rest. Then..." I shook my head slowly, feeling a sigh growing in my chest. "Then we can figure some of this out."

"All right," Loren whispered. Her voice was quiet enough I almost missed it entirely. She drooped further, curling up against Brendon's side.

Jake's eyes were on mine in the rearview mirror when I glanced back again. He didn't seem thrilled with the idea of adding demis to our number. I couldn't entirely blame him - we didn't know anything about these demis.

But looking at them, I didn't get any sort of inclination that they were waiting to attack us, that they were anything but victims. After all, the illusionist had left them behind, bound and relic-less in a motel room. Stuffed them into the bathroom and jammed the door, according to Keira's muted whisper.

It was a risk. I knew that. But it was one worth taking, if they were really the victims they claimed to be.

The conversation fell away as we drove on. No one was in a chatty mood, and I wasn't about to force it. I just turned the radio up, scanning futilely for something a bit more tasteful to listen to.

Keira's stomach growling was the first thing to break the silence. Her cheeks flushed in an instant. Shifting uncomfortably, she half-turned, as though looking out the window would hide the sound or make it less obvious it was her. I shot her a sidelong grin, fixing my eyes onto hers so that she *knew* that I knew. She just scowled, obstinately facing away.

The sound of my turn signal cut across the generic pop music station I'd found. I slid onto the exit ramp smoothly, seeing the gentle stirring of my passengers from the corner of my eye. They didn't say anything, although Loren made a face.

God bless highway signs. The McDonald's was right at the foot of the exit ramp, just a quick turn-off away. I eyed the others again as I turned in, quickly steering us towards a parking spot. With how beaten and bedraggled the two newcomers looked, there was no way they'd be going into the lobby, and I didn't want to risk one of the clerks peering in and seeing them through the windows, either.

"Just grab me something," Keira said, leaning back against her seat. "I don't care what." Her voice was quiet, growing more sleepy by the second. I wondered if she tired out from using her powers, just like Jake and I, or if her abilities were passive enough she could get away with it. I'd have to ask her later. In the meantime, I just forced a smile onto my face, leveraging myself out of the seat and back into the frigid morning air.

I zipped my jacket up as I crossed the parking lot, trying not to look too guilty. Feeling more than a little awkward, I straightened my clothes - and saw a second later that even the blood speckling my shirt from the demi I'd stabbed had vanished. Not so much as a trace of what I'd done remained. The thought didn't sit well with me - and I realized with a jolt that I had no idea where Jake's gun had ended up. Knowing Keira, she'd probably just pocketed it. Shaking my head and trying to ignore the guilty whispers in the back of my mind, I pushed my way inside the store.

In the end, it was so mundane it hurt. The world made no sense anymore. There was no *way* it was right to wake up to a panicked phone call, cross half the state before first light to go murder a handful of other people and save a few others, only to waltz into a fast food place like nothing was wrong. No one gave me a second look. Even the clerk only glanced at me for long enough to take my order, her eyes still misty with sleep.

A chuckle slipped from between my lips. Looking at it a different way, though, this was how it had all begun, wasn't it? Me at a McDonald's, in the midst of two worlds violently colliding. I half expected Aedan to come running around a corner, glaring at me with poorly hidden hatred and a tray of burgers in his hands.

For a single second, I was left to wonder *why* exactly Aedan had been working as a burger-boy in the first place. For as big a deal as he was, for as many people as were chasing him, it didn't make a whole lot of sense for him to be holding down a fast food job. But even as the thoughts crossed my mind, the sleepy-eyed girl called my number, shoving a sack of food into my hands. The frigid air wiped the questions from my mind as I walked back outside, pulling the collar of my coat a little tighter.

The car was silent as I stepped back in - silent, but for the sound of snoring. I glanced in the mirror again, beginning to grin. Both of the new demis were fast asleep, huddled together like an island in the blood-soaked sea of my backseat. So much for them eating, then.

Keira snatched the bag from my hands, making a pleased noise, and plunged one hand into it as quietly as she could. I was already turning the engine over, putting us back on the road.

The McDonald's faded into the distance behind me - no murder, this time. A small victory, but I took what I could get.

The silence dragged on, broken only by the strains of whatever starlette was hot at the moment singing some sappy romance song.

Keira munched away on a McMuffin, her eyes sharp. Jake reached up over her shoulder. She ignored him. He made a face, kicking the back of her seat. Rolling her eyes, she plopped a sandwich down into his hand.

Exhaustion made the trip back seem far longer than the trip out. I'd planned on getting more than half a night's sleep, and my body was feeling the strain with every mile that passed under us. At one point, I considered asking Jake if his relic would let him steal my tiredness, rather than just granting it, but decided he'd only make fun of me. I bit my tongue, downing the coffee I'd bought along with the food, and kept driving.

At last, the roads around us turned more familiar. I recognized the names of the stores flashing past, the businesses and homes. It was still dark, but the sun was at the horizon, turning the sky a muted grey-blue shot through with orange. Swallowing a sigh and thanking whatever god was listening that we'd made it in one piece, I turned onto our exit.

"I'll just drop you two off?" I said, my voice hushed, and glanced over at Keira and Jake. Both were still awake, somehow. "It's kind of on the way. I guess." Cutting across to our old apartment complex *wasn't* on the way, but there was no sense in pointing it out.

"I...I think I should come with you," Keira said, her eyes flicking back towards the pair fast asleep in the backseat.

"Oh?"

"They're new here," she murmured. "And there's no telling what she's been through. I think putting her alone in a house full of strange demis might be too much." She shrugged. "At least I'm a girl."

I nodded slowly, staring out into the night. "I guess. I don't know how long they'll be here, though."

"I'm coming too."

At the new voice cutting across, both Keira and I looked up. Jake was pressed against the car door, the weight of Brendon pressed heavily against him and his arms folded, but his expression was firm.

I glanced at him, then back to the road. "You sure?"

"We don't know anything about them." His voice was quiet, carefully hushed. His eyes flicked to the pair alongside him. "No one should be hanging around alone until we know exactly what they're about."

"I really don't think they're dangerous," Keira said. "They were tied up with no relics. If that was a trap, it was a shitty trap."

"Even still."

"He's not wrong," I said, glancing over to Keira. "There's nothing wrong with being careful. He can come if he likes."

She made a face, but nodded. "Fine."

The run-down but steadily improving shape of our house loomed in the headlights as we turned down the drive. The tension in my shoulders eased. We'd made it - with only minimal injuries. I didn't like playing games like that, but we'd made it.

"Last stop," I called, raising my voice gently. "Everyone off." The huddled mass in the backseat started shifting, muttering darkly, and finally resolved into the shape of the two demis. I chuckled. "There's beds inside. Well...there's, like, two beds. And a couch. And some chairs. Go wild." I cracked the door a moment later, stepping out of the grease-scented air of the car and into the morning half-light.

Keira followed half a step behind me as we meandered up towards the house. The roof was done. That was good. The siding was still hell, a mess of moss-covered wood and rusted nails. I ran the sleeping arrangements over in my mind, trying to place where exactly I was going to put people. There was the living room, with its couch and chairs, and the bedrooms trailing off the hall that wound around the back...

"I think Loren gets your room. Sorry," I murmured. She'd taken one of the first rooms we'd put back together, stuffing a futon into the corner. She'd held onto our apartment, at least until the lease was up - she wasn't *crazed* about the idea of living with her older brother until she was thirty. But, the money that had gone into the house belonged to all of us, and she stayed over from time to time too.

"It's fine," she said, shrugging. "They probably need the sleep more than we do."

"You could just break lease."

She made a face again. "That's-"

"It's probably not as much money as you think," I pointed out, turning back towards the car. The others were stumbling out, trundling up the path of stepping stones towards the old house. "If we...Well, if we start having more people around, then it'd make more sense to centralize a little bit. And there's no sense in throwing money away on rent."

"You mean, stay here, where you can keep an eye on me."

I grinned. "I didn't say that."

Keira sighed. "You didn't have to. I'm fine, Jon."

"I know you are. I'm not *worried* about you. Just think on it."

Brendon and Loren eased past us, looking around with curiosity. "Where are we, exactly?" Loren said, shrinking closer to Brendon.

I shook my head, stepping past them and unlocking the door. "Like I said. Greenville. It's quiet."

"You weren't kidding," she whispered, giving the pine trees around us one more glance. The house was tucked in amidst them, half-hidden behind the forest and the underbrush until it seemed to appear from within them. It was clearly old, with the dark-stained siding favored by eras past, which didn't help. Despite how big the place was, it had a way of sneaking up on you. Just another reason why we'd liked it. The fact it had a full garage and plenty of bedrooms was an added bonus.

Door in hand, I waved to them. "In. Don't let out all the heat."

Loren made a beeline towards the door, pulling the threadbare sweatshirt jacket she wore a little tighter around herself, but Brendon hesitated.

"Meteromancy."

At the sound of his voice, I blinked, turning my eyes to him. "What, now?"

His ears glowed red in the growing light. "My focus. I have a weather-sense. And Loren-"

"Brendon!" she hissed, grabbing his arm.

"They're letting us into their house, Loren," he snapped. "It would be rude to not tell them *that* much."

"But, that's-"

"You can tell them, if you prefer," he said, holding her eyes with his own.

"What if it's a trap?" she whispered, her voice low enough that I could barely hear it.

"They had our foci in hand," Brendon whispered back, equally quiet. "And then they gave them back. If it's a trap, why bother?"

She drooped, her eyes falling to the ground in front of her. And then her gaze snapped up to meet mine a moment later. "I...I give people dreams," she whispered. "Good dreams. Or nightmares, sometimes."

I gave both of them a long, assessing look. My necklace was warm against my chest, keying to life as I reached for it, but their words rang true. There wasn't the slightest hint that they were lying to me. Finally, I nodded. "Fair enough. Jon Christensen. I do...word magic, I guess you could call it."

"Jacob Cooper. I make people sleep," Jake said, pushing past me. "I call the couch."

"Keira Christensen. I...um. I don't really know," Keira said, glancing to me. "I see demis, I guess. And relics. Foci."

Jake was staring at me, when I glanced back. He jerked his chin towards the demis. I nodded.

"A few things, then," I said quietly. "I need to know that we're safe. Do both of you confirm that you mean none of us any harm, that you're not pulling any game or any tricks?"

"Of course," Brendon said, his eyes widening. "I wouldn't- we wouldn't-"

"I don't want to hurt anyone," Loren whispered. "I never wanted any of that. I won't do anything."

Once again, I watched the both of them, and once again, their words rang true. I couldn't see even a trace of a lie to their words. Finally, licking my suddenly-dry lips once, I nodded. "All right. In you go, then."

Loren's eyes swept over us again, lingering, but Brendon nodded. "Right. Uh, well..." His eyes tightened. "Thanks. For what you did back there. For this." His head dropped, his shoulders slumping. "I don't know what we would have-"

"It's all good," I mumbled, thrown off balance by the emotion in his voice. "Everyone's tired. Bedrooms are that way, chairs are over there." I pointed down the narrow hallway that led to the few rooms we'd finished off. "Take your pick."

With a last glance towards the three of us, Brendon and Loren slipped off towards the rooms.

I made it as far as the kitchen, dropping myself into a chair with a groan. My head dropped down onto the counter, letting the cool formica sooth my headache. I could hear Jake and Keira, settling into their respective places for the rest of the morning. I didn't care where they slept. They were both adults. That much was on *them*.

There was a bottle of ibuprofen on the counter, dropped haphazardly among all the rest of the mess. I seized it, downing four pills dry, and tossed the bottle towards the couch. Jake caught it with a clatter and a quiet, satisfied murmur.

The countertop was cold against my cheek as I leaned back down, sliding my eyes closed.

CHAPTER TWENTY-SEVEN

The doorbell rang.

My eyes snapped open. I flinched, jerking against the counter. The light shining in through the window over the sink was bright - not full midday, but working its way towards it. I eased myself upright, still feeling the sleep seep through my mind. Somewhere off in another part of the house, I could hear the strident sound of two people snoring.

From my spot in the kitchen, though, I could see Jake and Keira stirring, lifting their heads and staring around groggily.

The doorbell rang again.

I was on my feet before the echoes had faded away fully, glancing around warily. Who would come visit us all the way out there? Who actually *cared*? Visions of Officer What's-His-Name flew through my mind, dark and unsettling. What did we do? Was it a rival crew, following us home? But then - why would they ring the damn doorbell?

I caught sight of a vehicle through the ragged curtains still hanging over one of the windows, fresh from the 70's. A truck - a truck I *recognized*.

"It's Greyson," I said, my voice carrying to where Jake and Keira sat, rubbing the sleep from their eyes. I was already halfway to the door by the time they nodded. He'd just keep ringing the damn bell until we woke up, I knew, and not everyone in the house needed a wake-up call.

His finger was poised over the button again, in fact, when I pulled the door open. "Morning," he said, leering at me. "Almost afternoon, in fact. Have a busy night?"

"We had a busy *morning*," I muttered, wincing at the light. Something pushed straight past me - his little dog, trotting in as though it owned the place. Greyson was right on Spike's heels, letting himself in without waiting for an invitation. I just sighed, sliding the door shut.

He was carrying something - a six pack, I saw as he reached up and set it down on the counter. And a plastic back full of something that went *clink*.

"Greyson, it's ten in the morning."

"It's never too early for a drink," he said, rolling his head until he could glare at me. " 'specially when you've had a night like that. You get 'em?"

"So you knew they were there," I said dryly. He was rummaging through my cupboards, pulling out glasses. The bottle of whiskey he unearthed from god-knows-where inside his coat stank up the kitchen as he uncorked it, putting a finger in each of the three cups.

" 'Course I did," he said, flopping down on one of the chairs with a tired groan. "Well, I was pretty sure. There's few things in this world that are certain."

"You didn't *tell* us there were other demis involved," I said, trying to keep the irritation from my voice. "It would have been nice to know."

"Shit, son. We're just now starting this little partnership," he said, lifting his glass to his lips. "You should be grateful I'm telling you anything at all. Drink, for fuck's sake."

Keira and Jake were sidling closer, yawning. "Morning, Greyson," Jake said, waving at the finder. Keira just nodded, her eyes round. Spike wound in between her ankles, doing all but nipping at her to get her attention.

I lifted the glass to my lips obligingly, wincing. A morning filled with hard liquor was *not* the appropriate cure for a night full of relic-burn.

"If we'd known there were other people, we could have gone in more carefully," Jake said, masking his yawn as he seized one of the glasses.

Greyson chuckled. "Should've been careful anyway. Don't just charge in. And, I wasn't *sure*. Didn't want to get your hopes up if something...well, if something went badly."

"If they died," I said, my mouth going dry.

His smile went crooked. "Right. That."

"Does that happen often?" Keira said quietly, joining in at last.

"You've seen this before, then."

The old man shrugged, leaning down to tousle his dog's ears. "Now and then. Been easier to spot as the years drag on. It's all that much clearer. Time was, I couldn't feel anyone if they didn't have their focus in hand. It's different, of late." His eyes flicked from face to face around the table, dead serious. "Like I told you. Some of 'em are just passing through to the markets, up across the Canadian border. Some are harvesting foci. Impossible to tell for sure, less you're standing there watching them go."

"Is that what was going on?" Keira said. She was pale, bone-white in the dimly lit kitchen. "H-Harvesting their...foci?" She spoke the word slowly, as though tasting the different term on her lips.

Greyson made a face. Jake was still dead silent, staring down at his cup. He lifted it without a word, taking another sip of the amber liquid.

"It could be," Jake said, his voice quiet. "From what I've seen, anyway. I...Well, I haven't been around all that much, but I'm not from the sticks." He swirled his drink, pursing his lips. "The stronger demis, the ones with offensive capabilities....they normally get killed. It's too risky to keep them around. Even if you take their focus away, you have to let them have access now and again. They'll just collapse, otherwise. It'd be too easy for them to just kill you when you did that."

"But a weather-reader and a dream-giver," I said, feeling the blood drain from my head and leave the world to spin slowly around me. "Those don't sound all that dangerous."

"Right," Jake said, his shoulders rising even as his head drooped, until he was nose-into his drink. "And, well. You can only have one focus, right?"

Greyson chuckled mirthlessly, still petting Spike. "Why waste your one magical gift on something weak, when you can just drag someone along and force them to do the boring utility work for you?"

"Oh." If what they were saying was true, then...I had a lot to think about. And Brendon and Loren had been in a worse situation than I'd thought. The suspicion had been there, in the back of my mind. I remembered Matt all too clearly, getting ready to bond Keira with Recon's glasses and take her along with them.

I'd seen it myself, hadn't I? The way I'd been pushed around, the disadvantage I'd been at when I'd thought my abilities limited to simple translation. I'd been at the mercy of each of them - Christian and Matt, at first, but even Aedan could have killed me without a second thought. That was just the way demi culture worked. Aedan had explained it, and Jake. The strong took what they wanted, and the only way to stop them was to be strong enough to tell them no.

It was just a reality of the world that that system fucked over the people who were unlucky enough to be left defenseless. I pressed a hand to my face, rubbing my eyes. "This is messed up," I whispered, shaking my head slowly. "So, what? They just troll through cities looking for people they can control, in addition to killing whoever they can find?"

"It's a smaller market," Jake said, almost hurriedly. As though he was ashamed. He should be, I realized, if he'd played any sort of role in the murdering and stealing. I pushed the thought away as quickly as I could. I'd known that Jake had been part of Matt's crew. I'd known that he'd done things in the past that we wouldn't approve of. He'd sworn it off, when he stayed, and so far his claims that he was looking for a more peaceful life seemed to be true. "There aren't that many people who want to play around with holding pets, and there aren't *that* many people with powers suitable for it."

"Just people like Brendon and Loren," I said, trying not to glare at him. "And Keira."

"You, too," Greyson said, taking another swig from his glass. His voice was still bright and cheery, despite the razor-sharp look in his eyes. I flinched, glancing over at him. He chuckled. "You're only a danger so long as you've got your voice, boy. All it'd take would be a few minutes with a knife, and that danger's gone. A lie detector'd be a damn useful tool in someone's crew."

"Oh," I said, sitting back a little lower. Keira had gone even paler. For a long moment, the only sound in the kitchen was the quiet click of Spike's toenails on the linoleum.

Finally, Greyson cleared his throat. "Anyway. Regardless, I don't like getting people's hopes up less I know something for sure. And, well." He shrugged. "Wanted to see how you'd react."

"You mean it was a test." The words came out wooden as I stared at the table, still chewing on everything they'd said.

"If you'd like to call it that. Like to know who I'm working with."

"I thought we'd showed you that already."

He chuckled. "Well, you had some pretty words for me. But words are just that. I prefer to see the actions you'll take when you're against the wall. Chasin' after that asshole was a pretty good show."

My legs still ached from that chase, but I just laughed hollowly. "Right. If you say so. I…" I shook my head slowly. "He came *this* close to getting away."

"But he didn't. So stop bitching, and take the good where you can get it." His hand slapped into my back a moment later, sending droplets of whiskey spattering across the table. He was already busy with the bottle, refilling our glasses. I eyed the liquor warily, my eyes drifting back up to him.

"So what now?" Keira's voice was soft, but firm. We stopped, glancing at her. She gripped her glass with both hands, her knuckles shining white against her skin. A crooked grin tugged at her lips, as she glanced up and saw us looking. "We've got two demis in our house now. What do we do now?"

"Well…I wasn't thinking they'd stay forever," I said slowly. "I'm sure they've got places to go back to. Things they'll want to do."

Both Greyson and Jake made noncommittal noises, in perfect synchronization. I stopped, my eyes flicking between the two of them.

"Not…always," Greyson said slowly. "Sometimes, sure. Lots of times, though, the ones what get taken or have their foci stolen are just the last survivors of a raid. Might be they've been missing too long. Police' would have questions, ones they can't answer. Might be the demis responsible offloaded some of their problems onto their victims, as it were."

I just took another sip of my drink, feeling it burn as it worked its way down my throat. It clinked softly against the table as I set it back down. "Oh."

"If you tell 'em to go, they'll probably go," Greyson said, as though adding it on at the end. "You don't *have* to keep them around."

Keira was making a face. I could see it from the corner of my eye, even as I mulled over their words. The memories of our first encounter, of exactly how close we'd come to being just another demi statistic, still rang in my mind.

For the first time, I could understand a little of why Aedan had come back to that McDonald's parking lot, why he'd charged back out of the woods knowing full well he wasn't equipped to fight Matt's crew. He *had* to have known he'd die - at best. He'd charged out anyway, buying me a chance to run for freedom.

He'd bought me a second chance. Could I really just close my doors and hunker down, pretending the rest of the world didn't exist?

"I...We need to decide this together," I heard myself say, my words ringing through the quiet little kitchen. "If we do something like this, it's going to put a target on our backs."

"It will," Greyson said, leaning back. His eyes were unreadable from behind his glass as he held it to his lips.

"You're fucking right, it will," Jake muttered. "Are you-"

"I, at least, don't think we should turn them away," I said, little louder than a whisper. The others were still sleeping - that was the logical, rational explanation. This wasn't a conversation they should be privy to. Not yet, not until we'd decided. "It's not right. That's why you sent us after them, after all."

Greyson shrugged. "Watched all sorts of people rummage through the state, over the years. Not like I could do anything, by my lonesome. Best to pretend it wasn't happening. That's the story. But, eh. I'm older now." He grinned, yellowed teeth glinting back at me. "Not so much to lose. Why not?"

Jake stared at the table still, his fingers drumming against the glass. "I...I don't know."

"I'm not sure either," Keira said quietly. "I...I'd rather not bring fights down on ourselves. But if we throw them out, what'll happen?"

"They'll either find a corner to call their own, like we've got here, or they'll join a new crew, if they can find one, or they'll get picked off again by the next wanderers who drift through," Jake said, no hesitation in his voice. Despite the iron in his tone, though, his eyes were dark.

"And what's the most likely outcome, there?" I said, smiling sidelong at him with absolutely no humor in the expression.

He made a face, lifting his cup, and didn't respond. There was no need for him to.

"Right," I said, dropping my eyes back to my drink.

The silence fell back over our table as we sat, taking turns petting Greyson's dog as he waddled from person to person.

"There's no need to advertise ourselves," I said quietly. "I'm not suggesting we become some sort of haven for everyone who's in trouble. Just...if we see someone in our territory, we step in. If we're able to. If it's safe enough. That's all I'm suggesting - and if people need a bit of time to get their feet under them, I think that's fine, within reason." My smile grew, just a touch. "I might need to come up with a proper script of questions, but we can at least make sure they're not here to kill us in our sleep."

No one spoke. You could have heard a pin drop as everyone stared at the table.

"Our territory," Jake said at long last, taking another sip. "You do realize that by staking some sort of claim, you'll rub every other crew around us the wrong way? And that they're probably going to be bigger and meaner than us?"

"Territory is a *loose* term," I said, glancing over at him. "I don't see anyone else clamoring for this spot."

He shrugged, his face long. "Even still."

"We'll share, if it comes to that," I said, holding his gaze. "No one's looking for a fight. If you're uncomfortable with this, Jake, then we don't have to-"

"No," he said with a quick jerk of his head. "No, that's...that's not what I'm saying." He frowned, scuffing his shoe against the floor tiles. "I...I think this is...I don't know. Stupid. Definitely. But, it might be *right*, too. I just want us to think ahead before we take this plunge."

"We're just letting two people stay here for a little bit," I said, leaning back.

He snorted. "For now. And when the next people come through, needing our help?"

I had to nod halfheartedly. "I...suppose you're right."

"But...yeah. They can stay," Jake said, his voice quiet. "I don't think I can argue with that much. Fair's fair."

Greyson nodded, downing the rest of his glass in one go. "Good. Now, if you don't mind my saying, I like a good, wholesome crowd around here. But if that's the way you're all thinking of taking this, you might *also* think about finding yourself some allies worth a damn." His beady eyes were sharp as he peered from face to face. "Right now you don't exactly have much going for you."

"I'll...figure something out," I said, holding his gaze. "I know it's a problem."

"Long as you're thinking about it," he said, refilling his cup. "Now drink, damn it, and let's move on from this piss-poor conversation. Cheer the hell up."

I forced a smile, nodding, and let some of the tension slide away. We were in an interesting position, sure. There were risks. But the risks were worth it, in my mind. We'd figure something out. I'd figure something out. Whatever that 'something' was. You didn't just abandon your own, and I couldn't stomach the idea of sitting by and letting people get hurt and killed in my own backyard.

Keira had picked up where the conversation fell off. She hadn't had the chance to interact with Greyson, after all. I let them chatter on about this and that. He was a finder, and she was....well, if she wasn't a finder, she was something *close*. Maybe he could help her. I chuckled into my drink. It would have been nice to have someone help *me* figure my stuff out, but it just hadn't worked out that way.

The sound of Loren and Brendon snoring away in their rooms rose in my ears as I drifted away from the table, thinking of exactly how we were going to deal with this mess we were in.

***

Our fears were confirmed soon enough. Once they woke, Brendon and Loren had quickly admitted that they were stuck. They'd been pulled right from their communities, the other demis they knew killed around them. No one would miss a few more strays. They'd just fade into the legions of missing people that filled the cities, assumed to have just run off or have gotten caught up in trouble they couldn't outrun.

With nowhere else to go, they seized on our offer of a place to live - at least for a little while. There were enough places in town looking for low-income labor that they could squeeze in here and there, and Greyson turned out to have a shocking array of forgeries on hand. He'd only chuckled, staring at the dazed looks in our eyes. "Folks pay me however they can, sometimes," he'd explained. "It pays to be prepared, I always said."

We weren't about to argue, not when it was keeping our crew fed. And little by little, hour by hour, the house was beginning to come together. It was a lot of time and a lot of sweat, but having extra hands made it easier. Loren had come into her own when it came to the work, in fact, showing an expertise with the equipment I hadn't expected of the slight woman. Her eyes were still shadowed, and she still didn't seem comfortable to stray all that far from Brendon. We didn't push the matter. They'd clearly been traveling together for a while before we'd killed their captors, and if she took comfort in him being there, it wasn't our place to comment.

Day after day, things started drifting towards a sort of normalcy again - just one with more faces. To my smug satisfaction - and the satisfaction of my bank account - Keira passed Jake her lease, packing the possessions she actually cared about into the house. I'd known she wouldn't want to stay in that apartment forever, not with everything that had happened there.

In the back of my mind, I knew that the peace couldn't last forever. The others were absolutely right - this was going to put a target on top of our heads. For the life of me, I just couldn't find a proper solution to that. Anyone who would actually be useful in a fight and could help defend us was going to already be signed on to one of the other crews, fighting *against* us. I could do a lot, sure, and having Jake on our side was great. He'd happily taken one of Greyson's forgeries, settling into an office job in our town's meager business district. The thought of him leaving was worrying. Without him, it would be just me who could do *anything* to defend us, after all.

Our best hope was to find people we could pick off from other crews, people who would be willing to entertain our dreams of peace like Jake was. The only other possibility that presented itself to me was to find other people who were relic-compatible and *create* our own army.

I wasn't comfortable with that, even if I had a clue where to begin, and I didn't. What, was I supposed to give Keira's loud, boisterous friend Cathy a relic and tell her to go start killing people? How would something like that ever, *ever* work?

I hadn't found a solution. And with every day that passed, no solution there, the stress grew a little more. I just tried to push it away, to mixed success. It worked reasonably during the day, with the light of the sun and the sound of other voices pressed in around me. I could focus on that, instead of the problems that everyone else seemed to be expecting me to solve. Somewhere along the line, I'd become the group's spokesperson, and I was *not* comfortable with it.

At night, though, the fears circled around me, squeezing in tighter and tighter until I woke covered in sweat, certain that I could hear footsteps in the hall. Sometimes I'd be certain it was a rival crew, here to kill us. Sometimes, I couldn't shake the feeling that I'd come around the corner to see a dark-haired man, blood dripping down his filthy shirt from where I'd sunk a knife into his neck.

Nights like that, it was all I could do to keep the contents of my stomach firmly in place, to keep the guilt down. I'd never wanted to kill. I'd never expected to have to bear that burden. It didn't seem to care - I'd wound up carrying it all the same.

It was one of those Saturday mornings, holding a cup of coffee and taking swigs in the useless attempt to wash the taste of vomit from my mouth, when I'd slipped from the house and out into the cold. I wasn't going to go far. It was still early, with the morning light still dim and the sunrise in full blossom down on the horizon. But it had just snowed, the first of the season and a handful of weeks after Loren and Brendon had joined us.

The sound of the snow crunching under my feet helped, crystallizing my thoughts and making my fears seem at least a little farther away. The chill of the late-fall air helped even more. I swallowed my shivers, letting the nightmares drift a bit farther away. We just had to be careful. That was all we had to do. We could-

I stopped.

It had snowed, the whole night before. The first snow of the season was like that - it'd sweep in out of nowhere, transforming the world while you slept. Half-buried leaves poked out from under thin patches around the house, which was almost entirely obscured behind white-laden branches. Most of the dead leaves had come free in the winds and weight.

And now, peering through the suddenly-bare branches, I could see a low, bulbous shape. It was hard to make it out precisely, but I knew what it was. It was something that shouldn't be there.

A tent. There was a tent, halfway back into the woods where we wouldn't see it. Someone was here - and there was no one else around but our crew. The idea of them being mere campers, lost and bunking down in the woods, was laughable at best. They were here for us.

My heartbeat thundering in my ears, I took half a step back towards the house. And then I stopped.

Who would be here? Who would know, and who would stage such a half-hearted attack? If they were demis, they'd chosen to put themselves right in our backyard, hidden or no, and they'd done *nothing*. Greyson hadn't contacted me. The thought screamed in the back of my mind. He knew full well how much danger we were in, the stakes that were in play, and he hadn't said a *word* about other demis roaming through our territory. It wasn't like him.

Despite myself, I found I was stepping closer, picking my way through the snow as quietly as I could.

The tent looked old, run-down and barely able to support its own weight. It had collapsed entirely at one corner, in fact, the weathered brown fabric bent low around its poles by the weight of the snow that

237

had fallen off a tree onto it. Here and there, holes poked through the fabric.

I could hear the sound of someone snoring from inside it.

An idea grew in my mind, blossoming the closer I stepped to the tiny, decrepit shape. There were only a few reasons why Greyson would neglect to call me - and I wasn't foolish enough to entertain the idea that whoever was in the tent was a normal, mundane human.

I eased my phone from my pocket, keying the screen on. If I was wrong, then it would be a quick answer, and I could be off to rouse the others. If I was right...

The *Call* button lit up under my finger.

I held my breath, waiting for the call to go through. The soft buzz of it ringing vibrated through my hand.

And the sound of a cheap electronic ringtone blared out from inside the tent. I exhaled, leaning my head back and stared up at the sky.

It rang five times. Just when I'd thought it might go to voicemail, the tent erupted into jostling, rustling motion. The line connected.

"W-What?" Aedan snapped, fighting off a yawn. The sound of his voice was a few seconds off from the echo of him through the phone's speaker, discordant and jarring.

I just lifted my phone to my ear, eyes fixed on his horrible little tent. "What the hell are you doing in my backyard?"

The line went quiet. I counted to three in my head, ticking off the seconds of white noise.

And then he hung up.

The sound of a zipper being ripped open drew my eyes back to the tent. The flap on the end was open - and Aedan peered out through the gap. His eyes fixed on mine. A sigh rippled through his frame a moment later.

"Shit."

CHAPTER TWENTY-EIGHT

The fabric of the tent rustled, the zipper undoing farther. I could only stare, doing my best to process the sight in front of my eyes. Aedan climbed free, glaring at me all the while.

He looked...bad. That was the first thought that rose to my mind as I narrowed my eyes, leaning back on my heels. He'd always been thin and angular, sure, but there was a gaunt look to him that hadn't been there before. Dark circles ringed his eyes, like he hadn't been sleeping.

"Jonny," Aedan said, a smirk settling onto his face. I wasn't sure how much I believed it. "Well, this is awkward. I-"

"What are you doing, Aedan?"

He stopped, wrinkling his nose as he kicked at the snow between us with his worn-out sneakers. "Oh, you know. I was in the area, and I *know* how inept you can be. Thought I'd check in on you."

I stared at him, my eyes narrowing further. He didn't *seem* like he was lying - but Aedan knew how my relic worked, too. He was smart enough to know not to tell me an out-and-out lie. I was pretty sure my relic wouldn't throw a fit over a lie of omission.

"Really."

"I'm just looking out for you, Jonny," Aedan said, shoving his hands into his pockets and grinning at me.

"And that's why you're hiding from me?" I said, not bothering to try and keep the skepticism from my tone.

His smirk faltered. "W-Well, I didn't want you to think I was getting soft. You weren't supposed to see. Forgive me my weakness." He finished off with a jaunty wave, his green eyes sparkling innocently. I wasn't convinced.

Even less so when a single detail settled into my mind. "That's my sweatshirt."

It wasn't my imagination. Aedan was fair-skinned - he couldn't hide it. The reddish glow that settled over his cheeks stood out, even in the cold of the morning air. "T-That's not true. It's a grey sweatshirt, Jonny. What, do you think you own *every* grey sweatshirt in-"

"No, I remember," I said, glaring at him. "I put it away *last week* when the weather took a cold turn. If I go look in the closet, it'll be missing, won't it?"

"Please. Spare me your paranoia," Aedan said, lifting his chin stubbornly. But he didn't answer my question, and the flush in his cheeks didn't fade.

I didn't bother asking again. I just eased past him, ignoring his protests, and pulled the flap on his tent open.

"The hell?" Aedan snapped, grabbing at my arm. "That's not-"

"You've been stealing my beer?" I said, glaring at him. "And that cereal - I was blaming Spike, dammit. You've been letting a *dog* take the blame for your pilfering. New low, Aedan."

"Oh, fuck off. It was one box, Jonny. You'll be fine, and so will your damn dog."

"Greyson's dog. And it's Jon," I muttered, but it was hard to stay focused on the argument.

I should be mad. I should be *furious*. I'd thought- Well, even if Aedan hadn't exactly been a friend, he'd been an ally. The notion of him sneaking onto our property and stealing from us hurt. The idea of him using us like that was stuck in my mind, loud and impossible to ignore.

And yet...Aedan had taken a fall jacket I wasn't using and some food. And *beer*, but that was just Aedan. There were plenty of things in the house he could have stolen if he'd broken in, things that were much more valuable. He hadn't. And if he was going to steal, it would be just as easy to steal from a store, wouldn't it? He'd come here.

"It's fucking cold," I muttered. I'd been planning on a quick walk to settle my nerves, not a prolonged interrogation. "I'm going inside."

"Oh," Aedan said, deflating instantly.

I took a step back towards the house, trying to follow the footprints I'd already left. He wasn't moving. I glanced back, rolling my eyes.

"Come on, then."

"Oh." Surprise colored his tone, transforming the word into something totally different from a few moments before. But when I started walking again, his footsteps echoed behind me.

He didn't say a word as we picked our way through the woods back towards the house. I hardly knew he was there, but for the sound of the snow crunching underfoot. His lonely little tent faded into the trees behind us, the flap drifting gently in the breeze.

I breathed a sigh of relief when the warmth of the house enveloped us. Aedan shut the door, kicking off his shoes without so much as slowing down as he beat a path towards the overstuffed thrift-store couch we'd found.

I didn't bother saying anything. I wasn't quite sure what was going on, what he was up to, but I didn't think he'd stolen out of any sense of malice. Besides, I was hungry. It was still early, and I hadn't been up for nearly long enough to deal with this shit. "Coffee's still in the pot," I said, even as I reached for the handle to refill my mug. It was going to be a two-pot day, I could already tell.

"Right." The word was half-hidden behind an enormous yawn. He'd been sleeping, after all. I rolled my eyes, reaching for the fridge. There'd be eggs or *something* I could throw together without it being too much of a pain.

The act of cooking was good. It let me think, let my thoughts work themselves through as I lost myself in the simple process of it. Before long, the smell of eggs and bacon filled the kitchen and living room, and I was pretty sure I could hear the house's other residents beginning to stir.

"If you want something, come and-" I began, glancing back over my shoulder, but stopped.

Aedan lay facedown on the couch, curled into the fabric as though trying to become one with it. His eyes were closed, and I could already hear a low, steady snore begin to echo around the living room.

Rolling my eyes, I took a step closer to shake him back awake. And then I stopped. He'd been sleeping, out there in the cold and snow. Judging from the look he had about him, it had been a while since he'd been able to really relax. If he was tired enough that he preferred sleeping to food, so be it. I slipped back to the stove, reaching for the pan.

"You made breakfast?" someone said, slipping around the corner. I glanced up. Jake crept out of the hallway, clad in shorts and rubbing the sleep from his eyes. A tired grin stretched across his face. "That's pretty-" He stopped. He'd caught sight of Aedan, then, lying fast asleep on the couch.

"He just showed up," I said, keeping my voice low. "Let him sleep for now, I think."

"But, like, did he say he was coming, or something?"

I chuckled. "He did not. Here. Take this." I shoved a plate into his hands, turning him back towards the hall.

"But, I want to-"

"Just go eat somewhere else," I said, fighting down my irritation.

Jake groaned gently, but when I elbowed him, he went. I heard him step to his door - and then he stopped. "Aedan's here," he said, his voice hushed.

"What?"

I groaned. Keira. She came bounding around the corner a moment later, her blue eyes wide. "Jake said-"

"Right over there. Breakfast?" I said, shaking my head.

"Sure," she murmured. She seemed frozen in place, her eyes fixed on our sleeping ally. "What's going on?"

"He was camped out back in a tent. And he's been stealing from the house."

"What? Why?"

"I wonder," I muttered. Keira didn't hear. She just eased over to the couch, sliding the blanket from the back of the bed. It fell over Aedan in a heavy wave of fabric. He didn't so much as twitch.

"Did he say anything?" my sister said, glancing back to me.

"He did not."

"Then why did-"

"I'll try and figure some of it out when he's up, all right?" I said, running a hand through my hair. "Just...let's let him be for now."

"Fine," she muttered, turning to the stove and shoveling herself a plateful. She plopped herself down at the table, her gaze flicking between Aedan and I stubbornly.

I knew she was hoping he'd wake up, spiting my request for her to leave. I could see it in her face, the way her eyes lost a bit of their obstinance with every second he slept. Finally, with her plate empty and Aedan still snoring, she set her plate down with a sigh. "Fine," she said, her voice quiet enough I could hardly hear it. "Just-"

"I'll let you know as soon as I figure anything out. Let's just keep the others away for now, okay?"

"Right," she whispered, flashing me a quick smile. Her eyes drifted back to the couch, lingering for a long moment - and then she was gone, grabbing her coat and slipping through the door without another word.

I leaned back against the counter, snagging another piece of bacon, and settled in. It looked like it would be a long wait.

***

My eyes slid open.

For a long moment, it was hard to process exactly what had woken me up. I was comfortable. There was no blaring alarm, no houseful of people screaming for attention. But then I pieced it together - the snoring had stopped.

I rolled over, picking myself up off the counter that had become my bed too often of late, and glanced back towards the bed. Aedan was moving, slowly pushing himself upright and pressing a hand to his face.

"Morning," I said dryly, unable to keep from grinning. "More like afternoon, I guess."

He blinked, slowly turning to face me. "Jonny." His too-green eyes fixed on me, his hair a halo of snarls and knots around his head. "What the fu-"

"There's food," I said, waving towards the fridge. I'd finally given up and thrown what I'd cooked into some tupperware, after he'd made it clear that he wasn't planning on getting up anytime soon. "If you want it heated up, the microwave's over there."

His eyes hovered on mine for a long, drawn-out moment. And then he pushed himself off the couch, all but throwing himself at the fridge.

Aedan didn't want the food heated up, it turned out. He didn't seem to notice how cold it was. It vanished down his throat all the same as he devoured the last of the eggs - and then set into the leftovers stacked inside the fridge.

"Slow down," I said, swallowing a chuckle. "It's not going anywhere."

"Fuck you." His curse was muted, lacking the vehemence it normally would have possessed.

"What's going on?"

He fell quiet at last, his eyes flicking towards the door.

I sighed. "Just talk to me. For once, Aedan, just fucking *talk*. Why

243

exactly are you here, hiding from us and stealing our stuff?"

"I'm not *hiding.*"

"It sure seemed like that, what with you parking yourself in a tent off in the woods rather than knocking on the front door."

"You...I didn't mean for you to find out. I'll go." His voice was low. He set the tupperware back onto the counter with a clatter, turning towards the door.

"Aedan," I snapped, pushing myself upright.

"It just hasn't all gone so smoothly, all right?" he said, his voice just a hair shy of a snarl as he turned to glare at me. "Winter's settling in and I- Well, I'm just not quite where I should have been. Give me a break."

"Where you're supposed to be?" I said, folding my arms and leaning back against the counter. "Where would that be? Why are you hiding out in some tent?" One after another, the mysteries were starting to make a little more sense. "Is that why you were working at McDonald's?"

"It was just simple money, okay?" Aedan said, glaring at me. "That's all it was supposed to be - something to get the winter started right. I didn't plan on you blowing my cover. It all just kind of fell to pieces, I guess. I thought...It'd only be fair for you to take a bit of responsibility, since it was you that messed everything up."

Places to live took money. Having money took holding down a job - or being able to turn a profit, as a demi. Neither of which were things Aedan could do with people hounding him and pursuing him from town to town. What he *could* do was freeze - or starve. Something in the set of his face and the anxious, desperate way he'd set into the food told me everything I needed to know on *that* front. I stifled a groan, pressing a hand to my forehead. My head ached. Already.

"You could have talked to me," I mumbled, trying to rub away the steadily building soreness. It wasn't working. "I wish you'd have *said* something, instead of just coming in and rifling through our stuff.

"Oh, yeah, you'd have *loved* that," Aedan said, throwing himself back down onto the couch with a sigh. "I can see it now - the look of altruistic joy all over your face as I come begging. Yeah, right. That's not how people work."

"We might have been able to do *something*," I said, fixing my eyes onto him even as my face reddened. "And either way it doesn't give you the right to just walk in here."

There was no real anger in my voice. It was just cereal and some beer and an old sweatshirt. We could replace all of it. But if he was in trouble, and he didn't want to so much as *ask* if we could help him...I sighed. It didn't bode well for his chances dealing with whatever happened to come at him next. He was too stubborn by half.

"Yeah, right, right," Aedan said, pulling a hand through his hair and trying to work some of the bed-head loose. "That's what you do now, isn't it? Saw your two new friends. What's their story?"

I knew enough about Aedan and the way he talked to recognize a subject change when one was waved in front of my face. I let it slide. He clearly didn't like talking about himself, and for someone who *seemed* to be older than he let on, he was more than a little embarrassed by how things had played out for him at the McDonald's. It wasn't his fault - I knew that, knew that if I'd walked on and kept my powers to myself, he'd probably have slipped right under their radar - but that didn't seem to matter to him.

Dwelling on it would only make it worse. So I forced a smile, jerking my chin towards the bedrooms. "Right. Loren and Brendon. Picked both of them up a few weeks ago. They'd been snagged by a three-man crew, taking them north."

His nose wrinkled. "Fuckers. Anything useful?"

I eyed him for a long, steady moment, unsure it was my place to be handing out their information to other demis. But it was *Aedan*. He was crazy, yeah, but he didn't seem the slightest bit interested in hunting other demis. "Both of them are fledglings. He's some sort of weather-worker, and she gives dreams at a touch."

"Well *that's* not worth much, is it?" Aedan muttered, his voice low enough that I was certain he hadn't intended for me to hear.

Even as I opened my mouth, getting ready to say something, a dark shape moved from within the mouth of the hallway. A wedge of light fell down across their face, highlighting their features.

Keira drifted closer, her steps unsure at first but gaining confidence as she inched into the living room. From the guilty look in her eyes as she glanced towards me, I knew she'd been eavesdropping. Fine. Whatever. Out of everything that had happened so far that morning, her listening in on me and Aedan was the least of our worries.

"You're here," she said, letting a smile creep onto her face. "When did you get here?"

Aedan perked up almost immediately, his spine straightening an inch. "A...A little bit ago. Was out east for a bit, across the border. Had to wander for a while."

"Oh. Why didn't you say anything?"

Aedan let a sigh tear from between his teeth, rolling his head to the side until he could glare at me. "Your brother asked the same thing. I was just looking in. Just passing through."

"Oh."

"What about you, eh? How's the relic going?"

Her smile widened. "I-I don't know. It's hard to tell, really. But when I looked at Brendon the other day, it was like I could see water dripping through his hair. There was lightning in his eyes. A-And Loren, she-"

She drifted on and on, expounding on all the various ways her abilities had grown in the weeks and months since we'd seen Aedan last. From the way they were talking, I could only assume that they'd conversed since I'd yelled at Aedan for giving her a relic. I just sighed, forcing the irritation down, and tried to pick up on as much as I could. She was growing - and quickly. More quickly that I would have expected, although it wasn't like I had a great deal of knowledge to draw on.

For his part, Aedan just let her chatter, rocking back and forth in his seat gently. His expression seemed innocent and amiable enough, but his eyes were razor-sharp. He was listening, then, and listening hard.

They both glanced up as I stood, crossing the room to the door in three quick steps.

"You're going out?" Keira said, straightening. "Why?"

"Just need a few things. And I have a phone call I need to make. I'll be back in a few minutes. No need to get up."

At my words, they both settled. That sounded too much like *chores*, I knew, and chores were boring. The conversation was already rising anew as I let the door click shut behind me.

The phone was dialing before I'd crossed half the distance to my car. It connected after a few rings.

"What?" Greyson said, his voice soaked through with annoyance.

"I'm just checking in. Aedan showed up this morning. Just so you know."

"What, you're just calling me about this now? He was at your damn house, so how did you not know that?" The annoyance was fast giving way to derision.

"He didn't exactly announce himself. It's fine. Whatever. I just wanted to make sure you knew he was here."

"Yep." Short and to the point - as usual. I gave up.

"Thanks, Greyson."

The phone line was already dead as I lowered the speaker from my ear. It made sense. Greyson had no reason to tell us our own friend was in town, at our house. He'd just thought Aedan would act a little *more* like our ally. So had I.

So be it. I popped the door on my car, sliding into the seat. The engine turned a moment later.

My mind spun, whirling this way and that as I eased up the road and into the parking lot of the Meijer near the center of town. It churned over the same questions as before - what we were going to do, how we were going to keep ourselves safe. Aedan's being here and his plight were just cherries on top of the shit sundae.

We'd need more food, if we had *him* sucking down a week's worth of leftovers before I could stop him. And drinks. And more beer. Definitely more beer.

I lingered on my way to the door, running my hands over the coats on the rack. He'd seemed at home in the clothes he'd stolen...but at the same time, he was easily a few inches shorter than I was, and skinnier besides. It didn't really *fit*, and besides, it would only be getting colder from here out. It wasn't like I wanted the asshole to freeze to death for want of a coat. Swallowing a curse at the thought of how much this little trip was going to cost me, I grabbed one and threw it in the cart.

The others looked up as I slid back into the house. Aedan and Keira sat in the living room, the TV on and playing reruns of something from the 80's. Brendon and Loren were nowhere in sight. They must have slipped out when they got the chance. Smart.

There was a question in Keira's eyes as I dropped the bags onto the counter. Aedan just stared, his gaze skeptical. He'd found Greyson's liquor, I saw with a fresh wave of irritation. The smell of it wafted across the room from where him and Keira sat.

Well, that saved me a bit of work, at least. I set the case of beer I'd bought down where they could see it, unloading the bags one after another beside it. The coat went on top.

"What's all that?" Keira said slowly, her eyes drifting to me. "Jon?"

"I don't want to see you skulking around again," I said, keeping my voice low. "If we'd had other demis here, if Brendon or Loren had been out there with a gun, you would have gotten *shot*. Or worse."

He snorted. "So?"

"So it's fucking stupid, and there's no point, and neither of them need to feel like they've murdered someone for absolutely no good reason."

"Fine."

I stopped myself, ready to launch into my next argument. He'd conceded that easier than I thought. "If you're in the area, you're always welcome to stay here. Just like Loren, just like Brendon." God, it hurt, having to lay it out in simple terms. But I knew that putting it clearly was the best way. "You can take this stuff. What's left when you decide to leave, anyway. Don't *starve*."

A humorless chuckle slipped past his lips. "It's been a bit. Not planning on it anytime soon."

Keira's face was white as she glanced back at Aedan, her eyes wide. He ignored her, staring at me.

"That's an awful lot of generosity. What's the catch, there, Jonny?" His smirk widened. "Nothing in life's ever free, right?"

"You're not wrong," I said, easing myself down onto my usual chair around the table. The beer was still within arms reach. I snagged one, popping the top open.

He scowled at me. "So?"

A crooked smile tugged at my lips. "So, you've told me half-truths and danced around actually answering damn near everything since the day we met. I want actual answers - and I want you to answer the questions I ask. Not just dodge or tell me what *you* want to share."

His eyes narrowed, fixed on me. I held his gaze, refusing to budge so much as an inch. He gave first. His eyes flicked over to the food on the counter, the coat and the supplies and the beer. I could see him doing the math in his head.

"Just be honest with us for a little while," I said softly. "That's all I'm asking. Then you can come crash here over the winter instead of freezing to death in the snow." I chuckled. "Assuming you don't have a horde of other demis on your tail. You don't, do you?"

"Don't be ridiculous," he mumbled, and then fell quiet. He held his silence for a long, weighted moment, a muscle in his jaw twitching. The clock above the sink ticked away, counting off the seconds of eerie quiet that had fallen over the kitchen. I was just about ready to launch into my next argument when he leaned over, snatching up Greyson's still half-full bottle of whiskey from where it sat on the counter, long since forgotten.

Keira and I both watched, mute and more than a little stunned, as he popped the cork from its stem. He didn't bother reaching for a glass. He just tipped it up, taking a gulp of liquor big enough that my headache started anew just thinking about it. A second gulp followed the first.

The glass bottle hit the coffee table beside the couch with a solid-sounding *clink*. Aedan paused another moment, wiping his mouth.

And then he turned to me, his gaze steady despite what he'd just drank. A smile plastered itself across his face, cold and cheap and entirely forced.

"Okay. What do you want to know?"

CHAPTER TWENTY-NINE

The room was eerily quiet. None of us moved. None of us spoke.

He'd actually agreed. I hadn't thought he would - it would be more like Aedan to scoff in my face, loading up his arms with the booze and whatever else he felt like taking, and stroll right on out the door. But there he sat, growing more red-faced by the second and tapping his fingers with impatience.

Finally, he made an irritated noise in the back of his throat. "For fuck's sake, Jon, would you-"

"Are you human?" I said, the words falling out before I could snatch them back. I could feel my ears start burning a single second later. "I-I mean, are you a demi? A normal one. It just seems-"

"Jesus fucking christ," Aedan muttered, dropping his head into his hands and scratching at his scalp. "*That's* how you start off? Yes, Jon. I'm a damn human."

"But you're so different. If you're a demi, then...I mean, for lack of a better term, what *are* you?"

"Don't be rude."

"It has nothing to do with being rude," I said, on the verge of snarling at him. He'd said he would be honest - I should have known he'd take 'honesty' to just be another word for 'combative.'

"What was all that with Matt?" Keira said, cutting me off with a sidelong glare. "You two knew each other. Clearly."

"Did. Once," Aedan said, reaching for his bottle again. I didn't stop him. The more drunk he got, the more he'd talk. If he could get drunk. I was beginning to worry about that. I hadn't thought someone as small as him would have such an ironclad stomach. "It didn't really work out." A crooked smile flashed across his face for an instant. "Friends usually don't."

"But why?" Keira said, leaning closer. "What happened?"

He sighed. "What usually does, girl. Especially when the friend is an unbonded human. They start by trying to help, then they try and *save* you. Then, they start getting curious." A low chuckle slipped from between his lips. "And then they get greedy. Wouldn't it help both of us, after all? I get to ditch the damn thing, and he gets to take it."

"Your relic? But he couldn't," I said slowly. The path back to the questions I actually wanted answered lay right in front of me. Keira had just taken us on a bit of a roundabout road to get there. The smug little curl to her lips told me she knew. "I remember - when Matt took your relic. Your knife. That *is* it, right?"

The couch shifted as Aedan leaned back, shaking his head. And then he lifted his shirt with his free hand, sliding loose the sheathed knife that had been taped against his chest. He set it down on the table with a clatter.

"That's it, all right. Same as before."

I shook my head slowly, trying not to stare at the worn, bloodstained blade. "But when Matt took it away from you...when Jake shot you, you didn't die."

He grinned, taking another hit from the bottle. I was feeling sick just *looking* at him. "I did not."

"Then what?" I snapped, getting more than a little irritated at his complete refusal to answer a question. "Don't dance around the questions again, Aedan. Come on. We deserve to know what's going on here. What's *really* going on."

"My relic follows some different rules. That's all," he said, masking a burp with one hand.

"Why?" Keira said, holding his gaze with her own. "Why is yours different? What's special? Can we really trust our relics to behave like you and Jake said, when things seem so...abnormal?"

"Don't...You don't have to worry about that," Aedan said, pressing his hand to his forehead. "Don't overthink this. Mine is...Well, my relic is different because it was created differently from yours, and because I wanted different things from it than you did."

I paused. "Created."

Aedan leaned forward in his seat. He didn't look at me. He just reached towards where I sat and snagged one of the beers off the counter.

Every inch of him radiated refusal. He *didn't* want to talk about this. Tough. We'd been kept in the dark long enough. I wasn't about to let him run from it. "As in, it was made differently."

"That's what created means, isn't it?" Aedan said, a bit of his old snark sneaking back into his tone.

Silence stretched out between us, filling the room with its heavy, deafening atmosphere.

"How...How old are you, exactly?" Keira said, her voice soft. "I mean, uh. I thought these things were ancient."

There was something else, though. Something lingering on the edge of my thoughts. "When we first met," I said slowly. "You said I was speaking the 'old tongue'. And you spoke some weird language, back during Matt's little visit. In the truck. Something old."

Aedan made a face, running his hand through his hair.

"Just spit it out and we won't ask you about it again," I said, fixing a smile on my face.

"Yes, you will," Aedan mumbled. "You've got to be fucking kidding me."

"Aedan-"

"Relics," he said, lifting his chin to meet my eyes. "You keep calling them that. Over and over and over. Jake and them, they call them foci. But you call them relics."

I hesitated. "Because you do. And, I don't know. It just seems-"

"Right. It seems like the *right* thing to call them," Aedan said flatly.

Keira nodded, sliding forward to lean her elbows on her knees. "Yeah."

He smiled mirthlessly. "That's because it *is* the right name. No one remembers, so they don't care. But it's how it should be."

"What do you mean, remem-"

"They're called relics because they're leftovers," Aedan said, talking over me effortlessly. "Artifacts. Antiques. The scraps left over when everything else burned away."

I fell silent, and Keira didn't so much as twitch. Aedan's cheeks were bright red, but he just glanced away. "Really, you lot are idiots," he muttered. "In this world, this *reality*, you all found magic toys and never wondered what exactly was going on?"

"We wondered, Aedan," I said, swallowing a groan. "You wouldn't tell us."

"You asked how old I was, Keira," Aedan said abruptly, ignoring me completely. His eyes bored into hers. She nodded, still silent. "Old. Old enough to remember when it wasn't just relics at work in the world."

Her brow furrowed. "What? Besides for relics? Like, other...magic?"

"You've got it. Real Harry Potter shit," Aedan said, downing the rest of his beer in one long swallow a moment later. He wiped his mouth on his sleeve, shrugging. "It was a thing."

I sat back hard, my mind whirling. "If you're making this up to make a joke at our expense, Aedan, I'll-"

"Damn it, Jon, what'd I just say?" Aedan snapped, glaring at me. "Don't be an idiot. You've got magic now. You've known the relics are old. Don't be surprised when this all goes back farther than you thought."

"Then what happened?" I said, trying and failing to keep the challenge from my tone. "Where is it? The history books would have a *field* day with this story, Aedan. They don't mention it. So where'd this magic go?

He grinned. "Well, t-that's the big fucking question, isn't it?"

I blinked. *That* wasn't the answer I'd expected. "W-What?"

"No one really knows, Jonny. There were theories." He reached for his knife, waving the blade around carelessly. I drew back, my eyes drifting from the weapon to his wide, slightly unfocused eyes. "All we know is this. There was, at one point, magic in the world. True magic. It wasn't there for everyone, and it wasn't all that strong even for most who had it, but it was *there*. And then, over the span of a mere handful of years..." He shrugged. "It went away. The magical font people had found inside themselves, disappeared. Dried up. Faded to nothing. Not sure how long ago it was exactly, anymore. Thousand years. Maybe a bit more. And all we're left with is folklore and legend."

Part of me wondered why this was relevant. Part of me was *sure* that he was doing exactly what I'd just accused him of, and making up fanciful stories to get around answering us properly.

And yet, my relic glowed warm and alive against my chest, and I couldn't see even a single lie standing out among his words. I just swallowed, trying to force my fear and confusion away, and put my mind back to listening. He didn't so much as slow down, even though I was sure both Keira and I looked more than a little shellshocked.

"See, here's the thing. It was right about the same time when people started discovering you could take magic and *trap* it," Aedan said, tapping his knife against his knee. His leg was bouncing, his foot dancing against the ground. "Force it into a container and seal it in."

"A relic," I said softly.

"I'm not giving you a damn trophy for stating the obvious. Relics. The months keep passing, and day by day, there's a little less magic in the air," Aedan said. He was spitting the words out faster and faster, like he was racing to be done. I wondered how many times he'd told this story.

I wondered if he'd told Matt, once upon a time.

"Now, some people started blaming the artificers," he said, glancing at me and away without slowing down at all. "Said it was their fault for putting magic in a jar. Said they were taking it away from everyone else."

"Weren't they?" Keira said. Her gaze was fixed on him.

He shrugged. "Who knows? The artificers said no. They *insisted* that it started long before anyone tried making a relic. They said that if magic was failing, relics were the only option left." His eyes were hard despite the way they drifted, not quite able to fix on mine. "In the end, didn't really matter who was right, did it?"

"What do you mean?" I said slowly. "I mean, I know there's nothing here *now*, so I can kind of guess, but-"

"It didn't take long for people to p-piece together that with magic beginning to fade…well…having a relic would be the only way to keep up with the other relic-wielders," Aedan said, sagging back against the couch. "People fucking *like* power. So they all started…scrambling for them. Making as many as they could. Arming their houses and families and guilds with what little was left. Trying to grab at straws." He grinned. It wasn't a nice expression. "Even if it was the cause of magic's decay, it didn't matter. No one was going to stop making relics. Not really."

Keira whistled, a soft, low sound. "Race to the bottom."

"You got it," Aedan said, chuckling as he reached for the bottle again. We waited as he took another sip.

"Does this all…I mean, I'm interested. I'm *really* interested," I said, feeling my cheeks warm. "Only, is this really the best time for-"

"Shut the fuck up, Jon. You want to know why things are different for me, you need to know the context. Won't mean a damn thing otherwise," he snapped, rolling his eyes. "I'm not telling this again, so *shut up and listen.* Anyway. Anyone with a scrap of skill was making the things. That's all fine and dandy. Only, there came a time when the last scraps of magic were drying up entirely. Was i-inevitable. Everyone knew."

"And no more new relics," Keira said quietly.

"No more relics," Aedan said, grinning crookedly at the bottle in his hand. "Not everyone w-was so willing to accept it, y'know. Not somethin' like that. Some people were late to the whole party, an' got to feeling a bit left out. They still wanted a relic or two of their own."

I shook my head. "But you said-"

"Said that the world's magic had dried up. Mostly. I know what I fuckin' said, Jon," Aedan snapped, glaring at me again. His mood changed faster than I could react to, like someone was flipping a switch. "Only, see, it wasn't like *all* magic went away, was it? Some people...well, some people still have a lil' bit left in 'em. Bit of a mana-well, like." There wasn't even an ounce of humor in his expression as he smirked. "And life's a little like magic, isnnit?"

My breath caught in my throat. I could see where he was going. The world around us was dark, filled with horrible things that I'd never have thought possible just a few short months before. I'd almost gotten used to the horrors we'd seen thus far. Almost. I should have expected no less of the times that came before, and yet, it still sent a dagger of anxiety straight down into my heart.

Keira was a statue across from us. "You mean, they-"

"Humans aren't that expensive. Weren't. I mean, it wasn't *simple,* but they were already takin' enough of us. Wasn't but the work of a moment to skim a few dozen souls off the top of the ship." He shrugged one shoulder, taking another sip. "Never saw 'em coming. Wasn't looking, till it was too late. Stupid. Fuckin' *stupid.*"

He paused a moment before plowing onward, but my mind was already drifting. As he spoke, his words growing ever more slurred but still filled with an undeniable *truth,* I just stared at the floor, nodding along. I could see it, see the images carried along with every syllable and phrase he spoke. They painted a picture, bringing his words to life as he meandered on.

I could see the ships, hulking wooden behemoths. I could feel the wood under my feet, smell the salt and the fear. The shot of pain as he stepped out into the sunlight again at last was a dagger in my eyes.

The taste of blood that hung in the air was overpowering as he continued, laying each turn and event out with shocking, matter-of-fact clarity. Keira was white as bone where she sat, her blue eyes perfectly round. I hardly noticed. I could see the compound stretching out in front of us, hear the quiet murmuring of voices around me slowly swelling as the other captives grew more uncomfortable by the second.

"They didn't know what was happening," I heard Aedan whisper. "They thought it was just another market, like any other. I knew better. My mother. S-She was a hedgewitch. Taught me pieces, when she could, when I could manage it. Could see it was different. See the one that fancied himself a mage. Ridiculous."

The story unfolded, image after image. I could see them - the symbols, painted against the stone of the ledge in front of them. Their language was different, unfamiliar, but I knew what they were for. Power, and binding, and knowledge. The fear bubbled up in me again, carried along by the thin, anxious thread in his voice hidden under the liquor.

It erupted in full as the first man was taken, dragged away from the others to stand barefoot on the stone. The mage murmured something, his words obscured by time and distance.

Screams rang in my ears as he staggered and fell, blood flowing from the gash the mage's knife had torn in his throat.

I knew that knife.

Still, Aedan continued. He seemed to be going on automatic, as though once he'd started he couldn't stop until it was done. His summary of events was no less clinical than it had been, but my mind filled in the gaps. I watched helplessly as the act was repeated over and over, the mage inspecting the blade with interest as each victim's body was dragged off to the side.

I could feel the guard take hold of my arm, latching on even as I tried to slink further back into the crowd. Feel my wrists light in pain as I struggled, the skin giving way under my bindings. See the mage, coated in blood and eyeing me with cold disinterest.

And I saw the stones, littered with symbols nearly obscured with the mess of my fellows but beginning to thrum with power.

"Knew it was close to being done," Aedan said, somewhere in front of me. "Knew a thing or two about spellwork, myself. More than that ass. There wasn't enough mana in the air to make a relic from scratch, no. Just enough to tie the thing shut. I-I thought, no. No, no, no. Wasn't ready to roll over. Not like *that*."

The blade gleamed in the mage's hand as he stepped closer, reaching out. There were symbols on it, too. His red-stained fingers were rough in my hair, pulling me higher and holding me still. "Had a little left in me. Was savin' it. D'nno what for. Just enough to reach out and touch their working. Coax it to listen."

I gasped, flinching as the blade sank into my neck, tearing a line of fire across my skin. And just like that, he was staring at me, right there in my living room. Keira hadn't so much as twitched. Aedan held my gaze a moment longer, swaying gently.

I shook my head slowly, swallowing over and over as bile rose in my throat. My head throbbed. "But...How did you-"

"That's an awful nice relic you've got there," Aedan said abruptly, waving towards my neck and the chain hanging around it. He had his knife back in his hand. "How'd you get yours, eh?"

I eyed the thing with newfound repulsion. The memory of it plunging into my throat was altogether too fresh. "Aedan, I don't think that's really-"

"Oh, I've sat here answering like a good, obedient type," Aedan said, spitting each syllable out with care. "You can answer me one."

I sighed, sliding my necklace free from my shirt and holding it in the palm of my hand. The intertwined rings stared up at me. "I...found it at a pawn shop. Hated the place. but I was out with my grandpa. He liked that store. He was sick. I wasn't supposed to know, but I did." A shrug slid through my shoulders. "We'd never really had a chance to get to know each other, even though we didn't live all that far apart. I was too young, I guess. He seemed happy when I was interested so..." I shrugged. "I made like I was interested in this. Better than baseball cards, at least. He bought it for me."

"Go on."

I glanced up at him, my brow furrowing. "Go on, what? I don't have a story like yours, Aedan. I still don't understand how you're alive, if you-"

"Let me guess, s-since you're all stuffy," Aedan snapped, a bit of life returning to his tone as he glared at me. "You said he was...sick. That you didn't know him very well." He held a hand to his face, hiding another burp. "Make you guilty?"

My ears were burning. "I-I guess. I *wanted* to talk to him. I wanted to understand him. I just didn't-" I stopped, blinking. "I didn't know how."

"An' there it is," Aedan said, his voice uncharacteristically soft. He was watching me, his gaze far sharper than it had any right to be. "You got all the tools you needed. Lucky you."

I could feel the heat washing off my face. "So what- you get what you ask for?"

He shrugged. "Sometimes. Some relics are more subtle about it t-than others. Anyway. You got communication skills. Me, well." A chuckle slipped from his throat. "Only really wanted one thing, didn't I? To be alive. To be alive and somewhere *else*."

"So that's it," Keira said at last. She was still pale, I saw, and her hands were trembling, but her eyes were fixed on him. "That's how it started. A-And, your relic-"

"It's mine b-by blood," Aedan said, holding it up again. The tip of the blade wobbled back and forth. "Seem to be...stuck with it. Kind of thing. Doesn't r-really know when to quit." His shoulder bobbed in another shrug. "Maybe it's the blood bond. Maybe it's that it was...was born to keep me going. Dunno. Didn't come with ins'ructions."

I opened my mouth, but nothing came out. I...didn't know anymore. There had been questions, things I'd wanted to ask, but somehow, he'd wiped all of them away in a few brief minutes. I just sat, letting the story I'd just been told churn back and forth in my mind.

I'd known Aedan was old. I just hadn't known he was *that* old. I'd put everything labeled 'relics' in a mental box, pushed it away and disregarded it as too old and unavailable. I should have known he'd be involved, somehow. "Then, you...I mean you didn't die," Keira said. Her voice was low enough I almost couldn't hear. "You bonded with the relic they were trying to make?"

Aedan burped, not bothering to try and hide it behind his hand. "Yep. Opened my eyes on the other side of the compound, butt-ass n-naked and scared as hell. Started running."

"And never stopped," I said, just as softly. "So you've been running for, what. A thousand years?"

"Oh, don't fuckin' ask me to count," Aedan said with a groan, pressing a hand to his forehead. "Didn't...I wasn't runnin' for *all* of it. Just most. That's just...life."

Keira sat back in her chair. Her face was still white, her eyes tight and dark. "Oh. I mean...that's...so you just-"

"*Are* you just running, though?" I whispered. There was no way they should have heard me, but they did. Both of them stopped, glancing over at me.

"Is he lying?" Keira said, folding her arms across her chest. She glared daggers at me, as though my contradicting him was some sort of personal attack.

I hesitated. "Well...no." He wasn't. I could see that. But there were memories flitting back and forth through my mind, hints that he might not be *entirely* truthful with that statement. Even if he wasn't lying, that didn't mean he was telling the whole truth, did it?

"You took my relic away from me, back in the truck," I said, my words growing in confidence second by second. "You *made* me give it to you. Like you were looking for something. And you collect relics. Why? They're no good to you. Unless - can you bond with more than one-"

"Don't be an ass," Aedan snapped. "Already told you that's not poss'ble. Told you earlier. Those're mine. Keep 'em away from enemies. Less people to kill."

"And that's it?"

His mouth shut with an audible *clack*. "Don't be suspicious, Jonny," he said, leaning back. A smirk grew across his face all the while. "I'm just bein' safe."

"You're looking for something," I said, holding his gaze with my own. "You are, aren't you? A relic. A specific one."

"Not...well, maybe," Aedan murmured, settling back on the couch. "Not really a specific *one*. Jus' a particular skillset."

"What do you mean? What possible use could you have for something like that?" Keira said. The angry tone had vanished from her voice somewhere along the line, right about the same time Aedan had caved to my questions.

"You said it earlier," I interrupted, cutting Aedan off before he could reply. He glared at me, but I kept going. "Matt wanted your relic. You said he thought it was a win-win. Why would he think that?"

Aedan chuckled, leaning back against the couch. His eyes were slits, his gaze fixed on mine, and the knife lay carelessly across his lap. His hand rested against it. The gesture looked completely natural on him, the product of centuries of habit. "Well, y'see, Jonny. Findin' a way to get free 'n give one of you this fucker'd just make m-my job that much easier, eh?" He grinned. There wasn't an ounce of amusement in the expression.

"Then I wouldn't have to keep looking."

CHAPTER THIRTY

Then he wouldn't have to keep looking. His words should have echoed around our living room, carrying with them all of the weight that settled over my thoughts at hearing them. They fell flat instead. Keira and I stared, mouths hanging ajar, and just...sat. Both of us were processing, trying to make sense of the story we'd heard.

I reached the end of my mental downward spiral first. "Wait. So....wait. Are you saying you're *trying* to get rid of your knife?"

He opened his mouth to reply. A burp slid out instead. Making a face and pressing a hand to his face, Aedan sighed. And then he let it fall. "Right."

"Your relic."

"Mmhm."

"You want to *no longer have it*."

The look Aedan gave me, cracking one eye, was no longer so friendly. "Am I stutterin'?"

Well, he *was*. But before I could say anything more, Keira was there, her words filling the gap I'd left. "You're trying to die."

A crooked grin spread across Aedan's face. "More or less."

Once again, we were left staring, gaping wordlessly. Aedan didn't seem to notice. He lifted his stolen beer higher, draining the last few drops from its depths, and set it down onto the end table with a clatter.

"So, what," I said at last. "*That's* what you're looking for? What you've been doing? Looking...looking for-"

"Lookin' for somethin' that would let me break up with it. Finally,"

Aedan said, waving the blade around again. "Or someone. I'm not picky."

I'd thought Keira was bone-white during his story. She'd gotten even paler. "I don't know if I'm okay with this," I said quietly, forcing myself not to glance her way. I didn't want to see the look on her face.

Aedan only chuckled, his laughter growing by the second. "I'm not askin' if you're ok with it, Jonny. Not like I've decided this on the fly. And thas' the old story, innit? Tired old immortal, wantin' to be done. Shouldn't be so shocked."

"It's not exactly the most original thing I've ever heard, no," I echoed softly.

His laughter grew louder still. "See? Who knows. Mayhap some've those stories was...was 'bout me. *Inspired*, like. Who knows. Could happen."

"So why were you so desperate to get away from Matt, then?" a razor-sharp voice snapped from alongside me. I glanced over, taken aback. I'd expected Keira to be shaken, or shellshocked, or sad. She was pale, yes - but there was only fire in her expression. "From what you've said, he was right. Win-win."

"Maybe. If he actually knew a damn way to do what...what he wanted," Aedan said, swallowing his laughter just long enough to waggle the tip of his knife at her. "Boy doesn't...well....didn't have th' first clue what he was doin'." He shrugged, unrepentant. "Let 'im try, once. For a while. Among others."

"But he couldn't-"

"It's a mystery," Aedan said, droning on as if I hadn't said a word. His face was red, his eyes unfocused, and he was leaning back against my couch as though it was all that was keeping him up. "Kill me, I pop out of it. Take it away from me, it jus' comes back." His smile went crooked. "After a week. Collapses *suck*." His gaze fixed on mine, then slid to Keira's. "Tried everythin'. So spare me your concerns."

I couldn't help the snort that slipped out. "And yet you still think you can find something to do it for you?"

"There were stories," he murmured, his voice suddenly quiet. "Somethin' that could do it. A relic that could silence other relics, maybe. Or one that could shatter bonds. Maybe it's sleepin'. There's *got* to be one. Maybe its owner doesn't know what they've...what they've got."

"Or maybe it's just a story."

Keira shot me an irritated look from the corner of her eye. I didn't so much as glance back her way. It needed to be said.

A sigh slipped from between Aedan's lips. "Maybe. Maybe. But, see, if'n it...if it *is* just a story, then there's just one shot left."

"If there's a different way, then why are you running around chasing legends?"

"Got to age out." His voice was low enough I almost missed it. "Relics...We're weaker, when we're old. Sometimes."

"Greyson isn't weak," Keira said, her words quiet. "He's stronger than us."

"*Sometimes.* An'...well, 'm thinkin' that if this thing's attached to my blood..." He shrugged. "Maybe it'll weaken with me."

"If you can get there," I said, the true meaning of his words sinking in at last. "But, Aedan, you're at least a thousand. That's old. Wouldn't it have-"

"Everytime I die."

I stopped, my words dying on my lips. He was yawning, no longer meeting my eyes at all, and his hold on his knife was more tenuous.

"I *reset*," he said at last, spitting the word out. "Thas' the big trick. I pop back. Right how I was *then*."

Just for a second, I could see another flash of it - green grass, and a brilliant sky overhead, and the heat of too many bodies pressed in around me.

I blinked, clearing the foreign images from my mind, and glanced down. My stolen sweatshirt was big on him, but I could just barely see the swollen, angry red skin and white tracks of half-healed scars dancing along his wrists like bracelets. My skin prickled in response, remembering the cut of the shackles.

He grabbed at his sleeves a moment later, pulling them the rest of the way down. His eyes glared daggers at me.

"But if all you have to do is make it until you're old, why have you been around for-"

"I've told you *enough*," Aedan snapped, his words lacking any real anger from behind the wobble of the liquor in him. "Thas' more'n fair for some cheap booze and a crappy shirt."

The shirt he'd stolen - he'd seemed happy enough with it before right then. "Aedan, just-"

"Told you m' life's story, what more do you want? Fuck off. I'm tired." He rolled over even as he spat the words at me, sinking back into the cushions and reaching for the blanket Keira had dumped onto him.

"But you *just-*" I stopped, abandoning the effort. He'd only woken up from his first nap a little bit ago. If he went back to sleep, it would be night before he woke up.

Of course, he *had* just pounded several beers and a substantial portion of a fifth of whiskey. Swallowing a groan, I inched over to the sink, fishing a bucket out from under the counter. It dropped silently to the carpet beside his head as I stalked past. "If you're going to be sick, get it in *there*. Not on my couch, not on my carpet."

"Mmm." He didn't even open his eyes - but he did manage to raise a middle finger in the direction of my voice.

Moments later, the soft sound of snoring rose from the couch for the second time that day.

Perfect.

Out of everything I'd hoped for out of my Saturday, this was about bottom on the list - but at least I wasn't having to call off work again. My office seemed to be used to flighty coders, and so long as I got my stuff done, they didn't really seem to mind. All the same, too much of my time and energy of late had gone to the whole *demi* situation, rather than *me*.

Forcing my complaints and whining back down, I threw my hands up, heading for the door.

Keira glanced up, her hair flying with the sudden motion. "Jon? What are you doing?"

"His stuff's all out there in the snow still," I muttered. "It'll get soaked. Since a lot of it seems to be *my* stuff, might as well go protect my property."

She was on her feet in an instant, bounding across the room in three steps to seize her coat off the wall. "I'll come too."

"Fine. Whatever."

She didn't say a word, despite my brisk, chilly tone. She was thinking about everything too. I could see it in her eyes, the tense set of her shoulders.

Both of us breathed a little easier as the door slid shut behind us, cutting off the steadily rising sound of Aedan snoring.

The crunch of snow underfoot was all we were left with. I stared at the path, tracing my steps back into the woods.

"So…" Keira started, but fell quiet a moment later.

I glanced over at her, a chuckle bubbling up. "I don't know, either."

"I want to help him, but I don't know how we're supposed to *do* that," she muttered, kicking at a clump of ice. It shattered into a thousand pieces, scattering across the flawless white.

"He seems to have his mind made up. If he's really that old...maybe it's up to him."

Her eyes flicked to mine again. "Do you believe him? What he said?"

I shrugged, letting my hand rise and clasp around my necklace. "I don't think he was lying. Beyond that...I don't know."

"Your relic didn't...zap you with electricity when he talked, or whatever it does?"

I raised an eyebrow at her. "How do you think my relic *works?*"

She stuck her tongue out at me, planting her elbow in my side. I skittered away, chuckling softly. It felt nice - to be normal, to play at that little bit of peace. After the morning we'd had, I appreciated every bit of fun I could find.

"Jon?"

I slowed, glancing over to her. She stood, halfway back in the trees. Her hand was pressed to her coat - I knew she kept her glasses on a fine, delicate chain, hanging down where no one could see them from within her jacket. Her lips were pursed, her eyes downcast.

"I...I don't really understand what's going on, but, I..." She hesitated a moment, her mouth hanging open. "I *saw* things. When Aedan was talking."

"A ship, right?" I said, my voice soft. "And a field of grass."

"Just like he was describing. It was like...there was a window in front of him, reflecting back at me. Just a reflection in the lens of my glasses." Her eyes flicked up to meet mine. "Does that mean-"

"I saw something too," I said softly. "Only, it was more like a dream, half-remembered images in my mind. It wasn't *solid*."

"What I saw was solid," Keira whispered.

I faltered, remembering too clearly what Aedan had told us. The pain, the fear, the blood. "Are you okay?"

"I'm...I'm fine. Do you think it was his relic, showing us?"

"What, Aedan's knife?" I said, swallowing a laugh. "Doesn't really seem like his type of skill, does it?" I shrugged. "He was telling us the story. I probably read into his words - and you probably...I don't know. Saw into his soul or something."

She made a face. "Oh, he's going to *love* that."

"He'll be fine," I said, offering her a wan smile.

"But, for both of us to have almost the same thing happen-"

"We're siblings, aren't we? Maybe it's just one of those things. We think in similar ways and all that."

A scoff slipped from her throat. "Don't lump me in with you."

A crooked smile crept onto my face. I just pulled my jacket tighter and jerked my chin for her to follow.

She sighed, but trudged after me. His tent was ahead, still half-buried under a snowdrift. "But will he?" she muttered, shoving her hands into her pockets. "Be fine, I mean. He's homeless and hungry."

Lifting my eyes to the sky and praying for a scrap of patience, I shrugged halfheartedly. "We'll make sure he doesn't starve. Anytime he can make it back here."

"I suppose."

Kicking the tent flap open, I plunged my hand in, finding his backpack waiting at my fingertips. I'd hardly ever seen Aedan without the thing. He must really have been off-balance, to have followed me back to the house and left it behind. I slung it over my shoulder without hesitation, pausing a moment at the surprising weight of it. Keira bundled up the rest of what was thrown inside, blankets and a pillow and assorted food he'd pilfered from our pantry.

Together, quiet at last as we wrestled with our own thoughts, the two of us made our way back to the house, step by snowy step.

***

We dumped the recovered possessions in the back room, still half-finished and filled with the detritus of our home repair. Both of us cast anxious glances out to the living room, but the only sound that drifted our way was the steady, unrelenting noise of Aedan snoring.

"He's relentless," I muttered.

Keira grinned. "He's hammered. Wouldn't notice if we brought a marching band through."

"What's going on?"

We glanced up as one, eyes fixed on the narrow door to the hallway beyond. Loren peered through, the light at her back casting the rest of her into shadow. Brendon hovered a few steps behind her. He smiled sheepishly, offering a tiny wave. Loren just glanced between us nervously.

"Morning," I said, straightening. "I mean, well. Afternoon."

"Not for that much longer," Loren said, her nose wrinkling. "There's someone on your couch."

"Ah. Yeah," Keira said, running a hand through her hair. "That's Aedan. He's kind of a friend."

The thin, tightly-wound woman didn't look appeased. "He's a demi, isn't he?"

I nodded. "Y-Yeah. Don't mind him. He just kind of comes and goes. It's...a bit of a long story."

Brendon stiffened, his eyes flicking to Keira's as she spoke the name. There was too much recognition there for my comfort. "Aedan. That's-"

I cleared my throat. "Right. He doesn't want word getting out, so it'll just be our secret. All right? He won't hurt you or anything like that." I shrugged. "Besides, if people come looking for him, they'll be fighting *us*, too."

Her face went pale as she straightened, her shoulders rolling back. "I-I mean, I don't know who you're thinking I'd talk to," she muttered. "I just think you should have at least warned us."

"We really didn't know he was coming either," I said dryly. "Sorry about that."

Her mouth slid open, like she was going to argue further, but Brendon chuckled behind her. The sound brought her up short. A bit of the tension slid from her frame, just like that. "Oh, fine," she said, her voice quiet. "Why not." She slipped from the room a moment later, offering me a thin, wary smile. A coffee mug was clutched between her hands. Brendon followed after a moment later, her constant shadow.

Keira and I exchanged a single look, long and simple and carrying in it all the irritation both of us felt at the situation that had been thrown in our laps.

She vanished into her room with a sigh and a shake of her head, trailing one last wistful glance towards the living room.

I glanced out, my gaze trailing after the three of them. Loren was heading from the door, staring out at the snow beyond, until she hesitated. Her head turned, just a fraction, eyeing Aedan as he slept on the couch. He'd already gotten himself wrapped in the blankets like a caterpillar in a cocoon, half-invisible under the plush fabric, but I could see the muscles in his neck tense, twitching over and over again.

"He's dreaming," she murmured, a crooked smile slipping onto her lips.

I made a face, finding it more than a little hard to share her humor.

"Probably...not anything good." Not between the alcohol and the memories we'd made him relieve. "Can you...see? What he's dreaming, I mean." I eyed her with more than a little curiosity. She was a dream-worker, or so she'd said, but that still meant next to nothing to me.

My hopes were dashed a moment later as she shook her head. "No. Nothing. I don't...that's not how I work," she whispered. I wasn't sure if her quiet was due to some sort of shame at her lack of abilities, or an attempt to let Aedan sleep. She shouldn't have worried. Even if she couldn't see into his dreams she was more useful than I'd been for years, and with as much whiskey as Aedan had downed, we could have held a rave in the house without waking him.

He twitched again. She leaned over, slipping her hand onto his shoulder. "I can't see. I'm not an oneiromancer - but I can impact them. Give dreams, change them. Take them away."

Aedan shivered at her touch, like her hand was frigid cold. But just as quickly as the movement rippled over his skin, he froze - and slowly, gradually, he relaxed against the couch.

"What are you showing him?" I said, glancing up to Loren. "Or, are you-"

"I can't see. Remember?" she said, flashing me the first honest smile she'd given me thus far. "Something happy. That's all I know." Her fingers slipped from his shirt as she stepped back, jamming her hands back into her pockets.

I chuckled. "Well...thanks, then. So that's it? Just like that?"

Her ears were red. She ducked her chin, not meeting my eyes. "I'm...I'm still learning. I've only had my focus a few months. I-I'm sorry."

That shame was back. I shook my head hurriedly. "No, no. I'm the one who should be sorry. I'm not trying to- you're fine. I just haven't seen you cast before."

"And now you have," she mumbled. Her face turned to the side, angling towards where Brendon waited by the door.

"You and Jake need to talk sometime," I said, forcing another smile away. "You two together would really be something."

"We've talked," Loren said, glancing up at me. There was an iron under her expression I hadn't seen before. A night full of firsts. "I think we'll get on just fine." When she looked over to Brendon again, he just smiled at her, zipping his coat up a little more.

I let them go, when they turned to the door and pushed their way out. That little conversation had been the longest conversation we'd had yet. Maybe she was settling in. I just watched them go. For once, it hadn't been Brendon carrying the lion's share of the conversation. In fact, he'd seemed oddly quiet, watching her work her focus.

I let the thought slip from my mind. It was a matter for another day, a day when I wasn't already pushed to my mental limits by horror stories and history. I still had Aedan around, for as long as he chose to stay.

And *I* still had things I needed to do, immortal guest or no. Hearing the door creak shut as the two other demis slipped outside, I ran a hand through my hair, the tasks I had yet to do lining up in front of my mind.

Pushing through into my room, I eased myself into my chair and stared at the wall, still seeing that long-forgotten scene play out behind my eyes.

CHAPTER THIRTY-ONE

Spreadsheets. One after another, after another. They scattered across my desktop, glimmering from my monitors and casting the room around me into harsh light. Lines of code marched past, dancing along the window folded neatly into what little space remained.

Work wasn't what I'd had in mind for my Saturday night, *that* much was for damn sure, but it needed doing. With how much time I'd been missing of late, spending my days seeing after our new demis and getting the house in line, I didn't have much of a choice. My phone glowed with notifications from alongside my keyboard.

Messages from my friends, no doubt. They'd been pestering me, growing more tired by the day of my deflecting them and stalling - but what was I supposed to do? Things had just been too hectic, and my life hadn't exactly been suitable for public viewing for a while. I couldn't justify dragging them into the same mess I was in. I tried to ignore the steady blinking of the light, to pretend I couldn't see it. I'd deal with it later. I needed to *work*. Right. To do my job, the one that kept me paid.

A crooked smile flickered across my lips. Well. The one that kept me paid, at least on the surface. We'd played some shell games, doing what we could to avoid *looking* like we'd just been handed a giant wad of cash, and while most of our legitimate savings had gone to the down payment on the house, we were still surviving just fine off Matt's windfall.

We were doing fine, but for how long? How long could we sustain ourselves? If we wound up attacking other crews roaming through the region like we had Loren and Brendon's captors, would we snag enough of a windfall from their pockets to keep us going? I bit my lip, furiously typing on as though I could somehow put my thoughts to rest by working hard enough. I'd been *asking* my boss for a raise for a while. Maybe, now that I knew what I was doing with my necklace a little better, I could-

My fingers froze, coming to a halt on my keyboard as I stared. What? What was *that* thought? Shame rose hot in my chest like bile. I hadn't been aware of my relic for *that* long - already, I was thinking something like *that*? The memory of accidentally enspelling Mason that long-past day at the gym surged in anew, filling me with a fresh round of guilt.

Even as the angel on my shoulder screamed and moaned, the devil nodded along sagely. It was only understandable, the little voice in the back of my head said. We were looking after more people now, weren't we? We'd taken on a lot of risk. A lot of burden. Shouldn't I use the tools I was given - for their sake? Was that so wrong?

Leaning back in my chair, the dark of the room pressing in around me, I suddenly wasn't so sure. It didn't seem so clear-cut as I'd thought before, with the light of day clearing away the doubts. Everything else had changed. Why shouldn't this, too?

Everything else. I shivered, remembering too well the feel of the knife in my hand, the buck of the pistol as it went off. The way they'd crumpled, eyes-

The chair creaked underneath me as I pushed myself upright, stalking from the room and leaving the horrible thoughts behind. One step at a time. I repeated the words to myself, chanting them in my head like a mantra. Don't bite off too much. Be reasonable. Don't get overwhelmed. Small steps. Little by little, it worked. The queasiness in my stomach faded. My head cleared, coming back to center as the chilly air of the house hit me in the face.

I paused. The chilly air? I had a *furnace*. A furnace I paid well to keep on, despite its age and the repairs it had plagued us with so far. It wasn't going to be hot in the house, but it shouldn't be *chilly*. When I glanced out the window alongside us, snow gleamed in the lights mounted against the front of the house. A blizzard. Of course it was a blizzard.

The back door was cracked. I glared at it, staring at the sliver of light showing from under the wood-and-metal slab, and sighed. Someone had left the door open. We'd *talked* about this, damn it. Idly, the thoughts in the back of my head giggled, pointing out that I sounded exactly like my father when I complained about something like that.

I crossed the room in two steps, my hand outstretched and my mouth dropping open as I drew in a great, shuddering breath. In a second, it would be a yell, and we'd have *another* talk.

And then I stopped.

Voices drifted in from outside, hushed and half-hidden behind the weight of the door. I hesitated, my fingertips brushing the doorknob. Slowly, a twinge of unease flickering through my gut, I glanced back.

The couch was empty. Aedan was up and about, although I had to grin at the thought of what his head must feel like. And I knew the speakers - a woman whose voice I knew as well as my own, and a young man whose strident tone was filled with sarcasm. There was an accent to his words, I realized. Just a hint of something different, something older, as though it had been rekindled by the day's events. Would it slide back into nothingness as the memory of his past faded, I wondered? Probably. Aedan didn't seem like the nostalgic type.

Rolling my eyes, I glared at the still-cracked door. They were letting our *heat* out. They weren't kids. They should know better. I should go out and join them, join in their conversation, and actually *shut* the damn thing.

But there was a cheerfulness to the words being passed between them, still too quiet for me to hear. Aedan had been so...dark, when he was telling us what had happened to him. Him being happy was better than the alternative - for as little time as I'd spent with him, I knew that a pissed-off Aedan was something that *no one* wanted around. And Keira's tone was alight with curiosity, firing off one snow-shrouded question after another.

Swallowing a sigh, I eased away from the door, stepping back into the kitchen. No, there would be time enough for me to join in later. Aedan and I struggled enough keeping things *civil* in conversation, let alone pleasant. He'd left just enough of Greyson's whiskey in the bottle to fill a glass with a few fingers. I eyed it for a long moment, remembering him chugging the stuff straight from the neck, but shrugged. It was whiskey. Whatever bugs Aedan had, it had probably killed them. And I wanted a drink.

The thoughts still swirled behind my eyes as I leaned back in an overstuffed chair Keira had insisted on shoving into the corner, sipping from the clean glass I'd found. Loren and Brendon had vanished outside a few hours before. I'd heard them stomp out the door, laughing and kicking the powder around. Jake was still in his apartment. Greyson would call us if anything went wrong. All of that left me with a tiny scrap of what almost looked like peace. I settled further into the cloth of the chair, smiling.

And waited, still hearing the quiet lilt of conversation just beyond the edge of hearing.

After things being so hectic for so long, it felt good to just do...nothing. Every bone in my back thanked me for the break, offering the bill for all of the work we'd done on the house of late. I just leaned back further, sighing gently. The glass was cool in my hand, leaning against my leg and the side of the chair.

Fine. Let the rest of them throw the whole night away. I stared up at the ceiling for a single, long moment, hearing Keira laugh. It felt like I was torn, caught between two different worlds and two wildly different goals. For as much as one part of me wanted to sit, getting quietly drunk in the living room, the rest of me itched to get up, to move. Wrapping my hand a little more firmly around my glass, I stood, my joints popping, and turned towards my room with a groan.

The piercing shriek of the door creaking open brought me up short. I glanced back. Keira slipped in, her eyes fixed on the phone cradled in her hand. She offered me a tiny nod, just the faintest bit of acknowledgement, and continued on towards her room.

Aedan would be right behind her, I knew. "Shut the door," I called, pressing a hand to my face to mask a yawn. Bed sounded good. Really good. Today had been too much.

"Sit down, Jonny," the too-sharp voice said from behind me instead. I twitched, looking back before I could stop myself. Aedan grinned, throwing himself down - at the table, for once, abandoning the couch he'd occupied for most of the day.

I gave him a long, appraising look. His eyes were still a little unfocused, his cheeks a little red. That might have been the chill getting to him - or it could be his system burning off the last of the liquor. But even if he was still a touch on the buzzed side, the look in his eyes was entirely serious.

I sat down.

"Any reason you want to talk?" I said, leaning forward to rest my elbows on the table. "It's getting late."

"Yeah, yeah, I'll be out of your hair soon, so stop whining," Aedan said, rolling his eyes dramatically. "Look. What's your plan, here?" His eyes were sharper than they had any right to be as he stared at me.

I hesitated. "My plan? What do you mean?"

"Jesus Christ, Jon, what do you *think* I mean?" he said, shaking his head. "You're taking in strays, now?"

"Most strays are a bit cuter than you."

"I'm not talking about *me*, you prick. Those two."

"They have names, you know. Loren and Brendon."

"They're not even here right now. They'll be fine."

My hands curled up into fists, sliding closer to my body. "I couldn't just ignore them, Aedan. Greyson called, and..." I shrugged, staring at the table. "It didn't seem fair."

"It seemed to close to home, you mean."

"...Maybe."

He made an irritated noise in the back of his throat, dropping his head into his hands. When he looked back at me a moment later, I blinked. His irritation was there, yes, just as pointed as ever - but it was layered over the top of tolerant amusement. And worry. It was the concern that was enough to shut me up, letting him talk.

"You remember what I told you before, right?" he said, his voice low - low enough it wouldn't carry. "About rogues, and about cities?"

I just nodded slowly. "Cities are hell. That's what you said."

"And rogues are targets," he finished, folding his arms across his chest stubbornly. "Well, you're trainable, at least."

"No one bothered me for years, Aedan. I know it's a risk, but I think we're-"

"You were one demi, then."

I stopped. He eyed me again, his eyes dark and unreadable, and sighed. "The more demis you pack into one place, the better of a target you're going to look like, Jon. It'll be more and more appealing to anyone who's got the skills to look for you."

"Greyson's watching. He'd let us know if anyone's coming."

"If he *knows*. If someone else didn't pay him more to keep quiet. Or kill him."

"I don't think he'd do that," I said, shaking my head. "And he's too valuable to everyone alive."

"For now. How many demis are you thinking of cramming into this little shelter you're putting together? That's a lot of bait."

"I know it will be. But we have to do *something*."

"You don't *have* to."

"Then why'd you help me?" I snapped, glaring at him. "Back with Matt and them? You didn't 'have to', either."

He shut up, his mouth snapping closed. His eyes flicked away from mine. The flush in his cheeks said everything he wasn't.

"Don't tell me you wouldn't do the same," I muttered. He might try and act heartless, but I wasn't fooled.

He held his quiet for a long moment, kicking at the table leg to vent the irritation he couldn't quite push away. Finally, his hands slapped down flat on the wooden surface. "Your defenses here are a fucking joke," he said, his tone suddenly serious again. "If you're serious about this, Jonny, then man up and do it properly. Get some actual demis worth a damn. And fix the place up into something defensible, while you're at it."

The first words that bubbled up were immediately swallowed, forced right back down. No, what I *wanted* to say to that wasn't going to help. "We're trying," I settled for instead, doing my best not to spit the words at him. "Demis with fighting abilities don't exactly grow on trees."

"Unlike the refuse you're trying so hard to collect. Yeah, I know," Aedan said. A smirk curled at the corners of his lips as he stared at me. Despite his expression, though, that worry was still there in his voice - louder than ever. "I suppose...I might be able to help with that. Here and there."

I sat a little straighter in my chair. "You will?"

"No promises."

"I mean, sure, but what do you mean, you'll *help?* What are you going to-"

"In the meantime, unless something changes for you, you lot need to shape up, or you're going to get crushed the next time one of the prime crews comes to check on the region."

"Prime-"

"What have you got to your name, now?" he said, effortlessly steamrolling my attempts to ask a question. *Again.* I didn't know why I bothered anymore.

"Well, we have-"

"You, Keira, and Jake. Mr. Nyquil should be useful. And the two new lost puppies you took in are?"

"Dreams and weather," I snapped, forcing myself back into the conversation.

Aedan wrinkled his nose, sitting back a little. "Ah. Well, just because they're...uh...*different* abilities doesn't mean you can't put some sort of perimeter together. Get to it."

"Or what?" I said, holding his gaze with my own. "What did you mean, prime crews? I don't understand."

A sigh slipped between his teeth. "It's like I said, Jonny - weren't you listening, before? Crews and rogues."

"I get that."

"Cities, yeah, anything goes. Don't visit Chicago."

"I really wasn't planning on it."

"But out here, though," he continued, effortlessly ignoring me. "It's a quieter game. Strength lies in numbers - but numbers draw attention, which draws danger."

A scowl tugged at the corners of my lips. "Which is where we're at, yes. Was there something new to discuss?"

"There's a threshold you have to get past," he said, leaning back in his chair more fully. "Big enough that yeah, you've got a lot of eyes on you, but *also* big enough that you're too much of a pain for most of your neighbors to bother with. Too big for hunters to pick off.

I rolled the concept over in my mind, trying to make the piece fit with everything else he'd said, the way he'd painted our world as in the past. "I thought you said all of this was lawless. You made it sound like the wild west out here."

He chuckled. "It is. Sometimes. But people know when they've got a good thing going, and in the end..." A shrug rippled through his shoulders. "Everyone's after the same things. Money. Power. Can't get any of that if you're dead. So, sometimes, you get packs of demis that are big and mean enough none of the other kids want to come mess with their block."

I nodded slowly. "Prime crews."

"There's not really an official name for them. No one really gives enough of a shit to make it formal, and no one needs to. You just *know*."

The pit of my stomach churned, filling me with uneasiness. I understood perfectly well what Aedan was saying, what he was telling me to do. "You want us to make ourselves the tough kid."

He paused, watching me carefully. His green eyes were perfectly even, fixed on me, all traces of inebriation vanishing somewhere behind the serious mood that had settled over him. "Can't tell you if you should or not, Jonny. But the fact is, there are other crews in the region that view this kind of wide-open space as their hunting ground. Their territory."

"And they're not going to appreciate us picking them off every time they pass through."

"Figured that out all on your own, did you?"

"Who? Where?" I didn't add anything to the question, no detail or clarification.

Aedan pursed his lips, making a face. "There are a good number of little packs - crews of, oh, three, maybe four demis, who go pick off rogues."

"You know that's not what I'm talking about."

"There's a big one to the north," he said at last, all hints that he was talking around the question dropping away. "In Ontario. They're based out of Toronto, but they keep an outpost just across the border to the north."

"They said there was a market up there," I said, my voice low. "When...Well, when we got Loren and Brendon."

His head bobbed in a nod. "Right. Them. Leader's a guy who...well, he goes by Noah. Got himself a relic that saps at your willpower, makes you slow. Like you're drunk." He chuckled. "Not unlike your Jake guy, in some ways. Closer, though…" He shrugged again. "Detroit's a bit of a mess. Not as bad as Chicago or some of the western cities, at least, but there's still a good three or four crews going at it on your average week." A laugh slipped from his chest. "Not like there's much there to destroy, after all. But, the crew usually on top's one led by a demi called Carl. He's a phase shifter."

"Carl," I echoed softly. "Those two? Those are the big players?"

Aedan made another face. "There's...just some general instability on the west side of the state. They've all got their heads too far up their own asses to talk to each other, and with the way the population's been growing out there, there have been a lot of demis pouring in over the last few decades."

"I…" I began, but hesitated. "You know a lot about all this. And you're *telling* me a lot."

"Of course I know a fucking lot about it," he muttered darkly. "How exactly am I supposed to keep away from everyone if I don't know what they're up to?"

"Without talking to anyone?" It wasn't that I *doubted* him - it was just entirely unlike Aedan to be so forthcoming. Or so knowledgeable. "I didn't think you were on speaking terms with many of these crews."

His grin was positively feral. When his shoulders slid back, his arms rising in a languid stretch, the outline of his knife showed against the fabric of his shirt. "Oh, they talked to me."

Lovely.

"So what do we do?" I said, trying to tear my mind away from the thought of Aedan cutting his way across the country. Across the world, from what it sounded like. "From what you're saying, it sounds like we stand a good chance of pissing off the biggest, baddest players around."

The look he fixed me was full of tolerant derision. "Oh, there's always a bigger fish."

"What?"

"I'll see what I can do about shoring up your body count," Aedan said, tapping the tip of his knife against the table. "*You,* just worry about making yourselves as big and tough as you can. Be the bully on the street."

I half-shrugged. "Not really interested in being the bully."

His eyes bored into mine. "Get interested. At some point, one of the crews is going to come check you out. Feel out how much of a threat you are." He didn't blink. Neither did I. "If they don't think you're a force to be reckoned with, they'll just get rid of you."

Oh. I swallowed hard, trying not to look like I was doing so. "I see."

A crooked smile flashed onto his face for a single moment. "If you can make yourselves look strong enough to get them to slow down and talk, to try and negotiate territory lines, you stand a halfway decent chance of coming out of this on peaceable terms with them."

"Right," I whispered.

His hand slammed down onto my shoulder a moment later in what was probably supposed to seem like a comforting slap. "Cheer up, Jonny. You'll be fine."

"Jon."

"I'll try to hang a bit closer," he said, his old swagger creeping back in with every passing heartbeat. "I know you guys are hopeless without me around to clean up things for you. Ah, I'm such a softie."

"You just want free beer."

His ears flushed faintly red, but he only rolled his eyes. "Keep yourself in one piece. It would be a pain to have to find somewhere else to crash over the winter."

"Right," I said, glaring at him. "Oh, I understand. Just see about getting us some help. I'm more than aware of how many eyes are going to be on us."

"I'll see what I can wrangle up. You're asking a lot, you know." He patted the backpack that sat alongside the couch, sending a soft jingle of metal through the room. "I wouldn't turn these babies loose for just anyone, you know." That smirk was back. "It's because you're so hopeless."

"Boast all you want, just get us our help."

"Fine. But just be aware, Jon," he said. I froze. All of the humor had dropped from his expression. His voice was still bright and lilting, filled with sickly-sweet cheer, but his eyes had gone hard. The smirk he wore suddenly looked all too forced. "If I do this for you, if I'm out there putting my own neck on the line, for you and your strays, then there will be a debt between you and I. I might need your help in the future - and I'd expect you to return the favor."

A shiver ran down my spine. His accent was back, stronger than ever, and there was something in the way he was looking at me. Calculating. Assessing. Like I was a tool. It was there for a single instant, and then gone just as quickly as it had appeared.

"If you manage to find demis who actually *want* to help this whole thing going, then I'll happily owe you a favor," I managed, staring at him. "I won't kill anyone for you. I mean…unless they deserve it, I guess." My stomach twisted at how easily the words came to my lips. Everything was *fucked*, wasn't it?

He grinned, the plastic fakeness sliding from his face again. "Oh, I'm sure it won't be anything like that. It's just one of those *things*. Needed to be said."

"Right." Even as I forced the word out, my thoughts were spinning. So much new information - again. I didn't know where to begin, what I should ask. Of course, that was assuming that Aedan would answer anything in the first place. But, he seemed to be in a chatty mood. I should make the most of it.

But it was impossible to resist the fatigue, the steady ache in my skull. Reading lies took energy too, I realized - the willpower to sit and stare, to focus in on the tiniest indicators in how they held themselves, how they talked, how they moved. I'd been reading Aedan all day, and it was starting to wear on me.

He watched me stand, wordless. I pressed a hand to my face, muffling my yawn. "Look. It's been wonderful hearing about all these fun details for the *first time ever*, but I didn't spend the whole day napping. I'm out. Let me...I just need some time to process."

"I don't care how much time you take to process," he said, his lip curling in a sneer. "It's your fucking problem if someone comes to check in on you before you're ready."

"I know." I bit back the rest of the words that wanted to surge out alongside the quick, sullen response. Aedan was right. It hurt, and I didn't like him jabbing at me, but we were playing with fire. "We'll be ready. Should...Should we talk to the primes? Ahead of time? Take the initiative?" I hesitated, my hands on the back of the chair I'd been sitting in. "Is that something you *do?*"

"Probably be best, yeah," Aedan said, his tone still perfectly casual. As he talked, he leaned back in his chair until it stood on two legs, snagging one of the beer cans still sitting on the counter.

"Those are still warm," I said, feeling the need to point it out.

"Don't care."

"...Okay, then. Don't burn the house down, please. Seriously. I'm going to bed."

"Dig the sand out of your crack and lighten up. Go get your beauty sleep," he said, smirking up at me. The can hissed a moment later as he popped it open.

Whatever. I just ran a hand through my hair, feeling the ache worsen, and made for my bedroom. For my *bed*. It had never sounded so appealing in my life.

The last thing I heard before the door shut behind me was the sound of the refrigerator opening.

CHAPTER THIRTY-TWO

My eyes slid open. Light streamed in through the window, a sharp reminder that if I didn't get up, the day would be half gone before I knew it.

I wasn't entirely sure that I cared - but all the same, I found myself slowly rising, forcing my legs out into the harsh, unforgiving chill of the morning air.

My routine was simple. I wasn't a breakfast person, and I wasn't the type to spend all morning lounging around in my pajamas, either. I'd gotten most of my actual work done the night before, sure, but that didn't mean a dozen other things hadn't lined themselves up, waiting not-so-patiently for my attention over the weekend.

The smell of coffee rose over the kitchen, warm and enticing as I let myself settle into a chair. The only sounds in the house were the steady drip of coffee and the shockingly rough snores coming from the room Loren had claimed. I smiled, swallowing a chuckle. One could never tell.

My hastily-quelled laughter died off a moment later as I blinked away the last bit of sleep, letting my eyes settle on the table. More accurately, at what rested *on* the table.

A single sheet of paper. Even as I saw it, the rest of the pieces dropped into place - who had arrived, yesterday. The answers he'd given us. And the talk we'd had, the night before. A quick glance confirmed what my ears were telling me. The snoring that had plagued the house all night was gone. Aedan wasn't lying on the couch where he'd crashed. His blanket was mashed up into a bundle at the armrest, his pillow shoved to the side.

It wasn't just that. His backpack was gone - along with the rest of the food I'd bought. And my beer. "God damn it," I whispered. I hadn't expected him to hang around forever - it was *Aedan* - but I hadn't thought he'd vanish in the span of a night, without so much as a goodbye. Hell, I hadn't thought he'd even had a-

Oh, *hell* no. I sprang to my feet, hurling myself at the nearest window out to the front driveway, but pressed a hand to my chest a moment later. My poor, bloodstained sedan still sat in its parking spot, pressed up close against the house. Good. *Good.* At least he hadn't stolen my car.

It had snowed for hours, while we talked. And through the thick coating of white, I could see a solitary pair of footprints, plowing a trail through the snow out towards the main road.

My head pounded. Numb, I turned back to the table, reaching for the note he'd left. The lettering stared up at me, surprisingly refined and written in a cursive thick enough I had to stare at it for a long, hard moment.

Don't bother calling. I'm not up for hearing you bitch at me. Your couch sucks, by the way. I had a spring sticking into my back half the night.

I'm going to do you a solid. I'll get you your people, so just sit back and be a good leader. I know it's a stretch of the imagination. You. A leader. But that's just how life goes, so wipe your tears and give it a go. If you actually give put some effort in, you might even keep most of your demis alive.

A faint, nearly-invisible line meandered down, hovering over the next line - as though Aedan had sat with his pen at the ready for some time, staring down at the page. My pulse accelerated gently. When the line continued, each letter was carved into the paper fiercely. Here and there, he'd stuck the tip of the pen straight through.

You've said a lot of things, about what's 'right' and how you 'couldn't just ignore what's happening.' You've taken a lot of risks. I get it. I do. People are inherently good, I think.

I nearly dropped the sheet, hearing a chuckle bubble up from my throat. Aedan, waxing philosophical at me? Him? But I forced my humor down, reading on, and little by little my amusement died.

They want what's best. We try and help each other. But the truth is, Jonny, that the world's pretty fucked, and in general, people will take the easy road if it shows up. The selfish one. No one sets out to take the shitty road. It's no one's life goal. It just kind of happens.

I'm not thrilled that you're choosing this way to go. I think you're pissing up the wrong tree, and considering how much blood I've put into keeping you alive, I consider my investment at this point to be all but shot. But that's on you. Don't get yourself killed. If you can make it work, well, kudos to fucking you.

But you're not the first person I've seen set out with good intentions. Most of them wind up acting just like the rest, given a few years and a bit of temptation. It's hard to say no when it's all so easy. And in the end, they're monsters just like all the rest.

Matt started out with the best of intentions, too. Knew him a lot longer than I've known you. Didn't stop me from doing what needed doing.

Don't be a Matt.

Anyway. If I were you, and if you're serious about this whole making-a-crew thing, then I wasn't kidding. You're going to have Canada and Detroit breathing down your necks before long. Get ready for that - and don't let them get the jump on you. If you're not going to go through with all this, well, you need to figure that shit out. Now.

Your beer still sucks.

That was all there was - no goodbye, no *thanks* for the 'bad' beer he'd nonetheless stolen, not even his name scrawled at the bottom. I could nearly read his mind - *Why bother?* he'd no doubt been thinking.

The coffeepot buzzed that it was done, with the welcoming scent of the brew seeping inch by inch across the kitchen. I didn't move. My eyes were still fixed on that sheet, on the letter he'd left behind. He was helping us - but there was a threat in his words. Not even a subtle one. I tried not to let the uneasiness creep up on me. If I was going to turn our little crew into another batch of hunters like all the rest, well, I *wouldn't* have gone after Loren and Brendon. I wouldn't have put us in danger like that for nothing.

But as hard as I tried, the doubts still lingered in the back of my mind. The temptation, the promise of power right there under my fingertips if I only reached out and took it. And in the end, it wasn't just me I had to worry about, was it? If even one bad apple wound up in the crew, if they weren't as committed to our idealism as we were, it would be a divide that we'd have a hard time recovering from.

And I found I couldn't push aside Aedan's warning quite so easily.

The coffeepot quietly chimed a second time as I stood motionless in front of the table, staring down at the note.

***

It turned out, getting ourselves ready for visitors wasn't quite so easy a task. What did that even *mean?* I called Greyson as soon as it was late enough to be decent, that day Aedan left, and he assured me he'd seen no movement out of the southeast. He'd told me in no uncertain terms, in fact, along with some colorful terms for how little I must think of him if he wasn't already watching for that. My ears had been red when he hung up on me.

The first meeting we held was filled with an almost palpable air of awkwardness, sitting around the house's living room. Loren and Brendon had taken the couch, him sprawled comfortably across most of the cushions and her sitting bolt upright with her usual poise. Jake lounged in the overstuffed armchair, his feet propped up on the coffee table I'd told him a dozen times wasn't a footrest. And Keira and I waited on the far side, plopped down in hastily-turned kitchen chairs.

We talked, back and forth. Discussed our goals, our plans. What we wanted, what we hoped for. That was what the whole thing was about, wasn't it? Talking - and coming to some sort of agreement.

The good news, I quickly discovered, was that everyone was truly interested in one thing, probably the most *important* thing - in us all staying alive, and not winding up shot and relic-stripped in the forest. Not that that *really* needed saying, but, well. It proved to be one of the only things we agreed on. That fact became more apparent with every line that was said.

I'd expected them all to have similar arguments, to have issues about the same facets of our little mission. I was shocked when that wasn't at all the case.

"I'm not sure about this," Loren said, her voice quiet. Keira and I sat a little taller. It had been a few minutes since anyone had spoken. The dreamworker's back was ramrod-straight, her hands pressed against her knees so that every bone in her body was stiffened. Her eyes stared down at the ground, lost in some other world. "I-I mean, I want to help. I do. But isn't it safer to stay quiet? To stay unseen?"

"They helped *us.*" I was surprised that it was Brendon who spoke up next. The two were rarely seen without each other, and I wasn't quite sure that I'd ever heard him contradict her. From the way her chin snapped over, turning a few inches to face him, I could tell she had the same reaction I did. "How can we argue, when we'd be…" He swallowed hard, his eyes darkening. "When we'd be dead, if they hadn't stepped in."

"I..I know," Loren whispered, a bit of the steel in her expression crumbling. "I'm not saying-"

"They don't have to stay here, though, do they?" Brendon said, glancing up at me. There was a pleading note in his eyes, echoed in every word he spoke. "It shouldn't *have* to be a long-term thing. I don't know how I feel about strangers coming into the house over and over again. Strange demis. People we don't *know*."

I nodded slowly, holding his gaze. "People who could use us."

The relief on his face was nearly painful to look at. "Right. Yeah. That."

I'd never asked Brendon about his past, about where he'd been before we'd found him. I'd never asked Loren, either. They'd passed my little inquisition, and given what I knew about the darker sides of demi culture, it was more than likely a pretty unfortunate story. Loren simply slid her hand onto his leg. Her fingers tensed, squeezing gently. Comfortingly. It left me staring for a long moment, taken aback by the reversal of their roles over the last week or two.

I blinked away the last of the doubt, latching onto my words again and drawing breath to continue, when Jake spoke at last.

"Help them or not, I'm not sure how good an idea it is to tangle with the primes," he said, his hands folded in his lap. He didn't look at me as he spoke. Keira and I watched anyway, mute, and let him churn through his words. "We're…" His voice died away again as he hesitated, staring down at the floor. "We're only a few people, here. They could stomp us flat without really trying."

He wasn't *wrong*. We both knew that. "Aedan says he's going to try and find us some help. And we're certainly going to keep looking for our own."

"That's fine, but it's *him*," he snapped. "How reliable are you expecting him to be? You can't negotiate with the big crews, Jon. They don't listen. Why would they? They have the oomph to do whatever they want."

"But what are they gaining from holding control over a stretch of deserted forest?" Keira said, joining into the conversation abruptly. Her eyes flashed, locked onto Jake. "Sure, they could, but *why*?"

"Because it's *theirs*," he snapped. "People tend to get possessive."

"We just have to be enough of a threat to them that they think they'll lose more than they might gain," I said, trying to keep my voice level. Jake's gaze flicked back to mine, tearing free of Keira at last. She sagged alongside me like her strings had been cut. "I don't know what the right answer is either, Jake."

"Then why are we jumping headlong into this?"

"No one's jumping into anything," I said even more carefully, holding my hands up. "We're just talking."

"I just...the last thing we need is to piss them off and put ourselves on their shit lists," he muttered, leaning back in his chair.

Given the way Matt's crew had treated him, it wasn't entirely unexpected that he didn't like the idea of buddying up with any of the big players. I bit back my retort, resting my elbows on the table, and tried to find a way to get all of their arguments to line up. A way to get them to all agree, to find a middle ground.

As far as I could see, there wasn't one.

"We don't have to decide anything right now," I said at last, letting a sigh slide between my teeth. It wasn't what I wanted to be saying - more than anything, it felt like I was turning tail and running headlong away from the argument. But driving a wedge between the few demis we had wasn't the right way to work out our issue. "Why don't we all just stew on the argument for a little bit, and...we'll come back to it."

"Fine," Jake said. A muscle popped in his neck, twitching despite his languid, carefree pose, and his jaw was clenched tight. But he just closed his eyes, sliding an arm over his face, and put an earbud in with his other hand.

"Yeah," Brendon said, bobbing his head in agreement. He stared at the ground, his face bone-white, and didn't so much as glance our way. "Yeah, that's...let's do that." Loren's hand still rested on his leg, a constant presence. She looked towards me. She didn't say anything, but nodded once. Her skin was pale, too, but her gaze was razor sharp.

There was nothing I could say to stop them as the pair rose, wordless and quiet, and paced from the room. Jake hadn't moved, and might well have been asleep for all the acknowledgment he gave them. A soft sigh was enough to draw my eye, just in time to see Keira push herself back from the table, sliding away.

I forced a smile, seeing the corners of her lips curl up in response, and then she was gone.

I'd wanted *answers*. I should have known that it wouldn't be nearly that simple. The fact that all of them seemed totally and completely content with treating me as their leader, their spokesman, was even more concerning. I just had to....figure something out. Right.

Reaching into my pocket, I slid out the maps I'd printed off and grabbed the sharpie sitting on the table. Greyson had been more helpful than the rest of *them*, at least, and he had more specifics than Aedan did. He hadn't been happy about me soaking his mind for a good hour on his Sunday, but I think he knew that it was for a good cause. The maps were already covered with symbols, dots and lines and anything I could think of to label our surroundings.

At the center of it all was our house, alone in the woods. Surrounded on all sides by people who would as soon kill us as stop to say hi. A bead of sweat slowly dripped down the back of my neck, but I gripped my marker all the tighter.

I would figure this out. One way or another.

CHAPTER THIRTY-THREE

A branch cracked underfoot, half-hidden under the dusty covering of snow and frost that clung to everything in sight. I froze, feeling the blood drain from my face. The forest was silent on every side, balsam trees littering the ground with pine needles as far as I could see in every direction. I'd been doing my damndest to step carefully, to *not* tromp around like an elephant and give away my position to everyone who might be looking.

That hadn't gone so well.

I wanted to swear, but that'd only give away my position worse than I already had. I pressed tight to the truck of the nearest tree, leaning against it and keeping my feet perfectly still. My ears strained, reaching for the slightest flicker of sound, even the faintest warning that someone else was near.

Only the soft sound of birdsong overhead drifted down to me.

My heartbeat thrummed in my ears as I counted off the seconds. Five. Ten. Twenty.

As a full minute slipped past, a bit of the tension faded. I was an idiot, yeah, but they hadn't noticed me. So it was fine. Probably. My lips were pressed into a thin line as I eased back out from behind my cover, creeping on.

Damn it, they had to be somewhere out here. The forest was only so big, and there could only be so many places they could hide. My fingers stretched towards my pocket, towards where my gun *should* be.

I'd finally caved. Aedan was right, and Keira had cornered me a

288

month ago, only a bit after after he'd vanished into the early morning air. She'd told me in no uncertain terms that I was going to wind up dead one of these days if I kept playing around like I had been. It was hard to argue with her when she put it like *that*.

It wasn't big, and it wasn't fancy. I wasn't rich, after all. But it would put a hole in someone who was trying to kill me, and I supposed that would have to be good enough.

I could still feel Officer Baldwin's eyes on me, staring from the back of the office when I'd brought it in to register it. He hadn't said a word, and neither had I. I hadn't so much as *looked* at him, as much as I could manage. None of that changed the holes his stare bored in me, fixed on the back of my neck as I forced my way through the paperwork as quickly as humanly possible.

He still thought I was human trash, then, or something of the kind. Not that I couldn't blame him. If I'd been in his shoes, seeing a man's sister beaten half to death and him with a gunshot wound in him, I'd be more than a little suspicious myself. But I wasn't that kind of person, damn it. I *wasn't*.

Unless he remembered what I'd done, the way I'd shifted his attentions off of me. A shiver ran down my spine. No. If he remembered, he would have come after me long ago. And everyone knew magic didn't exist. It was hardly the first thing his mind would jump to, if he actually realized something was off.

His stare didn't stop me from getting the gun, as much as it made me worried. I'd scurried out minutes later, clutching the hard-sided case, and closed the door on him and his accusing eyes.

Already, I was getting used to carrying it. Its weight had grown familiar, much to my growing distaste. And its absence right then was a constant reminder that even though it might be the simpler answer sometimes, that didn't make it the *best* one.

Demis in the woods. My mind raced through the scenario. Their positions were unknown. Maybe they'd be armed, maybe not. There was no way to be sure. The others were nothing if not creative, I knew, and there were no rules.

I fixed my eyes back on the trees, forcing my mind to settle back into the present. There were others out there, that was all I needed to know - and they were looking for me every bit as hard as I was looking for them. I couldn't let them get the jump on me.

Something shrieked, halfway across the forest. I froze, my head snapping over to zero in on the sound. Animals - birds, complaining at something. A crooked smile tugged at my lips. Someone else wasn't entirely graceful either, it seemed. And they were still a good ways off. Picking my feet up a little more, I started to move. It would be a little louder than I wanted, but I could use a bit more speed if I was going to catch them.

Ice splintered under my feet. I glanced down, shock overcoming my satisfaction for a long, pointed moment, and plunged through the fragile layer of glass coating the puddle below. I had a single second to grit my teeth, adrenaline flooding my system, before my foot plunged into the congealed mess of mud and frigid water underneath.

I sank in instantly, the sole of my boot vanishing into the mud. And, pulling hard on it a second later to free myself, I was reminded that clay was all-too-common around here. It wasn't going to come so easily. Swearing more loudly, I braced hard, doing my best to get myself out without losing my boot in the process.

Half bent-over, staring down at the puddle, I froze. Someone had...covered it with leaves. Buried it well enough to pass a quick inspection. Someone had-

The crunch of snow under their feet was the only warning I got. Throwing myself to the ground, I felt the rush of air where my head had been. My hands sank into the mud just like my feet had, coating my gloves in an instant.

"God damn it," I muttered, adrenaline rushing through my system and giving me the edge I'd been lacking before. The mud came free with a disgustingly poignant sucking sound, letting me stumble back in time to avoid the second blow that came hammering my way.

Brendon lurched, overbalancing as he hit empty air instead of my head. The bat he held in his hands slammed into the ground, leaving speckles of blue chalk across the white snow.

An irritated noise slipped from the back of his throat. His eyes were fixed on mine, filled with single minded intensity.

I gasped for breath, trying to refill my lungs as quickly as I could after my touch-and-go. "Don't-"

He closed the gap between him and I before I could get another word out, coming at me with more energy than grace. My words came out a formless wheeze as we tumbled, hitting the ground hard. The bat bounced off into the trees, gone forever. One of his hands was over my mouth a heartbeat later, keeping anything else I might have tried to say from escaping. The other one fumbled at his jacket, reaching for one of the pockets.

Shit. I thrashed madly, trying to worm out from under him, but he was bigger than I was. At least if I could keep him from going for a weapon, maybe I could keep this going. I couldn't lose. Not here, not like *this*. I'd never live it down. He cursed softly, plunging his hand deeper into his coat.

And losing a bit of his hold in the process. I seized on the thin chance I was given, my eyes lighting up. "Stop," I said, forcing the word out as loudly and clearly as I could past the half of his hand that was still clasped over my mouth.

He froze. My gut unclenched a fraction. Good. He was listening. But- not *entirely*. There was still too much resistance, too much feedback for him to be going quietly. And his eyes were still fixed on mine, filled with that icy, frigid intensity.

"Take your hand off me."

His eyes stayed locked on mine. His hand didn't move. I faltered, suddenly unsure. Was this a ploy? Was he trying to play a trick on me? No, I decided immediately, seeing sweat glimmer to life across his temple. He was fighting - and fighting *hard*.

"Take your hand *off* me," I repeated, more firmly.

His palm twitched. It slid a quarter of an inch away, every movement slow and painful, before jerking to a stop again.

Why was he fighting so hard? Where was all of that stubbornness coming from? I'd beaten Matt's crew, and I'd been *killing* them.

I'd also been in real danger then, I was forced to admit. Losing would have meant dying. Here, in the little skirmish Loren had suggested, losing just meant returning to the house humiliated. Certainly not a goal, but hardly enough to compare to a life-or-death situation.

"Brendon," I said, my words coming a little more clearly without his hand fully across my lips. "Hands off. Stand up." A dull ache in the back of my skull warned that the harder he fought me, the harder I'd have to press to force him. I had a lot of strength to my name, but not unlimited. He wouldn't be my only opponent.

His hand finally slid free at last. His face crumpled at the motion, like he was acknowledging that he'd finally lost. I slowly pushed myself backwards, sympathetic but not about to lose. "Nod if you have a knife in that pocket."

Brendon's face glowed bright red with the sheer effort he was putting into resisting, but slowly, he nodded.

I sighed. "Fine. Take it and eliminate yourself."

They'd decided that I wasn't allowed to arm myself, to pick a 'weapon' and coat it in chalk and dust. It would be *unfair*, they said. I already had an edge on them, they said. There wasn't really a good way for me to protest, and their argument that it'd be good practice for me made sense. But, it meant that this fight was harder than it had to be.

His arm trembled, fighting for every inch as he strained against my command, but inexorably, it slid towards his pocket. The stick he pulled free wasn't much of a 'knife', but it was close enough to pass muster without actually running a risk of killing anyone. The whole length of it was slathered with blue chalk.

A tiny corner of my mind applauded my care with words as the stick arced towards his chest. If I wasn't careful, he might *actually* try and cut himself with it, and the national forest we'd co-opted for our game wasn't really set up for first aid. I'd done well, I thought with only a hint of smugness.

Something crunched, deep in the forest behind us. I froze, spinning in my seat, and scanned the treeline. Footsteps. It had sounded like footsteps, I was *sure* of it.

"Did you hear that?" I whispered, my voice only a little louder than a breath.

"Y-Yeah," Brendon panted, still fighting to keep from slapping the stick against his jacket.

Another crack - more footsteps. From a different direction, this time. A chill ran down my spine. "Are they working together, do you think?"

"Probably." The word came out a whine.

I glanced back over my shoulder. "Stop that, for now. Sit still. Help me look." We were *supposed* to all work independently. Even Brendon had agreed, although we all knew that there wouldn't be much he could accomplish on his own. Meteorologists just weren't all that useful in a fight. If Loren and Jake were cooperating, though…

Another stick breaking underfoot, from another direction. We shrank back a little closer, peering off into the branches. "Three of them?" I whispered. "That doesn't-"

A dog barked, somewhere nearby, the low sound of a working dog. My blood chilled. "It's not them," I breathed.

"There. See?" he murmured in my ear, pointing over my shoulder.

He hardly needed to. I could see them too, the dark figures moving through the treeline. *Lots* of figures. Here and there, the gleam of metal showed bright in the midmorning light.

I didn't ask who they were, and neither did he. The answer was clear enough - we'd been sitting here, pulling on our abilities one after another as we tried to get in a bit of practice. Had we made ourselves too apparent? Had we drawn in a crew passing through, who'd managed to find us somehow?

My hand settled onto Brendon's shoulder, tugging him deeper under our cover as he leaned forward. The trees would do a passable job of hiding us - but if they had dogs, there was only so much that hiding would do. They'd just hunt us down, dragging us out, and then...

Why hadn't Greyson warned us? The thought hung in my mind, crystal-clear through the fog that I suddenly realized was sliding deeper and deeper. We all had phones, and they were all still on. The old man certainly didn't love being our advance scout, but he'd never complained about giving me a phone call before. He'd done it in the past. So why not now?

"It's them," I said, trying to keep my voice low despite the adrenaline coursing through my system."

Brendon's head shook wildly. "I don't *care* who it is, we need to-"

"It's Jake. Jake and Loren."

"W-What?"

A muted sigh slipped out of my throat before I could hold it back. "This is a dream. A hallucination. They're close. Don't look at it." Loren had shown me a dream once. I'd been awake, which gave the images she'd filtered into my head a foggy, unreal quality, and yet...Together with Jake, I'd known she'd be stronger.

This, though. I could hear the barking of the dogs, smell the cigarette smoke off the coats of the figures walking past. If this was a dream, it was good. Very good.

"You're crazy," Brendon said, glancing back at me with wide eyes. "You can't be serious."

Muffling a curse under my breath, I grabbed his wrist, towing him out from behind the tree we'd claimed. We still had a few moments, if they were real,but not long. If they were fake, then Jake and Loren were close, and we had even less time. We needed to be clear before then. He fought for a second, resisting my tug, but gave in at last.

"I'll lure them in. I just need you to go handle them when I make a distraction," I said, my lips pressed to his ear.

"*What?*"

"You didn't make a single sound, before. When you attacked me. You're good at this. I'm fuck-all clumsy. And they're going to want to catch me." I flashed him a wry smile. "I'll be a good distraction, I think."

"I...I don't know if I can. If they catch me, I can't-"

"Then don't let them catch you," I said, forcing as much intensity into the words as I could at a whisper. I understood. I'd watched, seen the envy in his eyes as the rest of us played with this or that ability, honed a skill or polished a tactic. More than any of us, Brendon was entirely aware that his powers weren't exactly useful. Even Loren found a way to fit in, to match off with someone else and put her focus to work. Brendon was floundering.

He could deal with whatever personal issues and battles he had - on his own time. Sure, being able to tell us that it was going to snow next week wasn't the best help in a fight, but if nothing else he was another hand holding a gun if a shooting war broke out. We needed to find a way to jam a bit of confidence back into him.

Brendon didn't fight as I towed him a bit farther away, hardly daring to look at where the illusions paced. I *hoped* they were illusions. I was banking awful hard on Greyson not totally abandoning us.

"I-I guess," he said, his voice little more than a whisper. "I guess I can try."

"Good. I don't know how far they can reach," I said, forcing the words out as quickly as I could. "Jake's not a new demi, at least, but Loren's still fresh. Maybe they haven't figured out their synergy or whatever. Just...get clear of their range, and then get in behind them. Break their illusion, and I'll step in. I don't know if I can cast through this." I hesitated a moment longer, my arm still on his shoulder. "You got this?"

"Yeah."

I didn't say anything else. I just patted his shoulder gently, the sound vanishing among the boughs around us, and gave him the tiniest hint of a push.

He slipped off into the underbrush, glancing back and fixing me with unsure eyes for a single second. The shadows took him a moment later. I blinked slowly, still staring at where he'd been. He really *was* quiet.

But the other demis around me weren't - the ones that I was still hoping were an illusion. I swallowed hard, running through scenarios in my mind. I just needed to keep their attentions for a few minutes, to give Brendon time to circle around without them catching on. If they were just dreams, then Loren and Jake would seize any chance they had at getting the jump on me. If they were demis, *actual* demis, then they'd certainly leap just as hard for what they saw as a rogue demi out by themself.

Either way, it meant that I had to take the initiative - and that first step.

Praying that I wasn't making some terrible mistake, I slid my foot over a few inches, bringing it down on one of the myriad branches lying fallen under the tree.

The crack rang through the still air, echoing across the national forest.

I was off before the last reverberations died away, pushing away as quietly as I could. If these were dreams, then there was no reason to think that either of my friends was actually where the demis appeared to be. It might just be a shroud to draw my attention, leaving them walking invisibly where they would. But it was all I had to go on - and they'd make for the sound regardless

My breath came ragged in my throat as I raced on, minding each and every step in a haze of adrenaline-fueled detail. Distance. I needed distance from wherever they were.

Someone was behind me - a figure. I could hear them, hear the crunch of their boots on the snow. They were running, chasing. Great. They were after me. So much for my notion of stealth. I gave it one last go, curling back around a scrub of juniper and pine and slipping back the way I'd come.

All I had to do to win was get my voice around them. The thought echoed through my mind, a single fact that I clung to. But if this was a dream, could I force myself to talk? Was I even running?

They were closing in, whoever they were, my attempts at stealth disregarded. The fact that no one had shot me yet meant that my guess was probably right, at least, and these *weren't* foreign hostiles. And there was no way I could outrun them. The aching in my leg told me that much, still tight and painful where a bullet had torn through the muscle only a short few months before.

"Both of you!" I cried, raising my voice. "Stop-"

I tripped, falling headlong over a root buried in the soil as a wave of exhaustion pressed down onto my shoulders. I couldn't move, could hardly keep my eyes open under the weight of it. Jake. Bastard. He must've followed the sound of my voice, zeroing in on me once I'd presented a target. I tried to force air through my lungs, but it just seemed like so much *work*. Easier to lie there, to let my eyes slip closed.

I wasn't in the forest anymore, I realized. I lay on the carpet in the living room, threadbare and plain. And in front of me-

Jake crouched down by an end table, a crooked grin on his face. "Nice."

"You think?" A second voice, shy and with a smile coloring every syllable. Loren slipped out from behind Jake. Her lips curled up proudly, despite the way her hands shook. They were clasped in front of her chest - folded tight around her focus, no doubt.

I glared at Jake, my eyes narrowing. "Fucker."

"You want to do it?" Jake said, glancing up at Loren. "He'd probably forgive *you*."

"M-Me? What, you want me to-"

"Here." He held his 'knife' up for her, brushing the chalky dust from his hands. "Hurry up. We don't have all day. My show comes on in, like, 45 minutes."

Waiting on the far side of the room from where I lay, the TV set flicked on obediently. In a different situation, I might have thought it funny.

"Put that down," I wheezed, forcing the words out at last. A rush of satisfaction washed through my mind. "Put it down and sit down."

Loren laughed. The sound was different than I'd expected, small and thin but filled with surprise.

Jake groaned, glancing back over his shoulder at her. "What? What's that, now? Would you just stab the bastard already?"

"Oh, he's- he's just trying to give orders," she said, clasping her hand around the clean end of the stick.

"Is he, now," Jake said, amusement soaking through his voice.

She bobbed her head once in a nod, matching his smile, and then held the stick-knife out. "I can...I guess I can handle it."

That smile still clung to her lips, but I wasn't fooled. She was even paler than usual, and the trembling was getting worse. Jake couldn't be much better - but I didn't know how much of his fatigue he was hiding, or how much she was wiping away with the dream.

"Put it down," I snapped, glaring at her as she stepped closer. I put every ounce of strength I had into the words, but it was hard to convince myself that she'd listen. Not given what she'd said, the dream state she appeared to have jammed me into.

She only giggled again, her confidence growing as my words died away.

The tiny, smug grin that was growing on her face fell away in a wave of surprise as Jake bellowed angrily. She whirled on one foot, her hair flying out behind her, and stumbled away unsteadily.

A gasp slipped between my teeth as the world spun around me, tilting dangerously. The colors melted, shapes blurring and fading out to fog - and then my house vanished, leaving only trees and underbrush where tables and chairs had been. Jake had fallen to the snow-dusted leaves covering the ground, rolling madly.

Brendon was already there, though, his stick-knife clutched in one hand. The chalk-coated wood plunged into the dirt where Jake had been moments before, leaving a stain of blue behind. He tore it free with an angry noise, kicking off towards Jake again.

Jake twisted, caught for one horrible moment as he lifted himself off the ground. Half of him wanted to run, stretching out to break into a dash. He had to know that Brendon couldn't hurt him at range. The other half of him seemed to want to bring his abilities to bear before this could turn into something requiring actual *effort*. Even as he straightened, his head still turned, his too-wide eyes fixing on Brendon.

All of it just meant that when the weather-reader lunged, his arm snapping out, Jake was altogether too off-balance to do more than lurch to one side, making an irritated noise in the back of his throat.

Brendon's 'knife' slapped across Jake's front, staining his jacket with blue dust. "Out!" the man gasped, the start of a smile twitching at his lips. "You're out!"

Jake opened his mouth like he was going to argue, his eyebrows settling angrily, but something in Brendon's expression seemed to convince him it wasn't worth it. He dropped with a sigh, leaning back against a tree.

I was smiling too, I realized, a soft chuckling bubbling from my lips as Brendon turned back towards the woman creeping away. She held the stick-knife Jake had given her out like a shield, pointed towards Brendon as he advanced.

"Loren," he said, beginning to chuckle.

"No."

"You don't know how to use that," Brendon said, creeping another step closer. He was still grinning.

She snorted, the sound undignified enough that I jumped. "And you do?"

Loren was just starting to laugh as he lunged in, swinging wildly. She was right - he had no clue how to use a knife, clearly. Neither did she, though. The two batted at each other like teenagers fighting with pop bottles, laughing as though it was the most fun they'd had in years. Chalk dust flew, splattering against trees and branches and anything but *them*.

I let them go, creeping back into the treeline. Both of them were distracted. I wasn't going to *interrupt*. They were having too much fun for me to ruin it so easily. But that didn't mean I was going to sit around and wait for them to decide who could come after me, either. My eyes still fixed on them, watching carefully, I started into a slow circle, slipping behind a bush. After they settled their fight, all I had to do was-

An arm wrapped around me, a gloved hand pressing itself over my mouth. I flinched, the cry that threatened to slip out muffled to nothing behind it. Something slammed into my stomach a heartbeat later. Hard.

My cry dissolved into a sneeze. Dust filled my nostrils - chalk dust. Chalk dust that rose from the green cloud of the stuff rising from my stomach.

Keira slipped around me, one eye sliding closed in a wink and her finger pressing to her lips. She was wearing her glasses, the lenses sending glimmers of light across the forest floor.

I shook my head, glaring. "You little-"

"Shh," she murmured, flashing me a crooked smile as she turned back to the still-dueling pair.

She'd been watching us the whole time, I realized - keeping one eye on the brilliant gleam of our relics, tracking us back and forth across the forest. Staying a safe distance away until the rest of us were too distracted. I chuckled, pressing a hand to my mouth as I flopped to the ground with a puff of green dust. *Bitch.*

Both Loren and Brendon were red-faced by then, their blows beginning to slow as more of their energy went into laughter than their fight. It wasn't *quite* what I'd expected, from the final showdown of our little match, but there'd be time to work out their technique later. And we could probably set them up with guns, if they really needed weapons.

Loren stumbled with a surprised cry, her eyes going wide. Brendon didn't wait for a better chance. His arm lashed down a moment later, leaving a blue streak down her side.

"Damn it, Brendon!" she cried, the same instant as he bellowed "Yes!" for the world to hear. Both went right back to laughter a moment later. Loren sat herself upright with a weary sigh, glaring at him with bemused tolerance. He turned on his heel, facing back to where I'd been waiting-

-And was greeted by Keira, just as I'd been a few brief moments before. There was no problem with *her* form as she brought her arm up, throwing her wrist into a block and sending his instinctive blow wide. Her 'knife' drove in before he could recover. Green blossomed in a dusty cloud, drifting off the line painted down his front.

Just like that, it was done.

***

"That's cheating," Brendon muttered, kicking at a stick as we trudged back up the lonely little path.

"Stop whining," Keira said. Her chin was high, her eyes gleaming with barely-contained satisfaction. She'd pulled her hair back, tying it into a tail that swished behind her with every swaggering step she took. She'd won, and even if she hadn't *said* anything, she knew it - and so did everyone else. "It was a good game."

"A game where *only you* had no fog of war," Jake muttered under his breath.

"And you could have knocked me out in a second, so stop *whining*," she said, her voice taking on a bit more of an edge as she elbowed him. "Jesus Christ, you're a bunch of babies."

Brendon launched back in where Jake left off, wheedling and picking at her. There was no real venom to his words, though - he was doing it as much to get a reaction out of her as anything, I knew.

Someone stepped closer. I glanced up. Jake sidled over, his hands still shoved into his pockets casually. "You've been practicing," I murmured, my voice just low enough to carry to him.

He shrugged. "Seemed best."

"You and Loren? Is, that, uh-"

A laugh slipped out of him before he could bite it back. "Her? Hardly. But hey. You work with what you've got." His eyes flashed up to mine. "Someone's got to.

I flushed. The meaning hidden under his words was clear. After our impromptu meeting, we'd let the whole matter lie. I'd been meaning to call a repeat of that little gathering for a full two weeks. We needed to decide *something*.

I was still trying to ignore the other truth that I hadn't quite faced yet - that if we *didn't* decide anything, I'd have to make the decision for us. I wasn't quite ready to deal with that just yet. Part of me still shied away from the responsibility, from the burden of carrying the consequences on my own shoulders. Bad enough when it was just me and Keira. With the rest of everyone starting to pile on, my stress levels were through the roof.

Jake sighed. I glanced up again, realizing a moment later that his eyes were still on my face. He was watching - knowingly. "Just fucking great," he muttered. "We're so screwed."

My face flushed to read in an instant. Before I could say a word or try and reassure him, he stepped ahead, catching up with Keira in two long strides. Loren and Brendon were back to chuckling quietly, their earlier exuberance beginning to fade.

I'd taken two steps, falling in behind them, when a sound split the quiet of the forest. I jumped - we all jumped. The others spun, instinctively facing back towards me.

Slowly, reassuringly, I held up a hand. "It's just my phone," I said, letting my hand slide into my pocket. The tension bled from their shoulders, even if their eyes stayed on me, pinning me to the tree trucks around us. Swallowing a chuckle, I smiled at them, shaking my head.

My good humor died in an instant as I pulled the phone from my pocket, catching sight of the caller ID.

Greyson.

The bottom dropped out of my stomach. I stared down at the screen, frozen in place. The old finder knew what we were looking for from him, and as much fun as he seemed to have at my expense, he wasn't the sort to play around.

Maybe he was just calling to ask if we wanted to go get drunk with him. Maybe he'd had an idea. Maybe it was something purely casual, nothing at all to be worried over.

It didn't even sound convincing in my own head.

My thumb tapped the *Accept* button, the speaker at my ear before the screen finished changing to the open line. "It's Jon. What's up?" I tried to keep my voice light, as though I could somehow force reality to follow suit if I just tried hard enough.

His gruff, stern voice quashed those hopes a moment later. "This ain't some courting call. Don't sound so hopeful."

The others slowed, glancing back as they realized I wasn't following. I just stayed where I was, my free hand shoved down into my pocket for warmth. Keira's green chalk still coated my jacket. My eyes were fixed on it, unable to look away. "What is it, then?" I said softly.

I heard him sigh, the soft clink of something glass against wood echoing across the line a moment later. "Early warning. Got the usual movement - locals, back and forth, all that."

"And something else."

"Wouldn't be calling you otherwise. Got a car, moving north. Not terribly close yet, but it'll be here in an hour or two. Movin' quick. Real quick - and right for us."

"Hostile? How many? Do you know what rel- what foci they have?" It wasn't worth getting the old man off on another rant about 'usin' the damn right word'. He'd enjoyed lecturing me at every turn on the matter.

"Can't really tell. Too far to get a good reading on 'em. Thinkin' it's only one or two. Probably two. Haven't felt too many abilities kick off around em, and they're not meandering at all." He hesitated, as though he was rolling something over in his mind. "Haven't felt any demis die around em. So..."

"So they might not be hostile," I finished for him.

"Maybe. Anyway. You all still playin' that dumb war game you lot came up with?"

I winced. "Ah- no. Just finished. We're about to head back." Talking about our impromptu contest just felt wrong - too normal to follow up an announcement like Greyson had made. "We'll be on our way in just a few minutes."

"Fine. If I was you, I'd hurry."

He hung up the phone before I could say another word. I was left staring at the blank screen, torn between shock at his words and irritation at the realization that I'd probably never get to finish a phone call the normal way again.

When I looked up, the others were staring back at me, mute and motionless. I forced my smile back into place, keeping my back straight. It was all that was keeping me up.

"Back to the car, I think. Now."

CHAPTER THIRTY-FOUR

"What did he say?"

I spared Brendon a glance, my eyes flicking up to meet his in the rearview mirror as we accelerated out onto the highway. "Like I said. He just said someone was coming, and that they were close."

"Oh," the weather-reader said, his voice quiet. "Do you think-"

"I don't know any more than you do." As hard as I tried to keep my irritation from my voice, it crept back in little by little. I couldn't blame the man for having questions, really - I had plenty of them myself. But I just didn't *know*, and being asked a dozen things back to back to back just rubbed it in my face. "Shit," I muttered, my fingers tightening on the wheel. "We should have started reaching out to the other crews weeks ago."

"You don't know it's them," Keira said. Her hand gripped the handle molded into the door, the skin showing white around her knuckles. "It could be.....I don't know."

"There's no one else who'd just drop in to say hi. And Greyson said they were coming up from the south."

She nodded slowly. "You think it's Detroit, then."

"Stands to reason, doesn't it?"

"Marketeers are closer, if they came from their northern outpost. Probably." Jake's voice cut across the quiet of the car, bringing Keira and I to a halt. A smile tugged at his lips when we glanced back to him, small and humorless. "That's *Ontario*. Start learning this shit already."

"Already trying," I said. It was hard to stay truly angry with my mind racing a mile a minute. "They might be closer, but they're coming from the *south*. So let's just...stick with what we know."

He shrugged, leaning back against the seat. I wasn't fooled. His skin was pale, and a muscle twitched in his jaw. "Whatever. Stop driving like my grandma and let's go."

I was already ten over the limit. I didn't bother pointing it out. I just slid the accelerator down a little harder, watching the asphalt and trees fly past on either side.

"We could run."

I blinked, looking back over my shoulder for a split second. It was Jake again - and the tone of his voice was entirely different from what it had been mere moments before. He met my eyes, though, holding my gaze levelly. "It's an option. I'm just saying."

"If we run, we're giving up on this whole idea," Loren said. Her voice was little more than a whisper. "Is that what we want to do?"

Keira snorted, tugging her ponytail tighter. "Where would we even go? We've got nowhere to run *to*. And a wandering crew will draw just as much attention as a stationary one. That's not a fix."

Brendon didn't say a word. He just sat in the backseat, his eyes glued to mine in the mirror. Every muscle in his body was tense, his back ramrod straight.

"Greyson said there were only a few of them," I said, forcing myself to look back at the road. "One or two. Something like that. There are five of us."

"And Greyson," Keira muttered.

I glared over at her. "Who won't be helping us in a fight, so it doesn't mean a damn."

Her ears glowed red. She nodded, half-shrugging. "Guess so. Just saying."

"The crews aren't going to send lightweights to talk to us," Jake said. "If they're looking to visit our home turf, they're not going to go down easily."

"I know," I said, feeling a sigh ripple through my chest. "We'll have to stay on top of them. But they don't know what our powers are, either. It should be easy to get a voice-hold on them."

"If they want to talk," Brendon muttered, speaking at last.

I grimaced. "Well. Yeah."

"This isn't helping," Keira said, twisting so that she could see everyone in the car at once. "Freaking out and working ourselves up isn't going to help anything. Let's just get back, get our stuff together, and see what happens. All right? Greyson said we had a bit of time, didn't he?"

"An hour or two, at the way they're moving," I said. "That was half an hour ago, though."

"Oh." She fell quiet after that, but I could still see the wheels turning in her head. We weren't going to get much in the way of downtime, if they were that close - and we'd spent the morning horsing around in the national forest, playing with our abilities and tiring ourselves out. If I'd *known* we'd have visitors in the afternoon, I would never have gone along with the whole war-games idea.

"We'll be fine," I said instead, turning my eyes back to the road. "Keira's right. Just think of what you need to get done when we get back. We won't have long."

The others nodded. The car fell into blissful quiet after that, solemn and still. My thoughts still raced, swirling and circling around the fact that I'd let this happen. Our indecision had left us vulnerable. We could have been scouting, researching, exploring. We could have reached out to the crews already, finding our footing - good or bad. We'd know where we stood.

But dwelling on the matter wouldn't help us, right then. I stared at the road instead, coaxing a few more miles per hour out of my poor, tired car as we raced towards home.

***

The house was dark and quiet as we crept up the driveway, each of us staring around with wide, fearful eyes. I couldn't shake the fears in the back of my mind, the notion that somehow they'd managed to beat us home. It had hung heavy in my thoughts for the last ten minutes, the possibility of walking headlong into a trap.

"Anything?" I murmured softly, creeping foot by foot up the gravel drive.

"Nothing," Keira whispered from the passenger seat. Her glasses were on. She'd pressed her face to the glass of her window, peering out. Loren and Brendon were doing the same from the backseat, although with much less benefit. Jake sat slouched alongside them, trying to look disinterested, but the pocket of his jacket trembled as he fidgeted. "I don't see anything," Keira reiterated, turning to glance at me.

"And there's no car," I said, sliding up to my parking spot. "I don't think they're here."

"Are you sure?" Loren said, the words slipping out as though on automatic. Her hand slipped up to her mouth a moment later, her face going red.

I smiled mirthlessly. "No, I'm not sure. But let's go in - together."

They all nodded, frozen in place. Waiting for me to step out, I realized. Wonderful. Cracking the door and wincing as the frigid early-winter air slapped me in the face, I eased myself towards the house. The car doors slammed as they followed behind like lost puppies.

When I unlocked the door, sliding it open with a creak, the house was every bit as dark and quiet as it had seemed from the outside. We dispersed room by room, each of us looking for any sign of unwelcome guests - and each of us trying not to look like that's what we were doing. Somehow, it felt like acknowledging that we didn't feel secure in our own home would forever take away any sense of safety the place brought us.

Finally, I stepped back into the kitchen, finding the others waiting there too. "It's clear," I said softly. "Let's stop playing around. They probably aren't that far off, even if we made it here first. Go get ready."

They hesitated a moment, looking around at each other, and then slipped off to their rooms. I turned to the hall, clenching and unclenching my fingers.

Get ready? How, exactly, were we supposed to do that? There was no magic trick that was going to somehow keep the enemy demis away, and everything we needed was contained in our relics.

All the same, I felt better when the little safe in my room popped open, letting me grab the pistol inside. I slipped it into its holster under my coat, zipping the jacket back up nervously. I could use it, at least. I just hoped I wouldn't have to. My leg twinged sympathetically, like the memory of the *last* time I'd gotten in a gunfight was reasserting itself.

And then I slipped back out into the living room. The clock ticked on the wall, each second sounding off with a crack that echoed around the kitchen. The others were close - I could hear them shifting, moving quietly about in their own rooms. Trying to keep my bones from creaking, I eased myself down into one of the chairs.

And waited.

The seconds drifted away, spinning into minutes as the last dregs of the morning slipped into afternoon. Trying to keep my fingers from tapping against the table, I made a pot of coffee. It didn't help. With a cup of the stuff in me, it just made me jittery on top of nervous. But I felt better, clutching the warm cup between my palms.

And still we waited.

At some point, Jake took up his place on the couch, turning the TV on and leaving it playing low and soft enough that none of us could complain about the noise. Even with it on, though, he stared out the window, his eyes flicking this way and that as he watched for any signs of movement.

Some part of me wondered if I shouldn't set some of our demis to keeping watch, if we wouldn't be better served by distributing ourselves around the property. But the rest of me knew the truth - if a fight was coming, then we'd be better served staying together. It was good that Jake and Loren had found some sort of partnership that worked for the both of them. We might need it.

The sound of tires rolling against gravel was enough to sit me bolt upright, flying out of my seat entirely a moment later. Jake wasn't far behind - and within moments of the sound echoing around the living room, Loren and Brendon came bounding out from around the corner of the hallway that led to their room.

Keira was the last to emerge, her every step slow and measured. She clutched a knife in one hand, tucking it away and out of sight somewhere inside her jacket. I didn't like the sight of her armed, but I knew that whether or not I liked it wasn't important. I still remembered the sight of her blocking Brendon's attack, slashing her mock blade across his chest. She'd improved - and I didn't have to wonder too hard where she'd picked up her new tricks.

Aedan hadn't offered to teach *me* while he'd been at the house, I thought sourly.

Keira wasn't the only one who was armed. Brendon and Loren both had their hands in their pockets, clutching handles I could barely see. My knife block had some open slots, I noted, trying not to glare. Those knives were *nice*. They didn't need to get stuck in random demis. Jake wasn't bothering to hide the gun he held at his side, staring back at me without a shred of shame in his eyes.

Fine. Let him have his gun. I stepped towards the door, my heart pounding in my chest. The car wasn't moving anymore - and as I slid the door open, pushing back out into the cold, the engine turned off.

I could see it ahead, the back half of the car sticking far enough past the corner of the house that it was just barely in sight. It was as run-down as mine was, I saw, a bit of humor rising despite the gravity of the situation. There was more bond-o than actual paint, in places, and where there wasn't the body of it was a wonderful shade of rust. The bumper was held on by what looked like coat hangers.

The slam of a car door reminded me that I wasn't heading out to ogle their car - we needed to handle this situation. Whatever it turned into. Keira's hand slid up to my shoulder, squeezing for a single second before falling free again. She was there, and so were the others, filing out behind me one after another.

Taking a deep breath and lifting my chin high in a futile show of composure, I stepped out of the shadows and towards our guests.

CHAPTER THIRTY-FIVE

The snow-covered gravel crunched underfoot as I stepped forward. My anxiety grew with every step, building to a point that burned hot and furious in my chest. My lips slid apart, my breath waiting to bellow a command at the slightest sight of danger.

When I came around the corner, though, I was left facing two demis standing alongside their car. I froze, dragging my eyes across them as though I could suck in every scrap of information there was to be had just from looking. From the sudden halt of her footsteps I knew that Keira was doing the same - but at least *she* might actually have some success.

I could only stare at the two men, one of whom looked to be little more than a boy. The older one might have been my age, or a year or two younger. Both him and the teenager had the same golden-brown hair, the same nose. The resemblance was too much to be coincidental.

And none of it did the slightest bit to reassure me.

"That's close enough," I said, shoving my hands into my pockets. It wasn't a command - I didn't want to give myself away quite so easily - but I filled it with every ounce of iron I could.

The pair of demis jumped, glancing up. The younger one nearly toppled over, caught on a patch of ice, but clung to the car for support. For a long, silent moment we were like statues, staring back at each other.

"Oh," the older one said. His brown eyes fixed on mine, pausing for a second before sliding to Keira, and then on to our companions.

"Wow. Uh, hi."

"Can we help you?" I said, folding my arms across my chest. Keira elbowed me. She didn't have to say a word - *Don't ruin this with stupid aggression.* Her message came across crystal clear.

He only ran a hand through his hair, glancing over to what had to be his brother. "Uh...sorry, I guess I just didn't expect the full welcome."

"Well, we're glad you decided to come talk," I said. The words echoed hollowly in my ears, like someone else was talking. "We wanted to talk to you, too."

"You did?" the demi said. His brow furrowed, his eyes narrowing as he glared at me. "You knew we were coming?"

"We...have our sources," I said, choosing my words carefully. I didn't know quite how public Greyson wanted his involvement with us to be, but broadcasting his presence for the world to hear just sounded like a bad idea. "We got word you were heading our way."

"Oh. Good. I was a little worried that we might catch you off guard," he said, letting his lips curl up in the tiniest fraction of a smile.

"I wouldn't say we were really expecting you," I said dryly. "But our...friend, I guess, warned us you were coming."

Their eyes lit up. The younger one shifted from foot to foot, his eyes dancing between each of us, but seemed content to let his brother handle the talking. And for his part, the older demi nodded along, his smile growing. "Did he? Good. I wasn't sure he would."

A chuckle slid between my lips. "We've got our scouting covered. Anyway. I'm glad you're visiting, and that we can...have this conversation." I was glad that we could talk, that they were approaching us head-on rather than coming in guns blazing, trying to wipe us from the face of the Earth. The words I left unsaid hung in the air between us. "I was really hoping that we could come to some sort of understanding."

It wasn't so small anymore. The older one grinned, relief plain on his face. "Really? Ah, that's great. So do we. We were...I wasn't sure what we were going to be walking into. But...good." He glanced to his younger brother for a single second before his eyes flicked back to me. "And- we can really stay?"

I blinked. It was my turn to stare at him, my brow wrinkling as I tried to work through what he'd said. "Excuse me?"

Keira was making a strange noise. I didn't have time to look at her and see what her problem was. The demi was matching my stare with his own, the excitement of a few moments before fading. "W-What? I was just asking if we could-"

"You want to *stay?*" I said, repeating the words as though they'd make sense if I said them out loud. It wasn't helping. I shook my head instead, my eyes narrowing. "How'd you find us, anyway?"

"I...Well, he- We got your address," the demi said, his words coming more slowly. "We were given it. And told to come check in with you here. I'm sorry, I thought-"

Before he could say another word, the sound of Keira's laughter cut across the conversation. The demi stopped in a second, flinching away from us. His hand went to his brother's arm, dragging him a step away. But Keira only held her hand up, waving it back and forth hurriedly.

"Where exactly did Aedan find you two?" she said, glancing over to me.

Realization flooded in a second after her words hit me. Aedan. *Duh.* With everything going on, all the pressure and the stress, I'd been so fixated on the idea that we were vulnerable and just *waiting* for one of the bigger crews to pounce on us. It had never occurred to me that Aedan might be faster on the punch than they were.

"Down in Indiana," the older one said. He didn't look any more reassured, and he was still poised like he might run off at the slightest disturbance, but he was still *there*. "He said there was a place up north. Somewhere we might be safer."

I ran a hand through my hair, letting a ragged sigh slip out. "That's- Okay. Yeah. Sorry. I got a bit confused, that's all. Just a bit of a misunderstanding." Behind me, I could hear Brendon let out an equally tense noise. He'd been just as wound up as I was, clearly.

The demi's face fell. "Then...we can't? Is this the wrong place?"

"No, no," I said, waving my hand hurriedly. "I just- I just thought you were someone else. Yeah. No. You're rogues, then?"

He nodded slowly, still staring at me with that damn impassive expression. "Something like that, yeah. I'm Tyler, by the way. Morgan. Tyler Morgan."

"Jon Christensen," I said, holding him with my stare. Somehow, it didn't seem like shaking hands was the right thing to do. He nodded once more, even more slowly. His hand still clutched the elbow of the young man standing next to him. I jerked my chin in his direction, not taking my eyes off Tyler. "Whos' this?"

"Kai," the teenager said, jumping as though I'd shocked him. "Kai

Morgan."

"My little brother," Tyler said quietly, as though that wasn't totally obvious already.

Wonderful. Perfect. I fought off the urge to run my hand through my hair again, feeling all too clearly the pressure of everyone standing at my back. "And you're both demis, yes?"

There was a moment of hesitation, a poignant pause that passed between the two brothers. Kai bounced on his heels, his eyes alight with energy, but faltered at something in Tyler's expression.

"Yeah," the older demi said at last, looking back to me with a ghost of a smile. "We are now."

"Okay, so what- wait, *now?*" I said, shaking my head as his words sank in. "What's that supposed to mean?" This was probably the time for a bit of subtlety, a bit of diplomacy. I'd need it, if we were negotiating with the big boys soon - but all the same, I wasn't quite sure I could find it in me to be diplomatic when faced with the mess Aedan had dumped in my lap.

"He gave me this," Kai said, jumping in before Tyler could say a word. His wrist shot up, fast enough that I heard everyone behind me flinch. I stayed where I was, willing myself not to move, and glimpsed the gold-and-ruby bracelet clasped against his skin.

"Kai!" Tyler snapped, grabbing his brother's arm. "What the hell did I say?"

"Not to- oh," Kai muttered, his face going brilliantly red in the same time it took his to drop his arm to his side, stepping closer to his brother. His eyes flicked up to mine, almost guiltily.

"No one here will take your foci," I said, doing my best to sound more reassuring than I felt. "But, uh. Yeah. Probably not a good idea to go waving it around." I gave Kai an inspecting look - he couldn't have been older than eighteen or nineteen, and from the way he was acting...I looked back to Tyler. "Is he new?"

The older demi hesitated, his lips gently parted, and drew back half a step. Kai stumbled with him, pulled along by the hand latched around his elbow. "Yeah," Tyler said at last, still staring at me. "I didn't...I never expected to be able to give him a focus. We only had the one, in our family."

"Most families only have one," Jake said. I glanced back, caught off guard by the normally-disinterested man's words. He only kicked at a clump of ice on the ground, pursing his lips unhappily.

"But that guy had lots. What, was he collecting them or something?" Kai said, his voice brightening again.

I groaned. "So...Aedan. He gave you a relic?"

"A - He gave Kai a focus. Pulled a box right out of his backpack and started tossing them at us." Tyler's eyes were every bit as cold as his brother's were excited. "If this is some sort of a trick, I swear to god, I'll-"

"If you thought it was a trick, why did you come?" I said, cutting him off before he could ramp himself up. This was old territory, ground I'd covered enough times in the last few months that I was beginning to get tired of it. "You didn't have to."

"Well..." he said, a bit of his anger seeping away. "I guess...that's just it, isn't it? It doesn't make any *sense*." A crooked smile tugged at his lips, humorless. "What, someone's just going around handing out foci, and he didn't even stop to see what bond Kai wound up with? Just threw it at us, made us memorize an address, and walked out?" He shook his head. "That doesn't sound like a hunter. It sounds like an *idiot*." Tyler hesitated another moment. "But...there were already some demis getting curious about me. Poking around. It wasn't safe for us anymore. I thought...why not at least look?"

"There were demis starting to ask questions?" I said, standing a little straighter. "Did they follow you, any of them?"

Tyler was shaking his head before I'd finished the sentence. "No. No, I took Kai and left before they could figure too much out. They wouldn't have known to follow us."

"You *think*," someone murmured from behind me. Loren. Her voice was quiet, filled with all the tension that had finally started to bleed to nothing.

I eyed the demi carefully, rolling his words around in my mind, but I couldn't see any trace of a lie in what he said. He was nervous, sure, but so was I. "Here's what we're going to do," I said, keeping my voice neutral and calm. "I'm going to ask you some questions - alone. And then I'm going to ask Kai some questions."

Tyler stiffened. "What do you mean, questions? And if you think I'm going to leave you alone with him, you're-"

"No one will hurt him. But you two can't just stumble in off the freeway, telling wild stories, and expect us to trust you at the drop of a hat." I fell quiet for a second, letting my words hang between us. "If you want us to trust you, return the favor for a little bit." A shrug slipped across my shoulders. "We need to make sure your intentions are as good as you say. If you're honest with us, then we'll talk about what happens next. About you two staying."

"It's fine, Tyler," Kai said, glancing over at his brother. A smirk touched the corners of his lips. "If they try anything, I'll-"

"Don't even think about it," Tyler snapped, glaring at the younger demi. "You've had that thing for a *week*. Don't get a fat head."

Kai deflated visibly, crumpling in on himself as his brother stared him down. "...Fine," he muttered at last.

Tyler sighed, the sound filled with exhaustion. "And you swear you won't try anything?" he said, his eyes flicking to mine. "He can wait in the car. We can go stand over there." I saw the look he shot my entourage. "But I don't want them near him."

"Tough fucking titties," Jake muttered under his breath, scowling darkly. His scowl only deepened as I sighed, glancing over to him. "No. Fuck no, Jon. We don't know them."

"Jake's right," Brendon said, inching closer.

"It's going to be fine, okay?" I snapped, my ears filled with their arguments and murmures and the thoughts in the back of my head that they were *right*. "Going to have to do this somehow. It'll be fine. Just wait over there. We'll go stand by the trees. See? Everyone can still see everyone." Good god, it felt like kitten herding sometimes, trying to get everyone to cooperate, but finally they all nodded.

"Fine," Tyler said, the last bit of resistance seeping from his tone. "Go wait in the car, Kai."

"But-"

"Now."

"Fine," the younger demi muttered, glaring at me with venom in his brown eyes. Without another word he tromped over to the sedan, hurling himself inside and slamming the door.

"What did you want to ask?" Tyler said, tearing his eyes away from his brother at last.

I jerked my chin, motioning towards the treeline. "Like I said. I just want to make sure that you're not here to play tricks or hurt anyone. I'm going to ask you some stuff, and you're going to answer me. Honestly." I smiled. "If you lie, I'll know."

"Fine. Ask whatever you want," he said, crossing his arms across his chest as he came to a halt. Drawn up to his full height, he was almost taller than me. Almost.

"Is anyone following you?"

"What? No. I already told you, they're not."

"What's your goal here?"

He paused, settling back on his heels. "I want somewhere safe. Somewhere Kai and I don't have to watch over our shoulders every second. And the last place wasn't cutting it anymore, like I said."

My gaze danced across his form, searching for any hint of a lie, but I found nothing. Slowly, my hand slid to my chest, instinctively resting against the fabric of my jacket. The necklace hanging around my neck was warm against my skin underneath the layers.

Tyler scowled again. "Is that all you-"

"Do you have *any* other reason for visiting here?" I interrupted, rolling over his attempt at cutting into the conversation. "Any sort of ulterior motive?"

"Of course not," he said, his tone a hair shy of a scoff. "I'm not-"

"You clearly don't trust us. So why are you here, if our offer is so suspicious?"

Again, he paused. His words came more slowly when he spoke again, his eyes downcast. "Because I didn't have a ton of ideas on my own. Because Kai deserves to have a focus of his own, and not be left waiting for me to die on the off-chance he can inherit mine. Because something like this..." He shook his head, still staring at the snow. "It would be a dream, if it actually worked. If you can make it work."

His words rang true. I swallowed hard, feeling my ears begin to burn. "We're still kind of working all that out. Don't hope for too much. We're not through the worst of it yet."

Tyler chuckled. "I know. That guy was pretty explicit about *that*."

Despite the gravity of the situation, I found myself starting to laugh. "Ah, yeah. He can be like that. Skinny guy, red hair?"

He nodded. "Right. Him."

"What exactly did he tell you, anyway?" Part of me didn't want to know - but it was important that I knew what I was dealing with.

The other demi only shrugged. "Told me there was a crew looking for new demis. Strong and weak both - but strong would be better. Told me if I was willing to fight for it, there'd be a focus for Kai in the mix." His gaze flicked over to the car, to where the younger man sat in the passenger seat, half in shadow but clearly glowering. "It was worth a try."

"Right," I said softly. "What power did he wind up with?"

Tyler's eyes snapped back to mine. It wasn't as innocent a question as the others, I knew, and there was an almost-instinctive resistance there in the demi's stare. But it crumbled with every second that passed, until at last he sighed. "Fire," he mumbled. "Kai got fire. I'm...I don't know how to teach him. It's too early to say how much he got."

"Fire," I said, forcing myself to keep a straight face. "Uh. And he's, uh. Can he control it, yet?"

Tyler's wince told me everything I needed to know. "We'll work on it," I said, shoving my hands into my pockets to hide my suddenly-sweaty palms. "We'll *definitely* work on that." I didn't have much experience with the other demibloods, and I was used to being pretty much the most inexperienced one on the block. But something told me that having an untrained, un-mentored fire mage running around would be a bad idea. A really, really bad idea.

Tyler just made another face, running a hand through his hair. It hung around his face in limp waves falling just past his earlobes. It was greasy, I noted dispassionately. They'd been pushing hard to get here. Probably for longer than that. "I'm doing my best," he said, his voice little more than a whisper.

"And you?"

He scowled again. "What? What about me?"

It was all I could do to keep from rolling my eyes. "Your focus."

"Oh. Uh. Well." He raised one hand, his pointer finger trembling slightly, and brushed his hair back from his ear. A tiny black gemstone earring sat perched near the top of the cartilage, right where it would be out of sight. "Sound," he whispered. "I manipulate sound. The amplitude. The direction. Big or small."

"And you're not new." The words slipped out on automatic, my mouth working all on its own while my brain spun on overdrive.

He shook his head sharply, just once. "No. I've..." He glanced back towards the car again. "I've had it for a bit more than five years," he whispered. The sound rang perfectly in my ears, either through his power or my own adrenaline-fueled senses. "From dad."

"I see," I said, unable to find any tactful way to follow *that* up.

I wasn't done yet. We went back and forth, trading questions and answers almost more quickly than I could follow. This was the first time we'd tried something like this - taking in demis off the street, willingly allowing them to join the group without any prompting. Jake had had enough motive for me to give him the benefit of the doubt, after Matt's crew tried to off him. Brendon and Loren had both been themselves captives. It was hard to argue they'd put themselves in that position.

Tyler and Kai? They had none of those excuses to fall back on. I fired off every question I could think of, from their motives to their history and back to how long they planned on staying. I was repeating myself - I *knew* I was repeating myself - and yet I couldn't stop. I could only come at the same set of questions from as many directions as I could think of, trying to catch the demi out in a lie or a twist, a play on words that concealed his true intentions.

No matter what I tried, nothing changed. My relic was a constant, warm presence against my chest, keeping out the cold of the winter day around us, and only honesty showed in his words. A slow, building ache in the back of my mind reminded me that I'd already spent the day playing around, and I still had to go through all this again with Kai. There was a limit to how paranoid I could be, at least at first.

"All right," I said at last.

Tyler jumped, blinking slowly as my words hung between us. "All right?"

"All right, I believe you," I said, letting a tiny, crooked smile tug at the corners of my lips at last. "I can't make any guarantees, but so long as you stick with what you've said and play honest, I think there could be a place here for you."

His hand whipped up, pressing to his face, but I saw it - the tiniest flash of a smile, broad and earnest, spreading from ear to ear before his hand obscured it entirely. "That's- I mean, that's good," he said. From the way his voice warped, twisting softly, I knew he was fighting to get himself under control.

"I still have to talk to Kai," I said, hating to have to bring him down at all but knowing that I shouldn't let them go without being as thorough as possible. "Not that I doubt him, but-"

"No. No, I understand," he said, shaking his head hurriedly. "Should I-"

"If you want to wait here, you can trade places with him in the car. Otherwise, one of the others could-"

"I'll stay here."

No big surprise. I couldn't picture the man walking away and leaving his little brother in a crowd of still-strange demis. I just nodded, half-turning, and started back for the car.

***

By the end of it, my head was on fire. The slightest sound burned in my eardrums, like the worst hangover I'd had in my life was condensed down into one fiery, regret-filled evening. I thought about complaining, about moaning and whining about the pain, but when faced with the two newcomers, it was hard to let a bad mood stick.

We'd gone through the same questions, the same repeated lines of inquiry and drills back and forth to see if I could get Kai to stumble. He hadn't. He'd stuck to his story just like his older brother - but even with his honesty, I could see the truth of his inexperience shining through. Kai was new. *Very* new. Twice, he'd held his hand out, his eyes lighting up, and I'd seen sparks glimmering against the skin there.

So far, I'd managed to stomp out that line of thinking. He needed to learn - but he needed to learn in a more controlled environment than 'trying to show off in front of a new, older demi you want on your good side.' We'd put so many hours into the house. I much preferred to have it un-charred.

With every second, the sounds of their voices grew a little softer. The others were taking them around, showing them the property and the house. A tiny groan slipped between my lips at the thought of having to find homes for two new demis. Homes, and places to sleep, and jobs...the list went on and on. The house was big, sure - we'd opened up each of its four bedrooms, and there was an attic that we could *probably* convert into another, but we were going to run out of space all too quickly.

We needed to find a better way to do this. If this was even what we wanted to do. The others had fixed me with looks from afar as I questioned the little brother. No one had actually said it, but everyone was thinking the same thing. If we kept taking in demis, then the whole matter of how we approached the prime crews was going to get answered *for* us.

It was a problem, and one we'd have to worry about. But we had more people. The knot in my chest loosened, just a little, as I lifted the phone to my ear. The house stared back at me, filled with light and life.

The line clicked. "What?" Aedan snapped. "Don't waste my time."

"Hello to you too," I said dryly.

"I'm hanging up."

"Next time you send people, Aedan?" I said, forcing the words out before he could shut me off. "Could you call? You could even just text.

That'd be great. I think you scared Greyson."

The only noise on the line for a long moment was the sound of Aedan laughing. "It's good for the old fucker. Gives his heart a workout. Did you like 'em?"

"What?"

"The two. Not bad, eh?"

"Oh. Yeah. I think they'll help. Thank you." It took everything I had to spit the words out. I knew before I said anything that actually *thanking* Aedan would just make him even more insufferable.

Sure enough, when he spoke again, I could almost hear him preening himself. "Right, right. I'm the best, I know. Didn't think I'd be so fast, did you?"

I chuckled hollowly. "I did not. Which is why I'd *really* appreciate it if you could-"

"Yeah, okay. I'll think about it. See ya."

"Aedan, just-"

The line went dead. I swore under my breath, glaring daggers at the phone, but he was gone. If he ever let me actually finish a phone conversation, the world might just end. I thought about calling him back - briefly - but that wouldn't change anything.

The sound of the others' voices rose, Keira's polite laughter cutting across the rest. I wouldn't be alone for long. And with new demis hanging around, I knew it wasn't a good idea to remain apart for longer than necessary.

A smile crept onto my face as I turned back towards the ongoing tour. A lot was changing, yes. But for once, it almost seemed like things were changing for the *better*. I wasn't quite sure how to feel about that, but right in that moment, it was enough.

My steps were a little lighter as I made my way back to the others.

CHAPTER THIRTY-SIX

"Right. So, then, uh...I just-"

A blast of air cut off the words I'd been about to say - a warning to *focus*, or else he'd lose it. No need to warn him. Kai was bound and determined to figure this out on his own, clearly.

We'd put our collective feet down that he *was* going to figure it out, at least. One week. That was all the time it had taken to realize that Kai was a very narrow inch away from being a full-scale walking disaster.

He was a good kid. Somehow. I was sure of it. He meant well, and he seemed earnest enough about how things played out. He didn't freak out too badly when Tyler glared at him, or told him what to do. But clearly, he'd been sitting on the sidelines watching Tyler figure out his relic for far too long. Getting one of his own might have been too much, too quickly.

He didn't *mean* to set the kitchen on fire, when he'd attempted to show off to Loren. The candle he'd tried to light had remained blissfully cold and still. The roll of paper towel next to it, however, proved far more receptive to the notion of 'fire'. I'd been halfway across the living room when it had all started, seeing only his stunned face as the flames shot up with shocking ease.

We'd need a new set of dish towels. And probably a new coat of stain for the cabinets. And Kai might have needed a new pair of pants after that.

It hadn't stopped him from trying again the next day, when Jake had slipped out for a cigarette. Jake was lucky. The cigarette took the brunt of the force, rather than his face. His eyebrows would regrow, in time.

Tyler had done his best. He'd gone pale each and every time Kai fiddled around with his relic, dragging his little brother outside by the ear. But expecting the new demi not to experiment with the new toy that had been thrown into his lap was just too much.

Which was why I'd told Kai that he could experiment all he wanted - outside. After that, it was in all of our best interests to try and help him figure it out. We all wanted our home intact.

"That's fine. It's fine," I said, wiping a hand across my face to try and clear away the soot. His latest attempt hadn't had heat so much as smoke and grit.

"Sorry," Kai said, glancing up at me sheepishly. "I'll figure it out."

"He'd better figure it out," I heard someone mutter behind me, their voice low enough I wasn't entirely sure I'd heard. I glanced back, my brow furrowing. The others were nearby, all of them watching - but it was Brendon who had spoken. He glared at Kai for a moment longer, kicking at the snow, before turning away with a sigh. Within seconds he'd vanished around the back of the house.

"One more time." The sound of Kai's voice, filled with equal parts eagerness and stubbornness, was enough to bring me spinning back around to face him. Tyler stood only a few feet away, stepping in with one hand raised, but at Kai's announcement, he winced and skittered back.

Kai's right hand rose with an unnerving confidence. His left hand clasped around the gold-and-ruby chain of his relic. His brow furrowed as he stared into the campfire ring out back he'd declared 'his', the intensity of his glare growing by the second. The logs had long since been hurled out of its bounds, leaving only char-spotted dirt and ash behind.

"Easy, now," I said, forcing my attention back to him. We were all standing well back, thoroughly *behind* Kai. That didn't necessarily mean we were safe, but it certainly appeared to be the safest place to be. "We don't need an explosion. Just a steady flame."

"I know," he muttered, his eyes narrowing further at my words.

"Kai," Tyler said, and I could hear the sigh in his voice.

"I *know.*"

A quiet shuffling behind me warned me someone was moving - Keira, slipping farther away. She could recognize the petulant tone in his voice too, then. I smothered a smile, inching back as the wisdom of her decision made itself all too clear.

"Right...then I'll...just..." Kai breathed, his fingertips curling in.

He didn't get another word out as the air in the fire ring crackled to life. My ears rang with the sound of his magic going off. A fresh round of ash and muck splattered against Tyler's coat a heartbeat later. The older demi just flinched, his eyes squeezing shut momentarily, and glared at his little brother with good-natured tolerance. "You're still thinking too big, Kai. Take it down a few notches. It's just fire."

"Fire is big."

"It doesn't have to be," Keira muttered, slinking forward again now that it seemed the blowing-things-up portion was done for the time being.

I nodded slowly. "Maybe...we're going about this wrong."

That stopped them. Both Kai and Tyler paused, glancing back to me, and I could see the question in their eyes. "What do you mean?" Kai asked at last. The look he gave me was still filled with frustration, the irritation he had to be feeling just under the surface, but there was a begrudging respect there too. I got the feeling him and Tyler had had *words* about Kai, and me, and the crew they were being welcomed to. The young man had never quite gone so far as to argue with me.

Pulling the collar on my coat a little higher against the cold, I just nodded towards the fire pit. "You're all worried about starting a fire. Maybe it's better if you worry about putting one out."

He blinked. And then his head tilted to one side. "Can I do that?"

I stopped myself from chuckling just in time. "Hell if I know. Maybe?"

"It's worth trying," Tyler muttered, turning back towards the house. One hand drifted down his jacket, like a feeble attempt at wiping the grit and mess off himself. "I'll see if I can find some matches."

"There's lighter fluid in the garage," I called after him. He only nodded in response, vanishing through the door a moment later. I couldn't stop myself from smiling. He could try being a *little* less obvious with his relief.

"Serious, though," Kai said. I glanced back at him. He stared up at me, his expression a little sheepish. "Is that a thing? Uh...do you *get* more than one power? Does that count?"

Oh, god, he really *was* new. I stared at him, internally warring between pity and amusement. Is that was it was like for Aedan, when I'd been hanging off his arm?

It had probably been worse. I'd been even more clueless than Kai was - at least he had his brother's example to follow. *He'd* known about relics and demis for years, probably. But there was a difference between knowing they existed and having one of your own. Surreptitiously, I brushed my fingers across my necklace, takin comfort in the feel of it against my skin.

"Aedan always tells me it depends on what you want from it," I said, keeping my tone carefully neutral.

"Aedan? Who's that?"

Loren sighed, her exasperation finally shining through. "The man who gave you that focus," she said. She stood stiff-backed half a dozen paces away, staring after where Brendon had vanished.

"Oh. Him."

"Him," I echoed, my smile growing. "Anyway. It's not like a different power, is it? Just sort of...the opposite." I shrugged. "Give it a try, I guess."

The creak of the door announced Tyler's return. He trudged down the path from the side of the house, a pack of matches clutched in one hand and a bottle of lighter fluid in the other. "All right," he said, his voice weary. "I swear to fucking god, Kai, if you blow this up and get embers all over me, I'll-"

"I won't!" his little brother cried, just a note shy of a whine.

Tyler didn't look convinced. He kept muttering as he built the fire back up, glaring pointedly at Kai. Within seconds they were arguing again.

"Did you ever talk to Greyson?" someone said at my elbow. I flinched, looking over a moment later. Keira waited at my side, a knit hat pulled over her dark hair. A tiny smile tugged at her lips as my eyes met hers. "He wanted to talk to you."

"I called him back," I muttered. "Wasn't important enough he left a message, was it?"

"But important enough he called," she said, not backing down an inch. Her blue-eyed gaze was perfectly level. "So what was it?"

I ran a hand through my hair, my nose wrinkling. "About what you'd expect."

"He's getting annoyed."

"Pretty much." I shrugged. "We're growing a little bit. We stand out more. He doesn't love that. But he knew what he was getting into, at least. Mostly."

"Right, right. *Mostly.*"

I elbowed her. She jumped away, laughing, but her humor died off within seconds. "And, uh. What exactly *are* we getting into? Have you decided anything?"

An irritated noise slipped from the back of my throat. "It's not *my* decision."

"You're the leader. It kind of is."

"Who the fuck decided *that?*"

"You did, when you suggested Jake stay around. When you started collecting allies." She held my stare with her own, entirely unapologetic. "It's not a bad thing, Jon. But we should decide something soon. A plan. I don't think anyone wants to *run*, but we need to stay out front of all of this."

"I know," I mumbled. "I'm working on it."

"Work faster."

"I already asked Greyson for some contacts," I said, a little louder. "I mean, he doesn't know *names*, but he can at least tell us where to start looking."

"Good."

"What about you? I see that knife you've got in your jacket," I said, folding my arms and glaring at Keira. "And I saw the way you've been moving. What, is he giving you lessons, now?"

Her ears flushed to red. "I need to be able to defend myself too, Jon. Don't be mad."

"I'm not mad. But when'd he find time to do that? And, what, you couldn't be bothered to invite me?" A crooked smile tugged at the corners of my lips. "I'd like to know how to fight like a crazy person too, you know."

"If you ask *really nicely*, maybe he'll show you the next time he comes around," she said, her chin lifting. "Rather than just getting in a pissing match with him, that is."

"I-" I began, but stopped. Something had echoed around the treeline - a dull, hollow sound, on the very edge of my hearing. "What was that?"

Keira's eyebrows pulled together. "What was what?"

"Look. I'll figure it all out. Soon. I promise," I said, glancing around. My hand slipped up to pat her shoulder reassuringly.

She only glared at me, tight-lipped. "And where are we going to put everyone?"

"We're managing, aren't we?"

"For now."

"And when we're not, I'll...figure something out."

She snorted. "Right."

"Just go keep an eye on Kai, all right?" I said, fixing my eyes on her again. She stiffened, her mouth dropping open - no doubt to argue being saddled with the unstable new demi. I only chuckled, already turning away. "I'll worry about all that."

Her angry, indrawn breath echoed in my ears as I slipped away, but Loren stepped past me as I moved on. A quick smile flashed across her lips, there and gone in a single instant. I only nodded, continuing on towards the back yard. I was *sure* I'd heard something.

Sure enough, when I rounded the last corner into the yard, I was greeted by the sight of Brendon standing against the side of the house, all the way on the far side. His face was red, and I could see sweat drenching his hair from where I was.

His arms were down at his side, trembling with barely-restrained force, and his eyes were squeezed shut. A wisp of air slipped between his lips as a groan. One hand was clutched into a fist, wrapped around something.

A second later, the last of the tension bled from his frame, and he slumped like his strings had been cut.

I crept forward, taking another step, but before I could make it any farther he exploded into motion.

A dull, hollow thud echoed around the yard as his clenched fist slammed into the side of the house - hard. Something dripped from his grasp. His forehead hit the boards a moment later. He leaned into the siding, panting.

"Does the house really deserve your abuse?" I said mildly, taking a step closer.

He flinched, his spine straightening. His whole frame quivered, like he hadn't even know I was there. "Jon."

"That's my name," I said, flashing him a quick grin. He didn't return it.

"What's wrong?" he said. Each word was a little brighter than the one before it, like he was forcing life back into his voice. "Did something happen?"

"No, no," I said, shaking my head quickly. "Nothing like that, no. Just heard something."

"Oh. Well, sorry," Brendon said, glancing away. "I just- needed some air. There's nothing to see here."

I eyed the siding again. "Are you going to keep beating up the house if I walk away now?"

"Sorry."

"I'm not *worried* about the house."

"Worry about Kai. He'll burn it down, if we're not careful." He stiffened as the last word escaped, hanging in the air between us. Even still, there was no shame in his expression, no regret. He stared at me, eyes wide. His palm dripped blood from around whatever he held. It gathered underneath him, a tiny red blotch amid the sea of white.

I shook my head again, the movement slow and deliberate. "He's learning. It takes time. But he'll get there."

"And what if he doesn't?" Brendon snapped, his eyes flashing over to meet mine. "What if he never-" He stopped, the words vanishing mid-sentence. Just like that, all of his energy and exuberance from a few moments before was gone. "What if he never changes?" he said, picking his words more carefully.

"You don't like them being here."

"I don't…" Brendon began, but stopped. "I don't know. I guess not." His gaze dropped to the ground.

I shrugged. "They don't seem so bad, Brendon. Tyler seems nice. And Kai's a good kid." I just had to keep telling myself that. Maybe if I said it often enough, it would outweigh the stuff he'd blown up so far.

"We don't know the first thing about either of-"

"What's this really about?" I asked quietly.

He froze. For a long, still minute, he didn't say a word. The both of us just stood, staring at each other like picture-perfect statues. "If you want me to go, Jon, I'll go," he said at last. His voice was thin, lashing out with a bite I'd never heard from the weather-reader before. "Just say the word. I won't hang around."

"Wait, what?" I said, my surprise overcoming my concern in an instant. "What's that about leaving, now?"

"I'm doing my best, damn it. I can do better. I promise. But you don't have to- If you want me to-"

"Do you think I want you to *leave?* I said, interrupting his stuttering, rambling mess. "What the fuck? What's going on, Brendon?"

"I…I don't-"

"Seriously. Get talking."

"I'm trying, okay?" he said, the words falling out of him. "I'm working on it. I know I'm just a burden right now, but if you give me just a bit of time, I can-"

"You're talking about your relic," I said slowly, leaning back on my heels. "I mean, your focus. Whatever."

His face was glowing bright red by then. "I...I'll figure it out. I swear, Jon."

"I know you will," I said, working harder with every passing second to keep my confusion from my voice. "I'm not worried about it. I've been there, Brendon. You think being a translator is any better than a meteorologist?"

My mind picked up the pieces one after another, splicing together the mishmash of scenes since he'd joined our little crew. I'd known he was sensitive about his lack of power. I hadn't thought having new demis join the crew would send him into a meltdown. "It's just going to take time," I finished weakly, trying to smile at him. He still didn't return the gesture.

"Right," he said tonelessly, looking away. "Then...I should keep working. Thanks for the concern."

I winced. It wasn't right, seeing the normally-bright man so put out over all this, but there was a wall behind his expression that I didn't think would go away so easily. If I pushed him, if I tried to verbally slap some sense into him, he'd probably just lock down even harder.

His back was already turned to me. He stalked off, heading deeper into the woods over where Aedan had been camping. I watched him go, wordless.

I wasn't a damn psychologist. It was bad enough people were expecting me to make *plans* - I didn't have the first clue how to help him come to terms with his relic.

A light went on in my mind. I didn't know - but maybe I knew someone who *would* know how.

Turning on my heel, I accelerated back towards the front of the house - and nearly ran headlong into Loren.

The tiny, delicate woman crept from around the corner, right in my path as I charged forward. I caught myself just in time, grabbing hold of her shoulders before I could bowl her over entirely. "Shit, Loren," I said, trying not to scowl. "Give a guy a little warning."

"Sorry," she whispered.

Something in my mind screamed to stop - the set of her shoulders, the tired look in her eyes. The way her hands were clasped together in front of her. The fact that even that couldn't keep her from trembling.

I paused. "How long were you eavesdropping?"

She didn't bother arguing with my assessment of the matter, although her shoulders rose another inch. "Long enough," she mumbled. And then her eyes snapped up to meet mine. "Jon. Please. I need to-"

"Do you know what all that's about?"

Her cheeks flushed gently at my blunt words. She hesitated, glancing back to where Brendon had vanished. And then she looked back to me. "I...yes."

"Please, for the love of god, help me out a little here."

"Don't be too harsh on him," Loren said, little more than a whisper. "Please. He's really trying."

"I wasn't going to *do* anything in the first place," I snapped. "I was just trying to deal with *Kai*, and the crews who are ogling us, and all of the other demis who probably want to murder us in our sleep, and Christ, Loren, I didn't sign up for another piece of drama. So if you can do anything-"

"I don't know the full story." When she spoke, talking right over the top of me, I quieted. Her arm was folded across her front, like she was holding herself together, and her words were soft enough I nearly lost them entirely. "I-I mean, his story. I don't know all that much."

"But."

Her eyes dropped to the ground. "But when I was...taken, Brendon was already with them. They were moving him north. They didn't like us talking to each other all that much, but..." She shrugged. "I picked up pieces here and there."

"Pieces that told you what?" I asked, resisting the urge to fidget. It wasn't my place to hurry her - but I really wished she'd hurry up.

"He was in a crew before the hunters. I mean...I was too." The corners of her lip twisted in what looked like pain for a split second, there and then gone. "But my crew got killed."

I paused. Her implications were clear. "And Brendon's...didn't?"

She didn't say a word. She just looked up at me, her arms squeezing a little tighter about herself.

"Shit," I muttered, running a hand through my hair as I worked through what she'd said. If Brendon's crew wasn't killed by the hunters, then... "Did the hunters catch them off guard? Are they still looking? We can get you two back to-"

"You know they're not looking," Loren said, every word biting and chilled.

The knot wrapped around my heart twisted a little tighter. "...Right."

"Try not to take Brendon's...sensitivity...personally," Loren said, still holding my gaze. "He's trying. Really."

"No one's going to force him out, Loren. Believe me."

"Even when the crew is full of other demis? Ones more useful?" she said, her voice low. "Even when he's taking up a bed and eating the food that could go to someone contributing? Even when having one more focus here makes us an even more appealing target?" A wry smile tugged at her lips, small and dark. "Even when his focus is worth its weight in gold to the right buyer?"

"Loren. Stop," I said, shaking my head once. Quickly. Like I was trying to wipe away her words, drive them from the air itself. "No one said *anything* like that. And that's not the point. No one is going to turn on Brendon." I swallowed hard, trying to bring some moisture back to my suddenly-dry mouth. "I promise. Really."

She nodded slowly, shifting from foot to foot. "...All right."

"You believe me, don't you?"

Her eyes flashed up to meet mine. "I...yes. I do." A tiny, hesitant smile appeared on her lips and was gone in an instant. "Call me a fool, but I do. Sometimes I think you're the fool."

I laughed nervously. "M-Maybe. But, uh. Yeah. Can you...talk to Brendon? Things might have sucked in the past, but I'm not- No one's going to try something like that."

Her head turned as she glanced towards where he'd vanished into the trees. "Yeah. I think I will."

"I'm going to go find Keira," I said, offering her a quick smile.

She turned back to me, confusion plain in her eyes. "What? Keira? Why do you want-"

"She's got the glasses, doesn't she?" I said, rocking back and forth on my heels. "She can see relics. I think maybe she can read them, too. Maybe she can read Brendon's contract."

"And help him figure his focus out."

"Right."

A glimmer of life crept back into her eyes. "It's a good idea. We didn't have an appraiser, in my crew, and..." Her voice faltered, before picking back up a moment later. "The hunters didn't have one either. Just at the market."

"So no one's tried it yet."

Loren shook her head, glancing off into the woods again. "Not so far as I know," she whispered.

"Then it's about time. You good?"

"Yeah," she murmured, flashing a smile at me. "Thanks. I'll go...I'll see about him."

Lifting my hand, I patted her shoulder. "Thanks. I'll go-"

Another resounding crack lashed out from the front of the house. I winced. So did Loren. Kai was at it again, clearly. The thought did *not* fill me with confidence. "I'll go find Keira," I said, not bothering to keep the weariness out of my voice.

"Better you than me."

"What?" I said, half-turning back to her, but she'd made it halfway to the treeline already.

Swallowing a chuckle - and a fresh wave of dread as Kai let loose another focus-fueled firecracker - I made my way back out front.

It was just one more thing. One more worry, one more detail to work out. That was all. I fixed it in my mind, latching on to the notion that everything was fine. Just *fine*. They were all little problems, right?

Except that together they made one giant fucking problem, and I wasn't sure I had that many miracles shoved up my ass to pull out and fix everything.

"Jon!" I heard Kai cry, his voice filled with pure, unadulterated excitement. "Look what I figured out how to do!"

Shit. I was already around the corner - it was too late to hide.

There was only forward.

Forcing a smile and hiding my suddenly-sweaty hands in my pockets, I walked on.

CHAPTER THIRTY-SEVEN

Gunfire erupted across the yard, splitting the air with its deafening crack. I flinched, caught off guard for what seemed like the hundredth time that day. The earplugs I was wearing were *supposed* to help filter it out. And, well, it was better than nothing - but that didn't mean I couldn't hear it.

The sound of gunshots had never bothered me in the past. Of course, I hadn't been shot before, either.

"Don't you dare drop it," a voice across from me said. I glanced up. Jake glared back at me from across the massive log carried between us.

"I'm not going to drop it." I'd do my best, anyway. My fingers burned from the strain of holding it up, and jumping every few seconds wasn't helping matters any.

"Right." His tone was scornful. We staggered on, step after stumbling step through the snow.

The sound of giggling drifted over to the two of us. Swallowing my irritation, I let my eyes wander to the source.

Keira and Loren stood side by side, both holding pistols. Keira was showing Loren something, holding the weapon out so the smaller woman could see. Loren bobbed her head in a nod, flashing Keira a tiny smile, and lifted her gun. I flinched as another shot echoed off the house.

"You can put it down now," Jake said, his tone derisive. I forced myself to look ahead again. We were already at our destination - and he was half-crouched to set the log down, scowling up at me. "Unless you *like* holding it."

As if. I stooped low, resting the log against all the others we'd lined up so far. And then I stood with a groan, brushing the dirt and grime from my hands. "One more down."

"Can that be enough?" Jake said, rubbing his hands together. "We've been at this all morning."

"It's definitely at least time for a *switch*," I said, twisting to stare over at the two women.

"We switched twenty minutes ago," Keira said, not bothering to look my way. "You've got twenty more to go. Stop crying."

"It's our turn, though," Jake said, a whine entering his tone. "Seriously. We agreed to trade off at eleven, and it's eleven."

"Eleven thirty."

"You can't just change things on your own!"

Loren giggled, glancing back over her shoulder at him. "It's just a few logs."

Jake straightened, folding his arms. "It was *just a few logs* two hours ago. Now it's more than that." Despite his words, a bit of the bite had left his tone.

I just shook my head, patting his shoulder and moving towards the stack of firewood. Jake wasn't wrong, and we'd been at it a while. We'd agreed - the house wasn't ready to deal with anything major. It needed some adjustment in case anything happened. It had to be defensible.

Of course, the rest of the world didn't care that assault from magical renegades was a possibility, and we didn't want to terrify the pizza delivery driver. People would start asking questions if we turned the property into a bunker. So we also had to keep at least a semblance of normalcy to everything.

Thankfully, being in the north, no one would bat an eye at there being some stacks of firewood around a house - and wood was as effective at stopping bullets as concrete, we'd decided. The only downside was that we had to drag the damn stuff out of the forest ourselves. And split it. And stack it.

All together, it turned what should have been a quick morning's work into a sweaty, exhausting mess. I was going to ache all night, I just *knew* it.

But as much as we argued, I didn't think it would make a difference. And with a row of solid, unsplit logs forming a low barrier along one side of the lawn, that just left the heap of smaller pieces we'd spent the first few hours chopping up. I trudged towards it with a sigh, still feeling the burn in my arms from the last bit we'd carried.

The sound of tires rolling up the driveway was pure bliss. I straightened, coming to a halt, and heard Jake's relieved sigh from behind me. A pickup crept towards us - Jake's truck, stolen from Recon all those weeks and months ago. It sagged low on the suspension. Given the impressive load of brick they'd stacked into the back, I didn't have to wonder why.

The girls turned too, putting their guns down at last. All of us pulled together into a cluster as Tyler slid from the driver's seat. Brendon and Kai followed close on his heels, smiling and generally looking energetic enough to make me feel sick.

"Great," I said, forcing a smile as I came to a stop. "More stuff to carry."

"Did you run into any problems?" Keira said, elbowing me.

Tyler shook his head. "They had a lot of questions, that's all."

"Probably 'cause it's winter," Kai muttered under his breath. "What kind of assholes buy a load of brick in *winter?*"

"Just tell 'em we're getting it when it's cheap," Jake said, smirking at the younger man. "They don't need to know, and once you give them the money, they won't care."

"How about here?" Tyler said, looking straight past his brother and fixing his eyes on me. "Going well?"

I turned, pursing my lips and eyeing our handiwork. "I...think so?"

The house lay in the midst of all the chaos, just as stout as ever. Our hard work had paid off, though. It didn't look like it was going to fall down anymore, and at a glance you might even consider it halfway respectable. The garage out front would be a weakness, but with the log piles, the sides would be decently fortified. A good three of our demis could take cover on either side, sheltering from whatever came our way.

"It'll do," I said, tearing my eyes off it and glancing back to Tyler. "With a few brick 'retaining walls', I think it'll be perfect.

"No, no," he said, a rare smile flashing across his face. "They're barriers for our garden-to-be, Jon. Come on."

"Right. That."

"We could plant some trees in spring," Loren said, her eyes lighting up. "They'd make a nice barrier. And it'd be pretty."

Brendon chuckled. "We're in a forest."

She made a face at him, her chin lifting stubbornly. "So? I like trees."

He scoffed. She smacked his arm. Before I knew it, both of them were laughing, the sound soft and low.

The rest of the group was devolving, settling into chatting, idling clusters of people. I leaned against the truck, eyeing the load of brick unhappily. My arms still felt like leaden weights.

I jumped as a hand settled onto my shoulder. Keira slid past, rolling her eyes. "Go play with the guns, Jon," she said, shaking her head. "You need the practice. We'll take our turn."

"What?" Loren said, tearing her eyes off Brendon. "Oh, right. Yeah." Her mousy brown hair bouncing with the motion, she hurried after Keira.

"I'm a perfectly fine shot," I called after them, scowling.

Keira snorted. Actually *snorted* at me. "Right. Of course you are."

"Don't argue," Jake muttered. "Come on, dude. Do not argue."

"Do we have to carry all this by hand?" I heard Kai say from behind me, unwillingness etched into every syllable.

I smothered my smile behind a hand, taking Keira's pistol from the folding table we'd set up at our makeshift range. At least living in the middle of nowhere meant we didn't have neighbors getting in a huff over our shooting.

"There's a sledge out back. Go get it," Tyler said. The tailgate creaked open.

"Oh. Yeah."

The sound of his footsteps crunching through the snow drifted past as I lifted the gun, seeing the row of pop cans appear in front of my sights. It wasn't high-tech, but for a homemade shooting range, it did fine.

A gunshot rang out from beside me. Jake was faster than I, apparently. I jumped, making a face and hoping that he hadn't seen. His laughter said otherwise.

"Hurry up, Jon," he said. "And stop freaking out."

"I'm fine," I muttered, taking aim.

Right as I fired, someone dropped something. A load of brick, it sounded like. I flinched, squeezing hard - and watched the shot go wide. My target sat right where it had been, whole and untouched.

"Told you," Keira said from somewhere behind me.

"Just go carry the firewood," I muttered, feeling my cheeks burn.

Loren's laughter was drowned out by the roar as we started firing again.

***

My eyes snapped open.

For a long moment, I could only lay in place, staring up at the still-grungy ceiling of my room. My heart pounded, my blood rushing through my ears. Sleep clouded my veins, making it hard to think, but little by little it faded.

Why, though? The thought hung in my mind, demanding an answer. Something had woken me up - and after the day we'd spent carrying and lifting and building, I'd quite enjoyed the idea of sleeping.

I lay where I was, motionless, and let the tendrils of sleep tug at me again. Right. It was probably just a nightmare, another scene playing out in the back of my mind. If I couldn't remember what it was, well, that was a blessing. One that was becoming increasingly rare as time went on.

I'd just about managed to convince myself of that, falling back into the blissful waves of unconsciousness, when I heard it - a door shutting. And then footsteps.

My eyes slid open again, awareness returning. Damn it. Someone was up - and they were being loud. I could tell they were *trying* to be quiet, judging from the uneven set of their steps and the way every door was opened at a snail's pace, but it was an old house. The floors creaked. The doors creaked. Hell, sometimes when you stood *still* the place creaked.

And none of it changed the fact that someone was creeping around my house at....I glanced over, forcing my tired, aching body to cooperate. Three AM. They were sneaking around my house at three AM, and nothing good happened at three in the morning.

A groan slipped between my lips, soft and pained, but I eased myself upright, throwing the covers off. The floor was cold enough under my feet to make me wince. But I crossed to the door, easing it open. A shrill whine accompanied the motion.

On the other side, Tyler froze, staring back at me.

"Tyler," I said, keeping my voice as low as I could. Relief washed over me, the notion that someone had decided to break in slipping away. "It's early. What are you-" I stopped, ice flooding my veins. He had a hand in the pocket of his jacket, wrapped around something - a metal-and-wood grip I could just see a corner of. His eyes were fixed on mine, wide and terrified. Like he was scared of *me*. There weren't

335

too many options for what he might be clutching. "Are you actually going to pull a gun on me?" I said, speaking slowly and carefully. Somehow, I knew this wasn't the time for an aggressive lead-in.

"If you try and order me, I-I'll-"

"Tyler." Something was wrong. Logically, I knew that taking control was the best solution. But he wasn't lying when he made his threat, and it was still *Tyler*. Something was wrong, that much was clear, but the man's hands were shaking. I held my hands up instead, taking what I hoped was a comforting pose. "It's me. *Just* me. What's going on?"

"Where is he?"

His single, terse line was enough to bring me up short. I stopped, blinking away my confusion. "What? What do you mean?"

"I swear to god, if you don't tell me what's going on, I'll-"

"I'm the one who wants to know what's going on," I said, raising my voice a hair. I didn't want to wake the others up, not yet. There was too much risk of someone coming in swinging. A light went on in my mind at his words, though. "Where is who? You mean-" I shook my head, still holding his gaze with my own. "Did something happen to Kai?"

His arms spasmed, like he was twitching. His hands flexed in his coat pockets. "I- I don't-"

"Tyler, no one here did anything," I said, stepping closer. He let me. I breathed a sigh of relief. With the last of the sleepy fog leaving my mind, my thoughts had kicked into high gear. Tyler and Kai were still new, after all. They'd joined our crew, but it wasn't like we'd actually done anything together. And, assuming Tyler knew anything about the world of demis - which he seemed to - that made us the logical group to suspect if something went wrong. In his mind, anyway. Probably. "If something happened, then you need to let us help."

Tyler's lips parted, like he was about to say something. His golden hair hung in unkempt waves, still mussed from the night of sleep we'd had interrupted. And then his shoulders drooped. The hand in his pocket slumped free, apparently giving up on whatever fears he'd clung to. "He wasn't there when I woke up," he said, little more than a whisper. "I-I just thought maybe he'd gotten up to use the bathroom, but he never came back. And now-"

"And now you can't find him anywhere," I finished.

Tyler nodded, his eyes shadowed orbs. "If you did anything, I'll-"

"Give it a rest," I snapped, pushing past him. "What, do you think we stuffed him in the garage? How would that even make sense?"

"O-Oh. Yeah. I guess." The first hints of something like shame slipped into his voice.

I kept going, slipping down the hallway towards the main area. The floor continued its creaking under my feet. "If we kidnapped Kai, we'd have kidnapped you too. Don't you think?"

"I guess."

Not exactly the enthusiastic show of agreement I'd hoped for, but it would do. I peeked around the corner into the living room in the meantime. "His coat's gone, Tyler. And his boots."

"What?" Tyler pushed past me, his eyes wide.

"Didn't you check *that*?"

"I...I didn't think to," he muttered.

It was all I could do to fight back my groan. The guy was more stressed than I thought. "Well, maybe he just went for a walk."

"At three in the morning?"

"I don't know, Tyler. He's not in here. So let's go look."

He hesitated, drawing back. "Should...Maybe we should wake up-"

"Do *you* want to explain to Jake why you dragged him out of bed at three AM?" I said dryly.

Tyler winced. "I...no."

I reached for my own boots, pulling them on, and Tyler grabbed for his coat. My thoughts whirled, options flying around in my head. I was worried, yeah, and if there really was something wrong, then we'd go and rouse the team. But Greyson would have called us if trouble crept up. He wouldn't leave us to get surprised.

Assuming we could trust Greyson.

I just pasted a smile onto my face, pushing the worries aside, and stepped out into the snow alongside Tyler.

My ears screamed their complaint almost immediately, protesting the rough transition from the warmth of my bed to the frigid chill of the night air. I stomped onward, no longer worrying so much about waking anyone up - only to be stopped by a hand on my arm a few paces out.

"Quiet," Tyler said. He stood in place, clinging to my arm.

Standing would only make us colder, which really wasn't a priority for me. But his eyes were slitted, only a glimmer showing they were open at all, and his expression was serious. Biting back an irritated sigh, I stopped.

"Hold your breath."

All right, *that* was too much. "What the hell do you-"

"Jon."

My lips smacked together. I glared at him, my eyes narrowed, but he wasn't looking anymore. He'd shut his eyes, rocking gently back and forth on his heels. Fine. I'd play along, even if it irked to have *everyone* giving me orders. I drew in a breath and held it, letting the quiet of the night rise up around us.

As if my instinct, his hand drifted up, coming to rest against the tiny, almost-forgotten stud set in his ear. He didn't move, didn't breathe - but his eyelids tensed, twitching like he was in pain.

It was all I could do to keep from exhaling or letting out the gasp that fought to get out. I'd thought I was imagining it - but no, his relic was glowing, ever so slightly. The light grew stronger, letting slip just how hard he must be drawing off its power. The lines of his face were thrown into harsh relief by the hazy light. Dark circles ringed his eyes, and the first signs of creases were beginning to form crow's feet between his eyebrows.

I opened my mouth, ready to say something and his request for quiet be damned, when his eyes snapped open.

"Explosions," he said.

A shiver ran down my spine. "What? I don't hear anything."

Tyler's face was bone-white. "I hear explosions. It's Kai. Someone's attacking."

"But Greyson didn't say anything about-"

"Come on!" Without waiting, he broke into a run, tearing off into the woods.

I hesitated for a moment longer, glancing back towards the house. This was my last chance - if we were going to get the team together, it'd be better to do that *before* we wound up stranded and alone in the forest.

But Tyler wasn't going to wait for me to get ready. He was already nearly-invisible among the trees, and gaining distance fast.

Greyson hadn't called me. No one else had voiced any concerns about demis approaching. And given the way that Tyler was reacting, I had my own suspicions about what was going on.

Biting my tongue and forcing all the words back down, I lifted my snow-covered boots and raced after him.

Trees zipped past, one after another after another. Running through snow is *hard*. I was winded after just a few minutes. Tyler couldn't be much better off, but he showed no signs of slowing. And before long, I could hear it too - a constant, repetitive banging, as though someone was throwing firecrackers against the pavement. It came and went in waves, a little louder every time as we closed the gap. Within minutes it was visible. Plumes of fire flared between the trunks, bursting to life and fading out in embers that sizzled against the snow.

Each breath came ragged, deafening in my ears. But I could see the last row of trees approaching, the last barrier between us and Kai. Whatever was happening, whatever was going on-

Tyler exploded through the trees, not so much as hesitating.

And then he skidded to a stop, his eyes going wide.

A few paces behind, I was late to the show. By the time I got there, Kai had already turned around, lowering his hands. Embers fell like snow in every direction. Soot coated his arms to the elbow, and the trees encircling the clearing were blackened.

"T-Tyler," he said, his eyes going wide. "W-What are you-"

"Where are they?" Tyler said, crossing to his brother's side. His hand landed on Kai's shoulder, holding the younger man close. He spun in a circle, staring at the trees. "How many?"

"Tyler," I said, pressing a hand to my face. "That's...I think you should-"

"How many what?" Kai said, wrinkling his nose. "Look, I'm sorry. I know it's late, but I really wanted to-"

Tyler's mouth hung open for a moment longer, the words he'd been about to say still clinging to his lips. I could *see* the recognition, the lightbulb going on in his mind. "There's no one, is there," he said at last, the faintest hint of chagrin coloring his words.

"I'm really sorry. I didn't mean to wake you up."

"You're not being attacked."

"What? No!"

Tyler's lips flapped, a tiny, pained noise slipping from his throat. "So...what. You just decided to...to sneak out in the middle of the night?"

"Look, I knew you'd-"

"Without telling anyone?"

"It's really not that big a-"

"To throw fireballs around the forest?"

I winced. Tyler's arms had come up at some point during his lecture, folding across his chest. There was anger in his eyes - real anger, as he glared down at his little brother. "Hey. Tyler. It's cold out here. Why

don't we all head back and-"

"You never let me do anything."

I stopped. Kai's voice had been quiet enough I almost missed it. Even if I had, there's no way Tyler would - and its tone was openly mutinous.

"So you thought you'd just go behind my back and do it anyway?" Tyler snapped. "Jesus, Kai, you're not ten. You're supposed to be an adult."

"Funny, since you never act like it."

"This isn't a game!" Tyler spun on his heel, his teeth gritted. "Damn it. You could have burned yourself. You could have started a forest fire. And if other demis were looking, you just put a beacon on top of the whole damn crew."

"That won't happen!" Kai cried. "I'm good! Better than you think! I can put fires out. Really. And would you stop jumping at shadows for five fucking minutes?"

"Don't you swear at me."

"Oh, but *you* can-"

"Both of you, enough," I snapped, finally raising my voice enough to be heard.

They stopped, jumping as though startled. As though they'd forgotten I was there at all, I thought sourly.

"Jon," Tyler said. His face was beet red, and his eyes still glimmered with anger. "I-I'm sorry I woke you up. I know you've got work soon. See, Kai? Do you *see* that the things you do have impact?"

"It's not my fault I want to learn how to use my own damn-"

"I said *enough.*" I pulled my coat around me a bit tighter, kicking at the snow. Work. Right. I'd have just about enough time to climb back into bed before my alarm went off, at this rate. "Both of you. Work it out somewhere a little warmer. Kai, stop sneaking around lighting things on fire. Tyler, calm down."

Both of them stared at me, not saying a word. I threw my hands up. "Or stay out here and freeze! Knock your socks off. *I'm* going back inside."

But when I turned back the way we'd come, trudging along the tracks we'd left, something hit me from behind. Kai, I saw a moment later as he all but ran back the way we'd come. His lips curled down in the biggest scowl I'd ever seen on the younger man's face, and the tips of his golden-brown hair were singed in places. I stopped, letting him

340

accelerate towards the house.

"I'm really sorry," Tyler said, coming up alongside me. Kai was already a distant shape, rapidly vanishing into the night. "I didn't- Christ, for something like *this*, I nearly-"

"You didn't know."

"I should have guessed," he muttered. "He just doesn't understand. I don't know how to get through to him."

"Probably not by screaming at him," I said dryly.

"I know. I do. I just...I don't know. I'm thrilled he's got a relic, but-"

"He's excited," I said, glancing over at Tyler. His face was in shadow, the trees still passing by overhead. "Can you really blame him?" I shrugged, unable to keep a smile from flashing across my lips. "I mean, I was excited too, when I figured out I could do more. After we got past the whole people-trying-to-kill-us deal, anyway." It felt wrong to admit, but there it was. On some level, it *was* fun.

"I know."

Drawing in breath, I hesitated. There were a lot of things that I instinctively knew one shouldn't ask. There were a lot of horrible things out there in the world, and most of the people who'd wound up in our crew had probably seen the worst of the worst. Even still, after tonight, I wasn't quite sure that I wanted to let things sit without so much as broaching the topic.

"You two...you would have been on your own for a while before this, wouldn't you," I said, picking my words carefully.

Tyler's steps slowed. And then he picked up the pace, pushing up alongside me again. "I guess. I mean, it was mostly just me."

"And your dad gave you the, uh, focus?" I said, fixing my eyes on the footsteps ahead. "That...must have been hard." Relics weren't something that could just be passed down from person to person on a whim. If Tyler had inherited the relic, then there were consequences that went along with it.

He nodded, the motion slight. "Yeah. It was hard," he echoed. "Kai...he knew, some of it. I didn't think we'd ever be in a situation to give him his own focus. I didn't want to get his hopes up. I didn't want him to do anything stupid."

Thoughts of Matt flashed through my mind - forever caught chasing after a dream, interfering in a world where he didn't really belong. "I understand. I really do."

"He doesn't understand how badly things can go."

341

"I get that. But him learning how to use his focus is a good thing. He *should* be learning how to set things on fire." I shrugged. "Just maybe not out here. That's the thing, though. If you make him feel like he can't ever use his focus-"

"Then he'll do it behind my back."

I smiled. "Right."

Tyler sighed. We walked in silence, picking our way through the snow. Finally, he shook his head. "Damn it. I know."

I could hear the rest of it - the words he wasn't saying, the frustrations and fear written into every fiber of his being. He wasn't putting any of it to words, but his body was singing it for the world to hear. And given what he'd told me, I could figure the rest of it out.

His father, the lone demi in the family. He'd probably lectured Tyler, told him all about the dangers. Dangers which Tyler had no doubt seen, after he'd gotten the relic for his own. He was just a rogue, after all, stranded apart from anything by way of allies. With a younger brother to look after.

I could sympathize with how he had to feel, but continuing this way wasn't sustainable. And even if he'd been alone before, he wasn't now. It was time for him to relax a little, after what had to have been years of stress and watching over his shoulder.

He jumped as I cleared my throat. "Well...I think you should-"

"I'll apologize to him when I get back," Tyler mumbled.

I grinned. "I didn't say it."

"I just don't like it."

"I know."

"He still shouldn't have snuck out."

I ran a hand through my hair. "He really shouldn't have." I pursed my lips, seeing the edge of the forest ahead. "It's not going to work coming from you, though. I'll talk to Jake. Or Loren. Maybe someone can slip something into their conversations, subtly. Bring him down a few notches." Both of them had seen more than Tyler and I, and they were that much more removed from the whole mess. Maybe it wouldn't be so personal.

The trees thinned around us, parting entirely as we stepped into the yard. Kai had already vanished, disappearing into the warmth. I reached over, clapping Tyler on the shoulder. "We'll figure it out. And maybe we can set up some proper practice sessions. None of us know enough about each other's abilities, I think. I for *sure* didn't know you could hear like that."

Tyler chuckled. Whether it was from actual amusement or his entertaining my pathetic attempt to lighten the mood, I didn't know. But his expression wasn't so grim, afterward.

The house glowed, brilliant against the night as we walked towards home.

CHAPTER THIRTY-EIGHT

I stared out the window, glaring at the snow as it slowly drifted down out of the sky. The house was warm, thankfully. On any other night it would have been pleasure to sit there, watching the white flakes pile up around our cars.

Not tonight. Not right then. My mood was a different matter entirely.

Greyson's words still rang in my ears, his irritated voice lingering in my mind. "Don't know how many you've got the old bastard rounding up," he'd said. "Not sure how many people you think we *need* hangin' round these parts. But there's another carload north-bound. Meandering a bit."

"Like they might not be coming straight here?"

"Hell if I know," he snapped. "You're the one that's got his number on speed dial. Figure it out. But if they keep coming like they are, you've got a few hours and then visitors."

"How many?"

He'd sighed, the sound rich and filled with frustration. "Hard to say, like I've told you before. Harder when they're packed together. But there's more of 'em than last time, I can tell you that much."

I hadn't gotten much more information out of him. I didn't get the impression there was much more for him to give. He'd just groaned a few more times, making irritated noise after noise, and hung up.

Which left me sitting, stewing on the predicament Aedan had left me in. I'd asked him to *call*, damn it.

Of course, part of me knew that was almost certainly why he hadn't. Aedan might look young, but he had all the stubborn grumpiness of any old man - and he seemed to enjoy making my life more difficult. I only swallowed a groan of my own, pulling my cell from my pocket, and rounded up the stragglers of our group yet again.

They waited behind me, talking in low voices as I stared out towards the main road. Even if something were go to wrong, they'd have to come up that way. Circling around would take hours - and in the snow and ice, it wouldn't be so easy regardless. We'd need to be careful in the spring, I realized. Scouts, maybe. We could take shifts, if we knew other demis were in the area. Or maybe cameras.

Cameras. *Right.* That would work - if I wanted to wind up like all the other paranoid hermits, living out in the sticks to avoid the fluoride and big brother. *That* wouldn't tip any of the other demis off that something was wrong. Maybe I could gut some trail cameras or something. I chewed on my lip, leaning forward onto my elbows, and let the possibilities flow.

The smell of smoke brought me out of it in an instant. I flinched, spinning around, but the low sound of Kai's laughter beat me to it. He sat in the kitchen - over the tile floor, per Tyler's hissed instructions, which I appreciated. I couldn't afford to replace any more carpet this month. The younger demi held his hands cupped in front of his chest. A flame glimmered there, resting in the bowl of skin. It flickered and danced as though blown by a nonexistent breeze.

Jake only shook his head. He'd thrown himself down on the couch, entirely absorbed in something on his phone. Or, I'd *thought* he was entirely absorbed. "Fucking hell, Kai, could you not-"

"I've got it," the fire-worker said, grinning down at the red-and-orange blossom he held. "Really. Don't worry."

"If I have to go get the fire extinguisher again, I'm going to shove it straight up your-"

"It's *fine.*"

Loren only snorted. She sat in one of the overstuffed armchairs within arm's reach of Brendon. The both of them had been quiet all week, keeping their thoughts to themselves ever since Brendon's moment of crisis. He hadn't pulled himself out of his funk - but both him and Tyler had given Kai a break, which I was prepared to accept as 'good enough'.

Keira settled deeper into her chair at the table, wrinkling her nose.

She was tired - it showed in the shadows under her eyes, the way she let her weight fall slack and limp to the tabletop. She had good reason to be. She'd been working with Brendon every chance she got, ever since I'd asked her to help. She complained now and again, in private, but I think even she knew it was a good thing for her to be doing. She was still learning herself, after all, and helping Brendon push his limits pushed her own, too.

I might have wished she'd tired herself out a little less, given the day had turned out to be full of activity, but you couldn't always get what you wanted. I just leaned forward, nearly touching my nose to the glass of the window, and let the pair of entwined rings hanging from my neck slide back and forth between my fingers.

My other hand was wrapped around my gun, feeling its presence ready and waiting under my coat. I wouldn't have thought it could become so comforting, or that it would happen in so little time.

A shiver ran down my spine. I'd seen...no. Nothing. The only thing I could see from my vantage point were the woods between us and the road, fading minute by minute into twilight as the evening took over in full.

But- There. I wasn't imagining it.

A glimmer of light shone between the tree trunks, casting a pale glow onto the asphalt of the main road. A car. Someone was coming.

I tried to force myself to calm down, to keep myself from getting so worked up. We were still a long way off, and the house sat back from the road a long way beside. It was probably just someone coming home from work - or an afternoon spent in town. There were so many possible explanations that it was hardly worth getting worried over.

All the same, not even an ounce of surprise slipped through my mind as the dark shape of the vehicle emerged between the densely-packed trees - and turned down our driveway.

"Someone's here," I said, my voice low. The rest of the conversations died off instantly.

"Now?" Loren said. She sat perfectly still, her spine ramrod-straight, but I could hear the quiver in her voice.

"Now," I said softly. "Next batch?"

"Maybe," Jake said, glancing over at me. "Maybe it's the primes, just a bit late."

"That could be too," I said, keeping my voice level. "We won't know without talking to them. Everyone be careful, and stay awake. Let's not let anyone get the best of us, okay?"

A quiet murmur went around, passed from voice to voice. I couldn't pick out any specific speakers, but I got the gist of it perfectly clearly - 'Worry about yourself.' Right.

The headlights inched closer, drawn inexorably up the driveway towards the house. If I strained my ears, leaning closer to the window, I could hear the purr of the engine and the slow crunch of the snow-covered gravel under its tires.

It was time. I pushed myself upright, feeling every bone in my body creak. It had already been a long day. I had a job, damn it. I'd been busy. I hadn't signed up for being bothered at all hours of the day and night be anyone who was passing by.

But they were in our driveway - and I didn't think it was a coincidence. I let my fingers linger on the grip of the pistol for a moment longer, taking a shred of comfort from its presence, and then pulled my coat tighter about me. "Let's go, then," I said, glancing at the others.

The light on the eave helped a little. I flicked it on as I went past, casting the snow out front into dim relief. It was nothing against the force of the headlights shining at us. I held a hand up, trying to shade my eyes, and saw the motion reflected by everyone who had followed me out.

It was an SUV - pointed right at us, sitting in the driveway. We stood, frozen like deer in its headlights, and stared. Whoever it was, they stared right back.

"Wonderful," Jake muttered. I could hear the wince in his voice, the strain. "You'd think they'd have the common courtesy to-"

Right as he spoke, the headlights flicked off, casting us into darkness. I blinked away the sudden blindness, waiting desperately for my vision to return. "Damn it," I muttered under my breath.

"You're fine," I heard Keira murmur from alongside me. Despite the casual words, though, her tone was entirely serious.

The slamming of car doors brought our conversation to a halt. Shoes crunched into the snow. A lot of shoes. Our group inched apart, spacing out as if by instinct.

Still blinking furiously, I counted the figures that emerged from the murky darkness. Five. No. Seven. I eyed the SUV with dismay. They'd really packed into the thing, hadn't they?

"Are you Jon?" one of them said, stepping out front. My eyes finally adjusted, revealing a stocky, well-built man standing at the head of the column. His brown hair was neatly trimmed - and his eyes were dark orbs in the twilight, fixed on mine.

I stared at him for a long moment, debating exactly what he was going for, but then nodded. "I am, yeah. Can I ask what all this is about?" I waved a hand towards his friends as I spoke, not breaking eye contact with him. If he'd spoken first, then that put him as the natural pick for their leader. I wasn't about to back down in this first meeting.

He smiled, his teeth glinting white in the pathetic lighting. "Good! Good. We're..." He gestured towards his fellows, shrugging tolerantly. "We talked to a fellow, said you might be looking for help up in these parts." He tilted his head slowly to one side, still watching me. "Name of Aedan?"

Behind me, I could hear Jake swearing under his breath. Brendon wasn't far behind. His boot scuffed against the gravel, echoing around the yard.

I just nodded slowly, fighting back a sigh. "Right. Of course he did." How *just like* Aedan. When I talked to him next, we were going to have words about the games he played.

"Is that a problem?"

"No, no," I said, shaking my head swiftly. "That's...no."

"Oh, good." His smile didn't falter. He glanced over to the group behind me, his own friends milling about behind him. "Looks like you've got a fair number already, though."

"The more the merrier, right?" I said, smiling blandly. I was too tired to act nice. "You're not so small a group yourself. So, what. You want to hang around?"

He shrugged again. "We're all safer together."

One of his friends muttered darkly, hissing something under his breath as he zipped his coat higher. I didn't hear every word, but Tyler shifted uncomfortably behind me. I glanced back, meeting the man's eyes.

Tyler looked to me, his expression unreadable. "It's a bit cold out here," he murmured, his words soft. A translation. I glanced back to the newcomers.

"Davis, knock it off," the demi's leader said, rolling his eyes. "Sorry about him."

"It's fine," I said mildly. "It is night, after all."

"Right. Ah- I'm sorry," he said, rubbing his hands together. "I'm being rude. Aedan said to look for a Jon. That's you?"

My head bobbed in a slow nod.

His hand flattened against his chest. "I'm Glenn. This is my crew - we're out of the west side, mostly. Outside Grand Rapids. But..." His lips pressed into a thin line. "It's been more and more unstable, lately. We're kind of looking for a bit of a change." His eyes were still fixed on mine. "Thought you might do it for us."

Something was off. Something was *wrong*, tearing at his words. Not a lie, not as such. My relic hadn't complained about anything he'd said - and yet, I couldn't shake the feeling that something wasn't right. I tore my eyes off him, inclining my head gently towards the others standing behind him. "And them? We'll need a little more to work with than *that*."

"Right. Right. Well, that's Davis, of course," he said, flashing me a quick smile and gesturing towards the one who'd muttered before. "And we've got Carter over there. Leon. Amber and Nox, there on the end, and this is Ryan." He rattled off one name after another, pointing to each of his demis nearly faster than I could follow. The named slid past in a blur, completely out of reach of my memory.

"Right," I said slowly, eyeing them. Seven. There were *seven* of them - and I had to question all of them? I could already feel the headache I was going to wind up with, by the end of the night. I'd better find a way to cut straight to the chase with the questions I picked.

I tried not to think about the second half of it - that if something went wrong, I might have to try and hold *seven* enemy demis. Demis who were fresh, ready and raring to go. My headache loomed higher.

Turning back to his crew, I settled for inspecting his fellows. Their names were long gone, vanished along with whatever polite niceties he was spouting off, and there wasn't much I could glean from appearances. They all looked like normal, average-

I froze. *Most* of them were completely average people, ranging from their twenties to their thirties, staring back at me with varying levels of wariness or boredom. I said 'most', because all the way in the back, one with a mop of brown hair nearly obscuring his glasses stared right back at me. It was hard to get a good read on him through the murky twilight, but his eyes were wide with what looked like shock. And nervousness.

That didn't mean anything, I told myself. I was being stupid. Aedan had sent them - as much of an ass as he was, he wouldn't knowingly send us trouble. There were limits to how much of a jackass he would be. Probably. If they were nervous, it was probably because they were approaching a rival crew, asking to join forces. It was enough to put anyone on edge.

I forced my smile back onto my face, turning my attention back towards Glenn - but not before I saw the brown-haired demi creep closer to his neighbor, a woman with pitch-black hair flowing past her shoulders, and begin murmuring in her ear.

"I know this isn't exactly a normal thing, what you're trying to do here, but I think that's good," Glenn was saying, a lazy smile spread across his face. "I'm hopeful that some good will come of all this, you know?" Still, not a single word showed as a lie. I stared at him, focusing as hard as I could, but found only truth in his words.

And I still couldn't relax.

"Yes, I...think it'll be good," I heard myself say, still glancing from face to face. The woman's eyes had snapped to mine, somewhere along the line. She hardly moved - just sat back, slouching on her heels, and folded her arms across her chest. But I couldn't help feeling like she was staring straight down into my soul.

"So...how's this work, then?" Glenn said, a bit of sheepish anxiety sliding into his voice for the first time. He ran a hand through his hair, half-shrugging. "I haven't ever really done something like this-"

"I need to talk to each of your demis," I said, forcing myself back to the present. "Alone. We have to be careful, you know."

He pursed his lips, still watching me. "I have to look after my own, too. I can't let you-"

"I'm just one person," I said, shaking my head. "Is that such a risk? Don't you trust them?"

Glenn hesitated. I saw his lips part, his eyes narrow as he glared at me. He wasn't happy. I mean, I wouldn't be happy either, if I'd been told that I had to give a rival demi my people, one after another. I tried not to take it personally. "Fine," he said at last. "I suppose that's fair."

"Good," I murmured, my gaze sweeping over the lot of them again. How was I supposed to work this? There were seven of them. Should I question them right then and there? If I did, and something was wrong, I'd never get a grip on all of them in time. And we didn't know what abilities their relics had.

If a fight broke out between us - seven versus seven, standing mere feet away from each other - then people would die. It was as simple as that.

We needed a holding area, I realized. Somewhere to isolate the new demis from each other. I hadn't planned on having a crew as big as this show up. There was the garage, but if they were trouble, I didn't want to destroy my house. Sheds, maybe. Enough of them to-

Enough of them to turn our place into a miniature prison, I thought sourly. No, that wouldn't work.

I'd figure it out later. Right then, we just needed to get moving before something went wrong. "We're going to split up," I said, forcing my eyes back to Glenn's crew. His mouth slid open, his brow furrowing as a question rose to his lips, but I pressed on. "I'll take you one at a time. Why don't-"

"I'll go," the woman said, rolling her eyes as she stepped out of the group. "Let's just get this shit over with already."

Glenn looked over at her, his expression unreadable. "Are you sure you-"

"I've got it," she said, glowering. "No big." Her friend shifted behind her, nowhere near as comfortable.

I gave her a long, assessing look, sweeping from her beat-up, mud-stained green jacket down to the soles of her boots. She stared right back, not flinching so much as an inch. She was only one person, I decided - even if something went wrong, I could handle one person.

"Fine," I said, letting a sigh slip between my lips. "You're with me, then. You three." I pointed towards the three men sitting on the far end, her glasses-wearing friend in the middle. "Over by the trees. Jake. Loren."

My friends stiffened, hearing me say their names. I hadn't set anyone to guard Kai, when I'd been questioning Tyler. Granted, there were seven of them instead of two, and that changed things - but it still was enough to tell them that I wasn't quite comfortable with the situation that was playing out. The pair slipped past me with one last look, creeping closer to the three newcomers and ushering them away.

I watched them go for as long as I could, finally turning back to the remainder. "The rest of you, you can wait around the side of the house. Tyler. Kai."

The brothers were already moving, Tyler fixing the trio of new demis with a wary look. The newcomers weren't arguing, at least - they just glanced at Glenn, hiding their scowls, and filed away with the two.

And left me with the woman.

"We'll go over here," I said, looking to the far side of the house. I wanted to be somewhere alone - somewhere the others couldn't hear what she said. I wanted each of their answers to be honest and genuine. To hear what they really thought, not what they thought would be consistent.

Keira and Brendon hesitated, caught in the middle. I caught Keira's eye, held her gaze. "Just...keep an eye on things," I said, my voice tight. She hesitated a moment longer, then nodded, sliding her hand around Brendon's elbow. She'd understand, if she was paying half an ounce of attention. She could see when people were casting - I'd expect her and Brendon to keep watch, making sure both of the groups were behaving.

I hoped she'd keep half an eye on me, too. Not that I was *worried*. It was one person. I could handle that. Probably.

It didn't keep my heartbeat from slowly accelerating as we stepped out of the light, fading further into the shadows.

"All right," I said carefully, once we'd gone far enough the others wouldn't overhear. "I'm just going to ask you some questions. Basic stuff. Why you're here, what you're after, any motives you and your friends might have. Answer me honestly. If you don't, I'll know."

"Yeah. About that," she said, rolling her head until she was staring right at me. Her eyes were hazel, I realized, showing more green than brown against the black of her hair and the half-light. The look in them was intense enough to hold me still and quiet, pinned in place. "We should talk. Right now."

"W-What?" I said at last, finding my voice. "I'm just going to-"

"You don't realize it yet," she said, not so much as blinking, "but this is about to go sideways."

I froze. Her words rang true - without even the unease I'd felt from Glenn. "Explain."

A humorless smile twitched at the corners of her lips. It didn't reach her eyes. "If you listen to me carefully, then maybe you'll make it out of this alive and with your focus."

My heartbeat thundered in my ears. "But not for free."

Her smile twisted, going crooked. "The choice is yours."

CHAPTER THIRTY-NINE

I stared at the woman. She stared right back, her hazel eyes unreadable. My mind raced, thoughts whirling past at a hundred miles an hour. *Amber*, they said, digging the thought out of the chaos that had become the last few minutes. *Glenn said her name was Amber.*

"Start talking," I said, hearing my voice tremble despite my best efforts. "What's going on? And what do you want? What are you after?"

I'd hardly gotten the words out when she shook her head, folding her arms across her chest. Her jacket shifted - and I could see the imprint of a gun, under the fabric. "We don't have time for drawn-out negotiations," she said flatly. "What I want is simple. I want to leave here together with Nox. We'll go on our way, no trouble."

"Nox," I said, still watching her from the corner of my eye. "That's-"

She groaned, tapping her foot impatiently. "My partner. It's not *important.*"

"The guy with the brown hair and glasses who was whispering to you?"

"You think?" she snapped.

I stared at her for a long moment still, rolling her words over in my head. "What's going on? Why would Aedan send you if-"

"You didn't really buy that, did you? What's going on is that Glenn and the rest aren't so peaceable," Amber said, spitting the words out as quickly as she could while still keeping her voice low. Even as she spoke, she glanced back towards the corner of the house, as though watching for anyone listening in.

My eyes narrowed. "And you expect me to believe you'd just turn on them at the drop of a hat. Right as soon as you guys get out of the car, first thing you do. Betray your friends." I might be an idiot, but I wasn't *stupid.*

A low chuckle slipped out of her. "Oh, they're not my friends."

I blinked. "They're not."

"Do they *look* like my friends?"

"You all showed up in a car together," I said, fighting to keep myself still. "You sure look like friends to me."

"It's just a job. Nothing more. I don't owe them anything, and I won't die for them. Their plan's not going to work, not with you reading the lies behind all their words."

The blood slowly drained from my face. "W-What? What are you-"

"Don't fucking lie to me," she snapped, her head whipping back around until her eyes pinned me in place again. "I know what you can do. You're not fooled by them."

I swallowed hard, my mouth going dry. "How...how exactly did you-" I froze. "That guy. Nox. He was-"

"He heard it. Yeah. Knew the plan was fucked right then and there." A humorless smile played across her lips. "And that's that." Her hands crept towards her pockets.

"Don't do that," I said, lacing my words with the barest hint of a command. "I know you have a gun."

Amber flinched, but her hands stayed where they were for a long, still moment. A few seconds later, she let them fall slack to her sides again. "Come on. If you-"

"If what you're saying is true, you were perfectly happy to be killing me and everyone else here a few minutes ago," I said, fighting desperately to keep from yelling. "So you'll excuse me if I'm not exactly trusting you." But all while she was speaking, my relic burned warm and soothing against my chest. She was telling the truth - or if she was being misleading, she was doing it so well I couldn't pick up even the slightest hint of a falsehood.

"It's just a job," she said, rolling her eyes. "Jobs change. I already got paid. So who the fuck cares? I'd rather live."

"A job," I heard myself say. The world around me was beginning to go hollow, like I was watching everything happen from a distance. There were seven of them. *Seven.* And now, *this* was happening? "From who? Who's paying you? And what did they want?"

"You." She said the word simply and plainly, and fell quiet. Her eyes were sharp, her expression carefully neutral.

A shiver ran down my spine. "Me?"

"Did I stutter? So if you don't mind, let's leave the chatter for another time. Never, maybe. But you might want to actually deal with the problem at hand."

"W-Wait. Who-"

"You've got words, right?" she said, ignoring me completely. "Nox said something about you *holding* people. He wasn't quite sure, with what he got. Can you handle yourself in all this? Do you have some sort of weapon?"

The weight of my gun was right where it should be as I slid my hand into my jacket, feeling a shiver of relief. "Uh. Yeah. I can-"

"Good. Then you're on your own," she said, glaring at me. "I'm taking Nox and we're leaving. Have fun."

I grabbed her arm as she turned to go. "You're not leaving that easily," I hissed, pulling her back.

She spun on me, her chin coming up and her eyes flashing dangerously. "Try that again and I'll-"

"What are their relics?" I snapped. "Who are the most dangerous? Give me something to work with here." Christ. There were seven of them. And they were at our *house.* "And if you think you're just going to take all that information about me, about *us*, and walk away into the night scot-free, then you're-"

"Then I'm absolutely right," she said, venom lacing every syllable. "You're not going to do a damn thing about it. Worry about people who are actual problems and you might live longer."

Her fingers twitched, dancing down by her side. I shuddered, feeling my hand fly from her arm. She grinned mirthlessly, her eyes shadowed, and turned away.

"Amber," I snapped, reaching for her again, but she spun out of my reach. "Just give me a *little* more to go on. What are they going to do? What are their abilities? Come *on.*"

It was a small motion - just a flick of her hand. Her eyes dropped. There was a watch strapped to her wrist - the leather band old and worn, every bit as scuffed and dirt-stained as her jacket. Her eyes tightened, and then her hand fell back to her side. "Look. I don't have all day to give you a goddamn lesson. Any minute, Glenn's going to-"

355

A sound from the far side of the building brought her up short, her head snapping around. It was hard to see in the murky half-light from the house, but her skin looked distinctly more pale than it had before. Snow. Snow and gravel. Footsteps. Someone was coming.

I tensed, my fingers inching towards my gun, but she shot me a look. I froze. A bead of sweat dripped down the back of my neck. In that moment, with an enemy demi standing right next to me and a whole gang of them in my driveway, all I could think of was how much it had hurt to get shot. I licked my lips slowly, letting my hand slide into my pocket.

Glenn stepped around the corner of the house, half-leaning like he was peeking. A smile flashed across his face as he saw both of us looking back. "Oh! Sorry. Didn't mean to interrupt. Just wondered if everything was going all right."

He wasn't lying, I noted sourly. Of course, it probably *wasn't* a lie. That didn't make it the whole and complete truth, either. My relic had some weaknesses I needed to come to terms with.

"We were just talking," I said, forcing a smile. "Sorry about the wait - we just like to be thorough. But it should only take another few minutes."

He kept walking, bobbing his head in a nod. "Of course, right. Well, I understand. Just wanted to check in on how my colleague was doing." His eyes twinkled with humor as he smiled at the black-haired woman beside me. "I guess we're just used to dealing with more rough-and-tumble types, eh, Amber?"

"Right," she said, her gravelly voice low. She was smiling too - but the expression didn't quite reach her eyes. And her posture was stiff, her limbs rigid and tense. Her fingers curled into fists at her side as Glenn stepped closer, every bit as amiable as ever.

Should I hold Glenn, order him into submission? I could do it - but if that happened, it would spark off a fight with all of the other demis in the yard. There was no way I could kill him without them hearing. I didn't have the powers some demis did. And he was fresh, his powers untapped. It might be difficult.

I inched away, feeling my heartbeat accelerate as he kept coming. But the wall of the house was behind me, rigid and ungiving, and I had nowhere to run. Not without it becoming very, very apparent I wasn't comfortable around him.

Even still, I needed to do *something*. I opened my mouth, the command to stop rising in my throat. Amber's eyes flicked over to mine, widening, like she was trying to tell me something-

-And Glenn's hand landed on my shoulder a moment later.

"I'll leave you two be," he said, smiling warmly as he patted my shoulder. "Take all the time you need. Just give her back in one piece, you hear?"

I smiled, matching his expression as a peaceful calm settled over our little corner. "Right- ah, well, in truth, we were just finishing, I think."

Amber's eyes widened, just a fraction more. She didn't blink. It hardly looked like she was breathing.

Glenn's brow furrowed. His gaze flicked between me and her, his fingers squeezing my shoulder gently. "What? Are you sure?"

I shrugged, my smile growing. "I think so, yeah. I mean, what more is there to discuss?" I looked to Amber, running over our conversation in my head. She'd been up-front with me about everything, after all, and her story seemed solid. They were looking for a new home, somewhere they could be safe. A fresh start.

Who was I to tell them no?

Her lips parted, the corners curling down gently and then they squeezed shut a heartbeat later, pressing into a thin, tight line. "It's been a good talk," she said, forcing a smile at last. "Very...good."

"Well, I'm glad to hear that," Glenn said, beginning to chuckle. "If you're set with Amber, then, I can call Leon, maybe, or-"

"I think we're good," I said, nodding more firmly. "You guys have been nothing but honest since the minute you showed up. It's fucking cold out here. Let's not drag it out, eh?"

He beamed. "I couldn't have put it better myself."

The two of us were smiling still as we turned as one, trudging back towards the corner of the house. His hand patted my shoulder once more, companionably, and then he let me go.

Amber followed a few steps behind. I could see her from the corner of my eye. Her eyes were still wide, and she still had that nervous, unease set to her face for some reason. But it faded a little more with every second, hidden behind a carefully neutral facade. The light from the front door cast her face into brighter relief as we slipped back into the front yard. She wore a tiny, bland smile by then.

Well, if she wanted to be unhappy, that was her business, wasn't it? I couldn't think what she had to be upset about - she was getting a new home, after all. But she only slipped out from behind Glenn and I, making a beeline back for her friend's side. I furrowed my brow. He was staring at me, his eyes unreadable behind his glasses. His name flickered at the back of my mind, but I couldn't seem to grab hold of it. I pursed my lips. It was going to bother me.

"Who's next?" I heard someone say. I looked over. Keira was standing by Brendon, her hands at her sides. Her pale eyes glowed in the half-light, fixed on mine. "Was that...did it go okay?"

I shrugged again, turning towards her. "It went fine. Just fine. Nothing unexpected!"

Glenn chuckled beside me. "Did you think there would be?"

"We just have to be careful," I said, giving him a quick look before turning back to Keira with a smile. "Anyway. I see no reason to keep all of us out here in the cold. Why don't we get them inside, see where we can bunk down some newcomers?"

"What?" she said, straightening. The others were coming to attention too. I could see Jake from the corner of my eye, glaring at me with confusion plain in his eyes. "You don't want to talk to anyone else? You, uh...you don't have anything you want to ask them about?"

"I think we can figure that out as tonight presses on, don't you?" She was being too cautious. Not that I minded that, by and large, but she could at least pretend to trust me in front of all the others. If I was the leader, then they should let me lead. "It's *cold*, Keira."

Loren was motionless, her skin glowing red against the frigid air. Her eyes flicked to Brendon - then back to me. He crept away from Keira, inching towards her, but didn't seem to be able to tear his eyes off Glenn and I.

I could see other movement, too - Amber and her friend. They'd pulled closer together, with him half-sheltered behind her protective shoulder. Her lips were pressed into a thin line again, and I didn't miss the way her hand lingered in front of him like a shield.

Her eyes flicked to mine. Something dark flickered there, almost...regretful. I blinked, pausing for a second. Regretful? Why would she be upset?

What was wrong? It didn't make any *sense*.

"We don't have much by the way of stuff," Glenn said, breaking through my fugue. "Really, I think we just need somewhere to bunk down, at least until we can get on our feet."

"We can put one or two of the guys in Brendon's room, can't we?" I said, tearing my eyes off Amber. The thoughts still whirled in the back of my head, but I couldn't quite catch any of them. I was left with a sour feeling in the pit of my stomach, not feeling quite right but unable to figure out *why*. I didn't like it.

"Jon, I'm not-"

"Keira. Please."

Her mouth shut with a snap. She glared at me, like daggers boring holes straight through me, but didn't say another word. Tyler slipped closer, tugging Kai behind him. "Jon, why don't we-"

"This is what we wanted," I said, my brow wrinkling in confusion. "It's a good thing."

"Of course it is," Loren said, her voice thin. A smile crept onto her face, small and tight. "But don't you think we should at least-"

The sound of the back hatch on the SUV cut her off. I glanced over. Glenn was at the back, fiddling with the set of keys. "Like I said, we don't have much," he said, glancing over at me. "But, think you could give me a hand with the bags while the others go check out the inside?"

"Sure. No problem." I let my smile grow again as I turned to the car, putting the others behind me.

Glenn nodded, patting me on the shoulder again as I came into range. "Good. It's over on this side."

The back hatch on the SUV hung overhead, just a few steps ahead. It was black against the dark of the night, hidden in shadows. My steps slowed.

Something...was wrong. I stopped.

Glenn glanced back. "Something wrong, Jon?"

I glanced over at him, my mouth sliding open. "Uh...no?"

His head tilted to one side. "Then...it's just over here."

There was something in his hands - I couldn't quite see it, with the shadows around the back of the SUV, but he kept turning it over and over. Like he was nervous. Why was he nervous? I stared at him, my confusion growing by the second. It was long and narrow, encased in plastic. Like an epipen or something, I mused, feeling the world spin peacefully around me. That was weird.

"Jon," Keira hissed. "I need to-"

"It's fine!" Glenn said, waving at her cheerily. "We'll be in in just a second. Really!"

Why was he in such a hurry? I curled and uncurled the fingers in my hand, my eyes shifting between Glenn and Keira nervously. Something wasn't right.

Something was very, very wrong.

Amber was still watching me. She hadn't moved, hadn't twitched. Her hand was still in front of her friend, like a shield.

Nox. She'd said his name was Nox. When...had she told me that?

The conversation we'd had, that I *thought* we'd had, crumbled away to nothing as I stared at the two of them. I shuddered, twitching as my mind rebelled against the wrongness of it. All of the polite, perfectly manufactured lines that he'd jammed into my head somehow...they faded, leaving behind only the cold, hard truth.

The truth that Amber had told me - about Glenn, and about his crew.

The world around me slowed, adrenaline shooting through my veins as I stiffened. He was right there, just a sparse few feet ahead of me. The rest of his crew was close - so very close. And mine might as well be miles away.

My lips parted, the command rising on my breath, but it was so slow. I could already see the recognition in his eyes, the way his expression tightened. His fingers clenched around the syringe he held, gripping its plastic case more tightly.

The scene around me resumed in a blur of motion as he lunged, hurling himself across the distance between us.

CHAPTER FORTY

Time slowed to a crawl as Glenn surged towards me. His jaw was clenched, his eyes fixed on me - but my thoughts were blissfully, peacefully blank.

Shit.

One thought screamed in the bank of my mind, blaring through the quiet of the moment and drowning out my doubts. I didn't know what powers Glenn had, but whatever he'd done to me, to my mind, I couldn't let him do it again.

And I couldn't let him-

My breath came in a ragged, indrawn gasp as I threw myself to the side. His hand thrust past me, that syringe clutched like a knife. I slammed into the corner of the car hard, the air leaving me in a rush.

"Shit!" I heard him say, his voice little more than a gasp itself.

"Jon!" Keira cried, from somewhere in the rest of the yard. "What's going on?"

"Go!" one of the other demis bellowed, their voice blasting apart the meager calm that was left. The sound of yelling rose, carried on a dozen voices just out of sight.

I couldn't spare a look their way. Glenn's hand had snapped out - his free hand. It settled around my wrist, pulling me back as tried to run. I whipped around, fixing my eyes on his. "Sto-"

The word fell apart halfway through my saying it, melting into limp, shapeless syllables. I shuddered, my other hand rising to press against my face. What...what was-

What was I doing?

"Careful, there," I heard Glenn say. His voice was cheerful and bright, as casual as a friend. "There's a bit of ice back here. Don't fall, now."

"R-Right," I said tonelessly, shifting away from him so I could get more of a grip on the car. Good thing he'd been there to catch me. Glenn didn't let go of my wrist, though. If anything, he clung all the tighter, pulling me in closer and closer and-

Wait - what? My thoughts froze, crystallized by the continued sounds of yelling that drifted over to the two of us. That didn't-

"Jon!" Keira screamed again. "God *damn* it! Tyler!" Her voice warped, like she was turning away.

I'd started moving when she bellowed my name, though, twisting and yanking hard. The veneer he'd laid over my thoughts cracked more easily, with my sister's help. I couldn't sit around stewing on it, musing about his relic and the powers he had. I needed to get *free*.

I turned myself away fast enough that when he lashed out again, his fist arcing towards me, it caught my shoulder instead of my jaw. A grunt slipped between my teeth, pained and low. My gun. I had a gun in my jacket. I just had to get to it - which wasn't going to be easy, when he had my arm in his hold.

"Let go of me," I rasped, forcing the words out at last. "Sit down."

His eyes widened, his lips parting gently as my relic seared to life - and then I felt the magic take hold. It lashed out against my mind, straining with feedback as he struggled for every inch, but I just bit my tongue until the taste of blood filled my mouth.

He crumpled to the ground a moment later, the energy leaving his limbs like his strings had been cut - but not before he tumbled forward. It was kind of like sitting - if you considered 'falling' to be applicable. I didn't have the time to swear before his left hand slammed into my leg.

I winced, feeling all too clearly the razor-sharp pain of something sinking through the denim of my jeans. Glenn fell away a heartbeat later, his hands falling clear - and the syringe he'd stabbed into my thigh stayed behind, right where he'd left it.

My eyes widened slowly, infinitesimally, as I stared down at what he'd stuck into my leg. A single second - that was all it took. Just a heartbeat, and I swiped down hard with my hand, instinctively knocking it free like I would a bug clinging to my pants. A surge of pain reminded me that it wasn't a bug, and I could have handled its removal more gracefully.

But a second was still a second. The pain faded behind a numb, calming wave that swept over me. I could almost feel it traveling through my veins, wiping away the adrenaline and leaving only deadness behind. The coppery tang of blood still filled my mouth. I clung to it, letting the pain of my tongue and my leg be my anchors against the tides.

Glenn sat right where he was, right where I'd told him to - but he was smiling, and his hand drifted towards the pocket of his coat.

"Sit still," I said, my words painfully slow. "Don't touch it."

The first cracks of gunfire from the yard sent me shying back, half-falling until I landed on the gravel across from where Glenn sat. He leaned forward, his eyes fixed on me. "Sit *still*," I snapped, reeling. His image spun in front of me, dancing in my eyes.

Another gunshot. And then another. Each one sent a shiver of fear through my heart like a physical blow. I plunged my hand into my pocket, feeling the comforting weight of the pistol tucked underneath, but it was so heavy. Every movement felt like it was padded with wool, painfully slow and difficult. Sweat dripped down the back of my neck, cold in the frigid air. Focusing all my energy in on Glenn, sitting right in front of me, I pulled it free at last.

His eyes widened. Behind us, on the other side of the van, there was only the sound of screaming and fighting - but right there, it was just the two of us, alone.

My arms shook as I pointed the gun at him, hearing the crack of Kai's explosions ring in my ear. He'd needed to learn how to use his fire - I'd just hoped to give him a more peaceful way to practice. Glenn stared back at me, his face going pale. The pit of my stomach churned at the sight. I pulled the trigger anyway.

The bang of the gun when it went off was deafening, hot and bright and in my face. My eyes squeezed shut in complaint.

But when they snapped open a scant few moments later, Glenn was right where he'd been - unbloodied and whole, although bone-white.

The air between us shimmered, like I was looking at him through a layer of water. A smile blossomed across his face instantly, wide and full of relief.

"Fucking *hell*," I said, hearing my words come out a moan as the world tilted dangerously. I needed to get up - to get back to the others. I had no idea what was happening out there, but they were fighting.

They needed help - and *I* needed help, too.

A flicker of movement from the corner of my eye drew my attention, though. The woman from before - Amber. She stood, halfway out from the rest of her group. Her hand was thrown in our direction, even as she glanced back over her shoulder with a twitch of black hair.

Was it her, then? I'd...god *damn* it, I'd hoped that maybe she'd actually planned on switching sides, on helping us. I should have known that when that scheme fell through, ruined by Glenn's perfectly-timed appearance, she'd go straight back to their side. We could have used another friendly demi helping us. Or at least not helping *them*.

Another surge of movement, showing hazily through the murk that the world was slowly becoming. Tyler. Right. Keira had called for him - and where was she? A fresh note of panic sounded off, deep within my chest. I couldn't see her.

Amber stiffened, bracing at Tyler's approach. His teeth were gritted as he ran, casting one last look back over his shoulder to where he'd come from. A heartbeat later, his head snapped back around to stare at her.

A deafening roar exploded out across the yard between him and her, sending plumes of gravel flying up from the drive with the sheer force of the vibration. She was right at the epicenter of the eruption, frozen and alone. My mouth slid open, my eyes tightening in the fraction of a second I had. She might have been an ally. She might have-

Might have, but wasn't. The corner of my brain still capable of rational thought clamped down hard - right as Amber moved.

Her hands flying out in front of her, she braced, leaning into the force of the vibrations. The air around her thickened, taking on that same watery, blurred quality. Any doubts I had as to who was responsible for blocking the bullet meant for Glenn vanished as I saw that shell appear around her.

The ground around Tyler erupted, tearing itself apart, but he didn't slow. The demi skidded past in a hail of gravel, sliding free.

As though my thought had awoken him, the sound of Glenn scrabbling against the gravel brought my head snapping back around. He was shifting, fighting against my relic - and with my eyes on the fight building by the second, I was distracted.

He slipped free, a victorious light shining in his eyes as he leapt for the gun in my hand.

A hand latched around my collar, yanking me backwards. Hard. My feet slid out from under me in a second as I tumbled back. My hands clenched around the gun, my pulse thundering in my ears.

Tyler's eyes were wild, his mouth hanging open, but his gaze was fixed on Glenn as he let me go. His lips moved. I could read the words *not so fast* flying off them, crystal clear with every motion he took, but not even a flicker of sound reached my ears.

Glenn bellowed in pain, though, throwing his hands over his ears. In the instant I'd had before he moved, I saw the dark wetness of blood just beginning to flow down the sides of his head. A humorless smile slipped across my face. He'd tried to drug me. He'd come here to kill us. I wasn't about to feel bad for him.

But as I sucked in a fresh breath of air, another command rising to my lips, I stopped. As helpful as Tyler was, he'd put me in a bit of a conundrum. Should I command our now-deaf enemy? Shoot him? Would he even hear me, with his eardrums clearly blown out and useless? If I shot him, would Amber just stop me again?

With a dozen different possibilities whirling through my mind and the pressing need to do *something* growing with every second that passed, I found my body moving all on its own.

There was no thought involved. No carefully crafted plan, no care given to what might be best. I just latched onto the plastic-encased syringe, wrapping my hand around it and praying that I hadn't bent the needle, and slammed it down into his leg in a cruel parody of the move he'd tried.

He thrashed, taking a swipe at me, but I leaned away and let his fist sail through empty air. With every second that passed his movements had a little less energy.

I staggered free as he crumpled to the ground, twitching gently. I didn't know how much was left in the syringe, after I'd taken the first stab at it, but he was down, and that would have to be enough.

Tyler hauled me upright, his hand latched around my arm. "Jon! Are you-"

"F-Fine," I said, trying to keep my words from slurring. It was getting harder to string the syllables together, let alone do it while trying to walk. "W-What's-"

"Come on," he hissed, giving me one last tug and turning away from the van. In a second he was gone, tearing back off towards his little brother and the other demis. I lurched again, my balance gone just as quickly as he'd departed, and swallowed a curse. One foot in front of the other. Right. I remembered how to do this.

At the first step I took, though, venturing beyond the edge of the van and back into the yard, a spray of shrapnel tore across the gravel in front of me. I crumpled back behind cover, the ice in my veins overcoming the blur of the drugs in my system for an instant. Shit. Right. They had guns. I brought my pistol back around, feeling my palms sweat against the smooth metal, and leaned out as carefully as I could.

No sooner had I inched out than another barrage of gunfire began. I tucked myself farther behind the van, cursing under my breath.

I'd seen a little bit, in the brief glance I'd gotten. The plans we'd made were there in my mind, faint memories half-hidden behind my drug-addled thoughts. I'd...I'd split our people. Loren and Jake. Tyler and Kai. And that left-

Brendon skidded around the corner, tripping headlong. The ground behind him melted under his feet, sucking at the soles of his shoes and trying to pull him in. "Shit. Shit. Shit," I could hear him moan all the while, the words barely audible. He stumbled, hitting the ground. I was on him a moment later, doing what little I could to pull him farther behind the vehicle. The van was low enough to the ground to provide a *bit* of shelter. It was as good as we were going to get.

My breath caught in my throat. When he crawled closer, when I pulled, a dark smear of wet redness appeared across the snowy ground. "B-Brendon," I whispered. "You're-"

"It's my arm. Just my arm," he said, forcing a smile. I wasn't convinced. The agony was there in his eyes, hiding underneath the cheerful facade. His jacket was soaked through with blood. "What the *fuck* is going on?"

He was trembling, quivering with nervous, pent-up energy - and was too close to breaking under the pressure, I realized. That couldn't happen. We needed everyone to be together. I was sure of that, even if the ground wasn't entirely stable underneath me anymore.

His eyes widened as he stared at me. "Jon? What's wrong with you?"

I just shoved my gun at him, forcing it into his chest grip-first until he was forced to take it from me. "Yours."

"What the hell am I going to do with-"

"I'll figure something out. Pick them off." If I couldn't see straight, I couldn't shoot straight, either, and that wasn't going to be useful. We'd find another way out of this.

"T-That might not be so easy. They've got some sort of-"

"The woman. I know. She's-"

"Not just her, man. They're all pissed off, now. It's not so simple."

I paused. All of them, then. Right. Dimly, my mind processed Brendon's words, coupled together with what little I'd seen of the other demis. Amber had...some sort of barrier. Glenn messed with my mind. From what she'd said, her little friend Nox had been able to...gauge my abilities, somehow. Was he like Keira? Was it different?

She'd said he'd "heard" me - and that he hadn't gotten everything. Keira was different. I knew that much from talking to her. When she looked at someone, more and more, she could tell a lot.

Keira. We needed her. I needed her, to tell me what I was dealing with. If any of us could do it, it would be her. "Where's Keira?" I said, forcing the words out.

"I don't fucking know," Brendon muttered, leaning out again. He'd no sooner left the safety of our cover when another three shots rang out. He threw himself back in, his chin rising. I could see him swallow apprehensively. Tyler just sat where he was, eyes closed pensively. "We need to-"

"Stop shooting!" I screamed, forcing the words as loud as I could. "Sit down and-" I gasped, crumpling. My relic seared hot against my chest, hotter than I'd ever felt it before. The gunfire stopped. A round of confused cries went up around the yard. For a single moment, an eerie, impossible calm settled over the scene.

And then the shots resumed, one after another. I could see a fresh spray of plastic shards as the bullets tore into the side of the house. *Our* house. God damn it, we'd just put new siding on it last month. The little thoughts in the back of my mind shrieked that now was *not* the time. The rest of me was too busy trying to catch my breath, letting go of the relic's magic.

Well, that didn't work. I pushed myself back upright, feeling the blur settle across my vision again. Was it the drugs? Was it the fact that there were seven of them, and they were fighting? Was it the fact that I was trying to blanket my powers across a battlefield, rather than picking out individual people?

Whatever it was, I didn't have the strength to do something like that again. I bit my lip, running through things in my head again. "All...right. We need to-"

My words died as something cold settled against my legs - something cold and wet. Mud. We were sitting in mud, suddenly, sinking deeper and deeper into the muck. I threw myself upright, pulling myself free of the sticky mess, and Brendon was right alongside me.

"One of their demis," Brendon said, his voice shaking gently. "Jake's got two of them under, and Loren's confusing a third, but this one's making it hard."

Two asleep, one disoriented. And Glenn behind us, moaning gently in his half-sleep. I nodded, swaying gently. Tyler grabbed me, holding me steady. "What the fuck is wrong with you?"

"Have to move," I muttered, pulling my shoes free again. "Know we're here. Need the others."

"How do you figure we're supposed to-"

"Kai!" I screamed, forcing the words out as loud as I could. "Think big!"

I could almost hear the collective hiss from all of our friends taking in one, prolonged indrawn breath. The other demis faltered, hesitating. I crept away from Brendon, peering out from around the far side of the van - which now sat even lower against the drive, half-sunk in the mud.

Our nice, even groups had dispersed, somewhere along the line. Jake *did* have two of them on the ground, blissfully unconscious and removed from the fight. But Jake's arms were shaking, and as I watched he fell to one knee, hidden behind the corner of the house where he couldn't get shot.

The crackle of energy building was all the warning I got that Kai had heard my command. He was there, on the far side, creeping out of the treeline - with Keira beside him. A knot in my chest eased, coming untied. Sparks crackled around his open palm, coalescing as his bracelet glowed.

The other demis were clustered in the front yard, pulled into a narrow group. Three of them. They flinched, spinning as one to face Kai as he hurled the fireball in his palm at them.

Amber moved first, shoving the others aside and launching herself forward. Palms-out, she kicked one foot behind her to brace against, standing like a wall against the approaching flames.

The air around her quivered, blurring and distorting. I gaped, caught off guard for a single second. That too? What the hell was she *doing*?

The flames hesitated, caught in horrible stillness for a single second. And then they curled in on themselves, roaring to life in a hideous surge of heat, and exploded back towards Kai.

He gaped. That was all there was - his face, his eyes wide and unbelieving, cast into brilliant relief by the force of the light from his fireball, coming back for vengeance. He didn't move. I didn't blame him. I wasn't sure I'd be able to move, in his boots.

Luckily for him, he wasn't alone. Keira was there, moving before I could process exactly what was happening. The air around Amber had no sooner rippled when she grabbed him by the collar, bellowing wordlessly. Her eyes were wide, too, but it looked like her 'flight' reaction was stronger than 'fight'.

Whatever sound Kai made vanished behind the din of the fireball as it cascaded back in, exploding in rivulets of embers - against the side of my house. My heart froze as I stared, blinking away shock, but the flames fell away. There wasn't enough heat there to light the building itself off. Yet.

The dizziness grew worse by the second, strengthened by the fear that swept deeper across my gut. I forced my way through it, latching onto the fragments of reason I could find. I couldn't control the whole lot of them, not from where I was. That much had become clear. That didn't mean I was useless, I told myself. I just had to do what I could. Creeping forward, I peered out from around the cover I had, trying to find a target. The only one I could find was Amber - and the huddled form of Nox behind her, staring at me. His glasses glinted red with the dying remnants of the embers, hiding his expression.

Fine. They weren't exactly who I wanted to pick as my first targets, but I'd take who I could get. "Sit down!" I bellowed, narrowing my eyes as I locked onto Amber's slender form. "Hands on the ground!"

But the first syllable was no sooner out of my mouth when Amber wheeled. Nox was already shuddering, crumpling even lower to the ground. I saw his mouth moving all the same, forcing out words. Amber's legs gave out from under her as my spell took hold with a delightfully solid latch of magic, but her head came up.

Again - *Again*, the air around her shimmered, and I was left to reel as my own distorted voice came shrieking back to me. I shook away the momentary confusion, grabbing the back of Brendon's shirt. He'd fallen to the ground too, pressing his hands to the dirt. "Stop that," I snapped, my frustration overflowing. "This...this isn't working. We need to get back to the others. Can you cover us?"

"Y-Yeah," he stammered, lurching dangerously but rising, pressed flat against the side of the SUV. My gun was still clenched in his hands. "I think so."

Tyler rose alongside him, grim-faced and quiet, nodding along.

"Don't think," I muttered darkly. "Just do it."

"Yeah."

"Come on. On three," I whispered, my voice low. He nodded. I turned back to the rest of our friends. They were half visible, tucked against the house. If we could get there, if we could get around the house, we'd be safe.

My poor siding.

"One. Two. Three!" My legs pumped under me as I threw myself out from our hiding place, charging back towards Keira and Kai. Jake and Loren would be past them. They would. They had to be - there wasn't another option that I was willing to accept.

The gravel between the van and the house erupted with shards of snow and stone under my feet as I ran, putting every ounce of concentration I had into staying upright. I had a single, pointed moment to realize what was about to happen before a line of fire lanced across my leg - my *other* leg, the one that hadn't been ventilated by Matt's crew.

At least they'd match.

The ground rose up under me, but I caught myself, teeth gritted. We were so close. Tyler raced out front, making a beeline for his brother. Brendon was hot on my heels, firing round after round towards where the other three lurked. My heart leapt - until I saw one of the other demis lunge forward. His short-cropped black hair swayed with the force of the motion as he thrust a hand towards us, palm wide.

The ground under us caved in, hardened clay and soil turning to mud instantly. Him. It was *him*. My eyes locked on him as I tumbled, sinking into the mess. "Amber! Sit down!" I bellowed, willing my voice to reach, carrying it across the distance.

She was watching Brendon - one hand held in front of her all the while, shielding her and Nox from the hail of bullets. They hung like snowflakes in front of her, caught in midair. Given the way she'd acted before, I'd known that she'd be watching out for him. Her friend, who didn't seem to have a whole lot going for in in the focus category. A crooked smile tugged at my lips. And with her hands tied-

Her eyes widened as my magic took hold again, dropping her onto her ass. "Don't move!" I bellowed, even louder. She could shield Nox there. Fine. But her companions...that was a different matter.

The mud-bender had a single instant to gape, his mouth falling open, before Brendon's gunfire tore across his chest. He hit the ground with a wet, sickening noise, twitching gently and trying to curl in on himself.

The fact that Brendon had stopped firing told me everything I needed to know. There was no need for me to look at his gun to know that the slide would be locked back, the magazine emptied. Keira's hands latched around my arms before I could pull myself from the mud, dragging me free.

"Fucking- work with me- here," she grunted, her voice distorting with exertion. She didn't need to tell me twice. As the first round of angry cries rang out from where Amber and the other demis stood, I was already tumbling to the ground alongside Keira - and Brendon, and Tyler, and Kai. I breathed a sigh of relief.

"Where's-"

"Jake's around the other side of the house," Keira said, her voice toneless. "He's got two of them knocked out - they're behind that pair over there - but it's turned into a cluster. They're pinned. Loren's helping him keep the pair locked down." Her eyes tightened. "But I don't know how much longer they can keep them totally unconscious. Not with all this."

I swallowed hard, watching the numbers line up through the haze of my thoughts. Two sleeping there - and like Keira said, I could see them start to twitch. Glenn made three. Amber and Nox made five. The goddamn mud-bender made six. And the last one-

Keira's hand slammed down onto the top of my head as I peeked up, pushing me right back down. Just in time - I heard the crackle of *something* go flying past. Something that made my skin sear with its passing, and left a black scorch mark against the wood of the house.

I sat back down. "What the *fuck* was-"

"I can't get a good enough look at him to see," Keira snapped. "Not really."

"Give me that," I heard Brendon mutter. I glanced over just in time to see him pry a gun from Kai's hands.

A groan slipped between my lips. Jake must have given it to him. Wonderful. "Kai, just...keep casting." It was about the last thing that I *wanted*, but he'd be effective with cover fire if nothing else.

As the steady sound of gunfire resumed, carried on by Brendon's methodical stubbornness and accompanied by the relentless firecracker-bang of Kai's magic, I looked back to Keira. Her fingers were wrapped around the hilt of a knife she'd pulled from somewhere. I saw her swallow, the action too apprehensive to miss.

My eyes narrowed. "How much of their relics are you seeing, these days?"

"Enough," she muttered, glancing back towards the house. "Glances and...details. Little by little. But we don't have enough ammo. They're going to push in. Maybe I can go get-"

"Tell me what we're working with, damn it."

Her head snapped back around, eyes flashing dangerously. "Earth and mud," she snapped, pointing to the fallen body of the mud-bender. Her finger danced along, picking out person after person. "He's got...numbness? Maybe some sort of paralysis. The other asshole on the ground's got some sort of...metamorphosis. I think. I have *no idea* what she's doing, I just see a wall of light when she starts casting. Her little friend, it's something to do with...communication, I guess. It's not a fucking science, Jon."

"Communication," I said, my eyes lighting up. "Wait. That doesn't-" I stopped. It didn't make sense. Amber had known what I could do. Nox had told her. That was what she'd *said*. I'd thought he might be an appraiser or whatever they were called, like Keira was practicing for. If his powers were something related to communications, that whole school of thought was ruined.

Unless. A thought lanced through my head like a bolt of lightning. I sat upright, earning myself another slap back down and an irritated noise from Keira. "Would you fucking start ordering them around or something useful?" she growled.

I ignored her. I'd *tried* that. Without getting a clear line of sight on them, it would just drain all of my energy out in seconds, trying to keep that many people under. It wasn't feasible. And to zero in on Amber, I'd need to put myself right in the line of *whatever* that guy was doing. For all I knew, the mud-bender was still clinging to life, too, waiting to dick me over.

But maybe there was a different way.

Folding myself deeper in on myself, peering around the corner of the house, I cast an anxious glance towards the enemy crew.

Sure enough, a fresh spray of gunfire spattered across the siding, along with another blast of energy. I threw myself back, my heart thundering dully.

But Nox was looking, now. I'd seen his eyes fixed on mine, his bone-white face drawn and anxious.

Keira had said he'd *heard* me. Keira had said he had a communications-based relic. That narrowed things down considerably - and gave me an idea.

Feeling like an absolute ass, I slid my eyes shut, squeezing them as tightly as I could. *If this keeps up we'll all wind up dead,* I thought, focusing in on the words until they shone as clearly in my mind as I could. *We'll run out of ammo first, but there's more of us than you, now. We're all fucked.* A deep, shuddering breath slid through my lungs. This had better work. This needed to work. *But if we work together, we can all make it out of this. And you two can turn a nice profit, somehow, I'm sure.* I couldn't quite keep the sardonic smile from settling across my lips. *That was the plan, right? Why ruin a good thing?*

Leaning back against the house, my eyes slid open. I counted off the seconds in my head, ticking off the numbers one through ten. And then I glanced back towards the enemy crew, putting my utmost faith in the belief that I wasn't about to have my face blown off.

Nox stared right back at me, unmoving. His lips moved, just the faintest flutter. Behind him, I could see the other two, just beginning to twitch, to push themselves upright. "Shit," I whispered, tearing my gaze off them long enough to scan the far side of the house.

There. I could see them in the deepest part of the shadows - Loren and Jake, peeking towards the crew just like I'd been. Well. Loren was, I amended. Jake...My heart sank. Jake had one hand pressed to his shoulder - and even in the dark of their corner, I could see the dark of blood seeping out. He hadn't escaped their gunfire after all. *Fuck.*

Loren pulled him back to shelter even as I watched - and from the corner of my eye, I could still see Nox staring at me. *We will make it worth your while,* I forced out, emblazoning the words in my mind's eye. If I was wrong...god, if I was wrong, then I was wasting the little bit of time Jake had bought us.

But a heartbeat later, he turned to Amber, his lips moving furiously.

Her head snapped up at whatever he was saying, her spine stiffening. The air around them shimmered still, bullets bouncing back

towards our group one after another from the surface of her spell.
And then she spun, glaring at me.

CHAPTER FORTY-ONE

My pulse froze, ice flooding through my veins, as Amber stared at me. Her hazel eyes bored into mine, narrowing second by second.

Had my message gotten through? The possibilities ran through my mind, varying from her pulling out that gun I knew she had in her jacket and shooting me all the way to her maybe, *maybe* being willing to work together with us.

But her friend was right beside her, his adam's apple bobbing as he swallowed. My eyes flicked to him - and then back to Amber. The other two demis were stumbling to their feet, muttering words I couldn't hear over the ringing of my ears. We were out of time to play around.

The woman's lips pressed into a thin, tight line. And then she nodded incrementally, the motion slight enough that I might have imagined it entirely.

My hand squeezed against my leg, doing what little it could to blot out the agony. It wasn't a bad wound, I was pretty sure - I could still move it, unlike what Matt's crew had done to me. Just a graze. Probably. That didn't mean it didn't hurt. "Don't shoot the woman or her friend with the glasses," I said, my voice low enough that the enemy demis couldn't hear me. Probably.

Brendon's head snapped around, and the others weren't far behind. Kai gaped openly, his hands falling still for a long moment. "Keep going," I snapped, glaring at him.

The weather-seer grabbed my shoulder a moment later, forcing me to look at him. "What the hell do you mean, don't shoot them?"

"They're not committed. They're mercenaries," I said, breaking loose and peering back towards Glenn's crew. Another bolt of energy glanced off the side of the house, sending a pile of firewood cascading to the ground. I swore under my breath, pulling back in. The others crowded in behind me, trying to get a look of their own. "The woman - she tried to back out, when this all started. When she knew I wasn't going to buy their lies."

Keira groaned, pressing in against the side of the house. I could see the gleam of a knife in her hands. "Jon, just because she says that, it doesn't mean-"

"She wasn't lying," I said, leaning back and trying to calm my racing heart. Between the pain in my leg and the last dregs of the sedative in my system, it was increasingly hard to string a sentence together. "Not through any of it. Not like Glenn. was"

"If you knew he was lying, why did you-"

"Just trust me, all right?" I snapped. "Worry about the others."

"They're moving away," Tyler said. We stopped, glancing over at him. He sat halfway back in the shadows of the trees, tucked in behind a massive pine that obscured him entirely. A wry smile tugged at his lips. "Footsteps. I can hear them."

Risking taking a bullet or bolt of energy to the face, I hazarded a glance. He was right. They weren't *far*, but Amber and Nox had slid to the side enough to be kitty-corner to their supposed comrades. Her eyes flicked to me again, tightening.

"Don't do anything," I repeated, more insistently. "Not to her. Worry about the guy with the...the electricity."

"That's not electricity," Keira murmured, shaking her head.

I ground my teeth together. "Whatever the fuck it is. It doesn't matter. Worry about *him*."

"What are you-"

"On my signal. Who still has a gun?" I glanced around, spotting Kai's pistol hanging from his pocket, momentarily forgotten. The young man was a few paces ahead of us, crouched behind a tarped pile of shingles and sparking off blast after blast. "Kai!"

He glanced back, his face pale and drawn. His hair was matted with sweat. His eyes lit up in a split second of recognition. His gun skidded across the gravel a moment later, tossed back towards where we hid.

Probably not the recommended way to pass a gun, but I'd take it. It was in my hands in a second. I stared at Amber. She stared right back, impassive. Her friends clambered to their feet beside her, shaking away the last dregs of whatever Jake and Loren had done. The dream-worker was just a distant shape on the far side of the house, a slender fraction of her face peering around the corner at us.

"Can you talk to Jake?" I murmured, glancing at Tyler.

He paused. "I...maybe? I don't know."

"See if you can. If he's got anything in him still, use it now. They don't have to be out. Just take the edge off their sharpness."

"I'll try," he muttered, eyes dropping to the ground. His lips moved, even after he'd finished talking. I couldn't hear even the slightest murmur of noise from him. We'd just have to trust that it was working. I took a deep breath, resetting my grip on the gun. I had no angle on them from our hiding place. We'd have to-

Keira grabbed my shoulder. I was swaying. "Are you sure you should be-"

"One of you, be ready to shoot that bastard as soon as I occupy the woman," I said, not bothering to look at the others.

"Do any of us still have ammuni-"

"Figure it out. Come on." Feeling my pulse thundering, I hurled myself out from behind our hiding place, back out into the open.

The house was still a mess - and we were still working on it. The driveway was nothing if not cluttered, with my car and Jake's pulled into the drive. Keira's lurked in the yard. We'd built up the place a little - thank god - but thanks to that, we had a good variety of options for shelter. I offered a silent prayer of thanks for the 'landscaping' we'd done. Ugly, yes, but useful.

Most of us were out of rounds. I had to hope that they were, too.

Behind me, the sound of their footsteps across the gravel rang dully in the cold air. I had a single second to take in everything - the sight of Loren holding Jake upright across the yard, the way the other demis all sagged like someone had dosed them, the man with spiky, gelled blond hair whose eyes fixed on mine despite the sudden weariness that clouded them.

A blast of white light exploded towards me, engulfing me before I could twitch away. His partners behind him were just starting to move, to react, but they couldn't keep up. I stiffened, biting off a pained cry as my nerves erupted into fire. Every inch of my skin hurt, like fingernails across a sunburn times a thousand. I was certain I was burning away, crisping up like a potato chip - but when my eyes slit the tiniest fraction, my skin was whole and unblemished.

With that fragile window of vision, I could see Amber, too - and I saw her nod again, the motion even smaller than it had been the first time.

Her hand snapped up, precisely in time with mine. The pain helped, putting a note of desperation into my every act. The barrel of the gun wobbled, winding haphazardly back and forth, and her eyes narrowed.

The crack of it firing was loud enough to deafen. I staggered back half a step, gritting my teeth against the shock of it, and tumbled back out of the line of fire. Amber hadn't so much as twitched. Her fingers were arched in front of her, tightened - and a single bullet hung in thin air between them.

I'd seen her intentions plain enough, when she'd put herself away from the others without turning and running entirely. She didn't want to *look* like she was betraying them, like she was turning sides. She didn't trust that we'd win, and so she was playing both sides. Part of me wanted to be irritated with that. Somehow, I just couldn't be.

My leg gave out from under me, sending me to the ground in a heap of limbs, but I couldn't keep the satisfaction from my voice as I glared at the blond bastard. "S-Stop," I gasped, eyes locked on his. The woman couldn't block my voice - not while she had bullets to deal with. That was my theory, anyway.

He froze, hands outstretched. The pain started to dwindle, second after second. A smile tugged at the corners of my lips. "That's right," I said, licking my lips as sensation slowly returned. "Eyes on me. Hands down. There's no need to cast, is there?"

He didn't blink. Slowly, his attention still locked on me, he lowered his hands. The pain slipped away, the remnants just a pale shadow of what it had been.

A muted bellow was all the warning I got that there was more going on than just him and the pair. My head whipped to the side, just in time to see one of the other two demis leaping into the fray. His eyes were fixed on mine, blue and narrowed - and his *arms*. They were massive, swelling by the second with what looked like rock erupting across his skin. It was like he was-

I hurled myself to the side, throwing my arms up just in time, and took the punch that was aimed at my face on the shoulder instead - my shoulder which immediately went numb. Something inside it popped disconcertingly. My face smashed into the gravel driveway as I skidded, the air leaving me in a ragged gasp. What little control I had over my magic vanished alongside it, no matter how hard I grasped at the fragments.

The crack of a gun told me that my momentary distraction had been enough. I didn't see who had fired - but the sound of it was distant enough I had to bet that Jake had been holding out on us. No great surprise. The blond man's eyes widened, horror sliding across his face and etching in there. He hit the ground a moment later, shuddering. Within seconds, he was still.

One more down. That left-

The stone-covered man was still there, still right on top of me. My eyes snapped to him, coming back in for another blow in the moment of distraction I'd given him. "N-No, st-"

His fist slammed across my cheek. My words died as the taste of blood filled my mouth for the second time that night. I rolled clear, scrabbling for inches to put myself a little bit farther away from the demi. He'd gotten even *bigger*, somehow, like some sort of shapeshifter.

He was still staring at me, teeth bared. Tyler was there, dragging me back, but the stone-shifter pressed in still. My legs wobbled as I pushed myself upright, teetering. I couldn't run. He lunged forward, swinging wildly, and-

The demi reeled, bellowing in pain, as an explosion split the air between him and I. I winced. Right in his *face*. Bastard deserved it, but even still, that had to hurt.

Kai surged in, taking up the gap left by my absence.

I could feel Tyler's hands stiffen on my shoulders. "Kai! What are you-"

The younger demi's fingers snapped, his arm whipping across. The blast that cracked out wasn't big, but it was up close and personal enough to send the shifter stumbling back. His stone-laced fists swiped wildly, instinctively lashing out.

My heart froze, seeing the raw force contained there. But Kai only ducked under the blow, skittering behind the shifter before he could turn. Another blast of fire erupted a moment later.

It wasn't enough, though, I saw, anxiety building. The layer of stone or whatever it was that was blossoming across the demi's skin was just too thick. Kai couldn't break in.

"Look at me!" I snapped, forcing myself a little straighter as I glared at the shifter. He stiffened, his head snapping over to face me. My head pounded, aching with every second. It was too much. He was strong, and fresh, and I was tired and my head hurt. But just for a little bit, maybe I could-"

Tyler surged past me, one fist upraised. Invisible waves crackled from it, shaking the air with a low thrum. I winced. It was an honorable thought - but entirely useless. The guy was made of *stone*. How was he expecting to stop that?

His eyes widened before he could get past me. He hit the gravel hard, crumpling right beside me.

The last demi. He stalked away from Nox and Amber with one finger outstretched towardsTyler - whose eyes twitched, straining to see who had joined the fight. Besides for that, he was still enough I might have thought him dead.

A curse slipped from my lips. "You! Let-" A cough rippled from my chest, along with the fresh taste of blood. I could feel it, dribbling from my nose. I was going to hit my limit, soon. And-

The shifter broke loose with a roar, tearing away from my grip and spinning back towards Kai. The younger man twitched away, as light on his feet as any boxer, but I wasn't fooled. The bruises coating his skin were new, and painful-looking. And he was beginning to look more grey than just pale. He was too new for something like this, for this sort of prolonged use of his relic.

It would help if the other two would actually *commit*. But - no. They were still backing away, their eyes fixed on the SUV. I twisted, casting a look towards where Loren and Jake waited. "Can you- do you think you can-"

Loren didn't wait for me to finish. She was pale, too, and I didn't know how much control she'd have without Jake by her side, but she dropped her partner to the gravel without so much as a word. He grunted, making a face, but his eyes focused in on Amber and Nox. Loren slipped closer, dashing forward until she could crouch beside my poor, much-abused car. Getting covered in blood wasn't enough, apparently. Now it was going to get used as a backstop. Wonderful.

But Amber and Nox stiffened, drawing closer together. A second later they both staggered, throwing themselves down behind the SUV. All the way down - with their hands pressed to their heads. Loren's dreams weren't so good, this time, it seemed.

Fine. Good enough. At least they were contained. Two left. Only two. We could do two. Kai and the shifter were still dancing, trading blows - and making every bit as little progress as they had been before. I could hardly follow the bigger man with my eyes, his skin distorting with every passing second as the hardened layer spread thicker and thicker. He was too fast. It wasn't fair. No one that big and strong should be *fast* too.

If not him, then that only left one more option. "Hey, there. You," I rasped, my headache returning in all its glory as I stared at the final demi. He glanced over at me, flinching a second after as he realized I was looking at him. "Don't move. It's fine. Don't cast any spells or anything." My voice was quiet. I wasn't entirely sure I'd be able to summon the strength to yell at him. It didn't seem to matter. "Actually, scratch that. Come closer. Slowly."

He twisted, twitching like he was fighting against my hold, but I kept my eyes fixed on his. Smooth and steady, that was the trick. No panicked commands, no bellowed orders issued with adrenaline high in my veins. Just calm, even commands. *Oily*, I had to keep myself from saying. More than ever, my power just felt...wrong. Dirty. Like cheating. I could see the fear in his eyes, the feel the resistance he was trying to give. But there were only two left. There was no one else to distract me - and I couldn't let him go.

"Closer," I murmured as he shuddered to a stop a few steps away. He had a knife - I could see it clutched in one hand. He had a gun, too, shoved in his belt - but the slide was locked back, the grip hollow. Empty. One of the others must have taken it. A sigh slipped between my teeth.

A stray blast of fire glanced off my car. I winced. Damn it, Kai. His brother was already pushing himself upright, his arms wobbling dangerously but growing steadier by the second. The paralysis had worn off. Or whatever it was.

The paralyzer could see it in my expression. What was coming. He fought all the harder. I wasn't sure I'd have the strength to stand. I didn't close my eyes, didn't look away. That would have just made it worse, like I was running from it. As horrible as this was, they had attacked us - and these powers were mine. I had to accept that.

My voice was a whisper as I fed him line after line, watching the horror build in his expression. His limbs quivered as he fought. The paired rings burned against my skin, growing hotter the more he resisted. I'd have sworn I could see the glow of them light up the demi's face.

No matter how hard he fought, it didn't matter. Not with me right in front of him, not with everything they'd tried to do. His arms raised, twisting inwards.

A fresh patch of red blossomed in the snow. His body tumbled down a painfully short while later.

I sagged, letting my weight droop as the resistance fell off. There. I'd done it. That only left-

The shifter, who even then charged Kai. His fist had swollen to deadly proportions, big and heavy enough that the *thought* of getting hit with it was enough to make me wince. One good whack, and he'd break most of the bones in Kai's body.

My head pounded, blood dribbling down my lips from the nosebleed that continued relentlessly. Damn it, I needed to get better at all this - but controlling people wasn't so easy. That was becoming apparent. I needed to practice. One more. I could do one more.

"You- look at-" I began, but stopped. It wasn't going to get heard, not over the sudden whine that had kicked into high intensity.

Tyler. He'd stepped out from behind us, holding his phone out to one side and his hand to the other. A song blared from its speaker, loud and full of as much bass as the tiny speaker could muster. More, in fact. Much more. I'd only known the man a short time, but the pure rage on his face was unmistakable. The air itself shook, quivering with the force of the vibrations that were building.

I realized what he was trying to do at the same instant as the sound died away, falling off.

When it returned, it exploded out in a cacophony of noise, bursting out from under the shifter's armor and seething through the cracks Tyler had found. Distantly, hidden under the din, I could hear the demi scream - and the sound of stone, hitting the gravel driveway.

Kai didn't hesitate. Blood coated his face - and his arms, and his jacket - but as his opponent's armor shattered, he moved. The snap of his fingers was lost to the chaos. The blast of fire and raw energy that lashed out between them was not.

I winced, drawing back as my eyes rebelled. Spots covered my vision. The world washed to white as my eyes fought to adjust.

When they settled, letting me slit my eyelids open again, the shifter was already on the ground. His front was blackened, the armor coating his face and chest blown away. Only the barest fragments of it remained between him and the ground.

A knife plunged into his neck a heartbeat later, putting an end to his twitching. Keira stumbled back, straightening and glancing from side to side wildly as though looking for the next attack.

There wasn't one. The forest was quiet again, the yard littered with the rapidly cooling bodies of the demis who'd tried to slide past our guard.

A flicker of movement caught my attention, just on the corner of my vision. I glanced over. Amber had stumbled to her feet, despite the desperate way she swayed. She had Nox's jacket gripped in one hand, towing him behind her as she stumbled away.

"Both of you," I said, thankful that the noise had died away at last. It meant that I didn't have to yell. I wasn't sure I could, with the way my head was pounding. Someone grabbed my shoulder, discreetly propping me up from behind. Brendon. He was pale, but offered me a tiny smile. I returned it, looking back to the pair. "Don't run. Sit down." I stared at them a moment longer. "And give me your...your foci."

Both of them flinched. "You said we could go," Amber spat, even as her hands trembled. She was fighting, resisting. I inched closer, feeling Brendon move with me. My leg burned with every stumbling step. "If we didn't fight you, we could go. That was the *deal*."

"Your crew tried to kill us," I said, glaring right back. "I don't think you can claim the moral high ground here."

Her eyes tightened further. She was stuck, and she knew it. It wasn't like demis had *rules*. Fair and unfair were just childrens' tools, irrelevant to the realities of the world. We could kill them right then and there, and no one would even know, let alone care.

My ears roared, the rush of blood filling them as my relic screamed its complaint. I was winning, though. Amber was glaring daggers at me, yes, but her left hand slowly slid to her right sleeve. A second later, she was unbuckling a glove. I eyed it, trying not to let my interest show. It looked old-fashioned, which was hardly surprising. Fingerless, and sewn from dark-stained leather..

Nox wasn't putting up the same fight. His eyes were already glassy and fixed on mine. A crystal pendant hung from a cord in his fist, held out towards me. It was intricately carved, worked into the shape of what looked like an owl.

I stepped forward, doing my best not to fall over as my bullet-grazed leg quivered underneath me, and scooped both of them up. Brendon had his arm under my shoulder a moment later, tugging me farther away and out of arm's reach. Each breath he took was a ragged gasp, filled with pain of its own.

Amber didn't try and snatch them back. She glared at me, fury burning in her expression. "So. What now, then?" she snapped, the tension in her voice betraying the internal struggle that had just begun in her body. "You going to just take them, or are you planning on finishing what you started?"

"No one's killing you today," I said, leaning back on my heels. It was hard to keep the weariness from my voice, to find the energy to deal with the both of them. But if I didn't, I knew what would happen. Already, Tyler and Jake scowled at the pair, inching closer.

As angry as I was, as *furious* as I was that they'd been part of a crew here to kill us, I'd made a deal. I forced a smile instead, staring down the length of my nose at then. "No one's...we're not going to kill you," I said, folding my arms.

Her lips twitched into a frown, something unreadable flickering across her face. "What, then?"

A mirthless chuckle slipped out before I could stop it. "If you're honest with us, then you can go. Later. But right now? With you two here to kill us, hired by *someone* to come after me?"

Keira shifted, making a surprised noise in the back of her throat. I winced. I...hadn't exactly told her that, yet. Pushing it from my mind, I focused in on the pair, watching their every movement for any sign of deception.

"Right now, we have some questions you're going to answer."

CHAPTER FORTY-TWO

The yard went quiet. For a long moment, no one moved. We just stared at each other, letting my words fade out into the frozen air.

And then Amber thrust her hand out - her bare hand - pointing towards the back of the SUV. "You've still got that bastard. You can *keep* him. Ask him what you want to know."

"I'm asking you," I said, narrowing my eyes. "It's just a few questions, right?"

She didn't bother gratifying me with a response. She just leaned to the side and spat pointedly into the snow. The whole time, her eyes stayed fixed on mine.

"Ew," I heard Kai mutter behind me, only to get shushed by Tyler a second later.

"Will he wake up at all?" I said, unmoving. "You were here for me, weren't you? Were you going to-"

She rolled her eyes, flopping back and landing on the snow with a *whump*. "Capture, not kill. Well. Ideally." A smirk crossed her face and vanished behind an impassive facade again. "If something went wrong, disposal was a secondary goal. According to him, anyway."

"Fucking great," I said, bobbing my head in a hopeless imitation of a nod. It was all I could do. "So-"

"So, he's out, not dead."

"How long?"

Amber made a face. "Dunno. That dose was supposed to last a day or so. But-"

"But I took a chunk of that to the leg," I said wearily, still feeling my head spin.

She grinned, not a trace of humor in the expression. "That. And he's bigger than you."

"So we've got a few hours, then," I said, my tone pointedly cheerful.

Her grin faltered. "That's...you can't possibly be-"

"What are your rel- foci?" I interrupted, letting my gaze slide between her and her friend. He'd stayed quiet the whole time, his eyes fixed on me and almost perfectly round. He was white as bone, although his hands shook. I forced away the wave of shame that rose at the sight. Yes, they were suffering. Yes, I was putting both of them through a lot of tension by taking away their relics. But it was necessary. It wasn't like I was going to let either of them collapse.

They froze. Nox glanced at Amber, his lips parting gently, but her scowl only deepened. "That's not-"

"What are your foci?" I repeated, this time lacing a trace of a command into my words. My head pounded. I ignored it.

"Mind-reading," Nox said, the words sliding straight out of him.

Amber's eyes flicked to him, her eyes tightening, but it wasn't like we'd left much of an option to her. "Force battery," she said, the words low and soft.

I furrowed my brow, my words falling away. "You what, now? You're going to have to explain that to me."

She rolled her eyes, wrinkling her nose, but I only stared, not budging a single inch. "It's simple. I store and release energy. In the short-term, anyway."

"Like when you blocked those bullets."

"Real genius, aren't you?"

Someone behind me was snickering. I didn't bothering turning to see who. "Fine. And the rest of them?"

"What *was* that Glenn did?" Keira said, stepping forward. She didn't so much as hesitate, despite the chilly look Amber was giving her. "I mean, no offense, Jon, but he had you in the palm of his hand."

Amber paused, a bit of the easy confidence leaving her face. "I...I dont..."

"I don't remember," Nox said, his voice low. "I can't...I know I *know*, but I just can't-"

"It's something to do with memories," I said, thinking back to the scene between Amber and I, the conversation he'd interrupted. "When he touched me. I...something changed." My eyes flicked to Keira. "Think...maybe you could figure it out a little more?"

She made a face, telling me exactly how little she appreciated being sent away, but there was no real fight in her. "Probably shouldn't leave him lying over there all alone," she murmured, nodding begrudgingly.

"Go with her, Tyler?" I said, a question in my voice as I glanced to him. The audiomage was still attached to his brother, trying not to look like he was hovering while Kai wiped blood from his face.

Tyler glared at me, opening his mouth - to refuse, no doubt. But I wouldn't have asked him to leave if it wasn't important, and he had to know that. Jake was worn through and still bleeding from the wound in his shoulder. Brendon wouldn't be any help at all if Glenn wasn't actually asleep, and we couldn't risk Glenn mind-controlling someone and running off into the night with them as a consolation prize.

This whole mind-control business *sucked*. For the first time, I could appreciate a little of what some of our opponents had been thinking and feeling.

"So he didn't tell you *anything?*" I said, forcing my attention back to Amber and Nox. They hadn't moved, hadn't tried to run. Not that they could, while I held their relics, but they'd wisely decided not to try and attack me to get them back. For the time being, at least.

They both shook their heads, staring at me impassively. "Not that I can remember," Amber said, her voice suddenly quiet.

A sudden wave of unease washed over me. "Wait- If he could mess with people's memories like this...if he did this to you two, were the-" I faltered, my voice catching, but collected myself and pushed on. "How many others on your team did he enchant into working for him?"

"I don't think he'd do...something like..." Nox said, but his face fell halfway through the sentence.

"He already messed with *our* memories, didn't he?" Amber snapped, glancing over at him. And then she stiffened, the blood draining from her face. Her hand plunged into her pants pocket a second later.

"Stop that," I hissed, pinning her in place before she could so much as twitch. "Your guns. Give them to me. And your knives. Any weapons. On the ground." A fresh trickle of blood slipped from my nostrils. I wiped it away, trying and failing to make the action look nonchalant.

"I'm...I wasn't," Amber said, twitching, but her hands were already moving, sliding from her jeans and into her coat.

Three guns and two knives. That was the pile she left on the snow. Nox only had one small, pathetic-looking pistol. They had more ammunition left than their fellows, whose guns lay emptied and abandoned in the driveway, I noted dispassionately. They really hadn't committed to the fight.

"I was going for my phone," Amber said, folding her arms over her chest again and glaring at me with undisguised venom. "Not a fucking *gun.*"

"You should probably say that," Kai muttered from under one of the lights. His eyes were on Tyler, who was even then dragging Glenn's limp, motionless body over to the rest of the group.

I shot him a look, but tried to keep my attention on the pair. "And why do you want your phone? Who exactly are you going to call?"

She snorted. "Who the fuck calls people anymore? We have these things called *data plans* on phones these days." Slowly, exaggerating the motion, she slipped two fingers into her back pocket and pulled her phone free. "I...I just have a bad feeling. I need to check something." Her eyes were on Glenn as she spoke. He snored away, completely unaware of the danger he was in.

"I've got some zip-ties somewhere," Jake said. Keira and I looked at the same motion. He sat on the gravel by the corner of the house, one hand pressed to his shoulder. It didn't look like a bad wound, at least, but it would need to be looked at. With a sinking feeling, I realized I was going to be left in the position of explaining away a bunch of gunshot wounds yet again. "In my bag." A smirk slipped onto his face. "Can't be too careful."

"Sit," Loren snapped, pushing him back down as he tried to stand up. "I'll find them. I'll be back in a minute. *Don't* move." She was swaying herself, as she stalked towards the front door of the house, but she didn't fall.

"Fucking *asshole.*" Ambers's low, hissed curse brought me turning back to her. She stared down at her phone, her face white. "That little...I'm going to-"

I caught her shoulder, stepping forward to meet her as she lunged towards Glenn. "*Hey.* Back the fuck off."

She stumbled back at my push, her furious glare flashing to me, but Nox grabbed her shoulder. "Amber, a-are you serious?" His face was bone-white.

"The account's empty," she snapped, looking to him. "Nothing ever got deposited."

He blinked, his eyes widening behind his glasses. "Then, you're saying he-"

"Check yours," she muttered, kicking at the gravel. "*Fuck.*"

The rest of us huddled a little closer together, feeling the bite of the wind, but didn't say a word as the telepath pulled his own phone out and started madly navigating through menus. He was as silent as we were - but his face said everything he wasn't.

Amber swore again, making to throw her phone against the side of the house, but her fingers curled more tightly around it. Her gaze settled on Glenn a moment later. "Give me ten minutes alone with him. Just ten. Fuck, I'll take five."

"But- How?" Nox said, his voice rising into a whine. "I *know* we got paid. I *looked.*"

"He can play with memories," I said, keeping my voice carefully neutral. "Do you have to ask? Is this a surprise?" As much as it sucked for the two of them, it brought up a lot of other questions, ones that were more disturbing. How many of the others were being played? How many of them were unwilling, unknowing slaves?"

"Fuck," I heard Keira whisper alongside me, her voice too low for the others to hear. She was working through the same mental path, then.

I swallowed hard, glancing back towards our companions. Everyone was tired, and hurt, and bleeding. Jake and Kai needed to get patched up, and my leg was still oozing and screaming in pain. "Someone needs to get them to a hospital," I said quietly. "But maybe now you'll be a little more willing to talk to me?"

Amber scoffed. "I'll tell you whatever I've got, but it's not much. I wasn't lying." Her eyes flicked over to Jake. "And, you can't actually be talking about going to a hospital."

I paused. "I mean...we can't just let them bleed out."

"Where's your healer?"

The others were shifting uncomfortably behind me. "We...haven't gotten that far, yet," I said, my tone only *slightly* sheepish. "This is kind of a new thing."

"Well, you'd better damn well get on that," Amber snapped. "What, are you *trying* to get yourself arrested or watched? Jesus Christ."

"I can help. A little," Loren said, slipping back towards Jake. His bag was in her hands, ready and waiting. Her eyes lingered on me - on my leg. "But you should let me look at that."

"In a bit."

Her lips pressed together into a thin line. "If it gets infected, you'll-"

I sighed. "I know. In a few minutes. I think there's a first aid kit in the garage."

"Right," she said, only a note of irritation lurking in her voice as she turned away for a second time.

Amber and Nox stayed right where they were as Loren slipped past, accelerating with every step. "So what now?" Amber said quietly. She licked her lips. They were both looking more uncomfortable by the second, I saw with a touch of dismay. Damn it, I just wanted to keep them from coming after us. I didn't want to actually *hurt* them.

"We talked about Glenn," I said, shoving my hands deeper into my pockets. "Or as much as we know. How'd you two come into the picture? What was this job all-"

"It's not so complicated," Amber snapped, a bit of energy coming back into her voice. "Those of us who live like this, for hire, well, the crews around us know who we are. Word got out that he was looking. Money was good. So we showed up." She kicked Glenn in the small of the back. I didn't stop her. "Didn't ask for details. Never do. This fucker just gave us the instructions and a pile of money." She kicked him again. "Or so we *thought*."

"Don't kill him," I said dryly. "We've still got questions."

"I'm not killing him," she said, kicking him again. "Not yet."

I sighed. "And what else-"

"He didn't give out all the details," Amber said, leaning back with a groan and stepping away from him. Loren was already outside again, clutching the zip ties in one hand. Keira inched closer, pulling Glenn's jacket open. I didn't stop her. Getting his relic off him was something we should have done long before. "There was no reason for him to. So, sorry, asshole, but I don't know anything more for you."

"Nothing?"

"I...I got a little more," her friend said, creeping up alongside her. She cast a look his way, her eyes dark and unreadable, but he only shrugged. "I didn't...I can't dig too deep in someone's mind without them knowing, usually, but he wasn't always as careful as he could have been."

So I was right. He was a mind-reader. Great. The voices in the back of my head were rising again, crowing for my attention, but he was already continuing.

"H-He was doing it for someone else. Someone important. He seemed convinced that this job was going to be his gateway to greatness. Something to put him on the map for the region. I don't know." Starting strong, he ended with a sigh, his words dwindling. "He knew what I could do. He tried to shield himself." A crooked smile tugged at Nox's lips. "Most people do. But it's impossible to be careful all the time."

"And you got something," I said, perking up.

He shrugged again. "A face. A woman, a little older. Maybe...29? 30? Blonde. Kinda hot, but kinda scary, too. Glenn called her Anke."

A chill ran down my spine. We had a name at last, someone to blame for the day's fight and our injuries. A woman, a *demi*. A little older, and blonde...the details ran through my head, solidifying and imprinting themselves in my memory.

And something itched at the back of my mind. Anke. That name. I recognized that name. Only, I couldn't-

"Anke," someone said. Their voice was thin, filled with pain. I glanced back, finding Jake limping closer. Loren was at his side, trying to get a look at the wound in his shoulder, but he wasn't so much as looking her way. "You're sure?"

"What's that mean?" Brendon said, speaking up at last. His face was pale. Clearly, he'd picked up on the tension in the group. His eyes flitted between Keira, Jake, and I. "Who's Anke?"

"I don't know," I whispered. "But-"

"Another demi. Big deal," Jake said, shaking his head. "Runs one of the prime crews, out east. That's what I've heard, anyway." His amendment at the end was hurried, like he was catching himself. "Heard Matt talk about her, after I signed on." His eyes flicked to mine, a hint of shame there. "He wasn't as tight-lipped with his crew as Glenn, apparently."

"Right," I said, the memory igniting and rushing in to wipe away my confusion. "Matt said something about her. Back with that whole mess between him and Aedan."

"She tried to weasel her way into the crew for the hunt. Offered him demis," Jake said, finally letting Loren shove him to the ground. "He kept turning her away."

"And now she's sending crews after us," I said, my mouth going dry.

He only nodded, making a face.

I didn't have all the pieces. This was still too confusing by far, and there was still too much I wasn't sure of. But I didn't have to have all the pieces to understand the direction it was leading.

"All right," I muttered, hunching my shoulders a little higher. "Will you two promise to behave?"

"You have our fucking foci," Amber said, just a hair shy of a snarl.

"We're not going to fight," Nox said quickly, edging out in front of her.

A crooked smile tugged at the corners of my lips. He just looked so *nervous*. "Do either of you have anything on you by way of a weapon?"

She snorted again. "I could bludgeon you to death with my cell phone."

"Amber," Nox hissed.

"No."

"Fine," I said, glaring at her. No hint of a lie showed in her words, in the irritated set of her shoulders. "Tyler. Brendon. See them inside. It's fucking cold. The rest of you…" I glanced at Kai, at Jake. "Get patched up, get the relics everyone dropped. Let me know if I need to make a Meijer run to get anything. If we're not going to the hospital."

"I think we should be able to manage," Loren whispered, still eyeing Jake's shoulder. "But *you* should really-"

"I'll be in in just a minute. I need to make a call."

"Great," Keira muttered.

"What?" Nox said, glancing between her and I with a worried look on his face.

"Don't worry about it," I said, already digging in my pocket. "Just go on."

Neither of them looked even the slightest bit happy - not that I could blame them, when I could still feel the weight of their glove and necklace in the inner pocket of my jacket where I'd stashed them, safely out of reach. Their weapons lay in the snow at my feet. I gathered them up into a untidy heap, straightening with a groan.

A woman stared back at me, her face hidden in shadows from where she stood in the treeline. Her outline blurred into the murk, dark hair and a dark jacket.

Adrenaline shot down my spine. I lurched, grabbing for one of Amber's guns. It was frigid in my hand, awkward and unfamiliar.

When I brought it up, my arms trembling and unsteady, she was gone.

"Keira!" I cried, spinning. She froze in her tracks halfway to the house, her head snapping back around. "There's someone else here. Can you-"

"Looking," she said, her voice low and sharp, and pushed out in front of me.

I just gripped the gun a little tighter, feeling the world spin around me. More? We should have looked for stragglers. We should have called Greyson, had him poke around. I'd thought Amber would have told me, if there were others. Or Nox, if not her. He seemed more wishy-washy.

My pulse accelerated slowly. No. Amber and Nox were *mad*. Glenn and his crew had cheated them, or so it had seemed. Neither of them had been lying, when they did their little search. They were furious with their old companions. They wouldn't have shielded them.

But if it wasn't any of their crew, then who was-

"I don't see anyone," Keira said, a bit of the tension slipping from her shoulders. Her eyes flicked back to mine, masked by the glasses. "Where were they?"

"Right there," I said, stepping forward, but stopped. The snow was a mess, all torn up by the force of our attacks and the people running every which way. Even if there had been someone standing in the trees, there was no way I'd be able to pick their tracks out. "They were right there," I said a little softer.

"I don't see any other relics around us," Keira said, her tone careful. "The forest is dark."

"Is it the trees? Are they blocking your view, or something?"

A smirk tugged at the corners of her lips. "That isn't a problem anymore."

"Oh."

She sighed, turning back to me. "Jon, you're tired. You're bleeding. And if I heard right, you got injected with something - *after* that asshole tinkered with your memories. Are you sure you're not just-"

"She was right there, Keira."

My sister held her ground for a long moment, biting her lips as she stared at me. "All right," she said finally. "You can call Greyson after you call Aedan. But hurry up, will you? It really *is* cold."

I keyed my phone again, still watching the trees. "Fine."

She folded her arms, tucking her fingers under her armpits, but didn't bother continuing.

The phone had only been ringing for a few seconds when it connected. I blinked, having to grip the case a little more tightly to avoid dropping it.

"Jonny. Missed me that much?"

"Hi. Question. Who exactly have you been talking to about our little group here?" I said, trying to keep from yelling at him.

He hesitated for a long, quiet moment. "What? Fuck, Jonny, that's no way to thank me. I'm not a complete goddamn idiot, you know. I wouldn't go throwing something like this around. Like I said, you're an investment."

"Yeah, well, somehow someone found out - someone who shouldn't have."

Another pause - longer, this time. "What happened?"

I ran a hand through my hair, still scanning the woods. "Seven demis, Aedan. Naming *you* as the one who sent them - and no, they weren't friendly."

"Shit," I heard him mutter, the sound low and muffled. "So why is this *my-*"

"Someone hired them, Aedan. We've got a few of the crew - two of them deserted, and their leader is sleeping off his own drugs right now." I hesitated. The words stuck in my throat. "They say someone named Anke paid them to come. For me, they said. What the fuck is-"

"You've got to be fucking kidding me."

I stopped. Something in his words told me that he wasn't talking to me. A sigh came through the speaker, long and low and filled with irritation. "You've got some of them, you said?"

"Yeah."

"Their leader?"

"Yeah. What are you-"

"Don't kill them. I'm on my way."

"Wait, what? How long are we supposed to be-"

"Stop crying. I'll be there tomorrow. Well, probably not *tomorrow*, but soon. A few days at most."

Oh, *that* didn't make sense. That didn't make sense at all. "What do you mean? I didn't expect you to be that near."

Aedan chuckled, the sound tinny and canned. "Said I'd hang closer. But, uh. I was kind of coming your direction anyway."

The uneasy feeling in the pit of my stomach wasn't getting any better. "Uh...Why, exactly? Not that I'm not *thrilled* to see you, but-"

"Don't bother acting, Jon. But, well, I was kind of going to warn you about some stuff that's coming." He made a noise, like he was shifting. "Didn't really want to tell you this over the phone."

"Yes, why bother giving warning for some *stuff that's coming*," I said dryly. "Why would you ever want to do that, when you could just surprise us with it instead?"

"Stop whining. Anyway. Uh. I hear some rumblings that the Marketeers are beginning to move. That some of them are making to come south."

I stopped, freezing in place. "By that, you mean-"

"Ontario. One of the primes in the region."

"Shit."

"You knew it was coming," he said, a hint of humor slipping back into his voice. "Still, I'll hang out, just in case."

"Yeah. Uh." I cleared my throat, my thoughts whirling. Shit. *Shit.* I'd hoped for more time. I don't know *why* I'd hoped for more - it wasn't like we'd had much before now   but I had. "Soon, you said."

"Soon as I can. Don't kill them."

He hung up without another word. I couldn't even be angry. My mind was too busy.

The woman in the woods was a problem, and I needed to call Greyson - but right then, there were more important matters on my mind. With one last glance and a wary tightening of my hand on the pistol, I gathered the rest of the weapons into my arms and slipped inside.

I had a safe in my room - not big enough for everything, but I needed *somewhere* to put my gun. I shoved it and the other firearms in, hesitating for a long moment before tucking the two captured relics in on top. I'd need to make sure we got all of the relics off the fallen in the front yard.

In the meantime, I pushed into the living room, stepping right past Jake and Loren at the kitchen table. Amber and Nox stood on the far side, tucked into a corner and looking nothing but uncomfortable. I didn't care.

They turned at the sound of my approach. I stalked right up to them, staring Amber in the eye. "You two are mercenaries, right?"

She scowled at me, eyes narrowing. "That's what I said."

"And you just finished your last job. A job you didn't get paid for."

Her expression darkened further. "Are you trying to piss me off?"

I smiled thinly, feeling my pulse thunder in my ears. The others wouldn't be happy - but we were out of time and desperately in need of options.

"Want a new one?"

CHAPTER FORTY-THREE

I could almost hear the indrawn gasp from my friends at my words. I didn't look. My eyes were fixed on Amber, locked on hers so tightly I wasn't even blinking. She matched me stare for stare, her hazel eyes narrowing.

"What are you playing at?" she said finally, sitting back on her heels.

I smiled humorlessly. "Just what it sounds like. We've got a problem coming, and we're going to need all hands on deck. Your friends put *my* friends out of commission, at least for the immediate future. So I'm open to trying new things if you are."

"What's going on?" Keira said, slipping up alongside me. The others weren't far behind, wordlessly watching. Amber didn't twitch, but her eyes flicked to Keira.

"I talked to Aedan," I said, still fixated on Amber. She was listening, even if she was trying to look nonchalant. "He said that one of the primes is starting to make noise like they're moving. Like they're coming here."

"Could they wait a little bit?" Jake snapped. His voice was laced with pain. Loren was at his side, making a face and wiping at the hole in his shoulder with something strong-smelling.

"Do you know how to do that?" I said, unable to hold myself back.

Loren only glanced my way. "Well enough."

Amber sighed. The sound was enough to catch me off guard. "Give me that," she snapped. "Go see to him." She waved at Brendon, who lingered near the door. "He probably won't die if you fuck it up."

"Don't even *think* about touching me," Jake said, stiffening.

She only smacked his arm, sending a shudder of pain through his frame. "Don't be a baby. Sit still." She was digging through her jacket a moment later. I started, making to stop her, but caught myself. She'd given up all her weapons - she'd said so, and my relic had agreed. Right then, I saw no hints that she was holding back on me.

Jake grimaced, a pained noise slipping from his throat, but her movements with the antiseptic were quick and practiced. "You're picking another fight, then," she said, glancing my way for an instant and then back to Jake. "Did I hear that right?"

"Ontario," I said heavily. "Probably soon. Aedan said he's a few days out." I hesitated, not sure how much I should tell her. "He...wants to talk to the two of you. And Glenn."

Her eyes darkened, tightening. "That's the Wanderer?"

Not a title I'd hard used for him before, but impossible to mistake. "Right."

"Fucking great," she muttered. "And what exactly does *he* want with us?"

"What do you think?"

Suddenly, she didn't look quite as confident as she had before. "So. Uh. You're not starting small, are you? Don't you want to stay under the radar at least a *little?*"

"Wouldn't really do much good, would it? We're not going anywhere. We're not *looking* for a fight, either."

She snorted. "Right."

"So, what do you think?"

"About what?"

I glared at her. "About taking the job."

"She tried to kill us," Tyler said, his voice quiet. He had a wad of cloth in his hand, working on Kai, who sat at the table, trying not to wince. "You're letting her in just like that?"

"It's one possibility," I said.

Keira didn't argue - and neither did Jake. I could see the looks on their faces, all the proof I needed that they understood as well as I did. Nox was mute and wordless on the floor across the room, his shoulders tight.

If he was really a telepath - and my relic hadn't argued when he said he was - then there was no telling how much information he'd managed to scoop off the top of our thoughts with us unaware. None of us had been guarding our thoughts. Hell, I didn't know what that even meant, or how to do it. He could have information on all of our relics. Our home. Aedan.

Information like that would be worth a fortune, if he found the right buyer. And all of it would lead straight back to us. Letting him go free, no strings attached, was a risk that we just couldn't take. I just wasn't happy with the alternatives that presented themselves.

"What's the pay?"

I looked up, caught off guard enough that for once I was wordless. "W-What?"

Amber sniffed unhappily. "The pay. What are you offering? Was there something *confusing* about that question?"

I leaned back, running a hand through my hair. I hadn't quite thought that far. "Uh. Well, if you hang around, help us fight off whatever might be coming, you can...you can have the foci off your old crew." I chuckled darkly. "You can have Glenn, once Aedan's finished."

Her eyes narrowed, her chin raised stubbornly. "I was thinking I'd be taking those regardless. You promised to make my turning traitor worth my while - unless Nox was lying to me."

"I wasn't!" he said hurriedly, straightening and twisting to face her.

Amber rolled her eyes, shaking her head gently. "Damn it, Nox, I know that."

"Oh."

My irritation grew by the second. "You're not really in a position to negotiate, you know," I snapped, folding my arms. "You're lucky we're even willing to make this offer in the first place."

"You want our help, don't you?" Amber said, turning back to me. Her eyes were sharp. *Too* sharp. She knew exactly what she was doing - and I had no doubt that she was reading me like a book. "Well, put your money where your mouth is."

I swallowed a groan, glaring at her. For a second, I wanted to tell her to take her greedy grabbing and stuff it. But when it got right down to it, what options did we have? If I wanted their help willingly, then I had to win them over - or use their relics as leverage. The thought was enough to make me feel sick.

Nox was watching me. He *knew*. I scowled.

If I wasn't willing to turn them into slaves, then all I could do was work with them or set them free. And we needed their help. Badly. All in all, I didn't have a lot of options.

"We have a few other foci," I said at last, the words sliding out unhappily. "A few. From a trio of hunters we cleared out."

"Three, huh?" she said. Her eyes were fixed on mine, the expression hidden behind a world-class pokerface. "To go up against a Prime? Anything good?"

"Acid and illusion," I said, spitting each word out. "And electricity."

She snorted. "Not *bad*, but nothing to write home about, is it?"

"There's no telling what the next owner might wind up with," Keira pointed out, her voice quiet. "They could turn out to be something special still."

"Or they might not," Amber snapped.

"We, uh," I began, feeling my face slowly redden. Shit. I didn't have another option. "We could promise you another relic. Focus. From our...reserve stash. If there's actually a fight." I pursed my lips, staring at them. "If the primes don't come, you're stuck with the three."

Keira's head snapped around, her gaze fixing on me. She knew what 'reserve stash' I was talking about. Thankfully, if she objected, she kept it to herself.

Hoping that Aedan would react as gracefully was a different matter entirely.

"Nox gets a cut too," Amber said, drawing my attention back to her. One finger tapped against her arm, like she was irritated - but it was a more contemplative gesture than I'd seen from her before.

For a second, Nox looked like he might object, his mouth falling open. And then it snapped shut again. He sat right where he was, looking for all the world like he was trying to melt into the furniture and vanish.

"No. You can share," I said, glaring. "It's *plenty* to set you up right."

She sniffed, rolling her eyes, but didn't argue. At least she knew when to stop, I thought sourly.

Aedan was going to kill me. I already knew it. Damn it, we needed the help. It was the only reason I'd do something like bargain off his relics. "Do we have a deal?" I said, forcing myself to focus. Every sound echoed in my mind, and my leg was on fire. I wanted to be done with this already. Swallowing hard, I thrust my hand out, ready and waiting.

Amber looked down the length of her nose at it, like my hand was covered in something foul. "Don't expect me to touch you," she snarled, turning away from Jake so that she didn't have to look at me. "It's not like I have a choice, do I?"

"I'm just trying to make the best of this," I said quietly.

Her hazel eyes fixed on mine over her shoulder, dark and narrowed. Neither of us dared mention the *after*. "Fine. Deal. Now give me my-"

"Neither of you get your foci. Not now, not until the primes show up," I interrupted. "If they show up. If they don't, then we'll give them back with your payment."

"I can't *wait* that long," she hissed, spitting each word at me. Her fists were balled up at her sides, her arms rigid. "Are you really going to-"

"You won't collapse," I said, giving my head a quick, decisive shake. My eyes never left hers. "I promise. We won't let that happen."

She only held her stare, her lips pressed together tightly. "Fine. Then get out of my way and let me work."

That was about as good as I was going to get, I knew. Backing away slowly, I let her go. She turned back to Jake with an irritated noise, not sparing me another look.

Loren snagged my hand a moment later. "That leg. Sit *down*." For someone who'd been frigid and shy when we'd first met, she was getting pushy. I could only follow as she pushed and pulled, manhandling me into a chair.

Amber's eyes stayed fixed on my back the whole way, peering from the corner of her vision. They bored holes in my back as I leaned against the chair, letting the world turn into a hazy blur.

***

"So, like...how long have you guys been here?"

"I mean, Keira and I are *from* here. So....forever, I guess."

"Oh. Damn. What's that like?"

"What?" I said, glancing over. The room was dark, faintly illuminated by the moon through the window. He'd pulled the shades back, letting the light shine in. I hadn't had the energy to argue with him.

Bunking down the two new demis was an...interesting debate. They weren't allies, but they weren't precisely enemies, either. They didn't have their relics - and we'd made it very clear that if they attacked anyone, if they tried to take hostages or play games, they'd never have them again. Nox had been pale enough that I thought he might faint entirely. Amber just glared, her expression darkening by the second.

We'd stuffed Glenn into the garage where he probably wouldn't freeze to death, zip-tied and drugged to the gills. The pair were more complicated. No one had trusted them alone - but no one really wanted to sleep with them around, either. Finally, we'd split them up, putting Tyler and Kai out in the living room as a makeshift watch.

Which left me to deal with Nox.

"You know. Being here all the time. Isn't that boring?" He quivered with pent-up energy, wearing an old t-shirt and gym shorts. His glasses rested on the windowsill in easy reach. The whole thing was giving me more than a few flashbacks to middle school sleepovers. I wasn't sure I liked it.

"I don't know what part of this you think is boring," I muttered instead, rolling over. The floor was hard underneath me. The fact I was sleeping on the floor didn't help. I had a bed - a decent bed, considering the shape of the house. But on the floor, he couldn't get past me without waking me up, and I decided being practical was more important than being comfortable right then. "It's been a shitshow for months."

"Yeah. I guess." He folded his arms around his midsection, glancing back out the window. His fingers twitched, tapping against his elbows. "I didn't think it'd feel like *this*."

I sighed, rolling back over so that I could get a better look at him. "What, now?"

"My skin. It's- It's like there are ants. All over my skin." He shook his head, his shoulders sliding up a few inches. "Weird. Didn't think that would be a-a thing."

It was impossible to keep the note of concern from my voice. "Are...you okay?"

"I've never been deprived before," he muttered, pressing a hand to his forehead. "I mean, I've heard stories. Amber's mentioned it, now and again. If I asked. Didn't think it'd feel like *this*."

"...Sorry," I mumbled, my eyes dropping to the floor. It was our fault - my fault that he was hurting, that he was in discomfort. I could put an end to it, then and there. But-

"It's fine. Yeah. This is fine," Nox said, his voice a little stronger. I paused, looking up. He was staring right back at me, a smile tugging at his lips. It only looked a little forced. "I mean, I understand. I get it."

"Right."

"A-Anyway. It seems like a nice town, and all."

Good god, was he intending to talk *all* night? I could understand him being a little wired, after everything that had happened, and me taking his relic away probably wasn't helping matters any. But I'd been looking forward to actually sleeping and being able to put my thoughts together ahead of whatever was coming.

"It is," I said, flopping onto my back with a groan. "Nice enough, anyway."

"Are you going to kill us?"

His words were quiet, and matter-of-fact enough to bring me up short. I lifted my head again. He was staring out the window, not so much as glancing my way.

"What, now?" I said, blinking away my confusion. It wasn't working.

"I'm not stupid. She's not, either. Everyone's got secrets they want to hide." His voice didn't change. He spoke simply and clearly, as though it was a conversation he'd had a thousand times before.

I stayed where I was, slowly raising myself up to my elbows. "It's not what I want," I said at last. "And if everything goes well...I'll do my best to find a way that doesn't leave us...there." Somehow, I couldn't bring myself to lie and promise that we wouldn't. There was no way of telling how things would wind up.

He nodded, still peering out into the night, eyes narrowed as though that would let him see without his glasses. "Right. I try not to look, you know."

"Is that so."

"People already don't like being listened to. So I do my best." A crooked smile tugged at his lips, vanishing again a moment later. "If that changes anything."

"And when you're attacking a group of enemy demis?" I said dryly. "Are you telling me you still wouldn't try and get a peek at their thoughts *then?*"

"Well. No. I definitely would."

"And you were." It wasn't a question - there was no getting around the simple truth of it.

"I suppose. But I wouldn't *now.*" Nox *did* look back to me at that, his face shadowed against the dim light outside. "I just...yeah. I just thought you should know."

I bobbed my head in a slow nod, unable to argue with the earnest set of his expression. The man was like a puppy dog, dying to please.

"Been with Amber long, have you?" I managed, desperate to change the subject. Having such a matter-of-fact talk about killing my conversation partner was turning out to be one of the most uncomfortable experiences of my life.

That half-hearted smile he wore erupted into a full grin. "Couple years. Maybe, three? No. Four. She was hired to take out a convoy, out west. Someone kidnapped the wrong demi." He shrugged. "Only I was there, too."

And she took him in - like we'd taken in Brendon and Loren? A bit of the weight eased from my shoulders. She was still a weapon-for-hire, then, but maybe there was a bit of a soul to be found yet. Maybe.

"She's not so bad."

I glanced up. His brow had furrowed, his smile vanishing as quickly as it had appeared. I shrugged noncommittally. "I'm sure."

"Really. Probably. I mean, she's *prickly*, but-"

"Will she stick to the deal?" I said, my words pointed and blunt.

He froze. I pinned him in place with my stare, waiting. Finally, he nodded, all of his earlier flightiness disappearing somewhere under the serious set of his lips. "Yeah. She will. Or she'll come at you straight, if there's a problem. If something happens to change things."

"Great," I said with a groan, flopping right back down. I'd piled blankets up underneath me in a heap. They didn't do much. I could still feel every seam in the floor beneath my shoulderblades. "Just lovely."

Honesty was good. If he was right, anyway. I didn't think he was lying - but then again, my head pounded with every word he said, and exhaustion tugged at the corners of my senses. I wasn't exactly in the best of conditions to judge him. Besides, if his trust of her was based out of blind infatuation for the woman who'd saved him, his judgement of her wasn't exactly objective.

I could hear him rustling again, shifting on my bed. "Do you think we'll-"

"Go to bed, Nox," I said, letting a sigh ripple out under the words. Nox. What a ridiculous name. Part of me wanted to ask what it was about, to get the story I was sure waited behind it. The rest of me just wanted *sleep*.

"Night," he muttered. The bedsprings groaned gently as he rolled over again, falling silent.

It had all sounded so good, when I started. I'd set up a little camp, a base for us to work out of. Somewhere I could keep Keira and I safe - and Jake, after he'd straightened up. Somewhere along the line, things had gone crazy.

And now...Now *they'd* finally taken notice. I swallowed hard.

The pain of my leg and my head and the exhaustion and the traces of drugs still running through my system - they helped in ways I hadn't thought they would. They were enough to keep me distracted, to keep me from dwelling on what the next week would bring.

But I already knew it wouldn't be enough to keep the nightmares away as I gave in, slipping into the murky dark of sleep.

CHAPTER FORTY-FOUR

"What's that, now?"

I groaned, masking the sound behind my hand. Oh, Greyson did *not* sound happy. I should have expected it - I *did* expect it - and even still, the sour note in his voice was enough to send chills down my spine.

"Aedan called. He-"

"Yeah, I heard that part," he snapped. "You said-"

"It sounds like we've been noticed," I said. Interrupting him wasn't exactly the best of plans, normally, but I was running short on time and patience. "Aedan's heading back this way. Should be here tomorrow, maybe. Maybe the day after. But he seemed to think that the primes would be moving soon."

"Yeah, I bet they are." His words were still laced with sarcasm. I winced. "So what are you expectin' from me, exactly? Miracles? Should I start shittin' rainbows and sproutin' wings and-"

"Just give us a head-up when a group of them crosses into your range," I said, tempting fate by interrupting him yet *again*. "Aedan didn't give us all that exact a window. If you can give us at least a little bit of a head start, that would be huge."

"...Yeah, I s'ppose. And then-"

"And then go radio silent."

The line went quiet for a long, uneasy moment. I shifted from foot to foot, staring at the snow underfoot. It had blizzarded. Again. Amber stood a few paces away, pointedly glaring off into the trees. I didn't care if she heard - unlike her partner, *she* wasn't going to be listening in on my thoughts.

"Try explainin' that one to me again," Greyson said finally, his voice low.

I smiled, the expression more like a grimace. "If the primes are coming to visit, then they won't come alone. They'll be equipped, ready and set to dig us out of our encampment."

"If they're lookin' for a fight."

"I don't think we can afford to assume they're not."

Another pause. "Well, you're not wrong."

"If they've got a finder with them, if they know you're here...there's no reason for you to make your association with us clear."

I could hear him shifting on the other end, like he was scratching at his beard. "Don't get me wrong, kid, I'm not suggesting I put myself out on a limb for you, but aren't you going to at least try and convince me I should be helpin'? It'd be best for you."

I chuckled. "We brought this one on ourselves. Just giving us the information at the start's a big help. And the last thing we need is them sending assassins to go find you while we're occupied."

"Ah, well. Suppose that's fair enough." His words were low, his tone grudging.

"Careful, Greyson. It's almost sounding like you *want* to help us," I said, a lilt slipping into my tone.

"Don't get cocky, boy. I've put a lot of risk into keepin' you alive and out of sight since you found that there trinket. I don't want to see all that thrown away in a stupid pissing match."

"You sound like Aedan."

"What's that, now?"

"If something happens and we need you, we'll call," I said, raising my voice. "Other than that, just take care of yourself. All right?"

"Fair enough."

"Keep us informed, then."

Good lord, it felt amazing to actually hold a normal conversation. Like we were actual *adults*. I slid my phone back into my pocket, swallowing a sigh.

Amber shifted, turning to face me. "Can we go in already?"

I glanced out to the trees. "We still need to finish the last barricade. And I'd like to see if we can set some booby traps or something. I don't know. We'll try some stuff." I raised one eyebrow, staring at her. "Unless there's something else you'd prefer to be doing?"

"No." She spat the word at me, tight and low, and stalked towards the treeline.

I hesitated, watching her go. Her face was...very red. It didn't look like the normal flushed cheeks I'd expect to see from the chill, and it wasn't like anything had happened to embarrass her. If anything, it looked more like she was running a fever.

The pit of my stomach twisted a little tighter. I'd heard Nox shift, whining in his sleep. Whatever was happening to the two of them, it seemed to come and go in waves, little by little. But as the hours dragged on, the effect being 'deprived' was having on them was more and more noticeable.

Several days. Aedan had said a collapse would take several days, on average. I fixed his words in my mind. They were uncomfortable, yes. Maybe in a bit of pain. But I couldn't trust that they wouldn't turn around and kill us, given the chance. Not yet, not like that. We couldn't afford the risk.

"Jon!"

I froze, glancing back over my shoulder at the call. From the corner of my eye I could see Amber stop, her shoulders drooping gently.

Keira slogged through the snow towards us, bundled up in a thick jacket with a scarf thrown around her neck. She was smiling - at me, *and* at Amber, I noted with more than a little surprise. Then again, Amber and Loren had bunked down in Keira's room while I'd had Nox. I was still trying to push the thought of what conversations they might have had from my mind.

"Did you call him?" she said as she reached me, only a little breathless. She flashed a quick grin towards Amber, who inclined her head incrementally.

I nodded. "Yeah. He knows the drill."

"Oh. Good. Then, what are you two-"

"Jon wanted to play with booby traps," Amber droned, her tone pointedly flat. "We already plugged the bullet holes in the siding and built another retaining wall."

Keira's brow furrowed. "What? Why are you- It's too cold for all that, Jon."

"The cold doesn't matter," I said, shifting back a step as Keira inched closer to Amber. I couldn't shake the feeling that the whole tenor of the conversation had shifted.

"It does too matter. If you make yourselves sick out here, they'll stomp all over us," Keira snapped, folding her arms.

Amber chuckled softly. "Listen to your sister, Jon."

"Quiet," I muttered, glaring at her from the corner of my eye. She only smirked, her eyes drifting away. I didn't miss the fine sheen of sweat on her temples, though.

"The others have put together what we've got on the major crews," Keira said, shaking her head as she changed subjects. "Rather than freezing our asses off out here, why don't we look at *that?*"

"Fine. Whatever."

"Cool," Amber said, her words rippling with a sigh as she turned back towards the house. "Sounds like something an actual intelligent person would do."

Keira chuckled, right at her side in a second. I glared at their backs, my brow furrowing.

I couldn't shake a single, fundamental truth - Amber was a mercenary. A killer. Someone who would do whatever was asked of her, for the right price. She might seem pleasant enough, like this, but that didn't change what she was. The thought of her having sucked up to Keira, like Nox had warmed to me, wasn't a comforting one.

As I stared, though, they were already halfway back to the house. Shivering against the chill of the breeze, I followed in their tracks, watching the two of them walking side-by-side.

***

"Sit down."

A resounding *whoomph* of butts hitting seats - and in some cases, the floor - echoed throughout the room. I sighed, leaning back against the wall in the hallway. Practicing had seemed like a good idea, at first. It just wasn't working out like I'd planned. "Jake, take off your shirt."

"What?" I heard him snap. The sound was muffled, garbled behind what I knew was a shirt coming off even as he protested. I winced. He'd be mad at me later, but there was no getting around it. It had to be something he didn't want to do, after all. I just hoped he'd forgive me after it was done.

With the primes bearing down on us - supposedly - we were out of time to sit around on our asses. I'd been hopeful about getting a look at the woods, but with Keira shutting that notion down, we had to settle for what we could do.

The sound of the television was a low rumble, the one allowance I'd given them for agreeing to help me. Besides, I couldn't expect to be working in perfect silence constantly. I needed to be ready for any eventuality.

Kai laughed, a smug, amused noise. "Damn, dude, you should really work out a little more."

"Kai, go do the dishes," I snapped, knowing that Jake's face would be screwed up in anger and frustration even if I couldn't see it.

The floorboards creaked as Kai stood. I could feel him fighting the command, resisting. "What? Why do *I* have to-"

"Because you made the mess," Tyler muttered.

"Yeah, but we *all-*"

"Now, Kai," I snapped, putting a little more power into the command. The faucet turned on a second later, the rush of the water against dirty plates rising to join the mindless soap playing on the TV.

"Anything?" Keira said. She sat across from me in the hall, her arms folded across the chest. She could keep an eye on the others from that position. On Nox and Amber, who were somewhere out in the mix.

I sighed. "I don't know. I mean, I can *feel* them all. I can feel the strain." My hand lifted, cradling the rings that hung from my neck. They pulsated with warmth, and there in the darkened hallway, I could see them casting a dim glow across the walls around us.

Keira hesitated. "But."

"But it's not like before," I muttered.

Being attacked by Glenn's crew had changed things - for us, but for *me*, too. I'd been trusting my abilities to be enough, to keep us safe. But when I'd drawn on them, pulling at their gang, they'd failed me. Or at least, they hadn't worked like I'd wanted them to.

Practice makes perfect, I'd always been told. And we were nearly out of time - so flexing my magical muscles had seemed like the perfect way to kill some time before Aedan got back and sent everything into chaos again.

Only, something was different.

"Then, you-"

"I could do this all day," I said with a groan, leaning my head back against the wall.

"I don't *want* to do this all day," Kai called from the kitchen. "Like, seriously, can I-"

"Keep going."

"Can we change something?" Keira said, ignoring Kai and I entirely. "Are we missing something, some detail that was different?"

"I couldn't see them, and there were, what, a handful of other demis actually conscious?" I said, glancing over at her. "I can't see them now, and there are more of them. I don't *know*."

"It's still probably good for you to at least practice like this," Tyler said, walking over.

"Sit down."

He made an irritated noise in the back of his throat, but his frame lowered obediently to the floor.

I glanced back, peering around the corner. "Sorry."

Tyler only sniffed, rolling his eyes.

It wasn't like I *wanted* to make him frustrated or annoyed with me, but if they were going along willingly, then I couldn't trust that it was really a realistic simulation. So forcing them to do stuff they weren't actually interested in was the only way I could think of to make this work.

And still, it wasn't enough.

I'd just opened my mouth, drawing breath for the next round of commands - the front porch was looking a little snowy - when a strident sound split the silence of the room. We all flinched.

Keira plunged a hand into her pocket, biting her lip. "Damn. Sorry."

"It's fine," I muttered, closing my eyes and letting go of my relic at the same moment. "This isn't working. Let me...I'll just keep thinking."

"Fine," Kai said, shutting the faucet off without a moment's hesitation. "This is fine, yeah. Glad to help."

"Hi! Yeah, we're just- You're what, now?" Keira said, her eyes widening a moment later. "No, I mean- that's fine. Yeah!"

Her words were plastic and forced enough for the rest of us to stop. I half-turned, watching her push herself upright and begin to pace. Despite her cheerful tone, her lips were curled down in a scowl.

In three quick steps she'd crossed the room, sliding into the bathroom and away from the noise of all of us.

"What do you think that was about?" Tyler said, leaning over to glance at me.

I shrugged, still staring over where she'd vanished. "I...don't really know."

"Oh," he said, his shoulders settling a little. "Do you think-"

"It didn't sound like Aedan or Greyson," I said, arching one eyebrow as I tore my gaze away from her and looked back to him. "Besides, there's no reason they'd call *her* if something was wrong."

411

"You're right," he muttered. He didn't look appeased, though. His eyes were dark, and as I watched he shoved his hands into his pockets. I could see his jacket quiver from his fidgeting even still.

A few short moments later, the door burst back open. Keira stalked out into the living room, her face a carefully neutral mask. "Catherine decided it's time she saw the place," she said, spitting every word out.

I blinked. "What? No. She can come over- after. After this is all settled."

"That's what I *tried* to tell her, but she wasn't exactly listening. She said she's already halfway here. Pulled the place up on Google Maps and just started coming."

I bit off a curse. "And I bet-"

"Of *course* she's not coming alone."

"Of course," I echoed, lifting a hand to pinch the bridge of my nose. The headache that hadn't quite shown its face yet was appearing in full. "Okay. Um. We've still got some beer, and we can order a pizza or something, and-"

"Is someone coming over?" Kai said, unable to contain himself any longer. I'd seen the way his eyes had lit up at the mention of 'beer' and 'pizza'.

Loren and Brendon didn't look so excited. They sat where they were, frozen in careful wariness. "What's going on?" Brendon said at last, glancing to me. Loren pressed a little tighter into his side, wordless.

"We've got some guests coming over for the evening," I said, forcing the words out. "I'd really hoped- I'd wanted to get a little more done, but looks like that's not going to happen. They're...they're not demis. So-"

"They're human?" Amber said, speaking for the first time in hours. Her words were low and cutting, slicing across our conversation and bringing it to a halt. "Mundanes?"

A sigh slipped out before I could hold it back. "Yup. It'll be fun!" Biting off the sarcastic quip, I cast a tired glance around the room. "Shit. Uh...can we hide some of these guns and knives? It's like an armory in here." I wasn't exaggerating. Polished steel gleamed from every counter, resting on every end table and footrest. Boxes of ammunition were piled in the corners - no one wanted a repeat of running out. Making that mistake once was enough.

Tyler was doing the same - and pushed himself upright a moment later. "Fuck. Kai, can you-"

"On it!"

It was amazing how quickly our weaponry evaporated, vanishing inside jacket pockets and closets before I could really get things straight in my mind. We'd just have to hope that no one went poking around *too* hard.

Through all the chaos, I kept half an eye on Amber and Nox. I still didn't quite put it past them to try and pull something when we weren't looking, and this was an opportunity if ever there was one.

She was watching me too, I noticed. Her hazel eyes were narrowed, fixed on mine, and from the way they tightened I could only guess she'd been watching for a while. "This is a mistake," she muttered, watching me tuck her knife into the lining of my coat.

I paused. "What, now?"

"Mundanes. Here. Are you guys idiots? Are you *trying* to let everything slip?"

A crooked smile tugged at my lips. "What do you care?"

"I care because I don't want to get caught in the middle when the primes start thinking you're playing too casual with our secrets," she snapped. "They don't normally work together. They *will*, if you give them a reason to. Like letting mundanes figure out something funny's going on here. They'll be on us in a goddamn second if they think you're going to break secrecy."

"I...It'll be fine. I'll make sure of it."

She only snorted, shaking her head. "Right. Because you're a fucking paragon of capability. Be careful. That's all I'm saying."

Before I could say another word she stalked off, arms crossed over her chest. Nox watched her go from his seat in the corner, eyes wide and dancing between her and I, but made no move to follow.

Keira's voice cut through my thoughts, putting an end to whatever I would have said in response. "Jon! Where do you want to keep the extra magazines?"

"I'm coming," I called back, taking a step away, and tore my eyes off the other demis at last.

***

"Kind of a shitheap, isn't it?"

I winced. Mason had never been the diplomatic type. He meant well. I had to believe that. But the look he gave the ceiling was more derisive than curious, sweeping across the beams and sliding down to the floor with an assessing gleam.

"It's a work in progress," I demurred, seeing Keira's eyes ignite.

"Don't be a dick," Cathy said with a giggle, smacking him on the shoulder. Mason grinned. Both of them cradled beers in their lap - like the rest of everyone. Cathy had brought her friend Jessica, a short, quiet girl with a sharp glare and plain brown hair. She'd also brought Mason, who'd invited Dirk. They'd even managed to get our friend Kevin to leave his house long enough to socialize, which I thought was impressive.

It was all pretty much what I'd expected. Ours was a small town, after all, and there was only one school. We'd gone through high school together, and unlike me, they'd never bothered with college. 'Bumming around someone's house and drinking' was pretty much par for the course so far as our relationship went.

They'd hesitated, when they first saw our new 'friends'. And looked to me, more than a few questions in their eyes. We'd hand-waved and made excuses about friends of the family and college connections and splitting rent. Mason and the others had accepted our explanations. Probably.

With them all crowding in, though, it left our living room as full as I'd ever seen it. The sound of all of them laughing and yelling at each other was enough to send me cringing back to the corner of the room, but I couldn't very well leave. The others hadn't seen me for a while, after all.

Besides, so long as they were in here together, I knew they wouldn't wander. The last thing I needed was one of them happening across the drugged, sleeping form of Glenn, wrapped in blankets and locked in the shed for the night.

"How's the leg holding up now?" Dirk said, draping an arm over my shoulder as he leered at me. "Still giving it a workout? Next time he pisses you off, Keira, aim a little higher. You missed his-"

"My leg's fine," I snapped, glaring at him. It was - that leg, anyway. My other leg was still wrapped tight with bandages, hidden away under my jeans. The stitches Brendon had put in me under Amber's watchful eye stretched and pulled painfully with the slightest motion.

Jason only grinned all the wider, his one-armed hug becoming more of a headlock with every passing second. "Right, right. Look, man, you going to keep hiding out here? You get a hideaway of your very own and you're holding out on the rest of us?"

"It's not a party house, Dirk," I said dryly, shrugging free.

"Told you," Kevin muttered. He kept to himself, like usual, tucked into the corner and watching the rest of the party go on around him.

"What's that supposed to mean?" I said, wrinkling my nose.

He chuckled. "You've never been the frat-guy type. Thought you'd have got this place in order a little better, though, have to say." His eyes were sharp. The corners of his mouth curled up in a tiny, knowing grin.

"You should've seen it when we started," Keira said, leaning in to gesture towards him with her drink. "Jesus. There were bird nests in the attic, a-and mice. Everywhere. So many mice."

"Oh, hell no," I heard Jessica say behind her, her feet rising from the carpet as she curled into a tighter ball on the couch.

Keira rolled her eyes. "They're not here *now*, Jess. Stop bitching."

I smiled, nodding along, but the others had launched into their own conversations again. Loren and the other demis lingered around the corners of the room, breaking in with their own pieces of conversation when they could, but there was a distance in their eyes that was impossible to deny. They weren't comfortable, and I couldn't blame them. These weren't their friends, after all.

Watching them laugh and joke amongst themselves, going back to blissfully ignoring me, I couldn't quite shake the feeling that they weren't entirely *my* friends, not anymore. They were prattling on about jobs and girls and bosses, their favorite TV shows that got canceled and the horrible cliffhanger the newest blockbuster movie left them on.

I liked all that stuff too. I still needed *entertainment*. But with the mess my life had become, I couldn't quite bring myself to focus on any of it. It wasn't important, not compared with everything else I had going on.

Chuckling softly to myself, I wondered if this was what my parents had always lectured me on - 'becoming an adult'. Not likely. I didn't think they'd ever thought their darling son and daughter would be readying an army of makeshift superheroes to stand up against the local 'government'. If the primes could be considered a government, anyway.

No, everything we were dealing with was so far beyond normal that it was about all I could do to smile and nod, plastering a sufficiently cheerful expression onto my face and agreeing with the group often enough to pass inspection. I'd outgrown them. The thought hurt.

Left watching the others, an outsider in my own home, I was distant enough from the conversation to notice it in time - the way Amber inched away, creeping to the outskirts of the group. She was good, I realized. She'd pulled her hair back, running a braid through the black sheen of it to make herself a little more presentable. When she smiled, only the soft thrum of the relic around my neck gave any warning that her interest was anything but genuine.

Like I'd suspected, she was an actor. I glared at her, my eyes narrowing, and she shot me a quick, smug wink in response. She was on her feet moments later, turning towards the door and reaching for her coat. The other demis stiffened, their eyes snapping to me.

Our friends took notice of her moving away, too. "Something the matter?" Cathy said, her eyebrows furrowing. "It's cold out there. And dark. So what's up?"

"Need a smoke," Amber said, waving a hand dismissively. "Lend me one, Jake?"

The sleepworker had been silent through the whole evening, caught in place while Mason talked his ear off. Turning up the television hadn't seemed to help. Glaring daggers at our mercenary ally, he held the pack out begrudgingly. She snatched one free with easy grace, smiling at him. To everyone else, it probably looked like an ordinary exchange between friends.

From the glares the other demis were giving me, *they* knew it wasn't anything of the kind. "Right now?" I said, bringing her up short as she went for the door. "But we're having so much fun."

"When you need it, you need it," she fired back, drifting closer to the portal.

"Once isn't a problem. Why don't you smoke in here?" I had to force the words through my gritted teeth, but they slipped out.

"What? That's gross," Cathy protested, perking up at my words. "That stuff gives you cancer. No way."

"You heard her, Jon. Can't do that." Amber reached for the door, casting a smirk at me over her shoulder. It snapped open, letting cold air wash over the room. My friends muttered their complaints, shooting irritated glares her way.

Bitch. She knew that I couldn't order her to stay, not with everyone watching. It would look altogether too weird to have me commanding her not to smoke. There was nothing I could think of to say to keep her there - nothing that I hadn't already said, not in the half-second I had before she was gone.

The storm door clicked shut, bringing an end to my thoughts.

Jake shifted uncomfortably, glancing my way. He still held the pack in his hand, and I could see his thoughts working - if anyone was going to go after her, he had the best excuse. None of us but him smoked, after all. And just as clearly, I could see that he wanted no part of going out in the cold. He was wearing a too-large sweatshirt, but I knew that his shoulder was still a mess of stitches under it. He'd be in pain every second he was out in the frigid cold.

I jerked my head in a refusal, swallowing a groan as I pushed myself upright.

"Jon?" Jason said, glancing up at me with confusion in his eyes. "*Now* what are you-"

"Need another beer," I muttered, rattling my empty can at him.

"Oh." The last glimmer of interest left his eyes at my excuse. He turned back to the conversation at hand, paying me not another second's mind. Neither did anyone else.

I slipped into the kitchen - and through it, winding around the outside of the living room until I could get in the side hall. There were a pair of slippers waiting at the back door, remnants of a summer long since past. I glared at them as I pulled them on, muttering darkly under my breath.

The door made only the slightest click as I pulled it shut. Hopefully none of the others would hear the sound. Judging from the dull roar emanating from the living room, that wouldn't be a problem.

Kicking unhappily at the snow, I began the long trudge around the side of the house.

My jacket flopped awkwardly around me. I was pointedly aware of it, and of the weight tucked into a pocket that was causing the awkwardness. I still had my pistol, at least. Amber still didn't have her relic, and unless she'd nabbed a weapon from someone in-between our twice-nightly lie checks, she should be unarmed.

Even still, having the gun on me made me much happier.

It took me a long moment to spot her as I came around to the front of the house. The porch we had was small and narrow, but we'd managed to squeeze a bench onto it back before the snow fell. Amber sat on the very corner, huddled in the shadow where she couldn't be seen through the windows. Her hands were clenched into fists. The knuckles gleamed white under the lamps mounted on the siding.

I heard her groan, saw her head lift at my approach just far enough that she could glare at me. "Fucking great."

"Are you trying to get yourself shot?" I snapped, warring with my frustration. "Where do you get off thinking you can just run off and do whatever you want?"

"Screw you. If I'm working for you, have an ounce of faith."

"Faith is earned. All you've done so far is sit around and bitch."

"You're a fucking *idiot*."

I stopped, seeing the venom in her eyes. It wasn't enough to quell my anger, though. "Excuse me? What the hell are you talking about?"

"Do you really think this is going to work?"

"*What are you-*"

"This." Amber punctuated the low hiss with a pointed finger, her hand sweeping out to the side to thrust towards the window. "Humans. Mundanes. In your *house*? Living alongside you like everything's fine?" She laughed hollowly. "You've even got a fucking job."

I stepped closer, fighting to keep my voice quiet. "We need to eat somehow. You've *enjoyed* eating."

"Of course you need *work*," she said, just a hair shy of a scoff. "But with the focus you've got? Your talents?" She shook her head. "You could have whatever you wanted, if you just used it. And you're here playing house, instead."

"I think we're doing pretty well for ourselves," I said, eyes narrowing. "I don't need to *use* people to survive. We're not all killers."

"In case you were wondering, no, I didn't want your input," she snapped. "So take it and go fuck yourself with it." Her hands clenched more tightly. "If you're trying to shame me, it won't work. I don't care.

"So why are you out here, then?" I asked, my scowl deepening. "What game are you up to."

"Theres- There's no game," Amber muttered, a bit of the vehemence leaving her expression. It was like she'd tired herself out, like her outburst had been her parting blow. "You heard what I said. I just needed a smoke."

Her lie was plain enough I could have seen it even without my magic screaming its unhappiness. "You're not smoking," I said, glancing sidelong at her. "In fact..." I nudged the wooden boards of the deck with my foot. A tiny white cylinder lay there, nearly invisible against the dusting of snow that had made it to the porch. It was bent and torn, like someone had crumpled it in their hand. "Let's not lie."

"None of your goddamn business," she snapped. Her momentary resurgence vanished just as quickly as it had come. She slumped, leaning forward and bracing her elbows on her knees. Her hands cradled her face, resolutely facing ahead still.

I paused, a bit of my anger fading. She was shaking. It was a tiny motion, almost invisible in the half-dark. But every quiver of her hands was reflected in the waves of her black hair, gleaming and twitching gently.

"Are you all right?" I said, tentatively.

"I'm fine."

"It's your relic, isn't it?" My eyes widened as I stared at her, the realization ringing true. "You're deprived. I...Nox looked uncomfortable, but he didn't-"

"Nox hasn't had his trinket for more than a fistful of years," she said, spitting the words at me. She stared out into the dark, her fingers digging white marks into her cheeks. "Don't give me that shit."

New confusion circled in the back of my mind. "And...that makes a difference?"

"Excuse me?" she said, her nose wrinkling as she glared at me. The whole expression was close enough to what I'd given her a few minutes before that I had to fight to keep myself from laughing. Somehow I knew that wouldn't go over well. "A-Are you an idiot?"

"I'm...I'm new," I mumbled, my eyes dropping to the wooden boards. "Give me a break." My curiosity was winning out over my politeness. "So, uh. It's, like-"

"It's worse for old-bloods than the newbies, you asshole," she spat. "It..." She shook her head more vigorously. "It feels like someone's filled me with steam and left me to cook. And someone *else* is sandpapering my skin. And-"

"I-I think I get it," I stammered, cutting her off before she could launch into an even more vivid description. "Sorry."

"Don't lie to me," she said, her voice soft.

"I'm not...I.." I began, but my words fell away just as quickly as I'd started. From her perspective, it'd be hard for her to find anything I said on the matter plausible. I was the one hurting her, after all.

She'd turned away again by the time I looked back, planting her feet against the wooden boards. "Just leave me alone. I'm not calling for help. You took my phone, and my knife, and my guns. What more do you want?" She ran a hand through her hair, smoothing her ponytail.

"Just let me be."

"You looked fine a minute ago," I mumbled.

"That's how it works," she said, still looking down. "So, please, *please* just-"

"Lean forward."

"What, now?" Amber said, glancing up at me as I stepped up alongside her. Her lip curled back in a sneer. "Don't think just because you've got a few beers in you you can-"

"Jesus Christ, just shut up," I snapped, the sympathy she'd managed to work out of me fast-disappearing. "Put your arms down."

Her eyes stayed fixed on me for a long moment, wary and dark. Another shudder slipped through her frame. Finally, begrudgingly, she leaned forward, letting her hands drop down to rest against her knees.

I slipped a hand into my pocket, pursing my lips. The little thoughts in the back of my mind were screaming by then, blaring that I was being stupid and reckless and *stupid*. But I knew the flip side of it. If we wanted to win Amber and Nox's trust, then we were going to have to be willing to let them trust us, too. Fighting with enemies at our backs would be worse than not having them there.

Praying I wasn't making a huge mistake, I slid the glove from my pocket and brushed aside the hair hanging down her back. Before she could twitch I laid it flat in the small of her back. I wasn't entirely sure that it'd work through her jacket, but I wasn't about to try and strip her, either.

The shiver that rippled down her spine at the touch of it was enough to answer *that* question for me. I flinched, making to pull back, but she shook her head.

"Just...Just give me a minute," Amber whispered. She didn't beg, or plead, or even thank me. She just sat where she was, still as a statue.

I sighed. And then I shifted, sitting down on the bench beside her. It wasn't instantaneous, then. I could tell that much from the look on her face, the exhaustion still etched into every line of her being. "Sorry," I mumbled again. "I didn't...we're just trying to be safe. You and Nox are-"

"Shut the fuck up."

"Right."

For her part, she did as I'd asked. She didn't thrash, or try and grab at the glove. Little by little, her breathing slowed. I just waited, counting off the minutes as the others screamed and laughed in the house behind us.

"Didn't think you had it on you." When she spoke at last, her tone was worlds apart from what it'd been, enough so that I wasn't entirely sure I'd heard right.

I chuckled. "Well, that was kind of the point, wasn't it?" I'd fetched it from my safe, after I'd seen Nox starting to twitch with spasms of pain. We weren't in this to be cruel. That wasn't the point.

"I see."

"I was serious," I said, glancing over at her. She ignored me, staring out into the night still. "We don't intend on letting either of you collapse. We just...we just needed to be careful."

"Happy now?"

I let my breath slide out between my teeth. "We'll...we'll be more careful, I think. Now that I know it's hurting you like this." A crooked smile flashed across my face. "It's not helpful to anyone if you two are falling apart."

"Ah." She fell quiet again, and I didn't press the point. A bit of color was returning to her face, more with every second that the relic stayed resting against her back.

She twitched. I faltered, glancing over. Was she feeling well enough to fight back? Was she - No, I amended a moment later. She'd just lifted her chin, her shoulders rising gently as she stared out into the black.

"It's starting to snow."

"Isn't it always," I said, with something like a chuckle bubbling up.

"It's nice."

"Right. So they say." I wasn't convinced. Mostly it meant a lot of shoveling, and a lot of icy roads to drive on, and a messy, muddy slop come spring. But, well, it was one of those things everyone had their own opinion on, and who was I to argue otherwise?

"Is it worth it?"

I glanced over, furrowing my brow in confusion yet again at the blunt, quiet question. "What? What do you mean?"

Her hazel eyes were unfocused, watching the flakes drop to the ground all around us. One danced into our shelter as I stared, clinging to her eyelash. She blinked, and it was gone. "This. Your life here. Your friends. Is it worth it?"

"Well, yeah, I mean-"

"Worth lying to them? Worth putting them in danger?" Her face turned towards mine, slow enough that I couldn't possibly take it as an attack. She watched me from the corner of her eye, her expression unreadable. "If the primes attacked today, they'd all be dead. Or worse." The corners of her lips tightened. "Is it worth it?"

"I-" I began, but stopped. I'd been so ready to say yes, to affirm it offhand. But, that's how Keira had gotten mixed up in all this, wasn't it? What if tomorrow it was Catherine? Jason? Our parents?

I didn't know how to answer her. And so I just fell quiet, letting my fingers slide over the stitched leather of her glove. After a moment, as though recognizing that she wasn't going to get a response, she turned her face away again.

"You have a nice home," she murmured, her words whisper-quiet.

I bobbed my head in a nod, unable to muster up the words to reply.

Together we sat in the cold, the laughter of my friends echoing in my ears, and watched the snow fall.

CHAPTER FORTY-FIVE

"I don't know that I'm okay with this."

I glanced over at the muted whisper, meeting Jake's eyes. He stood, arms folded across his chest, and just glared right back at me.

"It'll be fine," I murmured, shrugging helplessly. "Trust me."

"They all came here trying to *kill* us not two days ago. And now you're going to waltz around with them like it's all fine?"

"We can't keep them locked in their rooms forever."

"Sure, we can," he said, smiling crookedly. "We've got that bastard over in the shed, don't we? It's a big enough shed. They could be bunkmates."

"Glenn was their leader. These two are-"

"Don't you dare call them victims," Jake snapped, rolling his eyes. "Jesus Christ, she's got you wrapped around her finger, doesn't she?"

I bit off the rest of my sentence, hastily amending what I'd been about to say. "I-I mean, they got screwed too. Yeah, they're not allies like Brendon and Loren, or the brothers. But-"

"They're only allies because you're paying them."

"That's still kind of an ally, isn't it?"

"Jon?" I heard someone call from the other room. "You about ready?"

"Coming!" I called, before turning back to Jake. "Look. We don't have time for this," I said, reaching out to pat his shoulder. He didn't look appeased, but he didn't pull away, either. "You can come with. It'll be fun."

"Don't *want* to go tromp around in the snow all day."

"Tough. Come on." I turned away, not looking to see if he was following. He trudged into line behind me, his footsteps echoing off the concrete floor of the garage.

The others were waiting in the living room, circled around the kitchen table. I cast half a glance at the surface, where printouts from Google Maps and whatever local geologic charts Keira could find were scattered haphazardly.

"Good?" I said, finding the others staring at me. They were wearing coats and boots - all but Brendon,. Keira, and Loren, who were firmly sitting in their chairs.

"Let's get this over with," Tyler mumbled, stepping towards the door. "Kai-"

"I'm coming," his brother called, his eyes bright. I hesitating, recognizing the look on his face. Unless I was mistaken, he was viewing our day in the woods as an opportunity to pull one over on Tyler. I made a mental note to pick a corner of the forest *far away* from the younger demi to survey.

Nox scurried over to the pair of them, every bit as bright as Kai with a knit cap pulled down low over his ears. He'd perked up, I noted with more than a little relief. Both of them had.

I'd learned my lesson. It wasn't my goal to punish either of them, when it came right down to it, and I wasn't trying to hurt them. We'd left off the whole notion of complete separation from their relics. They stayed in my watchful care - and Jake stayed close enough to them that he could black both of them out if there was an issue - but we made sure they could gain access to their relics often enough that they wouldn't suffer. Nox hadn't asked, but I'd seen the tension bleed from his frame the minute he'd gotten that owl back into his hands.

Amber stood a little straighter, too. She fell in behind me, expressionless. "Whatever. If you think it'll help."

"Did you make sure-"

"He's still sleeping. He'll be out for another hour or two, without the counteragent," she said, glancing back over her shoulder.

"Good," I said, nodding once. Keeping Glenn under and out of the way had been our next concern, after Amber and Nox were controlled. The last thing we needed was him waking up and causing more problems, toying with the memories of our demis and planning his escape. I'd worried. Aedan had wanted him alive, but if he was a

424

danger, there wasn't exactly a lot I could do to keep him from his fate.

When I'd mentioned it to Nox, though, his face had lit up like a lightbulb. He'd plunged back into the SUV, pulling loose a side panel and whisking a baggie out from inside. "It was supposed to be a bit of a trip," he'd said, with a hint of apology in his eyes as he glanced to me. "So we had some extra."

Any other day, I'd have been hurt. Offended. Taken it personally. Those drugs were meant for me, after all. But it was the solution to our problem, and I'd take it. We dosed Glenn to oblivion and back, happily.

So I just nodded, acknowledging her words, and slipped out into the cold.

"You guys good?" I said, glancing towards Tyler, Kai, and Nox. They nodded back. "You know what we're doing?"

"We've got it," Kai said, rolling his eyes.

"We'll keep an eye out for anything we can use," Tyler said, his eyes flicking up to meet mine. "But...what are you expecting to find?"

"It's pretty much a forest," Nox said, wrinkling his nose as he glanced out into the trees around us. "I mean-"

"I'm not expecting miracles," I said with a sigh. "But we've got a little bit of time, right now. Practice a little, maybe."

"You could use it," Tyler said with a chuckle.

"Shut up."

I swallowed my irritation, watching Kai scoop up a fistful of snow. Hadn't even taken five minutes, had it? Not that I was surprised. It was hard to get them to take something like scouting and mapping seriously.

With the primes bearing down on us, it was our time to get everything in line. Keira and Brendon had a line open to Greyson, pumping him for whatever information he could give us last-minute. His powers were still something of a mystery, but she'd seen the first glimpses of something in his pin. Numbers, she said. Clouds of calculations, floating through the sky of his mind. How she 'saw' that, I had no idea, but she'd been confident. So behind they stayed.

Which left me with *them*.

"So," I said, glancing over to Amber as we took our first steps towards the treeline.

She glared back at me. "What?"

Jake muttered darkly under his breath, something about her and her snark, but I shot him a look. He quieted. "You've been all over the state, haven't you?"

A snort slipped between her lips. "The state? Think bigger."

"The country, then."

"Better."

"How many primes do we have to deal with?" I said, a bit of the confidence leaving my voice. "Uh...I mean, the others said we had, like, one in Detroit, and one on the west side of the state, and one up north, but-"

"Ontario's the big player around here," she said, scowling down at the snow. "Which you'd know if you had a lick of sense and actually paid *attention*."

Right back to this, were we? "I'm trying."

"Trying? Don't give me that."

"This is all new to me," I said, forcing the words out between gritted teeth. "So, yeah. I'm doing the best I can."

"You don't look new. You don't *cast* like you're new. You're sitting here with a gang like you've been building your crew for ten years. So don't try and lie to me."

"Oh, he's not lying," Jake muttered.

I made an irritated noise in the back of my throat, my eyes slipping over to meet his, but he turned away. I'd seen the crooked smile flash across his face.

Amber groaned, straightening her spine and letting her head slide back. "Jesus. I just wanted to get *paid*."

I chuckled. "And now you're here. You'll get paid."

"And if you go and start a war with the folks who actually buy relics around here, how far am I going to have to go to cash in?" she snapped.

"Not my problem."

"Oh, it'll be your problem when I-" She stopped, her steps coming to a halt as she froze.

I faltered. "Come on. We need to-"

"Quiet."

"What?" Jake said, easing up alongside us from the position he'd taken up a few steps back. "What are you-"

"Shut the hell up," she said, her tone sharp. His scowl deepened, but he shut up.

I could hear it too, then. The sound that had set her off - Tires, rumbling against the snow.

"Shit," I muttered, spinning on my heels to face back towards the

426

main road. It was harder, with all the trees coated in white, but I could see the car coming up the gravel drive. Fast.

Amber went still, her eyes fixed on the car. "Is that-"

"Great. He's here. Can we go inside, already?" Jake said, his tone bordering on whining again. "My feet are wet."

"I told you to wear the right boots," I muttered, but he was already plunging back through our footprints towards the back door of the house. Amber hesitated another moment, her gaze flicking up to meet mine. And then she shrugged, turning to follow him.

I watched the car, though. I couldn't shake the sick feeling in the pit of my stomach, the questions that lurked around every corner. Maybe it was the primes. Maybe they'd slipped through, somehow, given Greyson's perimeter the slip. I'd had absolute confidence in the finder for so long - right until I saw that woman standing on the edge of the treeline, staring back at me.

If she could get through, with even Greyson insisting he'd felt no other demis around us, then who was to say others couldn't do the same thing? Could I really trust that we were safe?

The car looked like it was on its last legs, though old, mostly rusted through, and with a whine in the sound of its engine that was a sure-fire death rattle. If the primes were halfway as powerful as everyone said they were, they wouldn't be caught dead driving something like that. I forced myself to relax, trudging around the side of the house towards the driveway. Tyler, Nox, and Kai were on their way back too, with the audiomage looking exactly as wary as his younger brother wasn't.

A door slammed shut. I glanced back for a split second, checking to make sure I still had Amber and Jake behind me, and kept going.

Aedan was stretching when I came around the corner of the house, his arms stick-thin and reaching for the skies. At the sound of our footsteps, his eyes flicked open, fixing on mine. "Jonny," he said, a smile slipping onto his face. I wasn't fooled. I could see the worry in it, the grey circles under his eyes. He'd been running himself hard again.

"You made it," I said, offering him a nod and letting the matter of my name slide.

"Looks like. Wasn't quite sure I would. Last truck I nabbed shit the bed with a good twelve hours still to go." He slapped the roof of the car, leering down at it. "Good thing this bad boy still has lots of miles left in it."

I winced, trying to ignore the clear implications of grand theft auto being thrown at me. "...Right. So-"

"This one of them?" he said, coming back to serious so quickly I thought I might get whiplash. His eyes were fixed on Amber. Just for a second, it seemed like she stiffened, faltering in the face of his intensity.

"*She's* one of them, yes," I said, my hand twitching up as though to grab her shoulder. She didn't move, though. Her nostrils flared gently as she took in the sight of him, her eyes widening. I smothered a grim smile behind a hand. She recognized him, then - or she knew enough of the stories to guess.

"Fine. Whatever. There are more?"

I waved a hand towards the other group still approaching. "Ah, one more over there. Nox. Fellow with the glasses. And-"

"Which one's their leader?" Aedan said, his eyes fixed on the slight form of the mind reader. The others crept closer, nudging Nox onward. He'd stopped in place, glancing between Amber and Aedan nervously.

I ran a hand through my hair. "Glenn. He's- He's not here right now. We've got him in the garage. Uh...Tyler?" I glanced over to the soundmage. "Can you go get him? Take someone with you. And can someone-"

"I've got the wake-up juice right here," Loren said, plunging her hand into her coat pocket. The vial she pulled out was tiny in comparison to the bottles we'd been drugging the demi from. It was a one-time dose, after all.

I eyed her, my eyes narrowing. "How long have you been carrying that around?"

Her ears colored red, but she only shrugged. "It seemed best."

"Yes, yes, this is all quite amusing," Aedan snapped, folding his arms. "Now do you all want to cut the shit? We need to get down to business." I didn't like the way his eyes settled onto Amber before sliding to Nox, cold and unfeeling.

"Fine," I muttered. "Come inside, at least."

His lips pressed into a thin line, but he didn't argue when I stalked over and held the door to the house open. One after another, our group filed through. Amber didn't look at me at all. Nox was white as a ghost, but offered me a wan smile. I let the door slide shut behind me as I eased into the warmth.

"You." Aedan's voice brought me back to attentiveness. He jabbed a finger at Nox, pointing to one of the kitchen chairs a moment later.

"Sit."

Nox froze, his eyes flitting madly back and forth behind his glasses. "W-What? What do you-"

"Just sit, will you?" Aedan snapped. His head turned far enough that he could glare at me. "Tell me you at least disarmed them, Jonny?" His voice held all the saccharine sweetness I would have expected from him.

I stepped past Amber, who stood caught in place between Jake and Brendon. Neither seemed particularly interested in letting her go to Nox's aid, even if they hadn't actually put hands on her yet. The mind-reader took a seat like he was told, brown eyes wide. Trying to look casual, I leaned against the counter as I turned back to Aedan. "Of course we did. No weapons, and I've got their relics."

"Perfect," he muttered, letting his hand slide into his pocket. I flinched as he pulled it free a moment later - with a knife clutched in his grasp.

"Aedan, that's-"

"So. Jon tells me you were hired to come kill. To come *steal*." Aedan didn't even acknowledge I'd spoken. His attentions slid between Nox and Amber. The knife slowly turned over and over in his fingers, smooth as butter.

"I-I mean, we already talked to Jon," Nox said, holding his hands up placatingly. "We told him what we know. I don't-"

In a single, fluid motion, Aedan flicked the knife back into his grasp. The blade glinted dully in the harsh fluorescent light of the kitchen.

Nox stiffened. "I- That is, I'd be glad to tell you too," he said, the words falling out of him in a rush.

Aedan only nodded, still staring down at him. "Get to it."

"Stop bullying the kid," Amber snapped.

I shivered. Aedan turned around, half-sitting on the edge of the table. His free hand reached out, settling onto Nox's head. He ruffled the mind-reader's hair, perfectly comfortable. "Oh? Did you have something to say?"

"That bastard stiffed us too," Amber said, glaring daggers at Aedan. "We're not in this to protect him. So there's no need for the show."

Aedan chuckled. "I think-"

"Seriously, Aedan, put the knife away," I said with a sigh. "It's not helping."

"I'll decide what is or isn't helping," Aedan muttered, shooting me a look over his shoulder. But the tip of his knife dropped, coming to rest on the tabletop in front of Nox. "Fine. Talk."

"We were hired in southwest Indiana. Glenn was trying to fill out his crew in a hurry. The pay was good - too good, really, but it's been a while since we had a gig," Amber spat. "He told us, someone was paying good to go snatch a local crew leader out of his nest." She shrugged. "It wasn't anything we hadn't done before. Pay was good, like I said. So yeah."

Aedan scowled across the room at her. "And?"

Her eyes narrowed, fixed on the knifeblade. It wandered, meandering from the table's surface to drag across Nox's arm. He flinched, shivering. Aedan didn't so much as glance his way.

"And what?" she forced out at last.

"And, what else?"

She made a frustrated noise in the back of her throat. "I don't know what you're-"

"I heard the name Anke in his mind," Nox croaked, his eyes fixed on the blade. "T-That's all. He seemed to think she was important."

The blade paused. I glanced up. Aedan's eyes were fixed on Nox, still ice-cold. "Oh? Read his thoughts, did you?"

Nox's hands trembled, but his gaze stayed locked on Aedan's. "She was paying. Really well. Well enough that Glenn was willing to scrape together an impromptu crew for a raid. H-He was convinced that this was going to be his big break. Something like that."

"What did she look like?" Aedan said, still glaring.

Nox paused, his brow furrowing, but plowed on a heartbeat later. "I-I don't know. It's not really precise." His eyes flicked to mine. "Like I told Jon. Maybe...mid 30's? Blonde? Scary-looking?"

Aedan sighed. "Well, that's Anke, all right."

"You mentioned her before," I said, easing myself upright. "Back with Matt. She-"

"Don't worry your little head over it, Jonny," he snapped. "She's my business."

Anger blossomed in my chest. "We have people who are *gunshot* because of her, Aedan. We could all have died. I'd say it's our fucking business."

Nox let out a tiny, pained noise. My eyes dropped, drawn to the line of blood trickling down his arm. Aedan's hands were tensed, his knuckles showing white through the skin.

"Aedan," I snapped, at the same moment I heard Amber snarl something muted and dangerous.

He didn't move, didn't ease up. His knife dug in another quarter of an inch. "Don't get ahead of yourself, Jonny," he said, his eyes tightening before dropping back down to Nox. "Now. You're going to tell me everything. How much she paid you. What she's going to do with the information. Why she's picking at Jon's crew."

The mind-reader flinched back, trying to slide away, but Aedan grabbed him, pinning him in place. "I-I don't know," Nox stammered, shaking his head violently. "I never saw her. And...and Glenn-"

"Aedan, give me the knife," I snapped, crossing to the table in three quick steps.

A wave of irritation swept across Aedan's face, but his body was turning before he could argue. The knife slapped down into my hand, hilt-first. I backed away a second later.

His lips curled down in a scowl. "What the fuck are you doing? Don't you *ever* give me orders, Jonny. I didn't get you out of that forest so you could-"

"Everyone just calm the fuck down," I said, leaning against a chair. I held onto the knife, though. There was still too much anger in Aedan's eyes, and although Amber had relaxed a fraction in her seat at my intervention, she still looked like she might leap up at any moment.

"R-Really," Nox said, sliding a few inches further away. His hand slapped down across the gash in his arm. Red dripped past his fingers. "I-I'm not hiding anything. I don't know. I just-"

"Right," Aedan muttered darkly. "Picture of reliability, you,"

"You've got Glenn," Amber spat, enunciating each word clearly. "So don't go cutting on-"

Her words were interrupted by a blast of cold air, and the sudden return of Tyler. Loren was with him - and Glenn staggered along between the both of them, suspended by the iron-tight hold they had on his arms.

"Much better," Aedan said, pushing himself upright. All of the tension of a moment before was gone, wiped clean as he stared at the rival demi. "This is the ringleader, is he?"

"He's still probably a little groggy," Loren said, her eyes flicking to mine. "I didn't give him all of it. It didn't seem like a good idea to have him walking around totally in control."

"No, no," I said, waving my hands. "That's a good thought."

"Le' go've me," Glenn slurred, shaking his head. Tyler only snorted, dumping the demi into one of the kitchen chairs. His drowsy eyes flicked up a moment later as he peered across the table at Amber. "Y-You. Huh. Din't....There was somethin' you weren't s'pposed to figure out. You-"

Whatever he was about to say, it vanished a moment later as her fist plowed into his nose. He yelped, reeling and pressing his hands to his face.

"Well, I *found out*, you prick," she snarled. "Where's my damn money?"

I had my hand on her shoulder a moment later, pulling her away before she could go in for round two. "Hey. That's enough."

"Like hell it's enough," she muttered, her eyes narrowing.

I tugged her away anyway, letting Aedan push past. "Come on, Amber. Just-"

"I can have him after?" she said, glaring over her shoulder at me.

I hesitated for a split second, glancing over at Aedan. He rolled his eyes, but only shrugged at me. I chuckled. "Sure."

"...Fine," she muttered, knocking my hand clear and throwing herself down in a chair nearby. "But I mean it. Follow through this time."

"Right, right."

"If you two don't mind shutting up, I'd like to actually hear him," Aedan snapped, grabbing Glenn by the shoulder. His fingers dug into the demi's shoulder hard enough he yelped again.

I quieted at the look in his eyes. They were filled with the same smug confidence as always, but this time it overlaid a nervousness that ran deep. I understood. Things were finally beginning to happen, to come together, and if they went *badly*, our future would be grim.

"Now. Let's talk, you and I, shall we?" Aedan's voice brought me back to the present. He'd pulled a second knife from god only knew where, gleaming brilliant silver in the light. Glenn was trying to stare at it, but his eyes wouldn't focus. Aedan kicked him, bringing his eyes snapping back front and center. "Anke hired you. Where'd she find you?"

Glenn furrowed his brow, shaking his head slowly. "N-No. She s-said...somethin'. She said she'd stab me if I-"

He screamed. I winced. I hadn't even seen Aedan move, but by the time I blinked, there was a line of red running down Glenn's cheek.

432

"I have a knife too, you know," Aedan said, his tone conversational. He crouched down so that him and Glenn were eye to eye. "And I'm *here*. What did she tell you, exactly?"

A flicker of motion out of the corner of my eye caught my attention. I glanced over. Amber was fidgeting, squirming in her seat. Her eyes darted up to meet mine, and then drifted away again.

It didn't take me long to figure out what her problem was. She kept glancing towards Nox, then to Aedan, and back to me. Nox still sat at the table where he'd been left. His hand was pressed to his arm, the skin white with the pressure he was putting on it. He stared at Aedan, wide-eyed, as the immortal began the process of getting his answers out of Glenn.

He was too paralyzed with fear to move, I realized - and being in arm's reach of Aedan meant he was in the line of fire should anything happen. Swallowing a sigh, I eased myself upright again, slipping across to the table.

Aedan didn't so much as look up as I stepped closer. Nox, on the other hand, flinched so hard at the touch of my hand on his shoulder that I thought his glasses might fall off.

I didn't say a word. I just jerked my chin, motioning for him to follow me. He surged out of his seat, relief plain on his face.

Amber grabbed him as soon as he was within reach of her, pulling him closer. A look passed between them, like she was sizing him up. And then her shoulders drooped, a sigh slipping from her throat.

A thought occurred to me. "Uh...Nox, if I give you your relic back, do you think you can help Aedan?"

"What?" Nox said, his eyes going round again.

"What?" Aedan snapped.

I shrugged. "He'll be distracted. And I can tell if Nox lies to us."

"It's a good idea," Jake called from his seat in the living room. I wasn't fooled. He was staring out the window, but his fingers tapped rapid-fire in his lap. The sooner Aedan got his questions, the sooner this whole chapter could be over. I knew without him saying another word where his priorities lay.

Nox licked his lips, his gaze flicking back and forth between Aedan and I. "I....I can try," he squeaked out at last, his hands folded in his lap. "I-I mean, yes. I can- It shouldn't be a problem."

"And all we have to do is tolerate a snoop in our minds," Aedan muttered.

I sighed. "Aedan-"

"Fine. Fine!" he said, throwing his hands up. Glenn's eyes followed the motion of the blade, his head lolling to the side. "Whatever. Get to it."

Knowing Aedan, he wouldn't be waiting around if I wasted any time. I didn't wait for another invitation. I was vertical and off towards my room before he could say another word, flashing one last glance towards Nox and Amber.

She still had him by the arm, and she didn't look happy, but she didn't look like she was about to lunge at someone anymore. I offered her a tiny smile before I vanished around the corner.

The sound of Glenn bellowing in pain chased me down the hall, wiping away my fleeting victory.

CHAPTER FORTY-SIX

The living room was quiet. Eerily so, after the yelling and bellowing that had filled it so shortly before. I sagged against the worn, threadbare fabric of my couch, letting the tension bleed out of my shoulders.

"Maybe....maybe you could try something with your fingers?" I heard Keira say behind me at the kitchen table. Her and Brendon had been there since Amber had dragged Glenn away. After she'd got some paper towel to mop up the droplets of blood. And some disinfectant. My sister leaned closer to Brendon even as she spoke, peering through her glasses at him.

Brendon scowled, leaning away. "I've *tried* that. It doesn't work."

Keira pursed her lips, her eyes narrowing further. "Really? You can't, like, shoot lightning from your fingertips like Storm from-"

"No."

"Oh. Well...all right. Maybe if you-"

Brendon let out an exasperated sigh, cutting off Keira as she waggled her fingers meaningfully. "I've tried all that, okay? It's not right. Something's off. Didn't you say you saw something else in my relic?"

"I know what I said. But do you feel anything? We've been at this god knows how long," Keira said, finally throwing her hands up.

Brendon's shoulders slumped a little lower. "I-I know. I'm trying. I really am."

She groaned softly. "That's...that's not what I meant. We'll figure it out, Brendon."

"Right," he muttered. And then he cleared his throat. "I thought...I thought I could feel it get a little warm, when I was talking to Jake about the other crews in the region. Maybe he could-"

"No," Jake called from his perch on the overstuffed chair across the room. He slouched a few inches lower, vanishing from sight. "My show's on. Go away."

"Jake," Keira snapped, her head whipping around with a snap of dark hair. "Don't you want to help?"

"Already helped," Jake said, raising his voice a little more. "You heard him. It was warm. Victory."

"But nothing happened," Brendon said, a plaintive note entering his tone. "I still didn't *do* anything."

"After my show."

"Fine," Keira muttered, pressing a hand to her face. "Just fine."

Tearing my eyes off them, I let myself sag a little deeper into the couch. No matter how hard I tried, I couldn't quite drown out the sound of them bickering, but I could certainly do my best.

Amber was gone, for the moment. So was Aedan, and so were Tyler and Kai. The thought wasn't entirely a comfortable one, especially when the thought of *why* they were gone slipped through my mind again. I pushed away the queasiness. I'd promised Amber, and she deserved it. Besides, it wasn't like Glenn actually deserved even the slightest bit of sympathy from me.

Aedan and the others hadn't wanted to leave her alone with her former employer, even if she'd shown only honesty in proclaiming her hatred of him. She hadn't argued when they'd informed her they were coming along.

But a smile had spread across her face when I handed her glove back to her. The others weren't thrilled, but there were three of them and one of her. She'd been true to her word, and we'd promised her this much. If we were to be allies, it was time to start trusting each other a little.

They'd pushed Glenn out into the cold, caught in the middle of their little group. The storm door shut with a final-sounding slam behind them.

I could still see Glenn sitting in the kitchen chair when I closed my eyes, though. See the red that dripped down his skin, the way his shoulders had shaken. Aedan hadn't hurt him - not really. Just roughed him up a little. He'd talked readily enough after he felt the first touch of pain, and Nox dug any scraps of information he was hiding out of his mind. The slender man was even more pale than usual, but he'd done well.

And now we knew what they were doing here.

"You're thinking about it," Loren said, pulling me out of my reverie as she threw herself down onto the couch opposite me. "Aren't you?"

I smiled humorlessly. "Aren't *you?*"

"Well. Yeah. But people like him aren't worth losing sleep over, Jon," she said, her voice quiet. "They do...horrible things. They would have done the same to you, if they had the chance. So don't....don't worry about him."

"I know that. I do."

She chuckled. "Do you think Aedan's satisfied?"

Running a hand through my hair, I sighed. "Him? No. But we got about as much as we could have hoped for."

"What do you think she's after?" Loren said, her brow furrowing delicately. "That's what Glenn said, wasn't it? That she hired him?"

"Anke? I'm more worried about the fact Glenn seemed to think he wasn't the only one she approached," I said heavily. "And she was poking around with Matt's crew too, wasn't she? She's interested in something. There's no arguing that." My pulse had thundered as the crew leader had rambled on, talking about the friends he'd heard from. The stories they'd told of the blond woman approaching them, making an offer.

Anke was making the rounds, and Glenn was just the latest figure she'd made a connection with.

"You think?" Loren said softly, leaning back against the arm of the couch. There was no sarcasm in her voice, just quiet concern.

A crooked smile tugged at my lips again. "Three guesses what she's after, eh? Aedan *said* people like to chase after him."

"But Aedan wasn't even here."

"Ah...yeah," I said, shaking my head slowly. "I don't know. It's just a theory. I don't know what he was even *after*, without Aedan here."

"Power."

I flinched, glancing up. Nox sat in the very corner of his room, nursing the remnants of a mug of coffee that he'd chugged down after popping six ibuprofen. He'd been perfectly quiet for so long I'd nearly forgotten he was there.

"Power," I said, keeping my voice as neutral as I could. "What's that mean?"

His eyes flicked up to meet mine behind his glasses. "He seemed to think...this was his big break. Something like that. That after he did this job, he was on the ins. That Anke would rely on him. That he could join her crew.

I paused. "Her crew."

Nox's head bobbed in agreement. "Right."

"Of *course* she has a crew."

"That'd only make sense, wouldn't it?" Jake said. I glanced over. He was leaning back in his seat, his head tilted just far enough back for him to shoot me a scathing look. "Matt said she was trying to get her demis in on his team. That implies that she *has* demis. And it sounds like she's a big deal."

I reached up to pinch the bridge of my nose. "Right."

"He seemed to think that doing all this was worth the risk," Nox said softly. "The risk of cobbling together mercenaries into his crew. Of going out and attacking you guys."

"And none of you spotted that he was full of shit," Brendon said, breaking free of the muttered conversation him and Keira were sharing. He chortled. "Real smart."

Nox's face was slowly starting to glow. "I...I didn't-" He scowled at Brendon. "He messed with our memories. It's not our fault."

"Jon broke out of his web," Brendon said, leaning back in his seat and crossing his arms. "*He* could do it."

"That's- That doesn't mean anything."

"Enough, both of you," I said, letting my hand slide across my forehead. "We were lucky I could break free. Maybe it was because Amber had talked to me first. Maybe I wasn't entirely convinced. Either way, we made it."

Nox and Brendon both fell quiet, staring at the floor with scowls on their faces. I just settled back into my seat, relaxing a little once it became clear neither of them was going to try to kill the other.

I could still see Glenn staring at me from my memories, his eyes blank and confused. My question hung in the air between us, frozen in place alongside the coppery tang of blood and the glinting light off Aedan's knife. *What are you after? What do you want?*

He'd only shaken his head slowly, the confusion still there.

A place of my own, he'd said. *Control. Territory. What everyone wants.* His gaze had been fixed on mine, even as he slumped deeper into his chair.

Don't you?

I'd never thought about it like that before. When all of this had started, I'd been interested in staying alive. Then, after Keira had been dragged into our mess, I'd wanted somewhere the two of us could be safe together.

But what did I want *now?* After we'd come so far, after so much blood had been shed. What were we doing? What was it for?

The frigid gust of air that washed through the room as the door slammed open was enough to bring me out of my questioning thoughts. I snapped upright in my chair, shuddering and shivering against the chill. "God damn it, Aedan, would you shut that?" I snapped, glaring across the room through slitted eyes.

Aedan tromped in, kicking the snow from his boots. Well. My boots, from two years ago. They mostly fit. "Again with the bitching. There any coffee left?"

"No," Nox muttered, lifting his mug to his lips.

The others filed back in behind the immortal - Amber first, with Tyler and Kai keeping a watchful eye on her as they brought up the rear. Tyler looked like he might be sick. Kai did too, with a distinctive greenish tinge to his complexion, but he wore a smile.

I cast a tentative glance towards Amber. "Did you...uh, is Glenn-"

"Oh, he's dead," she said, stripping off her jacket as she stepped the rest of the way in. A knit scarf hung around her neck in circlets. I recognized it from Keira's room. "Don't worry about *that*."

"You should've seen her," Kai said, his eyes lighting up. "Just put a hand on his chest and *pushed*. Like, this sort of blurry wall, kind of. Against him. The more he struggled, the brighter the wall was, until-"

"That's enough," Tyler said, pressing a hand to his lips.

I gave him a long, assessing look. "Bathroom's that way," I said at last, motioning towards the hall.

He waved me off. "I'm fine. Really. That was just...More than I expected."

"It was fine," Amber said, flashing a sardonic grin my way. "I was nice."

"Not nice enough to use a gun," Tyler muttered.

She laughed. "Well. No." Without even trying to come up with an excuse, she slipped over to the kitchen table and flopped down next to Keira and Brendon. "What's all this?"

"I'm trying to learn about the primes," Brendon said, his voice low. "I...just thought it might help."

"You know all about that stuff, right?" Keira said, her tone brightening. "You told me those stories. Why don't you-"

"What a pain," I heard Amber murmur under her breath. But even though her nose wrinkled like she was smelling something distasteful, when I really looked at her, I didn't think she looked all that bothered. With a groan, she pulled one of the maps closer, grabbing a pen.

Brendon's eyes were fixed over her shoulder as she started scrawling. He hardly even seemed to notice what she was saying, much less what she was writing. And he *didn't* look happy. I glanced back surreptitiously.

Jake and Loren sat side by side in the far corner of the room, talking in hushed voices. Even as I watched, Jake flicked one finger out. Loren's hands were clasped in her lap. From the way she was fidgeting, bouncing from side to side, she was probably trying to look casual. It wasn't working. Following her gaze, I spotted Kai right as he let out the biggest yawn I'd ever seen from the young man.

Perfect. I smothered a smile behind my hand, biting my lip before I could let out a laugh and ruin their whole game. Well, it was good for us to be practicing. All of us.

The nagging thought in the back of my mind surged to life again, poking at me with reminders that I still hadn't figured out what was wrong with my powers. That I still had no idea why my relic had faltered when fighting Glenn's crew, but had been so strong against our own allies.

A sharp, biting creak of old, tired wood brought me back down to earth. I flinched, looking over in time to see Tyler settle down onto the other end of the couch. He still looked bothered and more than a little green, but he offered me a tiny smile. His eyes flicked back and forth between Kai and the nightmare duo, and his smile grew.

Well, at least he had a sense of humor about it. I groaned, shaking my head, and turned away from them. "I'm...sorry about all this, by the way," I said, keeping my voice low enough the others wouldn't hear.

Tyler paused, glancing away from the show being put on for us. "What? I don't understand."

I inclined my head in the tiniest fraction of a nod, gesturing towards the other demis around us. "I...we took you in. Them, too. And then it went to shit just this quickly, didn't it?"

His smile went wistful for an instant before vanishing entirely. "Yeah, I suppose it did." He lifted a hand, running it through his mud-brown hair.

"It really wasn't my intention to start a war at the first opportunity," I said, a little more fervently. "Really. It wasn't."

He rolled his eyes, beginning to laugh. "Sure. I mean, I don't think you're *looking* for problems. But you can't just set up base in one spot with your very own crew and expect nothing to happen. You know that."

"I do. Even still. I'm sorry it fell apart this quickly."

Tyler shook his head slowly, his gaze sliding back to the others. "Oh, I don't think it's over. I'm not ready to throw in the towel, anyway. So don't apologize."

"Sorry."

"What did I just say?" Tyler turned away, wiping his smile from his face with one hand. "Ah. Well. I knew this was going to be a fight. Your friend there didn't lie, you know." He jerked his chin towards Aedan, who'd pulled a chair up next to Keira.

I chuckled softly. "Well, there's a first time for anything." As I watched, Keira turned away from Brendon and Amber, reaching into the bag she'd tossed under the table. A knife gleamed in her hand when she pulled it back out, showing it to Aedan. He grinned. My chuckle faded into a groan.

"Aedan said we'd probably have to fight. So no, I'm not shocked," Tyler said, turning back to me. He was still talking quietly enough that the others wouldn't hear. "I've...I haven't had my focus all that long, I know. But I saw a little of the stuff that was going on. I didn't want any part of that. That's why we left. Once you've got the eyes of a crew on you, you're stuck. I didn't want that."

"I know," I muttered, staring at the ground. "Sor-"

"Knock it off. Anyway. I stayed separate from all that mess, once I realized the sorts of things that some of the crews think are 'normal'. I wanted to make sure Kai didn't get dragged into all that." He tilted his head to one side, slowly lifting his shoulders in a shrug. "We might be fighting now, but I still think this is the best shot I've seen for keeping him going straight."

I nodded, letting his words hang in the air between us. "Maybe."

"That's all I want," he said, his voice dropping even lower. "If I can get Kai a place he can be safe, I don't mind using the gifts I was given.

I'll hold up my end of the bargain we made." When he fell quiet after that, he seemed to settle, sprawling out so that his arm hung off the edge of the couch. He didn't say a word, and I let him hold his silence. The others were loud enough for the whole group.

My gaze did drift to him one last time, though. Part of me was curious, even if I'd never ask it. Sound. Tyler had been given sound, the capability to blow things apart through the force of his magic. To whisper in someone's ear, or blow their eardrum out. And I remembered Aedans words, too.

What sort of wish had Tyler made, I wondered? What had he asked for?

The sound of a phone ringing interrupted my train of thought. The others hesitated, glancing up at the disruption, but resumed their conversations a moment later. I muttered a curse, digging in my pocket to get at my phone. The ringtone was wearing on my very last nerve. I'd thought Catherine and the others had gotten their fill of social time during their last visit, but clearly they-

The sight of the word 'Greyson' glaring up at me from the screen put an end to that line of thinking. Along with every other word in my head.

"Are you going to answer it?" Tyler's voice brought me up short. I glanced up, torn away from my sudden fear, and found him staring back. The phone in my hand screamed on. His eyes tightened. "Jon?"

I flipped the phone open, turning away from him without a word. "Hey. Greyson," I said, staring at the carpet.

All conversation around me had come to a stop. I heard that much, even as Greyson's gravelly toners came through the earpiece.

"Jon. Everything good over there?" he said. I wasn't fooled. His words were casual enough, but there was a tension behind them that was impossible to deny.

"Yeah. What's up?" I said, matching him lie for lie. If he wanted to play this the cheerful route, so be it.

"Ah. Well…"

I sighed, letting a long, ragged gasp of air slide out. "How many, Greyson?"

From the corner of my eye, I could see Keira rise from her seat. Aedan put a hand on her shoulder, holding her in place. I didn't get up.

Greyson chuckled, the sound dark and mirthless. "Oh, just two of 'em."

I wrinkled my brow. "What? Two?" The thoughts circled in my head. That...wasn't what we'd planned on. I'd expected them to come with an army. *Two* was just...well, I'd expected them to come prepared. "You're sure?"

"They're the only ones I can feel," Greyson said, and I could almost hear him nodding. "Now, ain't any guarantees in life, but that's about as good as I can do for you lot. I'll keep an eye on them, let you know—"

"You'll do what we talked about, and lay low," I snapped, feeling my pulse accelerate. "They might not know you're with us. They might not know you *exist*. So let's not give them a reason to figure it out."

"Feel kinda useless sittin' on my thumb over here," he grumbled. The clink of glass echoed in my ear.

I smiled. "Just...enjoy your drink, and if you feel them coming, run. But I don't think they'll come after you if you play it smart."

"Ain't worried about me. I've seen this before."

I glanced over to the rest of the room, regretting my decision almost immediately. They were all *staring*. "Don't worry about us either," I said instead, turning away before they gave me a heart attack. "We've got a good group put together. We'll be fine. And if there are only two of them..." I shrugged. "Maybe they're here to talk. That's not how you start out a fight."

Greyson was silent for a long, brooding moment. "S'ppose," he said at last. "Guess so. Only, don't go assumin' anything. Be damn stupid if your batch got blown to pieces, and all. Who'd bring me booze?"

"You're all heart," I said dryly. "Now, go...I don't know. Hide. Lay low. Maybe you could take your relic off, hide your—"

"And not be able to see 'em coming? Boy, stop talking like a goddamn fool," Greyson snapped. "I'll be fine."

I could hear him winding up, hear the goodbye in his tone. "How long?" I said, spitting the words out before he could hang up. "And where?"

"Two hours. Maybe. They're comin' pretty fast," Greyson said, a bit of the tension leaving his voice. "Maybe less. And looks like this batch is from Ontario."

"Like Aedan said."

"Seems. Keep eyes to the south, though. Been seein' strange activity out of Detroit, too."

All of the adrenaline that had finally been bleeding out of my system rushed back. "What? Them too? You're kidding me."

"They're not *here*. And I don't feel any of them beatin' a path to get here, either. I just feel...movement. Can't give you more than that.

I ran a hand through my hair, forcing myself to calm down. "Right. Yeah. Okay. Well…"

"Don't be a dumbass," Greyson said. "Bullets go in the bad guys, not you."

I chuckled. "So they keep telling me. Go hide."

When I hung up the phone, turning around, they were all staring at me still. I froze, pinned under the intensity of their collective gazes.

"Uh," I managed at last, swallowing hard. "Yeah. Pretty much what you heard. We're in the last stretch, here. Everyone remember what you're doing?"

They all nodded at me, wordless. We'd practiced. Trained. We had no intentions of going down without so much as fighting.

"About that time, is it?" Aedan drawled, leaning back so he could see me. "Was I right?"

"You were right," I said, hating every word. Sure enough, his lips curled up in a twisted grin. At least he didn't *gloat*.

"How long?" he said instead, still watching me.

"Couple of hours. Probably." A sigh slipped from person to person around the living room. I made a face. "We've still got a little bit of time left. Let's not get too freaked out. And Greyson said there were only two of them."

"Two," Amber said. I glanced over. Her brow was furrowed, her eyes dark. "That doesn't seem right."

"I agree, but it's what he said. Two demis."

"Their leadership," Aedan said, stretching his arms out before pushing himself up out of his chair. "Or whoever they've sent as their representatives, anyway. We'll know soon enough." His eyes flicked to the side, meeting Keira's. "Jonny's right. We might as well make the most of the time until they show up. Shall we?"

As I watched, he slid a blunted knife back out of his pocket, handing it to her hilt-first. She swallowed hard, her blue eyes flying from Aedan to me, but took it and stood. Together, they slid out of the house, leaving a blast of cold air in their wake as the door shut.

When I turned around, the others were following suit one after another. Kai sat in the corner, staring with feverish intent into his palm. I could see the dim flashes of red that lit up the walls every second or two. Brendon stared down at the maps and notes Keira had put in front of him, bone white.

Swallowing a sigh before it could escape, I turned to the rest. "If they're coming, we should be ready," I said, locking eyes with Nox and Amber before turning to Jake and Tyler. "Greyson said there were two. I don't know that we should play around with finding out if he was right.

"We'll start patrolling," Tyler said. He looked to Jake, who looked to Loren, who nodded.

It would be enough. It would be. I tried to convince myself of that, even while my pulse slowly started thundering in my ears. The others weren't waiting for my approval. They were already stepping outside, leaving only a few of us standing in the warmth. Myself. Nox and Amber. Kai slipped out to follow his brother with one last glance in my direction. Brendon stared at his notes with feverish intensity, his hand starting to quiver.

"We'll be fine," I said softly. He glanced up, pausing when he saw me looking back. I smiled. "We will."

"I don't know how to help," he said. Even as he spoke, his eyes dropped back down to the notes. "I don't...I knew I wouldn't be able to figure it out."

"Brendon," I snapped. "Can you hold a gun?"

His whole frame jerked as his gaze lifted, flicking back to meet mine. "W-What? I mean-"

"You're not useless, so stop acting like you are," I said, leaning back onto my heels. "Yeah, you don't know much about your relic yet. We're working on it. Let's focus on the now."

I saw him swallow, his adam's apple bobbing up and down. "Right," he said hoarsely. "You're right."

"Go arm up," I said, patting him on the shoulder. My pistol was a comforting weight under my jacket as I moved. I'd been carrying it around more and more, with everything that had been going on, and that turned out to have been a good decision. "Then come back."

He blinked. "What? What are you thinking?"

"You're the one who's spent the most time looking at all this stuff," I said, sweeping a hand out to indicate the mess of papers. "Looks like we're out of time. So you're going to help me see if we can close up any loose ends."

"Oh."

He was just standing there, looking at me. I glanced up, meeting his rounded eyes for a second. Whatever spell had frozen him in place, that seemed to break it. Muttering something too soft for me to hear, he turned on his heel and vanished before I could say anything else.

***

"And you're sure?" I said, furrowing my brow.

Brendon shook his head furiously. "No. Of course I'm not sure." His finger tapped down onto the map we'd drawn of the land around the house, tracing out the property line. We'd been at it for a good hour and a half - long enough for the hand-drawn lines to have sunk thoroughly into my memory. "But if they were going to come at us from one direction or another, they'd come from the north, wouldn't they?"

I fixed my eyes on the map, feeling my confusion grow deeper by the second. "Would they?"

He sighed, blinking at me. "Yes. They would. I think. I don't know, Jon, I'm just guessing."

"But you're sure."

His mouth snapped back shut as he glared at me. I lifted a hand to my face, hiding my smile behind my palm. "Sorry. Couldn't resist. Ah...I guess what you're saying makes sense."

I really wasn't so sure. But with him that adamant, I wasn't going to push the point. It wasn't like I had any better ideas. I ran my hand along the edge of the table, my mind racing at a hundred miles an hour. "We can...get word to Tyler and them, then. Have them focus on that area. Keep an eye out." I bit my lip. "We need some way to talk. Walkie-talkies or something."

"They've got phones," Brendon said, a hint of derision entering his voice for the first time. "I think they'll be fine, don't you?"

"It's not the same," I muttered, scowling at the map. "But, uh....I guess." I glanced down to the notes Amber and Jake had put together. "You've read those, right?" My finger trailed down a list of names, neatly penciled in one after another. "Which of these would *you* bring, if you were launching an attack? Any threats?"

"So you don't buy Greyson's story," Brendon said, the tiniest hint of a smile tugging at his lips. "About there being two of them."

I shook my head slowly. "I...I don't know. I don't think he's lying to us." Not that I could tell, over the phone. I'd been taking my relic for granted, I realized. Coming to rely too much on it to tell me what was and wasn't true. "But he might not have the full picture. There might be more going on than he knows about. And, well. If *I* was going to visit an enemy crew, one that might be hostile, I sure wouldn't go with only two demis."

"True," Brendon said with a groan. "True. Then...maybe you could ask Aedan? I think he probably knows more than I do about it."

I glanced over my shoulder, casting a wary look through the front window. I couldn't see Aedan and Keira - but I could hear the noises of whatever training session they've started. The sound of metal on metal, punctuated by the occasional grunt or the slam of someone being thrown into the side of the building. And all too clearly, I remembered the way I'd ordered him around earlier.

"No," I said, shaking my head. "No, I think I'm good."

Brendon chuckled. The sound caught me off guard for a second, the sudden relief of the tension in the room. "Well, yeah. I can understand *that*. He's going to get back at you for that, you know."

"I know,' I muttered, kicking at the floor.

"Anyway. Uh...yeah. So, if I was putting a crew together for a raid..." Brendon said, grabbing at the sheets madly and starting to flip through. "I....would probably go for-"

The sound of my ringtone split the quiet of the room for the second time that night. We both froze.

"Greyson," I said, swallowing a sigh. "I *told* him to stay out of it." I wasn't surprised, though. The older man was nothing if not stubborn.

I pulled the phone from my pocket, hitting the *accept call* button on automatic as I put it up to my ear. Brendon was staring back at me, tapping his finger against the tabletop. "I thought I told you not to call?" I said, doing my best to keep my voice level and not snap at our Finder.

There was a long, pregnant silence. I could hear the indrawn breath of someone on the other end, like they were startled. "Am I speaking to Jonathan Christensen?" they said at last. Male. Generic tone. Their voice reeked with all the smooth, oily sweetness of a telemarketer. I bit back a curse, scowling. I'd been declining junk calls for weeks. Now that I'd accepted, they'd probably call twice as often.

"Look. Whatever you're selling, I don't want any," I said, rolling my eyes. "I know it's your job. But could you just put me on whatever do-not-call list you've-"

"Oh, I think there's a misunderstanding," whoever was on the other end said. I could hear the smile in his voice. "I'm afraid I'm not selling anything today. I'm really very sorry. Only, am I speaking to Mr. Christensen? Because I have important matters to discuss with him."

"Yes," I snapped, throwing my head back. "You've reached *Mr. Christensen*, so you can go ahead and cross my number off your list. Forever."

"Good, good. Are you free?"

I stopped, wrinkling my brow. It had been a long day, and I was more than a little tired, but the pieces were beginning to sink in. He had the right voice, but the rest of the conversation...

"Who is this?" I said at last, stock-still in my chair. "How did you get this number?"

"I believe we can discuss all that later, don't you?" they said, still bright and cheery. "It's been a long drive, you know, and I'd hate to think my colleague and I went to all this trouble without even getting to see you or any of your demis."

His words slammed into my ears like punches. I just blinked, feeling the shock wash over my skin. Finally, knowing he was waiting for a response - and knowing I couldn't let myself be seen as weak and flighty from the very start - I forced a smile onto my face.

"My apologies. I...was confused."

Brendon drew closer, his eyes growing wider by the second. I shot him a glance, unable to offer him any sort of comfort. "But...we've been expecting you," I said, tearing my eyes off my ally. It was a struggle to keep my tone light, to not let the fear show or snap at him. That wouldn't be the way to start, I knew. Not at all. I kept a conversational note in my voice instead, like we were just business colleagues, like he was a new acquaintance come to visit and not an enemy leader here to launch an attack.

"Welcome to Greenville."

CHAPTER FORTY-SEVEN

My greeting hung in the air. I couldn't find it in myself to say anything else, to add onto my meager attempt at civility.

The sound of laughter on the other end of the line precluded any attempt I might have given. "Yes, yes. Thank you. I can't say we've ever come this direction before. Nice place. Quiet. Peaceful."

It might just have been my imagination, but it seemed like a bit of the pleasantness had left his voice. The threat hidden in his words was impossible to ignore. I licked my suddenly-dry lips, doing my damndest to hold onto what little confidence I could.

"It is," I said, gripping the phone more tightly. "It's very nice. I'd offer to show you around, but I don't think that's why you're here."

Again, he laughed. "No, I'm afraid it's not, Mr. Christensen."

"It's Jon." I was *not* old enough to be a mister, and hearing him call me that was as unsettling as Aedan calling me Jonny was irritating.

"Jon, then," the man on the other end said. "I didn't know if you-"

"And your name?" I said, cutting him off. "I'd like to know who I'm speaking to."

"Of course. Entirely reasonable," he said, as smooth and polished as ever. "My name is Noah Wilson, Jon. A pleasure to finally speak to you."

"Right," I said sourly. "So. How exactly did you get my phone number, and-" I caught myself, grinding to a halt before I could finish my sentence. I was still confused, and more than a little worried, but if he was calling me on my cell phone then he was giving up on the idea of catching us unawares. Either they knew we had Greyson, and were trying to lull us into a false sense of security, or...

Or they weren't here looking for a fight. In which case, we needed to figure out what the hell was going on, *before* we started a war we didn't want in the first place.

"And, uh, why exactly have you come all the way here?" I amended hastily, falling back on what little I could remember of my presentations back in school. Public speaking had never been my forte, and talking to a rival demi from a crew probably more powerful than ours gave the conversation a level of risk far beyond a student's fear of his classmates. I was proud, though. My voice had only the tiniest quiver in it, small enough I was sure Noah wouldn't hear it. "I'm sure you're quite busy up in Canada. You *are* from the crew based out of Ontario, yes?"

"You've been watching, I take it?"

"Of course we are," I said wearily. "We'd be stupid to not."

"Well, yes. All the same, it's good to see you had at least *that* much sense," Noah said. He'd managed to wrestle his laughter into check, but I could still hear it underlying his words. "The reports I heard were...well. I'm relieved to hear that they weren't entirely accurate."

Someone else was there with him. I could hear them snickering. My grip on the phone tightened further, until I thought I could feel the entire thing flex a hair. Before I could say a word, though, Noah cut back in as though realizing their misstep. "Pardon me, pardon me. In any case, we've come quite a long way. Are you free to meet somewhere? We'd simply love to have a chance to talk to you. We have business that should be discussed."

"Business," I said flatly, leaning back on my heels. "What's that supposed to mean? Why should I go anywhere near you and whatever friends you brought? I have no intention of letting you-"

"Oh, really. We've come to talk. It's rare to see new crews crop up, but not unheard of. We'd thought that region just desolate emptiness, even if it's a part of our territory. Just a hunting ground, really. We've come to talk, not to kill." *For now.* He didn't say it, but I heard the words all the same.

The phone was still pressed to my ear. I hesitated, feeling the slow draw of air across my lips as I breathed in.

If this was a trap, then going to talk to them would put me right in the middle of the enemy's plans. I knew better than to hope I'd survive a mistake like that.

If this *wasn't*, though, and they were really here for some sort of truce deal, then choosing to ignore their offer would just start a fight. If I was wrong, and we went into a war we shouldn't have? The thought sickened me. Every wound, every death, would be on my shoulders.

My left hand slid up, grasping at the rings that hung around my neck as though searching for the faintest hint of warmth. They hung cold and heavy in my touch, dead and without even the tiniest fragment of magic. I knew the necklace wouldn't help me, wouldn't help my decision. Aedan had said it, after all, that fateful night months past. Relics and technology weren't compatible. Noah and I were talking so comfortably, and yet, there was no way I was going to be able to glean the truth in his words from the lies.

To do that, I needed to get closer.

Greyson had said there were two of them. I latched onto the thought, letting it circle in my mind. Two. Noah - and his colleague, laughing in the background. That much added up, so far as I could tell.

I could handle two. Somehow. If we had a shot at peace, or a guarantee of war, I owed it to the others to give the peaceful outcome the best shot I possibly could.

"Fine," I heard a voice saying. Distantly, I recognized it as my own. "Let's talk."

"Good," Noah said. I could hear his voice light up, like he was talking through a smile. "Very good. Now, there's a park on the west side of town with a-"

"No," I said, shaking my head violently. "Not there." I knew the park they were talking about, and there was nothing *wrong* with it, but the thought of them picking a location and me meekly driving over repulsed me. I didn't trust them - not even close. For all I knew, they'd have set booby traps all over the place. Like we'd tried our best to do around the house, I thought with a humorless smile. "Ah...we live a few miles out of town on-"

"I don't believe your land is the best place to hold negotiations of this importance, hmm?" Noah said, a disapproving lilt in his voice. "Somewhere more neutral would be better. Which was why-"

"Fine," I said, not bothering to sound surprised. I hadn't expected him to come to the house, not really. He wasn't stupid either, then. Well, at least I tried. "I understand." My mind raced. I *did* understand, but it didn't mean that I was willing to just roll over and do whatever he wanted, either. We needed another option. An independent location, somewhere that wasn't associated with us but which Noah wouldn't have been able to case.

A crooked smile tugged at my lips. "Then, if I might suggest..."

***

I set the phone down with a sigh. The others were staring, white-faced and ashen.

"Jon?" Brendon said hesitantly. "Are you...you can't possibly be-"

"We're not going to be stupid about this," I said, holding his gaze with my own. "Let's be careful. But at the same time, I think we have to at least hear what they have to say."

"And if it's a trap?" Jake called. He'd muted his soap opera at some point, even if he hadn't actually turned in his seat to look at me. "What then?"

"Then, there are only two of them."

"You *think* there are only two of them," he snapped, leaning back to glare at the ceiling. "If you're wrong, they'll kill you. If you're lucky."

"Then I'd better not be wrong," I said, feeling my heart thunder in my chest. He *did* turn around at that, narrowing his eyes at me. I smiled back as best I could. "Let's call the others back in. We need to talk."

Jake sighed dramatically, turning his glare on Brendon. "Go find Tyler and them, will you?"

The weather-seer froze for a second, pinned in place by the scathing intensity of it, but stumbled upright.

"Aedan!" Jake bellowed a heartbeat later, not waiting for Brendon to make it as far as the door.

I waited. The sounds of hand-to-hand combat outside died off - and then the door creaked open.

"What?" Aedan snapped, leaning in. "Don't call me like a goddamn dog. I'll-"

"They're here," I said.

He froze perfectly in place, unmoving. "Oh. Ontario?" he said at last.

I chuckled sourly. "Who else?"

"Oh."

"We'll be meeting them in town. They're already close, so we need to go," I said, as much for my own benefit as Aedan's.

He straightened. "Okay, then. We might have to take a few cars to get everyone squeezed in, but-"

"We're not *all* going," I said. Keira slipped through the door behind him, going still as she heard enough of the conversation to get up to speed. "There are only two of them. If we show up with a full crew to ambush them, it'll just turn into a fight. Or they'll leave, and come back with friends."

Aedan's lips curled down in the start of a scowl. "If it's going to come to blows, we should go in with a full team from the start."

"I can't tell if they're lying," I said quietly. "I'm sorry. I wish I could. We can have you nearby, with a few others. But-"

"Nearby?" he snapped, just a hair shy of a snarl. "What, you're not even letting me in on the fun? If you think you can order me to the sidelines, Jonny-"

"Until we know what's going on, we don't want to spook them," I said, keeping my voice low and level. If I ramped up to match Aedan's...intensity, then it would just turn into a screaming match. We needed to be more together than that. "That means we cooperate on this. I'll go in, with my second." My eyes lingered on his, holding his gaze. "That can't be you, Aedan. You're too conspicuous, and too well-known. There's already too many unknowns here to mix you into that shitstorm. If we declare you part of this crew's leadership-"

"Then there's no telling how far the gossip will spread. And the hunters will zero in. I get it," he spat.

And there was no way to tell how Aedan would react to the Ontario demis. The last thing we needed was him stabbing one of them for looking at him wrong. I didn't say it - I knew better than to say it - but I was thinking it. And from the way his nose wrinkled, Aedan knew I was thinking it.

"Un-fucking believable," he muttered, his eyes narrowing further. "And just who are you planning on taking, then?"

I felt a mirthless chuckle rumble up from my chest. "Jake. Shoes. Coat."

"What?" I heard the sleep-worker say, raw disbelief coloring his words.

I glanced over. He was finally looking back at me, staring dumbly. "If anyone in this crew is my second, it's you. You've been here longer and you know more about the surrounding crews than anyone but Amber and Nox. And if they're trouble, you can lay them out flat before they try anything." I hoped. I'd seen how fast Jake could work, from our first encounter in the forest to the fight with Glenn's crew. I could only pray that those weren't flukes, and he could reproduce it.

He shook his head, more firmly. "Hell no. I'm not going anywhere near that shit. You're on your own." Despite his words, I could see his expression shifting little by little. His eyebrows lifted gently, even as his lips curled up the tiniest fraction. He'd been in the game long enough to recognize when he'd gotten a promotion, and if we won our spot from the Ontario crew, that'd put him at the top of a promising new hierarchy. I could almost see the calculations flying past behind his eyes.

"Go put your coat on," I snapped, turning away to hide my laugh. "We don't have time to argue this." It wasn't a command. He rose all the same, still putting on a stubborn show, but turned towards the coat rack by the door.

"Is this a good idea?" Keira said. She hung by Aedan's side, her eyes drifting up to meet mine. "I don't know if we should be jumping into this."

"It's a risk," I said, unable to argue that much. "But we can manage it. We'll play it careful, Keira."

"Okay," she said, little more than a whisper. Her blue eyes were too-bright, and filled with more worry than I liked to see. "Don't-" She swallowed hard. "Don't get in a fight by yourselves," she muttered, glancing away.

The door creaked open for the second time, letting in the rest of our scattered crew. They were already still and quiet, pale-faced despite the cold. I smiled mirthlessly. Brendon had filled them in, then.

I fixed my gaze on Tyler as soon as he was through the door. He froze, staring right back.

"They're in town," I said without preamble, holding his eyes. "I...someone needs to go deal with them. Jake and I'll handle it."

"I'm going too," Aedan muttered, pulling his coat a little tighter.

I groaned. "Aedan, I told you, you can't-"

"If I can't meet them face to face, then I'll stay nearby," he snapped. "You're going to get in over your head, Jonny. Don't get big ideas you can't back up."

The retort that rose to my lips died as I paused. He wasn't wrong. "Fine," I muttered. "But you're driving separately." Him hopping out of the car ahead of our meeting would be nothing if not conspicuous.

"Fine," Aedan said, rolling his eyes. "Whatever makes you happier."

Tyler shifted from foot to foot, rubbing a bit of warmth back into his hands. "Slow down. What exactly is going on?"

"Jake and I are heading to....negotiate," I said, frowning. "Or whatever they want to talk about."

"Don't forget about-"

"Jake, Aedan, and I. I'm leaving you in charge here."

Another hush went around the room, quieting the murmured conversations that had been growing anew. I watched their faces, pretending I couldn't feel the hint of anxiety that sprang up anew.

If I was to pick the person I'd trust most, it would be Keira. But she was among the newest demis we had, and even with her relic, there was just too much she didn't know. She'd be guessing, as much as anything.

Tyler was a new addition to the group, but he'd been gifted for longer. He knew more about the world we lived in than she did. And I'd seen him handle Kai often enough that I didn't worry if he could maintain control.

For his part, Tyler didn't flinch. He went a bit white, the last hints of color fleeing his skin, but only nodded once and cleared his throat. "I understand. What...What are you expecting us to do?"

"Just get ready," I said, zipping my coat up and reaching for my keys. "If this goes well, we'll call home soon, and maybe we'll have guests for dinner."

His eyes were dark, unblinking. "And if it doesn't?"

"Watch the forest. Don't let them get the jump on you. Be ready for anything," Jake said roughly, surprising all of us by cutting in.

Tyler nodded slowly. "All right," he murmured. And then he turned on his heel, spinning to face the others.

I smiled as he launched into them, picking the other demis out one after another. He knew what he was doing, at least, and at the rate he was going he'd have a perimeter set up in minutes. I was already heading for the door, hearing Aedan and Jake stepping into line behind me.

The chilled air slapped me in the face as I walked for the car, trying not to look like I was hurrying. It was just another wake-up call, a reminder that this wasn't some sort of dream. Or a nightmare.

My skin shivered as I grabbed the ice-cold handle of the car door. "You know where we're going?" I said, half-turning to face Aedan as he pulled his door open. "It's-"

"Yeah, I heard," he said, not so much as glancing my way. "You're an ass for picking it, you know."

I chuckled. "I know. Not too close. Don't get spotted."

"Don't get *shot*," he retorted, offering me a smirk a heartbeat before he flopped into the driver's seat. He slammed the door shut before I could respond.

Jake was already buckling himself in when I settled into the seat, sliding the key into the ignition. "You sure about this?" he said, looking out the window. "There's still time. We could-"

"It's no different now than it was before," I said, raising my voice over the sound of the engine roaring to life. I'd put the car in gear before it was at a normal idle, turning us out onto the drive. Aedan's lights shone through our rear window. "If we run off now, we'll just get scattered. No one *wanted* this space, before now. There was no one here. We'll never find a better home."

"I think they might disagree with you about the whole 'no one was here' thing," Jake said, making a face. "And there are always other homes."

I glanced at him sidelong, my foot resting against the brakes as we approached the main road. "We don't know that."

He snorted. "If I'm your second, then at least let me warn you," he muttered. "I did *not* volunteer for that kind of responsibility, by the way. Don't expect me to do your paperwork."

"We're not the army. We don't have paperwork."

"Can I get that in writing?"

I wasn't fooled. He was blustering, making faces and complaining like he always did, but his voice lacked the sourness of true irritation. He sounded angrier when someone asked him to take the damn trash out.

"I just know everyone wanted peace and quiet," I said, watching the skips start flying past under our tires. I felt like I was having the same conversation over and over, but it felt wrong to ignore the elephant in the room. "I feel like I lied to people, right now."

"Well, it makes a nice story, but it's just not realistic," Jake said, grabbing at the handle down alongside his seat. The seat back reclined with a *thump* a moment later, dropping him from sight. "Rather than pretending we could all braid daisies and skip through the fields together, let's let them know we're too much of a pain to deal with," he said. His hand dropped onto his face, blocking his eyes from sight. "That'll be enough."

"Right," I muttered. "So, are you-"

"You're already trashing all my carefully-laid plans for the evening," Jake snapped, half-turning towards the car door. "Don't make this worse by expecting me to actually talk to you."

Right. I swallowed a chuckle and turned my attention back to the road.

Aedan's headlights glinted in my vision, following us like a brilliant shadow as we sped onward.

***

The car groaned as I hit the brakes. The gleaming lights of the parking lot lit up the world ahead, drawing us in like a beacon.

Jake popped back up to upright as I turned us into the first open parking spot. For all he'd fussed and grumped about coming, his eyes were sharp as he stared at the building beyond.

It wasn't perfect - but we'd needed somewhere we could be among the masses and yet invisible, public and private. Somewhere we could meet without being afraid the other demis were going to up and attack us before we even knew what was going on.

A crooked smile crept onto my face as I stepped out of the car, looking towards the glowing red-and-gold shape of the McDonald's.

The fact Aedan couldn't follow us in without drawing undue attention - something even he'd think twice about - was just a side benefit.

"Ready?" I said, tearing my eyes off the building to look at Jake.

He nodded, masking a yawn behind his hand. He stepped a bit closer to me, though, and from the barely-visible outline of something tucked under his coat, I knew he'd come armed. So had I. I just hoped we wouldn't need it.

The sounds of the store washed over us as we stepped inside - the angry chirping of machines, the quiet murmur of voices, the scream of the drive-through alarm. All of it was drowned out with the stink of fryer grease and cooking beef.

Just like I remembered it. How comforting.

I stepped towards the smiling brunette behind the register, trying to get a look at the other customers without seeming like I was casing the place. "Uh. Hi," I muttered at last, flashing a quick smile to match hers.

It only took a few moments for me to stumble through an order, doing my best to keep my eyes on the cashier, and slide my debit card into the slot. Jake and I slid towards the pop machine as soon as the cups were in our hands, huddled together like damn gazelles listening for the lion in the bushes.

They were already there when we turned back around, sipping our drinks apprehensively.

I flinched at the sight of the two men, standing casually a few feet back. There was no doubting who they were, what their purpose was. Not when their eyes were fixed on us, razor-sharp and without even the slightest hint of fear.

"You're Noah, I take it," I said, forcing the words past my suddenly-numb lips. We couldn't start this off as the underdogs. We needed to establish our dominance early and often, if we were going to convince them we owned this part of the state. I stuck my hand out, willing my fingers not to shake. "I'm-"

"Mr. Christensen," Noah said, a wide, honest smile breaking across his face.

Something caught in my breath, echoed by a warning pang of heat from my necklace. It outlined the coldness of his eyes, the places where that smile didn't quite reach. There was nothing so honest about his expression, it seemed to say.

As though I needed it to tell me that.

"It's Jon," I said roughly, still holding my hand out.

"Jon, then," Noah said, taking my hand at last. "The silvertongue we've heard so much about."

He'd heard about us, then. About me. The statement sent off warning alarms through my mind. How? From whom? The other demis I'd dealt with had all wound up dead or part of the crew. So far as I knew, I told myself, feeling a chill run down my spine. The woman in the treeline flashed through my mind. Was it her? Were there others? Or was it someone from inside the crew?

I didn't like any of the possibilities. But I just forced a smile onto my face, every bit as fake as Noah's, and inclined my head in a nod.

"Uh...I guess?" I said, not having to try and summon up the uncertainty that filled my tone. I hadn't heard *that* title before. "Um...where should we-"

"There's a table in the back. It's a little quieter," Noah said, gesturing. I could see the table he meant, empty and deserted in the farthest corner of the restaurant.

He wanted me to lead the way, I realized. Gauging my reaction. Seeing how I'd feel, having him at my back. I swallowed a snort. For people who were supposed to be shrewd businessmen, they didn't seem all that subtle.

"Sounds good," I muttered, jerking my chin for Jake to follow. He hung back a step, keeping just enough space between himself and the others to watch them.

As I turned towards the table, biting back a sigh, I caught sight of him - Aedan, leaning against the side of his car in the lot. His eyes were fixed on mine, green and every bit as sharp as Noah's had been. He just waited, motionless and staring.

At least he knew better than to come charging in. I didn't dare try and wave or nod or signal at all. He'd know that. Probably.

Still, knowing that he was there, that we weren't totally and completely alone...it *did* make me feel a little better.

I set my cup down on the table, sliding onto the bench, and felt Jake sit beside me. My attention was fixed on Noah and his still-unnamed colleague. The demi had remained silent, letting Noah do the talking much as Jake had ceded the floor to me. But he was *big*. He stared at me from under short-cropped blond hair, cold and expressionless.

Wonderful.

"Well, then, Jon," Noah said, sitting down with a sigh. He laid his elbows on the table, settling in, and fixed me with another one of those winning smiles.

I smiled frigidly back, keeping my hands wrapped around my cup. I had a knife in my pants pocket, and a gun in my jacket. But with all the customers around us, all the bystanders, there was no way I could act. I had to trust that his intentions were as peaceful as he'd said. My fingers tightened against the plastic as he leaned closer, eyes fixed on mine.

"My colleague and I have a deal we'd like to discuss with you."

CHAPTER FORTY-EIGHT

"A deal," I said, staring across the table at the two men.

Noah's smile widened. "A deal."

A deal. I chewed on the idea, letting the words roll around and around in my head. We'd known that something was wrong, when they'd shown up with only two demis. That something was strange.

All the same, I couldn't quite buy into the idea that they'd traveled all this way, deep into enemy territory, just to make nice with us. Given my experiences with the world of demis so far, I just couldn't believe things would work out so smoothly.

But my relic lay quiet and calm against my chest, safely hidden under my shirt and jacket.

And so I leaned back, putting a bit more distance between myself and Noah. "I'm listening."

He was beginning to look more than a little smug. "Well, I guess I should start by telling you a bit about us, shouldn't I? Myself and my partner - oh, this is Ethan. Ethan Harding."

Ethan waved a hand in my general direction. His glare didn't falter, and he didn't say so much as a word.

"Nice to meet you," I said, beginning to falter under the intensity of his gaze. "This is Jake Cooper, by the way. One of my team."

"The pleasure is ours," Noah said, pulling my eyes back to him instantly. "We're here, Jon, as representatives of our crew. Normally, we range just beyond the Canadian border."

"The marketeers," I said before I could stop myself. Jake groaned beside me, the sound soft enough I was sure only I'd hear it.

Noah chuckled, shaking his head slowly. "Yes, that nickname really has clung to life, hasn't it? It's not a name we chose, but...if you like."

He leaned forward again, splaying his fingers out in front of him. "Our organization, Jon, goes beyond just one crew. It goes beyond just one country, even. We have connections, you see. Ties to crews in ten different countries, all around the world."

"I see," I said, lifting my drink to take a sip. I tried to make the action seem nonchalant. I wasn't sure it'd worked. "Impressive."

"We do well enough for ourselves," Noah said, waving a hand dismissively. "But you see, Jon, that the services we offer are really quite varied."

His hand flipped, resting palm-down against the table as he jabbed fingers out one after another.

"I believe you've heard of some of our wares, yes? We offer foci for sale, of course. They're a precious resource, after all, and for many crews, it's the only way to increase their ranks." His smile gleamed in the fluorescent light, oily and all too genuine. "Some are more interested in....rentals, we'll say."

"Slaves." I couldn't stop myself, and I didn't really want to. Even if I knew that we were best served by making peace, it needed to be said, damn it.

Noah shrugged. Ethan was a motionless wall beside him. "Such an unpleasant term. We prefer to view it as assisting these creatively gifted demis in finding long-term homes."

"Right," I muttered. I wanted to argue - I *really* wanted to argue - but there were limits to how much I could afford to piss them off.

"It's not just that, though!" Noah said, cutting back in smoothly through the gap I'd left him. "No, no. Everyone wants to earn a living, right? And with gifts like ours, there are just so many ways to do it. Our crews help to match crews who need a little extra help with the demis who can give it."

I nodded begrudgingly. "Mercenaries."

He beamed. "Ah, good! Yes, mercenaries. And finders, and appraisal services, and defensive contracts..." He trailed off at last, spreading his hands. "It's no small task, but we've always enjoyed a challenge."

"Is there a reason you're giving us the verbal tour?" Jake said at last, breaking free of his silence for a brief instant before continuing to suck at his drink.

Noah's smile went flint-hard. "Well, you see, I just wasn't sure if you understood." His hands dropped back to the table, folded neatly in front of him. "I want to make sure you well and truly *know* how big the toes you've chosen to step on are."

I shook my head. "We never meant to step on anyone's toes," I said, my pulse accelerating at the new, ominous tone in his voice. "We never wanted to interfere with your crew."

"And yet, you did interfere, didn't you?" Noah said, still staring at me with that polite little smile on his face. "You attacked demis on their way through our territory. You stole from them, and used the power to grow your own crew."

"We were just helping two people in need."

"You killed on our land. You're building your own little army, aren't you? Hardly the act of someone who wants to remain neutral."

I stopped, my words dying on my lips at the look in his eyes. It wasn't so subtle, anymore - we were on the defensive here. Like it or not, from their perspective, it probably *would* look like we were trying to steal land out from under them, and I didn't quite know how to get around that.

I wasn't sure there *was* a way around the truth of the matter, honestly.

"So why are you here?" I said, squeezing my drink a little harder. My knuckles stood out white against my skin. "If we're so hostile, why would you invite yourselves in for a talk?"

Noah chuckled, low and soft. "Well, Jon, like I said. We have a deal."

He paused, eyeing me as though expecting me to jump in with an interjection. I didn't. I wasn't quite sure what I *could* say, if I wanted to get us out of the damn restaurant alive.

When I didn't answer, he smiled again. "This whole region is a little...desolate, isn't it? If I'm being honest. There's just not a lot here. Not a lot of people, not a lot of wealth, and not a lot of demis. Just...forest."

"Pretty much," I said, my mouth going dry. "So-"

"So this whole gloomy forest has really just been our hunting ground, so far," Noah said, not hesitating as he plowed right over the top of me. "Somewhere for us to corner rogues, where no one will bother us. Somewhere outsiders have to pass through, if they're coming to sell their goods at the northern outpost."

He paused again, watching me. I gave the tiniest nod I could, not quite sure I could talk. His smirk grew.

"In short, Jon, your being here isn't a problem in and of itself," Noah said, pinning me in place with his stare. "The *problem* is a rival crew blossoming right under our asses."

"It's not our intention to come after you," I said, giving my head a quick shake.

"You already have."

"We didn't-"

"We can overlook your crew's existence," Noah interrupted, his eyes narrowing further, "If you were to continue to exist as a branch under our own control."

I stopped, his words flashing through my mind. "You want us to join your organization."

"In short."

"Just like that."

"There would be terms, of course," Noah said, his tone cheerful despite the iron underlying it. "Your crew would be independent, but beholden to ours."

"A puppet."

"If you want to think about it like that. We have to maintain order, you see."

I could feel my face flushing red as my frustrations rose. We hadn't come so far, done so much, just to hand control of ourselves over to an enemy crew. We'd be giving up on everything we'd gained.

But the possibility of peace was there. I bit back my complaints, doing my best not to glare at Noah.

Jake shifted uncomfortably beside me. "Like hell we'll-"

I kicked him under the table. He shut up. "Go on," I said, still staring at the pair.

A smirk flickered across Noah's face, like Jake's outburst hadn't been overlooked. "As a member of the fold, you are to stop attacking travelers immediately. It isn't your place to interfere with Marketeer business."

Turn a blind eye to everything they were doing, in other words. A fresh wave of anger flared up.

"There are other stipulations as well, of course," Noah continued, waving a hand as if to brush off the rest. "You'd be required to muster forces to assist the organization, as needed. And to properly coordinate your crew's integration, a representative would return to Ontario with us on a semi-permanent basis." His smile turned even more smug. "Someone with the skills I've heard you have would be requested, I'm certain. Most useful."

Jake muttered something under his breath, too quiet and angry to understand. I just stared.

"You want me to leave Greenville," I said, buying myself time while my thoughts raced past. "Let me guess - you'll send someone right down to take my place."

"Of course not," Noah said, shaking his head more firmly. "You have your own staff here, don't you?" His eyes flicked to Jake - whose lip curled up ever so slightly at being called my 'staff'. Noah chuckled. "I'm sure your crew will manage just fine in your absence."

He kept talking like this was already decided, like it was set in stone. I hated it. But as much as the thought of putting myself right in the center of their domain repulsed me, of making myself a hostage for the crew's safety, I couldn't entirely dismiss it offhand, either.

"What assurances do I have that you're not just saying all this?" I said. From the corner of my eye, I could see Jake's head snap around to fix on me. I ignored him. "How do I know you're not going to turn on them the minute I'm out of the picture?"

"You'll just have to trust me, won't you?" Noah said, tilting his head to one side. "Besides, we've really got nothing to gain by lying to you."

And as suspicious as I was of his intentions, so far as I could tell, he *wasn't* lying. His words had rung true, no falsehoods or deceit that I could find.

I swallowed hard, seeing the writing on the wall. It wasn't what I wanted. I *really* didn't like the idea of what he was proposing. And yet, if we could make it through without any violence…my going with them wasn't something we should reject without at least giving it consideration. Jake kicked me. I didn't turn.

"Of course, as a show of good faith, there are some bridges to mend," Noah said.

It was enough to bring my thoughts grinding to a halt. "What?"

"It's only fair, really. Whatever your reasons, you disrupted our business. The other branches will want to see that proper order was maintained."

My brow furrowed as I stared at him. "What do you mean?"

"You stole from us," Noah said, enunciating each syllable clearly.

"I'm willing to overlook that. Move past it, for the benefit of both our crews. But our stolen merchandise will have to be returned, naturally."

"...You've got to be kidding me." Only after a long moment did I recognize the voice that had spoken as my own.

Ethan stiffened in his seat, his head turning slowly so that his steely gaze was fixed on me.

Noah patted his shoulder reassuringly. "If something has happened, of course, we'd be more than willing to accept the foci alone. We're not unreasonable." He shrugged, turning back to me. "And, of course, we'll be waiving any payment to your crew for the services of your demis until the cancellation fees for the contracts you ruined with that little stunt are paid off."

"You expect me to hand you two of my people. Just like that," I said slowly. My right hand was frozen around my drink, locked into place, while my left balled into a fist in my lap.

Jake kicked me again. I stared right at Noah, ignoring his bone-white face.

"Come, now," he said, leaning forward onto his elbows. "That whole mess was only a month or two past, yes? They're hardly irreplaceable." His eyes were razor-sharp, despite his pleasant words.

He knew. I was completely certain of it - he knew *exactly* what he was asking of me, knew that he was sliding needles under my fingernails by even bringing the subject up. And that's why he'd demanded it. If I was greedy like Matt, he'd probably have ordered I hand over a pile of cash, instead.

He was just after whatever he thought was going to sufficiently kick us into submission.

Through the wave of sheer repulsion that washed over me, I hesitated. There it was - the decision point, the moment where we had to choose. And staring the two demis in the face, I wasn't so sure anymore that there was a way out that left our hands clean.

The sight of Brendon standing by that wall flashed through my mind, one bloodied fist clutching his relic. The sight of Loren side by side with Jake in the forest, grinning more openly than I'd seen from her since she arrived.

If I sold them right back to this asshole to protect our own skins, there'd be no way for me to face Aedan afterward. No way for me to claim I was in it for the right reasons, versus greed and power and the want to protect my own worthless skin.

Even if that meant fighting.

"This is a lot to think about," I heard myself say. My voice was carefully level, more controlled than I'd have thought possible. "I think a decision this important should be considered carefully."

"It should," Noah said, his smile starting to fade. "The opportunity you've been offered is...not insignificant." The good humor had slipped from his voice somewhere along the line - right about where I hadn't leapt at his offer, I thought with a crooked smile. He didn't return the gesture. "It will not be offered a second time, and the consequences for your crew for a hasty decision would be dire."

He talked pretty, but he wasn't bothering to mask his threats. The combination of subtlety and brute force was probably meant to leave me uncertain. I just felt tired, with a sick, queasy feeling lurking in the pit of my stomach.

"Right. That," I said, uncurling my fingers enough to let go of my cup and run a hand through my hair. "So....mind if we sleep on it? Talk amongst ourselves? Give it some proper thought?"

Noah frowned. The expression looked odd on the polished, refined man. "You're the leader of your crew, aren't you?"

"Uh....yes? I suppose?"

"If you speak for your people, then I'd think you'd be capable of making your own decisions."

"Give it a rest," Jake muttered, glaring darkly at the demi.

"Excuse me?" Noah said, his eyes narrowing as he turned to my companion.

"Don't mind him. Hasn't had his dinner yet. Always puts him in a bad mood," I said, glaring daggers at Jake until he looked away, scowling more deeply. A sigh slipped between my lips. "I understand where you're coming from. Really, I do. But I can't make a decision like this offhand." My eyes drifted back to meet Noah's. "There are hotels in town. Give us one night."

For a long, hard moment we stared at each other. His gaze was hard, unblinking. I matched it as best I could, willing him to listen.

One night. Given one night, we could pull ourselves together. We could run, maybe, like Jake had said, or at least buy ourselves more time. If things went to shit, it wouldn't just be the two of them here anymore. I knew that much. We just needed one night. I fixed every bit of sheepishness I could into my expression. We only had one shot to make this believable.

But his eyes darkened, narrowing further as his brows drew closer together.

Shit. He wasn't buying it. Not at *all.* The time for waiting was over. With one last wistful thought, I drew in a lungful of air.

But as my lips parted, readying a command, a leaden weight settled across my shoulders. I wilted like a dried-up flower, coming to rest with my elbows on the table.

"You're stubborn," I heard Noah said. His voice wasn't so refined, anymore. There was a coarse, tired aspect of it that hadn't shown through before. "I respect that. I really do. But it's unfortunate." His hand patted down onto my shoulder.

I wanted to move - to talk, to punch him in his devious, manipulative teeth. But right then, it all seemed like work. And I was tired, more exhausted than I'd been in my whole life. Moving was an impossible feat.

"Don't worry. I still think you'll come around," I heard him say. Metal scraped against the tile floor as his partner pushed away from the table, standing up in a slow, ponderous motion. "Someone with your talents is too valuable to throw away. You just need to see the big picture."

I sagged lower, feeling the wall of fog settle more thoroughly over my mind. "No matter. I really do think you'll see reason," Noah said, his voice distant. Something patted my side. His hand, reaching into my coat pocket. He slid my phone free, accompanied by a jingle of metal, and set it on the table in front of me. The sound of him patting it echoed through my ears. "When you've had enough, you know how to reach me."

The jingling rose with his hand, silenced in a single second as he leaned away and shoved his hands into his pockets. He'd taken something from me. I twitched, fighting against whatever he'd done, but scrounging up the energy was beyond me. I could only stare blankly at the table, mute and motionless.

The sound of the door was followed by a rush of cold air - and then only silence.

Jake's leg was warm against mine, still sitting on the bench next to me. He was still there, then. Distantly, the part of my mind still functioning screamed that we needed to move, that we needed to race home or call Greyson or Tyler or do something, *anything* but sit there.

With that horrible exhaustion sinking deeper and deeper into my skin with every passing second, though, I could only lean forward, resting my cheek against the smooth, cool surface of the table. I couldn't. It was useless to fight. Easier to wait, to sit and-

The doorbell rang again. I didn't so much as twitch, even when the cold breeze washed across the dining room. Footsteps rang in my ears, loud and sharp. Jake sighed beside me, the sound every bit as thin and weary as I felt.

Something grabbed my hair. A hand. It yanked me upright before I could muster up the nonexistent will to pull away, bringing me face to face with Aedan.

An *angry* Aedan. I had just long enough to make note of the fire in his green eyes before his open palm drove home into my cheek. Hard.

I gasped, the stinging pain flashing across my cheek overcoming even the fog for an instant.

"Wake the fuck *up*," I heard him snarl, dropping me back in my seat. I fell heavily onto the plastic bench. The sound of skin slapping skin cracked out beside me. Startled cries rose from the other customers, growing by the second.

The fog cleared with every breath I took, every pang of sore skin. I shook my head, blinking it away - in time to take another slap to the face.

"Seriously, Jon, I do not have time for your-"

"I'm up," I gasped, reeling. My hand snapped up to grab his wrist. I missed. His palm cracked across my cheek again.

"Really?" he said, pausing. And then he turned on Jake, smacking him one last time. "Then let's fucking *go* already."

All right, claiming I was totally up might have been a lie. I shook my head, like that was going to help me clear away the fog. "W-What?"

Aedan just made an irritated noise in the back of his throat and buried his hand in my jacket. I tumbled across the corner of the table a second later as he ripped me from my seat. My pained yelp didn't slow him down in the slightest. "Hurry *up*," he snapped, likewise pulling Jake to his feet. "We need to move. We're up shit creek here, boys."

"Le'go'me," Jake croaked, swiping for Aedan with an unsteady fist. The immortal just ducked the blow, dragging us onward.

My steps grew stronger with every footfall, until by the time we reached the door I almost felt like myself again. Jake's protests fell away as he likewise awakened from whatever Noah had done to us.

Aedan paused for the slightest fraction of a second, grinning over his shoulder. "Feel better?"

I wiped a hand across my face, a sick feeling growing in the pit of my stomach. "I...guess."

"Then come on." With one last tug he reached out, slamming the door open. The cold winter air blasted against my face.

"Greg?" a voice said behind us, filled with confusion. I glanced back, getting a single glimpse of the brunette behind the counter peering after us.

She vanished a moment later as Aedan plowed out into the night, pulling us in his wake.

CHAPTER FORTY-NINE

The cold air did wonders as I stumbled out into the quiet. Aedan's hand was wrapped around my forearm, towing me on.

"Where...what do you think they're doing?" I mumbled, swallowing hard. Jake staggered on alongside me, wordless.

Aedan snorted. "You're not stupid, Jonny. Wake the hell up. My car's over there."

"I *am* awake," I mumbled. "And I can drive. I'm right over-" I plunged my hand into my pocket as I spoke, and froze. My steps came grinding to a halt.

My keys were gone. And so was my car, I saw when I twisted to face where I'd parked.

"They-"

"Yeah, they stole your car," Aedan said, rolling his eyes. "Guess they didn't want you chasing them, if you managed to wake yourself up somehow. Like I said. I'm over there."

Shit. My stomach churned, roiling unhappily. It was my *car*. Sure, it was riddled with bullet holes after our last encounter, and the backseat still looked like someone had given birth on it, but it was mine. I'd *liked* it, damn it.

I stared at the parking space where it had sat, my eyes fixed on the empty spot as though I could will it back into existence. Aedan groaned, grabbing hold of my arm again. "Jesus fuck, Jon, it's gone. Come *on*."

Jake didn't say a word. He'd gone pale, somewhere in the distance between the table and the parking lot. I just bit back my complaints, letting Aedan lead us to the car. Jake didn't *have* to say anything. I already knew how bad this was, how big a mess we were in.

The car door creaked ominously as I pulled it open. I hesitated, staring at the frame that seemed to be as much rust as metal. Aedan was already throwing himself into the driver's seat, plunging the key into the ignition. He glared at me as the engine coughed and sputtered to life. "Sit down."

"Right," I muttered, remembering myself. It wasn't the time to worry about tetanus. Noah and Ethan had enspelled us, freezing us in place - and then took off with our car. It didn't take a genius to figure out they weren't the friendly figures we'd hoped for, and that meant nothing positive for the rest of our group.

The rest of the crew. My mind latched onto the thought as Aedan slammed the car into reverse, accelerating backwards out of the spot with a roar of tires. I grabbed my phone back out of my pocket. The screen tilted madly in my hands as we veered out onto the roadway.

My contact list glowed up at me from its surface. I grabbed hold of the oh-shit handle as we took another corner on two wheels. "Aedan, you might be immortal, but we're not," I snapped, glancing over at him. "Please don't-"

"Shut the hell up and let me drive," he spat. The engine roared even louder as he accelerated. To spite me, I was sure. Jake just clung to the back of my seat in a desperate bid to stay upright, his fingers brushing my shoulders.

"Whatever," I muttered, turning my attention back to my phone. My thumb jabbed down onto a name, and I slapped the phone up against my ear a second later.

Keira. If Noah and Ethan were setting out to 'convince' me that it was smarter to join their side than turn them down, there weren't too many options they'd have. The others needed to know. They needed to be ready.

Distantly, the little voice in the back of my mind whispered that there was no telling how long we'd sat around that table, dazed and listless. Long enough for Aedan to get suspicious and barge in, certainly. But I didn't *know*.

The call tone buzzed in my ear. My fingers danced against my leg, anxiety starting to blend together with fear in one seamless mass of dread. "Come on," I whispered, my eyes tightening on the road ahead as the trees whipped past with terrifying speed. "Pick up, damn it."

The line clicked. My heart leapt. "Keira. Are you-"

"*Keira Christensen's phone. I'm not here. Leave your-*"

"Fuck!" I snapped, tearing the phone from my ear and silencing the machine with a smash from my thumb.

Aedan didn't say a word, but I saw his hands tighten on the wheel. The engine roared louder.

I was too busy scrolling through the list of names to yell at him for driving like a madman. The fact that Keira hadn't answered her phone wasn't damning in and of itself. It *wasn't*. Maybe she was watching TV. Maybe it was on silent. Maybe she'd forgotten it somewhere. But it wasn't a good sign, either, and I needed to know they were all right.

Hitting the call button, I again lifted the phone to my ear. And again, I waited, my heart in my throat, as the sound of ringing played from the speaker. Tyler. Keira was my first choice, but I'd left Tyler in charge. He'd pick up if he saw me calling. He'd know it was serious. They couldn't *all* have lost their phones.

The seconds ticked away as I sat, gripping the phone more tightly with every ring. I didn't bother muttering this time. After the third chime, I already knew it was hopeless.

"*Tyler Morgan,*" the pre-recorded message sang out in a disconcertingly cheerful voice. "I can't get to the phone right now, so-*"

I ended the call before it could finish the greeting, dropping my phone in my lap and pressing a hand to my forehead.

"Shit," Aedan muttered.

Jake shifted in the backseat, pulling himself closer. "Nothing?"

I stared straight ahead, focusing on the road. "Nothing."

"Oh."

My fingers twitched. Should I call Greyson? They might be coming for him, if they knew he existed. Did they? My mind raced back through our conversation. My blood chilled. I'd...I'd said too much, hadn't I? They'd know. They'd have to know. And if they were half as good as they said they were, they'd have known before they came in the first place. It wasn't my fault. Probably. It was the only relief I could cling to.

No. Greyson would be watching. He'd know the risks, and he'd been in the game for a long time. He wasn't stupid. He knew to get himself out , if things started going south. He'd be pragmatic, like always. And without knowing what all of their powers were, I needed to keep myself apart from him as much as possible. It was the safest way.

Aedan's *shit* was right on the money. We were in trouble. There were only two of them, I reminded myself - but that didn't mean anything. They would have come prepared. They would have been ready for us to turn them down. Why, why hadn't I spoken just a little earlier? Why hadn't I gotten them under my control, and forestalled this entire series of events?

Because we hadn't *known*, I reminded myself. We didn't know what they were prepared to do.

I just hoped that we weren't too late, now that we *did* know.

"Can't you go any faster?" I found myself saying, glancing over at Aedan.

He grinned, the expression looking more like a grimace than anything. "Careful, Jonny. We're almost there."

"I know."

His eyes flicked to the side, meeting mine for a split second before refocusing on the road. "You ready?"

I didn't bother asking what for. I might be an idiot, but there were limits. "I... yeah."

"Really," he said, casting another look my way. "You're giving me tons of confidence here."

"I don't fucking know, Aedan," I snapped. "We're in too deep. The things he was saying, the ties they've got-"

"Woah, woah, woah," he said, cutting me off with a brisk shake of his head. "Get your head out of your ass, Jon. They're only human. Mostly. And they've got other shit that needs protecting. They wouldn't come down on a crew like yours with everything they've got. So stop panicking."

I glared at him, tight-lipped. "And what about tomorrow, Aedan? Next week? Next month? We can't afford to have an enemy like them." I ran a hand through my hair, feeling the panic building again. "Shit. We can't win a long-term fight like that. We need to-"

Aedan slammed the brakes. The words left me in a rush as I flew forward, hitting the seat belt hard. Jake careened into my seat back a moment later, letting out a strangled gasp.

"I'm dead serious, Jonny. You're not a fucking kid, so pull yourself together already," he snapped, shooting me a look that would cut glass. "Your crew expects you to be a grown-ass adult, so start acting like it." He hit the accelerator again. Jake and I lurched back into our seats.

Aedan turned to the road without a second glance. "We'll do what we have to do. Right?"

I swallowed hard. That *hurt*, damn it. I could still feel where the seat belt had cut into my skin. It'd probably bruise. But as much as I hadn't liked being thrown around like a doll, the pain helped. It sliced straight through the confusion and the terror, letting the 'now' shine through just a little.

"Yeah," I muttered, settling myself back into my seat. "I get it." I slid a hand into my jacket, feeling the weight of the gun still tucked within. "We'll...we'll figure it out."

"Right," Jake said from behind me. His voice was even more subdued than usual. I glanced back. His eyes were downcast, fixed in his lap, but his jaw was set. When he saw me looking, he made an irritated noise and looked away. "One step at a time."

I nodded. "Right. We've been here before, I guess." A crooked, mirthless smile crept onto my face. "Least I've got a gun."

"And a relic worth a damn," Aedan said from the driver's seat. "Finally."

I glared at him. He only smirked, keeping his eyes firmly on the road.

Shifting in my seat, I scowled. "It wasn't *that-*"

"Eyes sharp," he said, his eyes widening a fraction of an inch. "We're nearly there."

My words died on my lips as I spun, pressing myself back into my seat. He was right. The trees cleared from around us, growing more familiar by the second. In just a few moments, we'd be out of the thickest part of the forest, and in sight of the-

Aedan slammed on the brakes again. I hit the seat belt for a second time, wheezing painfully. Jake yelped from the backseat. Aedan didn't say a word. He just spun the wheel, turning us off the road and nestling us behind a copse of trees. I eyed the snow nervously as I leaned back, remembering what I'd seen of his rustbucket. We were getting into deeper drifts, and the only thing keeping us going was momentum.

I cleared my throat. "Uh, Aedan, I don't think we're really set up for off-roading."

"They're here."

At his terse, hissed words, I froze. "What?"

The car came sliding to a stop, half-hidden in the shadows off the drive. Aedan threw it into park, pulling his seat belt off in the same smooth motion. "Look. Over there."

My eyes followed his finger, pointing further up the drive towards the house. "I...I don't-"

And then I saw it. My breath caught in my throat as I stared, struck dumb by the sight of the van pulled up in our driveway.

It was a sizeable thing, with the rugged, dulled look that said it hadn't seen a coat of paint in far too many years. It *worked* for a living.

Whatever Noah and them had done, whatever games they were playing, they hadn't come alone. I grabbed for the handle, feeling the icy chill of adrenaline flood my veins again.

Aedan grabbed for my elbow like he was going to hold me inside the car, but I was already out. Jake was right behind me, wide-eyed and gaping. A single step away from the car filled my shoes with frigid snow. I didn't notice. I was too busy staring at the house.

It had been quiet in the car, with the purr of the engine and the windows around us to keep the noise out. Outside, without even that shelter between us and the night, I could hear everything.

Voices, from somewhere nearby. From the house. *Our* house. There were people there, on *our* land, in *our* house. The crackle of explosions and energy hummed just under the surface, ready and waiting. The air itself seemed to carry an odor, a strange, sharp tang I'd never smelled before. It made my nose tingle unpleasantly. At least I knew what magic smelled like now.

There were other demis here - and they were casting.

As though it had been waiting for me to finally get acclimated, a gunshot rang out. I stiffened. Another followed it - and another.

The first had been enough to send a shock through my senses, pulling me from my thoughts like a lightning bolt. I leapt forward, my hand plunging into my coat for where my own gun waited. "Shit. They're-"

A force snapped me back around, sending me off-balance and off-course. Aedan. His hand was still outstretched, poised in the air from where he'd hit me. I couldn't quite see his face in the darkened forest, but his whole frame quivered with tension.

But he'd *hit* me. "Aedan, why the hell are you wasting my time?" I snapped. I drew back all the while, half-turning towards the house again, but his arm latched around my neck in a headlock. I was taller than him - he had to reach up to do it - but his arm might as well have been made out of iron for all I could pull away.

"If you charge in there, what good is it going to do?" Aedan hissed. His face was inches from mine, just a mass of shadows. Jake inched closer. His pistol already gleamed in his hand, and his eyes were fixed on the house. "You need to *think*, Jon."

Someone yelled. I didn't recognize the voice, distorted by the distance and the pain that ran through its tones. I spun on my heel, twisting in Aedan's hold. He clung to me relentlessly, not giving an inch.

Abandoning my attempt, I turned just far enough to glare at him. "They're in trouble. We need to *go*. Jesus, Aedan, let me-"

"We don't know how many there are, or what we're up against," Aedan said, unblinking. "If you run in there like a chicken with your damn head cut off, you'll just get yourself killed before we have a chance to help. *Think*."

I faltered. It was impossible to argue with the intensity in his stare, or his logic. With adrenaline flooding my system, I could hardly think straight. And yet, here he was, just as cool and methodical as always. He'd always been like that, I realized. Sure, he was an unpredictable asshole, but he'd been every bit as together during our fight with Matt's crew as he was right then.

How many times had he died? The thought lanced across my mind, cutting right through my fear and dread. How many times had he raced headlong into a fight, only to pay the price? How many times had he chosen his path knowing that he'd die and be reborn at the end of it?

His stare was still locked onto mine, daring me to contradict him. I forced myself to calm down, to stop panting and gasping for breath like an animal. I'd known this was going to be a fight. It wasn't a surprise. I'd been hoping for a *little* more time, sure, but now that we knew we weren't going to get it...

It wasn't easy to push the fear away. I did the best I could, turning back towards the house once the nervous energy had faded the tiniest fraction. This time, Aedan let me.

I scanned the scene, urgency giving me new focus. The van. Distantly, shapes moved in the darkness. Ours? Theirs? I didn't know. Another gunshot, from farther away. More yelling. And a flash of fire, splitting the night with its brilliant glow. Kai.

He was still fighting. And so were the others, if there was this much noise. They hadn't given in. And we just had to find them. That was all.

One step at a time.

"The forest," I said, tearing my eyes off the house to eye Aedan and Jake. "We can circle around. Get a better view, maybe. Figure out what's going on." I fixed my gaze on Jake, locking stares with him. "Keep an eye on our asses. If we're heading that way, they might be too. Put them on the ground as soon as you see them. It's all on you. If-"

"If we shoot, they'll know where we are," Jake said. His voice was little more than a whisper. He understood the mess we were in, then. But his gaze was steady as he bobbed a nod. "I know. I'm good."

Aedan's hand clapped down on my shoulders. "Fucking great. Now let's stop wasting time."

"Right," I muttered.

It took everything I had to turn away from the house, to see the chaos that was building around our *home* and face the woods instead. But Aedan was right. The snow crunched underfoot as we broke into a run for the trees. I glanced back towards Aedan's car one last time, my mind racing. It wasn't too late, I told myself. It wasn't.

The sound of another gunshot followed us into the black.

CHAPTER FIFTY

We circled the house, clustered together in a pocket of humanity amidst the dark. It would have been quiet but for the sounds of fighting that still erupted every few moments. I tried not to let it bother me. I *tried* to stay focused. There was just no way I could pretend I was comfortable with the sound of gunfire and explosions and magic blasting out again and again around my house.

Even Aedan was quiet, for once. He clung close to my side, a knife gleaming dully in the fragments of light that reached us. I eyed it sidelong, the first glimmers of curiosity working their way out from under the fear. A gun would be more practical, I wanted to tell him. He could just *shoot* people, rather than trying to run up and stab them. But somehow, I knew it was hopeless. And having seen him with a knife, well. He could use whatever he wanted, in the end.

"Anything?" I heard Jake whisper from behind. His voice was nearly inaudible, but huddled so close, I heard it. "Can you see them?"

I stared towards the house. It was just a solid, dark shape against the black of the night, almost invisible entirely. But it was mine, and we'd spent the last few months hard at work on it. I knew every turn and every structure. My eyes traced the line of the attic, jutting out over the first floor. The windows for each of our rooms, empty and still. The mass of the garage, looming just around the corner.

"I...I can't see anything," I murmured, shaking my head slowly. "We need to be closer."

"They're probably up ahead, too," Jake muttered. I saw his hand clench around something hidden just out of sight in his pocket. "The marketeer bastards. I don't know if that's a good idea."

I opened my mouth to respond, but just as I started, a flicker of movement proved my earlier statement wrong. I *could* see something - people, in fact. How many was a mystery, and I knew better than to make guesses, but there were definitely people racing around the outside of our home.

A flash of light split the darkness, flaring from somewhere on the far side of the house. I flinched, seeing the movement echoed by Jake and Aedan both. It was brief, but enough.

Jake swore under his breath. "Who the hell are-"

"*Not* our friends," I said, a little more decisively. The figures were frozen in my mind, captured like a photograph. Dark-clothed, and holding...."They had guns," I said, dropping my voice lower again. "I didn't see what their relics might be. I mean, not like I would, but...Do you think-"

"Might be they're demis," Aedan said, his voice hushed. "I'm sure they've got a squad here."

I paused. The rest of his sentence hung between us, unsaid. "Or?"

He made a face, showing through in the scant moments of light. "I'm just thinking, that's all. Try it sometime, Jonny. Greyson only saw two of them."

"Crews normally have more people than relics," Jake said. I spun, catching myself before I could slip and fall on my ass. He shrugged briefly, still turning in a slow circle and scanning the trees. "From what I saw, anyway. With my brother. And Matt."

I glanced to Aedan. He nodded, turning away from me a second later. "It's possible."

"So, what?" I hissed, drawing closer. "You're suggesting some of them are demis, and some of them are just thugs? Something like that? But how are we supposed to know which are the goons?"

"It doesn't matter," Aedan snapped, a little more firmly. "They're all here for the same reason, right? Kill the lot of them. Now come on. We need to figure this shit out. Fast." There was a tension underlying his words that I didn't expect, a nervous energy to the way he flipped his knife over and over in his hand. The motion sent glimmers of light across the snow.

Another bellow split the silence, and this time, there was an inhuman, impossible resonance to it. I flinched, throwing myself upright. "That's Tyler."

"He's alive," Jake said, a heartbeat behind me.

Aedan made an irritated noise in the back of his throat. "Don't-"

I'd pushed on before he could grab hold of me. His hand whipped down just behind my shoulder, leaving a rush of air in its wake. I'd crossed half the distance to the house before I could think the better of it. They were in trouble - they were *alive*, but they were being attacked. We needed to help.

One of the lights on the side of the house was on. It cast the side yard into dim relief - and the figures waiting there. I hurled myself into the snow, wincing against the pain accompanying the brightness. We'd cleaned up as best we could, but the woods were still messy and filled with more brush than I really liked. Even if Aedan was being more careful than usual, there was no way he could argue we weren't hidden.

Slowly, doing my best not to make more noise than necessary, I lifted a hand and pushed one of the branches aside enough to see what was happening.

Keira. My eyes latched onto her, a nearly palpable relief washing through my chest at the sight of her crouched behind a row of firewood we'd stacked alongside the house. Something gleamed in her hand - a gun, I saw as she threw herself upright, firing off a quick burst. She must have been who we were hearing.

The returning fire was enough to send me cowering back to the ground, loud and fierce and longer by far than Keira's had been. I spun, twisting over onto my back, and saw the trio of men standing over in the driveway. They had guns too, I saw. Bigger guns. The sight was enough to dash all my newfound hope.

Keira only hurled herself back down behind the logpile, though. The sound of her swearing filled the air as the gunfire faded. I couldn't quite make out her words, but her meaning was clear.

When she popped back up, her gun held out just like we'd practiced, Tyler was there alongside her. His fingers snapped out in front of him. I couldn't hear the noise, but clearly, the armed men did. They reeled, one fumbling his gun to clap his hands over his ears.

It didn't stop one of them from standing and firing off another spray at the pair's hiding place. Both Keira and Tyler dropped from sight again.

They were in trouble, I knew. At least they had some sort of shelter, but with the enemy armed like that, I just didn't know how long they could hold out. Worse still, if Keira and Tyler were right there, by themselves, where was everyone else?

What had happened?

A fresh burst of gunfire reminded me that I wasn't in the position to sit and mull the question over. I slipped my palm around the grip of my pistol, glancing back over my shoulder to Aedan as I pushed myself up a little higher. He nodded, his lips pressed into a tight, unhappy line.

The sharp *crack* of a branch snapping send a shiver down my spine. I froze, coming grinding to a halt again moments before I would have thrown myself out into the open. A hand slapped down on my shoulder moments later. I spun, coming face to face with Jake.

He nodded out into the night, holding a finger to his lips. I could see his eyes twitch back and forth, scanning the darkness. He'd heard it too - a noise. A noise that told us we weren't alone, when I very much would have preferred to be.

My eyes were still screaming their complaint, thrown from darkness into light and back into darkness again. I squinted, peering out into the forest. And then I jumped as the shapes came into focus.

People. There were more people behind us. My mind raced, zeroing in on the quiet sounds of them creeping closer. Where had they come from? We hadn't seen them on our way over. But there was no denying that they *were* here, I told myself, eyes fixed on them. They must've had the same idea we did, to circle around and catch their quarry off-guard.

I glanced back towards Keira and Tyler, my anxiety growing. I wanted to help them, more than anything. But it didn't look like a small group approaching, either. It was hard to make out distinct shapes amid the trees, but I could already tell there'd be more than enough of them to come down on Keira and Tyler like a sack of bricks.

"They don't know we're here," Aedan breathed in my ear. "Yet."

I understood his message clearly, the words he wasn't saying and the anxiety that filled his eyes as he glanced back towards Keira and Tyler. The others were holding their own. It would be better for us to pick off the newcomers before they saw us, versus turning the fight into a free-for-all. I could accept the logic behind his plan, even if I didn't *like* it.

Swallowing my complaints, I only bobbed my head in a nod. Jake echoed the motion, still clutching his gun.

We turned as one, creeping out of the path the newcomers were taking. Each and every step was an act of patience and terror. If we made a sound, if we gave ourselves away, then we'd be in the same mess as Keira and Tyler.

But they were just as focused on our friends as we were on them, I saw with a note of satisfaction as they hurried through the treeline just a short distance away. They had eyes only for our two demis, and didn't give the trees around them more than a passing inspection.

There were five of them, I noted at last. Five. I quashed the whispers in my mind that reminded me there were only three of us. Three held rifles, like the men attacking Keira and Tyler. They looked for all the world like soldiers, dressed in rugged, dark kevlar and decked out for a fight. A bare-handed man stood in the front lines, his black hair long enough to pull back into a tight ponytail.

And all the way at the back, a woman trotted along. She held a pistol, just like us - but casually, with a careless ease that spoke to her complete comfort with the situation around us. My grip on my gun tightened further. They were well used to fighting, that much was clear. And if they were veterans, that probably made them demis.

"Come on," I murmured, pushing away my growing unease. "They're close enough." If we waited too long, I knew, then they'd be on top of Keira and Tyler regardless. Already, I could see two of them men slowing, taking better hold of their rifles.

"I've got the goons," Aedan said, leaning his head back far enough to flash a crooked grin in my direction. "Let's have some fun."

"Focus, damn it. Jake, can you-"

"Yeah, I see them," he muttered. "I'll do my best."

Not exactly the resounding show of confidence I'd been hoping for, but I couldn't exactly blame him, either. The last time he'd gotten in a real fight, he'd gotten shot - and the time before that, he'd lost to Aedan and I.

I just nodded, silently praying that he could keep things together long enough to finish this, and threw myself into a low crouch.

The snow flew past under my feet as I accelerated. Quiet. I had to be quiet, still, but fast. Not guns. Not yet. It wasn't time. Aedan vanished into the night from alongside me, just a blur of motion and then nothing. Jake's footsteps were a low, muted sound echoing off the trees.

Closer. I held my breath, willing myself to be quieter still. Closer. The group was slowing, the black-haired man murmuring something to the others in a low voice. I brought my gun up in a rush of adrenaline.

Now. I could-

The woman turned, spinning on her heel to face us. I froze, shock overcoming my nerves for a single instant. How did she- There was *no way* she should have been able to pick us out like that. But there she was, staring across the night at us with her mouth hanging open. My shock was perfectly reflected in the surprise plastered across her face.

Jake pushed out in front of me, recognizing the issue in the same instant as me. His hand whipped up, his fingers stretching towards her, but she was already calling something to her friend, ducking under cover. The sound of her pushing through the underbrush, no longer so stealthy, gave up our last hope of catching them by surprise.

A flicker of motion caught my attention, right in the corner of my eye. I spun - just in time to see the black-haired man whip his arm across his chest. *Something* trailed in its wake.

The gesture rang clear, etched into my vision. It was like- It was like he was throwing something.

Shit.

Before the thought was fully formed I'd hurled myself into the snow, rolling behind a tree. The branches where I'd been standing sheared off in the blink of an eye, a hideous hissing erupting through the forest. I didn't stop. I'd already rolled to my feet by the time the second attack hit, sending shards of bark cascading down around my head.

That *noise* - like air escaping a hose, compressed to the point of no return. I swallowed hard, swinging my gun back up to face the black-haired demi, and squeezed as hard as I could.

Nothing. No bang, no recoil, no bullet shooting forth towards the man trying to cut me apart. Just me standing there like an idiot, staring at the gun sitting in my hand with its slide half-open.

"Down!" Jake cried, his voice filled with as much energy as I'd ever heard from the man. His hand was on the scruff of my neck, grabbing hold of my jacket and towing me aside as another blast of air slammed into the tree beside me. His hand came up, his own gun at the ready.

The woman smiled.

I gasped as Jake's hand became an anchor instead of a guide. There was nothing I could do to keep myself upright as he tumbled on the icy ground, hitting the ground hard. The air left me in a rush as I joined him.

The sound of the woman's low, confident laughter rang out under the sound of gunfire from the house. Her friends were already turning, bringing those rifles up to bear. I tore my eyes off her long enough to sweep a quick look over the demi shooting air-blades at us and the soldiers.

"Hold!" I cried, still clutching my useless gun. Was it stupid for me to declare my presence? Maybe. But until I could figure out what in the damn thing had jammed, I didn't have another weapon that would be useful - and a gunshot wouldn't be any quieter anyway, I had to admit.

The flicker of doubt that accompanied my words hurt more than I liked to admit. My voice was all I had, my words. But the last time I'd tried to use it, it failed me. If that happened, what would we do? How would we-

I grimaced as the entwined rings of my necklace flared to life against my chest. I could feel the drain, the energy bleeding off me like an all-nighter packed into a few brief seconds. But I was ready, and it was...better. Manageable.

The wind-caller and the soldiers froze. I gritted my teeth, feeling them fight. There were four of them, and one of me. I couldn't hold them forever. "Jake," I hissed through my clenched jaw. "I need you to-"

A flash of light - that was all I saw. Just a glimmer of light reflecting from a length of steel, and a blur of motion. A scream tore across the night a heartbeat after.

Aedan wrapped himself more tightly around the soldier he'd leapt onto, seeming even smaller when compared to the looming grunt. His knife was buried in the soldier's neck, still glittering. He pulled it free without a word, driving it home a second time. A third.

Jake threw himself upright beside me, fast enough I flinched. His hands were outstretched - both of them. His fingers twitched as he reached towards the two demis.

The black-haired demi stumbled, pressing a hand to his face. And then he twisted towards Jake, his eyes going wide. His hand slipped up, eerily similar to how Jake was facing him.

Jake was faster. His gun was at the ready, his finger squeezing the trigger.

The woman was *there* as the first round went off, though, ready and waiting. She kicked her companion's feet out from under him, leaving him to fall to the ground as the bullets sailed harmlessly over his head.

Again, I gaped. There was no way. No way in *hell*. But the woman only glared back at me, no longer looking so amused, and the man was rolling back to his feet as I delayed. Throwing myself low again, I grabbed at the slide on my pistol, trying to force it to clear. The pistol was having none of my shit.

"Here," Jake muttered, tearing his eyes off the fight for just long enough to glance down at me. "Spare." He dug in his pocket, pulling free another gun. I took it gratefully, spinning back to the fight and shoving my own gun back into my pocket.

A round sailed over my head. I shuddered, ducking low again. "Sorry!" I heard Aedan call from the far side of our little clearing. The sound of a man screaming hid anything else he might have said.

The soldiers were his problem. He'd wanted them, he could deal with them. I just hoped he didn't wind up getting us shot. Beyond that, I couldn't spare any more time to check in on him. The wind-caller was back on his feet, even if he swayed gently. A crooked smile tugged at the corners of my lips. Jake was still at work, then.

But when I turned on the enemy demi, opening fire, I found myself hitting only empty air. The man stumbled back into the trees with his companion's hand on his elbow, escaping unscathed.

"St-" I began, raising my voice after them, but a coughing fit hit me halfway through the phrase. My command vanished in a garbled mess.

"Jesus, Jon, would you *hit* something?" Jake cried.

"I-I'm trying," I muttered, aghast. I wasn't normally that bad a shot. I wasn't a marksman, by any stretch of the imagination, but we couldn't be more than ten or fifteen yards from the two demis. I couldn't even fault Jake for being irritated.

And over it all, I heard Aedan let out an exasperated sigh. I scowled, pressing forward after the pair. I knew what he was upset about - we were being slow. It wasn't my *fault*, damn it. The woman was too goddamn-

I froze, my steps slowing a fraction. She was too lucky. There was no way someone could have so much good fortune, time and time again. And I hadn't seen her use a power, had I? So it was safe to assume it was something like that. Probably.

In the meantime, I glared at Jake. "What, that's your best?"

"They were *moving*," he snapped. "And it's dark. I can't hardly see my targets. Don't blame your bad aim on me, Jon."

"It's *dark*," I protested, inching forward all the while. "It's no better for me than it is for you."

"That's no-"

I twisted, spinning away from Jake as he glared back at me. Another crack, a sound that shouldn't be there. More footsteps. We weren't alone. How'd they manage to circle back so quickly? Or- was it someone else?

A flicker of movement. I reacted purely on instinct, bringing my gun up and firing in the same smooth motion. My ears rang from the din of it.

The world ahead of me erupted into a blurred, hazy mess. The bullet hung in midair, caught in place in front of my target. I froze, my thoughts racing. The others were luck and wind, right? This didn't look like either of those. This looked like-

Oh.

Ice shot through my veins as I hurled myself to the side, grabbing hold of Jake and dragging him along with me. The world ahead of us exploded a heartbeat later. The bullet sang as it careened back the other way, right through where my head would have been.

"Amber!" I yelped, raising my voice through the hoarse, raspy pain of my throat. "I-It's us! Don't shoot! Don't-"

"God damn it, Jon," I heard her snap. "You fucking shot first. Don't up and cry when I-"

"I know, I know," I said hurriedly. "Sorry. I'm sorry. I thought-" I shook my head, reality catching up with me. "They went that way. And-"

The fog and confusion that had settled over my mind cleared enough for the gunshots to finally register. The gunshots that had no doubt been continuing the whole time I was ogling the wind-caller and his lucky friend, I thought sourly. A quick glance showed me Aedan, two soldiers laid out in the snow at his feet. A third was backpedaling madly, nearly falling over himself in his hurry to get away.

"We saw them," someone else said. I looked up. Brendon crept out of the dark behind Amber, a gun in his hands and his face pale as a ghost. "W-We were going to come help. And then-"

"Give me a little warning next time if it's *you*, damn it," Amber muttered.

"Right," I said, easing myself back upright. Jake accepted Brendon's hand, letting the other demi pull him to his feet. "Look. We've been trying to deal with them, but nothing's working. It's like-" I stopped, the words dying on my lips.

"What, *you're* having problems? One for the fucking calendars,"

Amber muttered under her breath.

I only shook my head, glaring at him. My thoughts were whirling, racing along at a hundred miles an hour. "This is serious. Act like it. Anytime we get close to them, it's like they're one step ahead - or something goes wrong, for us. We can't touch either of them."

"Foci?" Amber said, the sarcasm finally leaving her voice. She stood a little straighter, folding her arms across her chest.

"One's shooting blades of air," Jake said, cutting in when I hesitated. "And the other..."

"Luck," I said, my voice low. "Or fortunes. Something like that. Manipulating them. I think. Look, maybe-"

"Fucking great,' I heard Amber mutter, her voice low. "That sounds like a blast."

"Listen. I think- if she's staying a step ahead, then we just have to be a step ahead of her, " I said, forcing the words out as quickly as I could. My eyes fixed onto Brendon. Little things he'd said pieced themselves together, stitching an image that gave me an idea.

He flinched, seeing the look I was giving him. "W-What?"

I continued staring right at him, drawing closer. The sound of gunfire rang out again - nearby. We were running out of time. The wind-caller and the lucky lady weren't going to just up and forget about us. "What you've been doing, Brendon. It's different. Why are you even out here? How'd you guys get separated?"

He ran a hand through his hair, shaking his head. "I...I don't..." He pursed his lips, his shoulders drooping. "It was just a feeling. Something didn't sit right. And then...I saw a strange car coming up the drive, and-"

"He grabbed me and yelled for the rest to scatter," Amber said, cutting over him as he faltered. She rolled her eyes. "We did our best, but...we wound up getting separated. Not a second too late, though. They came out shooting not a few moments later."

"It was just a feeling," Brendon muttered.

I closed the distance between us, grabbing him by the shoulder. "Right. It was just a feeling. But you've had odd hunches like this before, haven't you?"

He froze. I could see him breathing in and out slowly, staring at the ground. "W-What? What are you saying?"

"We have two demis, Brendon," I said, spitting the words out more quickly. "One shoots out compressed air. The other seems to manipulate fortune. She's fucking *lucky*. And Aedan's-"

"Right," Brendon muttered, casting a glance towards where Aedan and one of the soldiers still danced.

"I need you to worry about the lucky one," I said, enunciating each syllable clearly enough he couldn't possibly misunderstand. "Tell us where she's going. What she's doing. What are they doing right now, for example?"

He paled, standing out bone-white against the night. "I-I have absolutely no-"

My hand tightened against his shoulder. "Brendon!"

His chin snapped up at the sharp note in my voice, his eyes locking onto mine. There was still too much fear there for my comfort, but there was a little of *him* looking back, too. His lips tightened. "They can't let us plan. They can't let us get our balance. They....they could go find allies. But there aren't that many here - that van's not that big." The words poured out of him at last, like a dam had been broken. His eyes darted here and there, flitting between the van and the woods around us. "So they'd probably-"

His eyes widened. It was all the warning I got before he grabbed me, tossing the both of us to the ground. I could hear Amber and Jake yelling, with the distant sound of metal on metal telling me Aedan was still carving a path through the marketeers' thugs.

The tree beside me exploded into sawdust in the same instant as gunfire rained down into our clustered forms.

CHAPTER FIFTY-ONE

A gasp slipped between my lips as the world around us erupted into chaos.

From my position on the ground, the forest around me just looked like a mess of falling bark and shredded, ruined leaves. Again and again the air overhead roiled, seething with pent-up energy before slamming into the trees.

And then, out of nowhere, it stopped.

Amber pushed herself back to her feet, one haid upraised. The air around us blurred, thickening into a foggy, soupy mess. "Get the hell up," she spat, her arm trembling. "Get your shit together, *now*."

I didn't need to be told twice. I glared at Brendon. "Do your best," I hissed. "Keep us ahead of her." Even as I spoke, I leapt to my feet, sliding my free hand around the hilt of the knife tucked in my pocket. Aedan always had a dozen of the things lying around. I'd helped myself to a few.

Brendon's face went pale, but he nodded. I turned away, facing back towards the woods as the shield between us and our attackers shimmered and vanished.

I was ready, when the two figures reappeared from out of the dark. The black-haired man was out front again, one hand rising. His eyes were fixed on us, sliding across our gathered shapes. My relic burned against my chest as I strained, reaching for every scrap of power I could grab at.

The last time I'd tried to command them, I'd started coughing. I didn't think a second attempt would be any better. But I could still read their body language, couldn't I? That wasn't an attack. It should be fine.

Unless Lucky there could somehow help her friend's attacks. The thought was less than comforting.

I could only trust in my own abilities, though. When the man twitched, sending a hissing, nearly-invisible wave spraying towards us, I threw myself to the side. It tore through a sapling right behind where I'd stood instead.

Jake lunged forward - only to be caught by Brendon a heartbeat later. "No!" the seer cried, his eyes widening. "Not yet!" Jake stumbled back, shooting Brendon an irritated look, but I could understand Brendon's logic. My powers were something more easily stopped, after all. There wasn't anything like a coughing fit that could make Jake stop casting - nothing short of actual physical harm.

Amber surged in while we stared at each other, working through the mess. Her fingers twitched her and there, leaving foggy, blurred air in their wake. Wind and Luck weren't giving up so easily. They pressed closer, trying to find a gap in her defenses. She was holding, for the time being, but her left hand quivered. Maybe it was from pent-up energy. Maybe it was exhaustion. Either way, she couldn't continue forever.

"Jake- and Jon. Go," Brendon snapped. He huddled lower all the while, a dark shape in the foliage. In the brief moments of light, though, I could see his eyes. They were stretched wide, like he was trying to take in every last fragment and scrap of the fight going on in front of him. "Get the bastard. Amber-"

"I'll keep her busy," she muttered, fixing her eyes on the woman. I shivered. The woman, who had a gun. But, it was Amber, and out of all of us, she was probably in the least danger of getting shot.

My fingers tightened around my weapons as Brendon's command really sank in. Oh, good. I'd always *wanted* to be on the front lines. I cast a quick glance back into the darkness, catching sight of Aedan and the last thug still going at it. This one was good, or at least better than his fellows. I could see the red staining his clothes even across the distance, but he hadn't gone down yet.

Jake's palm slapped into the back of my shoulder, snapping me out of my thoughts. I nodded, meeting the look he gave me, and we turned back towards the two demis.

It was all I could do to keep going forward as we lunged back in, stumbling through the snow and doing our best not to fall on our asses. My gun was still jammed, still hanging uselessly open. I seized the slide as Jake pushed out ahead, forcing it the rest of the way open.

The sound of Jake firing into the night was enough of a shock for me to finally clear the jammed casing, half-falling over myself. He'd fired. Maybe he'd-

No. A quick glance confirmed that both Wind and Luck were still on their feet, although Wind looked less than confident all of a sudden. His fingers snapped. Jake reeled back, twisting madly, and the blast of air shot inches over his head. A lock of his hair fluttered down onto the snow.

I knew better than to harass Jake for his shitty aim, missing when we were that close. It was just bad luck. My arms came up as he fell back, his eyes drifting over to where Luck stood. Her eyes were fixed on us, narrowed and tense.

When I pulled the trigger again, a flash lit up the darkness - but the gun didn't buck, didn't recoil like it should have. And Wind stood right where he was, unbothered and unshot.

"God fucking-" I began, hissing under my breath, but bit off the curse. I could already see the bullet, lodged into the barrel. It'd take time to clear - time and equipment, neither of which we had. I hurled it into the snow, still muttering my frustrations, and took better hold of my knife.

"In, Jon!" Brendon yelled from behind. Luck's head snapped around, fixing on him, but Amber sent a ball of ice sailing for her head with frightening speed. Brendon skittered back farther as she swore, ducking.

It wasn't *Brendon* that was having to go one on one with people. For a split second, I thought about yelling something back, but thought the better of it a heartbeat later. Swallowing my complaints, I pushed back in.

Jake and Wind were already at it, swapping fumbled, awkward blows. Jake kept stumbling over himself, tripping over his own two feet. Wind was more comfortable, and certainly wasn't having the issues Jake was, but he kept looking over to Luck, to me, to Aedan. His eyes were tight, his lips pressed into a thin line.

He let out a hiss as I finally staggered close enough to take a swing for him. He jumped back, leaving my blade to sail through open air instead of his arm. Jake was there to fill in the gap, one hand rising.

"Not yet!" Brendon called. Jake twitched, freezing in place. I stabbed straight out, hoping to fill in the opening he'd left, but Brendon wasn't done. "Jon - circle left, then- No, I meant ri-"

An ice-cold chill shot through me as I twisted left - and found myself faced with Wind's open palm. The demi was *grinning*. Leering at me, like he'd won. The currents and eddies off his fingers set my hair to blowing ominously.

There was no time to swear. I just twisted, hurling myself to the side with every bit of speed I could muster. It was almost fast enough. My leg exploded in agony. Red dotted the snow underneath me.

"Jon!" I heard Brendon scream behind me. "I-I'm sorry! Are you-"

"Keep going!" I snapped, shooting a glance back over my shoulder as I pushed myself farther back. It was just superficial. I could still move it. I had to. "Don't stop!"

His eyes were wide, his face ashen, but he bobbed a curt nod. "U-Uh…"

Wind swept back in, bringing his arm across. I threw myself low, my breath catching in my throat. The blade of air swept over my head. *Just* over my head.

"Brendon!" I cried, doing my best not to shriek.

"Aedan!" I heard Brendon call. "Closer!"

"What?" Aedan snapped, his voice distant and low. Another clatter of metal rang out.

"Jon - down, then forward!"

I ducked again. Wind snarled as his blade sailed cleanly past me again. Forward, Brendon had said. Praying he was right, I lunged, my knife sliding out. I was no Aedan, but I could manage.

Or I *should* have been able to manage if my leg hadn't crumpled, pushed over the limit by a patch of ice. I hit the snowy ground with a gasp, rolling madly.

"Jake! Keep going!" Brendon called. I twisted, narrowly avoiding a gout of snow where Wind stabbed down again. Whatever Jake was doing, whatever Brendon was seeing, it was a mystery to me.

Forcing my breath back into check, I pushed myself upright, still clinging to my knife. Wind had already made it a few paces away, closing in on Jake - and his back was to me. I drew breath, my eyes lighting up.

And started sneezing madly, breathing in the delicate sawdust floating on the chilly air. Jake's groan rose over the desperate noise of it.

A shock ran down my spine as a gunshot rang out again - close. I spun, finding the bullet hanging in midair a few scant inches from my face. My blood froze.

Amber stepped past me. "Bitch," she muttered, glaring at Luck.

"In, Aedan!" Brendon bellowed.

Aedan's irritated snarl was drowned out by the clash of metal - at the same instant as the bullet held in Amber's control went flying back towards Luck.

She twitched, spinning at just the right moment. But even the darkness couldn't hide the spray of blood that shot across her cheek.

Not fatal - but it was a hit, and that was better than we'd been able to do so far. Brendon's plan crystallized in my mind, right as he raised his voice again. "One more time!"

Luck was visibly panting, flushed red from more than just the cold. She was trying to protect both of them, after all, and there were far more of us. Knowing how quickly I could get tired out from commanding people, I wasn't exactly surprised. But the harder we pressed them, the more she stretched herself thin trying to keep her friend Windy there safe, the more she left herself exposed.

She knew it, too. As Wind fell away, pressed by Jake and with Aedan accelerating towards his back, I saw her raise a hand to her face, holding her fingers against the blood dripping down her cheek. Her lips parted gently, even as her eyes flicked from face to face around her.

Wind rallied, driving Aedan back with an explosive surge and sending another torrent sweeping towards us, but Amber was there first. His attack dissipated into nothingness. Jake closed in on him a heartbeat later - and Aedan. The redheaded demi launched himself at Wind like a missile, blade-first. I could just make out the darkened shape of the last of the mundane thugs falling into the snow behind him.

Brendon whipped around, his eyes darting to Jake and I. "Now!"

I was moving before his voice faded. It was purely an instinctive action, the way I hurled myself at him. Words rose to my lips, ready and waiting, but it was hard to focus past the pain of my arm and the chaos around us. Words were hard, right then. It was easier to just throw myself at Wind, knife out and slashing.

For a single second, he seemed ready to fight. His hands came up -

and then the reality of what was happening seemed to click into place. Just as quickly as we'd leapt in, he stumbled back, twisting to look over his shoulder at Luck.

Jake was ready and waiting. He shouldered past me, more eager to leap in than I'd ever seen him before. Sitting and waiting for us to clear the way must have really gotten to him, I noted with more than a little amusement. Wind stumbled, pressing a hand to his forehead. I'd felt that exhaustion before. I knew how hard it was to deal with.

Amber wasn't looking. She'd turned away from Wind by the time Jake started casting, her gun snapping up. Her sights were squarely fixed on the woman. Luck shrieked as she started to fire. Shots peppered the trunks around her.

"God *damn* it!" Amber cried, rising from her crouch as the snow settled. I saw it too. Not a single round had found its mark.

"Tara - back!" I heard Wind cry, shaking his head furiously. He was gaining his footing again, somehow. Quick as could be, he threw himself behind a tree. "Cover me while I-"

Amber closed the gap between her and Tara before he could finish, tossing her gun to the side carelessly. The slide hung open and empty. Her fist was raised instead, cocked back and poised. Her hazel eyes were terrifying in their intensity, locked onto the lucky demi's.

A flicker of movement was the only warning I got. I lunged, surging forward in a blind rush, and got a hand on the back of Amber's jacket as the sound of her fist connecting with Tara's face cracked through the air.

Clutching the fabric for dear life, I braced my heels, throwing both of us into the snow. Her startled, angry cry echoed in my ears.

A gust of wind tore through where she'd stood a second later, slicing branches from trees and leaving winds to dance on the eddies. Amber stopped protesting.

I left her on the ground, forcing myself back upright for what seemed like the tenth time that night. The two enemy demis stood in front of us. Wind was trembling, shaking like a sapling in a storm. He was getting tired too, then. Served him right.

We couldn't hesitate. We had to press the attack, use the opportunity we were given. We outnumbered them. We could do this. As the thought passed through my mind, Jake dashed forward again. His eyes were latched onto Tara, as though him and the lucky demi were the only two people in the clearing. My heart leapt. He could get her. He *could.*

But as he lunged forward, Tara seemed to reach some sort of conclusion. Her eyes snapped back to us, stopping their ceaseless roaming.

Brandon let out a strangled cry, one hand thrusting out towards the two. "N-No! Don't let her-"

With Jake mere feet from her and closing fast, Tara skittered back, cowering behind her friend. He rallied, straightening heroically, and raised a hand. My hair rustled in the gathering wind.

Tara didn't stop. She was running by then, picking up speed as she gave up any semblance of stealth. Her face turned as she left her friend behind. There was a hint of something there, some unrecognizable emotion. Regret? Satisfaction? Or just cold calculation? I couldn't see, and before I could so much as take a breath she'd vanished into the darkness.

"Where are you-" Wind said, spinning on his heel as his head snapped around. He followed her flight for a single second, staring in disbelief after his friend's retreating form. And then the reality of what was happening set in.

He whirled back to face us. A half-dozen tornados compressed out of the winter air shot towards us. I flinched, drawing back, but they only blew through my jacket and set me to swaying for a too-brief moment.

Wind was tired. The realization was enough to set hope blossoming in my chest.

Amber didn't even try and block them. She didn't hesitate at all. As the demi's attacks slipped through our group, she'd crossed half the distance to him in three great strides.

Part of me sympathized, and I could see the same strain on Jake's face as his fingers tightened. Whoever this demi was, he'd clearly been thrown straight under the bus. Despite what had happened with Matt and his crew, Jake had become a valuable part of the team. My *second.* Who knew what could happen, if Wind there was given a shot? How many people could be salvaged from these battles?

But they were here to kill us. And from the way the demi's face tightened, his teeth gritted and his eyes narrowing, he wasn't of a mind to surrender. As much as I wished things were different, I just...I couldn't justify wasting the time it would take to feel out if he could be salvaged.

Jake's hesitation was even more brief than mine. As I gathered myself, drawing a suddenly-clear breath of air, he made an irritated noise. His eyes tightened

Wind crumpled, his expression slackening into bemused drowsiness. He tumbled into a snowdrift a second later, still shaking his head like he was trying to clear the fog.

I wrapped my hand around my knife more tightly. And then I took a step towards him.

Amber slipped from the shadows in front of me, appearing from thin air. With Jake taking the spotlight, I'd almost forgotten she was there.

Tyler had talked about her crushing the life straight out of Glenn, using her powers to put her former employer out of his misery. Apparently, she was feeling a bit more merciful towards the demi who'd clearly been discarded. And she'd found another gun from somewhere. Probably from the man himself.

The gunshot cracked across my eardrums, loud enough that I heard only ringing in its wake. I stopped.

Wind drooped, twitching for a long, drawn-out second. And then he crumpled, his legs going limp. He sagged back into the snow a heartbeat later, all of the fight gone.

Little by little, I could feel my muscles relax, too. Only exhaustion remained afterward. I slid my hand back into my pocket, letting go of my knife.

Amber didn't sit around staring at her kill. She spun on her heel, stalking back towards me. "There. Fucking finally. If I catch that bitch, I'll-"

"About that. She could come back," I said, risking her wrath and cutting her off. It was better than all of us getting shot. "Maybe we should move? Or go after her? Or the others." My pulse accelerated again. "They're fighting. We need to help. Now."

"I doubt she'll come back," Brendon said, shaking his head hurriedly. "I-I mean, if she felt strongly enough about the dangers of staying that she'd leave her friend to...to die, then why would she come back alone?"

"She might come back with friends, though," Jake muttered.

Brendon hesitated, glancing over to him. "Maybe...but I'm guessing her friends have their hands busy. For now."

I stepped closer, grabbing his shoulder. "And by that, you mean?"

"The rest of the crew is out there too," Jake murmured. "They're putting up a fight."

"Okay. So, like I said, we need to go *help* them. Before they get overrun," I said, turning towards the distant shape of the house. "We can-"

"Oh, hell no," Amber snapped, slamming her palm into my shoulder hard enough to bring me about. "Your kiddos there will be just fine. They've made it this long, haven't they?"

"I only saw Keira and Tyler," I protested, faltering a little under the anger in her eyes. "They can only hold out so long. And what are you suggesting as an alternative?"

"Now, now, kids. Play nice," I heard Aedan mutter. He was crouched over Wind's body, pawing through his clothes.

I winced. "Come on, Aedan. The guy's dead. Have a little respect."

Aedan kept right at it, not so much as looking my way. "If he's got a problem with it, he can always tell me to stop."

"Everyone went every fucking which-way," Amber said, bringing me back around to face her. She was quivering with rage, or fear, or exhaustion. I couldn't quite tell. "But I saw Nox just a few minutes before you assholes showed up. He took off deeper into the woods, with a whole gang on his tail." Her lips pressed into a thin line, like she was daring me to argue with her. "I'm *not* leaving him."

I stopped. Put like that, I could almost see the point she was trying to make. I was worried about Keira and Tyler, but at least Tyler had years of practice and experience with his relic under his belt. He had abilities, both offensive and defensive. Keira was good with a knife, if Aedan had taught her anything, and both her and Tyler could shoot. They had a good position. They probably *could* hold out for a decent length of time, by themselves.

Whereas all that Nox had going for him was his ability to stay just a little bit ahead of his pursuers. I didn't even know if he was armed. I mean, I couldn't picture Amber letting him wander off totally defenseless, but I was pretty sure she considered herself his defense. Without her there, I had no idea how qualified he was to look after himself.

The clearing exploded into brilliant magenta light, accompanied by the sound of the fallen demi disintegrating. Aedan's exhausted but satisfied sigh followed after it.

"Fine," I heard myself saying. My heart sank at the thought of giving in like that, but I plowed on anyway. "If we can get to him, *quickly*, then let's do it."

Jake hovered at my side, a silent shape, and Brendon wasn't far beyond him. I could see that neither was thrilled with the idea, but they weren't arguing with me, either. Kai and Loren were still unaccounted for, and I didn't like that. But they weren't with Keira and Tyler. If we were chasing after Nox and his new friends, maybe we'd find them.

That's what I told myself, anyway.

Amber nodded, a bit of the anxiety leaving her eyes. "Fine. Let's go, already." Shoving her newly claimed pistol into her pocket, she turned towards the woods. Jake and Brendon followed behind with a second's hesitation, shooting me cautious looks.

I just swallowed my sigh, taking a step after her.

The sound of something hitting the snow brought me up short. Something wet. Something *heavy*. I spun in place, adrenaline coursing through my veins as my pulse skyrocketed again.

And froze, staring towards Aedan's limp, motionless body.

CHAPTER FIFTY-TWO

I stared dumbly, caught in place like a statue. Aedan twitched, moving for the first time since I turned around. A groan reached my ears, low and filled with agony. Jake was perfectly still alongside me, every bit as dumbfounded. Brendon was no better, his elation at our victory fading with every passing second.

Ponderously slow, Aedan brought a hand down, the pale glimmer of his skin vanishing in the snow as he braced himself. When he levered himself up off the ground a few inches, the once-white powder coating the ground was stained red.

"Aedan," I said, an icy chill shivering down my spine. A blur of emotions flooded my mind - Fear, first, for my fallen friend. Relief crowded in after it. It was *Aedan*, after all. It wasn't like he could die. Dread slapped relief out of the way before it could fully sink in. He couldn't die, but he was hurt. That much was clear to see in the way he shivered, falling back into the snow, and the rising sound of him coughing. We didn't have a healer, a fact of which we'd been made all too clear. And there was no way we could patch him up so easily.

But it was *Aedan*, the little voice in the back of my head chimed. There was a simple way to heal him, wasn't there?

I pushed it aside, my stomach doing a backflip at the thought, and closed the distance between him and I. "Hey. Aedan. What's..." My words fell away when I took his shoulder, rolling him onto his back.

The jacket I'd bought him was as red and soaked as the snow underneath him - as was my grey sweatshirt, I saw when I pulled the fabric back tentatively.

"Bastards were faster than I thought," Aedan mumbled, coughing again. Red flecks dotted his teeth, spattering out with the motion.

"Quiet," I whispered, seeing the damage all too clearly. A tiny circle, that was all the gunshot wound looked like on his stomach. Just a little thing. But even though it looked small on the surface, I knew the damage inside was probably worse. My breath caught in my throat.

His eyes were still glued to mine, filled with pain and irritation in equal measure. There was no fear there, only resignation.

I had no idea when he'd gotten shot. Earlier in the fight, no doubt, while we were occupied with Wind and Luck. He'd taken out three of them - three that I'd *seen*, anyway. Them with guns, and him with a knife. I bit my lip, my heart sinking at the thought that we'd left him to deal with them alone.

His hand slid up, covering the wound even as I thought it. "Annoying," Aedan muttered, his voice rising fractionally. "Thought I c-could manage. Fuckers. Guess not."

"What's going on?" I heard Amber say, stepping closer. Her steps froze a few paces behind me. "Oh. Uh. What's…What are we going to-"

"Just let me think," I snapped, my hand clenching on his shoulder.

"Don't be ridiculous," Aedan said, shaking his head as another cough rattled his frame. "I'm not going to sit here and b-bleed out, Jonny." His right arm raised, his left still clutched around his stomach. His finger jabbed towards the prone form of Wind - or where Wind had been, anyway. A dark shape lay in the snow between us and the imprint of his body.

"The relic?" I said, my brow furrowing. He'd been shot. It was hardly the time to worry about something like *that.*

Aedan bobbed his head. "Mine. I-It's mine. Put it in my bag. It's mine." The words tumbled out of him one after another, oddly fervent.

Fine. If he wanted it so much, he could have it. Swallowing a sigh, I let go of him long enough to reach across the white and take hold of the thing. A comb, I saw when I pulled my hand back. Delicate, and intricately carved out of dark wood. Feathers were etched into its spine, nearly invisible in the night.

Aedan grabbed for it. I drew back, scowling at him. "Calm down. I'm putting it in your bag. Just sit still."

He returned my scowl with a frown, glaring daggers, but lay back. I pulled his bag closer, brushing the snow off the fabric. It was the work of a moment to pull the zipper open, shoving the comb in and sealing it off again.

Aedan seemed to let out a sigh at the sight, a bit of the fight leaving him. "Cool," he mumbled. "Good. Now. If you don't mind."

I shuddered, seeing the meaning in his eyes. "Fuck."

"Don't be a baby, Jonny."

I ran a hand through my hair, suddenly not as confident anymore. I'd killed before, as my nightmares kept reminding me. It wasn't like it was my first time, as much as I wished I could say otherwise.

Killing Aedan would be a kindness, the logical part of my brain whispered. He'd pop right back, hale and healthy and none the worse for it. It wasn't really killing him at all, was it?

The rest of me didn't *care* about logic. It looked down and saw a friend lying in the snow, red sliding down his chin, and rebelled at the thought of causing him any more pain.

But reality didn't care about what I wanted.

I raised my hand, staring down at the knife in it, and my stomach did another spin. No. I couldn't. There was no way I could-

"What's going on?" Amber said. Her voice was low and guarded, even while I could hear an anxious note running through it. "Look, can we-"

"If we kill him, he'll come back," Jake said, breaking his silence for the first time. His hand was latched on Amber's arm, drawing her back ever so slightly like he was trying to give me space. "It's his way."

"Oh," Amber said, blinking. "So those *weren't* just stories."

"Afraid not," Aedan said, the words dissolving behind another red-coated hack.

She made a face, her lips twisting unhappily. "Fuck. Well. Take this, then."

I flinched, drawing back as a gun was thrust into my face grip-first. Slowly, unsure, I took it, sliding my knife back into my pocket. Brendon made a noise in the back of his throat, like he was about to be sick.

"Come on, Jonny," Aedan whispered. "We're on a schedule, here."

Amber sighed. "Yes. Yes, we are. Do you need me to-"

"When you come out the other side, get moving," I said, ignoring her offer. It should be me. I needed to come to terms with it, eventually, after all. And it was just Aedan. "We'll take care of Nox, and then go back for Keira and Tyler. Since we don't know where you're going to pop back out, start looking for Kai and Loren. They're out there somewhere."

It wasn't my imagination. His nose wrinkled. He glared at me, managing to look disapproving through the blood. "They need help. Back a-at the house. They're-"

"We'll be there as soon as we can," I said, a little more firmly. "Trust me, I don't like it either."

"Shouldn't l-leave them."

"We're not."

"Are."

An exasperated sigh slid between my teeth. "We'll have Jake go back and do what he can, all right? Brendon can go too." That way no one has to go alone. Well, except Aedan.

"What?" Jake said, his head snapping up. Brendon didn't say a word. He just shifted unhappily, crossing his arms.

Aedan didn't look happy, still. His lips curled down in a scowl - but he nodded, the movement slight enough I nearly missed it.

His head tilted gently to the side as I crouched beside him, pressing the barrel of Amber's pistol against his temple. My pulse accelerated. His eyes were still fixed on mine, not a hint of fear there. A lock of hair slipped down, brushing against the cold steel.

My hands shook. It wasn't killing him. I repeated the thought to myself over and over. It was Aedan. He wouldn't die. He *couldn't* die. And he was suffering, left in agony every second I delayed. The faster I did what he needed, the faster he'd be free.

It sounded so easy. But it was nowhere near so simple, with him staring at me like that. I held my breath, my grip tightening.

"Going to have to g-grow a pair one of these days, Jonny," I heard him murmur. He was trembling, weakening rapidly, but his hand rose to wrap around the gun. His finger inched towards the trigger, curving onto mine.

I hated the thought of killing Aedan, even in passing, but I hated even more the thought of being too weak to do what needed doing. Letting him do the dirty work for me would be the same as losing. Pushing aside my doubts and fears, with the pressure of his finger against mine building, I silenced the voice and pulled the trigger.

My ears screamed, the sounds of the night wiped away behind the dull, endless ringing left in the gunshot's wake. I didn't look away.

That would have been giving in as much as refusing to kill him was. His hollow eyes stared at nothing, empty at last.

And then it began - the myriad cracks that spread, dancing across his skin like a dark spiderweb. I rose, stepping back. I hardly noticed when Amber took her gun back, pulling it out of my senseless hand. Within seconds, the clearing was aglow with magenta light.

Aedan was gone as quickly as it had started. His backpack crumbled away beside the dust that remained, rapidly vanishing entirely on the wind.

I just sat back on my heels, breathing hard, and tried to keep from throwing up.

Amber had no such patience, though. She latched onto my arm after no more than a few seconds, dragging me upright. "It's done. Time to get to work," she said. There was a soft note to her voice, just a hint of something gentle under the strain and impatience. "He's in trouble. I can't abandon him. He'll-"

"I get it," I said, swallowing hard. And then I glanced over to Jake and Brendon. "Like I told Aedan. Think you can-"

"You really want me to go back there," Jake said, still staring at me. "Leaving you alone out here."

"He's not alone," Amber said, fixing her glare onto him instead of me for a single, wonderful second.

"And Loren's out there too," Jake said, not giving in so easily. He didn't spare Amber so much as a look.

"You're telling me," Brendon muttered.

I groaned. "I'll...be fine. With you and Tyler together, I have to believe you can clean that up. And Amber and I are more than capable." Amber snorted. I sighed, hearing her derision even without her saying a word. "Aedan'll go look for Loren and Kai. He'll find them. They can't be that far."

"It's Aedan. Do you trust him to actually do it?"

"He's been doing this sort of thing for a long time," I said, holding his stare with my own.

"Whatever we're going to do, shit or get off the pot," Amber snapped.

I stared at Jake, tight-lipped. He shifted uncomfortably, casting a glance back towards the house, then to me. I had to wonder exactly what he was getting so anxious about. Was he taking the whole 'second' deal to heart, and just being worried about me?

The image of him and Loren sitting on the couch, tormenting Kai, flashed into my mind unasked. And now him, standing right next to Brendon. I swallowed a groan. Perfect. Just what we needed - a healthy dollop of drama for our little group, right when we needed both of them to get their heads into the game.

But as I opened my mouth, ready to say....something, something I hadn't quite decided yet, Jake pressed a hand to his face.

"Fine," he said, his voice hoarse. "Fine, I get it. I'm going."

It looked like it pained him, but Brendon nodded a second after.

"Thanks," I said, a little more gently. "As soon as we've got Nox in hand we'll go try and help Aedan."

"Fine." There was no anger in his voice, just quiet resignation. Jake turned on his heel before I could say another word, raising his hand in the tiniest of waves, and broke into a run. Within seconds he'd melted back into the dark between us and the house. Brendon stumbled on in his wake, not quite as graceful.

Amber had me in hand before I'd had a chance to turn back around. I yelped, nearly falling over as she started towing me away. "There. They're all set, aren't they? Now come on."

"Amber, I-"

"I said come *on*."

"I can walk," I protested, pulling my arm free. She let me go. Apparently, seeing that I was following her was enough. I straightened my jacket, settling my hand back around the knife in my pocket. Little by little, the bit of calm that we'd found ourselves in was fading. We were heading back into the thick of it, I knew. "So, uh. Where do you think he is?"

"I don't know," Amber said, her voice clipped.

"You don't-"

"I saw someone who looked kind of like him running off into the dark, with people following him," Amber snapped.

I rubbed my face, trying to keep my irritation in check. "That's it."

"It's Nox. They won't catch him, if he's paying attention. And we don't have to find him, either."

I hesitated, my steps slowing. "What do you mean?"

She cast a derisive glance back over her shoulder, eyeing the scene behind us. I followed suit, and groaned. The bodies of the mundane soldiers were left lying under the trees, red-soaked and limp. It looked- Well, it looked like we'd murdered a whole group of people. And since they weren't demis, I'd have to figure out something to do about it. In winter. Fucking great.

"It's a battlefield out here," Amber said, throwing her hand out. Her gun glinted with the motion, sending shards of light across the trees. "It'll put them on edge and let them know they're in danger. It's not going to work, not here."

"What's not going to work?"

She glanced back to me, the corners of her lips curling up in a grin. "Our trap."

"Oh." Yes, that sounded about right.

She turned away, leading me deeper into the dark. "We need somewhere where they won't be expecting it. It won't be far. Just need...to..." Her words trailed off as she cast an assessing glance around. "Up there."

I could see where she was talking about - a little grove, barely visible in the night. A row of pine trees on one side formed a barrier, while juniper nestled against the little path weaving its way along gave a bit of cover. If they came through here, they'd be bottlenecked right up the center. Even I had to admit that it looked like a pretty damn good little spot, considering our choices.

Amber picked her way forward, satisfaction radiating from her every pore. A groan slipped between her lips as she dropped to the ground, settling into a crouch behind the bushes. I followed suit, eyeing the woods around us warily. "So...uh. Not to doubt you, but what now? We just...wait?" I ran a hand through my hair. "I don't think we've got all night."

"Start calling him."

I blinked. "What?"

Amber sighed, then rolled her head back so that she could glare at me. "Nox is a reader. He's a good kid - normally, he'll leave you in peace. As much as he can." Her grin twisted, going crooked for a brief moment. "I've trained him on that much. But, well. Now's not 'normal', is it?"

The light went on in my head. "And you think he's reading."

She snorted. "Of course he is. He'll be reading everything in range, pushing as hard as he can. But it's not like he can keep doing that forever without getting tired. He's fucked, right now, and he knows it. Unless he can find a way out, that is. So be that way out. Call him."

"How do I-"

Even as I spoke, her eyes slid shut with a sense of finality that I couldn't argue with. She ignored me, dropping her chin down against her chest. Her gun lay in her lap, still clutched comfortably in her hand.

Oh. Well....all right.

Feeling like an absolute idiot, I gave one last glance around, and then shut my eyes. The little noises of the woods seemed that much louder when I wasn't looking - the owls overhead, cars out on the freeway...and the constant noises of fighting drifting over from the house.

Nox, I screamed in my head, focusing in on every sound like I was saying it out loud. *Uh...If you can hear me, we're....this way? Over here? Something like that?* Jesus Christ, I didn't know how any of this worked. Could he tell what direction I was in? Did I need to give him better instructions? *Amber's worried. So...hurry? Can you hear me?*

Only the night continued around us.

I sat back on my heels, my concentration slipping. Maybe Amber was just being crazy. Maybe Nox was too far away. Maybe I was doing it wrong.

I tried to disregard the other possibility, the one naggling at the back of my mind - the one that said maybe we were just too late. Maybe Nox was already down. Maybe they'd already pulled his necklace off, and-

I clenched my fists hard enough that my nails dug into my palms painfully. Nope, that wasn't it. We weren't too late. Everyone would make it through this mess fine.

Nox! I bellowed mentally, focusing my thoughts in with razor-sharp intensity. *Over this way, god damn it! Get over here, right now!*

I repeated the calls over and over, until the words seemed etched into the back of my mind. With every repetition the phrases I used grew more fervent and creative, until I was pulling out curses that would have made even Aedan blush.

A shiver ran down my spine. Someone was moving - a second later, I remembered it was only Amber beside me. She'd been so still, so focused, that I'd completely forgotten she was there.

But she was rising to her feet, still half-bent to stay hidden behind the juniper. My calls faltered as I looked to her, confused.

And then I heard it, too. The sound of snow crunching underfoot. Branches snapped. Someone was running, and they weren't bothering being careful. They weren't being stealthy.

"Ready," Amber murmured, her voice the barest trace of a whisper.

She crept to the end of the bushes. When she crouched there, her jacket muted green and worn to the fibers, I had a hard time picking her out even from a few feet away.

I bobbed my head in a nod, clutching my weapon a little more tightly. The taste of air was sweet as I drew in a breath and let it go, enjoying the feeling of breathing easily. Luck wasn't here, this time. I wouldn't let anyone interfere. Not again.

The sound of footsteps grew louder and louder. I shuddered. They were right on top of us. This was stupid. There were only two of us, and we didn't know how many there were of them.

What bad choices had I made in my life that led me here? The thought was rueful, but impossible to brush off. How, exactly, had I wound up hiding in the forest, waiting to murder people?

Amber pushed herself upright, abruptly enough that I twisted, gaping. Her lips were pressed into a thin line, filled with worry, but there was a victorious twist there that was brand new.

Nox burst through the last line of trees leading to our clearing a second later.

I'd never seen the younger man look so disheveled. His glasses had fallen off, somewhere along the line. His hair was a mess to boot, covered in bits of snow and dead leaves and twigs. The net effect looked something like a bird had tried to nest on his head. The wild, terror-stricken set of his eyes wiped away any humor I might have found in the moment.

He didn't hesitate. He tore a path straight down the center of our little clearing, snow flying with every footfall. Without slowing, he hurled himself into Amber's waiting arms.

She rocked back with the force of him hitting her, but only wrapped her left arm about his head to draw him in closer. Her right hand snapped up. There was nothing gentle in her expression as she turned her face away from him, I saw. Just cold, hard calculation.

"They're here," I heard her murmur. Her fingers began a steady, constant waggle, twisting and twining in the air. It quivered in response, slowly filling with fog.

I threw myself backwards, a little closer to them, and held my knife at the ready. I could hear it too - the sound of footsteps rising again, of branches snapping under the weight of bodies plowing through them.

Two dark shapes hurled out of the treeline, hot on Nox's heels.

Amber's low chuckle rang impossibly in my ears as she opened fire a heartbeat later.

CHAPTER FIFTY-THREE

Two of them. There were two demis, accelerating across the snow towards us. I flinched even as Amber started firing. Again and again, the sound screamed out from alongside me. I threw a hand up, covering my ear in a futile attempt to block the noise. At this rate, I was going to go deaf before long. Nox quivered, sliding free of her embrace and cowering behind her.

They scattered, though, throwing themselves behind trees and shelter as Amber unloaded at them. The sound of her muffled swearing drifted across the clearing with the stink of gunpowder as she stopped. Her magazine dropped clear of the grip. She plunged her hand into her pocket, pulling another one out in the same smooth motion.

Something groaned behind me, like trees bending in a windstorm. A shiver ran down my spine. That wasn't right. That wasn't right at *all*. Twisting, I turned back-

-And ducked, dropping to the snow yet again as a branch sailed through where my head had been.

"Amber!" I yelped. "Look out! The...The trees!" I sounded like an absolute idiot, but it was all I could say. There weren't other words that came to mind as I stared at the tree, half-bent towards me. The branch in question teetered madly, careening back around at a frightening clip.

Shit. Well, I didn't have to worry about figuring out what *one* of their powers was. I rolled, putting a little more distance between myself and it. The sound of it slamming into the snow behind me was far too close for comfort. I was on my feet a second later, doing my best to catch my breath.

Amber skittered back, dragging Nox along with her. He wasn't fighting. His eyes flicked back and forth across the woods, towards where the two demis were hiding.

I cleared my throat. "Both of you!" I called, raising my voice a little. "Come out! Guns down! No shooting!"

As the last syllable left my lips, an ache settled across my skull. I groaned, the sound escaping before I could hold it back. From the corner of my eye, I could see Amber twist to shoot me a look. I just crouched low, pushing myself halfway behind a tree. The pain grew with every second, bringing with it a dull, leaden exhaustion.

Amber stiffened. I saw it too - the flicker of movement from behind the trees. Someone twitched, sliding out from behind cover. She was on them a moment later, pouring rounds into them. A strangled cry rang through the clearing. A tree grabbed them a moment later - I blinked, rubbing my eyes, despite the pain still filling my head. Yes, a tree. It wrapped the figure in its branches, pulling them out of the way.

I released my relic a second later. It had worked, sure, but at what cost? It was just like it had been back with Glenn's crew, I realized. It was like my relic was *trying*, but just...couldn't. And it was draining me in the process.

For the first time, I well and truly sympathized with Brendon's plight. It was infuriating. There was no reason for my relic to be failing me. None at all. It was supposed to be a part of me, responding to what I asked of it - for it to be sleeping on the job just felt....wrong.

But the trees around us were roiling, lashing out again and again. I spun, narrowly avoiding another needle-laden branch to the face, and grabbed Amber's arm. "Come on," I said, breathless. "Let's...get closer, I guess." It was all I could think of, that maybe it was a simple matter of distance. I couldn't quite convince myself, even, but it was worth a try. There was only one of them left, after all.

Nox shivered as we slipped past, and then shook his head wildly. "N-No. Don't-"

My heart froze as a pair of figures slipped between the tree trunks, there and then gone. They were looking at us.

Two of them. Perfect. They'd found friends, then? Or had Amber's shots not landed?

"God damn it," Amber muttered next to me, all the confirmation I needed that she'd seen the demis too. Her hand tightened on her gun.

And then she pushed past me, taking the front again. "You've got the magic words, don't you? Keep trying," she snapped.

I couldn't even muster up the will to protest. She was right. And both of us knew that there was only so much ammunition she could hide in her jacket. We couldn't just treat this as a free-for-all shootout, not when there were other fights ahead of us before the end of this. If my powers weren't cooperating, then I needed to *make* them cooperate.

But when I turned back to the trees, I could only stare blankly into their branches and needles. "Uh," I started, the words little more than a murmur. "Where, exactly...did they..."

The forest was quiet and still, with the only noise being the groan of the trees around us. They leaned in, growing closer by the second. I didn't know how much control the plant-worker had over them, and I really didn't fancy the idea of finding out. Being crushed to death in a needle-filled hug did *not* sound like a pleasant way to go.

Amber shot me a look over her shoulder, her eyes narrowed. I cleared my throat. Right.

"Why don't you come out?" I said, raising my voice a little. My hand slipped up to my chest, laying flat over the interlaced rings. "Just...put your guns down, and come out. That sounds good, doesn't it?"

A wave of vertigo washed over me. I scanned the trees more anxiously, looking for the slightest flicker of movement. But whatever else the demi was doing, he was making them a hell of a sight barrier. I couldn't get even a glimpse of them - and my head pounded worse with every second I delayed. I spun, searching desperately. "Come on," I snapped, unable to keep the nonchalant, pleasant tone up. "Get out here already."

A hand brushed my shoulder. I flinched, spinning. My hand shot from my pocket, still clutching my knife. The blade came up, ready to stab into-

Nox. Nox stood beside me, seemingly unaware that he was about to be attacked. His eyes were fixed on the woods, blank and unfocused. "They're over there," he murmured, still not looking at me. "Right-"

They *did* move, then, like they'd heard him talk. I saw the flash of light, the gleam of the moon reflecting off gunmetal, and that was all I needed. Seizing Nox's arm, I pulled hard.

He yelped as I hurled him behind me, grabbing my shoulders to keep from falling. I gasped, clenching my jaw as another line of pain exploded across my forearm.

"You fuckers!" I heard Amber roar. From the corner of my eye I could see her launch herself at the edge of the clearing, straight for where the shot had come from. A stream of words flew from her lips, increasing in foulness with every syllable. I tuned her out, latching in on the tiny, pale patch of skin I could still see between the branches.

Found them.

"You," I snapped, raising my voice loud enough that he couldn't possibly miss me. "Walk towards the sound of my voice. No games."

The half-hidden outline of the person twitched, fighting for a single, eternal second. My relic hissed its complaint, taking another swig of my power - but it was manageable. What I'd expected. Even though they were fighting, it was quite enough for me to handle. My lips curled up into a smile, despite the gravity of the situation. Finally.

They slipped between the last set of branches a moment later, each step a stumbling, staggering battle. Oh, they were fighting, pushing back as hard as they could. Their body didn't seem to care. It was a man, I noted as dispassionately as I could. Tall and willowy, with auburn hair gelled into spikes. His eyes were fixed on mine. They were wide, with a tightness at the corners that told me he knew he was in trouble, but he wasn't panicked. Not yet. He thought he could still get away, then.

My fingers tightened around my knife.

Another crack of gunfire brought my chin up as I searched, finally latching onto the sight of Amber standing across the clearing from the other demi. Or from their body, anyway. They lay in a dark, damp puddle, twitching gently. Her chin was raised, a triumphant light in her eyes.

The plant-worker stumbled closer, the confidence leaving his face little by little as he realized he wasn't going to be able to escape. I slid my hand from my pocket.

And froze, my blood chilling as another gunshot rang out.

Amber. She was firing again, her smile fading - and the demi wasn't on the ground anymore. He was on his feet, ducking behind the trees. Trees which bristled with rows of needles, throwing themselves up in her way.

"No casting!" I snapped, more loudly. The trees froze, quivering in place, and slowly slumped back to their normal positions.

I was *sure* Amber had shot the demi. And from the confused look in her eyes, so was she. Again, he darted out of the darkness, raising a gun to point at her - and again, she fired. His leg exploded in red. He fell hard. His shriek was pained enough that there wasn't any doubt he'd been hit.

When Amber stepped forward, though, raising her pistol yet again, he rolled awkwardly, twisting away from her. A second later, he pushed himself to his feet.

A glitter of brass - that was all I saw, sliding out of his leg. And then he'd vanished into the trees.

Amber let out another curse, wiped away under the sound of another gunshot. But she'd been caught off guard as much as I was. The shot went wide, tearing through the trunk of a tree instead of the demi.

Her slide locked back again. Empty. Her eyes tightened, crow's feet appearing at the corners. Her hand twitched towards her jacket - and then curled into a fist, dropping to her side. She shoved her pistol back into a holster into the small of her back, muttering darkly to herself.

I flinched, realizing that the plant-bender was nearly on top of me. "Stand still, now," I said, twisting to face him. "That's close enough. Stay still."

He froze in place. The muscles in his neck twitched, the only sign of the internal struggle that I could *feel* was playing out inside him. But try as he might, I had him, and the warmth of my relic was a steady, comfortable pulse against my chest. He wasn't going anywhere.

Nox darted out from behind me, a cry slipping out of him. I saw it too, the figure lunging out of the trees towards Amber. I had his arm in hand before he could get away, towing him back to safety.

Amber's mouth dropped open at the sudden surge of movement, spinning to face the demi, but recovered in an instant. Her palm snapped up, ready and waiting for the bullet that screamed in a moment after. The air in front of her hand blurred ominously. The copper-plated projectile shivered to a stop, hanging in midair for a single, impossible second before ricocheting back towards the demi.

He didn't even bother trying to avoid it. I gaped, shocked to silence at the sight of his arm exploding.

It was better, that way. I didn't have to do anything at all to properly express the horror I felt as the skin around his arm roiled, churning and bubbling. The mangled bullet worked its way back out before our very eyes, dropping to the snowy ground in a splatter of red. The hole was already closed by the time I looked back.

"Stay still," I said, my eyes dancing between the plant-worker and his friend. I raised my voice just a hair, reaching out tentatively with my relic. Two was workable. I could do two. I could.

A wave of relief washed over me as both of them froze, pinned in place. The other demi's gaze flicked over to mine, irritation warring with confusion.

Amber's fist plowed into his cheek a moment later. He crumpled, beginning to fall - but her other hand hit the far side before he could hit the ground. The crunch of his neck snapping was every bit as loud as the gunshots had been. My relic released its hold on him as I exhaled, shaking my head.

Nox grabbed at me, lurching towards her. "No. No, he's- She's still-"

"I see," I muttered, pulling him back again. Even that wasn't enough, apparently. The demi rolled over, pushing himself upright with a groan. Amber was there before he could rise, her boot catching him in the ribs. He toppled again, gasping. She laid into him over and over, putting everything that she had into keeping him down. I winced.

And still he kept getting back up. He was battered more than I'd ever seen a person before, ands his gun was kicked out of reach, but over and over again he'd roll over, fixing her with a knowing, superior look.

Every time, Amber was breathing just a little bit harder. I paused, another command on my lips. But it wouldn't help. I could hold him still, but what difference would that make, if we didn't know-

"How," I said, tearing my eyes off him long enough to glare at the plant-worker. My arm was on fire, dripping blood into the snow. I clenched my other hand over it, trying to stem the blood. The demi froze, his face going white. "How do we kill your friend?" My head pounded, but I laced my words with just a trace of magic.

His lips pressed together into a thin line. "Just like you'd kill anyone."

A scowl curled into my face. "Fuck you. You know what I'm asking."

"Wouldn't you like to know."

Amber yelped. I spun, twisting to face her. Nox twitched, a second from lunging for her, but seemed to think the better of it. He'd only get in her way, I knew, and he seemed to know it too.

She'd gone in for another kick- only this time, the demi had grabbed back. She was flat on her back in the snow, gasping for her lost breath and kicking madly at him with her free foot. His fingers were latched around her ankle, pulling her closer.

Shit. If she was struggling, then I couldn't very well sit by and do *nothing*. My head screamed its reminders that one way or another, I couldn't keep going all night. I licked my suddenly-dry lips, all too aware that this was far from over.

But I couldn't let her get hurt.

"Now!" I snapped, glancing back to her friend. "Answer!" The relic around my neck burned a little hotter as I poured more power into the command, pushing harder. My eyes flicked back to the brawling pair all the while. "And *you*. Let her go."

The regenerator's hand slipped, his fingers going lip. Amber pulled free in an instant, aiming a kick straight for his face. His nose audibly crunched with the impact. A fresh gout of red coated his skin.

"H-Head," his friend stammered.

I paused, looking back at him. He was still fighting, quivering under my hold, but there was a defeated set to his shoulders that hadn't been there before. "Like a zombie?" I said, a touch incredulous. "Really? That's it?"

He shuddered, cringing away as he struggled. Nox was already moving. His head bobbed furiously as he took a step towards the pair. "Yeah. Yeah, that's- Amber! Can you-"

"I heard," Amber snapped, skittering back. "Shit." She wiped her gloved palm across her face. "Okay, then."

The demi kicked hard, propelling himself forward. His hand settled around the pistol he'd dropped earlier. I grabbed Nox yet again, ready to pull him out of danger. My mouth dropped open. One command. I could stop him if he tried anything. Probably. All the while, though, I could feel the plant-worker pushing, sapping my strength.

Enough was enough. I didn't want to waste my power, but keeping him around wasn't serving any purpose if we knew how to kill his friend. And his words had rang true to me. Near as I could tell he wasn't lying - that'd have to be good enough.

"Breathe," I said, dropping my voice lower so that it was just the plant-worker and I. He flinched, his eyes locked on mine. "Just...breathe easy. Calm down. Don't move."

From the corner of my eye I could see Amber roll, dodging another blow. Her hand settled around something I couldn't quite see, lost to the shadows and the snow.

The plant-worker shivered, still staring at me, and little by little his breathing slowed. "There," I whispered, inching closer. My hand slid from my pocket. "Just stand still, all right?"

My stomach churned unhappily at the thought of what I'd have to do *again*. Already, I could feel the bile rising, the hot taste of acid lingering in the back of my throat. I'd have nightmares again, I knew, after I'd finally managed to put the last behind me. I could have him do it to himself. Then I wouldn't have to *feel* it, to have my body remember the way his skin parted under the steel.

But his eyes were too wide, with fear growing in their depths, and it wasn't right. It wasn't fair for me to use my power to escape what needed doing and force that onto someone else. I gripped the hilt of my knife a little tighter, feeling the solid weight of it in my hand. It wasn't right, not when there were other options. Not when I could spare him that much, at least.

"Close your eyes," I murmured.

His breath came ragged, despite my earlier command. But his eyes slid shut.

Something slammed into a tree trunk, from where Amber and the regenerator fought. Something big, something heavy. Something *hard*. I couldn't bring myself to take my eyes off the plant-worker. Not as my hand came up, the blade gleaming in the night.

I'd seen Aedan do it so many times, it seemed. He was so good, so fast. It was a mercy, I realized. I tried to remember just the way he moved, the way he held his knife.

A breath of air slipped out of him as my knife cut home. I could feel it, the way his whole being seemed to...shudder. My hold on the necklace slipped away. I didn't need it anymore. He stumbled back, one hand rising to his neck. It made it halfway there before his legs gave out.

He hit the snow a second later. He didn't move.

Nox pushed past me, scarcely waiting for the snow to settle. I let him go, staring down at my hand. My fingers were spotted with red, despite my best efforts. It was from more than just my cut arm. I rubbed them against my pants, numb. It didn't help.

The mind-reader pulled the plant-worker's jacket open, pawing through his possessions much like Aedan had a few short minutes before. "Got to be...somewhere," I heard him mutter to himself.

Swallowing my distaste with his scavenging and the blood on my hands, I clenched my jaw, turning back towards where Amber and the other demi still fought. The two of them hadn't stopped, in fact.

He had a gun. The fact sent a fresh rush of adrenaline down my spine, jolting me straight back to wakefulness. He had a gun, and he was pointing it right at her. I could see the movement in his every muscle - the way the tendons in his arm tensed, his hand tightening. The front of the barrel wobbled, tilting this way and that as he started to squeeze.

He screamed a heartbeat later, stumbling to the side.

I blinked, sure that I'd seen things wrong - but, no. Amber had closed the gap between them, her teeth bared and her eyes wild. She clutched something in her hand. A tree branch, it looked like, as thick around as my wrist and a good two feet long. And she'd knocked the gun clear out of his hand with one brutal blow.

His wrist was broken. It hung at an odd angle, twisted and dangling. He screamed all the louder, stumbling away.

And then it shivered, turning back around. Before our very eyes, it was setting itself. Nox whispered a prayer from alongside me, his voice just a fragment of sound.

She wasn't done. As I watched, aghast, she lunged in. There was blood staining her jeans, and more than a few new ragged gashes had been torn into the fabric, but her steps were sure. Her foot flew in, sliding between the other demi's. In a second they were entwined, close enough to grapple - and then she kicked out hard, sending him stumbling back.

Her elbow slammed into his face a second later. He hit the ground with a pained roar.

Nox and I sat right where we were. We could help, I knew. We *should* help. Helping was better than just watching, after all. We were supposed to be allies.

But somehow, it didn't seem like she needed it. And the thought of putting myself any closer to the two of them was anything but appealing.

The question of helping or sitting by was resolved for us a brief second later. Amber twisted, her stance widening underneath her, and swung hard. Her arms flew over her head, the makeshift club she clutched shooting up to brush at the branches above.

And then it came screaming back down with a rush of air that carried all the way over to the two of us.

I winced, turning away at last as red splattered across the snow.

Nox chuckled, pushing himself upright as I shook my head, pressing a hand to my face. "Got him. You got him." He clutched something in his hand - a belt knife, it looked like, small enough to fit into the man's buckle. The plant-worker's body started to glow as I turned back around, eyeing the young man with more than a little unease. He sounded *far* too eager for all this.

But I couldn't entirely blame him, either. A weight lifted from my shoulders as he hurried forward, closer to Amber. She was still hitting the demi, still driving her club into his head over and over again. What was left of his head, anyway.

"You got him," I said, looking away again hurriedly.

"Let me. Take five," Nox said, his hand on her shoulder. She bobbed her head in a nod, tossing the branch off to the side carelessly. He'd dropped to his knees in the snow before it stopped rolling, repeating the same search he had just moments earlier. "If I heard right...it's..."

"Perfect," I said darkly, hearing the man's satisfied little laugh as he found the relic. "Now if you guys don't mind, we're not done. Let's not take five. We need to get moving or else someone else is going to die." I paused, biting my lip. Where to next? Had Aedan found Loren and Kai? Did they need help? Who should we-

"About that," Nox said, straightening with what sounded like a tired groan. "Uh. I don't think anyone's farther out there than we are now." He glanced down, making a face. "I think I ran too far. Sorry."

"You did what you had to," Amber said, her voice rough.

"Even still, we can't just leave Loren and Kai," I said, shooting him an irritated glare. I wasn't fooled - and I hadn't spoken mt question out loud. He was pilfering thoughts. "We should go find them, before we head back."

"Uh," Nox muttered, his head drooping farther. "I think...I can feel them back towards the others, anyway. I mean, not *with* them, but...close."

I stopped. "We were there. We didn't see them."

He shrugged. "It's a big house. You probably missed them. Or they might have been farther out still. It's okay."

"Fuck," I muttered, kicking at the snow. "Then-"

"We should get back anyway," Nox said, his eyes widening. "We're

not alone."

I paused. "That's...no, we're not. But what do you mean?"

He hesitated, for long enough that Amber's hand settled onto his shoulder. "What do you hear?" she said, wiping her other hand on her pants just like I had a few minutes before. From the way dark blotches stained her jeans, I got the feeling it wasn't the first time she'd done something like this.

Nox swallowed, his chin lifting, and he looked between Amber and I. "I just...I just felt them," he said, his voice growing stronger with every word. "Like they appeared out of nowhere. I-I don't get it, but..."

My pulse thundered in my ears. We'd wondered. We'd *thought* it sounded too good to be true, for the marketeers to show up with only two demis. And, after all, we knew for a fact they'd gotten more people past Greyson, somehow.

Even still, I wanted to hear him say it. "What are you saying, Nox?" I heard myself say.

He stared at me, his brown eyes dark. "The house," he said, sounding halfway composed again. "They're regrouping. With a few new friends, I think. All together. At the house."

Shit.

CHAPTER FIFTY-FOUR

No one spoke. No one so much as made a noise, let alone said a word as we raced back through the forest.

My legs ached, burning underneath me, and every step sent a shudder of pain through the wounds I'd sustained. My arm had stopped bleeding at last, which was a small relief. Covered in bruises and bloodstains, Amber couldn't feel much better, and I knew that Nox had been running for far longer than either of us.

None of us was really in the mood for a good late-night sprint. Even still, I didn't hear any complaining. Everyone knew what the stakes were.

I just focused on putting one foot in front of the other, keeping my footing in the snow as we raced back through the dark.

The night parted ahead of us in what seemed like mere moments, though. The forest around us made everything seem darker and more isolated, but we weren't *that* far. The thought was a tiny bit of comfort amidst the rest of the chaos around us.

The sight that greeted us as we sprinted towards the edge of the trees wiped away any such feelings of relief.

Nox was right. There were more of them - a whole second van, in fact, jammed in alongside the first. It was already empty and deserted. The 'soldiers' within hadn't gone far. They crouched behind the first vehicle, our trash cans, the firewood pile. Anywhere they could shelter, which included the artfully landscaped barricades we'd built.

Wonderful. I glared at the sight of one of them peering from around a brick half-wall.

Ahead, the plight our friends were in became all too clear.

My heart sank. We'd done so *well*. We killed three of their demis, after all, and sent another one fleeing. I'd thought we were winning handily.

Things hadn't gone so well for the rest of everyone.

My eyes were drawn to a flash of gunfire - and to Keira, half-hidden behind the corner of the building. She was right where she'd been, and the fact that she still appeared to be unhurt was enough to ease my worries a hair. She clutched her gun, leaning out as I watched to fire again, then ducked back behind cover. A spray of gunshots sent sparks flying across the brick she'd found for cover.

Gunshots and what looked suspiciously like icicles. I swallowed hard, moving to close the gap between us. A hand latched onto my collar a second later.

"Quiet," Amber whispered, her lips inches from my ear. "Not yet. Watch. *See.*"

Keira winced back from another volley. My heart froze in my chest. But Amber was right, I knew - we needed to get our feet under us again.

Tyler wasn't with her anymore. My eyes flicked this way and that, sudden panic flooding my chest. He'd been with her. So where-

There. He'd made it halfway out around the side of the house towards the driveway before taking cover behind an old oak in the yard. From where we stood, he was only a dozen paces away. I gauged the distance between us as cooly as I could, running over my chances of making it to him.

An almighty *bang* exploded from farther down the drive, drawing my eyes like a beacon. Kai. He...wasn't doing so well. I stared, my throat tightening. His skin was blistered and red, and the unmistakable black of soot coated his hair. Even from where I stood, I could see his hands shaking with exhaustion.

There was another man, further down the road - and his hands were smoking. I didn't think it was from anything Kai had done. His coat was singed about the hem, and his eyebrows were missing, but he leered across the driveway at our companion. His lips moved. I couldn't hear what he said, but Kai did. The teenager erupted again, cupping his hands until a ball of tightly-contained fire churned within.

When he threw it, though, the other demi only reached out lazily, snapping it out of the air with one hand. And then he opened his mouth, swallowing the fire whole as though it was nothing worse than cotton candy. Flames danced around his fingertips.

Shit. Another fire demi? I cast a wary eye towards my house - and saw for the first time the bits of char and soot staining the walls. *Shit.* Another magician who could burn the place down. Just what we needed. And from the look in Kai's eyes, his teeth gritted with unmistakable fury, our youngest friend wasn't taking the competition well. He was still learning, damn it. He didn't need to come face to face with a pro.

Nox's hand latched onto my elbow. The mind-reader dropped down alongside me, one finger jabbing out through the night. "There," he whispered, a thin line of fear running through his voice. "She needs help. She's in trouble, if- if no one-"

"I see her," I muttered, forcing the words out. And I did see her, now that Nox pointed her out - Loren, half-hidden in the shadows on the edge of the treeline. Now that I saw her, in fact, it was pretty clear that Kai was trying to get to her. Or had been, until he decided to take up a mirror face-off with the marketeers' pyromancer.

Loren was caught, in fact, pinned in place between two men. From the rifles they had slung around them, they weren't demis, at least. Not from what we'd seen so far that night. My heart sank. It would have been obvious even without an appraiser, after all. Just a matter of time, to watch which of our crew started casting and which didn't. They'd *know* which ones they could try and slice from our numbers.

Only, it wasn't going so smoothly for them. Loren's face was white against the darkness, and her eyes were so round I thought they might pop out of her head entirely, but her heels were dug into the snow. The men had hold of her, but they weren't moving.

Her lips were moving. Just a tiny amount, like she was whispering to them, but I could see it. And the men shuddered in response every time she said a word.

She was a dream-worker, who seemed to like to cast via touch. And they were holding onto her. A grim smile tugged at my lips. Probably not their smartest move ever. *Hold on,* I whispered silently, seeing the strain in every fiber of her being. *Just a little more.*

In all of the chaos and mess, I *hadn't* seen Brendon. Or Jake. I cursed under my breath. It was my fault. I'd told them to go looking. I just hadn't thought they'd be here. Now two of our demis were out in the woods, separated from the rest of the crew when we could really use all hands on deck.

"They'll get here," Nox said, patting my shoulder. "It'll be fine."

I just shot him a look, warring between irritation and appreciation. But with a fight breaking out, I couldn't blame him for digging around a little.

A flicker of movement caught the corner of my eye - a dark shape, slipping between the stacked wood and hastily built retaining walls. A knife gleamed in his hands as he crept closer to where Keira hid, step by step.

Well, at least Aedan hadn't bothered to listen to my instructions. Or maybe he had, and he'd just figured out that Loren and Kai were here. Regardless, I was glad to see him.

He darted out from under cover, making a break for where Keira cowered - and fell back, throwing his arms up around his head. Ice shattered against the stacked wood.

"Shit," I swore, twisting until I could catch sight of the demi who'd thrown the icicles. A woman with mud-brown hair pulled back into a ponytail, her eyes sharp and fixated on Aedan's hiding place. Frost cascaded across the wooden surface, blossoming into silvered flowers. Aedan scrambled back farther, lips pressed tightly together.

Aedan wasn't going to be able to help her - and neither could Tyler, if I was any judge of the situation. More than anything I wanted to run in and do what I could, but what *could* I do? I only had the stupid damn knife, and it was too loud for anyone to hear me if I called. There were too many of them, and with how my relic had been uncooperative of late, I couldn't afford to have it screw things up.

Above it all was the heavy, leaden exhaustion building in my shoulders, behind my eyes. I didn't want to waste what magic I could still muster. Keira was in danger, yes, but so was everyone. She was unhurt, and clutched a weapon in her hand. It was as good as I could ask for.

A pained bellow echoed across the drive. I flinched. Kai reeled, his arm thrown up over his face. The other pyromancer advanced all the while. Kai was going to lose. I knew it in an instant, saw the outcome spelled out in their every movement.

Tyler made a tiny, furious noise and hurled himself out from behind cover. The world ahead of him shuddered, the snow flying into the air and carrying pieces of gravel with it as he pulled desperately on whatever power he could muster.

But I saw the ice beginning to form around his feet - and the smirk on the lips of the frost mage.

"Fucking hell," I breathed. The words slid between my lips as I lunged. Every step was shuddering and painfully slow, my body protesting the idea of moving. Keira was out of reach. Loren was out of reach. Kai was out of reach. Aedan was...Aedan. But *Tyler*. I wasn't going to let him get turned into a popsicle while I watched.

He grunted when I grabbed him by the belt, planting my heels and pulling for all I was worth. The two of us hit a snowdrift rather than the gravel drive. It was a small blessing. I pulled us down behind the embankment a second later, letting the spears of ice sail harmlessly past.

A burst of motion erupted in the corner of my vision at the same moment. I flinched, drawing my arm up defensively, but froze. Aedan flew past, low enough to stay under the worst of the enemy's fire. A scowl curled across his face, but within seconds he'd crossed halfway to where Keira was caught.

Tyler thrashed in my hold, bringing my observations to an end. "Let- Let me go," he rasped, pinwheeling one arm. "Kai. He's...he can't possibly-"

"You can't help him like that," I said, bringing my weight to bear. The words flew out of me all on their own. "We're up shit creek, here."

He twitched another time or two, still trying to pull free, but grimaced. "I can take them. Just give me an opening, and-"

Someone touched my elbow. I jumped, gasping. Nox crouched beside us. Despite the chaos, with fireballs exploding just a short distance off and icicles sailing through the air, he seemed oddly at ease. Amber watched from over his shoulder, half-hidden behind Keira's car where it sat on the snow-covered lawn.

"Jesus Christ, Nox," I snapped, turning away. "Give me some warning. Don't just sneak up on me like that."

Another spray of gunfire ricocheted across the siding of our house. I cringed.

Another tug on my elbow.

I paused, blinking slowly, and glanced back towards Nox. He was eerily silent, letting the fight go on around us, but his eyes were fixed on mine. Slowly, pointedly, his face turned away.

I followed the motion with my eyes - and stopped.

The van that the marketeers had brought was pulled up right in our driveway, perfectly placed to dispense their goons. The second round of reinforcements they'd brought while Amber and I were off chasing after Nox had brought a van too. It sat crosswise behind the first, like they'd jumped out hastily.

The back doors were open. And I could see two figures crouched in the shadows between them, small and wary. One peered out around the side of the van, inching into the light.

One of their soldiers screamed. Aedan's knife stuck from his stomach. I swallowed hard, forcing the contents of my *own* stomach back down.

His fellows responded with a fresh barrage of rifle-fire. Dimly, distantly, I heard Keira cry out in surprise and fear. My blood chilled instantly.

We couldn't keep this up. We were picking away at their numbers, but our own forces wouldn't hold out forever.

I hesitated, feeling Nox's hand still on my elbow. Again, he directed me back towards the marketeers.

The two demis hiding behind the van....didn't look happy. Two women - I could tell that much. One was nearly motionless, panting for breath loud enough I could hear her now and again over the gunplay. And when the other one had leaned out, I recognized the silhouette of our too-lucky opponent. Thus far, she hadn't helped, at least. So far as I could tell. Her shoulders quivered like she was running on empty. Maybe she *couldn't*.

And Luck's hand was raised to her ear. A bejeweled phone case sparkled from between her fingers. She was calling someone.

"Nox," I whispered, sliding a little lower and glancing over to him. "What's she-"

"This is taking too long," he said, still staring at me. "And they've lost too many. Her wind-gifted partner. He wasn't supposed to die. Neither were their troops. And now, she hasn't heard from their other demis in a long time. Too long."

"They expected to roll over us that easily, did they?" Tyler muttered darkly. He inched back up, scanning the battlefield.

I got my hand on top of his head before he could clamber up fully, shoving him back down with a sigh. "There's no way of knowing exactly how much information they had. And-"

Nox lunged, pulling both Tyler and I down. A fireball sailed over our heads a moment later, escaping Kai's duel.

Keira screamed, the sound soaked through with pain. My heart froze. Throwing off Nox's arm, I surged up, twisting towards her - and found her tumbling back behind cover. Embers danced from her clothes, and sparks flew about her hair. She'd vanished behind the brick wall a second later.

"Can you get to her?" I asked, still staring at the place she'd been.

Nox went still. "What?"

My gaze dragged across to meet his. "Keira. Can you reach her? You're probably the one least likely to get hit, so-"

He bobbed his head in a nod, although he went a bit pale around the edges. Amber scowled from behind him. I had no doubt she'd heard everything, and probably didn't *appreciate* my enlisting him, but someone needed to help her. "Get there," I said, a little breathless. "Please."

He hesitated a moment longer, scanning the battlefield, and nodded again. A heartbeat later he'd gone.

Tyler pushed up again, rising over the snowbank. "Sit down," I muttered, grabbing his shoulder and forcing him back to his seat.

He spun on me, eyes flashing dangerously. "Jon, I swear to god, let me go."

"I need your help," I said, forcing every ounce of conviction into the words I could. "So sit down and *help* me."

"Go ask Aedan to-"

"I need *your* help," I snapped, a little more loudly. "Shut up and listen."

He shut up. He was still visibly agitated, and I couldn't blame him for that, but I tried to keep my stare as even and calm as I could. It was the only thing I could think of to bring him back to some sort of rational thought, like I could push my mood off onto him. Much to my relief, his shoulders settled a fraction of an inch. His legs went slack, even as his eyes twitched to follow another icicle's flight.

"Fine," he said at last. "What?"

Straight to the point, then. Good. I licked my suddenly-dry lips, praying that I wasn't just crazy. That I could make this work. "You can manipulate sounds, right?"

He scowled at me. "Don't act like an idiot."

"Even small ones?"

"Of course."

"And you can direct them?"

His eyes narrowed. "You know all this."

I nodded slowly, glancing back across the battlefield. My well was too empty to grab hold of everyone there, of that much I was completely certain. And with four demis on the field, alongside a nice little host of their thugs, well, sooner or later they'd wear us down.

Unless we could make it too expensive to keep going. The sight of Luck's face flashed through my mind again, tight-drawn and pale. They were almost there.

Grabbing hold of Tyler's shoulder, I leaned closer, whispering my plan into his ear. He went stock-still, perfectly motionless while I poured it out.

And then he swallowed. His adam's apple bobbed with the motion of it, rocking underneath his skin.

"Can you do it?" I said, drawing back.

He nodded slowly. His face had gone bone-white, no matter what confident words he'd said moments before. I swallowed a humorless laugh at the sight. *Welcome to my life.*

A burst of light interrupted the two of us. I wheeled, eyes going wide. The marketeers' pyromancer had had his fill, apparently. He'd belched out a great cloud of fire, spraying it towards Kai.

The teenager did his best. His hands came up, like he could brace against the wall of heat and flame. It swirled in response, twisting and twining about his fingers as he grabbed at it, but there was just too much. He vanished into the fires.

"Kai!" Tyler roared, instantly forgetting about our plan and everything I'd explained. His eyes were wide. I just held on, keeping him where he was. Kai was a fire-type demi. That had to give some sort of resistance to heat. It *had* to. And Tyler wouldn't have any protection at all.

A curtain of sparks erupted at the edge of the cloud. The flames dissipated in moments, leaving Kai to stumble out. His hair was blackened in patches, and it was becoming hard to find any unburned skin on him, but - my heart leapt. He was still upright.

Not for long. One long, unsteady step later and he tumbled, hitting the ground with a wet *thud*. His feet stuck out from behind another snowbank, twitching gently.

We'd never make it across to him in time. Not before their demis got there to finish what they'd started. My hand tightened on Tyler's shoulder. "That one," I said, a fresh urgency underlying my every word. I pointed towards one of the marketeers' soldiers in the back, standing with his rifle at the ready.

Tyler twisted to face me, his brow furrowed. I could almost *hear* the incredulous protest about to erupt from his mouth. I forced a mirthless smile instead, pointedly turning back towards the soldier.

And then I started to talk.

CHAPTER FIFTY-FIVE

The driveway was the very picture of chaos. I stared across it, my eyes latched onto the lone figure of the soldier standing all the way in the back.

He wasn't the last one, of course. The icicle-throwing woman and their pyromancer might have been the two demis taking the lead in the fight, but there were still a fair number of mundane soldiers milling about. Two still clung to Loren, the three of them frozen in a motionless tableau. A handful more cowered around the edge of the battle as close to the vans as they could get without getting screamed at. The covering fire they lay down made the whole situation even messier than it already was.

With the sounds of explosions and guns and yelling, I'd never be heard.

By myself.

"Listen to the sound of my voice," I whispered, my eyes tightening. No matter how hard I tried, it was going to come out like some cheap hypnotist's routine, and I'd given up bothering. "Turn towards your friend, the flame demi."

It felt...wrong, somehow. With as much distance as was between him and I, there was no way in hell my voice should have carried even if it was a normal, quiet night. It was *wrong* to whisper to someone halfway across the yard. But Tyler's breath hitched as I started speaking, and I saw his hands tighten until his knuckles stood out white against his skin. He'd make sure my words reached their target, I knew.

And the soldier stiffened, shuddering and shaking his head.

"Do it," I whispered, letting my hand slide up and come to rest against my relic. Its warmth was a comfort. I wasn't out of magic yet. I was still in the fight.

The rifleman twitched one last time, fighting back as hard as he could - but he was just a human, not a demi. He didn't have magic, and he couldn't understand what was happening to him. Not fully. I gritted my teeth, bearing down hard, and pushed straight past his resistance.

The barrel of his rifle came up to the ready - and he turned, sliding around to face the pyromancer.

Kai groaned, trying to push himself upright on unsteady arms. He made it halfway up before collapsing again. His jacket was blackened. Smoke rose from where he lay in a pile of soot-stained cloth and blistered skin.

The pyromancer laughed. The sound echoed off the front of the house, cold and confident and callous. His hand came up, angling towards Kai.

"Shoot him," I whispered, unable to keep the frigid chill from my voice.

Tyler shuddered. The motion was small enough I nearly missed it entirely.

My rifleman fired. Again and again I could feel the pull of the trigger under his finger, like a ghostly afterimage of his senses. Underlying it all was his ongoing resistance. I ignored it.

Bullets ripped across the rear of the battlefield. His aim was...passable. Not as good as I'd have hoped, given the comfortable way he'd held his rifle, but it wasn't like he was cooperating.

It was good enough. The pyromancer screamed in agony, lurching forward. Red sprayed from his shoulder where he'd been clipped once - twice. My heart leapt. Good. His good hand swung up, slapping against the wound. He spun in the same instant. Gone was his confident attitude, his cocky demeanor. His wide-eyed gaze scanned the battlefield, looking for our gunman.

My rifleman twitched. "Keep shooting," I whispered. "Don't let up. Empty your gun at him and the ice woman." It wouldn't last forever, I knew. We had to make the most of it, even if his accuracy was the sacrifice.

What little resistance he'd managed to put up before was fading, nearly gone entirely as he settled the gun against his shoulder, firing shot after shot. Cries went up around their group, confusion spreading like wildfire. From the corner of my eye, I saw Luck and her exhausted friend snap upright as though electrified.

But even though the pyromancer was hurt, the moment of surprise was gone. Before my thrall could drive another shot home he was off and running, half-stumbling and still clutching his shoulder. In seconds he was safely behind a brick half-wall, out of reach.

"Shit," I muttered. The rifleman twitched. I sighed, redoubling my hold on him.

That was one of them - but the others were still on their feet, and they'd move in before long. Kai was still on the ground. Amber inched closer, nearly invisible in the dark. Her eyes flicked towards the group of thugs still at it.

A new scream of pain interrupted the momentary lull in the fighting. My breath caught in my throat.

Aedan had closed the gap between him and Loren, in the brief distraction I'd bought him. His knife gleamed in the dark as he swung hard. One of the soldiers holding her fell away, still shrieking in pain. The sound of his body hitting the snow rang out a second later.

The other hesitated, but only for a second. As Aedan turned back around, lunging towards them, he slipped his arm around Loren's neck. She squeaked, the sound vanishing in an instant as he squeezed hard. His gun was at her temple before she could twitch.

Aedan froze, skidding to a stop. His eyes were fixed on the soldier's, as though searching for any sign of weakness. A breath slid between my lips, a tiny fragment of relief that he wasn't just going to charge in, damning Loren to whatever followed. The two were caught in place instead, staring like statues.

"The icicle-thrower," I whispered, forcing the words out and making myself turn away from Aedan's macabre staring contest. "Now. Do as I tell you." The rest of the fight was still ongoing. Couldn't get distracted.

The rifleman wheeled, turning to face the mud-haired woman - and I saw her eyes widen in response.

"Hey!" she cried, taking a step back. "What do you think you're-"

"Now," I murmured. The man opened fire in the same instant.

Her brief moment of warning had been enough, though. She was already off and running. But I heard her cry out in pain, stumbling hard as a round tore across the back of her calf.

"It's him!" another voice yelled. A woman's voice, and filled with exhaustion and fury in equal parts. "Like Noah said. It's him!"

I glanced over, my eyes drawn to the sound of her voice - and found the lucky demi - Tara, my mind whispered - staring right back at me. Her skin was pale, but her fingers curled into claws around the side of the van's door.

"He's the one doing it!" I heard her yell again, continuing on uninterrupted. "Stephan - Natalie! Either of you, I don't give a damn, but do something. Don't let him-"

"Shut her up," I whispered, hearing my words slide away from me on the tendrils of Tyler's power. My rifleman spun, bringing his gun up to the ready-

-And stiffened a second later.

I cringed, gaping at the sight of the six-inch icicle sprouting from his eye. His rifle dropped from unfeeling hands. His fingers quivered, spasming.

He crumpled a second later.

"Shit," I muttered, releasing my magic.

Tyler shifted beside me, shaking his head violently. "Damn. *Damn.*"

Well, so much for the idea of shutting Tara up. I bit my lip, scanning the fight for my next target.

The world exploded into light before I could more than turn. Light and *heat*. A scream slipped from my throat as my skin erupted into blinding, searing agony.

A hand latched onto my shoulder. Tyler. He pulled me down into the snow. I let him. The touch of frigid, mostly-frozen water against my face had never felt better.

"Stephan!" Tara screamed from somewhere far, far away. "Noah said not to-"

I rolled upright, letting the two argue back and forth. Every movement hurt, my skin aching at the slightest tension. I raised one hand gingerly, inspecting it. It glowed red, like I'd spent all day in the sun without any sunblock, but that was all. I wasn't dead. We weren't dead yet.

"I don't give a fuck, Tara!" someone bellowed right back. The pyromancer, if current events were any indication. "If he wants this asshole on his leash, he can come catch the bastard himself!"

Still arguing. Perfect.

Turning back towards the enemy demis, I flopped onto our

snowbank just far enough so that I could peer over the edge. "Tyler?"

"I got it," he muttered. His face was as red and bright as my hand. "I can't do this forever, though."

"I know." I did know. He didn't have to tell me - the exhaustion seeping into every word he spoke was all the warning I needed that he was beginning to run himself low. He'd been at it since long before the others and I joined in, after all. I smiled gently, raising my arm to point towards one of the soldiers on the other side of the fight - the soldier holding Loren. "Just a little more. That one."

"Got it."

I bobbed my head, already focusing in on the distant pair.

My head pounded, protesting every syllable I spoke as I whispered. But the man stiffened as my words slipped into his ear. My smile grew, going twisted at the sight of his eyes glazing over.

"Good. Keep listening to me. And now - let her go."

"He's doing it again!"

I caught myself a second before a curse slipped out. Tara's voice was strident enough to carry to the whole battlefield despite the pain lacing it, and when I glanced over, she was still watching me. I gauged my reserves, my mind racing. Did I have enough? Could I take control of her and put an end to the annoyance? And if I did that, would I still have enough left to be useful after?

The sight of the last two soldiers turning from the ice-thrower's side and sprinting towards Loren left a sour taste in my mouth. Before I could say another word they were on her. She flinched back, but there was nowhere for her to go. They held tight, taking a step towards the vans - and shuddered to a stop.

I exhaled slowly. Loren was still casting, then, but there was no way to tell how much she had left. She could run out at any minute, and then she'd be screwed. I searched desperately. Aedan had fallen back at some point, driven away from Loren and her captors by the still-constant gunfire. He inched closer, seeing the same thing I was. An icicle sent him cringing back, flying inches in front of his nose.

That left Amber. I seized on the idea, searching the battlefield, and groaned. She crouched over Kai, pulling his limp, still-smoking body into her arms as best she could. Her eyes flicked up to meet mine, but they were filled with resignation, not hope. She turned away before I could say a word, pulling the both of them low enough to be mostly out of sight.

I gripped my knife a little tighter, resting my hand on Tyler's shoulder. "A little more," I said, feeling the world spin underneath me. "Just a bit more."

He couldn't be feeling any better than I was, but he just nodded. "Right."

I opened my mouth, letting my gaze flit between the thugs and Tara. And then I stopped.

The two men holding Loren didn't look so polished and professional, anymore. They still had hands on her, but even from across the yard in the half-dark I could see their grips slackening. One raised a hand to his forehead, his mouth dropping open.

The sound of footsteps brought me spinning around, my arms flying up to a defensive pose.

Brendon sprinted past me, red-faced and panting but moving faster than I'd ever seen him move before. Jake jogged out of the shadows of the woods behind him, and even *he* looked rather more animated than his usual. His eyes were steady, fixed on the two soldiers, and their sudden lethargy made just a little more sense.

Aedan wasn't about to waste the opportunity they'd left him. He surged towards the clustered trio in a whirl of red hair, his knife sliding back out. It flashed in the dim light as he drove it home. The unlucky soldier shrieked, shuddering and giving up the last of his hold on our dream-worker.

Loren let out a strangled gasp, twisting hard, and pulled free of the last thug. Her elbow snapped up, connecting with his nose. The *crack* of it snapping was one of the most satisfying things I'd ever heard. She was running before the noise faded, sprinting across the yard towards the woods - and Brendon. Ice sprayed in her wake, razor-sharp and wickedly fast. She didn't slow.

I breathed a sigh of relief when she slipped out of the icicle-thrower's range, bolting headlong into Brendon's arms. He had her pulled closer to him in a second, his other hand coming up - with a gun. The ice demi's curses echoed across the yard as she ducked back behind cover.

"Good," I whispered, feeling a bit of life surge back through my veins. "Good, good." Amber and Kai settled down behind one of our cars in front of the garage as Brendon's shots died away. Safe. Nox and Keira were still crouched where they sat, peering out from behind a corner. Safe. Brendon and Jake and Loren were going to be fine, Tyler and I would live. And finally, we were all back in one place.

534

Luck was still staring at me. Her lips curled down, pure hatred radiating from every line of her expression as she glared. I stared right back, matching her look for look. They'd had us on the defensive for so long - now, it looked like we might have the opportunity to pay them back for some of it.

"Natalie!" she cried, even as I drew breath to call to our own demis. "Stephan!" She didn't say another word - I heard the message clearly enough, and so did their fighters. *Time to go.* They'd lost enough, and their moment was past. Time to retreat.

"Hell, no," I muttered, feeling my pulse accelerate. They'd come into our territory, our *home*, and tried to kill us. Kai was hurt, badly, and more than a few of us bore wounds that would be slow to heal. There was no way I'd let them just turn tail and run so easily.

The two enemy demis hesitated too, as though weighing her instructions - and then they turned, waving to the surviving mundanes. The whole lot of them stood as one, sprinting back towards the vans. The icicle-thrower limped at the back of the group, her teeth gritted. Her leg hung underneath her, covered in blood from ankle to knee.

"Get me her," I snapped, pointing at the ice demi. Natalie.

Tyler nodded, raising a hand. "Go," he whispered.

My eyes narrowed, still fixed on her back. "Stop running."

She stumbled, her steps faltering underneath her. She ground to a halt, trying and failing to resist my order. Her shoulders twisted - and her gaze met mine.

I tried to ignore the look in them, the mixture of fear and anger and resignation. I tried to just focus on what needed doing. "Take one of your icicles and-"

Her hands clapped up, slapping over her ears violently. The motion was enough to make me stop, caught off guard.

Tyler flinched, half-rising before I could continue. "I can't...I won't be able to-"

"Figure it out," I said, forcing myself to keep my voice level and calm. It was just her hands. It couldn't be that big a problem - but Tyler knew his powers best, and it wasn't a good sign that he seemed unhappy.

A muscle in his jaw flexed, but he nodded.

I kept talking, letting the words slide out of me on automatic. "Take your hands off your ears," I whispered. Only it wasn't a whisper, not anymore. I could hear the sound of my voice ramp up, escalating as

Tyler turned up whatever internal knob controlled the volume.

I hissed unhappily, my words falling away again. It wasn't working. I could feel it, the greasy way everything I said just slid away. They weren't my words, anymore. They were his, fueled by his magic and his control. Not mine.

And she was already gone. One of her companions had her slung over his shoulder, tossing both of them through the van's door and slamming it shut. The sound of the engine revving to life had a note of finality to it that was hard to argue.

"Fuck," I muttered, holding up a hand to wave Tyler off. "She's gone."

"We did good," he said, still scanning the fight. Stephan was a few feet behind Natalie, racing around the side. The few remaining soldiers piled into the passenger compartment, ducking and yelling as gunfire chased them in. One last, unlucky one went down hard, and I heard Brendon mutter something dark and satisfied. The others joined in as best they could, but everyone knew it was over. We'd made an enemy, and the war wasn't done, but the fight had reached its end.

The doors around the backside of the van twitched, moving at last. I blinked. Tara the Lucky had climbed in at some point, and was completely out of sight. All that remained was her hand, reaching out of the van and towards her exhausted friend.

But her friend hesitated, a sour look on her face, and didn't take the outstretched hand waiting to pull her in. She cast a look at me instead, glancing back through brown hair cropped to her shoulders. The irritated look on her face flickered, fading for a single instant - and leaving a smirk in its place. She slid her hand across her friend's, like she was getting a blessing from the lucky lady.

My brow furrowed. What? What was she doing?

The air around her shimmered, glazing over as though there was an arch behind her. And then she vanished from sight as though erased off the face of the planet.

I gaped, realizing for the first time how Noah had been able to pull off a stunt like hiding his demis from Greyson - and what her powers truly were. And then my blood froze, seeing a glimmer of movement from the far side of the battlefield.

The teleporter leaped back into reality - right alongside Nox and Keira.

I was moving before she'd so much as found her footing. The world lurched underneath me, tilting dangerously as I heaved myself upright. My legs pumped, pushing as hard as they could. But every step was fire, every movement of my tired and wounded limps almost more than I could take.

For a single, eternal moment, the teleporter hesitated. Her eyes flicked back and forth between Nox and Keira, like she was sizing them up.

Someone was yelling. It could have been me, or Amber, or Tyler, or Aedan. Maybe it was all of us.

Whatever decision she was trying to make, she reached it in a flurry of movement. Her fist sailed out in a single, surprisingly clean motion. Nox yelped, ducking wildly. Her punch whipped over his head. His eyes were wide. Whatever moment of warning he'd been given, it was enough to avoid her first blow. It didn't save him from her elbow, reversing direction instantly and smashing into his face. He fell away, blood flying from his lip.

Her knee came up sharply, bringing an end to any ideas he might have had. His eyes rolled back in his head. He crumpled into the snow a few seconds later.

The teleporter spun, not waiting to see him hit the ground. Her arm slid around Keira's neck before my sister could flinch away.

I was already stumbling forward, despite the pain and the distance. Everything I had went into keeping me moving, into closing the gap between the two of them and I.

It wasn't fast enough to keep the teleporter from leaping back, wrenching Keira along with her - and vanishing into another almost-visible archway.

It snapped shut a moment later, leaving only empty air where they'd stood.

"Jon!" The sound of her cry, half-choked off, brought me spinning back around. "Aedan!" The pair had re-emerged at the back of the van, right where Tara's arm waited. The lucky woman leaned out, grabbing hold of Keira's wrists as she thrashed. The look she shot my way was so smug as to be unbearable.

And then they pulled her into the van. The teleporter leapt up behind her. The doors shut with a final-sounding click.

My breath came ragged, echoing in my ears as I stumbled on. The tires spun, spraying gravel from under their treads, and started picking up speed.

Something shot out from behind our cars, accelerating like an Olympic sprinter. Aedan. He had to know that he couldn't outrun a car, not with all of us tired and hurt. He'd been going flat-out since this started. He'd *died*. None of it seemed to dissuade him. He bolted for the van, his legs flying underneath him. I kept running, gamely doing my best to keep up.

Neither of us would make it. The realization was like ash in my mouth, bitter and dry and cold. Even though we'd held our own, Noah would still win. He'd make sure of it.

The van's headlights blazed a path through the darkness, illuminating the trees on either side of the drive beyond the house. It bounced along, sliding past our cars towards the road beyond.

A shape. That was all I saw, at first - just a shape, lunging out from a nook alongside the house.

Amber's jacket shone green in the blinding light as she dove in front of the car, moving every bit as fast as Aedan had been. I gaped, unable to do more than stare. Snow sprayed under her feet. Without slowing she twisted, coming around to face the van head-on. Her hands snapped up, bracing in front of her like she was going to try and sumo wrestle the van.

And then the air between it and her blurred, thickening and curling in on itself until fog erased her from view entirely. The last I saw of her were her eyes, narrowed to slits, and the gleam of her teeth as she gritted them.

The van never touched its brakes. It slammed headlong into her, still accelerating.

The shriek and groan of metal twisting and breaking erupted into the night, filling the darkness with its screaming. The van shuddered, skidding. Dimly, I could see Amber reappear in front of it, sliding desperately backwards. Her legs shook, her heels digging into the snow and ice underfoot, but she stayed upright. The front of the van crumpled, chunks forced in on itself and tearing off entirely as the force she'd been hit with cascaded back to its source.

My hands were on fire. Distantly, I could feel my nails, pressing hard enough into my palms to break the skin. It was just an afterthought, something lodged in the back of my mind and out of sight as I stared, open-mouthed.

With one final groan and a *crunch*, the van settled back onto its frame, coming to rest at last.

Amber reached up, still silhouetted in the van's dying lights. She wiped her mouth with the back of her wrist. When her hand dropped back down to her side, the skin was stained red - and I could hear her low, pained cough from across the yard.

Aedan didn't slow. He raced straight for the back of the van, reaching it even as the side door slammed open. The marketeers' forces piled right back out of the van, running in three different directions for a single instant before remembering themselves. In eerie, tense silence, they sprinted for their other vehicle.

Aedan didn't so much as given them a second look. He had the back doors open as Stephan leapt into their new escape vehicle, turning the engine over.

Keira tumbled out. She held one hand to her forehead, nursing an egg that *had* to be painful, but seemed otherwise unhurt.

I kept running, breathing a sigh of relief at the sight of Aedan pulling Keira to her feet. My heart still pounded in my ears, thundering at the thought of what could have happened. What almost *did* happen.

I reached Amber right as her knees gave out, sending her to the ground. My arm slid behind her shoulders, breaking her fall.

"Damn," she muttered, one hand still pressed over her mouth. "Not a good idea."

"You're an idiot," I said, panting for breath. "You're a goddamn *idiot*. That was a *car*."

She raised her other hand, her glove securely strapped around it, and leaned forward to punch the ruined grill lightly. "Yeah, right. I showed it."

"You almost got *flattened*."

"Maybe."

I glanced down. Her tone was rueful, her confidence ebbing away at last. Another cough rattled her frame, accompanied by another wave of red splattering down onto her palm. Her eyes were heavily lidded, only the tiniest gleam left to show they were even open.

A smile tugged at the corners of my lips. "Thank you, though."

She snorted. A cough followed immediately after, like her body was punishing her for the motion. "Didn't do it for you."

It took everything I had not to roll my eyes. "I know."

The rest of the crew raced towards us, the snow crunching under their feet. Jake and Brendon were left behind, outlined against what little light remained. They turned to the house, stamping out the embers and fires that burned here and there. It was minor, I noted with satisfaction. We wouldn't lose our house. Probably. Repairing it enough to hide the night's battle...*that* was going to be rather more challenging.

But we were all here. The thought was a small comfort. I leaned back, letting my shoulders settle as I gazed out at the rest of our little family. Was that it, then? Was it over?

I paused. Something...wasn't right. With the others pulling closer, wrapping each other in exhausted, frightened embraces, I wanted more than anything to just sit down and let it be *done*.

But something wasn't right. Something was missing.

The tail lights of the marketeers' van were just a distant sight by then, finally turning out onto the main road and vanishing entirely. They were gone - all of them. Fire, and ice, and luck, and their teleporter. They'd escaped. The thought wasn't a welcome one.

The sight of Tara talking on her phone appeared in my thoughts, frozen in place. And her words, called to Stephan.

I scanned the yard gain, my heart sinking with every passing second, but the truth I already knew was confirmed instantly.

My car was nowhere in sight.

Amber shifted as I leaned away, turning to face me, but I just let go of her shoulders with a quick squeeze. Fresh adrenaline coursed through my system, bringing back all of the fear and tension that I'd just managed to beat.

Aedan glanced up as I stepped closer, closing the gap between us as quickly as I could without looking like I was panicking. I had to stay calm, for their sake. If they saw me freaking out, they'd freak out too - and with so many of them hurt, with so much damage that had been done, we had to keep our wits about us.

But I locked eyes with Aedan, finally letting the thoughts I'd been holding back burst loose in my head.

Noah wasn't here. And neither was Ethan. Neither of them had come - and yet, they'd taken my car from the McDonald's and vanished.

If they weren't here, then they were somewhere *else* in town. And there weren't many places they'd go.

"Aedan," I said, holding his stare and packing every ounce of conviction I could into my words. "Give me your keys."

CHAPTER FIFTY-SIX

"Hurry up."

Aedan glared over his shoulder at me, grabbing hold of the door frame. "I am hurrying."

I shot him a look, barely able to hold myself back. It was his fault. If he hadn't decided to plant his car behind a snowbank, we'd have been on our way minutes earlier. But he *had*, and we hadn't had time to find another car.

Not with Kai limp and whimpering, twitching at the slightest touch. Not with Amber on the verge of unconsciousness, pale and still coughing blood. The others weren't as poorly off as them, but everyone had their hands full.

I wanted to stay and help, to see that things went smoothly. More than anything, I wanted that. But I knew that we had more troubles still.

So I'd just waved Jake over, putting my shoulder against the bumper of Aedan's car, and pushed the rustbucket clear of its snowy nest. He'd been hanging around enough for me to get the picture - he wanted to come. I didn't miss the way his gaze drifted over towards the rest of our crew, still milling about in front of the house, but he didn't hesitate.

I climbed into the passenger's seat, and he was in the back before I'd gotten my seat belt all the way buckled.

All three of us lurched as Aedan slammed down onto the gas pedal, sending the car careening across the snow. Any other day I might have yelled at him, or clung to my seat for dear life. All of my attention was focused on the cell phone in my hands, on pushing one button after another.

The fact that this was exactly what we'd been doing only a few short hours before hadn't been lost on me. I just stared down at the screen, trying to do my best to hit the right keys with my fat fingers as we skidded out onto the main road.

Aedan didn't ask for directions. I'd never taken him there before, but he seemed to know exactly where to go. He'd been around for centuries longer than any of us. He'd know the way.

The electronic dial tone rang in my ears, monotone and mechanical. I sat as still as I could, bubbling with nerves just under the surface. Once. Twice.

Again.

Again.

"God *damn* it," I swore, pulling the phone from my ear and tossing it back into my pocket.

"Nothing?" Jake said, leaning closer behind me.

I shook my head. "Nothing."

"Oh."

Aedan groaned. The engine revved higher. "That doesn't mean anything."

I glared sidelong at him. "The hell it doesn't."

"I'm just saying. You asked Greyson to stay radio silent. So he is."

"But it's *me*."

He chuckled darkly. "Maybe he's got a bit of an attitude about being stuck in the corner and told to sit quietly."

"That doesn't seem likely," I muttered.

Aedan didn't bother answering. He just shrugged. He had to know it too - how unlikely his argument was. If he was actually trying to keep the two of us calm, then things really *were* fucked.

I just grabbed an old t-shirt Keira had thrown my way, our one interaction before we'd taken off, and started tearing it into strips. Contrary to every TV show and movie I'd ever seen, it wasn't such an easy task. The fabric resisted my every tug and pull. I didn't mind. Having something to focus on took my mind off worrying.

My leg burned as I wrapped the first strip of cloth around it, pulling as tightly as I dared. It was just a graze, I noted with relief. Nothing like what Matt's crew had done to me. I'd escape the hospital, as long as it didn't get infected. It had even stopped bleeding somewhere along the line.

"He's smart," Jake said from behind me. His voice was low, almost hushed. "He's been around a long time."

I wrapped the next strip of cloth a bit harder, wincing at the spear of pain that shot through my leg. "He's an old man."

"He's an old *demi*. He didn't get to be old by being stupid."

"There are two of them. Or more."

"You saw his house," Jake said, a little more insistently. "He's got himself cocooned pretty nicely. He could hold out for a long time, there."

I sighed. "Maybe."

Aedan glanced over, glowering through the dark at us. "Shut up and let me drive."

I fell quiet, hearing the tension in his voice. The roads weren't snowy, at least. It was a small blessing after everything else that had happened. We were still going faster than I'd have dared, and it seemed that with every second that passed we accelerated a little more. Pine trees whipped past on either side of the worn-down, broken-up pavement. The buildings of town were long since past, leaving us to the forest.

I hadn't been out to Greyson's place in weeks. We'd been coasting, since we found Brendon and Loren. Considering ourselves safe and secure, alone in our hiding place. I should have made time. I should have put some of our demis with him, made sure he wasn't alone. It had been a mistake to think that he was secure by himself.

My hands tightened around the cloth as I started working on the gash in my arm. Mistake or not, it didn't change anything.

The roar of the engine became a dull monotone, a bit of white noise that erased the miles from around us as we sped into the night. But even though there was a fair bit of distance between us, it wasn't without end. Before long, I sat a little straighter in my seat. It was hard to tell, with nothing but trees around us, but some of it was starting to look familiar.

"Aedan, I think-"

"I know," he muttered. I lurched, grabbing hold of the dash as he slammed on the brakes. Just like that, we were turning, skidding down the narrow drive that I just barely recognized.

The gate was gone. My eyes tightened as I stared at the driveway, recognition sending shivers of fear down my spine. Before, we'd found our way blocked by illusions and trickery, spells to stand in our way and keep us from coming in. But as Aedan accelerated up the drive, picking up speed again, that had all vanished. There was just us and the woods, pressing in as close on either side of the road as I remembered.

"Shit," I whispered, shaking my head slowly.

"Shit indeed," Aedan muttered darkly. "And- fucking *hell*."

He slammed the brakes again, sending Jake and I lurching for a second time.

I opened my mouth to complain, but stopped. I could see what he was talking about. The woods were still dark, even quieter and more gloomy than the forest around our house - up until the driveway ahead neared the looming shape I knew to be Greyson's house.

There, the dark was split by the flickering light of something aflame. My heart in my throat, I went for the door handle. It took two tries to find it - and a slam against the seat belt to realize that I was still buckled in - but a few seconds later saw me outside the car. Aedan and Jake slipped in alongside me. Jake quivered with pent-up energy. Aedan just seemed resigned.

He grabbed my arm as I bolted forward - the one covered in blood and bandages.

I hissed in pain, pulling free, but glanced back over my shoulder. "I know. Be careful. Got it."

A crooked smile tugged at his lips, and he nodded. Forcing myself to move slowly, to not race up the driveway like I wanted, I stepped out more gingerly.

The driveway hadn't been plowed. A few inches of snow rested along its hard-packed dirt surface. In its untouched white powder, the single set of tire tracks that moved up the road ahead of us were all too clear. I reached into my pocket, sliding my knife free again, and tried to ease the pounding in my head.

The sick feeling in the pit of my stomach worsened as we crept up. The woods were quiet - quieter than it should be. The only sound that filtered back to us was the low, crackling sound of flames. Even that was barely audible. Picking my way along the flattened spot left my a tire, I inched out from around a tree truck.

And froze.

My car sat in the driveway ahead, abandoned a mere stone's throw from Greyson's front porch. The frame was blackened, and it looked like they'd driven over nail strips at some point between the road and here. Worse still was the fact that the whole thing was ablaze, burning quietly in the night.

Dimly, I remembered Jake's words - and cast my thoughts back to Greyson's talk of 'enchantments' he'd taken as payments from his clients. He'd been able to activate his defenses, then. It was *something*.

"My car." I couldn't stop myself from whispering the words, staring forlornly at the sad, rapidly blackening shape of it. Sure, its backseat looked like a murder scene, and it had been peppered with more than a few bullets since this whole mess had begun, but it was *mine*. I'd liked it. I'd been *used* to it.

"Come on," Jake muttered, giving me a stern look as he pushed past. His eyes were on Greyson's house, not my car, and I knew he was right. It was just an old beater.

I tried to keep telling myself that as we stepped through the light of the blaze, shading our eyes from the sudden brightness.

"Quiet," I breathed, glancing at the others as we crept up the first of the stairs. They nodded, already silent. They'd heard it too.

The low, hushed sound of voices coming from inside Greyson's house. All of us knew the old man lived alone. Above it all rose the sound of Spike, Greyson's tiny little dog. The thing was barking, on and on and on with no signs of stopping. There was no sign of his other dogs. With any luck, they were with him - or they'd escaped, running off into the woods.

When we'd first visited the finder, I'd thought his house looked homemade, pieced together from whatever he'd had around at the time. That might have been, but as I snuck closer to the door, I had to appreciate his work ethic. The porch let out not even a creak when I gingerly pressed myself to the wall under his front window. The voices drifted out, plain to hear.

"What about-"

"I already looked there."

"Well, look again." The speaker was clearly not having a good time. His voice was laced with irritation - and tension. He wasn't happy. Not at all. And even from what little conversation I'd had with him so far, I could recognize Noah's voice.

Which meant his companion was almost certainly Ethan - and he didn't sound any happier than the marketeers' boss. "What about the kitchen?"

Spike's yips reached a new high. The dog's energy seemed

completely undaunted by their being in the house.

"What *about* it?" Noah said, an inch from becoming a snap.

"Did you find anything there?"

"Why would he keep his records in the kitchen?"

"Why do you think he'd keep anything in the living room?"

"I don't know, Ethan. Just...just keep looking."

Something groaned, like furniture shifting across the floor. Claws skittered across the wood, like Spike was running. The barking continued. "Why'd you have to-"

"Oh, don't give me that."

"Only, he could just *tell* us if you hadn't-"

"He had a gun, all right? What, did you want to get shot?"

"He's *old*."

"It's his own damn fault," Noah muttered, his voice low. "I didn't *mean* to."

I licked suddenly-dry lips, casting a look over at Jake. My second stared right back at me, wide-eyed. I might not know everything that was happening in there, but I was starting to hear enough to figure out what had happened.

And we were in trouble.

"Shouldn't we...I don't know," Ethan muttered, his voice nearly drowned out by Spike's desperate barks. "Ca-"

"Who are we going to call, Ethan?" Noah snapped, suddenly finding his energy again. "He should have known better than to play games and withhold information. It's on him. Not us."

Slowly, carefully, I lifted myself off the ground, peering through the window into Greyson's house. The interior was dark, still mostly shadowed despite Noah and Ethan's presence. There were a few lamps turned on here and there as they tried to cast light on whatever they were searching for, but that was all.

Keeping myself low enough that they *probably* wouldn't see me, I scanned the house. They stood in the living room. Noah dug through an end table, pulling sheafs of paper out and sifting through them. Ethan inched closer to the kitchen like he'd been ordered, but now and again his gaze flicked across to the entryway. He'd seemed like a strong, silent type back in the McDonald's, but his face was pale. And he paused every few moments to scowl at Noah.

"Shut that thing up, will you?" Noah said with a groan, slamming the drawer shut again. "I can't hear myself think."

"I don't know what you think he's going to have here," Ethan muttered under his breath. Spike yipped away, completely unbothered.

"Where else do you think he's going to keep anything he took as payment?" Noah snapped. "He's not an idiot. It's not going to be in the damn bank."

"It could be anywhere, though. Tara said-"

"I know what Tara said."

"We need to go."

Spike barked on. Noah hissed through his teeth. Something slammed shut - another drawer, if I was any judge. "I thought I told you to-"

"I've got it. It's just a damn dog," Ethan muttered. "Get yourself in check."

Steps rang out against the wooden floorboards of Greyson's place, heavy and solid. A shiver ran down my spine. Not that I didn't appreciate the fact that Ethan clearly wasn't in for some good old-fashioned animal abuse, but too late I realized what the alternative in his mind was.

Greyson's door creaked open, just a handful of paces away on the front porch. Spike zipped out through the crack, yipping in delight at his sudden and unexpected freedom. He raced straight to Jake, an unhesitating blur of white-and-brown fuzz.

I was already moving when Ethan froze, silhouetted in the door. My knife came up, aimed straight for his chest as I lunged.

His eyes narrowed. His chin dropped to his chest as he stiffened.

A startled gasp slipped between my teeth as I tilted dangerously, starting to tumble. The knife in my hands was suddenly a lead weight, an anchor pulling me back to the ground. I had a good grip on it - the adrenaline coursing through my veins made sure of that much - but there was nothing I could do to keep hold of the blade as it slipped between my fingers. It hit the decking with a *crunch*, putting a dent in the wood.

"Shit," I muttered, my eyes sliding back up to meet Ethan's. He was still gaping, pale-faced and staring at me in a moment of pure confusion.

Someone was moving from inside the house, drawn by the commotion. "Ethan? What-"

Ethan just scowled, making an irritated noise in the back of his throat, and swung hard. My eyes went wide. I ducked, my body moving entirely on its own, and his fist sailed over my head. *Inches* over my head. Hard. It slammed into the wooden railing, and I heard the unmistakable shriek of nails ripping free.

I rolled, past, pushing desperately to put more distance between him and I. I still had no idea what his powers were, but given what he'd just done to the poor railing, I really, really didn't want to find out. Jake and Aedan were both yelling behind me, crowding closer in the narrow space allotted by the porch. Over it all, Spike screamed still, barking like it was his sole goal in life.

I got a quick glimpse of the inside of Greyson's house as I ducked, just a flash. It didn't look much better than the outside had. He'd clearly fought. The walls were peppered with what looked suspiciously like the blasts from a shotgun, and sections were blackened here and there.

The whole thing was made all the worse by the fact that Noah and Ethan had clearly been pawing through his things. His possessions were *everywhere*. Couch cushions were torn open, shredded and left exposed with tufts of fuzz floating on the still air. Newspapers were thrown haphazardly about. Footstools were overturned.

I tuned it all out almost immediately, spotting the bigger concern I had - Noah. He spun on his heel at the sound of the commotion, his eyes going as wide as Ethan's had.

Shit, shit, shit. My head pounded, aching at the *thought* of having to cow the pair of them.

But as I gathered my breath, biting down hard on as much power as I could grab hold of, his eyes narrowed again.

I staggered, my mind going foggy. What was...what was I doing? Why was I charging him? It wasn't a good idea, at *all*. No. If we... I shook my head, desperately trying to work through what exactly was happening, but it was like my limbs were made of lead. If we'd beaten his squad, then...then we should have run. But that was useless too, wasn't it?

Noah was breathing hard, but a satisfied grin twisted the corners of his lips.

I had a single, confused second to stare at it before an ironclad grip settled around my wrist.

"Back off!" someone roared. Ethan. I caught sight of his face from the corner of my eye as he pulled mightily. A heartbeat later I was flying, careening towards the door. Fast. Too fast. Whatever corner of my mind was still processing things rationally noted that something was really, really *wrong*.

Of course, everything seemed normal enough as his hand slipped free of my wrist. Aedan's eyes widened in the fraction of a second we spent face to face. And then I slammed into him, both of us hitting the twisted, shattered wood of the railing hard.

Jake still stood alongside the door, a hand pressed to his face. His shoulders shook. With a groan, he spun, pulling a pistol from his pocket in the same smooth motion.

Noah laughed. He *laughed*, with the three of us standing there, with a gun pointed at him. "Attack me, then," he murmured, tilting his head to one side and fixing Jake with a beady stare. "If you think you can."

Jake's frame quivered again. I blinked, the fog falling clear from my own mind. Noah...he'd always made me feel lethargic, like I was just a zombie. But this...this was different. It was the total *opposite*. A shiver ran down my spine.

A roar slipped between Jake's lips. His pistol slipped from his fingers, falling to the deck with a clatter of polished metal. Without hesitating, without so much as taking a second to prepare, he hurled himself at Noah.

Who stood as casually as ever, perfectly balanced on the balls of his feet. With a *knife* in one hand.

"God *damn* it," I muttered under my breath, feeling my pulse accelerate. "Stop! Jake- stop!" It was becoming clear that putting us into a stupor wasn't the only trick that Noah had.

My relic burned against my skin, and my head groaned in reply. I gritted my teeth, clinging to every scrap of mana I could. It was relic versus relic, which was exactly what I hadn't wanted, but it wasn't like I'd been given a choice.

My relief was palpable as Jake skidded to a stop, his limbs still shaking. *He* wasn't fighting me, at least. His eyes flicked back, fixing on mine, and I could see the fear there. It was nearly wiped away, hidden underneath the blind fury that Noah had shoved down his throat, but I knew Jake well enough to spot it.

Noah was still pulling at him, though. It wasn't going to last. "See to Ethan," I hissed from the corner of my mouth, diving back into the house.

"What?" I heard Aedan cry behind me.

Jake was shaking his head by then, his lips parting. A muscle in his neck twitched.

I was faster. I lurched out in front of him as he leapt forward, managing to get my hand flat against his chest.

"Stop," I spat through my teeth. A wet, hot trickle had begun seeping down my face, oozing from my nose. That was bad. I *remembered* that. We were nearly out of time.

But Jake stopped. He took one long, deep breath. And then another. His eyes were fixed on mine.

They widened.

I jumped just in time. Noah's knife whipped through where I'd been a brief instant before, cutting the air with a horrifyingly crisp sound. He turned on a dime, spinning to face me with a scowl. I winced, the fog beginning to settle over my mind again.

Fuck. Biting my tongue and doing my best not to think about what exactly I was doing, I flipped the knife over in my hand. Years of twaddling practice in class were suddenly given a purpose I'd never, ever wanted.

And then I plunged my knife down into my already-wounded leg.

Waves of pain shot through me. I grimaced, feeling the world spin underneath me, but clung to the feeling. It was enough to ward off the blurred numbness. Almost. My leg was already hurt after all. That made it....*sort* of worth.

Blinking away tears, I glared at Noah, taking some amount of pleasure in the way the blood slowly drained from his face.

I froze a second later.

It was difficult, with the fog and the pain warring for control of my mind. All I wanted to do was sit down and wait for the hurting to stop. But over Noah's shoulder, half-hidden behind the end of Greyson's couch, I could see it. My eyes rebelled against the notion, insisting that I was just...seeing it wrong. That it was a mistake.

I knew it was nothing of the kind.

Poking half-out from behind the overstuffed furniture and the rough-hewn, homemade wooden table sitting at its end, I could see a pair of feet lying motionless on the ground. A pair of *legs*. Greyson's legs.

Red pooled underneath them, soaking through the worn-down carpeting. It was splashed across the couch, too, just a spattering. And it was smeared down the corner of the end table, jagged and sharp.

"You absolute fucking *bastard*," I breathed, my eyes widening. "What have you done?"

My blade came up. Whatever battle of relics had been going on between us, it was over. His hold on me evaporated, the mist burning away as my pain-filled mind coalesced down to a single, furious point of focus.

That was Greyson. Lying on the floor, in a puddle of blood.

"You're in here," I heard myself say, the words falling out entirely on automatic. "Looking through his things. Seeing what you can *steal*."

Noah smiled across the living room at me. "I warned you, Jon," he said, his tone still as bright as ever.

But I saw his smile flicker, beginning to fade.

"You attacked him. In his *home*," I said, my knuckles standing out white against the skin of my hands as I pointed the knife at him. "You left him *bleeding* while you rifled around for anything valuable."

He chuckled. "Really, Jon, what did you think-"

"Shut up," I spat, my hands beginning to shake. It wasn't the furious, wild rage that had overtaken Jake a few brief moments before. I could see him lingering all the same, hesitating. His hand twitched towards me, like he wasn't sure if he needed to grab hold. I shot him a look, pinning him in place. Aedan and Ethan continued their fight halfheartedly in the entryway, both giving only the thinnest of effort into making it look convincing. They were too busy watching us, I knew.

Noah spread his hands slowly. "It's not too late," he said, tilting his head again and fixing me with a knowing stare. "A lot's happened. I think we've both made some missteps, eh?" A winning smile flashed across his face, there and then gone again in an instant. "We can still move past it, Christensen. If you agree, now, I can call the rest of my crew. We can-"

"Still save him?" I snapped, raising myself another few inches. Noah was a polished man, normally, but he wasn't all that tall. I had a fair bit of height on him, when push came to shove, and I leveraged it for all I was worth. "What, you'll call a healer in, fix all the wrongs? Make it like it'd never happened?" One step, then another. Noah grew larger in my vision as I stalked closer.

I could see Greyson, at that point. See his skin, grey and wan. See the blow he'd taken, the blood coating his head. He lay still and quiet, looking smaller than I'd ever thought to see him. He'd always been so full of life, of sarcasm and whiskey and sass, that I'd almost forgotten that he was just an old man, tired and more fragile than he liked to seem.

Noah cleared his throat. I glanced back to him, my nerves singing. If he made the slightest motion, inched towards *anything*, I'd-

"It's possible, Jon," he said, folding his arms. His chin rose stubbornly into the air. "We can do that. I'll personally see to it that-"

"Shut the fuck up," I said woodenly. The words carried with them the ring of a command, almost instinctively. Blood trickled down my face as my nosebleed resumed in full. "And your damn crony too. Don't either of you fucking *move*."

Noah froze as though he'd been turned to a statue. The sounds of fighting from behind me came to an all-too-abrupt halt.

I just stared at him, a void torn open in my heart. I'd been too late. Damn it, why hadn't I figured it out sooner? We should have...we could have divvied ourselves up better. Sent someone to look over our finder, like we should have.

"You did this," I said, the words raw. "You came here, to his house, and attacked him out of nowhere." My eyes were fixed on his boring into his soul, and I could *see* it. My stomach churned, but I didn't stop. He stood frozen, caught motionless in my gaze. "You pushed through all his defenses, everything he'd put in your way."

The sight of it hung in my mind, clear as day. Noah and Ethan, racing up the drive in my car, my car that they'd *stolen*. I could smell the smoke from the fires his traps had ignited. Hear the sound of my own car's tires blowing out. There had been illusions, yes. And booby traps, and pitfalls, and half a dozen other wards meant to keep people away.

They'd come prepared. I could feel Noah's satisfaction, the way he'd burst through layer after layer, slicing through the onion that Greyson had made of his home until at last they'd come right through the front door.

"I-I didn't mean to," Noah said, finding himself long enough to stammer out the threadbare excuse. "I just-"

"You came across an old man with a gun," I said, spitting each syllable out. Greyson's face hadn't been afraid. It shone in Noah's memories, or his thoughts, or *whatever it was* I was seeing. He'd been resigned, yes, but our finder was nothing if not stubborn. He'd held the shotgun in his arms with rigid precision, aimed towards the two of them. Only every time he'd fired, the shot had gone....astray. It was Ethan's doing, I knew. Noah knew it, and his satisfaction rang true in every memory and thought.

"I-It's not what you think, Jon. Really, you're losing sight of what's important. If-"

"You hit him," I said, stepping closer again. Noah stopped, losing what little color remained in his face. "Not with your hands. You wouldn't be much of a demi if *that's* what you turned to. No. You lashed out, sucking the will right out of him."

And Greyson had fallen. The rest of the story was clear, told in pieces - the blood coating the corner of the table. The wound on his head. The blood spattering the carpet, the couch...all of it.

My heart ached, tearing a bit more in two with every second.

"I'm serious, Jon," Noah said, a bit of life returning to his voice. "We'll do it. We'll see to him, if you'll agree to our terms. It's not too late."

Aedan made a low, irritated noise behind me. "Jonny, he's-"

"Lying," I said, my voice soft. "He's lying." I didn't even need my relic for it. Every fiber of my being shrieked not to trust him. To never again trust him, to never again let him anywhere near anyone that we cared about.

But it was already too late.

A flicker of motion - I twitched, coming awake just in time to see Noah lunge for me. The blade in his hand gleamed. I blinked, my eyes going wide, and-

Aedan's hand snapped to my shoulder, his foot sliding between mine. In a second I was tumbling, falling out of control. The knife slid past, striking wildly and cutting a line across the desk beyond where I'd stood.

My mind raced, churning through thoughts at a hundred miles an hour. In the very corner of my vision lay Greyson, frozen in perfect relief. The sight was enough to crystallize my reactions further, bringing all of my anger and frustration to bear.

Noah made an irritated noise, pivoting on his foot and lunging back in - hard. Distantly, I could hear the chaos building. Someone was yelling. A few someones. My eyes were fixed on the marketeer, tracing over every motion he made.

A half-forgotten memory surfaced in the back of my mind, carrying with it the scene of a forest. Of a man, with a gun, pointing it at me - and the way I'd managed to dodge.

My relic burned against my chest, hot enough I half suspected there'd be a scar. I just gritted my teeth, pouring the last remaining dregs of power I had into it, and prayed it wouldn't steer me wrong. Trusting it was all I could do.

Noah twitched, the muscles in his wrist tightening. I shifted, my body moving on its own as my relic screamed an alarm.

A single, delicate line of fire tore across the side of my face, close enough to my eye that I really, *really* should have been having second thoughts of all this.

And just like that, his knife was beyond me - and I was inside his guard.

His lips parted. He knew he'd erred, then, even if he didn't understand how I'd done it. Good.

A roar from behind me was enough to know Ethan wasn't happy. And Jake's tired, strained gasp told me my friends weren't going to let it happen. Aedan hadn't stopped muttering under his breath since Noah attacked me. They'd be fine.

My fist slammed into Noah's cheek, as hard as I could muster. My other hand came around, the blade swinging up.

He stumbled back, though, finally going on the retreat. The tip of my knife cut a gash across his cheek, eerily similar to the one still burning across my own. His skin looked as pale and smooth as it had minutes before, but he was wincing.

I wasn't about to let him recover, let alone put any amount of distance between us. I closed on him doggedly, still completely focused. My eyes followed his hands, his chest, the way his gaze flicked back and forth.

It left me completely aware of what was happening when his arm curled back in, the point of his knife angling back. It was as plain as day, broadcast in every line of muscle and tendon.

I could almost see it - the way he'd catch me as I charged in. The point where his knife would slip into my skin, bringing me grinding to a halt.

"Jon!" I heard Aedan bellow from behind me. It almost sounded like there was fear in his voice. I would have chuckled to myself, if I had time. Fear. Aedan. Yeah, right.

In that single, endless second, I considered just ramming myself onto the blade. He couldn't very well stab me with it once it was stuck in me, and there was enough blind rage in my system still that it almost sounded like a good plan.

My arms came together instead, sliding into position. He wouldn't

554

touch me, I decided, beginning to move. I wouldn't give him the satisfaction - and I knew just how I'd have to weave past his guard.

One fist up, ready and waiting. Knock his arm to the side.

His skin was hot when I knocked his guard clear, covered in a sheen of sweat that clung to my wrist.

The other hand in. Not too fast. Not too slow. Right past his weapon, then *twist* to the side. I was letting the relic steer by then, giving it free reign to watch Noah and pick out what help it could find.

His eyes widened as I swung. His knife came up, a little higher, but I was ready. I'd seen it, I'd prepared for it, and-

A gunshot split through the single-minded haze of my thoughts. I flinched, completely caught off guard, and stumbled.

Shit.

I'd pushed off hard before Noah could take advantage of my distraction, skittering back defensively.

So was he, I saw as I recovered. He'd pulled back nearly to the far wall, pale-faced and sweating. Probably grateful for the reprieve, I thought sourly.

The echo of the gunshot still rang in my ears, keeping me disoriented. I shook my head, realizing for the first time how hard I was breathing, and froze.

The only one here with a gun was Jake, and he knew better than to fire into chaos like our fight had been. So why-

"That's *enough*," a voice cried, loud and sharp and entirely unfamiliar.

I spun, twisting towards the door. My pulse pounded, accelerating as a fresh jolt of adrenaline hit my veins.

And then I froze, gaping, and stared at the stranger standing in the doorway, his gun pointed at the ceiling.

CHAPTER FIFTY-SEVEN

I stared.

The man stared right back, his arm still upraised. The stink of gunpowder drifted across the distance between us, bright and strident and enough to make my nose twitch.

A strangled hiss tore across my ears. I twitched, breaking away from the newcomer and back towards Noah - as he lunged back towards me, his eyes narrowing.

The edges of my vision blurred. I sagged, holding myself upright by a thread as his power washed over me. I still had my knife, though, and *he* was nearly close enough. Fog or not, I lifted my blade, and-

A second gunshot set me to reeling, my hands thrown up over my ears. The sound of footsteps stomping over to the pair of us echoed in its wake. A hand slapped onto my shoulder before I could twitch away, yanking me backwards.

"I said, that's enough," the stranger bellowed again, and there was a sharp note to his voice that hadn't been there before. "I ain't telling you again."

Noah swung around, turning away from me long enough to fix an angry look at the man. "This isn't anything to do with you and your crew, Carl. Don't interfere. It's not-"

"The hell it's not," the man muttered. Carl. I let the name sink into my memory, etching it in alongside his face.

Noah's scowl grew. "It's *not.*"

"The others aren't so amused by all this," Carl said, continuing

556

straight past Noah's complaints. "Don't think anyone appreciated having you swagger into our backyard unasked, doing as you pleased."

The marketeer's face screwed up, like he was trying and failing to keep himself from sneering. "Is that a threat?"

"Not yet. But give it time."

Noah opened his mouth, drawing breath, but Carl cleared his throat. "Don't you have places to be? Your crew was taking off - at speed. I'd hate for you to get left behind."

I stared, doing my best to keep my mouth from falling open. Noah and the newcomer were nearly nose to nose, both glaring daggers.

It was strange, to see the normally-arrogant Noah come face-to-face with someone like that. He'd been so full of it back in the McDonald's, so puffed up on the idea of himself.

But he sniffed, pressing a hand to his face, and turned away. My surprise solidified in an instant. "Damn it. Ethan."

His larger, beefier friend hadn't stopped scowling since Carl walked in. Aedan still had him by the arm, looking around warily as events unfolded. One of my friend's eyes was starting to bruise, but his knife had a trickle of blood running down it.

That old, guarded look had slid down across his face at some point, like he was considering if he should run or hide. Both of us knew it was far too late for that.

Ethan pulled free of Aedan's hold with an irritated grunt, shooting the immortal a look that promised hell. "Get your damn hands off me."

Aedan rolled his eyes, throwing his hands up in the air - knife and all. "Oh, don't get your panties in a bunch."

Ethan flinched, drawing back before catching himself. Noah was already at the door, shoving past Carl and pushing out into the night beyond. Ethan hurried to follow, giving me one last furious look.

And then we were alone. I didn't know how Noah and Ethan were going to leave - they'd brought my car, after all, and left it burning - but I didn't much care if they froze to death figuring it out.

I'd nearly had them. I'd come *this close* to putting an end to the threat. My lips pressed together into a thin line. If Carl hadn't interfered, this would already be over.

Over. Another needle of anxiety slipped under my skin. Greyson. His chest rose and fell - I could see that much from where I stood - but slowly. Too slowly. And the cast of his skin...

My heart ached. Carl interfering or not, it had long since been too late.

I turned towards him instead, more than a little numb - and was pushed back by Carl as the tall, slender man stepped right in front of me.

"Well, well," I heard him murmur, his words little more than a whisper. They weren't meant for me, I knew. "Told you. I *told* you that you were gettin' too old for all this."

He was moving for Greyson. My blood chilled. I raised my hand, moving to grab him before he could get too close. "I don't know who you think you are, but-"

"Didn't you ever figure out you shouldn't keep secrets?" Carl said, his voice dropping lower. He stepped straight past me. When I grabbed for him, my fingers slid right through him. A shiver ran down my spine. I'd known he was a demi - but suddenly, that fact became all the more important.

He stopped beside Greyson, dropping into a crouch. His dark eyes swept up and down our finder's form, taking in the wounds. The blood.

"Not yet, eh?" he murmured. "Hold on a bit longer, then."

What? I inched closer, my pulse thundering in my ears. The way he said it - like he had hope. There was a note in his voice that wasn't just resignation. The thought was enough to set my hands to quivering.

Carl pushed himself upright again, groaning. "The things I do," I heard him mutter, shaking his head. And then he turned back towards the door.

I froze, entirely unsure what I should be doing. We needed to get him help. He was hurt, badly enough that I knew he was right on the verge of death - and I didn't know what to *do*. I could...we could call for help. But that would mean paramedics, and police, and people tromping all over Greyson's property. If they saw us, if they saw the house, they'd have questions. Ones we couldn't answer.

My hand slipped into my pocket a second after, fixing around my cell phone. To hell with it. We couldn't just let him die. We could-

"Hannah!" Carl roared from the doorway. I jumped, shocked back to stillness. From the corner of my eye, I could see Jake flinch, pulled out of his reverie just like I was.

Aedan drew a little closer to me, his eyes narrowed. "Just wait, Jonny," he said.

A scowl slipped onto my face. "Wait? We can't-"

"Hannah!" Carl bellowed for a second time. I winced. The sound of his voice was loud enough that pangs of pain shot through my aching, sore head. Blood still trickled down my face. I wiped it away as he wrinkled his nose, opening the door far enough to lean out. "Damn it, girl, would you-"

"I-I'm coming," I heard someone call in reply. Someone female. Their tone was carefully respectful, but all the same, I could hear the irritation under their words. "You said not to move until-"

"Don't give me excuses. Get in here."

Footsteps rang out against wood, hollow and booming. Someone was coming up the stairs. I hesitated, glancing towards Aedan and Jake. There were more of them. It wasn't just Carl. The realization that we weren't alone, and that we were quickly on the verge of being outnumbered by a strange crew, was not a comforting one.

But before I could say a word or gesture to the others, the door pushed open. A woman stepped through. Little more than a girl, I amended, biting my tongue and doing my best to keep from jumping. Her auburn hair was pulled back into a messy bun, escaping from its confines in a halo of strands. She froze at the sight of us, her brown eyes going wide. "Uh-"

"Quickly, damn it," Carl snapped. The tapping of his foot itched at the back of my mind, grating against my thoughts. "Didn't bring you all the way along just so you could sit in the car, girl."

"Right," she said, turning around. "What's...ah." She'd seen Greyson. I felt my hands clench into balls at my side. I didn't know quite what was going on, but there was a regret in her voice. Regret for Greyson, or for us...either way, I didn't like it.

Carl sniffed, crossing his arms. "Now, how's about you-"

"Move," she said, breaking into motion. "What happened to him?"

"We...think he fell," I said, feeling Carl's eyes on me. "We're not really sure, but-"

"Can you do anything?" the other man said, acting like he *hadn't* heard his girl ask me a question.

My fingers twitched. "...Anything? What, can you..." I stopped, my words falling away as a lump welled up in my throat. The first hints of hope were painfully sharp, but I knew better than to get my hopes up. "What are you doing?"

"I don't know," she said, her back to us. She crouched at Greyson's side, brushing his hair back carefully. "There's...a lot of damage. And he's been left here." Glancing back, she fixed me with a glare, sharp and pointed.

I shook my head hurriedly. "Not us. He's ours. We wouldn't-"

"No promises," she said, her voice low. "He's old. You *know* I can't fix everything."

Just as quickly as it had appeared, the hope blossoming in my chest vanished. "Stop poking around at my friend," I snapped, drawing myself upright. "I don't know who you people are or why you think you can walk in here. B-But, can you help him?" I hated to put it in words, to risk being told *no*, that I'd misunderstood. But I could read the scene as well as anyone. I stepped towards Hannah, reaching for her shoulder. "What exactly are you-"

A hand latched around my elbow, pulling me away. "None of that, now," Carl said. His voice was carefully neutral, brimming with a cheerfulness so fake it might have been plastic. "Let's let her work. You and I should talk, anyhow."

"Don't touch him," Jake spat from behind me. "Don't-"

"Let them be," Aedan said. *He* didn't seem worried at all. He stood, leaning against the wall, his arms crossed casually over his chest. Only the rapid-fire tapping of one finger against his arm ruined the act. "Sit down, Jake. We'll be fine here, Jonny. Go."

"But- I can't-"

"Come on," Carl said with a groan, dragging me onward. The door creaked open, sending another wave of frigid air through the cabin. "Let's talk."

I opened my mouth to continue protesting, but snapped it shut again. Aedan didn't seem worried - and if Hannah there could actually help, having me hovering over her shoulder wouldn't change anything. I'd just distract her. Greyson couldn't afford any delay.

So I let Carl pull me outside. The door shut with a final-sounding creak behind me, cutting off the low, irritated argument ongoing between Jake and Aedan.

As though he'd realized I wasn't fighting anymore, Carl let me go. We slipped down the front stairs of the porch, finally coming to rest on the snow-covered driveway. A bench sat on the very edge of the yard, equally covered in snow but sturdy-looking. It glowed in the firelight, lit in flickering, shadowed colors.

I stared at the source of the light, my frustrations bubbling up again. My car still burned where it sat, rapidly becoming little more than a hunk of twisted, soot-covered metal. Already portions of it were little more than embers.

Another car sat in the driveway, though, behind my poor, dead husk of a vehicle and Aedan's stolen junker. Two figures were sitting inside, their noses pressed to the glass. They opened the doors, about to jump out at us. I flinched, drawing back. A trap. It was-

Carl raised a hand, waving cheerily at the pair, and they stopped. "Just wait," he said, his voice raised enough to reach them. "Or go help Hannah. She could use a hand."

They hesitated a moment longer. I fixed them in my minds - one stocky and short, with plain, unremarkable brown hair cut into a plain, unremarkable haircut. The other was lanky and long, his black locks braided back in rows.

I could almost see the thoughts churning behind their eyes - Carl, who was clearly their leader, hanging out in the dark with a strange demi. Both of them shut their doors a second later, their eyes still fixed on us.

Carl sighed. "Fine. Whatever. Be like that." He reached down, pulling his sleeve over his hand and knocking the snow off the bench enough to sit. "Come on. Want one?"

I eyed the carton of cigarettes he offered me with distaste, shaking my head. "I'm good. Look. I don't know you. What the hell are you-" I caught myself, biting off the words hard. No, that was the wrong way to go about this. I couldn't help but be angry - if Carl hadn't interrupted me, I'd have killed Noah. But it sounded an awful lot like there was hope for Greyson yet, and they hadn't attacked us so far.

We should probably *not* make every crew we ran into an enemy. Not until we knew there wasn't another choice.

Carl was watching me, I realized. His face was in shadows, nearly invisible, but I saw him nod fractionally. "Good," he said. "Least you're not an idiot. 'Bout this, anyway."

Now that I'd slowed myself down long enough to actually think, I just...stared. The pieces were falling into place, bits of half-remembered conversation from months before and clues my mind must have secreted away. In the center of it all was Aedan, lounging against the wall of Greyson's house as though he didn't have a care in the world.

"You're Detroit, aren't you?" I said slowly, staring down at him.

He grinned, flicking his lighter. His face erupted into light, there and gone a brief second after. "Real genius, you are."

I sank onto the bench beside him, seeing the way he nudged his chin towards it. "Oh. Then- I mean, why are you here?" I swallowed hard. "We've been meaning to...to talk to you, but we thought…" I shook my head, still trying to sort through the jumble of feelings and irritations that were taking over my mind.

"Why did you stop me?" I said, more slowly. "Those people. Because of them, Greyson is...hurt."

"Badly," Carl said, bobbing his head in a nod. A thin coil of grey smoke drifted up into the night to join the black pouring off my dead car. "Might be Hannah can help. We'll see."

"They won't stop," I said, unable to keep a sharp edge from my tone. "They got *away*, now. They'll come back. They'll hurt us again. So why the hell did you-"

"Shit, kid. Don't give me that," Carl said, shooting me a look. "I think you've done decent so far, given the circumstances, but you can't just waltz into someone's territory to set up shop and not expect them to take offense. It might surprise you, but not everyone's okay with you just fuckin' with how things've been around here."

I stopped. His voice was still cheerful, but there was an edge in his words. His eyes were fixed on mine, carefully watchful.

He held the stare for a long, drawn-out moment, as though waiting for me to say something. And then he sighed, letting a cloud of smoke slip between his lips. "Anyway. To get back to what you said. Don't know that we really have a name, but sure. Heard a few months back that there was strange shit going on up this way, but we've had bigger issues. Didn't really care to deal with you lot."

Deal with us. The implicit threat hung pointedly in his word choice. I stopped, my chin dropping gently. Suddenly, being alone in the yard with him didn't seem like such a good idea.

But Aedan hadn't been worried. I clung to the thought. He wouldn't set me up. Probably.

"Ontario moving was a bit much," Carl said, shrugging. "They're ambitious. Should have expected they'd try something, of course. So we came to see what happened." His grin glowed in the half-light. "Kids were getting bored, anyway."

"You've been here?" I said slowly, trying to keep from scowl. "What, and you just *watched*?"

He shrugged again. "Wasn't our fight."

"It seemed to be your fight when you stopped me from putting an end to things," I said, forcing the words past my clenched teeth.

Carl snorted. "What, you think that've ended it? Don't be an idiot. You go and kill the marketeers' leadership, you'll just leave a void. They'd all go scrabbling to fill it and pick out the next head. That'd be a total pain for everyone involved. They'd come south, chipping away at the territory boundary and launching raids. They'd be trying to make themselves look good, and all. Be *strong*." His eyes were fixed on mine, watchful. "You wouldn't have lasted to summer."

I swallowed. Put like *that*, it almost made sense. "Oh."

"Oh," he echoed, a chuckle rippling up from his gut. "Had to keep things from getting out of hand entirely. Besides." His tone softened. His eyes drifted towards the cabin, to where I could see Jake silhouetted in the door's window. "Nathan felt Greyson go dark. Figured something had to be wrong."

"Yeah," I said, my voice dropping. "And he- do you think your friend can-"

"We'll see."

"Oh."

Carl shook his head, shifting in his seat. "Asses shouldn't've just come in swinging at him like that. It's not right. Not with him having been here longer than any of us. Should've had a little respect."

I risked glancing over at him. "And that's why?"

He took another long draw, letting my words hang between us. "Well, I'm not going to lie," he said. And then he started chuckling. "Thought it was pretty damn funny to see them all come in like big tough guys, only to get sent packing. Wish we had some popcorn for *that* one."

So he didn't like them either. A bit of the weight in my chest eased up. Aedan and Jake had been pretty clear about how the primes behaved, and I knew better than to relax. All the same, the acknowledgement that even *he* thought Noah's group was full of shit was a welcome one.

"Anyway. While my girl sees to the old bastard, you and I need to talk."

I flinched. His tone was hard again, cold and level. I looked over, finding him staring right back at me. "I thought we were."

"This? This is just getting to know each other. And now it's time we got down to business."

I nodded slowly, still pinned in place by the look he was giving me.

"All...right."

He leaned back, sliding the hand holding his cigarette down to rest on the bench beside him. "Have to be honest with you. Don't think anyone's really thrilled that you're here, kid."

"Jon."

"Didn't ask," he said, not missing a beat. "If you thought things were going to end here, well, you're wrong."

I nodded again. "I know. I didn't think this would be *it*."

"Well, at least you've got that much sense," Carl muttered, looking down. "Look. So far as my group's concerned, we've got bigger fish to fry."

"You mentioned something like that."

"And I meant it. With the west side in shambles, we've got to keep an eye out for runners. And Toledo's always an issue too, you know." His eyes flicked back up to meet mine. "Up to now, the north's just been a buffer between us and them. I like that. Buffer is good."

"We're not looking to start a fight," I said, shaking my head. "Really." It felt like I was treading the same ground I just had, before Noah tried to sell his asshole deal to me. I could only hope this wasn't going to be a repeat encounter.

"See, right now, I'm pretty convinced that you guys'll have your hands full," Carl said. A crooked grin tugged at his lips. "They're going to keep you too busy to *think* about starting anything with us. And, hey." He held his hands up. "If they're occupied with fightin' off you lot, they'll leave us alone."

I stopped, my retort falling away. Carl was still watching me. The man was way more observant than he looked. His words played over and over again in my mind, rolling off the tip of my tongue. It almost sounded like-

"Are you saying you'll let us stay up here?" I said, letting the question slip out.

Carl's grin widened. "I'm just being practical here. Make yourselves useful, yeah? Keep the north away, and let me worry about the real problems at hand." His head tilted to one side a fraction of an inch. "Do that for me, and I could be convinced to overlook your squatting here."

I sat back, my shoulders rising. The truth was, like it or not, we'd be dealing with the marketeers again regardless. It wasn't like I could turn him down and everything would magically go back to peace. And right then, he sounded halfway friendly.

He'd still be doing all of the normal things, the whispers in the back of my mind insisted. Killing, and stealing, and using his powers to take advantage of the masses. He'd still be a demi, the leader of a crew, doing all of the things that we'd found so abhorrent in the marketeers.

"Don't try and ship anyone across our territory," I heard myself saying. "Not under our nose."

He chuckled. "Do you really think you're in a position to make deals?"

My eyes tightened. I wasn't, and we both knew it. I could try and command him - but with how my head was spinning, I knew I was dangerously close to flat empty. And enspelling the leader of the southern primes didn't sound like a good idea even in my head. If he refused, there'd be nothing I could do to argue with him. And there was no telling how he'd react to my asking, either.

But he only sighed, rolling his eyes. "Not like I'll be able to do much business with Noah for a while anyway, eh?" he muttered darkly. "Not after getting in the way."

I hesitated. "I guess. He didn't look happy," I mumbled.

Carl snorted, shaking his head. "Oh, he'll be pissed off for months, I'm sure. It's his way. But it's a bit far for us to make the trip north, in any case, so it's not really an issue."

So he'd still be doing it - but at least it'd be out of sight. My stomach churned unhappily. We'd be ignoring everything that was going on around us, leaving people to do as they would. The thought didn't sit well with me. I just wasn't sure that we had another way out.

He lifted his cigarette, taking another puff. "So. Deal?"

Shit. He was expecting me to make a decision right then and there. I glanced back towards the house. Jake stood in the window still, ready and waiting.

But despite my trepidation, despite the worries that I had about what we'd be tacitly responsible for, it was a good deal. It was a chance for peace, with at least one of our neighbors. And so I nodded. "Deal," I whispered.

He pushed himself upright with a groan. "Fucking perfect. Pleasure doing business with you then, kid." Turning, he eyed the mess that had been left of my car. "Now. This is a bit of a shitshow, isn't it?"

"Yeah," I mumbled, rising to my feet unsteadily. My head pounded at the movement. "We'll...I'll figure something out." I didn't know how.

I needed a story, I realized. Something to tell, to explain away how Greyson had been injured. Why we'd been here. Why my *car* was here, on fire, and why our house was scorched and riddled with bullet holes.

"Do you have a cleaner?" Carl said. His tone was skeptical.

I blinked. "What?"

He sniffed. "Didn't think so. Then what're you going to do, huh?"

My face flushed. "I-I don't know, just yet, but I'll-"

"No."

My words died. It was just one word, but it cut right across the conversation like a knife.

Carl stared back at me, his lips tight. "Look. You can't keep doing this," he said at last. "Not now. Not like this. You've been playing fast and loose, and it's not going to work anymore."

"W-What are you-"

"Now, I'm not saying *no one* on the outside knows," he said, steamrolling my efforts at rejoining the conversation. "People aren't idiots. Some people know - the people that matter, mostly. The bigwigs, the old families. Hell, I'm pretty sure there's even some folks in the government who know what's really going on our there. But it ain't common knowledge, and you can't keep playing at exposing us. Primes are supposed to keep the secrecy, not be the ones spilling the beans."

I stopped. By his words...the implications were clear. The group he was lumping us into...A bit more of the weight lifted from my shoulders. He might just be serious about his deal, then.

"I'm open to suggestions," I said, my mouth dry.

He turned. "Damn it," he muttered, shaking his head. "How's this all my problem?"

"I'll manage somehow."

"Nathan here's good at blurring things," Carl said, waving towards his car and completely disregarding me again. The two figures inside jumped, like they'd been startled awake. "He can make it so that no one'll remember a thing. It'll be enough to get the old bastard looked after and buy us a little time. There are crews who see to this sort of thing, for a price."

I nodded slowly. "Mercenaries."

He snorted. "Better with a broom than a rifle, but sure. I'll give you their number. They're not cheap, but it's what you've got to do. And get someone who can keep the mundanes away from your claim, before you wind up doing something stupid."

My ears burned. I nodded again. "Right."

"I don't want to see you lot out here getting eyes on our kind again."

"Right," I mumbled.

"If you start lettin' stuff slip, I think you know what's going to happen. The marketeers won't be the only ones to come knocking."

"Yeah."

"You understand? Say it clear."

"I do," I said, swallowing and pulling my gaze up to meet his. "It's not my intention to make problems. I'll...we'll be more careful."

"Then we're good," he said, stretching his arms skyward. "Hannah's time is on me, by the way. Owed Greyson a favor from years back." He grinned horribly. "And now I don't."

I nodded, still more than a little cowed by his lecture and the fact that Greyson was still lying on the floor, bleeding. "She's a healer?"

"She is. Still learning, but she's not bad. Good kid She'll get there."

My fingers clenched against my legs, curling back into fists. "She didn't seem all that confident."

For a long, quiet moment, Carl didn't speak. He just stared at the embers of my car. When he spoke again, his voice was low and quiet. "Greyson's old. It might be an issue. There's no telling."

And neither of them wanted to get my hopes up. I just nodded. "Fine. Thank you."

"We'll see if he thanks me, if he makes it," Carl said, his grin returning. "Think the old coot liked having something over my head."

If he made it. A fresh wave of tension slammed into me.

Carl seemed to see it. It was broadcasted on my face, I knew. He just sighed, reaching over to pat my shoulder. "See to your people," he said, a little more gently. "Let *us* see to the finder for now."

He didn't wait for me to reply. He just turned away, waving to the two still sitting in the car, and started walking back towards the house. They leapt from the backseat in a second, clustering in behind him.

The cold air nipped at my cheeks, my neck. Within seconds they vanished into the house. The sound of voices from inside ramped up almost immediately.

I leaned back, shutting the sound out, and let my eyes slide shut. Every breath hurt. My head ached, and although the nosebleed appeared to have finally stopped, the taste of blood still filled my mouth.

I supposed we'd won. It didn't really feel like it.

Aedan's voice rose over the rest, irritated and as loud as ever. I winced. Him and Jake would be out in a second, I knew, tearing back towards me with some problem they'd want solved. They'd probably want an explanation for everything that had happened. Everyone was going to want an explanation.

Greyson was still an unknown. We'd still have to have our home fixed. It needed to look a *little* less like a war zone, if we were going to pass inspection. I wouldn't put it past Carl and the rest of the primes to come squish us like a bug if they thought we were being too risky.

The *other* primes. His words still echoed in my ears. I didn't think there was any sort of formal structure to demis out there, but it sure sounded like we'd been promoted. It was just going to be another problem, I knew, another issue that I'd have to deal with. A groan slipped between my lips at the thought of all of the work that waited down the road.

But we'd won. Kind of.

For the time being, I was ready to call that enough.

And so I sat on the bench, staring into the flames, and let the world spin madly around me for a little while longer.

CHAPTER FIFTY-EIGHT

"But why can't I-"

"You've only just stopped peeling, damn it. Just sit still for five fucking minutes."

I leaned away from the table, grimacing, and slid a hand down to pet Spike as he wound back and forth across my ankles. It was still early. I'd thought that would be enough to get me away from the others for at least a little while. I'd been wrong.

Kai squirmed, writhing in place where he sat on the couch. His brother sat across from him, his laptop open on his lap. I caught the way Tyler kept glaring at him over the screen.

I couldn't really blame Tyler for wanting Kai to sit still. Hannah had come back to the house with us, after things had settled down. She'd given him a once-over, just like the rest of us. Thanks to her, the gashes adorning my face, arm, and leg had closed up in record time. I was still a little miffed that she hadn't been around when I'd been shot by Matt's crew. Things would have been much, much more simple.

She'd been fast asleep on the couch by the end of it, completely drained, but Kai would live - without even the burn-scars I'd been sure he'd wind up with. Both him and his brother had been more than a little grateful for *that*.

Of course, then the peeling had begun, and the bleeding as old wounds reopened. And now he'd been told to give his body at least a *little* time to heal. He wasn't handling it all that gracefully. No one had expected him to.

"I'm *fine*," I heard Kai mutter darkly. And just like that, he and Tyler were off again, bickering back and forth.

I just pushed myself upright with a groan, still feeling the aches and pains in my limbs even if the wounds themselves had vanished. Hannah was good, but she wasn't perfect.

A sigh slipped out before I could bite it back. No, she wasn't perfect. And then I shook my head, forcing the thoughts away. It was enough. We'd make it be enough.

Something cracked from outside. A shiver ran down my spine. Gunfire. Ours, at least, rather than someone attacking. All the same, the sound wasn't a welcome one just then. Or ever, probably.

Tyler and Kai didn't so much as look up at me as I slipped towards the door. Neither of them had a job yet, which was why I was so shocked to see them up and awake before noon. Maybe they were actually going to do something productive with their day. Something *useful*.

I got my hand up in time - the only sound that escaped me was a low, half-smothered chuckler, rather than the full-bodied snort that had tried.

"Don't burn anything down," I said, grabbing for my keys.

"He won't be burning *anything*," Tyler said, his eyes flashing dangerously.

Kai let out a huff, dangerously close to a whine.

I winced. I'd seen the way Tyler's lips curled down in a scowl. "Hannah's orders," the audio-mage said, spitting each word out. "Not for another week."

"I feel fine. Really."

"Kai," Tyler snapped.

There was no telling how long they'd stay at it. The two were good additions, and I didn't mind having them there, but...well, if the last two weeks had been any indication, this argument wasn't going to end anytime soon.

The door slid open at my touch. I winced, squinting against the sudden and harsh light that flooded in. Well, it was a pleasant, bright day, at least. I'd take what I could get.

A few steps saw me to the corner of the house, and I could all too quickly spot the source of the noise - Amber and Nox, standing out in the front yard. Nox had a pistol in his hands, aiming across the driveway at a row of pop cans lazily propped on top of some firewood.

Amber leaned almost carelessly against a pile of brick that had wound up deposited onto the lawn beside him, picking at her fingernails. Greyson's two guard dogs lay at her feet, panting happily and completely unbothered by the gunfire. Somehow, I wasn't surprised.

"Anytime you're ready, Nox," she said, carefully cheerful.

"...right," he mumbled. His shoulders slid up as he drew in a great breath of air. The barrel of his gun quivered.

"Morning, you two," I said, raising my hand in a wave.

Nox flinched, jumping a good three inches at the sudden sound of my voice. To my horror, he twisted, turning to face the intrusion.

Amber was there in a second, her hand latching around his shoulder and turning him back and away from me. The gunshot rang out an instant later.

I froze, the blood draining from my face.

"Jesus, Nox," I heard her snap. "What the fuck was that?"

"Oh my god," Nox said, his voice rising. "I-I'm so sorry. Jon. Are you-"

"I'm fine," I said mildly, taking a deep breath. "Yeah. Let's not do that, okay?"

"R-Right. Fuck."

I was already turning - I'd heard the noise, the plastic *crack* that had hidden under the sound of the round firing.

A mirthless laugh escaped at the sight that awaited, the one I'd known I would find. At the sight of a tiny, twisted hole in the bumper of the car parked a little ways up the driveway. *My* car.

My original car had died, at long last. It had survived Matt's visit and Jake hotwiring it, my bleeding all over the backseat and frenzied trips halfway across the state at all hours of the day and night. But being hijacked by rival demis and set on fire was just too much. Understandably.

As much as I'd liked the damn thing, it was gone - and I'd been happy enough to go down to the meager lot in the next town over, armed with what savings I had left. I'd driven off with something almost-new and quite serviceable. If nothing else, it was free of bloodstains and bullet holes, a fact I was quite happy with.

Very happy with, in fact.

The sound of my teeth grinding together echoed in my skull as I stepped over, finally crouching down. Staring at it didn't change matters at all. There was a hole. In my car. My *brand new* car.

"Oh," I heard Nox said from behind me. "Crap."

Amber chuckled, the sound growing louder with every passing second. "Good job, Nox."

"*Crap*," he repeated, and even I could hear the sheepishness seeping in. "Uh. Jon. I'll find a way to-"

"Just go."

"Right. Sorry."

I glanced over as he broke into a run, tearing off towards the house. His face was beet red under his newly-purchased glasses.

Amber chuckled, a low, gravelly sound. "Sorry about that."

"Damn it," I muttered, running my thumb over the fresh wound on my bumper. "I haven't even had the damn thing a month."

"Well, at least it's over and done with. Now you don't have to worry about getting your first door ding," she said.

"I guess," I said, wrinkling my nose.

She snorted. "Anyway. You have fun, now."

I glared at her. "I'm going to *work*. I'm not going to have fun."

The corners of her lips curled up. "I know. Tough titties."

I kept glaring. She kept chuckling.

"Fine. Whatever," I muttered. And then I stopped, eyeing her sidelong.

Her and Nox were still here, despite it being two weeks after the Marketeers had come and gone. It wasn't unexpected. She'd pushed herself to the very limit of her powers with the stunt she'd pulled to save Keira. For almost four days, she'd been unconscious in Keira's bed, and it wasn't until the last few days that she'd been up and at it.

But here she was.

"Listen," I said, breaking eye contact with her at last. "I-I don't know what the two of you have planned, but…you might have figured out that we're probably still in trouble."

"You mean how you've got everyone's eyes on you, with most of your demis still being fledgelings," she said dryly. "Yeah. I noticed."

"Yeah. Anyway. We…" I swallowed hard, feeling my cheeks start to heat up. Damn it, I could already *see* her laughing at me. "We could really use your help around here. If you wanted to stay on."

Her laughter died - but the look she was giving me didn't ease up at all. "That would get expensive for you, you know."

I could feel my lips pressing together, my anxiety growing. "W-Well. I was hoping that maybe…" Amber was still *staring* at me. I summoned every last scrap of courage I could, funneling it into a last-ditch effort.

"I was hoping maybe you'd stay because you wanted to. The crew needs some demis like you two, someone to back up our...inexperience." I hesitated, remembering the embrace the two of them had shared back in the woods. "I-I know the house is getting a bit full, but we've still got the apartment, too. We could make sure you and Nox had your own room. A bit of privacy. And we're doing ok, financially. It would be a good deal for you. I'll make sure of it." I fell quiet at last, the words finally running out.

And still she stared at me. My heart froze. Damn it, I was an idiot. Someone like her? She probably got offers like that all the time. It was stupid to think she'd be interested in hanging around.

A low rumble brought me up short. It took me a long moment to realize it - she was laughing again.

"A private room?" she said, shaking her head derisively. "Don't give Nox any ideas. He doesn't need them."

I winced. From the look on her face, I'd clearly misread both the situation and their relationship. The thought...didn't really bother me, despite the way she was laughing. And her chin had lifted, a contemplative look settling over her face.

"I'm not against the idea of some stability, frankly," she murmured. "It's not as peaceful around these days as it used to be. There are too many groups on the move."

I blinked, my shoulders lifting. It almost sounded like she was thinking about it - and thinking seriously. "We'll be trying to stay out of trouble," I said, doing my best to keep from sounding like I was wheedling.

Amber snorted. "Not buying *that*."

"I guess," I muttered, my eyes dropping again.

"Still, it isn't every day you're offered the chance to join a prime at the ground level."

"I-I don't know if you could really call us a prime. Not yet."

"The crew from Detroit seemed to think you were. And I'm inclined to agree." Her voice was a little more neutral, a little more serious. When I looked up, she had her arms crossed, her expression grave. "And not everyone's going to like that. People are going to try and test you."

"Which is why we need you."

She groaned, sliding her eyes shut and shaking her head. "Damn it. Don't think it'll solve everything, okay?"

I raised one eyebrow. I could read the conversation well enough to see where things were going. "But you'll stay?"

One of her eyes snapped open, fixing on me. "I'll stay. Nox can decide on his own."

A smile tugged at the corners of my lips. I quashed it as soon as I realized. "You don't really think he'll go off on his own."

"I'm not done," Amber snapped. I fell silent, watching her. She sighed, still glaring at me. "I'm still getting paid. You're not getting our services for free that easily."

"You'll get housing with the crew. And food. I think-"

"Nope."

I glared at her. She smiled back, all saccharine sweetness. She had me trapped, and she knew it. "Fine," I said at last. "Greyson had all the documents for new identities and stuff." My heart sank, just a little. "Until...that whole mess is resolved, I think Brendon's handling it. You can talk to him." The man had really come into his own, delving through all of Greyson's haphazard files and notes like a starving man happening across a feast. Together, him and Loren had pieced together a bit of sense out of the chaos of the last few weeks.

"I don't think that'll be necessary," Amber said, her tone airy.

I paused. "You'll need a job, won't you?"

"We *have* jobs. We take them quite seriously."

She wasn't grinning anymore - it had long since become a leer. I scowled across the driveway at her. "You can't be serious."

"Your safety is our top priority."

"At least do the dishes." There was nothing I could do to keep the words from becoming a whine.

Her teeth gleamed as her smile grew. "Can't. I'm afraid it's not in the contract."

"You absolute-"

"Anyway, we're quite busy. Sorry about the car. We'll work through the payment later," Amber said, raising a hand in a jaunty wave as she turned away. She *winked* at me. I ground my teeth together, my frustrations rising, and knew there was absolutely nothing I could do to respond.

And at this rate, I was going to be late. Rolling my eyes and forcing myself to take a deep breath, I reached for the car door.

Amber vanished into the house as I slid into the driver's seat, still grinning to herself.

***

The road flew past under my tires as I sped away from my office. The sun settled lower on the horizon, pasting brilliant reds and golds across the sky. I yawned, reaching for the can of pop sitting in the cupholder, and fought to keep my eyes open.

Distantly, some part of my mind already knew that the whole 'job' thing wasn't going to work. Amber had said it before, back when the two of us sat watching the snow fall. Our worlds were different, mundanes and demis. My trying to keep both of them connected was just a time bomb waiting to go off - and until then, it left me exhausted and drained. Trying to keep a houseful of novice mages from burning the place down was a full-time job in and of itself.

All the same, I wasn't ready to let go of that bit of normalcy just yet. And we still had bills to pay. Thoughts of the *other* ways we could earn a living still turned my stomach. Not yet. We weren't to that point yet.

But it had nearly been more than I could bear, sitting in front of my computer screen and tapping away at the keyboard while time slipped by outside. I'd had complaints about my job in the past, of course - the fact that with the ceiling my career had it might as well have been a cave, the pointless bickering and gossip and politics that filled day-to-day office life, the bureaucratic bullshit. Somehow, the fact that there was so much more going on in my life made the irritations ten times worse.

I wasn't going to make it. The thought hung in my mind, whispering in my ears. I wouldn't be able to put up with it forever - and without a job, that was one less tie that I had to a normal life. I wasn't quite sure how I felt about that.

It was a worry for my future self. I gripped the wheel a little tighter, blinking away the momentary pain as street lights rose up around the road. The parking lot awaited, sticking in my vision as I turned into view. My stomach churned unhappily.

I wished this wasn't necessary, either. But it was, and no amount of wishing would change that.

Within minutes I'd parked and crossed from the chilled night air into the warmth of the building. It was getting late, but you couldn't have told from the bustle and activity still filling the broad, open structure. Families circled here and there, dragging children behind them. Nurses and the occasional doctor scurried around them, muttering to each other in quiet voices.

I knew where to go. As soon as I had my visitor badge in hand it was straight into the elevator, following the same path as always. It felt like I'd made the trip a dozen times in the last two weeks.

Despite all that, it still hurt to turn the corner into the room all the way at the end of the hall and come face-to-face with the dark, blanket-covered form of Greyson.

I turned towards the chair by his bedside, but it was occupied Hannah jumped to her feet at my approach. "Jon. Evening."

A smile tugged at my lips. "Don't get up." Her eyes were shadowed. Dark bags hung under them, and her skin was getting pale. "You're running yourself too hard. No one wants *you* hurt, too."

She hesitated. "Yes, well, I'm being careful." Her expression soured in an instant. "But...I apologize for my lack of progress."

"It's not your fault." I stepped towards Greyson's bed all the while, inspecting him.

She'd tried. She really had. But we'd been slow in getting to him, and even if she was a healer, she couldn't work miracles. That was what I told myself each and every day when I came to visit.

It didn't change the fact that Greyson hadn't woken up - and the doctors were increasingly doubtful that he would. They'd just given me vague answers and talked about how little we knew about the brain. I'd nodded past what little they'd said. It didn't matter.

We clung to hope all the same. They had medicine, but we had magic. It could do what they couldn't. It had to.

I forced a smile onto my face, glancing back to Hannah. "Be sure to thank Carl for us. I don't know what we'd do without you here." That was a lie. I *did* know what would happen to Greyson without even a chance of healing him. I just didn't want to think about it.

Her eyes widened fractionally, and she nodded. "Yes. Ah. Of course. It's our pleasure as neighbors, I'm sure."

"Right." That was a lie too, but I didn't call her on it. Carl had offered us Hannah's services, and I hadn't said no. All the same, I wasn't about to believe that it was done from the goodness of his heart. Carl was a pleasant enough type, I'd found, but he wasn't soft. He couldn't afford to be.

Hannah was here, helping to heal our crew and our wounded Finder, but that didn't mean that they weren't getting anything out of it. She was new. When I asked, she'd told me she'd only had her focus for a handful of years. Detroit was bigger than us, naturally, and I didn't doubt that they had more healers than just her.

Giving her to us, even temporarily, meant that she'd get the chance to learn more about her skills - and *they* could let the more experienced healers deal with their own injured. They were letting us train her. I didn't really mind, right then. I tried not to think about the second half of it, the part where Carl had eyes and ears on our crew from the inside. The southern prime's leader hadn't shown any signs of being hostile. Yet. That could always change.

"I-I'm just about done, for the day," Hannah said, turning away. Her backpack rested on the floor beside her chair. She seized it, stuffing her few possessions back into it. "I'll...I'll leave you two alone. I'm sorry to intrude."

I raised a hand. "You're not-"

It was too late. She'd already scurried out the door, vanishing down the hall. Shaking my head, I swallowed a sigh. The healer had been so skittish since Carl had left, so *respectful*. Where Loren had seemed fearful, this was more like she was worried about offending me. No matter what I said to her, it didn't seem to change - and the more I told her not to worry, the more flighty she got.

All things in time, I told myself, turning back to Greyson.

My eyes dropped to his wrist, as always. The gold chain clasped to his skin gleamed dully in the faint light. A knot in my chest eased. I'd worried that the nurses would take his relic while I wasn't here, at first. They hadn't shown the slightest bit of interest. I still worried. It would be too easy for someone to slip into the hospital, if they knew he was here. I tugged the blanket a little lower, obscuring it from sight, and tried not to think about it.

The door creaked. I flinched, turning more on instinct than anything to face it.

Officer Baldwin stood in the doorway, his eyes widening ever so slightly. "Didn't mean to scare you," he said, a chuckle rippling under his words. "Something got you jumpy?"

I shook my head, turning back to Greyson. My heartbeat accelerated, pulsing faster at the sight of him. Despite our limited encounters with each other, I could already tell that having him around wasn't good. "Sorry. Long day."

"I bet." Baldwin waited a moment, silent, and then I heard his footsteps ring out against the linoleum. "Heard you stopped by after work sometimes. Figured I'd drop in. How's he doing?"

"About like you'd expect," I muttered, glancing towards the machines they'd plugged him into. They beeped just as steadily as ever. Tearing my eyes away, I glanced back towards the officer. "Was there something I could help you with?"

"Got a call from the restaurant in town. Said they saw two men getting in a bit of an altercation, few weeks back," Baldwin said, shoving his hands down into his pockets. His eyes were fixed on mine, unblinking. "Saw it was you. Then I heard some strange stories about the old fellow, here." He chewed his lip slowly, still staring. "Can't say I liked to hear you were involved."

I winced. The McDonald's. Aedan - and his slapping. "Just a misunderstanding," I muttered, turning back towards Greyson.

"Heard someone was attacking you."

"It's a friend. It was just a joke."

"Manager said it was an old employee. Sort of a sketchy type."

"I really couldn't speak to that." Good god, he wasn't giving up.

Indeed, Baldwin rocked back on his heels, showing no signs of wanting to leave yet. His eyes flicked to Greyson, then back to me. "And Mr. Greyson, here? How'd this all happen, eh?" A humorless smile flashed onto his face. "Old man like that falls, all by himself, usually there's a different ending attached."

I shook my head, forcing my irritation back down. "He's just...a family friend. Someone who's taken care of me in the past." Not technically untrue, either, which made it my very favorite sort of lie.

"And you *just happened* to find him, knocked cold by a blow to the head."

"We were lucky, that's all. Him and I were- supposed to watch the game. Only he didn't show up. Wasn't answering his phone. I got worried."

"The game, eh? Which one?"

I stopped. Baldwin stood where he was, sliding his arms across his chest.

He knew. I could see it, plastered across his face - I'd toyed with his memory once before, back when I'd been shot and Keira had been injured. He remembered, somehow. Or, at least, he could remember enough to know that something was wrong.

Magic wasn't real. Everyone knew that. With that in mind, there should be no reason at all for him to be thinking anything out of the ordinary was going on. Sure, he'd maybe have some lingering doubts about my role in the whole business. But I hadn't planned on the way he was glaring at me, eyes narrowed.

"I recorded it," I said flatly. "Have I done something wrong?"

"Strange, that *you're* the one left with the power of attorney for him. It's odd, that's all."

"He doesn't have any surviving family." It had been a heartbreaking discovery, when the cleaners we'd hired came to fix the whole mess up. Sure, they'd carted away the wreck of my car, and they'd fixed the bullet holes in our siding, but they'd also set things up so that we could take care of our finder. "His wife passed two decades ago. They never had any children. I was the next best thing for him."

"Right, right." Baldwin didn't sound convinced, regardless of what he was saying. "I'm sure that's all true."

I turned towards the door, fighting down my irritation. Greyson had his relic, and Hannah had been here looking after him, and there was nothing else I could do. Normally I'd stay, sitting by his bedside and talking for a few minutes. I didn't know if it'd help, but I didn't have any better ideas, either. With Officer Asshole here riding me, though, I didn't want to hang around. "Was there anything you needed from me? Otherwise, I'm tired. I'd like to get home."

"I don't know what you're playing at." His words cut across the quiet between us, low and ominous. He stepped closer, creeping forward until the two of us stood nearly nose-to-nose. "I don't know what games are going on here, Mr. Christensen, but know this." His eyes were fixed on mine, hard and unflinching. "I'm not buying your shit. If I find anything going on that's even an inch out of line, *anything*, I will make damn sure that you live to regret it."

Despite myself, I hesitated. There was an iron in his words, a seriousness that was hard to just brush off. "Officer, I promise you there's nothing funny going on."

"You know, over the years, you learn when someone's lying to you."

"I'm not-"

"Take advantage of this old man in his time of suffering, and I will make you suffer. Understand?"

I swallowed. Baldwin hadn't moved so much as an inch. "It's not what you think," I said at last, shaking my head. "I'm here to help him. Nothing more. Nothing will happen."

His lip curled up in a sneer. "Right. See that it doesn't." With one last glance towards Greyson he turned towards the door, raising his hand in a wave. "Say hi to your sister for me."

I watched him go, mute and still. It was only after he'd turned the corner and vanished that I let my breath slide out.

He knew. He might not know exactly what was going on, but he *knew*. And clearly, he'd been watching me.

Carl's words echoed in my thoughts, circling back and forth. We needed secrecy. We *didn't* need a county sheriff coming after us, some misguided notion of justice on his mind. Gripping the chair in front of me tightly enough that my hands stopped quivering, I shook my head. We'd have to be more careful.

Greyson was every bit as unmoving as ever as I glanced to him, taking another deep breath. "Wake up, already," I whispered. He didn't respond. In time, Hannah could help him. Maybe. And until then, every day without him left us a little more vulnerable.

I waited in his room, thoughts of how much trouble we were in filling my mind, until I could be sure Baldwin was really gone.

It was a long, lonely wait.

CHAPTER FIFTY-NINE

Birds shrieked outside the windows. I glanced out, blinking away my surprise. Birds. Actual living things - which meant that maybe, just maybe, winter would be winding down soon. The thought was a happy one. Despite their arrival, though, the early-morning sky was as grey and dismal as it had been for months.

I turned back to my phone, flicking through post after post from our friends. Their lives were as mundane as always, according to the status updates that greeted me. A picture of their dinner from the night before. A political rant. Pictures of their kids. It was all so normal and commonplace that it hurt.

Bending my head down, I lifted my spoon, taking another mouthful of cereal. My eyes didn't twitch off the screen.

Something creaked from the hallway past the kitchen, towards the bedrooms. I paused, glancing up. The others *should* be gone. Most of them, anyway. Loren and Brendon both had jobs, and Jake wouldn't be flitting around the house without announcing himself. The TV wasn't on, anyway, which almost certainly meant he was nowhere near.

I lifted another spoonful to my lips, crunching down on the toasted wheat.

Another creak - and the sound of a door opening. I looked up again. This time, I was rewarded with the sight of Keira's door moving.

Right. She had the morning off. I could *almost* remember her telling me that, amid a flood of other information I'd pushed to the side as probably-not-important. Smiling to myself, I opened my mouth, picking up my spoon yet again.

Aedan slipped out of her room, holding a hand to his face to cover his yawn. He was bare-chested - and in fact, it was just the towel wrapped around his waist that kept him at all decent.

The 'good morning' that had been rising to my lips died, turning to ash in an instant.

He turned away, still yawning, and padded off further down the hall. The sound of the bathroom door opening drifted out.

Milk dripped onto the table in front of me, falling from my spoon.

Aedan had been gone. He'd taken off, shortly after things settled down, without even a word. It was like him, after all. No one had been surprised.

The sound of water running into water echoed across the kitchen.

He'd been *gone*. Until now, apparently.

Just as quickly as the sound had begun, it stopped. The toilet flushed a second after.

The puddle of milk in front of me grew steadily. I hardly noticed.

The door opened again, and just like that, Aedan stepped back down the hall. Without a second's hesitation, without turning to look or notice that I was there, he reached for the handle to Keira's door.

And then he was gone.

I let my hand fall back down, the spoon vanishing into the cereal. It was muffled, but I could hear someone giggling from inside Keira's room. Suddenly, I wasn't hungry anymore. As quickly as I could without running, I crossed the kitchen to the sink, rinsing my bowl out.

The sounds of them laughing vanished behind me as I escaped into the morning air.

***

I milled about outside for as long as I dared, seeing to the odd tasks that needed doing. There were plenty of them. We had barricades to repair, disguised as lumber piles and retaining walls. It had to *look* normal enough, if anyone were to come poking around. Anyone like Baldwin, the whispers in the back of my mind crooned. I ignored them as best I could.

The work was good. It kept my hands busy, kept me from thinking about all the ways things had gone wrong. Because we were fortunate, I knew, and we'd come through the worst of the conflict. This was our victory.

Eventually, though, there was no delaying the inevitable any longer.

I turned towards the house with a groan.

Aedan sat on the couch as I stepped through the door. The TV chirped away happily, playing whatever mindless channel Jake had left it switched to. "Morning, Jonny," he said, not looking over. "I made it back. Haven't you missed me?"

Hadn't I just. "I saw," I said, a chilled note in my voice. Damn it, Keira was an adult, but she was still my sister. There were things you just didn't *do*. "At least I don't have to worry about finding you a bed."

I caught it - the way his face went pale, just for a second. "Ah," he said, and he did glance over at last. And then he grinned. "Ahaha. Well. You see, Jonny-"

"Slap yourself, Aedan."

"W-What are you-"

His words died as his hand came across. The crack of skin against skin cut across the quiet of the kitchen. My relic warmed gently. Happily, I ventured.

Aedan spluttered, color returning to his cheeks in a rush. "Jonny, don't you dare-"

"Again."

Again, his arm came up. Again, his words were lost to garbled nonsense.

His eyes flashed dangerously as he spun towards me. "I swear to fucking god, Jonny, I'll-"

"Again. Harder."

My relic hummed. The third blow was hard enough to set Aedan rocking backwards, teetering. He grabbed the arm of the couch a second later, twisting to glare at me. He didn't say anything. He just scowled, the red imprint of a hand lighting up against his cheek.

I lowered myself into a chair, not bothering to hide my smirk. "So. How's life, Aedan?"

"The hell's wrong with you?" he snapped, raising his hand to cradle his cheek.

I raised an eyebrow. He rolled his eyes. "Fine. Whatever. Let's *not* talk about it, then."

"Perfect. So, what. You just run off without a word, then wander back in? Did you run out of beer?"

My tone was mocking. He scowled more deeply. "There was no telling if anyone tracked me, after all. Can't hang around forever, no matter how much you miss me."

"That's your best excuse?"

He raised his hands into the air in a helpless shrug. "I'm a busy man. I've got shit to do. Don't cry when I have to see to it."

I eyed him sidelong, not too sure. Aedan suited the title they'd given him, surely - he was a wanderer if ever I'd seen one. It shouldn't be a surprise for him to flit in and out of our lives as he pleased, wreaking havoc the whole way.

And yet, every time he'd come around, he wanted something. Food, or money, or a place to hide. He didn't do *anything* without a reason, no matter what he said. He liked to play the helpless, innocent traveler. That didn't mean I believed the act.

And he was still grinning, just a little, despite the glow of the handprint painted across his face.

"And you just happen to come back now."

He tilted his head, settling back in his seat. "Eh, well. Don't blame a man for doing what he has to." His eyes flicked towards her door. "I don't think *she* minds."

I winced. Her own choices aside, I really, *really* didn't need to know. And besides, I still wasn't convinced. It was something about the calculating look about him, the way he'd vanished and then swept back in without any sort of pleasantries. And, as near as I could tell, he hadn't raided my fridge yet. That was enough to cast doubt over his whole story, even if my relic didn't think he was out-and-out lying.

I opened my mouth, ready to pry an actual answer out of him, but the screech of the door cut me off.

"Jesus, it's cold out there," someone muttered. Tyler stepped the rest of the way inside, closing the outside world off a moment later. "Oh. Morning, Jon."

I just waved. Tyler's eyes flicked to Aedan. "Hey." And then he chuckled. He didn't say anything more, but from the way his grin widened, I knew he'd spotted the handprint still outlined against his cheek. Maybe he thought Aedan had it coming. Maybe he just didn't care - but whatever he was thinking, he kept it to himself.

Aedan raised his hand in the thinnest excuse for a greeting I'd ever seen, scowling at Tyler. He knew that Tyler knew.

"So," I said, forcing my amusement down. "No word?"

Tyler shrugged. "It looks like we're alone. For now, anyway." His eyes flicked to the windows. "With Greyson out of the picture...I'm not incredibly comfortable, of course. But no one's seen movement."

I nodded slowly, gauging the expression on his face. We were vulnerable without a finder. It was a risk - and a risk that none of our demis *had* to put up with. Deep down, I'd been worried that some of them would start splitting off, running away before things turned sour.

Tyler shook his head, his eyes still fixed on mine. "Calm down, Jon," he said, stepping past the couch towards the kitchen. "We'll manage. And he'll pull through this yet." The cabinets groaned as he pulled them open, reaching for the coffee.

"Was I being that obvious?"

"Yes," Aedan muttered, rolling his eyes.

"Oh." I stared at the floor, letting the smell of coffee wash over the room. "I just think-"

The sound of the floorboards creaking cut me off. I glanced up, seeing the action mirrored by Aedan.

Keira froze, three steps outside her bedroom. "Oh. You're up. All of you." Her hands dropped to her side, smoothing the pajama pants she still wore. "Uh. I should-"

"Coffee will be done soon," Tyler said. His voice rippled with barely-contained laughter. "Sit."

"Right," Keira mumbled, turning towards the couch. She stopped dead in her tracks after a single glance at Aedan.

"Aedan's back," I said, my tone bright and cheerful.

Her eyes flicked from him to me - and back to him. And then she sighed, her shoulders drooping a fraction of an inch. Her own face was more than a little red as she plopped down beside him on the couch, staring pointedly towards the coffee as it bubbled in the pot.

I chuckled along with whatever Tyler was saying, his report of the day's plans and the news he'd heard from the others. The gossip he shared, stories of spotting Jake and Brendon having hushed, hidden conversations out behind the garage the night before. Jokes about the colors Hannah's face had turned when Nox finally admitted to her that he was a telepath. It was completely absurd - all the sorts of things that would have been unthinkable a few months before.

But those had been a busy few months. And despite everything that had happened, it felt good to enjoy a little bit of normalcy. I knew it wouldn't last, not with the way things had gone. Not with the choices we'd made.

That just made it all the more important to enjoy it now.

Which was why I crossed to the counter and started pulling mugs out of the cabinet, grinning along with the others. Keira chattered away, the conversation flitting back and forth without waiting for my input. A flicker of movement caught my eye - Amber, peeking out from around the corner from the bedrooms, still rubbing the sleep from her eyes. I caught myself before I could grin at the sight, taking out an extra cup.

There was more Aedan wasn't saying. I knew it, knew for a fact that he wouldn't have shown back up without something on his mind. Part of me wanted to force it out of him, to *make* him spill the beans. It was rich of him to keep secrets, considering everything we'd just done.

But the others were smiling. They actually looked happy, and there hadn't been enough of that of late. With how hard we'd fought to reach this point, with all the pain and struggle we'd gone through, I certainly wasn't going to be the one to interrupt them.

I leaned back, letting the noise swell up around us even if I wasn't hearing a word they said. Aedan and his problems could wait.

We had what we needed.

Acknowledgments

We're back at the end of another one!

Truthfully, it's hard to overstate how big of a process writing each of these books is, and how grateful I am for the people who have been here helping me along the way. For any newcomers to Silvertongue, or to my fiction, each of the novels that I've written and published are released on a chapter-by-chapter basis, put into the world as a serial that is condensed and re-polished into the book it is now. As such, I've been incredibly fortunate to have had company as this story came to life.

As always, there are a few names and faces in particular that I'd like to mention and pull out.

For starters, I'd like to thank Potato, who spent an unreasonable amount of time helping me pull apart the shell of a blurb I'd written and splice it back together into something several times more awesome. He also has been a font of ideas and information for the world - particularly regarding ancient Ireland and the lore surrounding that region - which has been a massive help to me. Keep sending me help, and I'll keep sending you chonkers.

I couldn't possibly publish without again thanking Alex, aka Hydrael, for his advice and commiseration. It's been an incredibly satisfying experience being able to do all of this together with other authors! Thank you for letting me make use of your knowledge!

The logical next place for me to go in the circle of thanks would be to the folks who have been here following along chapter by chapter, reading and giving me feedback and help. Cz, and Faren, and Palm, and Westrion, and everyone who's been so dedicated from the very start. The problem is that there are so many people who have been a part of this that I know, *know* that I'd start forgetting people. My mind and memory being what it is, you know.

Instead, let me repeat the same tired old truth that I keep falling back on - without all of you who have been here, reading and sharing and enjoying, I wouldn't have found the stubbornness to finish my first book, let alone this beast. You've made it fun for me, and that's more important than anything. So thank you, to each of you who has been a part of this, and I hope to keep entertaining you in the months and years to come.

Moar words!

Interested in reading more? Looking for the next book?

Casey White's series are updated chapter-by-chapter on her websites:

http://inorai.com
www.reddit.com/r/inorai

31365542R00362

Made in the USA
Lexington, KY
19 February 2019